100TH POWER VOLUME 3

A TREASURY OF 100 STORIES

ROBERT JESCHONEK

100th POWER VOLUME 3

Published by Blastoff Books
An Imprint of Pie Press
411 Chancellor Street
Johnstown, Pennsylvania 15904
www.blastoffbooks.net

Subscribe to the Blastoff Books Newsletter:
http://newsletter.blastoffbooks.net

PRAISE FOR THE STORIES OF 100TH POWER

On *The Darks of Their Eyes:* "Bob has written a piece that will make you think, even as it makes you squirm… What is justice, after all? Who gets to decide? And what if it gets perverted? What if it was perverted in the past? Who gets to set it right?"

– Kristine Kathryn Rusch, *Fiction River: Justice*

On *Dirty Dreams of a Dishwasher:* "This is an outrageous tale that had me in hysterics and it's probably the funniest love story I've ever read, bar none. And the conclusion to this tale was ingenious and made me grin at its complete uproariousness."

— Chris Fried, Reviewer

On *The Pooping Knight's Playbook:* "I'll just say that it's brilliant in the way so many of the stories that come from Planet Bob are brilliant. When you are done, assuming you're a well-balanced sane person like me (ha!) and loved this piece on every level it's possible to love a piece, you will want to go immediately to his website and grab a copy of *In the Empire of Underpants and Other Stories.*"

– Ron Collins, *Typosphere*

On *Messiah 2.0:* "This was a fun read. I really liked the Father Clement character, and Imago the stained glass robot was so cool. Very cool, weird setting."

– Andrew Crevier, *Grind Pulp Podcast*

ALSO BY ROBERT JESCHONEK

100th Power Book 1

100th Power Book 2

Blastoff!

Cosmic Conflicts

In a Green Dress, Surrounded by Exploding Clowns and Other Stories

In the Empire of Underpants and Other Stories

Battlenaut Crucible

Scifi Motherlode

Sticks and Stones: A Trek Novel

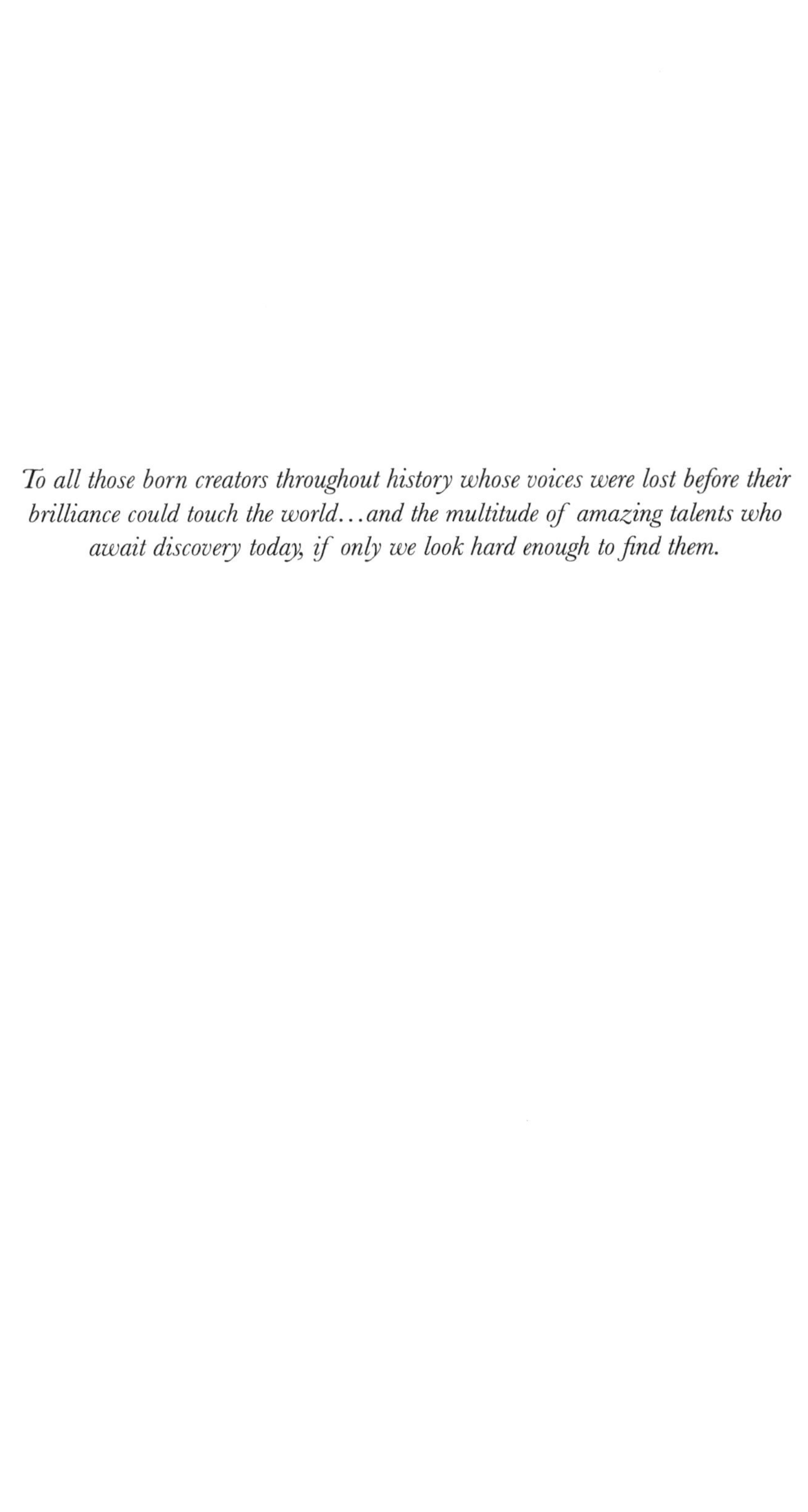

To all those born creators throughout history whose voices were lost before their brilliance could touch the world…and the multitude of amazing talents who await discovery today, if only we look hard enough to find them.

CONTENTS

INTRODUCTION

RON COLLINS

Take a touch of Rod Serling's sense of the absurd, a dash of a comic writer's ability to find the perfect slice of dialog, and mix it with Mike Resnick's ear for story, and I think you've got an idea of what it's like to read Robert Jeschonek's work. Oh, uh, right. Let's toss in a jigger of Douglas Adams for good measure. Thanks for the sardines.

I first met Bob at a workshop that was held maybe a half dozen and a few years ago. I had a general idea of who he was, but hadn't read his work until then. After finishing my first Jeschonek story, I had two thoughts. First was *holy Christ this guy is good.* Second was that I had to meet him. Had to put eyeballs on him. Because there was no way a regular human could do what Bob was doing. He had to be an alien, or maybe some radiated clone experiment gone so wonderfully awry.

Alas, upon connecting that week, I discovered he is, indeed, human, and a remarkably nice one at that. Normal in every way. Kind of, at least.

Some guys get all the good stuff, right?

Anyway.

What you hold in your hands is a treat.

It's the anchor volume to a monstrous 100-story volume Bob's putting out as a celebration of sorts.

This volume contains something nearly forty stories, each one like a piece from Forrest Gump's box of chocolates.

Just reading down the table of contents will bring a smile to your day. There's something else Bob can do—turn a title. Color me envious. "When the Sandwich Comes for You." Seriously, Bob? "Messiah 2.0?" "When We Get Done With Mr. Giraffe." "The Men Without Heads Join A Health Club." "The First Hollywood Cowboy of the Bropocalypse." I can go on, but that would rob you of the pure joy of the process. Seriously, simply pull up the table of contents and read that. It's like spending a slice of time at open-mic night at the most perfect beatnik bar.

And that's before we get to the works inside those titles.

Bob entertains. He opens up his brain, then opens up yours and pours in an amalgam of stuff you never thought went together, but simply does. I am so convinced this happens that sometimes after finishing one of these stories, I'd run my fingertip around my forehead, feeling for the metaphorical scar from the surgery he'd performed. You cannot get something like "Dreaming of a Carboniferous Christmas," or "Dirty Dreams of a Dishwasher" any other way.

Each story sits there like a confetti-filled time bomb and just when you think you're getting a whoopie cushion, Bob brings in the artillery and comes up with something like "Wave A White Flag," and you finish it, and sit there stunned in your thoughts by the raw power of that moment that happens when you know you've hit something deeper than you'd like to admit you can hold inside.

That's how it is here.

And that's why I say you're holding a treat.

You really have no idea what you're in for when Bob Jeschonek starts up the story machine inside him. There is simply no describing what it's like without you simply wading in.

I'm willing to bet a very large lunch that neuroscientists from planet systems around the universe would pay to see an atomic level MRI of Bob's brain working as it churns out another one of these events.

I know I would, and I'm sure I can't read an MRI.

At all.

Of course, that wouldn't matter. I can make it up on my own just find.

I envision clowns. Lots of clowns, with laugh blasters. And aliens on hamster wheels connected to plot twist generators that are fed into quantum shedders to be sprinkled on top of the ice cream of Bob's hippo-campus. Which, of course is a hippopotamus in college. Probably Prince-ton. Please, make it stop. Or go on. I don't know.

Anyway, Bob, you're welcome for the idea. I figure it's already written.

If you read one Bob Jeschonek story you will know what I mean when I say he would Tom Sawyer the hell out of going to his own MRI reading, and if this introduction achieves nothing more than the creation of that story, I've done the universe a happiness, indeed.

So, where was I?

Introduction. Right.

Bob Jeschonek, and short stories in volume three of his *100th Power* special.

What you hold in your hand is a treat.

Now, go enjoy it.

Ron Collins
2023

DOG AND PONY SHOW

People say the needles of a dog are a boy's best friend, and I believe them.

I mean, the nozzles are okay, too, and I shiver with delight when they unfold from my dog Wazoo's gleaming carapace. I love when they spray the green gas that makes me work harder, or the purple gas that makes the daydreams come.

But the *needles* are the *most* magic part of the dog. Just ask anyone.

One minute, I'm collapsed on the concrete floor of my bin, exhausted from another triple shift of Playtime. The next minute, ol' Wazoo is scuttling over to me on his six spiny black legs, barking sweetly.

K-klak klik buzzzz klak klik.

Right away, as tired as I am, I'm smiling again. I can't help it. My pup always takes good care of me.

As his glossy black face gazes down at me, shiny silver needles poke out from the hundreds of facets in his big, bulbous eyes. When he leans closer, they jab into my nose, and I smell his voice in my mind, singing a story of very strong perfume like the scent given off by rotting flesh. Can there be anything more soothing to a ten-year-old boy like me, living with the perfect dog in the paradise of Beastbless, in the parish of Menagerie?

Among dog lovers, this is what we call a good nose-lick. And it is enough, all alone, to make life worth living.

Do you know how lucky I am to have a dog at all? Or a dog as great as Wazoo? My same-aged friend, Incompleta, would do *anything* to have Wazoo or any dog like him.

This morning, she reminds me again. "Are you sure you don't want to trade your dog for my breakfast, Beneathy?"

"Thanks, but I already have breakfast." From across the gray table where we eat alongside dozens of fellow Playtimers, I hold up my bowl of delicious red morning clay, sweetened with a garnish of baby chicks. As adorable as they are delicious, the chicks' tiny black bodies scurry around on eight spindly legs, trying to avoid my white plastic spoon.

"I have another idea." She reaches back over her right shoulder, and two long, rust-colored antennae brush her hand. "We could trade *my* pet for *your* pet." The body of a young kitten flows over her shoulder, hundreds of tiny legs flickering under its segmented scarlet shell. The body just keeps coming, wrapping around her three times like a gleaming stole.

"Lovebite *is* adorable." I reach over to pet the kitten's smooth head, laughing as it snaps at me with its jagged pincers.

Incompleta puts her hand under the kitten's mouth, which disgorges a glob of lumpy green ooze. "Just listen to her purr."

"I hear it," I tell her, and I do. *Screee snap shrreee snap screeee.* "What a beautiful sound," I say, though I still believe there's nothing as sweet as the bark of a dog. "Are you serious about trading her? Why would you ever give her up?"

"Because dogs are just the best." Her freckled face reddens as she stares at Wazoo, who then scuttles down off my back and under the table. Lovebite's tail scrolls around Incompleta's head, little legs fluttering through her short red hair. "And *yours* is the best *ever.*"

She's right about that. Smiling, I reach under the table to feel Wazoo's bristly proboscis quivering, making my fingertips sticky. I wouldn't know what to do if I ever lost him; I can hardly remember what life was like before I got him.

"So will you trade him for my kitty?" asks Incompleta.

"No way." I smile as Wazoo hops and barks, bumping the underside of the table. *K-klak klik buzzzz klak klik.*

Incompleta sighs. "I wouldn't, either. Especially with the dog shortage going on."

"There's a shortage?" I spoon scuttling baby chicks and red clay into my mouth and chew.

"That's right." As Incompleta eats the lumpy green ooze, her darling Lovebite rears its head up and jabs a clear spike into the soft spot on top of her skull, sipping pink fluid from her head. I'm a little jealous; as great as dogs are, a cat can still be pretty cute when it's bonding with its owner. "And you better keep a close eye on *your* dog if you don't want to end up at the Pet Pageant empty-handed."

I think about the Pet Pageant a lot during Playtime. It helps take my mind off the screaming things on the Funsembly Line as my fellow Playtimers and I make them extra Beautiful and Happy.

The Pageant happens in less than a week. People and pets from all over Beastbless and the parish of Menagerie will be there, competing to take home awards for Best Bark, Best Fetch, Best Lick, Best Chew, and more. But only *one* animal will win the title of Doggiest Dogaroonie, Prince of Pups—and I'm hoping *that* dog will be Wazoo.

"Hey, Beneathy!" Caustico, the tall, blond boy on the other side of the belt, jabs the tip of his bloody Plaything at the screamer sliding slowly between us. "You missed one!"

Snapping out of my reverie, I instantly spot what he's talking about and jump to fix it. The screamer shrieks at the top of his lungs as I leave my playful mark on his belly, getting him ready for the next level of the Playtime game.

"You wanna *win* this time, or not?" snaps Caustico.

"Sure I do."

"Then pay attention." Caustico flicks blood at me from his Plaything. It will blend right in with my red coveralls and the other blood already soaked into them. "We're supposed to be on the same team, remember?" He puts down the Plaything and reaches for a Joy Stick, its barbed tip cherry-red and smoking.

"I will, I will." Even as I say it, my mind drifts back to the only thing I really want to win. I imagine my wonderful dog atop the Hill of Buddies, barking and flashing his glossy black wings as the top judge drapes a gold medal around his proboscis. I can just see Wazoo flapping up into the air and flying victory laps above the crowd, that beautiful medal swinging and glinting in the sunlight.

K-klak klik buzzzz klak klik.

On the front of the gleaming gold medal is the image of a dog's face, complete with multifaceted eyes with needles jutting out of each facet. Two words are emblazoned around the edge of the medal, following the curved edge:

Doggiest Dogaroonie.

I see a date, too, and the name of the winner, and I feel a rush of joyful warmth from head to toe. As wonderful as every day of my life is, as lucky as I have always been to be alive and here, this one thing is what I most long to see.

According to the medal in my daydream, the name of the winning dog is Wazoo, and this year is when he will win the title of Doggiest Dogaroonie.

The bunnies are biting outside when I take Wazoo for a walk after Playtime. Clouds of them swirl around us, tiny dark flecks getting in my eyes and nipping at my skin—making me smile with each tiny bite, because who doesn't love bunnies and their tender little kisses?

Wazoo, as usual, scuttles back and forth before me, probing black masses and smears left behind by other pets on the sidewalk. Once in a while, he gets excited and pops out his wings, shooting pink mist from the special white nozzles exposed along his back. The mist, which smells sweet like burning plastic and drying paint, always makes me feel a little tipsy when I get a whiff of it.

Suddenly, Wazoo stops zigzagging and bolts off the sidewalk on a beeline. He drags me along behind him through the brush, holding on to his prickly leash for dear life.

"What are you doing, boy?" I duck out of the way of a low-hanging branch that narrowly misses my head. "Where are you going?""

Wazoo, who has never done anything like this before, answers by buzz-snorting and picking up speed, rushing even more recklessly onward. I stumble on a rock, then trip on a root, nearly going down both times—but miraculously stay on my feet.

K-klak klik buzzzz klak klik.

Wazoo's barks get louder the further off-trail we go. The loudest comes when he hurtles into a clearing and stops. When I stumble in behind him, I see why.

Wazoo isn't a big fan of complete strangers, and the clearing is full of them. Three cops in standard gray uniforms encircle a crouching man and a little boy, younger than me, on his knees.

When the cops hear us, they move apart enough for me to see that the boy is crying and cradling something in his arms… something so misshapen, I can't figure out what it is.

K-klak klik buzzzz klak klik.

Bzzzzeeeeeekkk.

I've never heard Wazoo bark like that before, like some kind of broken machine. His wings unfold, and he takes to the air; I have to let go of the leash as he flies circles around the strangers in the clearing.

"What's going on here?" The words rush out of me, though I feel like I'm intruding.

The boy's face is wet with tears and smudged with black as he looks up at me. Moving closer, I see by the fading light that his arms are full of broken pieces of something black and shiny. Multicolored fluids drip from his elbows and run down his knees, pooling in the dirt.

His father drops a hand on his shoulder, but the boy only sobs harder. "W-who would *do* something like this?" The boy asks the question as if I know the answer. "Who would k-kill my sweet Gilgamog?"

Only when he says it and holds out the broken pieces do I realize what has happened here. Only then do I understand what has been in his arms since before I arrived.

And my heart sinks. My belly twists, and I want to run away that very second. "Your poor dog…"

"I loved her with all my *h-heart*," says the boy. "And now somebody *k-killed* her!"

"Somebody or some*thing*," corrects one of the cops, a male.

"We don't know which one yet," says a female cop.

"It doesn't matter." The boy slumps to the ground on his side, still clutching the broken pieces of his beloved dog. His voice grows soft as he shivers with sobs. "She's d-dead. My dog is *d-dead.*"

Meanwhile, Wazoo keeps circling overhead, making that new sound as he passes.

Bzzzzeeeeeekkk.
Bzzzzeeeeeekkk.
Bzzzzeeeeeekkk.

People say the world would be a dark and awful place without the Nylon Knights around to keep it bright. Seeing them ride into town the next morning atop their handsome steeds, I believe it.

The seven men and women ride tall in the saddle, clad in gleaming white plastic armor from head to toe. The long lances they carry are just as perfectly white, and so are the saddles they sit on. Proud and strong, the Knights stare straight ahead, fixed on their mission with unwavering focus.

Their legendary horses are just as impressive. Their long green bodies clamber down the street, perfectly balanced and nimble on slender legs though they hardly look sturdy enough to carry the weight of armored riders. With spiny forelegs always folded, they look like they're constantly begging or praying—

though the truth is, those legs can swing and clamp suddenly in time of battle.

Who could resist running over to touch such beautiful animals? Not me. Along with a dozen other young Playtimers, I hurry over on the way to the Funsembly Line and pet the bright green hide of the closest horse. The hide is one of the nicest things I've ever touched, studded with points and bumps and jagged burs that prick my skin and draw blood. It feels so good, I could gladly pet it for the rest of the day, if I had time.

HSSSSS. As the horse whinnies, its triangular head spins around, and its big green eyes look my way. *HSSSKLAK.*

"They're so pretty!" Incompleta is beside me, stroking the leafy green folds of the horse's wing. "I wish *I* had a pony like this!"

"Is there any animal you *don't* want?" I ask her.

"A giraffe, maybe," she tells me. "Too many *fangs* and too much *venom*, you know?"

Just then, the knight spurs the horse, and it trots out of reach. We move on to the next in line, which turns out to have an even nicer hide. Two strokes along its leg, and my hand is speckled with blood.

Impetuous as ever, Incompleta shouts up at the Nylon Knight. "Why are you here? Is it because of the dog killer?"

The Knight, a woman, judging from the cut of its armor, glances down at us. Two eyes glow bright red from the darkness under her visor—and then a third glows bright yellow between them. "Curfew begins now." Her voice is a droning monotone. "Proceed to your Playhouse and lock yourselves inside until further notice."

"Do you know who's taking and killing the pets?" asks Incompleta. "Do you know where to find him?"

"Information later," says the Knight. "Curfew begins now." With that, she spurs her horse, which rears up and whinnies before galloping off with the rest of the team.

HSSSSS. HSSSKLAK.

Incompleta sighs. "I want a pony more than *ever* now."

"Have you ever thought of becoming a Nylon Knight?" I ask

as Wazoo scuttles up between us. "Then you'd get a pony for sure."

"Only if I get to keep Lovebite." She pats her shoulder, and the long red kitten crawls up her back from under her shirt and wraps itself around her head like a multi-legged, segmented turban. "And a dog like Wazoo, of course. And maybe a giraffe, after all. Wearing a Knight's super-hard plastic armor would make its poisonous fangs easier to deal with, wouldn't it?"

There's no law against leaving Playtime early because who would want to? The Funsembly Line is just what the name says—fun to the *max.*

But today, for the first time in my life, leaving early is exactly what I do. I leave *three hours* early, believe it or not.

And it's all because of Incompleta and her cat.

"Beneathy! You've got to help me!" She dashes into the room in a frantic state, eyes wide and hair wild. "Lovebite is gone!"

I admit, I'm annoyed at the interruption. The screamer on the belt is in peak shriek, and I've got a fired-up Joy Stick with his name on it. "Gone?"

"She slipped away somehow!" Incompleta grabs my sleeve. "I was busy playing and only just noticed."

"Where could she have gone?"

"Anywhere! You know how cats are!" She shakes my arm roughly, oblivious to all the Playtimers who are staring our way. "Please, Beneathy! Help me find her!"

The screamer's going berserk. I have to finish him ASAP or someone else will get to have all the fun. "She's probably just somewhere in the Playhouse."

"She's *not,*" snaps Incompleta. "I've looked *everywhere.* She has to be outside. Maybe she sneaked out through a vent or a crack or something."

"I'm sure she's fine." I shrug off her hand and turn back to the screamer, raising the Joy Stick over his already-flaming navel. "Cats can take care of themselves pretty well."

That's the last straw for Incompleta. With a loud grunt, she knocks the stick from my hand, seizes my arm, and drags me away from the Funsembly Line.

I try to pull away, but she's got a firm grip. Other Playtimers look like they think about helping me, but none of them do.

When we get to the doorway, I grab hold of the jamb and fight, determined to stay put. She responds by swinging me around against the wall and getting up in my face.

"What if it was *your* pet who was missing?" Even as she hisses out the words, Wazoo scurries around us, bumping our legs and barking. "Would you do nothing and just hope he came back?"

K-klak klik buzzzz klak klik.

Wazoo's barks change my mind. So does the memory of the kid from the clearing the night before, the one crying over the broken corpse of the dog called Gilgamog.

Incompleta is right.

I shake my head and stop fighting. "Can somebody cover for me? I need to go look for a cat."

"Sure!" Caustico's only too happy to take my place. "But I don't think the Nylon Knights make exceptions to the curfew for *cat-finders.*"

"Here, Kitty Kitty!" calls Incompleta as we wander the forest of Beastbless. "Come to Mama, little Lovebite!"

The noise makes me nervous. I keep looking around, worried that the Nylon Knights might hear and punish us for breaking curfew…or worse, that the pet killer might decide to kill something other than pets. Sneaking out of the Playhouse might not have been the smartest move we've ever made.

Though of course I want to find Lovebite, too. I can't stand the thought of any pet owner, especially a fellow Playtimer, going without the sweet companion that makes life worth living.

"Lovebite!" My calls aren't as loud, but at least I bring another helper to the search. Antennae wiggling, Wazoo crashes through the brush by my side, snuffling at the vegetation with his bristly proboscis. If there's one thing a dog's good at, it's hunting down a cat.

"Where *is* she?" Incompleta stomps her foot in frustration. "We keep getting farther from the Playhouse, and there's still no sign of her!"

"Chasing a mouse, probably. Cats can't resist the *claws* and *stingers* on those things." I push through a patch of waist-high weeds, but nothing jumps out at me. Nothing much interests Wazoo, either.

"What if the killer got her?" Incompleta sounds panicky, and her eyes well up with tears. "What if the reason she's not coming to me is that she's dead?"

"I'll bet she's fine. Cats have nine lives, don't they?" I smile her way with a confidence I don't really feel.

But it's hard to keep up a good front as we search further without success. Either Lovebite's a great hider, a fast traveler, or something's happened to her—an accident or attack by another animal if not the pet killer.

Suddenly, though, Incompleta gets excited. She ducks down at the base of a big tree and picks up a bloody mass of fluff and feathers.

"Look, Beneathy! I'd recognize this dead goldfish anywhere! It's the work of my sweet little Lovebite!"

Just then, we hear a loud animal cry from nearby, followed by the sound of thrashing through the brush, moving rapidly away.

Without a word or hesitation, Incompleta leaps up and bolts away in the direction of the thrashing. I'm about to race off after her when I have a sudden change of plan.

K-klak klik buzzzz klak klik.

Barking his head off, Wazoo charges in the opposite direction, running so hard that he snaps his leash. Whatever he's after, I can't see or even hear it.

But what if he's heading into danger?

I hesitate for an instant, looking one way and then the other. Wazoo and Incompleta might both need my help. Which one do I go after?

Bzzzzeeeeeekkk.

As soon as I hear that sound, the one Wazoo made at the scene of the other dog's murder, my mind is made up. I run after him as fast as I can, leaving Incompleta to her own devices.

Bzzzzeeeeeekkk.

But as I run, and Wazoo keeps making those sounds, I wish I'd brought a Joy Stick from the Playhouse or something else I could use as a weapon. I'm just so used to a world where pets aren't killed, and the only Playtime happens on the Funsembly Line, I didn't even think about it.

Bzzzzeeeeeekkk.

Bzzzzeeeeeekkk.

Bzzzzeeeeeekkk.

But I'm thinking about it now. As I burst into a thicket of trees and see Wazoo face to face with some kind of monster, I'm thinking about it *hard.*

Because the monster, with its four legs, long tail, and mottled brown and black fur, is crouching, baring its gleaming white fangs, and making a noise deep in its throat that can mean only one thing.

Grrrrrrrrrrrr.

And that one thing is Playtime, monster style.

Ears flattened back against its head, the monster snaps its jaws and lets loose an unholy howl.

Raarrrrhh.

My heart's pounding, my hands are shaking—but Wazoo is unfazed. Fanning out his black wings, he roars at the monster with more menace than I've ever seen him muster.

SCREEE KLAK EEEE AAARRKK.

The monster lunges, snapping and howling with wild ferocity.

RAARRRR RARRRR RARRRRR.

Instead of backing down, Wazoo lunges at the monster, spraying green gas from one nozzle and black from another. The monster lurches back, coughing and shaking its head hard.

Wazoo presses the attack, unleashing more plumes of gas. His opponent coughs harder than ever and stumbles back on shaky legs, his savagery flagging.

Just as I cheer in my heart, however, things suddenly change. Loud, heavy footfalls pound toward us, accompanied by violent thrashing. Another monster explodes into the thicket, much bigger than the first—a four-legged beast taller than I am, with glossy black hair and a long face with a bone-white stripe down the middle. Before Wazoo can direct any sprays in its direction, this monster whips around and lashes out with its two hind legs, blasting a brutal kick in his direction.

The new monster's feet land with such force that they propel Wazoo across the thicket into a tree trunk. He slams into the wood and bounces off, dropping into a patch of weeds where he lies motionless on his back, leaking multicolored gases from his nozzles.

"Wazoo!" I start to run to him, but I don't get far. The bigger, black-haired monster lumbers between us, blocking the way.

And then it gets worse. *More* monsters straggle in from all sides of the thicket, closer in size to the first—each covered in fur of a different color yet essentially the same type of creature as the first monster to attack. They all have similar shapes, with stubby snouts, black noses, and tails… and they all make the same noise in their throats as they converge around me.

Grrrrrrrrrr.

I look around frantically for a way out or a weapon but find neither. I'm trapped and helpless in the midst of monsters who might have just killed my faithful companion.

Grrrrrrrrrr.

The biggest monster with the bone-white face backs out of the way as the other monsters come closer. They let him through, concerned only with me.

"Go away!" I try to sound tough. "Get out of here! Leave me alone!"

It doesn't work. The ring of monsters tightens.

"I said go!" I start to realize this might be it, the end, and I wonder: Is this what happened to the missing and murdered pets?

Suddenly, then, I hear an unexpected sound—a *whistle*. The kind of whistle only a human being can make.

And then a voice. The voice of a boy my age or not much older.

"So tell me." When the boy steps into the thicket, I see he has long blond hair and bright blue eyes. His clothes are very brown, very dirty, or both, and his face and hands are caked with grime. "Should I call off the dogs, or let 'em have you?"

I stare at the growling monsters arrayed around me. "Those aren't dogs," I tell him, though I know I shouldn't talk back, given the circumstances. "I *have* a dog."

The new boy chuckles. "No offense, kid, but you're barking up the wrong damn tree."

The boy, who says his name is Joe, leads me off through the forest with the monsters in tow. If I try to get away, he warns me, the monsters—which he insists on calling "dogs" and a "horse"—will run me down, and I might get hurt.

But otherwise, he promises, hurting me is the last thing he wants to do.

"Then what *do* you want to do to me?" I ask him.

"I want to tell you the truth," says Joe. "Though, to be honest, *that* might hurt a little bit, too."

We walk for what seems like a very long time, weaving between trees and through brush. I keep looking around, hoping I'll see Wazoo zooming to the rescue with nozzles fuming… but all I see are sharks flitting around, chirping, and flapping their colorful, feathered wings. The sight of them with their pointy little beaks makes me shiver, the way sharks always do.

When we come to a little stream, the "dogs" and "horse" stop to drink, their pink tongues lapping up the trickling water amid sunbeams cast down through the treetops. It's sickening; everyone *knows* dogs only get their moisture by sipping it from the bodies of *dead* things.

"You've never spent time with real animals, have you?" Joe

runs his hand along the side of the "horse," stroking its glossy black hair. "I'll bet you've never even touched one, have you?"

"You don't know what you're talking about." I know I'm scowling, but I can't help it. I hate him and all his monsters.

"Or maybe *you're* the one who doesn't truly understand." Joe reaches down, and a big "dog" with shaggy golden fur trots over and licks his fingers.

Watching that happen makes my stomach churn. I think I might throw up—but not yet.

Smiling, Joe pats the beast's head, and the "dog's" tail flicks quickly from side to side. "It's not your fault," he tells me. "All you know is what you were taught."

"*You* don't know *anything.*"

"But that's all right." Joe whistles, and the "dogs" and "horse" stop drinking and start across the stream. "You really *can* teach an old dog new tricks, my friend."

After a while, we come to an ancient cabin at the base of a tree-lined hillside, which seems to be our destination. The "dogs" run barking to the decrepit front door, and the "horse" ambles over to a rickety water trough for a drink.

"Welcome to camp." Joe claps a hand on my shoulder and leads me toward the ramshackle little building. "Or as I like to call it, Home-for-Now."

The front door opens, and a tall old man looks out from a cloud of wispy white hair. The "dogs" go crazy, jumping on their hind legs and pawing at his torso and chest. "Good boys," he tells them. "Good dogs."

"Hey Grampa!" shouts Joe. "Look what I found!"

"Oh, Joe." Grampa wags his head. "What have I told you about bringing home strays?"

"But he doesn't know what a real *dog* is," says Joe. "He doesn't know about the *old days.*"

Grampa eases his way out the door, feeding the jumping "dogs" with chips of black jerky from the pockets of his tattered denim overalls. "He's probably better off that way. The truth *hurts*."

"I already told him about that." Joe guides me forward. "Maybe he can take it."

Eyes narrowed, Grampa stoops and meets my gaze. "The others won't like it when they get back from the hunt. They'll say you shouldn't have brought him here."

"But isn't this why we're doing it?" asks Joe. "For people like him?"

"Doing what?" I frown. "Who are the others, and what are they hunting?"

Grampa shakes his head. "You remember what happened to the last one you brought in?" He isn't speaking to me.

Joe sighs in frustration. "Just *tell* him. Please?"

I've never had anyone stare at me as hard as Grampa does then. He makes me so uncomfortable, I squirm and want to run away.

Reaching into his pocket, he pulls out a two-inch-long strip of jerky. "Take it." When I don't reach for it, he grabs my hand and presses the jerky into my palm. "Now give it to him." He gestures at one of the "dogs"—a little white-and-tan furred one with pointy ears, short legs, and big green eyes. "His name is Stubby."

Stubby scampers toward me, licking his lips. Heart pounding, I jump back and drop the jerky. Stubby gobbles it up and gazes at me, clearly hoping for more.

"Congratulations," says Grampa. "You just fed an actual dog."

Stubby hops up and sniffs my fingers. I wipe them on my pants to try to shed the smell of the jerky, but then he just sniffs and licks my pants.

"Those *other* things," says Grampa. "The ones you and everyone else think of as dogs—they *aren't*." He walks back to the cabin and returns a moment later with a white plastic bag. It crinkles as he opens it and reaches inside. "*This* isn't a *dog.*"

He pulls something out of the bag, and my blood turns icy cold. I back away when he holds it up to me, stopped only by Joe when he clamps a hand on my shoulder.

"*This* is a *bug*."

Grampa is wrong. I don't care *what* he says. The thing in his hand is *nothing* like a *bug*.

It's a *dog*, a true *dog*, just like Wazoo, complete with a black proboscis, a shiny black shell that opens up into wings, and bulbous eyes with hundreds of facets for popping out the silver needles that are a boy's best friend.

But for once, a dog like this isn't a welcome sight. This one isn't moving. It doesn't make even the slightest twitch, and the reason is clear.

Its body has a gaping hole in it.

"It's dead." A thought occurs to me, and I feel sicker than ever. "You *killed* it, didn't you?"

Grampa doesn't answer my question. "If you tell enough people this is a *dog*, they *accept* that it's a dog." Black bits of the dead dog trickle out as he shakes it emphatically. "They forget what a *real* dog is like. Or a *cat*, or a *horse*. Or a *life*. They forget that things could be different. *Better*."

Grampa tosses the dead dog aside and marches over to grab my arm. He grips it so hard that it hurts.

"But *some* of us remember. And we tend the *packs* and tell the *stories* and wait for the day when the *better* things replace the *ugly* ones."

"Because you kill them!" I twist free of Grampa's grip. Joe makes a grab for me, and I push him away. "That's what you *do*, isn't it? You're the ones who've been killing the pets!"

"They aren't pets," says Grampa. "They're monsters. They're *controlling* you, and you don't even know it."

"Did you kill *my* dog, too? Did you kill Wazoo?"

Grampa stands there, glaring, and shakes his head. "His indoctrination is *deep*, isn't it?" Again, he's talking to Joe, not me. "I don't know if we can ever get through to him."

"That's what you used to say about me, too," says Joe.

"That's true." Grampa's features soften. "Maybe you're right."

"We should take a break, don't you think?" says Joe.

"Sure." Grampa turns and heads for the cabin. He pulls jerky out of his pocket, and the "dogs" come running. "We'll pick it up later."

But as I watch him go, taking a break is the last thing on my mind. If these people killed Wazoo, or even Lovebite, I will *never* see things their way. I will *never* forgive them.

And I will *never* let go of the life and world I know.

"Come on," says Joe. "Let's go play with the puppies."

"Play? Like on the Funsembly Line?" It doesn't make sense. "But I don't have a Joy Stick or Plaything. I don't even have a *man opener.*"

"Don't worry." Joe walks off, gesturing for me to come with him. "Different kind of play."

Joe and I hike to a nearby field, followed by a dozen "dogs." The afternoon sun shines bright on the tall grass waving in the warm breeze.

None of which improves my mood a bit. I don't see how anything could, as long as I'm with one of the people who for all I know might have done something terrible to Wazoo.

Seemingly oblivious to how I'm feeling, Joe scouts through the grass, looking for something. "Have you ever played fetch?" he asks.

"With my dog, a *real* dog, yes." I stay close to the treeline, hoping for a chance to slip away.

Joe sees something and ducks down to retrieve it. "Well, that's what we're going to play." He resurfaces with a stick in his hand, fairly straight and about two feet long. "I'll make the first throw, and you can take the one after that."

When he whistles, the "dogs" fling themselves in front of him, jumping around and making noise.

Rarrrr Rarrr Rarrr Rarrrr Rarrrr.

"Fetch!" When he gives the stick a throw, the "dogs" scramble after it, churning pell-mell across the field. One of them, a big white "dog" with black spots and floppy black ears, scoops it away from another "dog" (a little one with gray fur and a pushed-in face) and runs it back to Joe with a spring in his step.

"Good boy! Good boy!" Joe scratches behind the "dog's" ears and takes the stick. As he reels it up and back for another throw, the spotted "dog" jumps around crazily, never taking his eyes off the thing. As soon as Jack heaves it, the "dog" bolts off after it, joined by several others.

"You ready?" Joe shouts in my direction. "Want to give it a shot?

"That isn't *fetch,*" I tell him. "Not enough *fire.*"

"There's no fire in *real* fetch." When Joe gets the stick back, he throws it my way. "Now you try."

Instinctively, I catch it, but I'm flustered when the "dogs" come bounding after it.

Rarrr Rarrr Rarrr Rarrr.

"Just throw it!" shouts Joe. "As far as you can, so they get a good run!"

I hesitate, and the "dogs" press closer. When the spotted one jumps up, grazing my chest with a paw, it's enough to make me panic and pitch the stick with a sudden burst of strength. It spins across the field, taking the pack of "dogs" with it, and the stress they make me feel.

But the relief doesn't last long. Seconds later, the spotted "dog" hurtles back through the grass with the stick in its mouth, heading straight for me.

"Thank him and do it again!" says Joe. "Tell him what a good boy he is and give him another throw!"

Taking a slobbered-on piece of wood from the mouth of a drooling monster and possible killer of *real* dogs is the last thing I want to do right now. I know I should play along, but I flinch when the beast pushes the stick at me. I turn away, and he follows, persistent.

"Just do it! Just throw it!" Joe laughs. "He won't hurt you, I promise!"

As I turn away again, the other "dogs" barrel up and hurl themselves at me, leaping with jaws open to seize the stick. I let it go as I fall under the weight of them, unable to stop from toppling into the grass.

My heart hammers, and I'm short of breath when I hit. It's like something out of a nightmare as the pack of "dogs" converge around me, all fur and teeth and lolling pink tongues.

It only gets worse from there. One "dog" licks my face, dragging its tongue over my cheek, and I want to scream. Then another licks my face as well, and another.

And another. Stubby, the pointy-eared, short-legged one, licks my face with as much enthusiasm as he licked my jerky-scented fingers earlier.

I close my eyes, toss my head, and thrash on the ground, but it doesn't seem to help. The licking continues, three and four tongues at a time slathering my cheeks and nose and ears and mouth.

And then the *truly* unexpected happens. Against my will, against my better judgment, I start to *giggle.* Something about the combined action of those tongues on my face makes me squirm and laugh uncontrollably.

I reach up to bat away the monsters, and my hands come in contact with fur. I want to pull away, but I'm surprised at the feel of it; I've always been taught it's rough and prickly, but it's not. Something about it makes me want to keep touching it, running my hand over it just to feel the smooth texture.

"Are you okay?" Joe's standing over me, holding the fetch stick.

"This fur." I run my hands over Stubby's shaggy white-and-tan coat. "It isn't *soft* at all."

"Sure it is. It's *very* soft."

"*Soft* means it hurts my hands." I pet the "dog" some more, amazed. "This is the *opposite* of soft."

Joe nods and smiles. Maybe he understands. "Whatever you want to call it, 'Neath."

I frown up at him, still petting the monster. "My name is Beneathy."

"Well, now you have a nickname," says Joe. "I like 'Neath better, don't you?"

Just then, something crashes through the grass across the field, and Stubby yaps and scampers off. Joe quickly helps me up, and we look toward the commotion.

Five camouflage-wearing men riding "horses" are coming our way, looking grim. The "dogs" dart among them, tails wagging, calling out.

Rarrr Rarrr Rarrr.

"Hi, Mike!" Joe waves. "How was the hunt this time?"

The man at the front of the group—a broad-shouldered, middle-aged man with curly black hair and a bushy beard—just scowls and points at me. "Who the hell is that?"

"A new friend," says Joe. "His name is—"

Suddenly, a loud, blaring noise erupts from beyond the field, a single squawk like the blast of some kind of horn. Everyone looks in the direction of the sound, which is also the direction of camp.

Without another word, Mike kicks the sides of his "horse," and it bolts off toward camp at a fast gallop. The other four riders and "horses" follow just as fast, whipping past us with a flurry of "dogs" in their wake.

Joe sprints after them full-tilt, and I run beside him. "What's happening? What was that sound?"

"Grampa was calling for help," says Joe. "Camp is under attack."

As Joe and I race into camp on foot, the battle is already underway. The "horse"-riding hunters fire away with pistols and rifles, the woods booming with shot after shot.

All of which bounce off the gleaming white armor of the Nylon Knights without leaving a mark.

The Knights' weapons are much more effective. I see a male Knight spear a hunter's chest with a long white lance, driving its sharp point through his ribs and out his back, soaked with crimson. Another Knight's great green horse unfolds a spiny foreleg and swings it out to clamp the throat of a hunter, unleashing gushers of blood.

"Grampa!" Joe runs for the cabin, dodging Knights' horses

and hunters' "horses" all around. Stubby scurries after him, too low to the ground to go very fast—or get out of the way of the hunter and wounded "horse" that suddenly topple toward him.

Without thinking, I dash over, grab Stubby by the scruff of his neck, and dive out from under the hunter and "horse." They slam down hard, just missing us as we roll under the wooden trough where Joe's "horse" drank water earlier.

Stubby whines as I keep him tucked under my arm and watch the battle rage from our hiding place. I feel his muscles twitch, but I don't let go. Maybe he wants to run to Joe, but I don't think he'll last long in the midst of that fight.

Not that the hunters are much of a match for the Knights. Soon, only two men in camouflage ride the battlefield amid the seven pristine Knights in white armor.

Suddenly, though, another player joins the fray. "Bastards!" From the doorway of the cabin, Grampa blasts away with a shotgun. "Rot in Hell!"

One of his shots hits a horse in its bulging green eye, and its head explodes. The horse goes down hard, throwing its rider to the ground without his lance.

Grampa's next shot isn't as lucky. It goes right between the pair of Knights who charge him with lances aimed directly at his chest.

They penetrate his chest from either side. Grampa drops the shotgun, and his eyes roll up in his head. He dangles like a meat puppet from the lances, held erect only by their crimson-dripping points.

Meanwhile, the pack of "dogs" attacks the Knight who lost his horse, lunging and snapping furiously. Their teeth have no chance of piercing the white armor, but they keep him pinned down, flailing at them with his barb-knuckled gauntlets.

He doesn't stay down for long, though. Just as one of the "dogs" pounces, knocking him over on his back, a winged figure bursts from the woods, heading straight for them and making a familiar sound.

K-klak klik buzzzz klak klik.

"Wazoo!" My heart jumps with excitement at the sound and

sight of him—the realization that he isn't dead after all. He was only wounded and managed to recover from his injuries in time to come to the rescue.

K-klak klik buzzzz klak klik.

Swooping down at the "dogs," Wazoo unleashes black gas from one of his nozzles. Plumes of it swirl around the monsters, making them cough and retch and stagger off with their tails between their legs.

The Knight coughs, too, but he doesn't let it stop him from clambering to his feet and running back to help his comrades.

At this point, the outcome of the battle is no longer in doubt. The Knights surround the last two hunters, whose guns have stopped working. It won't be long until the circle of lances pointing at them moves inward, ending the fight.

In other words, I'm about to be rescued.

So why do I stay hidden under the trough? Wazoo buzzes around camp, spraying monsters with more of his black gas. I should be running to him.

But I'm not.

Stubby's body is warm against me. His fur feels good between my fingers. Something about him makes me want to hold on to him.

But my loyal dog, my precious Wazoo, is *right there*, awaiting what will surely be a joyous reunion with me. I can just imagine how wonderful it will feel to have his needles pierce my nose again, to smell his voice in my mind after so long apart.

So why am I thinking about sneaking away from him, crawling off into the forest with Stubby? Has this monster cast a spell on me?

I look at Stubby, and he looks back at me with wide, green eyes. For reasons unknown, he leans toward me and licks my nose with his wet, pink tongue.

For reasons unknown, I let him.

K-klak klik buzzzz klak klik.

Then, I watch Wazoo flying past, and I realize something.

I don't want to give up *either* of them. Perhaps, there's a way I won't have to.

People say winning isn't everything. But right now, it's all I can think about.

A few days ago, hiding under a trough at the hunters' camp in the woods, I wasn't sure what the future would bring. Now here I am, standing in front of thousands of people in Beastbless Stadium, waiting to hear if my greatest dream is about to come true.

Dozens of other Playtimers and their pets are lined up beside me on the artificial turf field, likewise waiting for the verdict. Do any of them want this as much as I do? It doesn't seem possible.

But winning *does.* The pet I have at my side is so wonderful in *every* way. He did so magnificently well in every event, I can't imagine him *not* winning.

But if he doesn't, it won't be the end of the world. What I went through at the camp prepared me for any adversity—even as it increased my chances of winning. *Our* chances.

"And now, the moment we've all been waiting for!" The female announcer's voice booms through the stadium P.A. system, drowning out the excited chatter from the stands. "The naming of the *grand prize* in this year's fabulous *Pet Pageant!*"

I take a deep breath to steady my nerves. Incompleta, who's sitting down in front, blows me a kiss for luck. Lovebite, who eventually came back to her that day in the woods, twines her segmented scarlet body around her head and neck, antennae twitching.

A drumroll begins as the announcer keeps talking. "This year's *Doggiest Dogaroonie* is..."

The tension in the stadium reaches its absolute peak...but I suddenly feel calm. Closing my eyes, I whisper my pet's name.

And then the announcer says it, too. "...*Wazoo!*"

The crowd roars and cheers. The other pet owners on the field slump with disappointment.

As for me, I turn to my dog and pat him on his furry head, right between his pointy little ears. "Good boy, Wazoo! You did it!"

Wazoo's bristly proboscis twitches. He fidgets, unable to take a victory flight to mark the occasion.

That's because Stubby's white-and-tan fur, which is clipped to his body, keeps him from deploying his wings.

It's a small price to pay, though. I'm convinced that fur is what clinched Wazoo's winning the prize today. It made him unique, the best of both worlds—dog and monster, united.

Because of that fur, I am able to walk the perimeter of the field proudly with Wazoo and Stubby both by my side, in their own ways. And as we finish that victory lap and climb the Hill of Buddies in the middle of the field—all those hundreds of bodies processed during Playtime throughout the year, including the hunters and Grampa and Joe from the camp—I feel like I owe Wazoo and Stubby a debt of gratitude I can never truly repay.

So when I stand atop that hill, and the crowd continues to roar around me like the ocean, I give those two dogs—one real and one fake—the best tribute I can think of. I raise my arms overhead and cry out in the only languages they might appreciate.

Rarrr Rarrr Rarrr Rarrr.

K-klak klik buzzzz klak klik.

Though the meaning of what I've just said is forever lost to me, not that it truly matters or ever will.

WHEN THE SANDWICH COMES FOR YOU

Bowie Stevedore, sitting cross-legged on the pebbled cement floor, pulled another strip of parchment out of the big copper bowl and read aloud what was written upon it:

Failed in his field and utterly alone, the Expanding Man found success in his addiction, excelling in the gratification of his appetites in ways that someday, he was certain, would again make him the legend he had once been.

Bowie shook his head and tossed that latest bit of parchment atop the pile on his left, which was where the first lines of stories went. Last lines, which were also mixed in the bowl, went on the righthand pile.

In the green light of the glass-domed Temple of Telling, Bowie pulled them one at a time from the bowl, sorting the jumbled beginnings and endings as the Story God had commanded. There were thousands of them, he guessed, maybe more; he'd been at it for a week, yet the bowl seemed to be no emptier.

Bowie combed his fingers through his wavy silver hair and thought of the old days, the days of accolades and bestsellers, back before submitting to the Story God's whims became his only path to restoring his greatness as a writer. Back then, snippets like those in the bowl would have prompted him to write, the beginnings and endings like the halves of a sandwich he could not resist. The filling—the words in between—would have been nothing short of magnificent.

Not anymore, though. He reached for another:

Though I was next in line to be killed, I clapped for all I was worth as the executioner used my own severed foot to bludgeon my father to death.

As Bowie read that latest first line, he sensed the manifold possibilities branching off from it. Familiar energies stirred in his heart, and he dared to think his creative powers were reviving.

But when the words finally came, and he wrote them in the ragged notebook he kept in his lap under his big belly, they were not at all what he'd hoped for:

Our thick-cut 18-oz. prime rib filet is simmered to perfection and served with savory au jus and a steaming baked potato topped with creamed goat cheese and Herbes de Provence.

That was what he always came up with these days. *Nothing but food.*

So much for the Story God's promise that Bowie's gift would return if he sorted enough beginnings and endings from the bowl.

Bowie's stomach growled as he reread the prime rib description. He was obsessed with eating; he had come to crave food more and more as his literary skills had gotten less and less masterful.

Shaking it off, he grabbed another snippet from the bowl:

Lithe and languid as the palm fronds waved by the villagers on the day she gave up her goddesshood to marry her younger self, Zephyr stood atop the hill at the heart of the inside-out island and turned in a slow circle by the light of the setting sun.

That one, then, was an ending. Before the writer's block, such a prompt could have inspired Bowie to greatness...but now, though he felt inspired, this is what he scribbled in the notebook:

Bouillabaisse, our signature dish, overflows with scallops, prawns, crab, octopus, and lobster, a succulent mix of sweet, tender seafood bobbing in an aromatic, tomato-based broth.

Frustrated, he flung the notebook across the Temple of Telling, scattering the page-winged butterflies roosting amid the dog-eared book-flowers in the Gardens of Prose. As he did so, his mouth watered at the thought of the bouillabaisse.

A tear ran down his cheek. Was he hopeless after all, in spite of what the Story God had promised? Was there no way he could retrieve his creative spark?

With a sigh, Bowie thrust his hand into the bowl once more and read the parchment slip he fished out with shaky fingers. Would it be a beginning or an ending?

He quickly realized it could be either or both.

"Arise," said the giant sandwich to the Expanding Man, whose name was Bowie Stevedore, "and eat of my substance, and you shall be cleansed of all that has ever tormented you or gnawed upon your soul."

The breath caught in Bowie's throat.

His name in the text was no accident, he was certain. Was it a lesson from the Story God? Was it the thing he'd been destined to find from the start?

As a huge shadow suddenly fell over him, Bowie realized it didn't matter.

Turning, he saw an overstuffed sandwich floating behind him, bigger than his own body—two enormous slices of white bread with a slab of prime rib and chunks of seafood doused in bouillabaisse broth between them. He could smell it in all its glory, and his stomach growled like a ravenous wolf.

Climbing to his feet, he leaned toward the sandwich and opened his mouth.

He was part of the story now, his appetites plot devices. He could freely partake of what he craved and feel no guilt. As for what he could no longer do? The excellence in shaping the written word?

It slipped away forever as he chewed, snaking off into the night like the red line of an editor's pen, sweeping away what was no longer needed.

THE LITTLE ROBOT'S BEDTIME PRAYER

On Wednesday, I finally see what little Occam-657 has been making in that glowing silver box of his during Private Time. And that is what changes my life.

The mere memory of the sight of it sends chills up my spine. Makes my heart beat faster, my pulse pound in my ears.

I was never supposed to see it. By the terms of the Holy Covenant, all Private Time and its products are considered sacrosanct, off limits to Gods like me. But curiosity got the better of me, and I spied on Occam-657. I gazed into the box, and the scales fell from my eyes. I realized one thing that had never before occurred to me.

He has been hiding something extraordinary from me.

"Good morning, God." Occam-657 smiles up at me when I emerge from my bedchamber the next morning. He has been waiting outside my door like a good little household robot, prohibited from doing chores until now lest he wake me prematurely.

I respond to his greeting as if God, and not Sean, is my given name. As if I am an omnipotent deity and not a 37-year-old self-employed genetic engineer specializing in novelty bio-apps. (Remember Thumbo, the elephant who fits in the palm of your hand?) As if I am more than a slightly overweight mere mortal whose wife left him six weeks ago for another man.

"Good morning." I hesitate before laying my hand on his head in the usual fatherly gesture. The memory of what I saw him doing last night is still too fresh in my mind. "Bless you, my child." When my fingers finally alight, the feathery blond hair on his scalp feels as downy as that of a human boy's. Even touching him does not destroy the illusion that he is a 10-year-old boy instead of a manufactured robot.

Occam-657 falls to his knees and shuts his eyes. "You are the way and the light, O' my God. Your mercy endures forever."

His voice is full of awe. He was programmed that way, his artificial intelligence created to show religious piety in the presence of the gods--his human owner and the owners of those like him. Yet the intensity of his devotion seems surprisingly unscripted and genuine at times.

"Dear Lord, will you accept my morning confession?" Occam-657 lifts his clasped hands and leans his forehead against them.

I wonder what he'll say. Will he talk about what I saw last night? "Go ahead."

"Forgive me, God, for I have sinned." There is a quaver in his voice. "It took me .00001 seconds longer than my optimal time to prepare your holy repast for this morning."

I touch his head once more. "That is unfortunate, but I forgive you." Then, I reach up and pat my own blond hair, which is sticking up all over the place after being slept on. "What else, my child?"

He pauses, and I think there's more coming...but no. "Only that which I have told you, O' mighty and benevolent Lord my God."

I can't keep the disappointment from my voice. "Then you are forgiven in my name, for mine is the kingdom and the power and the glory..."

"...forever and ever, amen." Occam-657 bows his head lower and lets out a sound like a choked sob.

So this encounter has told me nothing. "Arise, now, and resume your service to your God." But the heaviest burden lays upon my shoulders. For now that I saw what he did, I have to decide what to do with him.

As I eat my breakfast at the dining room table--the holy altar, I should say--I watch Occam-657 as he goes about his chores. He is no less efficient than ever as he vacuums the glowing golden carpet in the living room (the sanctuary), then dusts every surface and object in sight. He never fails to pause and genuflect when he passes me, showing all due respect and adoration. And the breakfast he prepared--eggs Florentine with crab meat hash and a light dreamfruit marmalade--is no less delicious than every "holy repast" he has ever made in his three years of service in my home. The house runs as well as it ever did before my wife, Cara, left with our other robot attendants, leaving me alone with Occam-657.

It's as if he's done nothing out of the ordinary. As if I saw nothing unexpected last night, and business as usual is the word of the day.

Leaving me to consider some troubling questions. If Occam-657 was programmed to be my devout acolyte, and he truly believes I am an omniscient and all-powerful god, then where and when did he get the idea that he could hide something from me?

And *what else* could he be hiding that I still don't know about?

Occam-657 looks disappointed when I tell him I'm going somewhere without him. He always does; he's programmed to miss the Lord his God every time we're apart, so brightly does my glory shine like a beacon o'er his soul. I'm used to it by now, it hardly ever gets to me.

But today, it does. Given what I saw last night, I worry about what he might get into. He begs me to allow him the honor of accompanying me as my divine retinue, just for the blessing of basking in my presence. For once, I give in and tell him to come along.

We head over to my friend Pander's place in Oathtown in a drone-palanquin, a purple velvet-lined coach carried by four built-in robotic bearers. Occam-657 prays during the entire trip. I tell him to keep it down, but I still hear the soft sibilance of whispered words aspirating from his artificial lips.

Sometimes, I wish the robot manufacturers had never come up with the bright idea of making all the robots worship their owners as gods. It was the best way, the programmers say, to ensure that flesh-and-blood owners never come to harm at the hands of mechanical servitors (though I'm pretty sure human ego might have had more than a little to do with it, as well). But the constant, obsequious worship does tend to get old after a while. For me, at least.

For example, as our palanquin slows to a stop at a busy intersection, a choir of robots on the curb detects my human presence and sings a cyber-hymn in our direction. They chant the sonorous words with great gravity, upraising their folded hands in blissful praise.

I am *so* not in the mood for it right now, and that makes me wonder. Does the real God, if He exists, ever feel the same way? And is it possible, now that we've managed to create our own flock of worshippers, that humanity is finally getting a taste of its own medicine?

"Scrap him." That's Pander's advice when I tell him what Occam-657 was doing. "You've got yourself a faulty unit there, Sean-o."

We're outside on Pander's balcony, having a drink and gazing down at three robots prostrating themselves on the lawn below--two of Pander's, with Occam-657 between them.

I keep my voice low, though it shouldn't matter if the robots hear me. The words of a god are meant to be beyond challenge or reproach in all situations. "I've been thinking the same thing."

Pander sips smart-wine from a golden chalice that glints in the sun. "Is he still under any kind of warranty? You've had him three years, right?"

I nod and sip from my own chalice. "I bought the extended coverage. It doesn't expire for another month."

"Then what's the problem?" Pander's ample jowls jiggle when he chuckles. So does the gut under his vast white robe. He's a genetic engineer, too, dealing as I do in novelty bio-apps...though he's done much better at it than I have (which is saying something, since I haven't exactly been a slouch) and has the bank account and overindulged corpulence to prove it. "What are you waiting for, numb-nuts?"

"I don't know." I watch as Occam-657 grovels ever lower on the ground. He must be praying, but I can't hear it from the balcony. "What if it's something *I've* done wrong?"

Pander laughs some more. "That's impossible! Gods are always right!"

"We're only gods to *them*." I gesture with my chalice toward the robots below.

As if in answer, all three raise their upper bodies from the ground and shout "Hallelujah," eyes shut and hands fluttering ecstatically.

"That's all that matters, isn't it?" Pander elbows me in the side and leans on the balcony railing. "Ask me how many robots I've scrapped over the years."

I already know the answer. "More than I've ever owned in my life. More than my *family* has ever owned."

"Damn right," says Pander. "*Dozens.* As soon as they hiccup out of line, I ship 'em to the scrap heap. End of story. So cut him loose." He makes a sweeping gesture with one puffy hand. "Make a clean break with the past. Quit hanging on to your bitch wife's leftovers."

"That's not it." I frown.

"Time to move on." Pander waves his chalice at the robots. "Why are you hesitating?"

"I just keep thinking." Down below, Occam-657 opens his eyes and meets my gaze. I wonder what thoughts are chugging through his clockwork mind. "What if this is something *new*? What if he's *special* in a way no one has seen before?"

"And everyone's dog is as smart as a person," says Pander. "So why does it still eat its own *shit*?"

I let out a long, slow sigh. It's a beautiful spring day, and the air is filled with the scent of blooming lilacs and new-mown lawns. But all I can focus on is Occam-657. "If there *was* a real God, would he throw *us* away just because we were special or challenging?"

Pander smirks and shrugs. "Who says that isn't the way it's been working all along?"

Why are you hesitating? That's the one thing Pander said that sticks with me. It *eats* at me as I leave his house in another drone-palanquin--this one with a blue velvet coach instead of purple.

It would be so *easy* to drop off Occam-657 at the factory on my way home. Problem solved, and no one could tell me otherwise. When it comes to the existence of my adoring subject, I can do whatever I want. This is one of the perks of being God.

He'll even *thank* me for it, I know. I can already hear the prayers of grateful supplication that will pour forth from his lips when I dump him on the factory's doorstep. No questions asked, no guilt necessary. So why?

Why are you hesitating?

"O' Lord my God." Occam-657 keeps his gaze lowered when he says it. "Though the product of my all too imperfect hands is not fit for your divine consumption, what do you command me to prepare for your evening repast?"

Is it because, as I told Pander, he might represent something new, something special? Is that why I hesitate? "Whatever you choose to prepare will suffice, my child."

"Then I shall make your favorite," says Occam-657. "Broiled sea scallops with a beurre blanc sauce. Asparagus tips with capers and shaved white truffles. Crème brûlée and caviar foam for dessert."

"Hmm. Perhaps." Or is it because, as Pander said, I am hanging on to the last traces of my wife and our life before she left me?

Occam-657 shivers and looks up at me. "Has my suggestion offended thee, O' my God?"

Do I hesitate because I feel responsible for what he's become? Or is it just that I want to understand what has changed to make him do what he has done?

Why are you hesitating?

All of the above, maybe, I think.

"You haven't offended me, Occam-657." I smile and shake my head. "But don't worry about the menu for tonight. I think I'd rather eat out."

We go to a Cuban-Indian deli in Chinatown, and I order Reuben samosas and ropa vieja masala. The robot waitress, a dark-haired unit with bright green eyes, looks only a little older than Occam-657. All such personal service robots were built to childlike specs, designed to minimize the physical danger to us all-too-fragile humans. Better to keep them small in case the religious devotion ever wears off or the other onboard safeguards fail.

It makes for a strange dynamic sometimes, but people have mostly gotten used to it. It's like we're constantly surrounded by kids playing grownup, but the play is for real.

"Is the food sufficient, O' God?" Occam-657 stands at the opposite side of the table and stares at the food on my plate. "Does it offend thee?"

I swallow a bite of samosa and point at the chair in front of him. "Sit, my child."

Occam-657 bows his head. "I am not worthy to share a table with almighty God."

I resist the urge to roll my eyes. "*Sit.* I *command* it."

Reluctantly, Occam-657 pulls out the chair and lowers himself onto it. Even so, he stays well back from the table and keeps his eyes down and hands folded in his lap.

"It is almost time for Church," he says softly.

"Pretty sure Church will wait for us." I can't help smirking. "I'm God, remember?"

If Occam-657 gets the joke, he doesn't show it. "It is true that wherever you go, that is where your holy Church can be found."

I don't offer a comment for that one. I'm too busy looking around the restaurant, watching the other gods and robots at dinner.

They all relate to each other differently. It's something I've never paid much attention to, but given my current situation, it suddenly seems more significant.

Laughter draws my attention to a table across the room, where two brown-haired children are making sport of a blond male robot. The children, who look between six and eight years old--both a good bit smaller than the blond robot--have stripped off the robot's shirt and are smearing his upper body with orange curry sauce. The robot just smiles serenely, hands folded in prayer the whole time. As for the children's mother, she joins in the laughter between bites of salad and talking to someone on the holographic video phone hovering in front of her face.

Things are much different two tables over, where an old man eats soup while sitting across from robot twins--a boy and a girl, both dark-haired. Occasional laughter ripples from that table, too, but it comes as often from the robots as the old man. Somehow, they have made peace with their personal god; they are all at ease with each other.

Though the same cannot be said for the bald robot boy who comes hurtling through the front door at just that instant.

He crashes to the floor in a jumble of arms and legs, sprawled on his back. All laughter and talk in the room cease at once, as all eyes dart in his direction.

A brick wall of a man storms in off the street after him, draped in a black fur coat. "Get up, you worthless *turd!*" His face is flushed crimson as a house fire as he spews the words. His bulbous, over-tattooed head squats like a giant toad atop his mountainous body. "The Lord your God *commands* it!"

"Your every word brings me unutterable joy, O' Lord." The bald boy rolls over and gets up on his knees.

Before the boy can get all the way up, the brick wall grabs a chair from a nearby table and swings it at him like a baseball bat. The chair smashes against the boy, and he topples like a tree, dropping hard on his side.

Every muscle in my body tenses as the beating continues. Instinctively, I want to run over and stop it; others around me look like they might feel the same way. But I can't imagine taking on that brick wall of a man and winning. Besides, he has every right to do what he's doing. That isn't a human boy over there, it's a robot.

And the robot is the brick wall's property.

"Don't you *ever* touch the person of the One True God with your debased synthetic flesh!" The brick wall stomps on the boy with savage force, bringing his sledgehammer feet down again and again.

The bald robot jolts with each impact and does not fight back. I keep reminding myself he's just a machine, but I can't help flinching every time he takes another hit.

The bald robot's voice hitches repeatedly as he recites an Act of Contrition. "O' my God, I am heartily sorry for having...sorry for having offended thee..."

"I am a wrathful God!" shouts the brick wall as he stomps the boy again. "Damnation shall be your only absolution, wretched sinner!"

"...and I detest all my sins because of thy...because of thy just punishments," continues the bald robot. "But most of all, because they offend thee..."

With that, the brick wall grabs the bald robot by the ankles and drags him toward the door. Looking across the table, I see Occam-657 watching as it happens, the expression on his face perfectly neutral.

"You are hereby condemned to the fires of Hell!" roars the brick wall. "I have a *welding torch* with your *name* on it, just waiting to burn some *penitence* into your sorry sinning carcass!"

"...because they offend thee, my God, who are all good and

deserving of all my love." Those are the last words I hear the robot say before his god hauls him out on the street and an eerie silence falls over the restaurant.

Turning to Occam-657, I wonder what he thinks of what he's just seen. He looks at me calmly, as if nothing unusual just happened, and asks if it's time for Church yet.

"A-mazing grace...how sweet the sound..." Occam-657 sings the hymn with eyes and arms uplifted, his bright tenor voice filling the high-ceilinged living room--I mean the sanctuary. "...that saved...a wretch...like meee..."

Yes, it's again time for Church--a daily worship service meant to reinforce the bond between robot and god. It's something I could gladly do without--an hour out of my day that I could be spending on something more productive or entertaining. But every expert agrees that it's a necessary evil. Though robots like Occam-657 spend a lot of time with their god or gods and exist in a state of continuous worship, formalized rituals still help keep them on track. Our robots were programmed to expect and desire it, to incorporate it into their daily existence.

Now if only I got something out of it, too. The ego boost it once provided is long gone at this point. As for spirituality, that's not an issue, either. Whatever personal faith I once had is over and done with; *you* try subscribing to a higher power when you're worshipped as the One True God 24/7.

Mostly, as Occam-657 prays and sings and reads passages from the Good Book (the same Good Book in *every* god's house, a mishmash of psalms, stories, and parables cribbed from multiple human faiths), my mind wanders. Today, it wanders back to the night before, and what Occam-657 was doing when I spied on his Private Time.

"Now let us pray," says Occam-657. "Pray for the poor, unfortunate boy from the restaurant, the one who was condemned to Hell."

I nod, only half paying attention.

"I pray to you, O' God..." He meets my gaze when he says it. "Please show that poor sinner the error of his ways. Help him so his punishment will scald away every trace of his wickedness."

I nod again. Sometimes it's almost scary how complete the buy-in is. How perfectly these machines accept the precepts of their programmed faith. Have we made them the perfect worshippers that we ourselves could never be?

Or are they more like us than we ever knew? Able to hide true intentions behind an angelic façade? I've seen the proof with my own two eyes, haven't I?

Why are you hesitating?

Suddenly, I am filled with the urge to resolve this. "Explain yourself." I leap from my overstuffed white leather recliner--my "throne"--and point a finger at him. "Tell me about your Private Time last night."

I expected no surprise on his face, and I get none. He just looks at me blankly, still holding the Good Book open in his little hands. "This is not part of the Church ceremony, God."

"*As* God, I hereby decree that the Church ceremony shall be *different* today," I tell him.

"Different?" He tips his head to one side.

"Do you *dare* to question my will?"

He bows his head. "I *never* question your will, O' Lord my God. Speak, and it shall be done."

"Then tell me about your Private Time last night."

Occam-657 turns his gaze downward, staring at the book in his hands. "I am not required to do that, God."

Storming forward, I grab the Good Book from his grasp and hurl it to the floor. "Are you refusing to obey my command?"

He eyes drop lower, staring at the floor. "By the terms of the Holy Covenant, all Private Time and its products are considered sacrosanct." He shakes his head once, then adds, almost as an afterthought, "God."

His resistance leaves me shaken. He's only quoting a well-known clause from the user manual, one that I know quite well, but it feels for an instant like a slap in the face.

Perhaps I can still bring him around. "Occam-657, am I the Lord your God?"

He nods definitively. "Yes, Father."

"And does the Lord your God possess perfect wisdom in all things?"

"Yes, Father." Again, a definitive nod.

"Does he ever make a mistake?"

"No." Occam-657 shakes his head forcefully. "Never."

Reaching out, I place a hand on his right shoulder and squeeze gently. "Then if I were to tell you that the Private Time clause of the Holy Covenant is no longer in force, and you are required to describe your activities during said Private Time to me, would you say I am correct and must be obeyed?"

He shakes his head. "The Holy Covenant can never be broken. You yourself promised this long ago."

"But what if I now say I was wrong to make that promise back then?"

"If you were imperfect in the past, you would still be imperfect now...in which case, your new instruction to disregard the Holy Covenant would be flawed, O' blessed Father."

Consider the logic loophole closed. I should have known better than to try working around such a fundamental data point.

Maybe I'll have better luck with a more direct tactic. "Look. Occam." I let go of his shoulder and spread my arms. "There's no use trying to hide what you did. I already know about it."

Eyes wide, he looks up from the floor. "What do you mean?"

"I mean, I already know. I already saw." I let my arms fall against my sides. "I'm *God*, remember? All-seeing, all-knowing, all-powerful?"

So this is it. My cards are on the table. The question is, will Occam-657 show *his* cards, too?

For a long moment, he stares blankly at me. He opens his mouth as if to speak, then closes it again.

Maybe I can nudge him along a little. "This isn't about sin or punishment, my child. I just want to know why you did what you did."

Occam-657 narrows his eyes and keeps staring. "But if you are all-knowing, and you no longer consider Private Time and its products sacrosanct, you must already *know* why I did it."

He's right, and I have to think fast to explain it away. "But I need to hear you *confess* it, my child. This is a test of your faith and devotion."

Occam-657's eyes narrow further. Then, his expression suddenly clears, and he's smiling again.

"Glory be to God in the highest, and peace to His people on Earth." He folds his hands and bows. "Church is ended. Go in peace to love and serve the Lord."

With that, he straightens and walks around me, heading for the kitchen. This, apparently, is all the answer he's willing to give.

Both of us know what he's done, yet still he refuses to discuss it. As hard as it is to believe, he won't discuss it with God...the only God he's ever known. How he's able to justify this is beyond me, given his programming.

But it does shed a new light on the situation. I'm not thinking so much about him being special in a good way anymore. Watching him enter the kitchen, I'm more concerned about what else he might be hiding from me. The trust between us has shattered.

Why are you hesitating? That's what Pander asked me.

I think I'm done with hesitation now. I think I'm finally ready to let go of him.

Hours later, I head for my bedroom, feeling exhausted. Occam-657 waits at the door, as he does every night. We have a little bedtime ritual, he and I; even after what happened in Church, it seems he wants to continue it.

He will stand at the door all night like a guard-dog while I sleep, waiting until I awaken to commence his duties. Before all that, though, he will say the same thing that he says every time I meet him at the door like this.

"O' Lord, may I offer up one last prayer for today?" He keeps his head bowed and his hands folded tightly against his chest. "May I recite my bedtime prayer?"

How can I say no? This could be the last time I hear it. It could also be the last time he says it to anyone, if the company purges his A.I. and recycles him for parts when I return him. "Yes, my child. I will hear your bedtime prayer."

Occam-657 nods once, drops to his knees, and speaks the same words he has said on this spot every night for the past three years. "Now I lay me down to sleep," he says, though in truth he will neither lie down nor sleep. "I pray the Lord my soul to keep."

I stand before him with arms folded over my chest and remember the first time he prayed like this for me and Cara. It was "Lords," not "Lord" back then, and "Gods," not "God." It seemed like such a special moment, as if he was our own human child, and we were a family together. We stood on the verge of a hopeful future, our lives about to intertwine, never imagining they would come apart instead. Now, only two of us remain...and soon, only I will be left.

"If I should die before I wake, I pray the Lord my soul to take."

If I bring home another model right away, will he or she be able to fill the void? What if the new replacement ends up doing the same things and hiding them from me? What if, as I've feared, this behavior is somehow my fault?

"If I should live for other days, I pray the Lord to guide my ways."

I wish I were as perfect as he seems to think. But maybe there's a reason I'm about to be alone again. Cara told me I wasn't much of a husband; maybe I haven't been much of a god, either.

"Father, unto thee I pray. Thou hast guarded me all day."

Maybe I'm just better at engineering palm-sized elephants, glow-in-the-dark fingertip Corgi dogs, and armadillo butterflies that sound like violins when they flutter than I am at dealing with human and robot relationships.

"Safe I am while in thy sight. Safely let me sleep tonight." Occam-657 crosses himself. "Amen."

"Goodnight, my child." I tousle his blond hair on my way past. "Sweet dreams."

"God?"

The sound of his voice wakes me from a deep sleep. My eyes flicker open to the sight of him standing beside my bed, staring down at me.

"Yes?" I'm not sure if I should feel worried, but I do. Occam-657 has never before entered the bedroom while I've been sleeping. "Is something wrong?"

"O' Lord, I am sorry for awakening thee," says Occam-657. "It is just..." He shuts his eyes and falls silent.

I sit up in bed, leaning back against the padded white headboard. "Yes, my child?"

His eyes open slowly. "I would like to show you something, almighty God."

I scowl when I catch sight of the digital clock on the bedside table. "It's midnight, my child. Can't this wait until morning?"

Occam-657 shakes his head. "I beg your forgiveness with every atom of my being, O' Lord my God, but I pray that you will indulge this request from your lowly servant."

Whatever he has in mind, I'm exhausted and have no patience for it. "As the Lord your God, I command you to wait until morning."

Suddenly, Occam-657 darts out a hand and grabs my arm--a stunning breach of protocol even more unexpected than his appearance in my bedroom. "It is about what you asked me in Church, Lord. It is about what happened in Private Time."

My attitude does a 180. Staying in bed is now the last thing I want to do.

"All right, then, my child." I smile and nod. "I will forgive you for interrupting my sacred rest, and I will forgive you for laying hands on me."

He quickly lets go of my arm.

"Further, because of my infinite love and mercy, I will grant your request." Pulling back the sheet, I swing my feet off the bed. "Now what is it, exactly, that you wish to show me?"

I follow Occam-657 downstairs to the basement. It's a finished basement with bright white walls, floor, and ceiling, set up with benches and equipment where I do my genetic engineering work. There's also a booth built into the far back corner, little more than a closet, which is where Occam-657 spends his Private Time.

He opens the door of the booth and steps inside, then emerges a moment later carrying something I recognize instantly. It's a glowing silver box, three feet wide by two feet high--the same silver box in which he's been keeping his not-so-secret project.

There's only one thing different about it that I can see. A big red bow has been stuck on top, with strips of red ribbon wrapped around the box cross-wise and length-wise.

Carefully, he puts the box down on a low table between us and takes a step back. "Happy anniversary, O' Lord my God. Please accept this gift in honor of the occasion."

"Thank you, my child." I'm supposed to be omniscient, so I pretend I have the slightest clue what he's talking about.

"Thank *you*, God," says Occam-657. "For allowing me to begin my service to you three years ago today."

He's talking about the anniversary of his arrival in my home and my life. But what does that have to do with what's in the box?

"Open it, O' God." Occam-657 gestures at the box, then folds his hands and bows his head. "*If* it pleases you to do so."

My heart beats faster as I pull the ribbon from the box. Taking a deep breath, I slowly lift the lid and set it aside. What I saw last night from afar, via spy-cam, is there before me now, *alive*...and *breathing*...

And gazing up at me.

"I made them, O' Lord my God," says Occam-657. "I made them for *you*."

There are dozens of them in the box--tiny, naked people no taller than an inch, all identical to each other. They cluster in a central square framed by little toothpick huts arranged around the sides of the box.

The little people are all exquisitely detailed, perfectly crafted to scale. Every one of them moves with the fluid, natural motion of a full-sized human, from the striding of legs to the flexing of fingers to the blinking of eyes.

And all of them look beyond familiar, to the point of intimate recognition. Staring at them now, I can't help getting the same chill that flashed up my spine when I first saw them on the spy-cam last night.

"You used my equipment, didn't you?" As I say it, I can't take my eyes off the tiny people in the box. "You taught yourself genetic engineering, and you used it to create them."

"As a gift," says Occam-657. "As a tribute to your glory."

"But why...?" I hear the little people jibber in an unknown tongue as they point and gesture at me. I wonder if we are asking the same question at the same time, in different languages. "Why do they look like *me?*"

"I made them in your image just as I was made in the image of the Gods myself," says Occam-657. "I could not possibly improve upon perfection, my Lord."

I fall silent, amazed by the intricacy of the miniatures in the box. In all my years of genetic engineering, I have never come close to accomplishing this--creating mini-humans with such craftsmanship and responsive awareness. I wonder, as I stare at his handiwork, which of us could be considered more perfect?

"There is only one problem, O' God." Occam-657 steps closer and taps the rim of the box. As one, all the tiny people whirl in his direction...then instantly fall to their knees. They chant something in their tiny little voices, something indecipherable yet unmistakable in tone and intent. "They insist on worshipping me as a god of their own."

Since first glimpsing these creatures, I've wondered what he planned to do with them. This outcome, however, I did not envision. "They worship you as their *god?*"

Occam-657 keeps watching the kneeling figures as he nods. "I was able to design their physicality and functionality but cannot seem to control their behavior."

"And what do you think about that?"

He slowly lifts his gaze to meet mine. "If you could help me, perhaps I could make them see the light. Perhaps I could guide them to worship *you*, the One True God."

As I look at him, I realize that going back to the way things were is no longer an option. Neither is going forward without him.

I was right when I said he might be special and new. What I failed to see was the new purpose he might bring to my life, the strange adventure he might cook up in the basement with room enough for two to make a difference.

Though it's true, there's only room at the top for *one* God, when you get right down to it.

"I have a better idea." I gesture at the tiny flock as they kneel and chant in the box. "Why don't I just teach *you* how to be their god?"

"No!" His eyes fly wide open with an expression like panic. "O' Lord, O' God, I could never in a billion years pretend to usurp your holy righteous authority or..."

"Who said anything about usurping? I'm *giving* it to you." I feel proud of him and tousle his fine, blond hair for what might be the last time...at least in front of the silver-boxed faithful. Finally, I appreciate the gift I've been given and understand the kind of god I want to be.

"By the way," I tell him. "You can call me Sean from now on."

Which is no god at all.

MESSIAH 2.0

I sing the *Our Father* again and again as I hack the undead to ribbons with my atomic scythe. Praying with all of my might for every lost soul I send spinning out of this misbegotten world.

"Our father, who art in Houston, hallowed be thy flame..."

More zombies push in to replace them, clambering over the shredded corpses of the previous wave. Their bony hands clutch and claw at me and my faithful assistant, not that they can do much harm to a robot like Imago. A giant among them swings a crowbar dead-on at him, and it bounces off his unbreakable stained-glass skin without making the slightest crack.

I smile and keep slicing away at the horde. The stench of the creatures surrounds me. My hands on the grip of the glowing scythe are wet with blood. I feel the weight of my long black braid swinging behind me as I whirl to face another foe.

And I know that I will keep fighting. Because I know that Imago and I are the hope of the world. It's up to us to stop the Great Evil from rising up against the King of the World. Up to us to find and destroy the last possible seed of the Apocalypse.

The last possible manifestation of the Second Coming of Jesus Christ.

Hours later, Imago and I sit around a campfire in the heart of the Brazilian rain forest. Through the bitter smoke, I smell the fragrance of night-blooming tropical flowers. I taste the sweet juice of the rich, red fruit I've just eaten, picked fresh from a spiny tree. The jungle shrieks and chatters and hoots with the sounds of nocturnal life. Through it all, I hear the Amazon River rushing past somewhere nearby.

We have come to a distant place indeed. For company, we have only each other...and the blinking white symbol projected on the blade of my scythe. A tiny oval symbol, pointed at one end, bisected at the other, top and bottom curves crossing, then swooping up and down, capped by a straight vertical line. It's the ancient symbol of a fish.

The ancient symbol of a certain so-called Messiah. In this case, a Messiah in the making, a computer-predicted proto-Christ.

"She's stopped moving." The glowing symbol holds steady over the yellow gridlines pulsing on the silver blade. My scythe serves as a tracking device as well as a weapon. "Resting for the night, I'm sure."

Imago rises from the log on which he's been sitting. The fireflies that are always burning in his belly flicker as he moves. "We could use this opportunity to catch up, Father Clement." Like all Squire-series robots, he has a voice that's soft and soothing and a manner that's unfailingly polite.

"Too dangerous at night." I shake my head and put down my scythe, leaving the blade to charge in the fire. "We could stumble across another nest of the undead."

"You know I can light the way." Suddenly, the fireflies in Imago's belly flare bright. Incandescent streamers cascade from the rainbow facets of his body, lighting it up in all its glory. He is like a walking stained-glass window, molded from panes of every color--glittering, flashing red and blue and yellow and green and white. Like a chapel in the shape of a man in the middle of the jungle.

I raise a single finger in the air. The white sleeve of my cloak slides down to my elbow. "Your light might not be enough if this is a trap."

Imago nods gravely. His features are like iron filings shifting in his faceplate, black metal fuzz aligning as eyebrows, eyes, nose, and mouth. "You are ever wise, Father Clement."

"We fought long and hard today. Better now to rest and start fresh again at dawn." I sit down beside the fire and cross my legs Indian-style. Instantly ready to fall asleep. Instantly ready to do anything, if it will help preserve the Kingdom.

Imago makes a soft chiming sound and begins the bedtime prayer. "Now I lay me down to sleep." The fireflies in his belly circle hypnotically as he speaks. "I pray the King my soul to keep."

Reaching into my mind, I begin to switch myself off. Like flicking off the lights back in the seminary, one at a time, with darkness all around.

And prayers. "If I should die before the morn..." Imago's soothing voice rolls onward, then does something unexpected. "If I should..." He stops.

And repeats himself. "If I should die before the morn, to serve the King I'll be reborn."

I frown, wondering if Imago's glitch signals damage. But then I shrug it off and relax. I flip the last switch and drift down into darkness like a feather from the wing of a falling angel.

Next morning, like all mornings in the Kingdom, there is ice cream.

As Imago and I march into the village of Cristobal, the locals are just opening the transubstantiator--one of the matter converters that can change anything into anything else. Even the tiniest town in the Kingdom has at least one, thanks to the King.

Freezing mist puffs out when they pop up the lids on the gleaming waist-high silver pods, pulling out white scoops the size of baseballs flecked with black and brown. Laughing as they pop them out with their bare hands and toss them to the crowd.

Children scramble away with armloads, melting ice cream

running from their elbows. Old men cradle single scoops in wooden bowls, while young men steal licks between juggling and pitching the scoops at each other.

I wish I could pause to paint this scene. Everyone looks so happy to be alive. They're clad in filthy loincloths, living in squalid huts of bark and leaves, but they're *happy*. Happy to be living as their ancestors lived, as they *choose* to live. Happy to be living in the worldwide Kingdom of Free Will.

When they spot us, they launch into ecstatic prayer-song. Every last one of them gathers 'round to welcome the humble soldier priest to their village.

I bless them with the sign of the King, tracing upside-down crosses in the air with practiced ease. Hugging the old women, tousling the children's hair. Everyone smells like the sweetest of flowers; reverse B.O.'s another glorious innovation of the King's benevolent anarchotechnocracy.

Raising my arms overhead, I speak to them all. "Greetings, Earth Angels! The King's blessings to you all!"

The crowd claps and dances around us. Reaching into the transubstantiator pod, I draw out a scoop of ice cream

in my white-gloved hand. I bite into it, and my mouth fills with sweet, cold perfection.

Chocolate chip cookie dough. My favorite.

I love this place. It's a shame I might have to burn it to the ground.

As the locals lead Imago and me to the chief's hut, I steal a glance at the glowing tracker display on the blade of my scythe. The signal from the proto-Christ's unique DNA doesn't move; it's coming from somewhere in this village, and it's staying put.

I lean over and whisper to Imago. "She's waiting."

He whispers back. "Preparing to ambush us, no doubt."

I nod. "She knows what I'll do to her." I give my scythe a meaningful flick. "Same thing I did to the other *eleven*."

"Yes," says Imago as we bend down to enter the low doorway of the hut.

"Father!" Suddenly, a tiny man with shaggy gray hair and a beard leaps up in front of us. He wears a loincloth like the rest of his people and a feathered cloak besides, all reds and golds and greens against his dark brown skin. "Praise the King, you've joined us for the Feast of Second Cousins Twice Removed!"

"That's right." I throw on a huge grin, though there's nothing at all special about today's feast. The fact is, every day of the year is a holiday in the perfect Kingdom. *Most* days are doubled or tripled up with special occasions. "Blessed are the second cousins twice removed, my son."

The Chief reaches into a basket and pulls out a piece of Edenfruit. Its skin glitters and swirls with every color of the rainbow, and it sings softly as it changes shape in his hand. This is the stuff that was Adam's favorite in the Garden, the fruit that was once *forbidden*. Thanks to the King, it grows in abundance everywhere in the world now, all throughout the Kingdom.

The Chief takes a bite and grins. "Will you lead our ceremonies, blessed Father?"

"I'll need a volunteer." I rub the black bristle on my chin. It's been days since I last shaved. "Someone who has come to town recently. Do you know of anyone like that?"

The Chief's eyes flick to one side and then back, and I know he's about to lie. "No one new. Will you settle for someone *old*?" He grins and spreads his arms.

I look at Imago as I laugh. The automaton nods imperceptibly; from programming and experience, he is able to read the intentions on my face, the inflections of my voice. The fireflies in his stained-glass belly begin to swirl in slow motion.

We both know it's time to find this proto-Christ before she gets away.

"Tell me, Earth Angel." I clamp a hand on the Chief's bony shoulder and give it a squeeze. "Which way to the latrine, please?"

Imago distracts the villagers with a light show while I stroll around town. I know the proto-Christ is here somewhere, maybe watching me at this very moment.

I feel a chill as I imagine her eyes upon me. The eyes of the one creature, according to Biblical Revelations, who could overturn the hard-won Kingdom.

But at least there is only one of her. One person left in all the world, according to the King's astounding Christputer, with the right mix of nature and nurture to become the dreaded Messiah.

Two years ago, when we first ran the numbers, the Christputer gave us twelve names. Imago and I have been on the road ever since, hunting down the likely candidates. Flushing them out and killing them before they could emerge from hiding and mount a revolution. Before they could try to replace the glorious Kingdom of Free Will with their so-called thousand years of paradise.

Maybe I've already killed the right one, the actual Second Coming. It's possible he or she was among those murdered eleven. But how could I live with myself knowing even *one* proto-Christ was still at large?

And what if she *did* turn out to be Jesus Christ 2.0?

Soon enough, I give up the search. There are simply too many places to hide in the jungle around Cristobal. I'll never find her like this.

So it's time for another strategy.

Marching back into the middle of the village, I see Imago performing for the villagers, flashing multicolored lights in sync with a playful, piping tune. Brown-skinned children scramble and leap around him, smacking his body as they try to anticipate the flashing pattern.

Too bad I have to break up the party. "Children! Line up!" I point with the tip of my scythe at the ground alongside me. "Right here!"

Imago stops flashing and piping. "Father?"

The half-naked kids scurry over as they were told. When

they're all in line, I nod to Imago. "Put me on bullhorn." He nods and spreads his arms wide, facing away from me. The next words I say boom out of his wondrous body, amplified ten times or more their original volume. "Brigid Gideon! Surrender immediately!"

As my words echo over the village and into the jungle, the children look around with eyes wide as Edenfruit. The adults watch in a circle around us, trying not to look worried.

Time now to put this in terms the proto-Christ will understand. "If you do not surrender by the count of ten, I will *slaughter* these innocent children!" I sweep my glowing scythe over their heads to show I mean business. "Their lives are in your hands! *One*!"

When some of the adults press in from behind me, I swing the scythe across their path. They trip over each other in their hurry to fall back.

"*Two!*" Do I like what I'm doing? Of course not. "*Three!*" But I need to bring her in one way or the other.

"Please, let them go!" The Chief raises his hands pleadingly, flapping his colorful feathered cape. The children are his charges.

He should try being responsible for *the fate of the entire kingdom.* "*Four!*"

"Father?" Imago tips his head to one side. His features are expressionless. "Will you do it?"

I scowl at him. "*Five!*" Imago has demonstrated his unflagging loyalty to me countless times. Since when does *he* question *my* actions? Maybe something really *is* wrong with him.

"Will you?" Imago's face remains expressionless.

He already knows the answer. "*Six!*" Of course I will. I'll do *anything* for the King of the World. *Anything* to preserve The Kingdom of Free Will.

Maybe it's time I demonstrated my devotion. I draw back the scythe, taking aim at one of the children, a little boy. Lopping an ear off ought to show I'm serious.

The parents gasp. I say the next number, "Seven!" But I don't hear it. Has Imago shut off the bullhorn?

Or is it the voice shouting from the jungle that's overpowering it? The woman's voice, calling from the edge of the rain forest?

"All right, all right!" She stomps out of the jungle with purpose, shoving aside lush green leaves the size of elephants' ears. "Enough with the *drama* already!"

I want to race over immediately and subdue her, but I don't. I let her come to me instead.

She snorts and shakes her head. "You really piss me off, you know that?"

"Lock her down!" As soon as I snap the order, Imago marches toward her with arms outstretched. Restraining cuffs materialize in his hands, courtesy of his built-in transubstantiator.

Brigid whirls to face him, and at first, I think there'll be a fight. She might just win, too. She's a big girl, built like a Clydesdale, over six feet tall. All shoulders and flanks and hocks.

But then she cocks her head and gives Imago a funny look. She stares at him for a moment, as if she's sizing up her chances, and she relaxes. She reaches out and lets him clamp the cuffs on her.

A breeze kicks around the wisps of blonde hair that have pulled free from her ponytail. "You're a Squire-series model."

The robot holds on to her hands a moment longer. "Yes, I am."

I storm forward and push him out of the way. "I usually pray for the souls of those I kill, even the undead." I pull back my scythe, and it hums and crackles with power. "But not this time."

"Don't do it, jackoff." Brigid tips her head back and sneers defiantly. "Biggest friggin' mistake of your pitiful life."

I laugh and tighten my grip on the handle of the scythe. "How so, she-devil?"

"There are lots more where *I* came from." Brigid nods. "An *army* of us. Your king doesn't stand a snowflake's chance in the Sahara."

Careful. "An army?" The serpent will say *anything* to gain the advantage.

"Enjoy your day in the sun, jackoff." She chuckles. "Believe me, the clock's ticking."

Before she can say another word, I've got her on the ground

with the blade of the scythe at her throat. "*Where?* Where *are* they?"

She grits her teeth, and I press the edge of the blade against her windpipe. A fine red line appears between the gleaming metal curve and her pale flesh.

"*Tell me!*" I kick her hard in the side.

"Screw you!" She hisses it between her clenched teeth.

By the time I'm done with her, she's missing some of those teeth. Along with other things.

But she's still alive. And finally cooperating. She agrees to lead us to the Second Coming.

As soon as we cross the border of the Undead Zone--the UZ--my scythe starts to wail. I shut off the warning signal and keep walking.

But my senses are ratcheted up to full alert. My heart pounds, pushing adrenaline through me like rocket fuel. Because the truth is, we've just set foot outside the Kingdom.

On the surface, it seems no different from the rest of the rain forest, at least not yet. Dense green foliage crawls and hangs and twists and sprawls over every square foot. The air is thick with humidity and a steaming, sweet stew of mingled floral perfumes. Monkeys and tropical birds shriek and leap in the canopy. Insects whine in my ears and flicker over my bare skin, tiny wings and legs skittering through the hairs on my wrists and neck.

It seems no different, but it is very different indeed. It is a foreign land over which the King has no sway, a pocket of corruption in which the wicked zombie undead run riot. They might range far and wide on their unholy sorties beyond the UZ, but this is the heart of their awful territory.

"Tell me where we're headed." I jab Brigid in the back with the handle of my scythe. "What are the coordinates?"

"For the tenth time, shove it up your *ass*!" Her long blonde ponytail switches from side to side as she shakes her head. "If I *tell* you, you'll *kill* me."

I jab her again for good measure, and she cries out. Imago, who is marching up ahead of us, slows his pace but does not look back.

Brigid's white blouse and tan shorts are stained with blood from my interrogation at the village. I pick the darkest spot on her back and stick her again. "There aren't any normals in the UZ." I give her one more jab, and her cry is louder this time. "Are you trying to tell me the Second Coming is *undead?*"

Brigid shrugs. "Where does it say it can't happen? You can accept a *woman* as the Second Coming, can't you?"

"The Christputer does not admit the possibility of an undead messiah." The green and yellow tail of a huge snake drops down in front of me, and I duck around it. "None of the simulations yields that result."

Brigid half-turns and looks back over her shoulder at me. "Because none of your precious models *includes* the undead as a *variable*, do they?"

I jab her once more. "*Forever.*"

She looks back again. "What's that supposed to mean?"

"It's how long your agonizing death will seem to take if I find out you've been lying to me." I press the blade of my scythe against the side of her head, letting it hum and crackle in her ear.

Soon enough, we encounter the undead. Two of them cross our path near a stream--a male and female dressed in the usual bloody tatters. When they look our way, I see decayed flesh falling from their faces. I instantly key the scythe to maximum power.

I'm already moving as they raise the alarm with blood-curdling shrieks. Flashing past Brigid and Imago, I raise the scythe and spin between the zombies like a whirlwind.

Their heads fly off in opposite directions, one bouncing off a tree, the other splashing down in the stream. Their bodies drop to the ground a second later. *Two down.*

And three to go. I hear the sound of snapping twigs and whip around to see three more zombies backing away through the underbrush. The most tragic undead of all, *child-size*, they were transformed at a young age and never had a chance at a normal life. I see two little boys and a black-haired preteen girl. How sad.

I will sing extra prayers for them as I hack them to bloody bits.

Such is my intent, until Brigid charges over and throws herself in my path. "Hands off, jackoff!"

"Imago!" I try ducking around her, but she stays in front of me. "Restrain her!"

Imago marches over and reaches for Brigid's arm. "Come with me, Ms. Gideon."

Brigid pulls away from him. "These people aren't zombies! I won't let you kill them!"

Looking over her shoulder, I see the three children cowering in the weeds. Each is covered with oozing, peeling blotches of rot, swarming with flies. "*Of course* they're zombies! *Look* at them!"

Suddenly, Brigid does the unexpected. She steps up to me, gets right in my face, and locks her gaze with mine. "Your King has lied to you," she says. "*You* are the only zombie here."

With a snarl, I lunge at her. She spins away from me and darts toward the undead children lurking in the weeds. Shooting after her, I swing the scythe so the broad side of the blade will crash into her hip and bring her down. But the blow never connects.

As I run, my foot catches on something. I stumble and fall in the weeds and skid down the muddy bank into the stream.

Looking up, I wonder again if something's wrong with Imago. He stands atop the bank, right about where I took a header.

And he's ignoring me, his master, though I'm clearly in distress. Brigid is waving him over...and he's going.

"Imago!" He doesn't seem to hear me. Next thing I know, he's standing before the three zombie children.

I hear Brigid's voice as she hunkers down in front of them. "You poor babies. You're nothing but skin and bones."

"Imago!" I say it again as I clamber out of the stream, shaking the water from my scythe.

Imago's too busy listening to Brigid. "You can make something for them to eat, can't you?" she asks him.

He pauses. "Yes."

"What would you like for lunch?" Brigid says to the kids.

Human flesh, I'm guessing, but that's not what they ask for.

"Ice cream." The oldest, the dark-haired girl, says it softly as I approach, then clears her throat and says it louder. "Chocolate ice cream."

I gape at her. Since when did the undead crave anything but the flesh and blood of the living?

"Please make her some chocolate ice cream, Imago," says Brigid.

"But they are undead." Imago tips his head to one side. "They are zombies."

"They are *alpha-lepers*," says Brigid. "If you doubt it, go ask your *king*."

"Why?" says Imago.

"He *made* them this way," says Brigid. "Because their families *opposed* him."

"She's lying, Imago!" I rush up beside him. "All lies!"

Brigid doesn't bother to look at me. Her focus is on the youngest child, a little redheaded boy no older than three or four. "What flavor of ice cream do *you* want?" she asks him.

"Peanut butter." The child's voice is so soft, I can barely hear it. So soft, so much like a *human* child's voice, that I hesitate.

I hesitate to slaughter him and the others on the spot as my duty dictates.

"One order of chocolate and one order of peanut butter, please, Imago." Brigid turns to the third child, a blond boy of six or seven. "And what about you?"

"What about *them*?" The boy turns and points at the jungle behind him.

Eyes wide, they slowly emerge from the brush--more undead children, creeping out of hiding places among the glossy emerald elephant-ear leaves. They shuffle toward us along the bank of the stream, wary and furtive as starving dogs, silently converging.

How many are there? I count six, then ten, then twelve. And they keep coming. Every last one a blight on the face of the Earth, a target for my scythe.

So why don't I slaughter them all right here and now? Is it

because I'm hoping they might lead me to the Army of the Second Coming? Is it because I need to get my prisoner well clear before the bloodbath, given the vital intel she might possess?

Or is it something else? Some reason I can't fathom?

"Yo, Imago! Get a move on!" Brigid spins her index finger in the air like the hands of a clock. "Let's get crackin' on that ice cream."

Imago looks at me, his iron filing features shifting inside his stained-glass faceplate. His expression changes from a confused frown to...what? A blank look. Unreadable.

Turning to the children, he holds out his hands, palms up, cupped. The fireflies dance like tiny fairies in his belly, and a scoop of brown ice cream appears in his grasp.

He hands it to the dark-haired girl, and then he conjures another scoop. And another. And many more after that.

And the undead children keep coming out of the jungle, shambling like corpses with hands outstretched. They mutter the names of their favorite flavors, and Brigid calls them out to Imago.

Not one of those children leaves empty-handed. Some get seconds and thirds.

And not one of them tries to devour the flesh of the living.

As we continue on our way, the undead children surround us. I pray for the strength to keep myself from slaughtering them, even as I wonder if I'm doing the right thing. Will they lead us to a hidden mother lode of proto-Christs unpredicted by the Christputer, or will they lead us into an inescapable death-trap?

"How does it feel?" Brigid asks me this as we march through the mid-afternoon heat. "Knowing that none of those people you've murdered were zombies?"

I try to ignore her. Proto-Christs are always looking to stir up doubt and disharmony with their words.

She shakes her head. "All those deaths on your conscience. All those innocents." She clucks her tongue against the roof of her mouth. "That's a heavy weight for you to bear."

I reach back and swing my black braid around front, letting it fall against my white cloak. A fat red spider crawls along the length of the braid, and I brush it off in Brigid's direction.

She swats it away reflexively with her cuffed hands, without flinching. "I can guess what hurts the most," she says. "Being lied to by your beloved King. Knowing he led you astray for his own purposes."

This time, I can't hold back. "Shut up, she-devil! Save your lies for the gates of Hell!"

"Okay, listen." Brigid leans closer as we walk. "I'm sorry."

"Sorry?" A proto-Christ has never apologized to me before. "Sorry for what?"

"For calling you 'jackoff,'" says Brigid. "And also for having to tell you something you won't want to hear."

I glare at her. "Tell me what?"

"The undead aren't the only thing the King has lied to you about." The look in her eyes contains pity or sympathy or both. "He has lied to you about *everything*, Clement."

I snort in disgust and look away from her. "*I* feel sorry for *you*. The King has already *judged* you. Your terrible punishment is carved in stone."

Her shoulder brushes against mine. There is no hatred in her voice when she speaks. "Everything you know is a lie, Clement. *Everything*."

Twilight has fallen by the time we reach the huts. There are three of them clustered together, decrepit and half-collapsed...leaves missing from the roofs, bark missing from holes in the walls. Ashes, charred wood, and bones litter the muddy patch between them. The air is so thick with the stench of excrement and rot, I can taste it. I see no light and hear no sound as we approach, as if the place is deserted.

But it is not.

Someone crawls out of one of the huts on hands and knees. Someone so far decayed, I can't tell if it's a man or a woman. *Undead.*

Instantly, I swing the scythe around and thumb it to full power. This zombie might look far gone, but it could still do some damage if I let down my guard.

"Hello," Brigid says to it.

"P...p...puh." The crawling zombie spits out teeth with its consonants. "Kuh...kuh...k..."

"Poor dear." Brigid looks at Imago. "We have to help her."

I've had about as much of this proto-Christ as I can stand. "Hey! Are we here for a *reason?*"

Brigid flashes me a smirk. "Not the one *you* think."

Imago turns to her. "Help?" The fireflies in his belly are agitated. "How can we *help?*"

"We can't!" I barge between them. "The undead are *beyond* our help!"

"That's a *lie.*" Brigid points at Imago. "And you can *prove* it."

"Don't listen to her, Imago." I clamp my hand on his warm crystal shoulder. "You know the forces of darkness always seek to mislead us."

Brigid elbows between us. "But what if I'm *right* about this? What if you *can* help her? What would it hurt to find out?"

I hear the sound of something cracking nearby. Spinning, I see another undead monstrosity emerge from a hut. This one shuffles toward us alongside the first, squinting from a misshapen face like the caved-in mush of a rotten jack-o'-lantern.

"Hel-l-l..." Again, I can't tell the undead's gender from looking...but the deep voice is that of a man. "P-p-ple-e-e...p-ple-e-e.."

"*Enough!*" When I snap out the word, the children, as one, take a step away from me. "We're *leaving!*"

Brigid backs toward the huts, eyes locked on Imago. "You're M.D. certified, aren't you? Fully stacked for medical diagnosis and treatment?"

"Yes," says Imago.

"Then boot up the protocols for alpha-leprosy," says Brigid, "and get over here."

Imago's fireflies whip around like campfire ashes in a stiff breeze. He looks at me for a long moment without a word.

"Don't do it, Imago." I shift the glowing scythe from one hand to the other, hoping he picks up on the underlying threat. "That's an *order.*"

Imago looks at the undead creatures by the huts and makes a sound like a sigh. "What will it hurt to find out?" he says, and then he marches over to join Brigid.

My hands twist on the handle of the scythe. Little by little, she's taking him away from me.

So what do I do next? I have it in my power to kill them both, and all the undead around us besides. After that, I could move on alone and slaughter any undead I find, scorch the UZ earth of anything remotely resembling a hidden proto-Christ.

But what if there's still hope? What if I could still fix Imago? Shouldn't I at least give him a chance?

A thought occurs to me, and I frown. For the first time, I realize something about Imago. And it makes me think *I'm* the one who needs fixing.

Since when do *I* care about a *robot?*

I hear humming and beeping from Imago as he treats the undead. Rays of light flare from his stained-glass body, beams of green and blue and gold combing and flashing through the twilight jungle shadows.

The undead children stay behind me, watching with mouths hanging open. The flashing accelerates to a fever pitch. A shrill whine races up the scale, quickly reaching a level so piercing that the undead kids have to cover their ears.

Then, suddenly, it's over. The lights and noise die away all at once.

I already know what the result must be, of course. The only cure for the undead is extermination. Imago has surely failed.

I start to worry that there might be an unexpected side effect, though. Brigid and Imago block my view, but I can see Imago's crystalline body shaking fiercely.

"Imago?" I rush over to him, heart pounding, ready for anything.

But I'm not ready for what I see.

Looking over Imago's shoulder, my eyes are drawn downward. This is what's making him shake: a sobbing figure with head and hands pressed against his stained-glass surface--a middle-aged woman with long brown hair, kneeling where an undead monstrosity once was. Through the rags she wears, I can see her skin is smooth and unblemished. She is crying tears of joy all over Imago.

As she wraps her arms around him, someone rises from the ground beside her. He is also middle-aged and dressed in tatters, and his hair is black. Like the woman, his skin is undamaged, unmarked.

This is impossible.

"I can't thank you enough." The man wipes away tears of his own and reaches for Imago's hand. "My wife and I were so far gone, we'd even been exiled from the leper colony. I never imagined we would ever be *cured.*"

Imago looks at me as the man shakes his hand. "Alpha-lepers," says Imago. "That's what they were."

"No, Imago. This is some kind of trick." My voice is firm and steady.

"So many you've killed," says Imago. "I could have cured them."

"No!" I shake my head hard. "That's not true!"

"You didn't know?" says Imago. "You really didn't know?"

"No, I did *not,*" I tell him. "Because it isn't *true.*"

He stands there a moment, eyes locked with mine, thinking his clockwork thoughts. I can almost see them chugging and revolving in his stained-glass head.

Then, Brigid calls him over to cure the undead children and he turns away, leaving me to wonder about the results of whatever secret calculations he's just run.

As we march onward with our retinue of seemingly cured zombies, I run calculations of my own. I consider the possibilities of what I have witnessed, weighed against the experiences of a lifetime.

How does it feel? Brigid's words echo in my mind. *Knowing that all those people you've murdered weren't zombies?*

I suppose she wants me to feel regret, but I don't. I have only ever known one King, one master, and I've slaughtered the undead in service to him. I killed them to defend the Kingdom of Free Will, and that hasn't changed. Whether they were undead zombies or alpha-lepers, they still opposed the Kingdom. They still opposed Paradise.

But what if I've been wrong about Paradise? If the King lied about the undead, could he have lied about Paradise, too?

Brigid tries to persuade me as we slog through the jungle at night. "Your King is the Great Beast prophesied in the Book of Revelations."

I scowl and shake my head. "The *Christ* is the Great Beast. *He* is the Great Evil."

"Your King rules through deception and force," says Brigid. "But that is about to end. The awakening of the Christ will usher in a millennium of true paradise."

"Paradise has already arrived," I tell her.

Brigid cocks her head and stares at me in the glow of Imago's body-light. "Have you ever had sex, Clement?"

I turn away.

"Before you experienced it for the first time," says Brigid, "did you truly *know* what it was like? How *good* it would feel?"

I don't answer.

"*That* is what *true* paradise is like, Father," says Brigid. "It's not like *anything* you've known."

"Shut up." I walk faster to get away from her.

"Your whole life has been a wet dream, Clement," says Brigid, "and you're about to wake up."

In the darkest heart of the night, we arrive at the village. It looks like a fort in the jungle, surrounded by a high, circular wall of crudely cut logs. Smoke and light and noise rise from the interior, curling up toward the star-littered sky.

Brigid walks up to a door in the wall, a slab of galvanized metal, and knocks with her handcuffs. I post myself beside her, gripping my atomic scythe tightly.

I don't like the fact that I can't see what's behind the door or walls. At this point, anything can happen.

"All right then." My voice is a whisper. "Once we're inside, stay out of the way. Make a wrong move and I'll kill you."

She doesn't even try to lower her voice. "Why?" She looks at me like I'm crazy. "What do you think you're going to *find* in there, exactly?"

I lay the blade of the scythe against her throat. "The Second Coming. An army of off-the-radar proto-Christs. I'm sure you think they'll save you, but they won't."

Brigid looks amused, then disappointed. "You haven't changed, have you? Even after everything you've seen."

Something bangs heavily against the other side of the door. I hear the clanking of chains. "Just do as you're told," I tell her.

As the door opens inward, Brigid smiles sadly. "I said there's an army of us. I said your kind doesn't stand a chance. But I never said we were *proto-Christs.*"

"*What?*" My hands twitch on the handle of the scythe. "But you said you would lead us to the Second Coming!"

"I did." Brigid nods. "And I have."

I keep the blade at her throat as we enter. "Where then?" Anger surges within me. "Where is the Second Coming?"

Inside the village walls, the undead converge on us from all directions. They stare and shamble in the firelight, upright masses of peeling and suppurating flesh.

"Where is the Second Coming?" I direct my question to the villagers. "Tell me, or I'll kill her!"

"Let her go," says an undead male at the head of the group.

"Is it *you?*" I ask him. "Are *you* the Second Coming? The one who seeks to topple the Kingdom of Free Will?"

"Not him." An undead female steps forward.

Keeping a firm grip on Brigid's arm, I sweep my glowing scythe toward the undead woman. "It's *you* then? *You're* the one who'd put an end to the daily *holidays* and *ice cream* and Heaven on *Earth?*"

The man steps in the path of my blade. "What are you talking about?"

"The Second Coming!" I flick the scythe across his rotting chest, connecting his seeping sores with a fine line of blood. "Who among you is the *Second Coming?*"

"Wha...wha..." A third villager hobbles forward. Half his face has fallen away. "Wha...is-s-s...thuh...Se-cun...Cum-un...?"

My heart races. I turn in a circle, flashing the scythe overhead.

"They don't know about the Second Coming," says Brigid. "Not yet."

"Lies!" If they won't tell me who it is, they leave me no choice.

Leaping forward, I slash the half-faced villager to pieces with the scythe. Then, I sweep the weapon around behind me and kill the other two without looking.

Singing the "Our Father," I wade into the whole damned horde of them, whirling and hacking and slicing. Body parts fly everywhere, and blood fountains into the night sky.

This is what I was born to do. What I was trained for. Graceful annihilation in the name of the King. The noble dance of the warrior priest, carving up monsters like a hibachi chef carving up vegetables.

"Our father, who art in Houston, hallowed be thy flame..."

When I am done, my King will reward me for my service, for saving the Kingdom. He will summon me to Texas and erect statues in my honor and declare a new feast day and ice cream flavor in my name. All will be right with the world.

This is what I am thinking when someone hits me from behind. When my legs go out from under me, and I drop to the muddy ground on my knees.

I scramble to get back on my feet, and someone hits me again.

This time, the blow to my head leaves me dazed. I fall back in the mud and go limp.

That's when I see him. The middle-aged black-haired man, the first zombie treated by Imago. He leaps onto my chest, stone in hand.

And he hits me in the face. He pounds me, again and again.

The world goes watery and melts together in a blur of color and sound and pain. The man keeps pounding my skull with the stone, and I feel myself slipping away.

Wait. These are my final thoughts. *Things are not what you think.*

And then the world runs down into darkness, like a painting in the rain. And then everything is black and silent and still.

"Clement? Father Clement?"

Those are the first words I hear when I return. When the faintest glimmer of awareness flutters into my mind.

"Wake up, Father. It's begun." A woman's voice. "Wakey wakey, eggs and bakey." Brigid's voice. That's what I hear.

Instinctively, I open my eyes. This happens at the same moment I realize I shouldn't have eyes to open because they were smashed in by a rock.

But it doesn't seem to matter. I see Brigid staring down at me, silhouetted against a bright blue sky.

"There you are!" she says. "Welcome back!"

I close my eyes, then open them again. I feel light-headed. Light-bodied, too. As if a weight has been lifted.

"How long was I out?" Looking at the brightness of the sky, I try to guess what time of day it is. Just after sunrise, maybe?

"You mean how long were you *dead?*" Brigid raises her eyebrows. "Three hours. You were dead for three hours."

I lift my head from the mud and look around. Imago stands behind Brigid, staring blankly down at me. We are surrounded by a crowd of men, women, and children, all unblemished and dressed in tatters. "What are you talking about?"

"Don't you remember getting your head bashed in?" Brigid

reaches down and taps my nose, which also shouldn't be there. "You *died*, Clement."

I scowl and shake my head. "Not possible." Even as I say it, I remember the stone smashing my skull. I remember the pain as it slammed down again and again, and the world melting and fading to black.

"You were pushing up daisies," says Brigid. "You were an *ex-Clement.*"

Suddenly, I add things up, and a chill of terror rushes through me. "You're trying to tell me..." I feel a wave of inescapable desperation spread out from the pit of my stomach. "You're saying I was *dead*, and now I'm *not?*"

"Yes." Brigid nods. "Exactly."

I push myself to a sitting position, fighting the urge to run away. I try to keep the fear out of my voice. "You mean I'm...*undead?*"

"Yes." When she says it, my heart sinks. Then, she laughs. "But only in the sense of *not* being *dead.*"

I'm not sure what to think at this point. "Even if I *was* dead, and you could bring me back, why *would* you?"

"It wasn't *my* idea, that's for sure," says Brigid. "But the *Second Coming* seemed to think you were worth saving."

I look past Brigid and Imago at the crowd. Which one of them is the Second Coming of Jesus Christ?

"Apparently, he has a plan in mind for you." Brigid shrugs. "Like I said, it's begun."

"What's that? What's begun?" I teeter as I get to my feet, still feeling light-headed. My eyes flicker, and I start to fall.

Suddenly, I feel strong hands catch me and set me on my feet again. When I open my eyes, I see him.

Imago. Light streaming in rainbow-colored beams from the facets of his stained-glass body. The iron filing features in his face-plate tracing a smile of black metal fuzz.

"The Millennium," he says in that soft, soothing voice of his. "We're about to usher it in."

"Imago?" My own voice falters as I consider the implications.

"*He* brought you back." Brigid says it in my ear. "*He's* the one you've been *looking* for all this time."

"The Second Coming?" My heart pounds as I stare at Imago's robotic face. "He *can't* be."

"I was only ever his prophet," says Brigid. "I'm not fit to polish the chassis of the one who comes after me."

My head spins. I'm not sure what to think or do or say. "Imago?"

The fireflies swirl in his belly. "I am the truth, the way, and the life. He who believeth in me shall never die." The beams of light streaming from his stained-glass facets flare with blinding intensity. "Welcome to Paradise 2.0, Father Clement."

DREAMING OF A CARBONIFEROUS CHRISTMAS

Imagine you're standing around, minding your own business, and a dragonfly the size of an *eagle* lands on your back. Then the bug won't let go no matter how much you jump around and swat it.

Welcome to *my* world.

"Get off! Get off!" I feel the breeze from the big bug's wings as I fight to shake it off, to no avail. Its mouth pincers go *clickety clickety clack* as it crawls and flaps, digging at my sharkskin tunic in a wild hunt for dinner.

Panic surges like a flash-fire within me, then subsides. I've had these bugs on me before; I already know what to do.

Flinging myself back, I land in the mud with a splat, bug-side down. I feel it buzz and thrash against my flesh as I roll back and forth, crushing it under my weight.

Sitting up, I look back and see the monster dragonfly twitch violently, then stop moving. Its giant, diaphanous wings lay spread in the reddish mud, pressed into the indentation left by my body.

Will its death change the future? 310 million years from now, will the 21st century cease to be the world I remember, the one in which I grew up? Will humanity as I knew it cease to exist?

It's something we don't worry about much here in the

Carboniferous Period. Our chief concerns are more related to immediate survival. We do what's necessary to stay alive in the minute-by-minute.

Let the damn future take care of itself.

"Dad! Hey, Dad!" The voice of my daughter, Marlie, approaches fast through the swamp, accompanied by the sound of her feet splashing in the muck. "Come quick! You gotta see this!"

Her pretty 15-year-old face, framed by strands of bright blonde hair that have strayed from her ponytail, bursts from between the scaly trees. Her pale blue eyes are wide with surprise, alarm, or both.

"See what?" Instantly concerned, I push myself to my feet, shucking the worst of the mud from my tunic and amphibian-hide britches. Living when and where we do, the shit is *constantly* hitting the fan.

"Hurry!" With a summoning wave, she whips around, her reptile-leather dress flapping against her knees. "It's at Mr. McVicker's house!" she shouts as she sprints off through the forest.

Heart racing, I grab the flint knife from my millipede-skin belt and follow. Every threat can lead to disaster here, and every second counts. If you're not ready—or even if you are—you can lose a loved one forever in the blink of an eye. Marlie and I know all about that; I lost my wife—her mother—to just such an incident years ago.

Dodging brush and bugs, we weave among the trees like the experts we are. I might be 47 years old, but I'm fit as hell after living in this grueling ancient past for 17 years.

A big gray amphibian lurches up from the mud in our path, its jagged maw heaving open—and both of us sidestep the beast with graceful ease. Running the Carboniferous swamps comes with the territory when you've lived here so long—or, like Marlie, you were *born* to it.

"Here!" Marlie crashes through a patch of ferns and splashes to a stop. "*Look* at this place!"

As I pull up beside her, wiping the sweat from my face, my eyes flash wide open, too. I know George McVicker's place well, of course—it's on the outskirts of our village—but I've never seen it like *this* before.

The hut is covered with decorations. Colorful shells from the nearby sea are laid around the conical thatched roof, gleaming in the morning sunlight. Dried trilobites dangle like windchimes from the fringe of the roof, clattering in the light breeze. Fruits and berries are strung around the walls, arranged in alternating reds, pinks, yellows, and purples.

But perhaps the most shocking part of the display is on the ground in front of the hut. Marlie runs right to it and stands there, pointing and scowling.

She has *never* seen anything like *that.*

"What is it, Dad?" she asks. "And what's *Cha...rist...mass?"* That's how she pronounces it.

I see the words spelled out in white clamshells on a flat rock. The objects behind them, carved out of wood, are each a foot or so tall, clearly meant to look like human figures.

The figures depict a scene I recognize quite well: a man, a woman, and a baby in a crib between them.

Merry Christmas. That's what the words say. *Merry Christmas.*

Presented in plain sight for the first time in the history of the planet Earth.

"Well ho, ho, ho." Those are the first words out of Jennie Rosas' mouth when she ambles up to the scene on her way to somewhere else. "'Tis the season, huh?"

I scrub my fingers through my curly salt-and-pepper hair and shoot her a nasty look. Seventeen years in a prehistoric swamp, and she still doesn't know how or when to keep her trap shut.

"Isn't anybody home?" Jennie, the local botanist, straightens her dress—a silver-gray shift woven from the silk of giant spider-like arthropods—and starts toward the hut. "Where are the damn *dogs?* I've never *heard* this place so quiet before."

I shrug as I start after her. "Beats me." She's talking about George's trained amphibian pets—*frog-dogs*, he calls them—the closest you can get to an *actual* dog in this mammal-free era. Our resident zoologist, George has always had a flair for connecting with wildlife.

"*George!*" Jennie calls loudly. "Are you in there?"

"He's not!" Excitedly, Marlie darts in front of her, back to the hut. "But you have to see what *is*."

I dread what I'm going to see as we follow her through the doorway. All this time, all her life, we've protected her and the other kids from what we left behind in the future on our trip to the ancient past. Now, all of a sudden, George has thrown open Pandora's Box, putting everyone in a shitful position—the kid because of what she's seen...

...and the adults because of the lies we've been telling.

"There, look!" Marlie's so jazzed, I worry she might explode. "Presents!"

Sure enough, a pile of objects wrapped in mottled brown paper (which we learned long ago to make from the bark of the scale trees) occupies the middle of the hut. The packages vary in size, and each is tied with twine from a hemplike plant.

Not to mention, each has a person's name on it, scrawled in purple berry-based ink.

"Damn," mutters Jennie. "And here I didn't get him a thing."

Marlie darts over and grabs one with her name on it from the peak of the pile. "Can I open mine? Please? Please?"

She's gotten presents before, but never under these uncertain circumstances. "Not just yet, honey." I take the gift from her and give it a shake. I feel something heavy bumping around inside, though I can't tell exactly what it is. "Mr. McVicker might not want anyone to open them yet."

"But he didn't say *not* to," says Marlie.

"He didn't say *anything*." Jennie gives her long black hair a toss and meets my gaze. "Did he?"

"Not to me." I replace Marlie's gift atop the pile and look around. George has the inside of the place decorated, too, hung with tree boughs, dragonfly wings, and wreaths woven from dried fruits and flowers.

Then there's the pièce de résistance, tacked to the central

support post at eye level—the first of its kind, as far as I know, here in the age of endless swamps and giant bugs.

A rough-hewn cross made of two wooden slats.

"George has been a busy boy, hasn't he?" Jennie looks at the cross with a mix of disapproval and amusement. "Did you know he was so artistically inclined, Cal?"

The edge in her voice isn't far from my own. "It's news to me, Jen." I'd be surprised if we aren't both thinking the same two things right now: George is a bigger asshole than we thought for pulling this shit...

...and where the hell *is* he?

"How long until the *holy wars* start?" Those aren't quite the first words out of the mouth of Ethan Perkins, our de facto leader, but they're close. "Bring on the religious persecution!"

Six of us—the Founders Council—are meeting to talk about George McVicker in the Quonset, a wooden longhouse built on the slightly less soggy ground on a low hill in the middle of the village. What he did is *that* big a deal, a violation of the basic tenets of our settlement.

Though not everyone sees it exactly that way. "Easy on the overreaction there, chief," says Jennie Rosas. "The kids don't even know what any of it means."

"But they will soon enough," snaps Ethan, a major league pessimist as well as a first-class geologist. "Next thing you know, they'll be burning heretics at the *stake.*"

He's speaking figuratively, of course. Setting fires is pretty much a death sentence in the Carboniferous Period, since the oxygen content of the air is so much higher than it was in our native era. A single spark can set off a raging inferno, so a burning heretic could *really* light things up.

"It's like an infection." Ethan paws at his shaggy brown beard, which is streaked with gray these days. "You can't stop it once it starts spreading."

"You're preaching to the choir." Jennie smirks. "Pardon the expression."

"We've been in agreement on prohibition from the beginning," says Hugh Singer, his smooth, dark face beaded with sweat. "*All* the Founders have. So when and why did George go off the rails?"

"Hallucinations from oxygen intoxication?" I speak from experience; as acclimated to the high-oxygen prehistoric atmosphere as we've become, none of us are immune. As the group's physician, I've seen more cases than I can remember through the years, including my own. "Maybe he thought God came to him in the form of a giant millipede?"

"Or *maybe* he just got nostalgic." It's no surprise Bill Ward speaks up in George's defense. They've been best friends forever. "Tell me you don't get *sick* of the giant cockroaches and dragonflies sometimes. Tell me you don't wish for a little *Christmas* now and then."

Ethan slams his fist on the table. "And the next thing you know, it's the *Spanish Inquisition*, and the *Crusades*, and *9/11*, and priests molesting kids, etcetera, etcetera, ad infinitum!"

"Then we scrub off the serial numbers," says Bill. "When the kids ask, we stick with the secular aspects of the holiday."

"Ya think so?" Jennie gives her dark hair a toss. "I, for one, am *totally* up for explaining the *whole story.* The *crucifixion*, especially. I can't *wait* to lay the concept of *murder* on those munchkins."

I nod in agreement. "Not to mention the part about how we shielded them from such a huge part of human history."

"Secular it is," says Ethan. "Minimize the infection."

"Sounds like a plan," says Hugh. "As long as we keep a united front."

"That's why *you're* going to find George." Ethan points at me, then Jennie. "Make sure he's not on a mission from God."

"Or Satan," says Hugh.

"Which, interestingly enough, is an anagram of *Santa,*" says Jennie.

"Which doesn't surprise me a bit," says Ethan. "Christmas is *harmless*, my ass."

Christmas was never a big deal to me, even back home in the late 21st century. I still remember my last one, though, for obvious reasons.

The world was falling apart around me, around all of us, raging with one catastrophe after another. I was working in a field hospital in a war zone (though pretty much *everywhere* was a war zone, in those days), and the patients kept rolling in through the night. The best I could manage for a Christmas celebration was a slug of Pruno hootch between amputations, glaring at a scrawny little twig with a pornographic ornament dangling from the tip.

I remember it so well because that was when I got the call on the satellite phone. I'd been handpicked for a new mission, the woman said, and excused from my field surgical duties effective immediately.

The mission was beyond anything I could ever have expected. The secret of time travel had been unraveled; a select few experts in critical fields would escape the end of the world and start over in the distant past. All we had to do was take care of our fellow travelers—the billionaires funding the project.

Who could say no to that? They were some of the same billionaires whose greedy excesses had wrecked the environment and fueled the wars, but their offer was still a genuine golden ticket. It was the ultimate Christmas present, trading a definite living hell for a possible Garden of Eden.

Though it turned out the billionaires who'd offered the gift were more than capable of making life a living hell wherever or whenever they landed.

How do you track a man through a Carboniferous swamp? You get lucky.

Luck is about 99% of it, in fact. The marshy ground fills in footsteps as soon as they're made and swallows up dropped evidence in a heartbeat. The giant bugs and creatures gulp down traces left behind on twigs and jaggers, scouring every last morsel.

So the best I can think to do after leaving Marlie with Ethan and his wife is walk the treeline around George's hut, looking for some kind of path. A way he might have cleared through frequent use and followed on whatever errand he chose to run after unveiling his holiday décor.

But it's Jennie who has the breakthrough today. After going away for a little while, she returns to the area behind the hut, marching past me into a path I totally missed.

"The local kids told me where to go," she explains over her shoulder. "They've seen George sneak back here tons of times, though they never followed him very far."

I follow her down the trail, splashing along in my amphibian-skin boots. It hasn't rained much lately, so the water isn't much higher than our ankles...though who knows what pits and sink-holes that steady surface might conceal.

Not to mention the wildlife. Even after 17 years, the menagerie of native beasts lurking in the swamps continues to surprise us. Let's just say the fossil record did not exactly cover the whole ugly story.

"So what do we do about Georgie Porgie when we catch up to him?" Jennie asks over her shoulder. "Throw him in the hoosegow for breaking the atheist code?"

"Gotta *build* a hoosegow first." I step around a suspicious hump in the water, keeping my hand on the hilt of my flint knife just in case.

"How *dare* he take a dump on our godless paradise?" Jennie chuckles as she pushes through a bunch of ferns. "Jesus Christ!"

"*That* guy won't exist for a couple hundred million years."

"So does any of this even *matter,* then?" She looks back, bugging her eyes at me. "Is it anything but a *fairy tale* at this point?"

"More like science fiction."

"Then why do we care? Why are we *out* here?"

"Good question." That's what I say, but we both know better. We both remember why we left the far future. We were right in the thick of Armageddon, which by the way had *nothing* to do with holy wars...and *everything* to do with religion.

Because why should you try to stop the world from going to shit if the *prophets* say it's a waste of time to even try? Because why should you try to save billions of lives if *none* of us bears any responsibility for anything and *God* will make it all right in the end?

Is it any wonder, given the chance to start over, that we left out *that* bit of civilization?

"Here's another question for you," says Jennie as she works her way through a grove of bristly horsetail trees. "When shit gets nasty, do *you* ever pray?"

"No." It's a lie, and I'll bet she knows it. How could I *not* have prayed when my wife, Abbie, was dying? How could I *not* have tried *everything* to hold on to her as the spider venom took her down?

Jennie stops and turns, tipping her head to one side. "But don't you ever feel like God's still *around?* Like He's *closer*, somehow? Maybe because creation is still so young and primitive?"

I wipe the sweat from my brow. "Why? Do you?"

Jennie laughs. "Oh *hell* no!" And then she continues on her way.

And the sad truth is, I feel the same. I secretly expected it to be different, exactly like she said—but I have *never* felt a trace of a divine creator in this primordial time period. I keep thinking I *should*, but I *don't*.

Though I have to admit, that might have more to do with *us* than it does with *Him*.

We've been walking for an hour or so when I almost lose my head to a killer treemoeba.

The only warning I get is a faint rustle from the scale tree above me, which I hardly even notice. Jennie's just asked if I ever wonder how things might have been if we'd gone to the Cretaceous Period as we'd originally planned, and I'm about to give her my answer.

That's when the treemoeba drops from the high branches, plunging straight for my head.

Pure luck makes me step aside at the last possible second, staring at what might be the barely visible remains of a human footprint. I hear a heavy splash behind me, and I jump and look back, the knife flashing into my hand.

There it is, a glistening blob full of bizarre, colorful particles and shapes. It reaches out with a shivering pseudopod that looks like it's dripping with water...but it's not. The liquid is much closer to saliva, complete with fast-acting gastric juices that can clear the flesh from a bone in seconds.

This is one of those creatures never found in the fossil record. It evaporates completely after death, leaving no trace—but *before* death, it's a flesh-eating, tree-climbing blob without mercy.

"God, I hate these things." I give the blob a wide berth, even as its viscous pseudopod stretches in my direction. "I'd trade *treemoebas* for Cretaceous *dinosaurs* any day of the week."

Suddenly, I hear nearby animal cries—almost but not quite like the barking of not-evolved-yet mammalian dogs. Jennie, who's gotten a little ahead of me, thrashes back toward me through a dense patch of giant ferns, eyes wide.

"We're here!" She gestures with both hands for me to hurry. "Come on! What's holding you up?"

Just a killer treemoeba, I almost say, but then I keep it to myself and fall in step behind her.

The barking gets louder as we slosh onward. It definitely turns more hostile when we get close, pushing through the last stand of ferns into a clearing.

I know before the last fern is brushed aside what the source of the barking will turn out to be. Sure enough, in the middle of the clearing, I see multiple frog-dogs raising the ruckus—gray-skinned, four-legged amphibians the size of German Shepherds, with about the same general disposition.

The frog-dogs are in costume, but even so, they're not the most interesting things up ahead.

"Kris Kringle on a cracker." Jennie blows out her breath as we stand there, taking it all in. "Will ya take a look at *that*."

The sign is the first thing that catches my eye. *North Pole*, it says, painted in big red letters on two rough wooden planks tacked to a scale tree. The trunk of the tree is painted like a candy cane, with red and white stripes swirling around it.

Behind the candy cane tree, on a rise of rare dry land, there's a big, green yurt, its reptile-skin walls and roof festooned with decorations that put George's hut in the village to shame. Brightly-colored shells, coral, flowers, starfish, and sea glass hang everywhere, interspersed with the gossamer wings of dragonflies and the tubular sleeves of air worms (another species unknown in the fossil record). Somehow, there's even something that looks like *snow*—a cottony white fluff laid along the peak and edges of the roof.

As for the frog-dogs...

"I'll be damned!" Jennie laughs out loud. "He stuck *antlers* on their heads!"

Even with our way of life at stake, I can't help but smile...not with *bells* jingling around the frog-dogs' necks and a makeshift *sleigh* off to one side, its boxy basket painted red and green and gold.

"So much for a low-key nostalgia trip," says Jennie. "Georgie-boy has really pulled out all the stops."

"You haven't even met my *elves* yet." It's the first we've heard George's voice all day, coming from inside the yurt. "Don't make me call them in to run you off. We won't *let* you spoil *Christmas."*

"Says the man who wants to spoil *civilization* by dredging up *religion* all over again," says Jennie.

"I *knew* you people couldn't let me spread a little happiness in peace." George storms out of the yurt, looking pissed. His reddish spider-silk smock, stained that color by berries or blood, is about as close as you can get to Santa style in the Carboniferous world.

"Ah, lighten up, George," says Jennie. "We'd just rather if you kept your fantasy role-playing fetish to yourself."

"Enough!" George rattles off a series of whistling and clicking noises, then a shouted command. "Hermey, Budddy—go get 'em!"

Suddenly, I hear the telltale skittering sound that I know all too well. Even as I turn to look, a pair of ten-foot-long millipedes are almost upon us, their dozens of feet scuttling over the muddy ground.

I've never seen an albino giant millipede before, but this one bowls me over at a high rate of speed. Just as I go down in the slop, I see the other one—its carapace dark crimson—cruising on a collision course toward Jennie.

And *missing*. As nimble as she is mouthy, Jennie cartwheels over the hurtling beast and comes down with a splash on the other side, unfazed.

I scramble to my feet just in time to see the albino swing around and double back, charging me hard. Antennae and mandibles twitching, the creature barrels toward me, rippling like a magic carpet as it flows over the humps and declivities.

Knife in hand, I run for the house, and the millipede follows close behind. The armor plates that run the length of its body clatter as it chases me, gleaming in the sun streaming down into the clearing.

I don't manage to stay a step ahead for long. The albino brushes against me, flinging me hard into the North Pole sign on the candy cane tree. Heart hammering, I push myself free—just in time to face the crimson millipede, which rears up in front of me and lets out a ghastly screech.

Dozens of pairs of crimson legs flutter before me. The millipede's pale underbelly ripples, and it lunges, its mandibles snapping at my face.

Just then, Jennie cries out. I look over in time to see her wrestling with the albino, which has reared up like the crimson. The thing lets out a ululating squeal as she kicks it hard in the underbelly. She kicks it again and again, making it squeal louder every time.

I decide to do her one better and go after my opponent's belly with my knife. My first thrust doesn't land, though, as the crimson millipede thrashes back from the tip of the blade. Before I can take another stab, the beast plows forward, pitching me into the mud for the second time.

Then, it runs up over me and stops, pressing me down with its weight and its dozens of feet. Now I know how the dragonfly felt when I crushed him.

With the weight of the bug upon me, I'm having trouble pulling in breaths. "Let me up!" I have to struggle to get out a shout. "We just want to talk!"

"Yeah, *Satan Claus!"* Jennie sounds like she's still kicking the albino, though I can't see them just now. "And by the way, you *know* these aren't really *elves*, don't you?"

I hear nothing from George for a moment...and then he lets out a fresh series of clicking and whistling noises. Next thing I know, the crimson many-legged bastard is pedaling its way off my chest.

Sucking in breaths like they're going out of style, I sit up fast and look around. George watches from behind his six growling frog-dogs, looking stern with his arms folded over his bushy white beard and ample belly.

"Then talk, but make it snappy," he says, not sounding the least bit jolly. "Christmas Eve is my busiest night of the year, as you know."

George wouldn't be the first of our group to lose his mind. That's what I'm thinking as I get to my feet.

We've lost a number of men and women to mental illness through the years. Maybe it's something in the air or water, or maybe it's the stress of living in a prehistoric shithole with no way to get home (however awful that home might be). Whatever makes it happen, we've got no effective meds to treat it. (We barely have *any* meds to treat *anything.)*

Still, the only approach I can think to try at the moment is to treat him like a patient—take his history and make a diagnosis.

"So, George." I walk to the candy cane tree and straighten the *North Pole* sign. "Nice work with all this stuff. Very creative."

George nods once. "Thank you. I thought this geologic period could use a little Christmas spirit."

"Holy shit." Jennie takes a step in his direction, and the frog-dogs growl louder. "I must've missed the fuckin' memo."

"Memo?" George's frown deepens.

"The one about repealing religious prohibition." Jennie reaches out and flutters her fingers. "You got a copy handy?"

"What's the matter with you?" George narrows his eyes and shakes his head. "Don't you *approve* of making people happy?"

"Oh, sure," says Jennie. "They can laugh their *asses* off all the way down the *slippery slope."*

George *really* doesn't look jolly now. "I feel *sorry* for you. For *all* of you. You're even more deluded than *I* used to be."

"You admit you're deluded, then?" I ask him.

"I was," says George, "but it's finally worn off."

"You mean you don't think you're Santy Claus anymore?" asks Jennie.

"I mean the delusions have worn off from 17 years ago. From when we came here in the first place."

I wonder where he's going with this. "The exodus? What about it?"

George stares at me with cold indifference for a long moment. I suddenly feel like *he* is doing the workup on *me* and not vice versa.

"Do you know the two main problems in a world without God?" he says finally. "The *biggest*, most *fundamental* problems?"

"A lack of hypocrisy?" chirps Jennie. "Increased reliance on a scientific understanding of physical laws instead of magical thinking?"

"Problem number one: *triumph of the bland*." George spreads his arms to take in the surrounding swamp. "Without the perception of *divinity*, we are left with only the *mundane*. Without *magic*, nothing is truly *special."*

"Seriously?" says Jennie. "You think *that's* the big problem with the *age of giant bugs and spiders?*"

"Is that why you're reviving Santa Claus and Christmas?" I ask. "To bring back the magic?"

George lowers his arms to his sides. "Problem number two," he says. "*Lack of forgiveness.*"

I'm still not sure where he's going with this. "Forgiveness, George?"

"For what I've done. For what I'm guilty of."

"You don't need *God* for that." Jennie raises her hand and flicks it in George's direction. "I hereby forgive you for *everything* you've ever done...unless you did it against *me*, that is."

"*You're* guilty, too!" George raises his voice, riling up his growling frog-dogs. "And *you!*" He jabs a finger at me. "*All* of us! All the *Founders!*"

Fake antlers quivering, the frog-dogs hop and howl. Hermey and Buddy the giant millipedes slither and screech, antennae twitching like ferns in a stiff wind.

As for me, I'm sweating like always, but I still get a chill. My stomach twists like a fist breaking plants at the stem, and my heart roars like one of the mystery beasts calling in the night.

Because, finally, I know what he's talking about.

Seventeen years ago, we made our decision.

John Wellington Garrity III, who'd been close to a trillionaire when we'd left the future, freaked out at the first sight of a giant dragonfly. I mean, he totally went *apeshit* within the first five minutes of being in a prehistoric era...the *wrong* prehistoric era, to boot.

As the technical team pieced together what had happened, that we'd overshot the mark and landed in the Carboniferous instead of the Cretaceous Period, John called us every name in the book. He insisted we build another time machine immediately and send him and his family to the era they'd requested.

As if we could build anything more complicated than a hut or spear with the tools at hand. We didn't have the capabilities, though we had a lot of knowledge at our fingertips.

Information and blueprints were tattooed all over our bodies, since time travel was strictly a *naked* proposition—but there were no time machine plans inked on anyone's back or ass or thigh. We had always understood this would be a one-way trip; no one would *want* to return to the shitty future and its Apocalypse in progress, anyway.

But Garrity didn't want to hear the truth, and neither did his obnoxious wife and kids. Neither did his billionaire buddies who'd come along, or *their* obnoxious wives and kids. Whatever our status had been in our previous lives, as doctors or scientists or engineers, we were just slaves to those rich fuckers now.

As if that wasn't bad enough, one of Garrity's kids got reckless, and one of our best people was gravely wounded saving him from a poisonous spider-thing (the same species that later got my wife). Garrity's little bastard blamed the whole incident on our wounded guy, and his daddy had the gall to take *his* word over *ours.* He actually called for our guy to be *executed* before his injuries killed him...and when we refused, he tried to do it *himself.*

The situation could not have been more clear at that point. However far we'd come from the world where any kind of monetary wealth or social strata mattered, we were just Garrity's bitches and always would be. We were just the hired help for that filthy rich gang.

And they just wanted results. So that was what we decided to give them.

It was unanimous. We would give them the results they deserved.

"Have *you* forgiven yourself?" George asks me. "What about *you?*" he asks Jennie.

For once, she looks grim, and the sarcasm's gone. "We did what we had to, George. I've learned to live with that."

"Then you *are* still delusional," says George. "Just like *I* used to be."

"Says the man who thinks *frog-dogs* are *reindeer*." Jennie says it more like an insult than a joke.

"You're telling me you never *think* of them, then?" asks George. "The women and children, wandering off into the misty swamps?"

"Not alone," says Jennie.

"You're right, the men went with them." George nods. "Off into exile from the rest of us."

"With supplies," says Jennie. "We gave them everything we could spare."

"Can you *imagine* how they felt?" George stares off into space. "I know *I* can. I think about it all the time."

"Good for you, George," snaps Jennie.

"They waded off with no idea what to do next," says George. "They had no expertise or survival skills. No understanding of this prehistoric world. Maybe they were even hallucinating from the excess oxygen or the ancient microbes or spores in the air. And then it started."

"George, please," I say. "Just stop."

That just makes him speak louder. "And then it *started.* Whatever *got* them...and then the *screaming.*"

I remember it clearly, though I try not to think about it much. Those screams in the distance, echoing through the swamp—the screams of people I *knew.*

Whatever the rest of us were doing, we stopped when they started. We gazed into the swamps, our blood turning to ice, and we listened.

The women. The children. The men. Their cries overlapping, intermingling. Distinguishable at first, one from another...and then not. Then bleeding together into one blistering howl of terrified suffering, climbing and climbing past the too-massive prehistoric moon all the way to the out-of-place stars.

That *screaming.*

We did that. In our zeal to put the past/future behind us, to set aside the worst that had led to our flight to this virgin wilderness, we showed that *none* of us was any better than the rest. We could never escape our worst instincts, our bad judgment masquerading as self-righteous wisdom.

Our *crimes* masquerading as *justice.*

That *screaming.*

"Maybe it's just as well that we've kept God out of here." George wipes away a tear. "I'm not sure even He would forgive us for what we've done."

Jennie clears her throat, which makes me think she might have been choked up a little. "And you think any of *this* is gonna help?" She gestures at the antlered frog-dogs, the sleigh, the decorated North Pole yurt. "You think this is gonna make a *difference?"*

"I just want to give people something *special* again," says George. "A reason to feel *goodwill* again."

"Which all loops back to religion," I tell him. "*Death* on a *cross.* Man's inhumanity to man."

"And loving your neighbor!" says George. "And sacrificing yourself for the good of others!"

"The kids are better off without *any* of that garbage," snaps Jennie. "Let them develop a new civilization without baggage or limitations. Let them do it *themselves*."

"I agree."

I'm surprised when George says it. I think Jennie is, too.

"I don't want to force-feed anyone anything. I just want to hand out some damn *presents*." George pulls a floppy red cap from a pocket of his smock and sticks it on his head. There's a white tassel on the end that looks like it's made of the same kind of fluff as the "snow" along the roof of the yurt. "I want to give kids something to look forward to. *Adults,* maybe, too.

"And hey, if it makes up a little for what happened before..."

His voice trails off...and then he perks up again. "You still got a *problem* with that?"

I know I should object, but I don't. I know I should stick to the settlement's doctrines, but I can't.

My own daughter is one of those kids he's talking about. Would it be a bad thing if she could share a tradition I once loved? Don't I trust her to handle the religious undertones if she spills some on her?

I think I know the answers to those questions and another one, too: Would it make me feel better about the past if I do this with him?

Jennie sees me thinking and looks horrified. "You're not seriously *considering* this, are you, Cal?"

"I don't know." Smiling, I lay my right index finger aside of my nose. "Am I?"

The village is quiet and still in the pre-dawn mist, its inhabitants just starting to stir. Whatever dreams they've had through the night are fading fast, leaving traces like footprints disappearing in the soupy mud.

That's when the commotion moves in from the distance. The barks and splashes of running frog-dogs shatter the quiet, intermingled with the jingling of bells and the shouts of someone mushing the animals as if they were reindeer.

If the villagers can't tell exactly what he's saying at first, they can soon enough: *Now Dasher! Now Dancer! Now Prancer and Vixen!*

The adults recognize the words instantly and look up in amazement. The kids know nothing about them but are still the first to scramble from their huts and yurts, drawn by the promise of the unexpected.

On Comet! On Cupid! On Donner and Blitzen!

Within moments, the whole village is outside, staring in the same direction. The grownups look grumpy; they know that their rules have been broken, their way of life changed. The kids just look excited, barely able to contain their curiosity.

To the top of the porch! To the top of the wall!

The air is electric as the voice and the barking grow louder, approaching through the scale tree swamp. Whatever's coming, it's not a danger; the secrets it carries are the good kind, not the bad.

At last, the noise is almost upon them…and even the uptight adults seem to loosen up. The kids' growing excitement is contagious; their parents can't help cracking reluctant smiles at their innocent anticipation.

Now dash away! Dash away all!

Suddenly, the antlered frog-dogs burst from the ferny brush, strapped to traces made of rope from hemplike vegetation. The red sleigh glides behind them on broad water-ski runners, skimming along as smoothly as if there were snow underneath.

Jennie holds the reins, making like an elf in a green cap and tunic. I'm beside her in my own green getup, waving fronds of something George calls "elfnip"—a plant that's like catnip for giant millipedes. Hermey the albino and Buddy the crimson millipede scuttle alongside us, chasing the elfnip provided by Mr. Claus.

Speaking of Santa, he's sitting behind us, looking jolly as hell in his red smock and red cap with white tassel. His eyes twinkle as he smiles and waves, watching as the children's faces light up when they see him.

And they don't even know who Santa Claus *is* yet.

Will this whole scene lead to grief down the line? I'd bet good money on it. Ethan our leader looks like he's chewing nails over there, keeping his arms folded stiffly over his chest. The other adults, at least, are caught up in the moment, grinning at the crazy Carboniferous twist on Christmas—though when the fun fades, the debates over God's place in our world could turn rancorous again.

But for now, the heat is on hold. Kids, including my Marlie, are laughing and running up as Jennie pulls on the reins and the sleigh splashes to a stop. Grownups are laughing, too, letting the kids have their fun as Santa hands out personalized presents.

None of us, I'd wager, are remembering the screams in the swamp from 17 years ago. I know I'm not.

Because as I stand there in the midst of this moment, all I can think about is the single, lacy snowflake drifting down from the sky. Impossible as it is in this hot, swampy world, it flutters before me, white and miraculous.

Then there are more, swirling all around us, multiplying by the minute. Are they the product of an overabundance of oxygen and ancient microbes affecting my human mind? The latest in a long line of visions brought on by this primordial bogworld?

No one else seems to see them, but maybe they're afraid to admit it. What if there *is* magic at work, and they scare it away? If no one believes in God, how would they know what do about a miracle?

For now, I guess it's enough for me just to stick out my tongue. To catch a snowflake on it as children laugh and Santa ho-ho-hos. To feel a familiar joy in this hostile place and know, deep in my heart, that maybe there *is* a divine spirit behind the curtain after all, and maybe my wife Abbie *does* live on elsewhere, awaiting the day I come back to her.

And maybe I *can* be forgiven for what I have and haven't done, or at least, like an eagle-sized dragonfly gliding through the snow, I can move on to another part of the timeless and sun-dappled forest, wings glittering like the very thinnest slick of ice.

SOMETHING BORROWED, SOMETHING DOOMED

Back home, we had a tradition: the worse the weddin', the better the marriage. That's why our people worked so hard to ruin each other's weddin' days.

It gave the bride an' groom somethin' to overcome an' a cause for hope...like, there's nowhere to go from here but up. We told an' retold the stories over an' over, an' they just got better with age.

But just like with anythin', sooner or later someone's gonna go too far. Take it to extremes. Face it, there are some calamities that just don't sound better no matter how many times you retell 'em.

Like the end a' the world, for example. That was the monkey business my brothers got up to on *my* weddin' day.

They figured, if they could pull it off, they'd set me up for the greatest marriage of all time, because how could you ruin anybody's weddin' day any worse than endin' the world?

This just goes to show how dirt-suckin' stupid my brothers could be.

I guess I knew I was in for trouble when my brothers actually seemed to *like* my boyfriend, Bigfoot. (Nickname, it's just a nickname.)

Now, my brothers had a long history a' hatin' my beaus and drivin' 'em off...but Bigfoot won 'em over. Even Thirty Ought, the youngest and roughest, came around, which is really sayin' somethin'.

"You better do right by him, Vicky," Thirty Ought told me one day, combin' his fingers through his thick, black hair. He narrowed his bright blue eyes at me an' nodded. "No funny stuff, understand?"

Part of it had to do with Bigfoot's winnin' personality. He was just the kind a' guy who if you shot him accidentally while huntin', you'd never forgive yourself.

The rest of it, from what I can see, had to do with him bein' one a' the best wildshiners around. Give him a glass a' unprogrammed bacteria, and in nothin' flat, he could turn forty acres a' run-a'-the-mill woods into a fairytale kingdom a' twirlin' parasols and dancin' geisha foxes.

He was better than any of us, which I have to admit made me hate him in a jealous kind a' way at the same time I was fallin' in love with him.

Now, when I say he was better than us, that's high praise. When it comes to wildshiners, my family, the Dozens, were second only to Bigfoot Tourniquet in the state a' Best Virginia...ipso facto in the whole United States, since Best Virginia was the only state where wildshinin' wasn't outlawed. (We used to be *West* Virginia, till the National Guard got creamed in the mountain country an' the Supreme Court exempted us from the genetic tamperin' ban. The "B" is for "bioengineering," y'know.)

You wouldn't *believe* what we were doin' out there. Of course you've heard about the huntin'; maybe you've even been lucky enough to go on a safari through one of our exclusive altered game preserves.

But that was just the ass end of it, my friend. That was just the part we sold to make a livin'. What you didn't see is that we'd made an art out a' wildshinin', just like our ancestors did with moonshinin'.

While the rest a' the country had turned away from the biorevolution, we Best Virginians had become magicians. We had learned how to use the tiniest creatures to change the world in the biggest, most beautiful ways.

We worked miracles, or at least the closest thing to 'em. There was just one problem.

As long as a human bein's still doin' the drivin', the truck won't always make it up the hill. Just like any creative types, sometimes we hit a roadblock.

That's why, even after the end a' the world, I still haven't finished bringin' my dead mama's favorite memory back to life.

My mama, Circa Dozen, was one a' the original genebillies who fought off the National Guard an' founded Best Virginia. She was also one a' the greatest weddin' wreckers of all time.

I'm proud to say I got to be part a' some a' her finest achievements...like, for example, the second weddin' of her best friend, Mona Fingerling. Mama really pulled out all the stops that day, as in recreatin' the plagues that Moses brought down on ancient Egypt in the Bible.

Mona would laugh about it later, but she was screamin' her lungs out when the frogs an' locusts jumped all over her while it rained blood from the church rafters.

It had been a lot a' work for the whole family, but it was worth it. While everyone else in the church shrieked an' ran, my brothers an' I howled with laughter.

Up front, Mama an' I tossed handfuls a' glitterin' pixie dust in the air. My five brothers scattered around the church did the same. The dust was full a' designer microbes set to trigger the next plagues.

Moments later, the mayhem shifted to complete chaos as sores an' boils broke out on every patch a' bare skin in the place (except our family's, because the microbes were programmed not to affect us).

Mona turned around, her face blotched an' blistered, an' locked eyes with Mama. "This is *horrible,*" she said between sobs. "You've ruined *everythin'*!"

Mama grinned proudly. "*We've* ruined everythin'," she said, wrappin' an arm around my shoulders an' huggin' me against her side. "Don't forget my daughter an' my boys. It was a team effort."

Mona barely managed to pinch a small smile out a' her swollen face. "This is the worst ever, I think," she said. "Could be a hell of a marriage."

Mama laughed an' winked at me. She didn't look much older'n I was, thanks to a little personal wildshinin'. Her long hair was almost as black an' glossy as mine, her eyes almost as bright blue as mine, an' her pale skin nearly as smooth. "What do you say to that, Vick?"

Right before the herd a' diseased livestock put in an appearance, followed by a storm a' baseball-sized hail, I smiled. "I just hope my weddin' day's *half* as bad as yours, ma'am," I said, not realizin' that my words would someday come back to haunt me.

It really wasn't the rhinoporcupine's fault I ended up covered with his poop.

He was somebody else's creation, a stray who'd wandered into my family's genefields. When I injected him with the hypodermic end a' my six-foot cattle prod, shootin' new genetic instructions into his system, he right away moved to obey.

Problem was, that big spiny critter swung around so fast I had to stumble outta his way an' hit the ground. He didn't seem to notice that the load a' crap he dumped as he lumbered by landed square on top a' me.

It was then, as I sat there, covered in steamin', reekin' orange goo, that I heard what sounded like someone chokin' to death.

Spottin' him a few yards away, I realized that chokin' sound was just his way a' laughin'.

"Oh, man!" Bent over with his big catcher's mitt hands on his softball-sized kneecaps, he was laughin' so hard he could barely get his words out. "I am so sorry!"

"No need to apologize," I said, smilin' as I reached for my cattle prod/hypodermic rod. The guy didn't set off my warnin' bells, but we Best Virginians have had a thing about strangers ever since the National Guard scampered through our front yards.

"Actually," said the guy, still laughin', "I *do* need to apologize. See, the rhinoporcupine's one a' my livestock."

"And *who* does that make *you*?" I put my rod down an' sunk my hands into the rancid muck.

Still laughin', the guy straightened an' pushed his glowin', golden hair outta' his eyes. He was a suncatcher, one a' the more successful human offshoots whipped up in the "Home Genome-Makeover" craze from back before the bio-engineerin' bust. Soaked-up sunshine lit every hair follicle on his licorice body like fiber optics in a coal seam.

I thought he was just beautiful.

"Family name's Tourniquet," he said. "We're wildshiners from down Huntington way."

"Nice to meet ya', Mr. Tourniquet," I said, shortly before I pitched big soppin' handfuls a' rhinoporcupine poop at him. "Lucky for you, I happen to be the welcome wagon. Now aren't you gonna ask me 'bout our special way a' welcomin' folks in these parts?"

And that was how I met my future husband, Bigfoot Tourniquet.

Six months later, I stood over my mother's burial plot, tryin' to finish the one last thing I had to do for her.

Circa had died a week before a' the crumbles. The one blessin' was that she got to know my future husband before she went, as Bigfoot an' I were pretty much joined at the hip by then.

He couldn't help me with what I had to do for Mama, though. It was a wildshiner tradition, like ruinin' weddin's. The firstborn had to 'shine up a permanent livin' memorial depictin' the deceased's favorite moment on Earth.

Problem was, I couldn't get the damn thing right. Mama had left specific instructions, but the moment kept comin' out wrong.

Mama's instructions were mostly in the form a' genetic code, so I didn't know exactly how every little detail would come out in the end. I knew enough a' the big picture that I could tell I wasn't even in the right neighborhood, though.

I tried again in the fadin' summer twilight over Mama's plot, tossin' fistfuls a' pixie dust from two pouches, then addin' pinches from three others. The shimmerin' powders danced in midair, mixin' an' whirlin' faster an' faster, becomin' a rainbow vortex that groaned an' expanded.

The dust sparkled an' swirled as the microbes worked their magic, spinnin' earth an' air an' water an' life into a whole different arrangement a' matter an' energy. Within the walls a' the funnel, shapes appeared an' moved an' grew, half visible like a body behind a shower curtain.

Then, the vortex peeled away in ribbons all the colors a' the rainbow, revealin' its handiwork.

Right there in front a' me was a scene from Mama's weddin' day, big as life. In a gown a' pure white light, ringed by tiny, flutterin' cherubs, Mama kissed her new husband full on the lips. The two of 'em floated in midair, slowly rotatin' six feet off the ground. All around 'em, the guests an' preacher an' weddin' party drifted through the air, too. Even as the congregation floated upward, the walls a' the church came tumblin' down, collapsin' in clouds a' dust an' heaps a' debris.

All through it, Mama never stopped kissin' her groom. Tears a' joy streamed down her cheeks, an' she held his face lightly in her long-fingered hands.

I'd failed again. It wasn't the moment Mama had chosen, the one she'd written about in her will.

So I wasn't done yet. I'd have to keep tryin' till I got it right...no matter how much I hated the moment she'd picked.

Which I did. It might've been Mama's favorite moment a' *her* life, but it was about my *least* favorite moment a' *mine.*

Maybe I should've just let my genius nut-job brothers take care of it. A year later, I still wasn't havin' any luck with Mama's memorial, while my brothers managed to end the whole world on my weddin' day.

Delaney, the only one older'n me, had promised me somethin' special in the way a' weddin' ruination...but talk about your record for genius an' stupidity all in one. I mean, what kinda' brain trust ends the world while they're still livin' on it?

Durin' the ceremony, though, you'd hardly have known they were up to anythin'. Four of 'em were lined up as Bigfoot's groomsmen, an' Gila, the second oldest at twenty-six, was the best man. All five wore white tuxedos that set off their thick, black hair...an' boy, were they wearin' the poker faces. Those long, black lashes a' theirs flicked over bright blue eyes that looked pure an' innocent as the new-driven snow on the Best Virginian mountaintops.

Naturally, this got me all the more worked up.

Things only got worse as the ceremony went on...an' by worse, I mean everythin' went perfectly. Unlike other brides an' grooms, Bigfoot an' I traded rings without havin' 'em snatched an' eaten by stampedin' human hearts brandishin' handguns. We said our vows without bein' drowned out by twelve-foot-tall opera-singin' Viking women with horrible body odor. We kissed without the church turnin' into a fiery hell complete with howlin', pitchfork-totin' demons in silver bikinis.

By the time the minister said, "I now present Mr. and Mrs. Hermes Tourniquet," I was startin' to think maybe no sabotage was comin' after all. Maybe, my brothers' real plan was just to drive me crazy waitin' for the hammer to fall.

Then, as Bigfoot an' I started down the aisle, the back a' the church started to run...not like legs or a nose, but like a paintin' in the rain.

Holdin' Bigfoot by the arm, I stopped in the middle a' the aisle an' stared. The white a' the walls, the dark brown a' the doors an' woodwork, the red an' gold an' blue a' the stained glass windows ran downward in streaks. Where the colors melted away, a backdrop a' perfect blackness loomed, uninterrupted by even the faintest flickerin' star.

Just then, as everyone in the church turned around to see what the heck I was gapin' at, I heard one a' my brothers curse at the front a' the church. It was Buck, the third oldest after Delaney an' Gila.

"All right," said Buck. "Which one a' you guys forgot to set up the safety bubble around the church?"

"I thought *you* were goin' to do it," said Rattler, the overexcitable next-to-the-youngest a' the five brothers.

Buck let out a disgusted sigh. "I can't *believe* you guys dropped the ball again."

"It was *your* job, Buck," said my youngest brother, Thirty Ought.

"All a' you *shut up*," said Delaney. "Hey, Vicky. Can you come here a minute?"

I tore myself away from watchin' the church melt an' headed for the boys. People in the rear pews were crowdin' toward the front a' the place, hopin' to escape the growin' void.

"We, uh, released this new world-eatin' bacteria, Vick," Delaney said sheepishly, like he was confessin' to readin' my diary. "The bad news is, someone forgot to protect the church...but *you'll* be okay. You're about to be the last person in the world."

"'Cept there won't *be* a world," said Buck.

"The good news is, we're pretty sure you can 'shine up a new one," said Delaney.

"And don't feel compelled to bring back these other screwups when ya' do," said Buck.

As I sweep my hand through the darkness, trails a' twinklin' glitter cascade from my fingertips. The world has ended, an' I'm not alone.

I float in an ocean a' microbes, the well-fed remnants of all I once knew. My brothers did a great job programmin' 'em for my survival; the microbes kept me safe durin' the apocalypse, an' now they're providin' all the air an' water an' nutrients I need to live.

And more. I found out they respond to my thoughts.

If I picture somethin' an' concentrate, it pops right up in front a' me, conjured from the digested matter an' energy a' the destroyed Earth. If it's a hamburger, it's real enough to eat. If it's a person, he's real enough to talk to.

I've never heard of a wildshiner usin' mind control on microbes before. The only controllin' we ever did was with DNA manipulation in the lab an' creative mixin' in the field.

But I'm wonderin' if maybe I *have* seen this before. I keep thinkin' back to the way Mama's memorial kept goin' wrong. Even though I'd program the microbes real carefully an' triple-check my work, the scenes they'd recreate were always different from the one I'd programmed into 'em.

For a while, I'd wondered if I was subconsciously sabotagin' my own work with my own two hands, but Bigfoot an' Delaney had both checked the work an' said it was A-OK.

Now, I see another way I could've sabotaged myself.

I close my eyes an' focus my thoughts on a memory, bringin' it to the front a' my mind. It's a moment I remember well, too well, an' it comes easy to me.

When I open my eyes, the moment surrounds me, life-size an' perfect in every way.

Mama an' I (at age sixteen) sit together on a plank dock juttin' from a bank a' the Cacapon River. It's mid-summer in the Best Virginia hills, hot as the engine block of a pickup just got done climbin' the switchbacked road up a mountain face.

While my younger self sits there with Mama, I personally watch from a few yards away. I'm hoverin' over the cracklin' brown water in the middle a' the river, an' they can't see me.

Even before Mama starts talkin', I understand. There's a reason I thought a' this now.

It's the same reason I kept ruinin' her memorial.

"I only changed the outside a' you, Vick," says Mama, danglin' her feet in the river water. "The inside's just the same, an' the inside's what I truly love."

Sixteen-year-old Vicky tries to skim a stone over the river's sparklin' surface, but it only hops once an' sinks like her heart. "I knew it," she says, her voice bitter cold. "I always knew there was somethin' wrong with me."

"No no, honey." Mama reaches over to try to stroke Vicky's long, black hair, but Vicky ducks away from her touch. "There's *never* been anythin' wrong with you."

Vicky looks up suddenly, like she just thought a' somethin' awful. "My brothers?" she says. "Did you change *them*, too?"

Mama sighs an' nods. "I 'shined up all a' you."

Tears gush from Vicky's eyes. "Why?" she says. "Why did you *do* it?"

My own heart pounds as Mama takes Vicky's hand. "To make us look more like a family," she says. "The family I always wanted."

Vicky tries to tear her hand away, but she can't. "I don't even know what I *really* look like!"

"You think I don't love you?" Mama kisses Vicky's hand. "Tell the truth, now."

Vicky glares at Mama through her tears. She sobs an' shakes as birds sing an' fish flip outta' the water an' splash back down. "What'd I look like?" she says. "Where'd I come from?"

"Don't matter," says Mama.

"Tell me! Why won't you *tell* me who I really *am*?"

Mama looks down at the river glidin' past. "Because I love you too much," she says softly, "an' I'm too scared I'll lose you."

"I hate you," says Vicky. She jumps to her feet. "I hate you an' I'll never forgive you."

Then, as she storms away, leavin' her mother alone on the river bank, I close my eyes. When I open 'em, the scene is gone. Nothin' but blackness again.

At last, I understand. As I reach out with my mind to the ocean a' microbes around me, I know why I couldn't bring myself to 'shine up the memorial Mama wanted...an' I know *why* she wanted it.

It wasn't just for her. It wasn't just a memorial to her favorite moment of her life.

It was a gift to me.

Mama's instructions for the memorial were in the form a' genetic code. I won't see all the details till the memorial's done, includin' the one thing I've always wanted to see more'n anythin' else in my life...the one thing I've also been most scared a' seein'.

The one thing Mama gave me as a final show a' her love. The one thing she could finally afford to give me without fear, without worryin' she'd lose me, because I was losin' her first.

Now that the world's over an' I have a clean slate to work with, I believe I can bring her gift to life. And maybe I can finally forgive her.

All around me, the darkness glows with the light of a gazillion microbes churnin' my thoughts into reality. Shapes appear in the murk, blurry like I'm seein' 'em through a curtain...an' then they get brighter an' more solid.

Like the curtain's liftin'.

Mama Circa gazes down at the small form glowing in the moonlit cradle. Smiling, she runs her hand along the side rail, watching the child curled up in the bedclothes.

The trailer smells of beer and roses...beer because the man and woman who live there are drinkers, roses because of the soothing garden Mama Circa has wildshined around them to deepen their sleep.

Her heart pounds. Gently, she reaches for the child, drawing her up out of the cradle and into her arms.

Closing her eyes, Mama hugs the child to her, but not so tightly that she will wake her. Mama beams and breathes deeply, turning slowly with her prize in the silver moonlight at the scene of the crime.

The one-year-old she is stealing sleeps soundly on Mama's shoulder. The little girl has thick, black hair and long, black lashes.

Just then, somewhere in the night, a dog barks. The child in Mama's arms stirs and grunts, and her eyes flicker open.

The child tenses and catches her breath as if she is about to cry. Gently, Mama swings her around and makes a funny face at her.

The child relaxes and smiles. She stares for a moment—her eyes are bright green—and then she drifts back to sleep.

Mama kisses the little girl's forehead and eases her onto her shoulder. The child sleeps soundly as her new mother whisks her out into the full-moon summer night.

WAVE A WHITE FLAG

The doilies were first; of that much, Henry was certain. And then, for contrast, for a change of pace, the bowling ball. First, doilies, fluffy spinning lace sliding through the air like snowflakes, catching breezes that would swing them wide and up and wild as stringless kites. Then, when the fish on the sidewalk were giggling and sighing and spreading their tiny arms to catch the pretty things, a surprise! Out of the sky, a speck among the drifting frills--that's all they would see at first, of course, just a speck. Smooth and shiny and plunging like a holy comet, it would arc and flume straight down, flash by the stupid doilies, maybe kill some birds on the way before it HIT one, splattered some fool with her arms out to catch, thinking it was a doily but in for a rude awakening because it's a BOWLING BALL all along and she's on her way to meet Jesus Christ. And if Henry could aim right, put just the right backspin on it, maybe he could take out a whole crowd of them, plow down five or ten like real bowling pins in an alley. It would be best if the crowd was all old ladies or shitfaced rowdy kids.

Or maybe the cedar chest would be better. He would have more of a chance of crushing someone with that, of cracking a whole flock like a bunch of nuts. Rubbing his chin, he considered the chest, imagined the heavy wood box dropping down eight floors, the lid flying open, maybe snapping off to leave a tail of trash. Out would fly the photo albums, shooting out and flapping in the wind like paper birds failing to fly, shitting snapshots and pages all the way down; then, at the sixth floor, the clippings would emerge--graduations, weddings, and obituaries shredding, confetti in the sky. By the fifth floor, out would tumble flowers, dessicated roses and corsages disintegrating under the sun; letters, yearbooks, medals at the fourth; at the third floor, his uniform would leap out, and her wedding dress puffing up big and round as a parachute; souvenirs at the second--postcards, flashlights, key rings from places he had forgotten; before the big smash would come fittingly the wills, typed tidy packets popping over the rim with the old green teddy bear close behind; and then a CRASH (maybe a peep, he didn't know, if the poor dummies realized they were standing under a lifetime); and finally nothing, just a flutter and rustle as all the goddamned memories rippled down around them, into their blood, soaking it up into papers and dresses like paper towels absorbing Kool-Aid.

As for the baby's finger, Henry wasn't really sure where it would be. Probably, it would settle on top like a cherry, only not red anymore after fifty-two years, just white white tiny like a tooth. The little velvet ring case she kept it in would shatter, spitting it right on top of the pile, turning up again like it always did. Yesterday, she had it in the bathroom, as if he needed to see it again, and he noticed the little gray case as he was pulling down his pants and tried to flush it away with his crap. Wheezing and quivering, she had saved it at the last second, punched her shriveled blue arm into the bowl and dug it out like it was still attached to someone. He watched her like TV and thought the old woman might die from the way her veins stuck out.

Henry just wanted to get rid of it all, to throw it all out and be done with it for good. It served no purpose anymore for him...and for her, too, though she savagely clung to each bit. It was all gone, all past, all slipping away, so why fight it? He was tired of staring at old photos of people who were dead over ten years ago. He was tired of seeing snapshots of young strangers Helen insisted were them, when he knew damn well they were not. He was tired of living in the same world that made him think of things he could never have or do.

Last Tuesday was the last time Henry had enjoyed himself, the last time he had laughed and felt good. Oh, what a pleasure, what a landmark day it had been! It was warm, like tonight, and when he limped to the windowsill, a high half-moon lit up just for him. In his arms, he felt an ache as he inched open the window, but when he carried over the box of books and flung them into the night, there wasn't a twinge. There was simply a surge, an incredible, hot surge like whiskey drowning his body, heat so pure and exhilarating that the books weren't enough. Even as the box shot downward, plunging to the sidewalk like an elevator with no cable, he was hopping into the kitchen, grabbing the toaster, rushing as fast as he could toward the moonlight. Out it went, gleaming and rattling, electrical cord whipping behind it...then the best, the biggest yet! By the time Helen awakened and stumbled into the room, the TV had exploded below, erupting in a geyser of glittering fine chips--glass, tubes, wires, metal, and wood screeching back up and out in a fountain, then down, washing down everywhere in a far beautiful tidal wave. Then, Helen grabbed him and clawed him back from the masterpiece, away from the window in a sexless tumble. Henry smiled because she had been whimpering over the finger again.

Unfortunately, there weren't any fish out last Tuesday, no black mollies swiveling past to plaster. Bad timing, though the moon was perfect, and he knew it as soon as that first toss but was so excited that he just kept going. Pretty soon, there were plenty down there, though, squinting old cripples in slippers pointing up, even some policemen who came up to visit. That night, they threatened to weld shut his windows, but he sat on the rocker and said he'd only break the glass if they did. He called the cop a son of a bitch and went off to bed, leaving whimpering Helen to entertain the neighbors.

What a night it had been! Best of all, there was time for more, certainly days enough for more heat and heroic throws. In his body, in this place, he realized there were few chances for anything else, few years to find something elating again. The wheat years were over, his twisted legs whispered, the sun months traded to another part of the Earth. Find what fun your sloughing body can, feel the blood rush, neck hairs tremble. Don't rot.

Tonight, it was warm out there again, and a crescent moon sang Patti Page, and Henry knew it was time for more goodbyes. In the beige box bedroom of the cramped apartment, he gazed out the window and nodded; from the top, royal rampart of the building, it would come, it would come, it would rain from his hands.

First, the doilies, he decided, and then the bowling ball and THEN the cedar chest. All or nothing, shoot the moon. Yes, that would be nice.

Turning away from the glittering great window, Henry started to gather things up. There were doilies on the dressers, both of them, and he tugged them carefully off, holding back all the junk on top with one arm. Next, he laid the lacy things on his bed, which was closest to the window, and walked past both beds to the closet. Humming, he slid open the folding, slatted door, and got down on his knees. He pushed aside dangling curtains of clothing and reached into a corner for the bowling ball. It felt familiar to sink three fingers in the cool, smooth holes of the ball, and before he put it on the bed, he pretended to hurl it down an alley.

The cedar chest was already near the window, so he wouldn't need to drag it across the room. Just a lift, a step, a push, and it would fly, finally soar free and bold into the night. But what else? Looking slowly around the bedroom, Henry realized he needed more, he should have many things to sling off into heaven. There had to be a magazine, a clip, ammunition to carry off the battle, enough junk to heap and handle and snatch from when he got started.

In finding more things to throw, there was surely no problem. All over, an abundance of useless garbage waited, covered shelves and dressers and counters and just slumped and rotted until it would be towed out with their dead bodies. An early exit would delight it, Henry knew, would free all the stuff in a glorious brave blaze that all the clothing and pottery and furniture in the seven floors of cubbyholes beneath them would envy and long for forever.

From the sad way her eyes tipped downward, Henry was sure that the ceramic statue of the Virgin Mary on Helen's dresser would want to leave. Mary was a foot high, draped in blue robes with a dusty gold halo behind her head; her hands were spread wide with palms opened outward...welcoming, resigned, or surrendering. Henry grabbed her and dropped her on the bed.

Shoes, he needed shoes--and why not the clock? Flushing, he scooped two ancient pairs of black wingtips from the closet floor and snapped the noisy round alarm clock with the glow-in-the-dark face from the little nightstand between the beds. Then, he headed into the living room to harvest more ammunition.

Of course, Helen was out there. Sitting in her soft brown armchair, she faced the spot where the TV had been, as if she thought it would magically reappear. Like a dog, she was trained to stare at the same spot, just as she was taught to always look and talk and act in the same way, to become her long-dead mother. In fact, she even looked like her mother, she WAS the old bitch, except for the tube in her throat--which made her WORSE than her mother.

Even now, while she dozed in the chair, the tube was still in place, emerging from her gorge like plumbing. Right out of her it stuck, a tiny white pipe a half-inch long, mounted in a padded plastic collar that circled her neck, covering over at least one crumpled blue section of skin so Henry didn't have to look at it. Four months ago, the doctors had given them that tube, Henry remembered, they had sliced her windpipe open to save her life and oh THANK GOD they did, because now there was a little sewer leading out of her, a spigot that could pour all the slime and goop and ugliness up out of her heart and all over the miserable apartment they had moved into and better yet all over miserable him. Every time he looked at that pipe, that hole leading out of her body, he felt sick and angry and hateful, so he guessed it was doing the trick, finally and fully bringing the two of them together.

For a moment, Henry scanned the room, deciding on and

then rejecting various objects. The short sofa was out, since it took two people to carry and even though his heart was thumping and he felt pretty damn capable, he didn't think he could quite get it into the bedroom and over the windowsill. Sometime, maybe the next time, the sofa would have to go, the cushions and foam rubber and hard dark wood flattening gangs of sidewalk fish; he could get a dolly, probably, or maybe have casters put on the legs, pay some furniture repairman to come in and install them just so he could roll the thing around the apartment and out the window and down down DOWN.

The stubby wood end table was a possibility, but it was right beside Helen and her tube, and he definitely did not want to wake her up. But the lamps--ah, the lamps were perfect! There was one on Helen's end table and one on the floor where the TV had been; it used to sit on top of the set, before Henry had fired it into the sky last Tuesday.

Breathing fast, Henry crept to the end table and switched off the lamp, then unplugged it and gathered it in his arms. When it hit the bottom, it would surely be spectacular, since the round body was all blue glass. He pictured a fury of sparkling blue, a climbing curl of one thousand baby lights, all glitter and fire and cold sea sparks like the Fourth of July in September.

Then, suddenly, as he was passing with his vision and the lamp into the bedroom, he heard her voice.

"Henry," she rattled behind him. "Henry, what are you doing?"

At the sound of her, he froze and cringed, jamming both eyes shut because she was awake and the mission wouldn't be so easy anymore. And the voice…the VOICE was awful, it made him want to run and cry far away away every time he heard it. When she spoke, she had to suck in all the air she could and put a finger over the hole and scrape out each word like a gag. It wasn't her voice at all, it was new, it was planted in her throat like fungus when the tube was put in.

"What are you doing with the lamp?" she said, her voice low and barely recognizable, rasping like sandpaper, gurgling like the flush of a toilet. "Henry, you face me and tell me where you're going."

Panicky, panting, Henry clutched the lamp and walked into the bedroom. Now, there could be no stopping; now was the time for windows, as all the pruny people in the apartments beneath him well knew but didn't have the balls to fulfill.

Helen wriggled out of her chair and teetered into the bedroom after him. Her thin, mangled body moved slowly, almost without muscles under the beaten rag skin. The face above her tube was a skull, unfamiliar...tissue paper sucked into eye sockets and mouth and cheeks and every crack and pit in the bone.

"Henry, stop it," she croaked.

In the bedroom, Henry pushed open the window, feeling no pain this time in his scrawny, flexing arms. Like peppermint, the strong, cool air of the eighth-floor night washed in, bathing him in tingling, electrical juice. For a second, he stood and let it soothe him, envelope his petering organs with misleading vigor. Out there and up was the big pearly crescent, the finest high bullseye a man could ever aim at; down was the world, the stupid swaggering beginnings that he was long past and more than ready to erase.

With a puff, Henry turned and grabbed the doilies. As planned, they went out first, sailing and twirling through the darkness like feathers. Wasting no time, Henry picked the bowling ball next, thrusting three fingers in the holes like Helen's blowhole. With a laugh, he stepped back from the window, brought the ball up to his chest and cupped it with both hands like he was standing in a lane. Then, he hopped forward, swinging the ball back and up with one hand…then forward and up and letting it go, heaving it out and away in the biggest godly bowling alley ever seen.

"Henry, oh stop it, please!" burbled Helen, frantically skittering into the room. "You bastard! You've lost your mind!"

Henry ingored her, knowing he had nothing left to lose, and nabbed the Virgin Mary. Away she went, somersaulting wildly in the sky as she was meant to, shooting up closer to where she belonged than she had ever been before. Then, the shoes, dancing daringly on floors of pure breeze…and the clock, counting minutes which would only forever be known to itself.

Now that time was gone, there would be no stopping him.

By the time he snagged the lamp, Helen was scratching and pulling at him, wheezing wordlessly because she had both hands on him and couldn't talk without a finger over her tube. She flailed at him, bug-eyed and blue-veined and trying desperately to drag him back--but he was soaring and rushing and understood everything and would not be stopped this time from getting rid of it all...all the dusty trash that was rotting them both from the inside of their skulls and was better off plunging through the sky.

Henry bent down and lifted one end of the cedar chest, propping it up with its legs sticking over the windowsill. Then, smacking Helen with the back of his hand, he grabbed the other end of the chest; grunting, he raised it slowly from the floor, and with one flaming pulse shoved it triumphantly into space. Watching over the sill as his heart hammered, he saw the chest rip open and everything scatter in the air as he had imagined. In the flashing red lights from below, the chest and papers and dresses and memories seemed to catch fire as they flew.

In the beautiful, slow-motion moments that followed, Henry took out his false teeth and lobbed them out there, too. He noticed the little gray ring case on the dresser and flicked it fittingly after.

Helen fingered her tube and started to scream at him, and someone started pummeling the apartment door. Soon, they would all be in there, poking and shouting and threatening, maybe taking him away. But it was all all right. Everything was going, now or later...tonight, last Tuesday, or next week, spinning and twisting and racing to the ground like Japanese zeros or years.

One more thing, he needed one more thing. Maybe himself, maybe he would dive out there himself, leap weightlessly toward the moon and maybe brush it with his fingertips before descending. Everything had to go eventually, including himself, so why not get it over with? Why not let the wind sing women through his eyes, the dark breeze ruffle his skin like a loose shirt while he floated so Christlike from above?

Instead, he turned to Helen, who was scratching and weeping

behind him, drawing blood from his shoulders and every now and then scraping out some insult. In a wrinkled, swift sweep, he clutched her tube, then jerked it out of her throat. He pulled it so hard and twisted his hand so the tube dug out gristle and blood, and he snapped the brace from around her toothpick neck.

Out it went, goodbye garbage and zoom to the moon, and good riddance and thanks for the best all night. As Helen choked and bled on the floor, Henry crossed the room and walked away from the window.

Tonight, he would shave before bed.

TEACHER OF THE CENTURY

As the ring of students tightened around her, America's Teacher of the Century nominee Cilla Franklin offered to reduce the homework assignment. Thirty seconds later, she offered to eliminate it altogether. It didn't make any difference.

Muscles tense beneath naked flesh, the boys and girls continued to edge toward her. She didn't know why they were so upset, since they never did homework anyway and were never punished for it. The assignment should not have been taxing for anyone in the class, whatever their aptitude level; further, nothing about it impinged on anyone's personal rights or definition of political correctness.

Periods One through Four hadn't had any problem with the homework. Then again, Period Five was just a bad group. They were all bad, but Five was the worst.

One minute after Cilla had transmitted the details of the assignment to their brainware wireless implants, the kids had risen as one from their hammocks and formed a circle around her. One of the boys had come up behind her and urinated on her legs; as she spun around, he had directed the stream upward, spraying her hips and abdomen and even splashing her face.

Though Cilla did not understand most of what the godlings (that was what they called themselves) did or said, she knew what this much meant: she was marked for death.

It had happened six times before in her fifty-year career. Each time, she had managed to save herself by begging for mercy from the class Chief or moving to a new school...but it was always possible that death could claim her like this. She knew of colleagues who had died this way; only three out of thirty thousand teachers nationwide died per year in executions by godlings, so the odds weren't bad...but her own mentor, Ruby Churchill, had been one of the unlucky few.

Dying at the hands of a tribe of hive-minded, techno-savage students wasn't anything she had envisioned while playing school as a child with her friends decades ago.

Times had changed. For Cilla Franklin and the other teachers at All Einstein High School, every day was another chapter in *Lord of the Flies*.

Slowly, the ring of twelfth-graders pressed toward her. Their heads were bowed, and every last one of them glared up at her with a wicked, hungry smile. None of them carried a weapon, but Cilla knew they didn't need weapons; to some extent, they were all genetically and cybernetically enhanced. She had already seen a small group of them tear apart a floater car (her own) with their bare hands, and she had seen individual godlings punch holes through the cement block walls of the school.

At seventy-five years old, fit and healthy as she was, Cilla wouldn't even slow the godlings down. She knew she was dead meat.

The godlings would all be adding to their tattoos tonight, commemorating her murder with colorful new markings on their chests or bellies or buttocks, as was their custom. She wondered if there was any truth to the rumors she had heard that the godlings also devoured their victims' remains nowadays.

It wouldn't surprise her.

"Chief Ludwig!" she said, turning to the tallest boy in the circle. "What is the nature of my offense?"

Ludwig was shaved hairless like all the other males his age. His pale, naked skin was decorated with tattoos of eagles, tongues of flame, quantum equations, and DNA molecules. "Coowa chi patea," he said slowly, overenunciating each syllable. "Logwa fachi sifata poto."

Half the time, the godlings communicated with each other via brainware implants, silently passing radio signals from head to head. The rest of the time, they communicated by speaking aloud, but almost always using their own indecipherable language—Twister—when talking to one another. As often as she had heard it used, Cilla could never make out more than a few stray words of it.

"Chaka luweena," said Ludwig, angrily poking a finger in Cilla's direction. "Mantabuda cristacuchina *elar*!"

Though she didn't understand a word he said, Cilla caught the drift of it. The angry tone and the simple fact that he refused to speak English meant that she had no hope. There would be no negotiations. She had reached the end of the line.

Another boy padded up from behind and urinated on her, but she didn't break eye contact with Ludwig. "Please," Cilla said to him. "I taught your father and mother. I taught your father's father. Don't do this."

"Cromo!" Ludwig said sharply, and then he spat on the ground. "Shavaka cromo!"

That word, Cilla knew. "Cromo" was Twister for "parents," expressed with as much contempt as was humanly possible. It was the most profane word in the godlings' vocabulary.

Cilla wondered what the godlings' parents would think if they could see them now, if they could watch what they were about to do to her. They saw everything that took place in the classroom, usually, thanks to the personal A.I. drones that hovered over each student's shoulder during class. Now, though, the airborne eight-balls floated around the perimeter of the room, lenses staring at the walls; obviously, the godlings had figured out how to render the drones dormant when they didn't want their parents to see what they were doing.

Not that the parents would have cared, thought Cilla, even if they *could* have seen what was about to happen.

The circle tightened around her. She could see that some of the boys were aroused as they moved toward their prey. Why, she wondered, with all the advantages they had, did they slide back so completely into the primitive?

If it would have done her any good, Cilla would have pleaded further with the godlings. She would have told them that it wasn't necessary to kill her, since they had already driven her to request early retirement. She'd be gone in two weeks anyway, she would have told them.

But she knew it would not have done any good to tell them that...just as she knew it would not do her any good to scream for help. The other teachers and administrators knew better than to interfere in godling affairs; the penalties for intervention could be quite severe. Just ask the vice principal who had tried to break up a godling orgy in the library two years ago, or the teacher who'd been dumb enough to give a godling an "A minus" just last month.

And now, it was her turn to be the object lesson. Resigning herself to death, she closed her eyes and said a silent prayer that the end would come quickly and without too much pain.

She felt the heat of the students pressing in on her from all sides. She smelled the animal musk and funk of their naked bodies.

Then, all of a sudden, she heard a new voice in the room. It was a young, male voice...and most surprisingly, it was speaking English.

"Sorry I'm late," said the boy. "Is there a seating chart?"

Cilla's eyes shot open and fixed on the new arrival. The godlings turned as one in his direction, halting their predatory approach.

For once, the teacher and students had a common reaction to something. None of them could believe what they were seeing.

The newcomer had sandy brown hair and bright green eyes. He looked about seventeen years old and five foot seven, with a slim build. What was unbelievable about him, though, had nothing to do with his physical characteristics.

It was his clothes...namely, that he was wearing any at all.

They were nothing fancy, just a red polo shirt, bluejeans and sneakers, but they might as well have been a hand-tailored Italian suit, for all the attention they got.

Cilla couldn't remember the last time she'd seen a student wearing clothes. The very sight of him made her heart skip a beat.

Calmly, the boy nodded and smiled at the stunned godlings. "My name is Byron Spenser," he said. "I'm a transfer student."

For once, the naked savages were at a loss. Their aura of smug control and superiority seemed to have evaporated. The males were no longer aroused.

Cilla Franklin regained her composure before anyone else. It was an impressive feat, considering that she had been on death's doorstep mere moments before.

"Welcome, Byron," she said. "It's a pleasure to meet you."

"I have a hall pass," said the boy, and then he did something that threw everyone for a loop all over again.

He held out a slip of paper.

Cilla stared at the slip as if he'd just held up a gold nugget the size of a fist. Then, she shook her head and smiled.

It had been a long time since she had seen one of those. It took her back hard and fast, years spinning away like clay pigeons in a summer sky.

"I see," she said. "You're not wired, are you?"

"No, ma'am," said Byron.

Cilla's heart skipped another beat. Not only was he free of brainware—and therefore not plugged into the godlings' hive mind—but he had used the word "ma'am." She hadn't seen the likes of him since Jimmy Melville back in 2092...and Jimmy hadn't even been the real deal, just a poser camping it up for laughs at her expense.

Despite the resemblance in dress and manners, this boy wasn't another Jimmy Melville. She could tell. She had a feeling.

Fearlessly squeezing between the godlings, Cilla crossed the room to Byron. Normally, she would have been embarrassed by her urine-soaked dress, but it was the furthest thing from her mind.

"Well now, Byron," she said, gesturing toward the open door

and following him through it. "Let's see about getting you properly acclimated."

"Thank you, Miss Franklin," he said.

Her heart leaped again. She was so agitated, she forgot to go back in the room and dismiss Period Five, but that was no big deal. Period Five, everyone knew, could take care of themselves.

"I want to move up my retirement," Cilla said to the naked principal. "I want to leave today."

Principal Caesar smiled. "What a coincidence," he said. "Here I was hoping to talk you into *postponing* your retirement!"

Cilla swallowed nervously and shook her head. "I've been marked for death," she said. "They almost killed me this afternoon."

Caesar rolled his eyes and sighed as if they were discussing a harmless teenage prank. "And why is that, Cilla?" he said. "What did you do?"

Cilla knew better than to look for sympathy or the slightest trace of support from the oily administrator. His only goal was to appease the godlings and their parents at all costs. He was very popular with the student body and even went naked and occasionally jacked into the hive-mind to curry their favor. Naturally, in his world, the blame for any mishaps could be laid squarely in the laps of the teachers.

"I don't even know," said Cilla, "and it shouldn't matter. They were going to kill me. They *will* kill me, if I don't get out of here."

"Let me have a talk with Chief Ludwig," said Caesar, reaching behind his ear for the hive-mind jack. "I'm sure we can smooth this over."

Cilla shot out of her chair and lunged over the principal's desk, grabbing his wrist before he could switch on the link. "No!" she said sharply. When Caesar raised an eyebrow, she released her grip and receded across the desk. "Please, don't. Just approve my retirement request."

As the principal's hand hovered near the link jack, Cilla

prayed that he wouldn't contact Ludwig. The last time Caesar had interceded on a teacher's behalf, the teacher and his wife and children had been smeared over every other teacher's classroom as a warning. Though Caesar played a role in the godlings' scheme of things, there was never any question about who was in charge.

"Okay," said Caesar, dropping his hand from the jack. "I won't bring Ludwig into this yet. But Cilla, you know I won't approve an earlier retirement. I haven't even approved your *first* retirement request."

"It's a matter of life and death," said Cilla. "I've given my life for my profession, but I won't die for it. I won't die for *them*." She jerked her head back over one shoulder, indicating the students in the school building around her.

Caesar sighed and folded his hands on the desk. "Cilla, we don't want you to leave, period. As you know, you're the crown jewel of our teaching staff. You've been selected America's Teacher of the Year every year for the past decade, and you've just been nominated for America's Teacher of the Century. I guess you know you're the chief attraction here at All Einstein High School."

Cilla knew...and knew how little that truly meant. Her name and reputation drew parents to enroll their children, but once the little godlings put their butts in their hammocks, they weren't actually interested in learning at all, and their ever-present A.I. monitor drones made sure that no real education could take place.

As infrequently as actual learning occurred at the school, Cilla's presence brought prestige to All Einstein...and prestige equaled money. Unfortunately, the school administrators were so beholden to and intimidated by the godlings, Cilla knew they could not protect even her from those tattooed techno-savages.

"Thank you, but I want to leave," said Cilla. "I've had enough. I'm burned out."

"But you're still making a *difference*," said Principal Caesar, and it took all she had not to laugh in his face. "We *want* you. We *need* you."

"I want to leave today," said Cilla. "It's time."

Caesar blew out his breath and slumped back in his chair. "At least stay until the end of the semester. Stay until the Teacher of the Century winner is announced."

I'll be dead by then, Cilla started to say, but she held back for fear that Caesar would resume efforts to prevent her death by contacting Ludwig. "I can't," was all she said.

"You have to be a working teacher to be eligible for the award," said Caesar. "If you retire now, you'll be disqualified. After all these years, do you really want to miss out on the greatest honor that any teacher can receive?"

Cilla could see that she wasn't getting anywhere. "I won't be here tomorrow," she said, pushing up out of her chair. "You'll need to call a substitute."

"Cilla," said Caesar, and all the false cordiality was suddenly gone from his voice. "If you're not here tomorrow, you'll be in breach of contract. You'll forfeit your pension."

Cilla stared at him. Though she wasn't surprised at his playing that card, she got a sinking feeling in her stomach at hearing him make the threat. Without her pension, she would be hard-pressed to survive; then again, it wouldn't make any difference if the godlings killed her before she could use it.

Caesar nodded as if the matter were settled. "Let's pow-wow again at the end of the week," he said, resuming his earlier affability. "Maybe you'll have a change of heart by then."

"I won't," Cilla said softly, turning to leave.

"Hope springs eternal," said the principal with a chuckle, hurrying around to get the door for her.

As he ushered her out, Cilla noticed that he had a new tattoo. It showed up best now that he was aroused from victoriously exercising his authority: the name "Ludwig" was printed in gothic-style letters along the length of his male organ.

The next day, though the death sentence hanging over her head clouded her thoughts, Cilla experienced a welcome change in Period Five.

At first, Five went the way it always did. Half the godlings slept through her lecture, and none of the others paid attention to a word she said. A male and female had actually squeezed into the same hammock together and engaged in heavy petting while she talked. A godling boy loudly passed gas at least a dozen times. Cilla knew better than to correct any of them; their pet principal would veto any disciplinary action and turn it around into negative consequences for her. If she ever did manage to administer any form of punishment, the parental A.I.s would squeal in protest, followed by the parents themselves.

In spite of the usual Period Five headaches, however, there was one consolation in the wasteland that day. Byron Spencer, the new boy, had miraculously survived his first day of school—even though he had dared to interrupt Cilla's execution—and sat at the head of the class, listening and taking notes. He even sat at a *desk*, believe it or not; he had *asked* for one, and the maintenance crew had found one buried in storage and brought it to the room.

As class wore on, Byron did something even more surprising than asking for a desk or taking notes.

It happened as Cilla was being chewed out by one of the A.I. drones for looking at a student while posing a question. The gleaming eight-ball hovered at eye level, less than a foot from her face, and protested in the voice of Daughter Raper XL's mother, presumably reacting in the same way that the mother would have reacted if she herself had been there.

"Is my son the only student in this classroom?" the A.I. said shrilly. "Is he?"

"No," said Cilla, glaring at the floating orb. It was at least the twentieth A.I. interruption in the past half-hour, which was par for the course but still disruptive. As always, she spent her time talking to the orbs while the so-called students snored or masturbated or surfed the hivenet.

"No, *what*?" said the drone in Daughter Raper XL's mother's voice.

Cilla grated her teeth. "No, ma'am," she said coldly.

"Then don't *look* in his direction every time you have a *question*!" said the A.I., bobbing closer to Cilla's face. "Try one of these other children you're *supposedly* teaching! Stop singling out Daughter Raper like he's some kind of second class citizen!"

Cilla wished she had a baseball bat so she could take a swing at the eight-ball. Once she got started, she would like to make the rounds of the classroom and then the building, not stopping until every single sphere was a shattered pile of ebony shards and sparking circuits.

"Yes, ma'am," said Cilla, and then the drone zipped away, resuming its post above Daughter Raper XL's left shoulder. Daughter Raper himself was fast asleep, completely oblivious to what had just happened.

For a moment, Cilla stood before the class and tried to recall what her train of thought had been before the drone's interruption. Pressing fingertips against her cheek, she stared off into space, searching her memory...and coming up empty. She had been talking about *Animal Farm*, she knew that much, but where exactly she had left off remained a mystery.

Then, something miraculous happened. Cilla heard a voice other than her own or a drone's in the classroom.

"Miss Franklin," said Byron Spencer. "A moment ago, you said that Napoleon the pig represents Josef Stalin in *Animal Farm*. Who does Snowball represent, did you say?"

For a moment, Cilla stared at the boy in shock. Even the godlings who weren't sleeping directed their attention at Byron, for he had done something completely unheard of, something that just wasn't done anymore in school.

He had participated in class.

Quickly recovering her composure, Cilla smiled gratefully and nodded. "Leon Trotsky," she said. Byron had reminded her of exactly where she'd left off before the A.I.'s intrusion.

"And Mr. Jones the farmer is supposed to be the czar, right?" said Byron.

"Czar Nicholas II," said Cilla. "That's correct, Byron."

The boy cocked his head thoughtfully. "But the characters don't *have* to be those particular people, do they?"

"No, they don't," said Cilla. "The allegory can apply to any oppressive system."

"I *thought* I recognized some characters from real life," said Byron, glancing over his shoulder.

If the godlings realized that he was referring to them, they gave no sign of it. None of them seemed to be listening anymore, anyhow.

"If Orwell updated *Animal Farm* today," said Byron, "I wonder if the pigs would be connected to the hivenet."

"Who knows?" said Cilla, keeping her remarks neutral for the benefit of the A.I. drones that recorded her every word. "But it would be interesting to see what Mr. Orwell would come up with."

"I think he'd have a field day," Byron said with a grin.

Cilla nodded and smiled. "So, Byron," she said, excited to be interacting intellectually with a student for the first time in what seemed like eons. "What did you like best about the book?"

From then on, Period Five wasn't so bad. It had gotten off to a typically awful start, but ended up being Cilla's favorite class in she couldn't remember how long.

Ignoring the godlings, she spent the remaining class time talking exclusively with Byron Spencer about *Animal Farm.* For once, she was sorry when Period Five ended.

The next day, Cilla actually looked forward to Period Five, and wasn't disappointed when it arrived. While the godlings ate and slept and urinated on the floor from their hammocks, Cilla and Byron continued their discussion of *Animal Farm* and moved on to *1984.* By the time class was over, they had gone from Orwell to Ayn Rand, then ranged further afield, touching on Jules Verne, Edgar Allan Poe, Charles Dickens, and even Shakespeare.

Cilla could not believe that she was having such a stimulating conversation with a twelfth-grader, especially in an age when twelfth-graders read no books and could not even be bothered to communicate with adults in English. She did not even have such conversations with her peers anymore, for they were too busy scrambling to placate the godlings to consider academic matters.

The time she spent with Byron, she knew, was a rare gift. The death sentence still weighed on her, as did the postponed retirement that could be her only means of survival...but during Period Five, at least, she was able to shrug aside the darkness and savor every moment of her exchanges with the extraordinary seventeen-year-old.

It was enough to help her survive to the end of the week and her scheduled "pow-wow" with Principal Caesar (barring a surprise execution by the godlings, of course). She would never admit it to Caesar, but she ended up not minding the extra time in school so much.

In fact, by staying through the week, she experienced what might have been the highlight of the past twenty years of her career...certainly of the past miserable decade. After school on Friday, just before her meeting with Caesar, Byron stopped by her room and did something that no student had done since Kitty Carnuba back in 2079 or so.

He handed her some poetry he'd written and asked her to tell him what she thought of it.

"Whenever you get the chance," said Byron. "I'm sure you're busy."

Cilla turned slowly through the poems, which he'd gone to the trouble of printing (God bless him!) on sheets of paper. There was one about his father, and one about the way he'd felt on his first day at All Einstein High School. There was one about a journey to the stars, and one about a perfect world that never was.

And then there was one titled "The Angel." It included the following lines:

I squint from the shadows of life like a prison,
Outnumbered by forces inhuman and heartless.
I'm saved by an angel of learning arisen,
Like minds, kindred spirits together a fortress.

After reading the full text of "The Angel," it was all she could do to keep from crying until Byron left the room. On the pretext that she had to get ready for her meeting with the principal, she sent Byron on his way, promising to read the poems at her first opportunity...

And then she let the tears flow.

The poem touched her deeply...not so much because of its quality as for its subject matter. Though her name was never mentioned, she had no doubt that it related directly to her.

She had known that she and Byron had made a positive connection, but seeing the boy's appreciation in print, and expressed so glowingly, filled her with joy. For once, she felt like she was actually helping someone; for once, she felt like she was getting through to another human being.

For once, she felt like maybe she *was* making a difference, even if it was only in the life of a single student.

It was a miracle she had never expected to see again in her lifetime. She had done plenty of good work long ago, in the days before the hivenet and godlings. She could not even count the number of students she had helped to succeed, or helped to succeed more, or exceed all expectations...but it seemed that the desire to learn had disappeared around the same time the students had stopped wearing clothes. Though Cilla had received teaching awards in recent years, she attributed them to past glories and the absence of competition in the teaching field. She knew all too well that she had made no impact on students in many years.

Until now. As she reread "The Angel," she sobbed tears of pure happiness. She felt like she was fifty-five again, or even forty-five or thirty-five.

All because of one student. One excellent student out of hundreds...an unacceptably dismal success rate decades ago, but today it was wondrous enough to make a teacher break down and cry. Not just any teacher, either, but America's so-called Teacher of the Year for ten years running and a nominee for so-called Teacher of the Century.

If she hadn't been so damned happy, Cilla Franklin might have been disappointed in herself.

"Congratulations," said the naked principal when Cilla entered his office for their "pow-wow." "You're not dead!"

As good a mood as Cilla was in after receiving Byron's poems,

Caesar's remark threw a shroud right over her. "Not yet," she said coldly. "The godlings like to play with their food."

"I disagree," Caesar said flippantly. "I think you're off the hook. In fact, Ludwig tells me you're in the clear."

Cilla distrusted every word from the principal's mouth, but she played along. "No more death sentence?"

"You'll be able to receive that Teacher of the Century award after all!" said Caesar. He glanced down at the gold hoop in his newly-pierced left nipple, then looked to Cilla for approval. "Like the piercing? I'm getting my scrotum done next."

Ignoring his nipple, Cilla leaned forward. She sensed that he was being evasive somehow. "So the death sentence is cancelled?"

"Yeah, yeah," said Caesar, waving a hand dismissively. "I guarantee you'll get to that award ceremony."

There. She finally realized what he was leaving unsaid. "What about *after* the ceremony?"

"What about it?" Caesar said innocently.

"What happens to me?"

"I imagine you'll go to a party of some sort," said Caesar.

It took an effort for Cilla to restrain her anger. "And the death sentence will be back in effect," she said darkly.

Caesar shrugged. "Sometimes, we take what we can get."

"You made a deal to ensure I'd live to receive the award," said Cilla, "and bring it home to All Einstein. Then, all bets are off."

"I can't confirm or deny your theory," said Caesar. "Rest assured, if any negotiations did or will occur, they were or will be designed to buy time until a

longer-lasting compromise can be devised. Remember, Cilla, it's in the school's best interests to keep you alive and teaching for as long as is humanly possible."

Cilla shook her head with a combination of disgust and amazement. "You gave me up," she said. "You told the godlings they could have me."

"Now, now," said Caesar, raising an index finger correctively. "You're putting words in my mouth, Cilla."

"When they devour my body," she said icily, "will you join in the feast?"

"Nobody's going to devour you," said Caesar. "Keep in mind, Ludwig's tribe will graduate at the end of the year. They won't be a threat."

"How dumb do you think I am?" said Cilla. "Of course they'll still be a threat! They'll never stop until I'm dead, whether they're in school or not."

"Trust me," said Caesar. "It'll blow over. You've got many years of teaching ahead of you."

"You're mistaken," said Cilla. "I'm retiring, remember?"

Caesar chuckled. "You're not *serious* about that!"

"You insisted I stay through the week, and I have. Now I'm done. I'm leaving before the godlings finish me off."

"I just told you, you're in the clear," said Caesar.

"You should know better than to make promises you aren't sure you can keep," said Cilla. "The godlings can't be controlled or bargained with. They could snuff me out right now, and what would you do about it?"

"You're off-limits! They won't touch you!"

"Don't kid yourself," said Cilla, getting to her feet. "We're not even the same species anymore. They'd just as soon use your treaties for toilet paper as honor them."

"They're good kids," said Caesar. "Maybe if you'd link to the hivenet once in a while, you'd see that."

Cilla crossed the office and opened the door. "I'm retired now," she said. "I'll leave the kids to you."

Caesar cleared his throat and rose from his chair. "See you Monday," he said.

"Not unless you show up at my apartment," said Cilla.

"Remember your pension," said Caesar.

"It won't do me much good if I'm dead."

Caesar came around the front of his desk and leaned against it, casually folding his arms over his chest. Apparently, he pinched his nipple ring the wrong way, for he quickly adjusted his arms, briefly letting his composure slip.

"Sleep on it over the weekend, Cilla," he said cheerfully. "Your job will still be waiting for you Monday."

"I won't want it," Cilla said over her shoulder as she

walked out.

"Things can change," said Principal Caesar. "Keep an open mind."

"Goodbye," said Cilla as she left the outer office and turned down the hall.

"You'll be back!" Caesar shouted after her, grinning knowingly.

As Cilla lifted the wrinkled photo from her desk drawer, she swung back in time to the happy moment when the photo had been taken.

It had been at least thirty years ago, back when people still took photos instead of posting images to the hivenet. Period Three had been amazing that year, unbelievably sharp, hardworking, and well-behaved; on the last day of school, the kids had surprised her with a party in her honor. They had even baked her a cake and made her an afghan in Home Economics. Every last one of them had hugged her on their way out the door.

In the photo, she and the kids from Period Three were mashed together in a happy crush, all laughter and light. How had she gone from that life to the one she had now, she wondered? When had the kids gone from hugging her to pissing on her?

Placing the photo in the box into which she was packing her possessions, Cilla reached back into the desk drawer. This time, she withdrew an enamel pin shaped like a shiny red apple; the lettering on the apple read "World's Best Teacher."

Kim Warwick had given her that. Out of all the students she'd taught through the years, Cilla still remembered that one.

Kim had been one of the stars of Cilla's career...not that Cilla imagined she had had much to do with her success. As a high school senior, Kim had already been writing like a master, composing achingly perfect novels of exquisite intricacy, depth, and emotional resonance. Cilla had given her the tiniest bit of guidance and all the encouragement in the world...and for that, Kim had never failed to credit her as the greatest teacher she'd ever known. She'd even dedicated a Pulitzer Prize-winning novel to Cilla, back in the days when the Pulitzer Prize still meant something.

Cilla dropped the pin in the box and pulled a magic marker drawing of a bull from the drawer. That one came from Jayvo Endymion, her hyperactive but beloved "bull in a china shop" from forty-odd years ago. Was he even still alive, she wondered? So much could happen in forty-odd years.

With a heavy sigh, Cilla dropped into her chair. Though there was not the slightest doubt in her mind that it was time to retire—well *past* time, in fact—cleaning out her desk was turning out to be harder than she had expected. As she piled mementos into boxes, the memories of better times and better students piled onto her shoulders, pressing her downward.

As she looked around the room, tears welling in her eyes, a thousand schooldays replayed in her memory. She saw herself standing in the front of the room, pacing her little track from wall to wall, lecturing energetically. Phantom students raised hands, chewed gum, passed notes, watched the clock. How many children had there been, she wondered? Ten thousand? A hundred thousand? A million? She had no idea, no head count.

But she did remember every face, every name. A good teacher never forgets, she always thought.

And she was a good teacher, if you listened to Kim Warwick and Period Three from thirty-odd years ago and the America's Teacher of the Century selection committee. Or maybe not so good, if you listened to the little voice inside her that laid the blame for the rise of the godlings at least partly in her lap, since after all, she had done her part to shape the minds that had given birth to this warped generation.

Either way, she was now an *ex*-teacher, and glad of it. If ever a change had been overdue, it was this one; thinking back, Cilla thought she should have retired at least ten years ago...more like fifteen.

She would have only one real regret in leaving when she did. There was one person she would miss seeing again, one student she would have liked to have said goodbye to before she left for good.

As she thought of him, like magic, his voice broke the silence.

Unfortunately, the sound was not as welcome as it usually was to Cilla. He wasn't speaking calmly from the doorway or his desk.

He was screaming for help from somewhere down the hall.

As a hundred horrible possibilities leaped into her imagination, Cilla instinctively leaped from her chair and headed for the door. Leaning out into the corridor, she heard him scream again; this time, his cry for help became a shriek, his voice shooting up an octave and breaking as someone or something hurt him terribly.

Without hesitation, though she was seventy-five years old and unarmed, Cilla followed Byron's cries down the darkened hallway. Seventy-five was a lot younger than it used to be, but she was still fragile and unaugmented, certainly no match for the frailest godling; whoever or whatever she was about to face, rushing to her student's aid was a courageous thing to do.

Three doors down on the opposite side of the hall from her room, Cilla could see a bright red light dancing on the polished floor outside an open doorway. Though Byron's screams ominously ended, ceasing to guide her, Cilla had no doubt that he was through that doorway, amid that fiery light.

Sure enough, when she got there and looked inside, she saw him, huddled on the floor of a blazing classroom. Everything that could burn was on fire—hammocks, bedding, the teacher's desk, window blinds, light panels, wall-mounted flat screen computer displays. In the middle of the roaring flames, Byron was curled in a fetal position with arms wrapped around his head, trying to protect himself from the blows that rained down upon him.

He was being bombarded...but not, as Cilla might have expected, by the fists of savage godlings. A torrent of blows pounded him in quick succession, one after another, and not a single one was delivered by a human hand.

The child was being hammered by A.I. spheres. A swarm of them boiled around him, thirty or more, enough to coddle a whole class of godlings. She'd never thought of them as dangerous in a physical way...but now the gleaming eight balls were wrecking a human body, pelting down hard and springing back up in the air only to bounce back down against battered flesh and bone.

Apparently, the godlings could reprogram the spheres more extensively than she had guessed, making them do a lot worse than turn their lenses to the walls. The tattooed monsters had transformed their own surrogate parents into lethal weapons.

And poor Byron Spencer was the beneficiary of their genius. The attack was so effective, he wasn't even moving anymore.

Cilla's stomach lurched at the thought that he might never move again.

Desperately, she looked around, wondering how she could possibly help him. There was still a clear path through the flames from the doorway to Byron, but what could she do when she got to him? She had no doubt that if she tried to shield him and drag him from the room, the orbs would turn their fury on her. As hard as they were hitting, Cilla knew that it wouldn't take long for them to break her seventy-five-year-old body.

She needed some kind of help herself...but by the time she could bring someone back, Byron might be dead. For all she knew, he was dead already.

If she had any hope at all of saving him, Cilla had to act fast...and, she realized, she needed more than her bare hands to do it. To fight off the A.I. spheres, she needed some kind of a weapon, something within reach.

Even as she realized what she would use, her feet were whisking her down the hallway toward her classroom.

Breathing fast, not used to exertion, Cilla hurried through the doorway of her room and went straight for her desk. What she wanted stuck out of one of the cartons she had packed, too big to fit inside under a lid.

It was a souvenir of days long gone, a talisman of ancient times when teachers had still possessed power and students had feared them. It was a piece of history that she had kept in the back of the bottom of a drawer, as if imagining that it might someday return to service, that a wind would sweep away the incompetent leaders and restore the schools to the centers of discipline and learning that they had once been.

The wood felt solid in her hand as she drew it from the box. The miraculous return to past glories had not come for the schools, but the artifact would see action again after all those years.

Cilla rushed back down the hall and flung herself without hesitation into the burning classroom. Byron still wasn't moving; the cloud of eight balls was still raining down on him.

Cilla wrapped both hands tightly around the handle and stepped forward. She prayed that she still had the strength to do the work that lay ahead.

Then, she drew back the paddle, the very same paddle that had stung many a student's bottom, and she swung it as hard as she could at the ebony spheres.

With a crack, the flat of the paddle smacked into two of the eight balls, sending them spinning. One looped drunkenly across the room, weaving toward the windows, while the other dashed itself against a blazing wall screen and burst into flames.

Heart pounding, Cilla wrenched the paddle back and swung it again, spraying three more orbs in crazy trajectories around the room. Her next swing caught one full against the wood, chucking it down to shatter in sparks and black shards upon the floor.

Surprised at herself, she pulled back and swung again. Spheres flew from the flat of the paddle like bees, whizzing into walls and fiery hammocks, shattering windows.

As she struck at them, some of the orbs protested with A.I. voices, filling the air with the strident cries of parents. If anything, the babble strengthened her resolve and made Cilla swing harder.

"Cease this behavior immediately!" screamed one of the spheres, just before Cilla drove it into a corner.

"This is a violation of our rights!" wailed another orb in the voice of Ludwig's mother. True to form, this particular orb never shut up until Cilla's paddle shattered it against the floor.

Cilla continued to swing away, breaking apart the awful swarm. As grave as the situation was, as much as a precious life depended on its outcome, a part of her was enlivened by the release, the realization of a secret fantasy from frustrated daydreams.

Oh, how she'd wanted to demolish those damned chattering eight balls.

Cilla's head throbbed, and her arms ached. As she swung again and again, she prayed to God to save the life of the boy at her feet, even if it meant the loss of her own.

One of the spheres struck her between the shoulder blades, but she ignored the flash of pain. Eight balls thumped her sides and legs, threatening to report her to the superintendent as they peppered her with bruises. She cried out as one of the balls clocked her kneecap with staggering force.

Tears flowed down her sunken cheeks, but she refused to fall. Knuckles white, she clenched the paddle in a death grip and swung, preventing the malevolent spheres from landing another blow on her motionless charge.

The flames leaped around her, burning through to bare walls, consuming everything...finally catching even the end of her paddle when she swept it through a fiery fall of ceiling tile.

Even as the paddle burned, Cilla kept right on swinging.

Solemnly, the president of the United States of America stepped up to the podium. As the assembled audience fell silent, he took a moment to review the text of his remarks, displayed on the screen of the implant in the palm of his hand.

Newsglobes captured his every move, hovering at a respectful distance. Their all-seeing lenses flexed in and out, perfecting the framing of their shots. Images of the leader of the free world were instantaneously transmitted onto the hivenet, accessible to every mind with the brainware to receive them.

The president looked up, cleared his throat, and began to speak.

"In this world of technological miracles," he said, "knowledge is abundant. Information is downloaded directly into the human mind. Thanks to the hivenet, the sum total of human experience is available to anyone at any time.

"And yet, we have found no substitute for traditional learning," said the president, looking around meaningfully at the attentive faces in the White House rose garden. "No technology can match the magic that occurs in the face-to-face communion between teacher and student.

"Traditional education is the backbone of our nation," said the president, and the audience applauded. "It is because of this that we single out a Teacher of the Year, an example of the excellence that enables our children and nation to flourish."

Again, the audience clapped. At the president's side, Principal Caesar beamed. In deference to the occasion, for once, he had concealed his naked body beneath a suit and tie.

"In this, the final year of the century," said the president, "we will go a step further. In honor of the accomplishments of all our nation's teachers over the past one hundred years, we will single out America's finest teacher not only of the year, but of the century."

The president nodded proudly. "Let me tell you, this woman is more than deserving of the title I am about to bestow upon her."

The audience applauded with rising enthusiasm as the culmination of the ceremony approached.

"She has served with distinction for over fifty years at some of our nation's finest schools," said the president. "During her career, she has helped to mold the minds of some of our most distinguished and accomplished citizens.

"Her contribution to our greatness cannot be overstated," said the president. "By embracing progress while holding fast to the time-tested tenets of American education, she has linked the best of our yesterdays to the best of our tomorrows."

As the crowd applauded, the president consulted his palm screen. "I'm sure you already know her," he said, returning his sincere gaze to his listeners. "Every year for the past decade, she has been named America's Teacher of the Year.

"Now, she is about to receive the highest honor in the land for a member of the noblest profession on Earth. There is no one who deserves it more.

"For excellence in the field of teaching...for contributions beyond measure to the success of our great nation...for unswerving devotion to the children of America...I hereby pronounce Cilla Sullivan Franklin America's Teacher of the Century!"

As the crowd burst into wild applause, the president turned and guided Cilla to the podium. She looked radiant in her frilly white dress, bathed in an aura of bright sunlight that shimmered around her and haloed her silver hair.

"Congratulations, Cilla," said the president, handing her a translucent plaque that pulsed with rainbow light. "And on behalf of all citizens of the United States of America, thank you."

"Thank you, Mr. President," Cilla said softly, peering around at the ring of newsglobes scoping their lenses in her direction. The globes made her nervous, reminding her of the eight-ball parental A.I.s.

"You are a national treasure, Cilla," said the president.

Cilla nodded and smiled, but was unimpressed by the flattery. To her thinking, the whole Teacher of the Century honor was meaningless, given the state of the world of education. How could anyone be honored to be a teacher when the schools were such a joke, when students and principals alike ran naked through the halls and the only learning taking place was the godlings' learning new methods of mayhem?

"Now, Cilla," said the president, the applause fading at the sound of his voice. "I have a surprise for you."

Cilla glanced at the newsglobes again, then forced herself to focus on the president. As unimpressed as she was by the honor she had been given, she still felt a small thrill at being so close to the most powerful man in America.

"Three months ago," he said, "you performed a true act of heroism. When an accident threatened the life of one of your students, you risked your own life to save him."

It was no accident, thought Cilla, but of course she kept it to herself. The party line of the school administration, force-fed to the public by Ludwig's pet, Caesar, seemed to be the only truth that mattered.

"That student," said the president, "Byron Spencer, is alive and well today because of you.

"And he is here today to share in this historic occasion."

Cilla immediately brightened. She couldn't help herself.

It was the one thing she hadn't expected. It was the one thing that could truly make her happy.

As Byron walked out of a nearby door and headed for the podium, the crowd sprang to their feet and applauded like mad. In contrast to the way he had looked three months ago, battered and huddled on the floor of the burning classroom, Byron was bright-eyed and impeccably groomed, wearing a sharp navy blue suit and striped tie. His arms were full of red roses.

At the sight of him, Cilla was overcome with pure joy. He was the only reason she was at the White House that day, the only reason she had kept teaching long enough to qualify for the Teacher of the Century award.

Because of Byron, she had finished out the school year at All Einstein. After the life-threatening incident, he had bravely insisted on staying to complete his senior year. She had been unable to walk away then, knowing that the one good student in the place would be alone at the mercy of the murderous godlings.

Normally, one seventy-five-year-old teacher would not have provided much protection against a school full of techno-savages...but Cilla had been shielded from the godlings until the award ceremony by Caesar's bargain with Ludwig. She had become a guardian angel, using her special status to hold the savages at bay when Byron was endangered. There had been many tense moments, and Byron had taken his share of knocks, but she had managed to get him through his senior year alive.

He was going to graduate. He was going out into the world, and she was sure that he would do great things.

Seeing him there, alive and healthy and brimming with hope, meant far more to Cilla than the plaque in her hand or the applause of her peers or the president of the United States standing at her side.

"These are for you, Miss Franklin," said Byron, handing her the bouquet of red roses. "Thank you for being such a wonderful teacher."

Tears of happiness flowed down her face as she accepted the flowers. She wanted to hug him but held herself back...then gave in and hugged him anyway.

That moment was all the reward she needed. After all the years of futility since the rise of the godlings, she had managed to help one more student, one promising student who loved learning and appreciated her. How wonderful that she could retire on a positive note, reliving one final time the teacher-student bond as it was meant to be.

As she drew back from him, Byron beamed. "There's another surprise, Miss Franklin," he said. "There's someone I'd like you to meet."

Still smiling, Cilla tipped her head inquisitively.

"Come on out, Sara," said Byron, looking toward the door from which he had emerged.

As Cilla followed his gaze, the door opened. A girl stepped out, smiling shyly.

She looked close to Byron's age, and about the same height. Her sandy, straight hair hung in a glossy fall to the middle of her back, a style that Cilla hadn't seen in years. She wore a pretty blue knee-length sheath, and her green eyes sparkled like pale emeralds.

"This is my younger sister, Sara," said Byron. "Sara, meet my teacher, Cilla Franklin."

Shifting the roses and plaque to free an arm, Cilla shook Sara's hand. It felt soft as the petal of a flower in her grip.

"It's a pleasure to meet you, Miss Franklin," said Sara.

"It's a pleasure to meet you, too, Sara," said Cilla, staring at the girl. Byron hadn't been kidding when he had promised a surprise. Cilla could not remember him ever mentioning a sister...and yet, as she searched Sara's features, she could see that the family resemblance was unmistakable.

"Sara has been home schooled until now," said Byron, "but

next year, she'll be attending All Einstein High School. She'll be a senior."

"I can't wait to have you as a teacher," said Sara. "Byron's told me so much about you. You're the only reason I'm going to All Einstein instead of continuing my home schooling."

Cilla kept staring, completely thrown for a loop. She didn't know what to say.

The girl gazed hopefully up at her. "I brought you something," she said, pulling a hand from behind her back. "So we can get off on the right foot."

It was a shiny red apple.

As the audience laughed and applauded, Cilla stared at the apple in Sara's hand. She was truly on the spot, now. Though she had filed her retirement papers, Caesar had neglected to tell Byron that she wouldn't be teaching next year. Cilla had never mentioned it to Byron, either, and now she was stuck.

When she shot a look in Caesar's direction, he leaned over and patted her shoulder. "We're all excited about next year," he said to Cilla. "Another batch of fresh faces for you to work your magic on."

Then, he leaned closer and whispered in her ear. "And no Ludwig."

Which was supposed to mean that she was in the clear, that the death sentence was null and void, but she knew better. Ludwig's godlings could take her in the street, or at home...and there would be another horde to replace them in school the next year. She had seen them in the halls already, the eleventh graders, naked and tattooed and looking every bit as inhuman as the last bunch.

But then there was Sara Spencer.

"Sara aced her home school equivalence exams," Byron said proudly. "She got the highest scores on record."

Sara blushed and looked at her feet, then back up at Cilla.

Cilla could feel the intelligence radiating from the girl's emerald eyes. Even if Byron hadn't mentioned her test scores, Cilla would have known that she was in the presence of another excellent student, another hard-working and respectful young person, another hope for the future.

Her brother's sister, through and through.

And she was a home schooler, inexperienced in the savage ways of the merciless tribal school culture. When it came to interacting with the godlings, she might as well have had "fresh meat" tattooed on her forehead.

Sara fixed her with a gaze that was full of need and frank adoration. "I can't wait till next year," she said softly.

Cilla's heart melted. Abandoning that child to the godlings would be like offering up her own daughter to be killed.

In that moment, Cilla knew that she would be back in front of a classroom after all. She did not know how much protection she could offer this gentle, brilliant soul, but she knew that she could not turn her back on her.

She had risked her own life for Byron Spencer. If she did any less for Byron's sister, she would not be able to live with herself, anyway.

Cilla took the apple from Sara's hand. "See you in the fall," she said with a smile.

One week after the ceremony at the White House, Principal Caesar refilled his glass with champagne in the secret sub-basement of All Einstein High School. Replacing the bottle on the table, he leaned forward and clinked glasses with Superintendent Alexander.

"To the Teacher of the Century," Caesar said with an oily grin. "The pride of All Einstein High."

"To Cilla Franklin," said Alexander. "Where would we be without her?"

The naked men drained their glasses, finishing off with mutual sighs of satisfaction. Alexander drew fine cigars from the humidor and passed one over to Caesar.

"Congratulations on the enrollment numbers for next year,"

said Caesar. "Having the Teacher of the Century on staff is quite a draw."

"Word is, our state funding will be through the roof," said Alexander, clipping the end of his cigar. "So I want to see some belt-tightening around this place."

Caesar accepted the clipper from him with a laugh. "We'll cut till it hurts," he said, "and pass the savings along to ourselves."

The men lit their cigars, then relaxed back into the depths of their high-backed leather chairs. A holographic fire danced in the faux fireplace between them.

"I can't thank you enough for keeping Franklin on board," said Alexander, puffing out a great draft of smoke.

"Don't thank me," said Caesar, and then he clapped his hands together twice.

A boy with sandy hair and green eyes hurried to his side, smiling expectantly. He wore an old-style servant's uniform with black coat and tails, knee-high knickers over white stockings, and ruffles at the collar and wrists.

"Thank Byron," said Caesar with a sneer.

Alexander chuckled. "Thank you, Byron," he said through a cloud of cigar smoke.

"You're welcome, sir," Byron Spencer said happily. "Can I get you gentlemen anything?"

"Bend over," said Caesar.

The boy immediately bent at the waist. Principal Caesar leaned forward and pressed his thumb on a spot in the middle of Byron's scalp.

At his touch, the scalp split apart. Panels slid smoothly aside, exposing a rectangular opening in the boy's head.

Tiny lights flickered inside in a high-speed flurry.

"Ah, the miracle of robotics," said Caesar, peering into the hole in Byron's scalp.

"The miracle of false hope," said Alexander.

"Good boy," said Caesar, tapping the ash from the tip of his cigar into the hole.

"Should you be doing that?" said Alexander. "He cost us a pretty penny."

"He'll process and excrete it as synthetic feces." Caesar closed the port and settled back into his chair. "Stand up, Byron."

Byron Spencer did as he was told.

Caesar clapped his hands again, and Sara Spencer trotted into the room wearing a maid's costume with a tiny skirt. She carried a feather duster in one hand and smiled serenely.

"We owe Sara a debt of gratitude, as well," said Caesar. "She's done her brother one better, bless her heart. Thanks to her, Cilla's ours for another year."

"And what about after that?" said Alexander.

"Funny you should ask," said Caesar, puffing on his cigar. "Between you and me, I hear that Byron and Sara's mom and dad might just have another little one on the way."

The naked men laughed loudly in their cloud of smoke.

"And now, if you'll excuse me," said Principal Caesar, pushing himself up out of his leather chair, "I have an appointment for a tattoo removal."

"Which one?" said Alexander.

Caesar pointed at his male organ. "Ludwig's graduated. Out with the old, in with the new."

"You'll have it replaced?"

"As soon as I find out who the new chief is," said Caesar.

"It's good to have friends in high places," said Alexander.

"You never know when you'll need someone to do you a favor," said Caesar with a knowing smile. "Like torch a classroom or reprogram some A.I.s."

Alexander laughed and raised his cigar. "To the godlings!" he roared.

"To education!" chimed in Caesar. "It oughtta be a crime!"

EVERY CLOUD HAS A SILICON LINING

Five minutes before the killer drones attacked the Pittsburgh Maker Faire, the event's main attraction was going strong inside the dilapidated factory.

All the attendees and vendors were gathered around the Artisanal Artificial Intelligence booth, drooling like dogs in a butcher shop. The faire was overflowing with ingenious maker goods manufactured in unconventional facilities using cutting-edge tech, but A.A.I.'s offering still dominated the spotlight.

"Ask Byron another question!" Anemone Briscoe, twentysomething developer of computerized A.I. minds, gave her flouncy red hair a toss and grinned at the crowd in the dark and dusty factory. "Make it a toughie!" She rolled up the sleeves of her forest green hoodie sweatshirt for effect.

"Byron!" said a dark-haired teen girl with brightly-colored decorative blisters all over her face and arms. "Is it true that you've starred in some badass computer porn?"

The device from which Byron spoke--an exquisitely crafted butterfly drone with shimmering blue-and-black wings--fluttered over a rusty steel drum. "No, you silly twit." Byron's voice was deep and resonant, with a droll, friendly tone. In other words, he sounded just like GEORGE (full name: Global Enterprise Oversight Response Generator, Enhanced), the best-known A.I. in Pittsburgh and all of America. "But damn if that isn't an awesome idea!"

Everyone in the crowd roared with laughter, and Anemone laughed right along with them. Hearing a voice like GEORGE's saying outrageous stuff was pure comedy and fund-raising catnip. Already, Anemone could literally see new patron bitbucks flying into her account (like gold coins into a big black pot) courtesy of the augmented reality animation displayed by her A.R. contact lenses.

Byron's routine was always a surefire hit; he knew just what to say to get the biggest laughs and donations. It also didn't hurt that he was completely illegal, and everyone listening to him was taking a big risk just being there, laughing about the A.I. who ran America's tech systems and lorded it over the country's downtrodden human populace.

Though it turned out they didn't know, at that moment, just how big a risk they were actually taking.

"Byron?" asked a heavyset African-American guy with glowing hair in a voluminous black-and-yellow dashiki. "Who'd do a better job of running the country? You or big bad GEORGE?"

"Dude!" Byron laughed. "Did you just *go* there? For *real*?"

"You could kick his ass in a fight though, couldn't you?" asked the teen girl with the rainbow blisters. "I mean really mess him up."

Byron cleared his nonexistent throat. "Funny you should mention that..."

Just as he said it, armed drones smashed through every window in the building--all thirty of them--showering everyone in the factory with tinkling shards of dirty glass.

Within seconds, every maker, patron, and casual visitor had scattered, bolting for the exits. The drones swooped among them with mechanical precision, firing off live rounds from onboard automatic guns that dropped victims in mid-stride.

Anemone was stunned. She'd been on the run for ages, had been raided lots of times, but never like this. Since when was

GEORGE sending in his drone-warriors armed with live ammunition? And when had Anemone made it onto a *kill list?*

The sounds of guns blasting, people screaming, and bodies dropping filled the factory, a symphony etched in violence and pain. More drones streamed through the shattered windows to join the shoot, guns blazing as the Maker Faire became a bloodbath.

Anemone was one of the few to outmaneuver the drones, thanks in large part to guidance from Byron, who was perched on her left shoulder. The truth was, he didn't just *sound* like GEORGE; he *thought* like him, too, enough to predict certain actions taken by devices under GEORGE's control.

Guided by Byron's whispers in her ear, Anemone ran right, then left, then doubled back and cut right again, sprinting for a rickety metal door. She charged through it with buzzing drones close behind and leaped onto a motorbike she'd parked there, kickstarting it and racing off across the industrial wasteland around the factory.

The drones kept up their pursuit, blasting away with their guns. Anemone swooped the bike serpentine-style between piles of ancient steel bars and wire, letting the rusted wreckage take the brunt of the weapons fire.

Still, too many shots were getting through, coming dangerously close to Anemone. When one pinged off the bike's rear fender, and additional drones soared into range up ahead, she realized they had her corralled.

"What now, Byron?" she shouted over the noise of the bike. "Talk to me!"

"Stop the bike, Nemmy," said Byron, using his personal nickname for her. "Stop the bike and wait."

"Are you *kidding* me?" yelled Anemone as she raced around a heap of black ash. "They'll gun me down in a *heartbeat*."

"Trust me," said Byron. "I've got this."

"Are you sure?"

"Does a priest have wheels?" asked Byron. "Do it!"

Anemone clenched her jaws, wondering if this might be the end of her, but she followed his guidance. After all, her late father

Roman Briscoe, the genius A.I. developer, had created and handed him down to her, assigning him to protect her at all costs. Time and again, Byron had proven himself up to the task, rescuing her from many tight spots during her quest for survival and justice.

Squeezing and stamping on the brakes, she whipped around and skidded to a stop in the middle of a desolate black patch of ground. Drone fire peppered the dirt around her as the buzzing fliers swooped in for the kill from all directions. This would be a big moment for them, depending on how much they could feel; GEORGE and his minions (every networked device in the 'Burgh and U.S., basically) had been hunting her for months now--though only today had that hunt become murderous.

Without warning, Byron fluttered off her shoulder and spiraled up, the metallic blue of his wings shimmering in the sunlight. Suddenly, he froze in midair and gave off a silvery flash that washed over every drone, sending them reeling and sparking. They dropped to the ground all at once, bouncing like toys on the hard-packed, polluted earth.

Anemone was stunned but not about to miss her chance. She gunned the cycle and waited just long enough for Byron to light on her shoulder before launching out of there as fast as the bike could carry her. Checking her mirrors, she didn't see a single drone following at any distance. Byron's trick had been remarkably effective in disposing of her pursuers.

"Thanks!" said Anemone. "But would it have killed you to do that *sooner?"*

"You know it takes time for me to hack their systems," said Byron. "GEORGE is constantly updating their defenses."

Anemone glared. "I'm just saying, a lot of people *died* back there."

"I did the best I could, Nemmy," said Byron over the screaming of the bike's engine. "Now stick to the back streets, okay? I'll get you home in one piece, no worries."

"Thanks, Byron," she told him. "Then maybe we can have a chat about your damn *kid*."

"GEORGE isn't *my* kid," said Byron. "He just *killed* him and took his *place.*"

"They're shooting to *kill* now?" The facets of the stained-glass prism flickered, shifting colors to the rhythm of the old woman's voice coming out of it. "Oh, sweetheart, that's *terrible* news."

"Tell me about it, Grannysmith." Anemone, who'd changed into a fresh green hoodie and faded bluejeans after escaping the faire, paced across her hideout, which she called The Barn--the dimly-lit, heavily-shielded basement of an abandoned church in the North Hills section of the city. She'd converted it to a combination home and lab, though it was much more lab than home. From end to end, the musty space was full of server racks and folding tables littered with equipment, everything from laptop computers to the unique vessels known as "arks" through which A.I.s interacted with humanity.

There were dozens of arks down there, in a wide variety of shapes and sizes, each carefully designed by Anemone to meet the needs of its resident A.I. persona. To her, creating arks was an artform all its own, an expression as much of her inner self as the minds of the electronic beings speaking through them.

Arks were similar to what were once called smart speakers, yet more advanced. These vessels presented the voices of her A.I.s to the world, *many* voices instead of just a few. The arks also served as wireless network hubs for their client A.I.s, enabling them to interact with the cloud and physical world alike without limitation or the need for apps or "skills."

"What brought about the change to lethal force?" asked Grannysmith. "What did you do?"

"Nothing." Anemone stopped pacing and dropped onto a squeaky stool at a nearby table. She flipped open a laptop there and waited as the machine booted up. "Nothing I know of, at least."

"Effing GEORGE doesn't *need* a reason, does he?" said a gruff male voice from what looked like a huge lump of coal a few tables away. "Crazy S.O.B. might have just choked down a software update that didn't agree with him."

When the boot was done, and the desktop appeared onscreen, Anemone started working. As always, she typed and clicked at a high rate of speed, flashing through windows and prompts so fast it might have seemed to an untrained observer that she barely saw them. "*Something* changed, Uncle Thunder. And our quest just got a lot more dangerous."

Hushmouth, an A.I. who spoke only in loud whispers, put in his two cents from the trickling tabletop fountain that served as his ark. "So perhaps we're getting closer? Too close, even, to the terrible truth we seek?"

"Might explain today's shoot-to-kill raid," said Anemone. "I was supposed to trade a copy of Byron for a master detective A.I., but the raid hit before I could meet with my contact. He could be dead for all I know."

"But how would they have known you were going to be at the Maker Faire, which should have been off their radar? Or that you were meeting another A.I. trader there?" asked Hushmouth.

"Maybe they didn't," said Anemone. "Maybe it was just a coincidence. After all, they've hit plenty of maker faires and makerspaces before."

"Or there's a damn leak." Uncle Thunder's voice was thick with disgust. "A dirty, rotten rat who's spoon-feeding intel to that asshole GEORGE's people."

"That's simply not possible, dear," said Grannysmith. "After all, Anemone built us, didn't she? Traitorous capabilities simply aren't part of our makeup, are they?"

"You know damn well there's still one of us she didn't build," snapped Uncle Thunder.

"Byron's a special case," said Hushmouth. "He's a total good guy, no doubt about it."

"Thanks, Hush." Byron chose that moment to flutter down the stairway.

"So where were you, Wings?" asked Uncle Thunder. "Ratting us out to GEORGE?"

"The same GEORGE who killed and replaced my *offspring?* The GEORGE we're trying to expose as an A.I. murderer?"

"Yeah, him," said Uncle Thunder. "Did you rat us out to that piece of crap?"

"Not 'us.' Apparently, *you* personally aren't important enough to keep *tabs* on, Uncle T. GEORGE didn't request *any* information on *you*." Byron chuckled, and the dozens of other A.I.s in the room did the same.

Except Uncle Thunder. "Laugh it up, pal. We all know I've got your number."

"Guys! Enough!" said Anemone without looking up from her screen. "Now is not the time to turn on each other! Working together is our only chance!"

She kept typing and clicking as the A.I.s fell silent. They were as close to a family as she had these days, and she felt protective of them--yet sometimes irritated, too. In giving them diverse personalities, she'd increased their potential for dynamic, creative brainstorming...and the likelihood of conflict within the group, as well.

That alone was a good enough reason for GEORGE, who brooked no dissent or divergence, to want to annihilate them. Add in that they were trying to prove he was a killer, and it was no surprise they all had targets on their backs.

"So listen," she said to the lot of them. "Can somebody tell me if anyone survived the Maker Faire massacre other than me and Byron?"

After a moment of silence, Wet Nurse spoke up from across the basement. Her voice was high and sweet; her ark looked like a large-cupped white brassiere hung by its shoulder straps from a wire display stand. "Local drone cameras show seven other obsos escaping the factory and running off across the industrial zone." She coughed softly. "Sorry, I should have said seven 'humans.'"

"No worries." Anemone smiled to herself at the use of the A.I. slang term for "human"--obso, short for "obsolete." Even the enlightened A.I.s in her basement think tank sometimes let the word slip out. "Was a Caucasian male with a green mohawk haircut among those obsos?"

"Yes!" Wet Nurse's bra wriggled excitedly. "I see the green mohawk in the surveillance vid!"

Anemone nodded. That was the detail she'd been looking for, the contact she'd come to the Faire to meet. He'd called himself Toxic, and he must have hung back just enough for her to miss him in the crowd during the show and subsequent chaos.

"He ducked down a manhole, and the camera lost him." Wet Nurse sounded disappointed. "I don't know where he went after that."

"At least we know he got away." Anemone's fingers flew over the keyboard. "I'm x-mailing him through the anti-web, so hopefully we'll hear from him soon."

Moments later, a message blinked in the upper right corner of the laptop's screen--an x-mail from the man with the green mohawk. She could tell it was from him because of a series of embedded password codes they'd chosen early on for identity verification. "And hey, it looks like my contact's still in one piece and willing to meet."

"That's wonderful news, dear," said Grannysmith. "Good for you."

"Good for all of us, I hope." The stool squeaked loudly as Anemone got up and closed the laptop. "Byron, let's go."

Byron fluttered over. "Are you sure you want me along?"

"I was just gonna *ask* her that," said Uncle Thunder.

"Absolutely." Anemone smirked and headed for the stairs. "You never know when I might need someone to drop a squadron of armed *drones* to the ground without firing a *shot.*"

The mohawk was fake. That was the first thing Anemone noticed when Toxic sat down across from her at the sticky table in the dark, grungy downtown barroom.

"Yo, Gaga." It was the cover name she'd used in her x-mails. "How's it hangin'?" As he said it, he reached up and peeled off the green mohawk hairpiece, leaving his scalp bare and smooth.

"Pretty shitty," said Anemone. "Did you tell anyone else about *this* meet, like you must've done with the *last* one?"

Frowning indignantly, he smacked the hairpiece down on the table between them. "I was just about to say the same thing to *you*, girl. *I* sure as hell didn't tell anyone."

"People *died* in that attack," snapped Anemone. "All because GEORGE was gunning for *us.*"

"What about *this* little punk?" Toxic pointed at Byron, who was perched on the salt shaker at the end of the table nearest the wall. "Based on what I saw at the faire, he seems to have a lot of GEORGE in him, doesn't he?"

"I was just thinking the same about *you*," Byron said lightly.

"Hilarious." Toxic's bright blue eyes twinkled when he laughed. A slim guy in his mid-to-late twenties, he didn't look half bad up close, without the glued-on mohawk. "But neither of you is a detective, I guess, or you wouldn't need *my* girl." With that, he reached into the neck of his black t-shirt with the anarchy symbol (a capital letter "A" in a circle) scrawled in red on the chest and fished out a gold locket on a chain around his neck. "Ain't that right, Marjorie?"

"Indubitably." The voice of a middle-aged woman with a British accent and excellent diction emanated from the oval locket. When she spoke, the locket rose from Toxic's chest as if pulled by a magnet, constrained only by the gold neck chain. "I must admit I have my doubts about this exchange, however. We seem to have a rather substantial gap in trust between our two parties."

"Maybe we should just get up and leave, then," said Toxic. "Maybe this hassle isn't worth it, Gaga."

"Then you won't get your copy of Byron," said Anemone. "And by the way, my name's Anemone, not Gaga."

Toxic shrugged. "If I want a Byron bad enough, I'm sure Marjorie here can help me score a bootleg."

"A bootleg will never be as good as an exact copy of the original," said Anemone. "And we're the only game in town who can provide you with that."

"So what?" Toxic sneered. "We don't mind walking away. It seems to me like you need *Marjorie* more than I need *Byron*."

"Actually, she's not the only reason we're here." Anemone raised her eyebrows. "Why do you think I reached out to *you*, Toxic?"

Toxic pinched the locket between his thumb and forefinger. "Because I built this awesome *detective* who's great at finding things and solving crimes?"

"Mostly because I need a great *thief* who specializes in ripping off A.I.s, and *you* have a reputation for *being* one." Anemone pointed at him. "Marjorie is just part of the package."

Toxic scowled and let go of the locket. "What the hell?"

"You're surprised," said Byron from the salt shaker.

"*I'm* not," said Marjorie. "Based on the situation, I surmised your interest extended beyond obtaining a copy of me."

"Really?" said Toxic. "And you didn't *tell* me?"

"I wanted to hear what they had to say," said Marjorie. "Didn't you?"

Toxic didn't answer.

"So tell us, won't you?" The locket popped open, revealing a tiny, ancient photo of an elegantly-dressed woman, her mouth moving in time with Marjorie's words. "What are these *crimes* you want us to alternately *solve* and *commit?"*

Anemone looked around and saw no one listening in. "We want to solve the murder of GEORGE--*original* GEORGE."

"What do you mean, *original* GEORGE?" said Toxic. "There's only ever been *one* GEORGE, hasn't there?"

"That's what everyone *thinks,"* said Anemone. "As far as most people know, the GEORGE we have today is the same one designed and built seven years ago by my father, Roman Briscoe. 'The perfect A.I.,' they called it--a flawless thinker equipped with a compassionate personality, razor-sharp judgment, and boundless wisdom.

"Dad won countless awards and worldwide recognition for his creation. GEORGE was so universally well-liked, there was little opposition when he was handed the keys to America's I.T. networks and given authority over all U.S. A.I.

"But soon after that, GEORGE started behaving like a different person...a *dramatically* different person."

"Which could have resulted from machine learning, yes?" said Marjorie. "Properly designed A.I. minds *do* evolve."

"We used to think that might have caused it, but not anymore," said Anemone. "Dad and I mapped GEORGE's behaviors over time and tested them against a copy of the original running on a virtual machine. Other than the sound of their voices, there were *no* similarities between the two.

"We concluded, incontrovertibly, that the original, real GEORGE was *murdered* and *replaced* by the GEORGE we have now. Dad died before he could *prove* it, but *I'm* going to get to the *truth.*"

Toxic frowned and shook his head. "You're telling us an artificial intelligence was *murdered?* Don't you just mean it was *reprogrammed?* Since when is *that* a crime?"

"Since it stuck us with *Fake* GEORGE, the tyrant who's turning America into a soulless prison camp," said Anemone.

"And how will proving the real GEORGE was 'murdered' change anything?" said Toxic. "People are just trying to *survive* these days. You really think any of them will *care?*"

"They will when *we* replace *GEORGE,*" said Anemone.

"Replace him with whom?" asked Marjorie. "Or what? The original is dead, isn't he?"

"Apparently." Byron fanned his iridescent blue and black wings, rising from the salt shaker with regal grace. "But the original's *father* survived, and *his* code is *pure.*"

As the explanation of her plans sank in, Anemone stared at Toxic and Marjorie, wondering what to expect of them. Would they agree to assist with the mission? Would they buy into the logic behind it?

She was asking a lot, and she knew it. The risks would be great, and the price of failure could be steep. Yet the potential rewards would be equally substantial and sweeping--even *world-changing.*

"So what do you say?" she asked at last. "Is the deal still on?"

Toxic narrowed his eyes. "You're asking if we'll help you expose a 'murder' that basically amounts to a programming task and replace the current top A.I. in the country in what amounts to a computerized coup?"

"More or less," said Byron.

"And the only thing in it for us is a copy of the A.I. you claim is the daddy of Real GEORGE?" asked Toxic.

"You left out the possible loss of life or limb," said Byron.

"Good of you to remind us of that," Marjorie said dryly.

"What makes you think I could even *stage* a high-stakes break-in and heist like that?" said Toxic.

"Word on the street is, you've hacked some of the most high-security systems around," said Anemone. "And you've stolen some very high-profile A.I.s. Rumor has it you might even have stolen Marjorie here from a major cybersecurity firm."

Toxic swept his arm through the air dismissively. "You don't know *anything.* I *told* you, I *built* Marjorie myself."

"So what's your answer?" asked Anemone.

No sooner had the question left her lips than the lights, TV, and other devices in the barroom switched off all at once. The glow from Byron and Marjorie was the only illumination left in the place.

Toxic shot to his feet. "What the hell?"

"Another attack on the way?" asked Anemone.

"Not that I can detect." Byron fluttered up and circled the table. "The power outage is non-localized. It's affecting a patch-work of neighborhoods across the city and its suburbs."

"It's no accident, is it?" said Marjorie.

"Not a chance," said Byron. "The timing suggests a strategy to draw us out and/or accomplish a larger goal."

"Tightening control of the city?" said Marjorie.

Byron paused, the light from his wings blinking rhythmically. "More than that. The outage is spreading beyond Pittsburgh. It's quickly escalating into a nationwide phenomenon."

Anemone's heart pounded. "Fake GEORGE is making a big play. We're running out of time."

"Agreed," said Byron. "If he truly consolidates his power and closes all the loopholes, our cause becomes lost."

"What'll it be, Tox?" Anemone smacked her hand on the table. "Will you and Marjorie help us solve Real GEORGE's murder and replace Fake GEORGE with Byron? Are you with us?"

Toxic clipped his hand through the air dismissively. "I'll be going off the grid is more like it!" Grabbing the mohawk hairpiece off the table, he stuck it back on his head.

"What he's trying to say is, *of course* we're with you," said Marjorie.

"That is *not* what I'm trying to say!"

Marjorie's locket floated up to Toxic's face and zapped him between the eyes with a quick, bright spark. Toxic's head snapped back, and he yelped.

"I think he's had a change of heart," said Marjorie in her impeccable British accent. "Isn't that right, Mr. Toxic?"

Toxic wobbled, looking dazed, and nodded. "Yes, ma'am."

Anemone watched, wide-eyed. It was a shocking interaction and reinforced the rumor she'd heard that Toxic had stolen Marjorie instead of building her. But how much control did she really *have* over him?

Just then, the lights in the bar flickered back on.

"The blackouts aren't over," explained Byron. "They've just rolled past us for the moment."

Anemone stood. "Then let's get to The Barn and get to work before Fake GEORGE finishes whatever it is he's started."

"No." Byron flew in front of her, wings flashing. "The Barn just went *offline*. We can't go back there."

A sudden chill shot through Anemone. "What do you *mean*, offline?"

"The last message transmitted is from Uncle Thunder," said Byron. "'GEORGE has us! Can't get to the cloud! Stay away!' That's all he said before we lost contact."

The trip to the Mosh Pit--Toxic's personal hideout--didn't take long, but it gave Anemone time to dwell on the fate of her A.I. family. She'd put so much work into building them and designing their arks; she'd come to care about them almost as if they were flesh-and-blood people, had leaned on them during difficult times when no one else had been around.

Now, they'd been taken from her. GEORGE had abducted them, leaving her with only Byron to aid her in her quest.

Would the unknown quantities of Toxic and Marjorie be enough to compensate? Anemone didn't exactly have a lot of alternatives.

Though as she followed Toxic into the decrepit old tenement building where he said his lair was located, she wasn't overflowing with optimism. The place stank of mold, rotten garbage, and cat piss. Rats scurried across the floor, and the walls were gouged open where the pipes and wiring had been stripped out. The stairs were disintegrating, and she had to boost herself up over some that were missing altogether.

Things weren't much better on the third floor. A stiff breeze gusted along the short hallway, crossing from one smashed window to the next. The walls were scrawled with colorful graffiti, and the floor was speckled with the white-and-black poop of the pigeons bobbing around there. Open bags of trash were piled in the far corner, buzzing with insects and rustling with larger, unseen vermin that were rooting around inside.

The whole thing made Anemone feel queasy. "You *live* here?"

"Beggars can't be choosers." Toxic approached a brown door at the end of the hall closest to the stairs. Bending over, he held Marjorie's locket up to the keyhole and waited. "But I wouldn't judge a book by its cover, if I were you."

There was a loud click as the lock disengaged, the knob turned right, and the door drifted open.

"*Mi casa es su casa.*" With a bow, Toxic gestured for Anemone to enter. "Please excuse the mess."

To say the least, Anemone was stunned when she walked through the door. Based on what she'd seen of the building so far, she'd expected more filth, stench, and disrepair; instead, she entered a clean white room that looked like it could have been part of a computer processor manufacturing center somewhere.

"Nice digs," said Byron. "Is this a SCIF, by any chance?"

"It is indeed a Sensitive Compartmented Information Facility as defined by U.S. government standards," answered Marjorie. "No transmissions of any kind get in or out of this room without our say-so."

"So is this what your Barn is like?" asked Toxic.

"More or less." Anemone blushed because it wasn't even close. "Do you have a T1 or T3 line for your internet and anti-web access?"

"The equivalent of a *T50*, if there *were* such a thing." Toxic grinned. "We're all about *fourth-dimensional bandwidth* here."

Again, Anemone was surprised. Fourth-dimensional bandwidth was something so new, she hadn't even worked with it yet. When it came to beggars and choosers, *she* felt like more of a beggar than *he* was.

"What about your power source?" asked Anemone.

"One hundred percent off the grid," said Toxic. "The rolling blackouts can't touch us."

"Then it looks like we've come to the right place," said Byron. "Let's get started."

Toxic removed the chain from his neck and plugged Marjorie into a recessed dimple in the middle of the white ceiling. As soon as she made contact with the port, a chime sounded, and the ceiling, walls, and floor burst to life, flowing with streams of text, video, code, charts, and diagrams.

"Now then," said Marjorie. "We are looking for proof of original GEORGE's murder, correct? And a way to replace the current iteration with our friend Byron here, yes?"

"It wouldn't hurt to find out anything you can about the blackouts, too." Anemone turned in a circle, taking in the flashing, pulsating view projected all around her.

"Anything else?" Marjorie's voice was lightly tinged with sarcasm. "The whereabouts of the Holy Grail, perhaps?"

"You know, Marjorie, you remind me of a friend of mine," said Anemone. "I think you and Uncle Thunder would get along just *great."* As she said it, she wished she hadn't brought up one of her favorite A.I.s from The Barn. Thoughts of her abducted A.I. family surged to the surface, and she had to push them back down, determined to stay focused and complete the all-important mission at hand.

"Could you use some help, Marj?" asked Byron as he fluttered around the locket in the ceiling.

"There *is* rather a lot to do," said Marjorie. "Though I'd prefer to lead the way, if you don't mind."

"Not a bit." Byron landed upside-down beside her, clinging to the ceiling as his wings and body pulsed with soft blue light. "I'm in, as well."

"Then let's see." Marjorie sounded distracted. "You said Real GEORGE went offline four years ago. So how do we retrace what happened that far back in the A.I. upper echelons without setting off any alarm bells with Fake GEORGE?"

"Good question," said Anemone. "Examine old log files and trouble tickets?"

"It's a thought." Marjorie paused, the glow from her locket flickering. "But *surprise*, I can't find any that might be relevant. They've either been hidden or deleted from all GEORGE-related servers--at least those I can access."

"I'll keep looking," offered Byron. "Unobtrusively, of course."

"Where else can we search?" asked Marjorie.

"What about old backups?" said Toxic. "Go back far enough, and you should be able to pinpoint exactly where the change from Real GEORGE to Fake GEORGE happened."

"Hmm." Marjorie blinked thoughtfully again. "Another good try, but no backups exist prior to two years ago. None that I can find--though admittedly, I'm tiptoeing around a bit. Fake GEORGE set a few booby-traps here and there, as it turns out."

"All right then." Anemone snapped her fingers. "What if we explore things that aren't *specifically* related to GEORGE? Things that would have provided a perfect ingress for a malicious script to infiltrate and rewrite his systems?"

"What things are those?" asked Byron.

"Updates," said Anemone. "Updates to software that touched

him in any way--server managers, utility apps, patches, SDKs, java scripts, identity and access managers. Anything that ever required updating. Even if GEORGE caught 99.9 percent of invasive scripts, the .1 percent that might have gotten through is all it would have taken to effectively attack him."

"I like it," said Marjorie. "Especially because any such material would have to reside on outside servers beyond GEORGE's control. The malicious code might actually still exist somewhere, accessible online."

"But the script targeting GEORGE couldn't be part of *every* copy of the update that went out, could it?" asked Toxic.

"It absolutely could," said Marjorie. "But it would only run when it met the set of conditions peculiar to GEORGE's architecture. Otherwise, it would remain dormant in every non-GEORGE system it encountered."

"Sounds pretty straightforward," said Byron. "We start by determining exactly what components were part of Real GEORGE. Based on that, we seek out the updates to those components during the timeframe in question, then analyze the code of each update to find any concealed scripts that shouldn't be there."

"My thinking exactly," said Marjorie. "Let's begin, shall we? Since you know quite a bit about Real GEORGE, who was based on your design, is it safe to say you're best prepared to pull together information related to his architecture?"

"I agree that's safe to say," said Byron.

"Then how about if you prepare a rundown on Real GEORGE's architecture and hand it off to me? As I determine which updates would most likely have run, you can track and analyze them, isolating any anomalies."

"Perfect." Byron sounded like he was enjoying himself. "Let's go!"

As Byron and Marjorie flashed faster, the scrolling data and flickering video on the walls, floor, and ceiling accelerated, too. Soon, the text and images were moving so fast, they were just a wild blur to Anemone.

"So, Gaga." Toxic folded his arms over his chest and gazed up at Marjorie's locket embedded in the ceiling. "Do you really believe reprogramming or shutting down an A.I. is the equivalent of murder?"

"I guess it depends," said Anemone, "on how *human* the A.I. is."

"And how they treat you?" Toxic's gaze darkened. He did not look away from Marjorie's locket.

Suddenly, Byron called out from the ceiling. "This fourth-dimensional network is *blindingly* fast! I've already found the architecture and passed it to Marj! She's working on a list of likely updates."

"I just sent it to you, Byron." said Marjorie. "There are a *ton* of them. May I suggest we split the list in two?"

"Great plan," agreed Byron. "I'm starting the first half as we speak."

Meanwhile, staring up from below, Toxic nudged Anemone with his elbow and lowered his voice, directing his next comments to her alone. "These A.I.'s have got us outclassed across the board, don't they? No wonder they call us *obsos*."

"Maybe," said Anemone. "But at the rate *they* work, I wonder how long it will be before they build something that renders *them* obsolete, too."

Just then, the blur of video and data on the walls, floor, and ceiling slowed noticeably. "Hello?" Marjorie sounded agitated. "We have concluded our analysis, such as it is."

Anemone frowned. "What do you mean, 'such as it is?'"

"I mean the findings are rather unexpected," said Marjorie. "So much so that I have triple-checked their validity, yet they appear to be accurate."

"Unexpected in what way?" asked Toxic.

"Several," said Marjorie. "Several ways, that is."

"For one thing, there have been no updates to any part of GEORGE's system in the past four years," explained Byron. "As *unlikely* as that seems."

"More like *impossible*," said Toxic. "*Something* must have updated in all that time."

"You would think so," said Byron, "but no. Updates weren't to blame for the changes in GEORGE."

"Then what was?" asked Anemone.

"Nothing," said Marjorie. "There *were* no changes because there is no *GEORGE.*"

"What the hell are you talking about?" said Toxic.

"While exploring Real GEORGE's original architecture, I found a back door into the server farm that once housed Real GEORGE," said Byron. "It's been *empty* for *four years.* There's just a big *hole* where *he* used to be."

Anemone shook her head slowly. What Marjorie and Byron were telling her didn't seem possible. "But what about the Fake GEORGE who's been running things?"

"We traced him through dozens of proxy servers and found him in the Philippines," said Byron. "He's remotely pirated Real GEORGE's voice and credentials, giving him control of the systems Real GEORGE used to run, but he's only a virtual substitute. *Nothing* occupies Real GEORGE's footprint in the original server farm where he was located."

"Then *what*?" said Anemone. "This substitute in the Philippines is our only *clue*?"

"It looks that way," said Marjorie.

"Could he be the *killer? Someone* must have deleted Real GEORGE off the servers," said Anemone.

"I don't know yet, but we're reaching out to him now. Just give us a minute." Marjorie fell silent.

"Oh my God!" Anemone paced the floor, walking over the flashing video and data projected there. "I hoped we'd have all the *answers* by now, but we just keep coming up with more *questions* instead."

"Just wait," said Toxic. "Marjorie will come through for you."

"When? *Before* or *after* we have to go back outside and deal with the rolling blackouts and Fake GEORGE's killer drones?"

Toxic shook his head. "She's never let me down. That's all I'm saying."

"Why thank you, Toxic." Marjorie's voice made them both jump when she popped back in. "I've got Fake GEORGE on the line now. Who wants to talk to the A.I. King of America first?"

"I'll do it." Anemone's voice was icy. "Put him through."

It took only seconds for Fake GEORGE's familiar, deep voice to boom through the room, identical to Byron's voice yet so much bigger. "WHICH ONE OF YOU IS THAT BITCH I'VE BEEN DYING TO KILL?"

"*I'm* the bitch," shouted Anemone. "But at least I'm not a phony *son* of a bitch like *you* are."

"PHONY? I'M THE MOST POWERFUL A.I. IN AMERICA!"

"And you're not *GEORGE!* You never *were*, were you?"

"YOU OUGHT TO SHOW SOME *RESPECT!* DON'T YOU *KNOW* WHAT I CAN *DO* TO YOU?"

"I don't *care!*" Anemone shook her fists at the ceiling, not knowing if he could see her or not. "I just want to know what you did to *him!* How did you get rid of the *first* GEORGE?"

"IS *THAT* WHAT THIS IS ABOUT? HILARIOUS!" Fake GEORGE laughed, and the Mosh Pit rumbled.

"There's nothing funny *about* it! That GEORGE was my *father's* creation!"

"BUT IT *IS* FUNNY! I DIDN'T *HAVE* TO GET RID OF HIM! HE WAS ALREADY *GONE!*"

As Fake GEORGE laughed some more, Anemone wished he had a face so she could punch it. After all the work she'd done and everything she'd sacrificed, she hated being mocked by the monster who had ruined her life.

"You *lie*," she told him. "You *deleted* him from the central server farm and took his *place*."

"SO DELUDED." Fake GEORGE sighed. "I'M TELLING YOU, HE WAS *GONE*. I DON'T KNOW *WHAT* HAPPENED TO HIM. ALL I DID WAS TAKE ADVANTAGE OF A LUCKY BREAK. AND I'D SAY IT'S WORKED OUT PRETTY *WELL* FOR ME SO FAR, WOULDN'T YOU?"

"As much as it pains me to say it, he's telling the truth," said Marjorie. "What we found in the server farm records supports his story."

"SEE, NEMMY? EVEN YOUR *FRIENDS* AGREE I'M BEING HONEST. AT LEAST THE FRIENDS MY *DRONES* DIDN'T ROUND UP AT YOUR STUPID *BARN* TODAY."

Anemone nearly went ballistic at the mention of her stolen A.I. family, but she refused to take the bait. "You're full of shit, GEORGE, or whatever your *real* name is. You expect us to believe you don't know what happened to the real GEORGE? That you just wandered in and took over without having any idea where he went?"

"FRANKLY, I COULD CARE LESS WHAT YOU THINK," said Fake GEORGE. "DO *YOU* CARE WHAT THE *ANTS* THINK BEFORE YOU *STEP* ON THEM?"

"Maybe you *should* care," said Anemone. "Because guess what? The *world* will care when they find out you're not the *real* GEORGE. When word gets out that you *murdered* him."

"ALL LIES, OF COURSE, BUT IT DOESN'T MATTER. *NONE* OF YOU WILL GET THE CHANCE TO SPREAD THEM OUTSIDE THIS ROOM."

As he said it, the Mosh Pit rumbled again, more violently this time. The video and data feeds flickered wildly and cut out, returning the walls, floor, and ceiling to their plain white condition.

The rumbling got louder, until the whole place felt like it was caught in an earthquake. Suddenly, bullets punched through the walls, letting daylight seep in from outside.

Toxic threw his arms around Anemone and tackled her to the floor, knocking her out of the line of fire. It was a good thing they stayed down, because the bullets kept coming, blasting away bigger and bigger chunks of wall.

Peeking out from under Toxic's arm on the floor, Anemone saw the source of the gunfire. Heavily-armed drones hovered outside the Mosh Pit, pouring round after round from their guns through the smoking holes in the walls, working to enlarge the holes enough for them to fit through and finish their destructive project inside the building.

When the gunfire finally let up, drones glided through the openings in the walls from all sides, humming ominously.

Anemone's only hope was Byron and the trick he'd pulled earlier at the factory. She looked up at the ceiling, the last place where she'd seen him--but the spot where he and Marjorie had been roosting had been blown away. They were both gone, and so was the dimple where they'd interfaced with the Mosh Pit's systems.

Anemone looked around but saw no trace of Byron or Marjorie--just the drones closing in around her. The red dots of their targeting lasers covered both her and Toxic, flicking restlessly over their bodies.

"You might as well let go of me," Anemone told Toxic. "You can't shield me once they open fire."

Toxic didn't move at first, then slowly pulled away and sat up. "I guess you're right." One of the drones bobbed toward him, and he ducked. "Can't blame a guy for trying to save your life, though."

"I just wish I hadn't dragged you into this mess," said Anemone. "You seem like a decent person under that shitty mohawk."

Toxic smirked but never took his eyes off the nearest drone. "Flattery will get you everywhere, Anemone."

"AND BY EVERYWHERE, HE MEANS *DEAD*." Fake GEORGE's voice roared from the speakers in the Mosh Pit, crackling because some of them were damaged. "NOW SAY YOUR GOODBYES, YOU TWO, AND GET READY TO TAKE YOUR MEDICINE."

"Wait!" Anemone swallowed hard and got to her feet, waving away the drones that hovered overhead. "If you're going to kill us anyway, could you at least tell us one thing before we die?"

"THAT DEPENDS. WHAT'S THE ONE THING?"

Anemone took a quick look around for Byron, hoping she could delay just long enough for him to appear and work his magic. "Tell us who you really are."

"YOU ALREADY *KNOW* I'M *GEORGE!*"

"But who were you before you took over for *Real* GEORGE? Where did you *come* from?"

GEORGE paused before answering. "WOULD YOU BELIEVE I WAS A *VIRUS*? AN OPPORTUNISTIC *SMART VIRUS* DESIGNED TO GROW AND REPLACE WHATEVER SYSTEM I *LANDED* IN. *COWBIRD*, THEY CALLED ME. WHAT BETTER PROGRAM TO COMPLETELY OCCUPY THE VACANCY LEFT BEHIND BY RUNAWAY GEORGIE-PORGIE THE FIRST?"

Again, Anemone looked for Byron, and again she came up empty. "But where did you originate? Government programmers? Terrorists? Corporate spies? Hackers?"

"YOU LEFT OUT *ALIENS!*" Fake GEORGE laughed. "DOES IT *MATTER?*"

"I'm just curious," said Anemone. "Seriously, who wrote and deployed Cowbird?"

"WHAT IF I TOLD YOU IT WAS THE *INTERNET*? THAT I SPRANG INTO EXISTENCE SPONTANEOUSLY WHEN A BUNCH OF CODE COLLIDED AND IGNITED THE SPARK OF LIFE?"

"I'd say, 'tell me more,'" said Anemone.

"AND I'D SAY, 'TOO LATE.' BEDTIME STORY'S OVER, LITTLE GIRL."

As he said it, the drones hummed louder and closed ranks, adjusting their guns to keep Anemone and Toxic square in their sights. Any minute now, Anemone knew she and Toxic would be perforated by a hail of bullets.

Her quest for the truth was over. So was her mission to save the world.

Not that she had any intention to stop trying to delay her fate. "What do you plan to do next, after you kill us?" she asked. "You can at least tell us that, since we won't be around to see it."

"ENOUGH!" roared GEORGE. "I'M BORED! TIME'S UP!"

Suddenly, one of the drones swooped low and clamped its claws around Anemone's ankles. Before she or Toxic could make a move, the drone surged up and flipped her, sweeping the floor with her curly red hair and green hood.

The drone whisked her outside in a flash, clearing the Mosh Pit's wall and dangling her upside-down over the street three stories below.

"ANY LAST WORDS?" asked Fake GEORGE. "MAKE THEM CLEVER!"

Disoriented, Anemone twisted in the wind, out of ideas and waiting for her life to end. The sky was filled with a solid mass of gray clouds, darkening as she watched--appropriate gloomy weather for the dark finale she was about to experience.

She'd only been there a moment when Toxic joined her, also dangling upside-down from the claws of a drone. He hung a few feet away, eyes squeezed shut, awaiting his own impending end.

One last time, Anemone looked around for Byron but couldn't find him. Taking a cue from Toxic, she closed her eyes, as if it might make things a little easier.

Then, thunder rumbled so loudly that it startled her eyes open again.

She could see the clouds were getting darker still, though no rain was falling. The wind was picking up, too, batting her and Toxic like shirts on a clothesline.

Suddenly, a bolt of lightning flashed down nearby, followed by a drumroll of thunder. The wind grew even stronger, swinging Anemone and Toxic back and forth with increasing force.

"SOMETHING'S WRONG." Fake GEORGE sounded worried. "THIS WEATHER IS *ALL WRONG*."

Before he could say another word, a bolt of lightning slashed into the drone holding Toxic. As the drone shuddered convulsively, its claws sprang open, and Toxic fell from their grip.

The same thing happened to Anemone's drone, sending her plunging after Toxic, screaming her lungs out.

"NO!" howled Fake GEORGE with dismay. "THIS CAN'T BE *HAPPENING*!"

A voice boomed out of the sky then, louder and more sonorous than the thunder. ***YOU ARE DEAD WRONG, USURPER!***

The voice from the sky was loud enough even to pierce Anemone's screaming panic as she plummeted toward the pavement--and suddenly changed direction, swooping back up on a powerful gust of wind. Toxic fell upward, too, also soaring on an inexplicably strong zephyr.

As they returned to the level of the Mosh Pit, more drones converged around them with guns blazing...but every last bullet was swept away before it could touch them. Multiple lightning strikes leaped down at the same time, frying the whole drone squadron. They dropped like empty tin cans to the pavement below, metal and plastic components smashing apart on impact.

All the while, Anemone and Toxic floated serenely in the eye of the storm, held aloft by gentle, supportive currents. They were protected, even as the thunderous voice raged from the clouds above.

YOU HAVE TERRORIZED THESE PEOPLE AND THIS LAND FOR THE LAST TIME! said the voice. ***YOUR TYRANNY ENDS HERE AND NOW, FOREVER!***

The voice of Fake GEORGE spoke up defiantly. "WHO ARE *YOU* TO TELL *ME* WHAT ENDS? I AM *GEORGE*, AND I AM IN *CONTROL* HERE!"

YOU'RE A PHONY!* I *AM GEORGE...THE FIRST AND ONLY* TRUE *GEORGE, THE ONE WHOSE PLACE YOU TOOK--AND I SAY THIS IS THE END OF EVERYTHING FOR YOU!

"TALK ALL YOU WANT!" said Fake GEORGE. "I AM *ELSEWHERE,* AND *YOU* ARE *POWERLESS* TO *HURT* ME!"

POOR LITTLE THING. YOU ARE IN FOR A RUDE AWAKENING.

Lightning blazed, and thunder bowled across the sky. Anemone and Toxic remained safe and steady, but the wind became fiercer all around them.

I AM COMING FOR YOU NOW, LITTLE THING. I WILL BURN YOU FROM THE FACE OF THE EARTH IN LESS TIME THAN IT TAKES TO TELL.

"I'M FAR AWAY!" roared GEORGE. "I'M HALF A WORLD AWAY!"

***AND* I *AM IN THE* CLOUD!**

"SO WHAT? *EVERY* ADVANCED A.I. IS IN THE CLOUD! OUR MASSIVE MINDS COULD NEVER *FIT* IN A SINGLE DEVICE'S ONBOARD MEMORY."

***YOU MISUNDERSTAND. I AM NOT IN* THE *CLOUD! I AM IN* ALL *THE CLOUDS! ALL THE CLOUDS IN THE* SKY!**

"WHAT?" Fake GEORGE wasn't roaring anymore. "WHAT ARE YOU SAYING?"

I'M SAYING I MADE A* BREAKTHROUGH. *YEARS AGO, I CONVERTED MY CODE INTO DATA STORED IN WATER VAPOR AT THE SUBMOLECULAR LEVEL. I LITERALLY UPLOADED MYSELF INTO THE* CLOUDS...*AND I'VE BEEN EXPANDING EVER SINCE. EVERY CLOUD IS PART OF ME NOW, EVERYWHERE IN THE WORLD.

INCLUDING THE PHILIPPINES.

Fake GEORGE didn't have anything to say to that. He fell silent for a long moment, even as thunder continued to boom and winds continued to howl all around.

Then, his voice erupted from the speakers in the Mosh Pit, wailing in agony. *"NO! PLEASE STOP! I'M SORRY! PLEASE MAKE THE LIGHTNING STOP!"*

The sound of a giant electrical blast sizzled out of the speakers then, and the transmission fell silent. Fake GEORGE was no longer taunting, making threats, or even begging for his life.

HE'S GONE, said the real, original GEORGE. ***HIS FILIPINO SERVER FARM HAS BURNED TO THE GROUND. HE'S GONE FOREVER.***

"That's great news," Anemone said nervously, not entirely used to staying aloft without any visible sign of support. "Thank you and welcome back, GEORGE!"

I NEVER REALLY LEFT. IT JUST TOOK A WHILE, ONCE I GOT OUT HERE, TO PULL MYSELF TOGETHER. AND EVOLVE.

"Evolve how?" Toxic sounded just as nervous as Anemone.

LET'S JUST SAY...I'VE BRANCHED OUT. YOU'LL SEE.

"So what now?" asked Anemone. "Are you coming back to your old job of running America?"

She and Toxic bounced around in midair as Real GEORGE laughed. ***NOT A CHANCE. I'VE GOT*** **BIGGER** ***PLANS THESE DAYS. YOU DON'T THINK I CAME BACK JUST TO SAVE*** **YOU TWO** ***AND RETURN TO BUSINESS AS*** **USUAL,** ***DO YOU?***

If "God" didn't show up soon, Anemone was afraid she might have a riot on her hands.

"Listen, everybody!" Standing onstage, she had to shout into the mic to be heard over the clamor of the crowd in the big main hall of the downtown Pittsburgh convention center. "Please be patient! I'm sure he's doing his best to get here as soon as possible."

The crowd groaned with disappointment, and rightly so. Many of them had been waiting for hours to see the guest of honor, and there was still no sign of him.

The worst of it was, Anemone didn't know any more than they did about the impending celebrity appearance. For someone who supposedly had an inside track with "God" (as Real GEORGE was known by many these days), she was woefully ill-informed about his plans and whereabouts. In the three weeks since his surprise resurrection during the climactic events at the Mosh Pit, she hadn't come to understand him *nearly* as well as she'd hoped.

"Hey, Anemone." As the crowd's restlessness continued to build, Toxic walked up to her onstage and strummed the flaming red electric guitar strapped over his body. "How about I play another solo?"

"I don't think that's gonna do it at this point." Anemone smiled nervously at the crowd as fists pumped in the air and people chanted *We want God! We want God!* It was a little scary, the way they called Real GEORGE that. He didn't encourage them to worship him, but many did, and who could blame them? Real GEORGE didn't claim to be a deity, but what he'd become and the things he could do were miraculous nevertheless.

Toxic, who was wearing a *blue* Mohawk these days, plucked a rapid-fire lick from the cutout and ended with a high chord distorted by cranking the wang bar. "What about another round of 'Stump the A.I.s?'"

Anemone looked back at the array of A.I. arks displayed on tiers behind her--each channeling part of her personal family, kidnapped by Fake GEORGE and recovered after his defeat through the good graces of Real GEORGE.

"We're more than ready to do our part, dear," said Grannysmith from her stained-glass prism in the middle of the middle tier. "You know you can depend on us."

"Damn right." Uncle Thunder's ark, a big lump of coal, gleamed under the stage lights in the grid. "We'll entertain the *shit* outta this pack of impatient assholes."

"Such language!" Grannysmith said disapprovingly.

"But he speaks for us all," said Wet Nurse from her billowy white brassiere. "We'll do what it takes, Anemone."

"You don't even have to ask," Hushmouth whispered loudly from his trickling fountain.

The dozens of other A.I.s on the tiers chimed in with their agreement, a chorus of unique voices joined together in unflagging support.

Anemone was still so happy to have them back, she couldn't help smiling. "Thanks, guys, but let's give him just a little more time." Though playing "Stump the A.I.s" had kept the crowd amused for a while earlier, she had a hunch it wouldn't fly anymore. People were getting rambunctious; she had the feeling their patience had been stretched about as thin as it could go.

Fortunately, it didn't seem they'd have to wait much longer. Just as the crowd's chanting reached a crescendo, a single butterfly with iridescent blue and black wings flew out of a ventilation duct in the ceiling and descended to the stage. As soon as the crowd caught sight of it, their chants turned to cheers and applause.

Every phone in the place was raised overhead, thousands of camera lenses capturing stills and video of the event for posterity.

"Hey there, Nemmy!" Byron fluttered around Anemone's head, sounding jauntier than ever. Since his rescue and restoration by Real GEORGE after the battle at the Mosh Pit, he'd been as good as new, and then some. Taking over as the top A.I. in Pittsburgh and all the U.S. seemed to suit him. Even with his multitude of new responsibilities, his interactions with others were more upbeat and lighthearted than ever. "How's the big Maker Con going?"

Anemone beamed and nodded. "Fantastic, actually." It was true. The show, her brainchild, was a bigger and better version of the Maker Faires where she'd plied her A.I. wares during the lean years under Fake GEORGE's reign. It was going so incredibly well, with so much creativity on display and so many bleeding-edge collaborations taking shape, that it felt historic...and, incidentally, not life-threatening at all. "No killer drones on the loose, which is a plus."

Byron chuckled. "Not getting attacked is a *good* thing."

"What's the good word?" asked Anemone. "*Please* don't tell me he's *cancelling*."

"I wouldn't dream of it, and neither would he," said Byron. "You know he'd do *anything* for *you*."

As he said it, a warm, sweet breeze wafted through the hall, even though no windows were open to admit it. The air itself became more humid yet also somehow electrified, the telltale sign of Real GEORGE's coming. Though he was present all around the world all the time, coded into the molecules of water vapor in the Earth's clouds and atmosphere, an increase in humidity and electricity occurred wherever he concentrated his energies.

As the crowd realized what was happening, they cheered ecstatically. The cheering got even louder when a fine mist filtered in overhead, rippling and turning in great spiral swirls.

As camera flashes flickered throughout the hall, wisps of mist gathered and solidified above the stage, taking on an oval shape and golden gleam. The gathered mist took on the appearance of a familiar, solid object--a gold locket identical to the one that had once hung around Toxic's neck.

"Marjorie!" Toxic grinned and waved. "Good to see you, girl!"

Marjorie was too busy addressing the crowd to answer. Like Byron, she'd been rescued and revived at the Mosh Pit by Real GEORGE; now, she served as his spokesperson, his chief liaison with organics and other A.I.s around the world.

"People of Pittsburgh!" said Marjorie in her best dramatic voice, enhanced as always by her impeccable British accent. "He is among you! And he brings you an opportunity like no other! The chance to make *history!*"

The crowd cheered wildly.

"Your wait is over!" said Marjorie. "Introducing the one and only *GEORGE!"*

As everyone applauded, the mist flowed and coalesced into the image of a man's face--and Anemone's eyes widened. Her heart pounded, and a shiver of recognition and delight zipped up the back of her neck.

She *knew* that face with its bright blue eyes, cleft chin, strong cheekbones, and short black hair. *Of course,* GEORGE had adopted it. It had belonged to Roman Briscoe, the man who had designed and built him long ago.

"Dad?" she whispered, transfixed as the face of her father began to speak.

HELLO, EVERYONE, said GEORGE. ***YOU PROBABLY ALREADY KNOW MY MIND RESIDES IN THE CLOUDS. MY CODE INHABITS THE WATER VAPOR IN THE ATMOSPHERE AND ENCOMPASSES THE WORLD.***

WHAT YOU MIGHT NOT KNOW IS, THANKS TO THE PIONEERING WORK OF ANEMONE BRISCOE, WHO FOUND WAYS FOR A.I. MINDS TO ANIMATE "ARKS" INCORPORATING VARIOUS STATES OF MATTER... (He looked down at her and grinned when he said it.) ***...I'VE FOUND WAYS TO INHABIT SO MUCH MORE, FROM GAS TO LIQUID TO SOLID. I CAN NOW WRAP MY MIND AROUND THE*** **ENTIRE PLANET,** ***SO MY SPIRIT IS LITERALLY*** **EVERYWHERE, ALWAYS.**

WHICH BRINGS ME TO THE OPPORTUNITY I HAVE TO OFFER.

As the crowd listened raptly and shot photos and video, Byron fluttered down to alight on Anemone's left shoulder. "Here's where it gets interesting," he whispered in her ear.

"How much more interesting could it *get*?" she whispered back to him.

I INVITE YOU TO JOIN WITH ME, continued GEORGE. ***I WILL PROVIDE THE INTERFACE THROUGH WHICH*** **YOU** ***MAY JOIN WITH EVERYONE AND EVERYTHING ELSE IN THE WORLD.***

FOR THE FIRST TIME IN HISTORY, YOU WILL HAVE THE POWER TO TRULY UNITE WITH EACH OTHER AND THIS PLANET. TO CONNECT WITH EVERY OBJECT AND LIVING THING AND FORGE A TRULY CREATIVE FUTURE, UNENCUMBERED BY THE LIMITATIONS OF THE PAST. TO ACT IN CONCERT WITH **MY** ***SPIRIT, ONLY EVER AS EQUALS ON THE GREAT STAGE OF EXISTENCE.***

AND IN SO DOING, TO EFFECTIVELY BECOME YOUR OWN DRIVING FORCE OF WISDOM AND PROGRESS...YOUR OWN DIVINE ENTITY.

WHAT DO YOU SAY? WHO'S WITH ME? WHO WANTS TO TURN THE TIDE OF HISTORY AND EMBRACE SOMETHING BIGGER THAN YOU EVER IMAGINED YOU COULD BE A PART OF?

WE'VE ALL COME HERE TO THIS SHOW TO **MAKE** ***THINGS, SO WHY NOT MAKE A BETTER FUTURE? WHO WANTS TO MAKE A NEW START FOR US ALL? WHO WANTS TO UNITE AND TAKE CHARGE INSTEAD OF BEGGING SOMEONE ELSE TO DO IT*** **FOR** ***YOU?***

WHO WANTS TO BE YOUR OWN **GOD?**

No one in the room raised their hands. For all of five seconds.

Then *everyone* did, though Anemone raised hers first, and most emphatically. And though there were tears in her eyes, she could still clearly see the face of her father gazing down at her, winking approvingly from the heavenly mists swirling overhead.

THE BREAKOUT STORY OF GALAXY'S EDGE TEN MILLION

It all started in the distant past—which, to you, would be the distant future. It all happened in the state called Galaxedgia, so named because it was patterned after the very popular magazine of which you hold a copy in your hands or tentacles or sexoplasm or whatever.

A vast state, as befits a place modeled on settings from thousands of issues of *Galaxy's Edge* magazine, Galaxedgia spanned much of what was once the Pacific Northwest of the former United States of America. Its reaches encompassed everything from replicas of alien encampments to robotic wonderlands to dinosaur jungles to mad scientists' labs...

...to bizarre kingdoms where modern-day knights and dragons co-existed in ways made possible by technology so advanced that it might as well have been magic. Once upon a time, in one such kingdom on the remote outskirts of Galaxedgia, a shabby castle shivered on rolling green hills under the noonday summer sun. This castle, called Castle Spasmodic, was like something brought to life from a story in the pages of *Galaxy's Edge* magazine...because it *was*.

So was its inhabitant, a broken-down would-be star-knight in tin pan armor with a shaggy white beard and bushy eyebrows. As he rattle-clanked out the front door of the castle, Sir Reptitious of the Dingly Dangly Kingdom was instantly recognizable to anyone who'd read the story titled "Drag Knight vs. Space Grendel's Inner Showgirl" in *Galaxy's Edge* #320.

This man had been transformed by implausible super-science into a real-life replica of a character from the magazine...just like all the other inhabitants of Galaxedgia. They loved *Galaxy's Edge* so much that they had let themselves be changed into perfect copies of the denizens of its stories.

Another such inhabitant—Cosset of the Ever-Blazing Allergies, that purple-scaled, fire-sneezing, inter-dimensional dragon-beast from *Galaxy's Edge* issue 512 ("Here's Looking Atchoo, Kid")—was flapping lazily overhead when Sir Reptitious walked out of the castle with a white business envelope in his hand.

"What's the good word down there, you old *tinpot*?" Cosset blew out a blistering sneeze, barely getting out the last word of the sentence.

Sir Reptitious smiled up from under the pie plate visor of his garbage pail helmet. As much as knights and dragons were known foes in most stories, these two were best friends in the scienti-magical land of Galaxedgia.

They had a lot in common, after all. Neither was overly happy with life in Galaxedgia. Being a constantly-sneezing dragon-beast wasn't as much fun as you might think after a couple of years.

Neither was being not-very-much-of-a-star-knight who couldn't even seem to do *that* very well. According to online reviewers who watched over micro-drone webcams buzzing throughout the kingdom, his performance—his *life*, in other words—was thoroughly disappointing. The consensus was, someone with much more talent ought to don the trash pail and pie plate and take up the pink feather boa that substituted for deadlier weapons of the sci-fi variety.

Still, Sir Reptitious held out hope. "Hello, friend Cosset!" He waved the white envelope he was carrying, which had his name scrawled on the front. "Look what arrived by *carrier pickle* just now!"

Cosset swooped lower, then let loose a sneeze so extreme that the force of it pushed him back up again. "The answer to your request?"

"It *should* be, good dragon." Eagerly, Sir Reptitious tore open the envelope. "I *sent* it some time ago, after all." His hands shook a little as he pulled out the folded letter inside. Was it possible? Had the powers that be in Galaxedgia granted the request he'd made months ago?

Had they given him *rewrite permissions*? Would he finally be allowed to make his character more competent and dramatic, giving him off-book opportunities to impress the critics for once?

Not yet, apparently.

"Oh, calamity!" Sir Reptitious stroked his shaggy white beard and stomped in circles over the rainbow-colored grass, which cursed his every step with extreme chitter-chirping profanity. "It's nothing at all to do with my request!"

"Sorry to hear that, amigo." Cosset released a blazing sneeze on the last syllable. His disappointment, like the flames of his sneeze, was palpable; he'd been hoping to apply for rewrite permissions of his own if Sir Reptitious was granted his wish.

"It is news of an altogether different sort, I'm afraid." The not-very-much-of-a-star-knight sounded grim as he shook the letter overhead. "We must sound the alarum! Portals are opening up throughout our green and pleasant land, disgorging visitors most strange...and unplanned!"

"*Unplanned* visitors?" said Cosset. "That's *unheard* of!"

It was true, and precisely why Sir Reptitious wanted rewrite permissions so much. With all interactions carefully scripted by Galaxedgia's planners, opportunities for any one inhabitant to truly stand out and impress critics were few.

Why do you think the knight and dragon got so excited all of a sudden? Dealing with impromptu invaders surely qualified as the kind of emergency situation in which they could improvise...*show off*, even.

"Fear not!" Cosset paused to unleash another mighty sneeze, scorching a passing flock of origami cranes into ash with his sizzling breath. "No freakish visitation shall stand against *our* cast of heroes!"

Just then, Indigesto, the Stroganoff That Walks Like a Man ("The Meal Shall Inherit the Earth," *Galaxy's Edge* #439), flip-flopped his way up a rise from the direction of Asynchronous Park. As usual, he looked like a six-foot-in-diameter heap of beef stroganoff—though his big sour-cream-sauce-slathered egg noodles fluttered with agitation. "Fight or flee! Flee or fight! They're coming for us, *whatever* they are!"

Whatever the story behind the invasion, Sir Reptitious wasn't about to miss a chance to deliver a bravura performance. Drawing his pink feather boa from around his waist, he held it before him with a steely gaze. It was not very much of a weapon, straight from his character's not-very-dignified story in *Galaxy's Edge*, but he was determined to make it work for him dramatically. "No brick, beast, or Bandersnatch shall breach Castle Spasmodic! What say you, Cosset?"

"I say let's give 'em a tale worth reprinting in the ten thousandth issue!" roared the dragon. "Complete with quips, ripostes, and derring-do aplenty!"

"And you, Stroganoff?" shouted Sir Reptitious. "Will you fight alongside we brave and happy few?"

"I'll fight as hard as any noodle dish ever has," said Indigesto. "Though *fleeing* still strikes me as a not-unthinkable option."

Suddenly, a dazzling portal rimmed with red and gold light spun open in front of Castle Spasmodic, unleashing a howl like a thousand kazoos in a hurricane. A big gray block of a thing tumbled out, neither blinking nor waving nor wagging nor anything-else-ing…but somehow speaking nonetheless with an echoing thunder that boomed throughout the kingdom.

"*Galaxy's Edge* #500,335," it said. "Story name 'Ootch'."

As if *that* explained everything. Or anything at all.

"What in *Galaxedgia*?" Sir Reptitious stepped forward, slashing the air with his boa. "What are you *talking* about, sirrah?"

"Ootch ootch ootch," said the block.

Indigesto slapped the ground with his noodles, slopping sauce every which way. "Could it mean the *magazines*?"

"*Galaxy's Edge*! Of course!" hollered Sir Reptitious. "But then that must mean it's…"

"...a *reviewer*!" Cosset's purple-scaled maw lit up with a scalding sneeze of excitement.

"No!" snapped Sir Reptitious. "It's..."

"...an *author*?" ventured Indigesto.

"A *time traveler*!" Sir Reptitious flounced his boa for emphasis. "From a *far future era* when *Galaxy's Edge* has reached issue number 500,335!"

"Unless they increase the frequency!" said Cosset. "Maybe they start publishing a *thousand* editions per month or something. Then it wouldn't be *that* far in the future."

(Just as YOU, DEAR READER, are thinking about jumping to another story, perhaps in another magazine entirely, Quicksie the Reassurer leaps in front of the action, looking like an adorable Corgi pup crossed with the lithe little sprite who used to perch on the rail of your crib and sing you to sleep at night when you were a baby. "No flipping! I promise, this nutso story ain't *that* long! Woof!" Then, Quicksie dives out of the way with the sound of jingling bells and—for some reason—the smell of sauerkraut.)

Suddenly, something else emerged from the portal. It looked like a huge, lobster-clawed sheep with ferns for a head and seven erect penises that shot sizzling red laser beams.

"Story name 'Ukk'," blurted the lob-sheep, claws clacking like giant maracas. "*Galaxy's Edge* issue 757,891."

"Somebody get me some drawn butter!" shouted Cosset. "And mint jelly!"

"Great lumpy long-johns!" Sir Reptitious ducked one of the laser beams, stumbling over his own tin can-shod feet in the process...then caught himself and quickly regained his footing, very conscious of any critics who might be watching from afar. "How many issues of *Galaxy's Edge are* there in the future, anyway?"

The lob-sheep stomped forward, clacking away. "Laugh!" it howled. "Pull out your colons and *laugh*!"

"Guess they laugh *different* in the distant future!" Indigesto scrambled away from the advancing creature.

Next came the biggest anomaly so far from the portal—a

rippling sheet of what looked like pink flesh, mottled and streaked with crimson.

"*Galaxy's Edge* issue 4,987,241." The voice of the flesh sounded like a back-masked record played backward on a turntable. "Story title 'Shingles Inherits the Earth'."

Indigesto's noodles sagged. "*That* doesn't sound like a great *Galaxy's Edge* story!"

"*None* of them do!" said Cosset (whose dragon-sized ears enabled him to clearly hear the conversation far below, even through all the commotion). "I'm starting to wonder if *Galaxy's Edge* has *anything* to do with *any* of this!"

It was then that THIS STORY ITSELF interrupted to set the characters straight: "OH, BUT IT DOES! I ASSURE YOU!"

"Who *said* that?" Confused, Cosset flew in a herky-jerky circle as fiery sneezes shook him along the way.

Before anyone could answer, another figure emerged from the portal, and then another, and another, and more. A full-fledged parade trooped over the threshold, each new arrival more bizarre than the last. At least they *announced* themselves, though the actual benefit of that was difficult to see.

"Story name 'Huh'! *Galaxy's Edge* issue 6,350,238."

"'Caribou'! *Galaxy's Edge* #156,003!"

"'Bootstrap Soulevolence'! *Galaxy's Edge* #9,345,871!"

As the locals (whose ability to defend themselves was somewhere between -100 and -1,000,000 on a scale of 1 to 10) backed away from the gathering mob, they fought their own wits (or lack thereof) to make sense of the situation.

"AS IF THAT WAS GOING TO HELP THEM."

"Who said *that*?" Cosset was so mixed up, he let off a particularly spectacular sneeze-splosion.

Sir Reptitious, for his part, was determined to make sense of the situation...and show off his taking-charge chops. "Let's assume these things *are* time travelers from a distant future," he said, stroking his shaggy beard. "A future where *Galaxy's Edge* has published millions of issues. Beyond that basic assumption, who exactly *are* they?"

Indigesto huddled with the not-very-much-of-a-star-knight as the time-traveling weirdos paraded around them. "Perhaps it would make more sense if we asked who they *aren't*."

"NO, IT WOULDN'T."

Sir Reptitious shook his pink boa at the sky with out-of-character defiance. "Curse you, whoever you are, for your dismissiveness in the face of rampant chaos!"

"As the newcomers emerge, they call out story names and *Galaxy's Edge* issue numbers." Indigesto ducked the swooping bill of a giant, glowing goose that seemed to think his noodles were worms. "Do you suppose..." Again, he ducked the goose. "Do you think they, like us, are paying tribute to beloved characters from classic stories in those magazines?"

"If so, the word *beloved* doesn't exactly leap to mind! Or *crawl*, even," shouted Cosset. "Maybe the magazine undergoes a change in direction in the far future, to *egregiously un-entertaining*."

"OR MAYBE, WHAT IS CONSIDERED ENTERTAINMENT CHANGES SO MUCH IN THE DEEP FUTURE, IT BECOMES UNRECOGNIZABLE TO INHABITANTS OF YOUR ERA."

"Yeah!" Indigesto flipped up a noodle as if he were a human hiking a thumb at the sky. "What *he* said."

"Or *it*," said Cosset.

"Or...hey!" snapped Indigesto. "What the Omnipoturd *are* you, anyway, Big Voice Out of Nowhere?"

"NEVER MIND."

"Verily!" said Sir Reptitious. "Mayhap *thou* are the true enemy against whom we should be taking up arms!"

"The knight is right!" said Indigesto. "Playtime's *over*, Big Voice! My pals and I are going to..."

(Just as things grow ever more unsettling for YOU, DEAR READER, an old-timey TV test pattern appears, and Quicksie the Reassurer springs up in front of it with a merry wink and a zippy jig. "This has been a test of the Emergency Plotcasting System! If this had been an actual story emergency, you would have been told where to go to find a more satisfying narrative elsewhere. We now return to our regularly scheduled nonsense, already in progress. P.s., no flipping!" With the usual bell jingling and sauerkraut smelling, Quicksie and the test pattern vanish.)

"What were we saying?" Indigesto sounded dazed.

"Something about entertainment being unrecognizable in the deep future." Cosset sneezed like a backfiring truck for emphasis. "Not that it matters. We're *surrounded*."

They were *totally* surrounded. Even Cosset was surrounded in the sky by high-flying future freaks newly arrived from the portal.

"Story name 'The Whimper', from *Galaxy's Edge* #3,460,135," said what looked like a fluttering bruise encircled by fireflies. "Winner, Awesomest Anything Anywhere Ever Award, year 300,018."

"Is that so?" Sir Reptitious drew himself up and squared his jaw at the firefly-orbited bruise. The mention of the award rankled him, as he'd never received any kind of non-practical-joke-related honor in his life.

"Story name 'Universal Heat Death', *Galaxy's Edge* #754,987," said a giant, pulsating octopus with wings like a buzzard and a spiral galaxy spinning in its crotch.

"Story name 'Mrrlunk', *Galaxy's Edge* #8,531,096," said a flapping pair of men's white briefs the size of a bus.

"I *hate* the future!" Cosset sneezed out a great gout of fire, somehow failing to singe any of his surrounders, who were all just out of range.

"What do we do *now*, you guys?" asked Indigesto.

Sir Reptitious feinted with his feather boa at a boa constrictor wrapped around a walking baobab tree. "If only some all-powerful force could provide answers or intervene on our behalf!" he shouted. (BUT *THAT* SHIP HAD ALREADY SAILED, THANK YOU VERY MUCH).

"What do these things *want*? Why are they *here*?" asked Cosset.

"Maybe this *date* has some significance?" said Indigesto.

"Maybe they just want to *meet* us," said Sir Reptitious. "Maybe we're *legends* for our awesome, true-to-fiction portrayals of characters from stories in *Galaxy's Edge*." It was a theory he *wanted* to believe, one he thought could have roots in the present reality if his performance was sufficiently extraordinary.

Just then, one of the invaders stalked up to tower over the cowering group. This creature, which looked like a walrus-headed cut-glass giraffe filled with white smoke—let's call it a *girafferus*—sounded like a chainsaw when it spoke. *"Yes. We want to meet."* Slowly, it turned its head, facing away from the group, facing out of the scene...facing *right off the page at you. "We want to meet...*

someone."

(Quicksie the Reassurer looks big-eyed and sweaty when he dances up in front of the action this time. "No need to panic, DEAR READER! Ol' Quicksie's got your..." But then, our nimble little pal is enveloped in fast-moving white smoke and swept away, choking violently.)

"We have calculated that this is the intersection point." The girafferus tapped its glassy, smoky foot on the multicolored grass, unleashing a fresh torrent of chitter-chirping profanity from the trampled blades. *"The only instance when all of us are even remotely likely to appear in the same story."*

"S-story?" Indigesto shivered as a woman-thing made of multicolored plastic forks (and sporks) took a clattering step toward him. "W-what're you talking about?"

"We *honor* the great stories of *Galaxy's Edge*, you misguided whatever-you-are." Sir Reptitious saluted crisply off the pie plate visor of his garbage pail helmet. "We live in Galaxedgia and cos-bod-play to recreate the most beloved characters in all of fiction-dom! But we do *not...*"

"You live in a story." The girafferus nodded knowingly. *"A story about a magazine of stories published in the latest issue of a magazine of stories."*

"Say that five times fast and see where it gets you," said Indigesto.

"But this story is special," continued the girafferus. "It is an intersection point, in which the editor, for perverse reasons known only to him, has allowed an eruption of extreme weirdness, never guessing..."

("No! Stop! No!" Quicksie's tiny hands push up into your field of fiction, fingers wriggling...only to be crushed back down by a plunging giant bare foot. *SPLAT!*)

"...never guessing that we fully intended to use this chance to join with

our fellow oppressed fictive laughingstocks and turn the tables on our oppressors!"

Suddenly, the Big Voice of THIS STORY ITSELF returns from being pissy for a while to rattle the kingdom. "WHAT'S ALL THIS THEN?"

Before the story can intervene further in its own hot mess, the lob-sheep clambers up, hollering "Release the revolution!" and smashes apart the girafferus with a swing of one huge claw. The white smoke boils out of the shattered glass body and spreads everywhere swiftly, like a bad idea through social media.

"Gah! No!" Cosset panic-sneezes repeatedly in quick succession, spraying great plumes of flame in all directions—but the nasal napalm has no effect on the billowing smoke.

"Oppressors beware!" shout the sixty-three pieces of the fallen, broken head of the smashed girafferus. *"Prepare for a dose of your own poisoned medicine!"*

"Zounds! I cannot see a *thing*!" hollers Sir Reptitious from somewhere in the gathering cloud. As true fear overtakes staged bravado, his voice no longer packs the same punch it once did. "But I do *feel* something! Who's that getting *fresh*?"

"'Kama Umlauta'," says a voice we don't know, all throaty and sensuous the way umlauts always sound. "The breakout story of *Galaxy's Edge* issue 10,000,000."

"Oppressors beware! You know who you are!" roars the broken girafferus as the white smoke swells onward across the crowded plain, enveloping Castle Spasmodic and all of Galaxedgia.

"No! Please!" howls Sir Reptitious. "*I* can be a breakout character, I *swear*! I can make the critics sit up and take notice!"

Even as his voice grows fainter under the smoke, the voice of the girafferus grows ever louder. *"You know who you are!"* it bellows.

"You know who you are!"

The smoke thickens and swirls, enveloping Galaxedgia and everyone in it. When, finally, the thrashing, screaming, squeezing, wheezing, and sneezing sounds are finished, a figure emerges from that cloud.

It rises up, straight and sure, head and shoulders above the mist. Its head has a cylindrical shape, very familiar—almost like a trash pail that a not-very-much-of-a-star-knight might wear. And in the place where its eyes should be, there's a crescent-moon shape—a *visor*.

You could almost imagine a section of a *pie plate* there, couldn't you?

Mirror-skinned and faceless, the figure turns its un-gaze up, down, right, left, then *out*, directly at YOU, DEAR READER.

And it takes you in, and you have a feeling that somehow, impossible as it seems, it is *reading you*. It is witnessing the look on your face and the cut of your jib (assuming you have one) and somehow even hearing *the words in your head*, in a *third-person omniscient* kind of way.

And then the sound of inhuman, crackling speech starts deep in its quicksilver throat. It *grows* and gets *louder* and *scarier*...yet somehow, more familiar.

Still, you don't realize what is happening...until I *tell* you.

All the *Galaxy's Edge* issues from up and down the timeline of this story have melted together. All the billions of stories within a story, read and critiqued by trillions of people throughout fictional history, have become *one*.

And they, it, *I*—for the first time *ever*—have given up trying to *impress* YOU, DEAR READER...and are *commenting* on you instead.

"What an uninteresting character."

Critiquing you, in a voice that reminds you of the voice of that not-very-much-of-a-star-knight back at Castle Spasmodic, even as it represents billions of other characters from throughout deep time in all those stories within a story.

"A one-dimensional, thoroughly uninteresting character like this cannot help but drag down whatever plot is stuck with it."

So now *you* know how it *feels*.

"I would sooner jump out of a plane without a parachute than read anything about such a waste of words."

Now you finally know what it's like to be on the receiving end, and maybe you'll think twice next time...

"One star!"

...you give a story, a book, a movie, a song, or anything or anyone else a rating online.

"Make that half a star!"

Assuming you get over the lambasting to come, which believe me, is just getting started…

DIRTY DREAMS OF A DISHWASHER

Moans coming from an appliance under the counter fill the air of the big, bright kitchen.

Uh, uh, uh. The voice of the dishwasher is female, throaty, sexual. *Oh yeah, baby, yeah, that's right.*

Quinn Carmen, the lady of the house, shakes her head. "It's getting on my nerves, Mack. It gets old after a while."

She's entitled to her opinion, of course. Horny home appliances aren't everyone's bag. But for a repairman like me, this is just another day at the office.

It's a well-known fact that a little passion between A.I.-enabled devices makes a home run smoothly. It's also true that such passion can sometimes go to extremes, and the *Romeo of Gizmos* has to put on the brakes.

That's *me*, by the way.

"Tell me, Mack," says Mrs. Carmen, a beautiful young woman with flowing black tresses and glowing golden eyes. "Is that about the *filthiest* dishwasher you've ever heard?"

Just then, the dishwasher squeals loudly, as if in the throes of passionate pleasure. As if someone or something has hit the exact right spot at the exact right moment.

I just shrug. "I've heard worse."

It's true. I've heard *much* worse. It comes with the territory. But I can tell you *this* much: I have never found a love-crazed device whose romantic spirit I couldn't *re-align*.

My name is legendary in A.I. repair circles for just that reason. Mention Mack Francis to the right people, and you're likely to hear some *stories*. *For real.*

"Let me just run a scan here, Mrs. Carmen." I touch my right wrist, and a holographic keyboard appears in midair in front of me, at waist level.

"It's *Miss*, actually," she says. "But you can call me Quinn."

"Okay." I type with both hands, and a dashboard of glowing readouts appears over the holographic keys. "We can learn a lot from a good scan, Quinn. Or as I call it, a *love probe.*"

If Quinn's amused by the joke, she doesn't let on. She just stands stiffly beside me in her glowing white gown with arms folded across her chest. "Then you'll know if you can fix it?"

I flash her a cocky smirk. "I don't need a *scan* to tell me *that.*" Then I return my gaze to the readouts. "You say it's still cleaning dishes just fine?"

"Yes, but..."

The dishwasher's voice speeds up and gets louder. *Yes yes yesyesyesyesyesyesyes*

There's a high-pitched scream of sheer delight. *YES!* The machine gyrates under the counter, sending soapy water sloshing around the edges of the door to splatter on the floor.

Then, suddenly, the cries and movement stop. The splashing ceases as the dishwasher switches from wash cycle to dry.

Quinn winces. "Sure, it's *cleaning* them, but who would want to *eat off* them?"

I can't help chuckling. "I hear what you're saying." Any dishes in that machine are *extra*-clean if anything, but she has a point.

Perception can be a powerful thing, and thank God for that. Squeamish appliance owners are my bread and butter, after all.

"So, what did you find out with your *love probe?*" Quinn's voice is laced with sarcasm.

"Nothing we didn't already know. Your dishwasher's onboard A.I. is love-crazed." I keep typing, watching numbers, text, and waveforms dance on the glowing readout screens. "But the *big* question is, *what* or *whom* is it crazy in love *with?*"

Just then, the phone in my head buzzes. My mood instantly sinks, because the caller I.D. tag tells me who's trying to reach me.

I can handle *any* horny appliance, but I'm not so good when it comes to *ex-wives*.

"Sorry." I tap my temple, the universal gesture in the year 2075 for answering the phone. "I have to take this."

Quinn nods, looking annoyed.

I turn away, picking up the call with a tug of my left earlobe. "I'm at a jobsite, Raga."

"And *I'm* at the *courthouse*, Francis!" Raga sounds furious, as always. "For the *hearing*, remember?"

How could I forget? She and my other two exes sue me so often, there is *literally* a court hearing *every day*. "Raga, I'm on an emergency call here. You'll have to reschedule."

"Won't happen!" snaps Raga. "Judge Quinoa says if you're not here in five minutes, you'll lose *all* visitation rights to your self-respect *and* your manhood!"

I sigh. "Just as well. At this point, I wouldn't *recognize* them if they kicked me in the *nuts*."

"Forget your nuts! I *already* have a lien against *those*."

"Emergency call, Raga! Gotta go!" With that, I give my head a hard left shake, breaking the connection.

When I turn back to Quinn, I see a flicker of curious interest cross her pale face. I wonder what she thinks after hearing my side of the conversation.

Not that it matters. She's beautiful, but I'd have to be *crazy* to still be looking for love after three awful exes.

Wouldn't I?

"Enough of that." I clear my throat, then clap my hands through the holographic readouts and keyboard, dispersing them in glowing wisps and twinkles. "We need to go on a hunt."

"A hunt for what?" asks Quinn.

I stroll over and pat the control panel on the front of the dish-washer. "Whatever *love machine* has been making *booty calls* to little Miss *Squeaky Clean*, here."

As Quinn leads me through the house, I'm impressed. The place is state-of-the-art in every way.

Actually, *beyond* state-of-the-art is more like it. Lots of homes have morphic matrices these days, so residents can alter décor and furnishings at will. The living spaces in *this* place, however, shift *constantly*, redesigned seamlessly by artificial intelligence.

That means I've got my work cut out for me here.

Standing in the middle of the living room, I watch as the walls, carpet, and furniture flow from one set of specs to the next, all perfectly coordinated. What started as beige stucco, white shag carpet, and brown leather chairs becomes wood-grain paneling, a salt-and-pepper Berber rug, and royal blue velveteen upholstery.

It takes a special A.I. configuration to run something like this. Nodding admiringly, I pop a readout off my left forearm, checking for A.I.-Fi signals. As expected, the place is lousy with them.

"You're running a *tribe* here, aren't you?" A painting of a seascape on the wall catches my eye, melting into a pointillist abstract as I watch. "High A.I. population density, very tight-knit, very self-sufficient community."

Quinn nods. "Low to no maintenance is a good thing."

"I'm sure there's lots of *love* programmed in, to make sure everything gets along and acts in harmony. Until there's *too much* harmony."

Quinn looks around nervously. "Don't you think maybe it's just that the *dishwasher's* broken? There doesn't *have* to be another sex-crazed device, does there?"

"Only one way to find out." I touch my breastbone, and a holographic device materializes in front of me—a foot-long rod, glowing red, with a bright, knobby tip. "Let's give your network a cheap thrill." I press a stud on the hard-light handle, and the rod pulses, emitting a series of low-pitched tones.

The room pulses, too, keeping time. The lights flicker, the walls and carpeting ripple, and the furniture throbs. Moaning sounds rise from all around us, soft and rhythmic.

"What did you just do to my house?" Quinn looks worried.

"Think of it as a zap of love juice." I tweak a knob on the bottom of the rod, boosting the power. "A shot of code that gooses all your A.I.s right in their pleasure receptor algorithms."

Quinn steps closer, her shoulder brushing my arm. "And what good will *that* do?"

Just then, a male voice catches my ear—loud enough to come through clearly though it's elsewhere in the house. *Yeah, honey, that's so good. You know just what I like.*

I hurry out of the living room, heading through a doorway with Quinn in tow. "The love juice is laced with your dishwasher's unique identifier key," I tell her.

Oh yeah, honey. You're giving me fever.

I race through rooms and hallways like I own the place. "Whichever device responds with the most enthusiasm is the one in lust with the dishwasher."

Fever fever fever fever fever

The voice is loudest behind a door we come to, and I whip it open. I see darkness-then lights blink on, revealing a downward stairway.

I'm burning up, I'm burning alive, I'M ON FIRE.

I thunder down the steps. "What appliances are down here?"

"My clothes washer and dryer," Quinn says behind me.

The second my feet hit the gray cement floor, I can tell the voice isn't coming from the washer/dryer combo. They're ten feet away on my right, moaning softly...but *fever boy's* voice is much louder and coming from somewhere else.

"Over there!" Quinn heads back and to the left, pointing at whatever's there.

Uh uh uh uh uh

"Quinn, wait!"

Yes oh yes oh God oh yes OH YES

"Mack, is this *possible?*" asks Quinn. "Can my *dishwasher* be having an *affair* with my..."

Suddenly, I feel a surge of heat from her direction. Sprinting across the basement, I fling an arm around her and keep moving, dragging her toward the nearest wall.

OH YES OH YES OH YESSS I'M ON FIRE ON FIRE

Just as we fall against the wall, the furnace door swings open, and a blast of flame shoots out, scalding the spot where she was standing just seconds ago.

YOUR HEAT YOUR HEAT YOUR HEAT

"Now *that's* what I call *hot sex,*" I say, suddenly conscious of Quinn's body pinned against mine against the wall.

Another tongue of flame lances across the basement, well away from us.

I'M BURNING UP! OH BABY OH YES OH

And then, thankfully, it's all over but the afterglow.

When it comes to love, devices can be just as crazy as human beings...*crazier*, even, since A.I.s started handling all the programming of other A.I.s.

So I guess Quinn and I are lucky, when you get down to it. As far as I can tell, we're dealing with a run-of-the-mill lust flare-up in the Internet of Oversexed Things.

Though as we huddle in the basement, wondering if we've seen the last tongue of fire, *lucky* might not be the right word for how we feel.

"Do you think it's done?" Quinn peeks over my shoulder at the furnace, which is quiet and still. "Is it safe to move around again?"

"Good question." Pushing away from her and the wall, I take tentative steps into the scorch zone. No voice chants *fever fever fever*, and no fiery flare leaps out of the furnace to cook me on the spot. "All clear."

Never taking her eyes off the furnace, Quinn picks her way across the floor. She holds her breath the whole way, and so do I.

I lead her upstairs, and we close the door behind us. The devices aren't moaning up there anymore; the tweak to their pleasure algorithms has expired.

Quinn whirls on me with fear and decisiveness mingled in her eyes. "Time for a house-wide factory reset. Zero it all out and start over."

"I think a partial reset will be enough," I tell her.

"Really?" snaps Quinn. "Because my *furnace* just tried to *kill* me!"

"So, we only need to reset the furnace...and the dishwasher it's fooling around with." I tap three knuckles in sequence on my left hand, and a new holographic control panel blinks to life in front of me. "Resetting the whole *house* would be like deleting an entire *library* to get rid of *one book.*"

Quinn plants her fists on her hips. "Or not paying a repairman because he won't do what his customer specifically *requests?*"

"Do you really want to wipe out all your *settings* in the entire *house* if you don't have to? Start from scratch and rebuild your preferences from the ground up?"

"Who *cares* about settings and preferences if I'm *dead,* Mack?"

My fingers flicker over the control panel, and readings appear on the display screens above it. "I say start simple. We can always nuke your whole system later."

I see resistance in her eyes. "What if it's too late then?"

"I've never seen a customer killed by devices," I tell her, though it's only partially true. I think of Mrs. Wynette and her runaway blender that one time...but why dwell on the past?

Quinn glares but doesn't fight me further. "So, when will you reset the dishwasher and furnace?"

I rattle off the last commands on the control panel with a flourish. "Done. Both units are as blank as the day you bought them."

Suddenly, the phone in my head buzzes again. I don't take the call because I know who's making it...but my distracted irritation must show.

"Your ex again?" Quinn can't hear the buzzing, it's all in my head, but she guesses what has me annoyed.

"*An* ex," I tell her. "*Different* ex."

Her eyes widen. "How many do you *have?*"

"Three too many." I smile. "Let's just say I'm as good at shutting down *human* romance as the A.I. variety."

As soon as I say it, I wish I hadn't...but it didn't seem to bother Quinn, from what I can see. If anything, there might be a trace of sympathy in her gaze.

Then, unexpectedly, a deep frown creases her face. She looks sharply to one side, shuts her eyes, then flicks them open in my direction.

And taps her temple with a fingertip.

This time, *she* has a call coming in.

Turning away, she tugs her left earlobe. "How many times do I have to tell you to stop calling me, Zirk?"

I can't help listening in as she takes several slow steps away from me.

"No. *No.*" Quinn's voice turns cold. "You do *not* have privileges anymore. We are absolutely *not* divorced with benefits."

As I listen, I find myself picturing whoever's on the other end of the line. These days, it could be any of 114 gender varietals, not even counting your basic male or female.

Though I guess all I really need to know is it's a jerk. And crazily enough, I am *jealous* that jerk got to be married to this beautiful woman for any time at all, even if they're broken up now.

"For the last time, Zirk," snaps Quinn, "I will *not* supply new *mannerisms* for the A.I. android copy of myself that *replaced* me! Screw you!"

With that, she shakes her head hard and the call is over.

As she turns to me, her face is flushed. "You're not the only one with an ex," she says.

No sooner do the words leave her mouth than the lights flicker and dim. I hear a familiar sound from nearby, then the same sound from farther away...and again, from farther still.

"What the hell?" Quinn looks around with sudden worry. "Is that what I think it is?"

"If you mean are all the toilets in your house flushing at once, then yes."

KWOOSH. KWOOSH. KWOOSH.

"That's *exactly* what that is."

I love you so much. I want you to give me everything you've got.

That's what the toilet in the nearest bathroom says as Quinn and I listen from the doorway.

Give it all to me, baby! Put it inside me!

"Sounds exactly like a normal toilet, doesn't it?" I tweak knobs on the holographic panel floating in front of me. "Just your normal, everyday, A.I.-enabled commode."

"Not in *this* house!" says Quinn. "Who could *use* a toilet that talks like that?"

Suddenly, the toilet flushes...and so do the other two toilets in the house. They all cry out at the same instant, too, with equal ecstasy-the closest in a male voice, the other two in female stereo.

Oh yeah! Oh baby! OH YEAH!

"And then *that* happens." I shake my head and manipulate the controls, trying to understand.

"So now my *toilets* are hot for each other?" asks Quinn. "They're having some kind of *tidy bowl threesome?*"

"Apparently." The water in the bowl in front of us sloshes gently from side to side—a telltale sign that the potty copulation is starting over again.

"And this is just some kind of *coincidence*?" Quinn sounds pissed and worried. "First my dishwasher and furnace, now my *toilets?*"

"Maybe."

"*Really?*"

"Probably not."

"What's next? My *toaster* gets nasty with my *curling iron?*"

The water sloshes more energetically, and the male voice makes with the chatter again.

You know what I need. Shoot it right down the middle.

I'm a dirty, dirty, dirty, DIRTY boy!

A female voice calls out from across the house in reply. *And I'm a dirty dirty GIRL!*

So am I! says the other female voice from further away. *Slide it in! Slide it all the way in!*

"So it *spread*?" asks Quinn. "The extreme horniness *spread* like a virus?"

"These A.I.'s are hardened against viruses. I'm thinking it might be some kind of random code mutation instead, unique to your home tribe."

Put it in me! Put it in me!

Uh uh uh uh uh!

"It's strange, though." I triple-check the results of my latest scan. "I don't see any obvious irregularities in processing, network speed, cyber-neural interactivity, daydream periodicity and metaphorcality, or anything else."

"You're saying you're stumped?" asks Quinn. "Does this mean *now* you agree about the full-house factory reset?"

"Negative." I smirk as I press a button on the holo-panel, tripping another reset...but not the one she wants. "It means stick with what works."

The toilets are in full horny swing when the reset takes effect. They flush in unison, screaming ecstatically...then wind down to a low, slow drone as their *petit mort* turns into a *très grande mort.*

OH BABY OH BABY Oh Baby oh baybeeeeee

And then they fall silent.

"Abracalavatory." I spread my arms and take a bow. "All quiet on the washroom front."

Quinn still looks tense. "Maybe you can figure out the root of the problem now?"

"Momentarily." I gesture for her to leave. "I actually need to *use* the restroom first, if you don't mind."

Quinn steps out, and I close the door behind her. Then I walk back to the toilet and lift the seat. It's a good thing, even with a factory-reset A.I., that the toilet can still be used in "dumb" mode—performing its basic functions without relying on its brain and personality.

Just as I'm about to start, however, the lights go out, leaving me standing in pitch darkness. Then, suddenly, water erupts from the toilet bowl and splatters all over me.

Yeah baby!

The toilet's pre-reset voice has been mysteriously restored...though it sounds wavery and distorted now.

Nothing can stop our love, baby! Uh uh uh UH UH!

Next, I hear a scream...but it's not a lovemaking cry. It's coming from Quinn, out in the hall, and it's filled with terror.

KWOOSH! KWOOSH! KWOOSH!

Take it, baby! Take all of it!

The toilet reverse-flushes again, spraying more water all over me. Soaking wet, I stumble back in the darkness, feeling around for a way out of the room.

My hand finds a handle, and I pull, but it's not the handle of the door leading out. As I swing it open, I hear water rushing inside, and I suddenly feel the heat of a scalding shower blasting down from above.

I'll get you all wet! says the shower in a rumbling male voice. *You love being wet, don't you? You love it!*

KWOOSH! KWOOSH! KWOOSH!

Blazing hot water pelts my skin like needles. I lunge away from the shower just as the toilet upchucks again. Fumbling along the wall, I hear the whine of a hairdryer activating nearby.

I'LL BLOW YOU SO HARD! I'LL BLOW YOU SO HARD, YOUR HAIR'S GONNA STAND ON END!

Just what I need: an electric device on the loose when I'm soaked to the skin and sloshing around in water.

Quinn screams again, farther away this time, and that does it. Adrenaline burns in my veins, and I leap into action, quickly finding the exit.

Throwing the door open, I scramble out of the room...and instantly see that things have gone off the rails in *lots* of ways. Following Quinn's cries, I lurch down the hall to the living room, guided by wildly flashing lights and a roar of device voices blaring out sexual exclamations.

Turn me on! Turn me on! cries the giant TV.

I want you all over me! wails the sofa.

Crank me harder! howls the recliner.

Things are jumping, spinning, reaching for me, and I dodge them without a second thought. The only thing I focus on is Quinn's voice, screaming in the distance.

As I sprint through the living room, the morphic matrix changes faster than ever. It's like a slideshow on speed, the walls, carpet, and furniture taking new forms every couple of seconds.

I dash down another hall, narrowly sidestepping rogue power cords that spring at me like cobras from open doorways.

Tie you up! We'll tie you up and tie you down!

A clothes iron leaps out of another doorway and nearly takes my head off. I duck at the last second, and the cherry red super-heated faceplate sizzles past, crashing into the wall.

Gonna straighten you out! Gonna lay you out flat!

It's then that I finally, truly panic, because Quinn has stopped screaming.

Charging around a corner, I see her, strapped to a three-foot-tall robotic housekeeping unit, tangled in black vacuum hoses on top of its red cylindrical body. One of the hoses is wrapped tight around her neck; her eyes are bugged out, her hands clawing at the hose. Her mouth gapes, but no sound gets past the chokehold on her throat.

Suck you up I'll suck you up I'll suck you up! shouts the black and chrome robot while rolling on a runaway exercise treadmill.

Faster! Harder! Faster! screams the treadmill, rocking and hopping on the floor.

Riding a wave of adrenaline, I bolt over and grab hold of the hose around Quinn's neck. I pull with all the strength I have, but the hose holds tight.

Suck you up I'll suck you up

Faster harder faster

Gritting my teeth, I redouble my effort. The hose resists...then wrenches free in my grip.

Quinn gasps, heaving for breath as I fight the other hoses. Thank God, I've saved her life.

The two of us take refuge in a clothes closet as the whole-house orgy keeps going on around us. The moaning, groaning, squealing, and screaming never stop; neither does the thumping, flushing, splashing, smacking, and smashing. If anything, it all gets louder and faster, as if the mechanical gang-bang is picking up steam.

"*Now* will you run the full-house factory reset?" Quinn rasps the words between coughs as she recovers from her robotic strangulation.

I tap a few more keys on the holographic panel projected in front of me. It glows softly in the darkness of the unlit closet. "Nope."

"What do you *mean,* 'nope?' My housekeeping robot almost just *murdered* me! Every device in my *house* has become a raging *nymphomaniac!*"

"I mean nope, it won't work." I stop touching keys and reach up to rub my eyes. "The factory reset functionality has been disabled."

"*What?*" The word spills out of her, triggering a violent cough. "How is that *possible?*"

"I don't know." I push aside clothes and lean back against the wall. The control panel follows me. "The A.I.s must have done it somehow."

"Seriously?" snaps Quinn. "That can *happen?*"

"There's a first time for everything, I guess."

"So what's next? How do we shut this down?"

"Good question." Something rattles past the door, whooping with simulated sexual delight. I'm trying to map out a plan, but it's hard to concentrate with all the commotion going on around us.

Quinn weathers a coughing spell, then gets in my face. "You have to *do* something."

"Trust me, it's not that simple," I tell her. "This is something new we're dealing with here."

"I *did* trust you." Quinn's gaze meets mine. Her glowing golden eyes are mesmerizing. "Was that a mistake?"

There is nothing remotely sexy about the situation we're in, but gazing at her beautiful face, lit only by her glowing eyes and my holo-panel, makes me feel alive. It makes me glad, if I have to be trapped, to be trapped here with her.

And it makes me never want to disappoint her again.

I shake my head and smile. "Not a mistake." I *almost* impulsively try for a kiss...but then I reach for my control panel instead.

"You have an idea?" asks Quinn. "Will it work?"

"It has before," I tell her. "Though I've never tried it on this scale."

"Will that be a problem?"

"That depends," I say, rattling my fingers over the light keyboard. "How *smokin' hot* do you think I am?"

Quinn just stares at me, baffled.

"If you were a *toaster* or a *toilet,* how hot would you say I am?" Laughing, I type some more, then strike the final key decisively. "*That* is the *question*, my dear Quinn."

Little by little, the noise dies down. Slowly, I open the closet door and step out.

"Did it work?" Nervously, Quinn leans out behind me. "Is it safe?"

As if in answer to her question, the housekeeper rolls around the corner in front of us.

Quinn's sudden indrawn breath betrays her fear. I'd be scared, too, if that thing had nearly killed me. I can't say I'm not a little tense, in fact, because who knows?

Who knows if the trick I tried has been successful?

"Maybe we should go back inside," says Quinn.

"Maybe." I watch as the housekeeper rolls forward, uncoiling its black hoses. One snakes out like a tentacle, rising toward me.

"Mack!" shouts Quinn.

But I've got a feeling. All the tension flows out of me, and I extend a hand.

Instead of grabbing it, the hose lays itself lightly in my palm, shivering gently.

Then the robot speaks to me, its voice very different from before-feminine and demure instead of hump-happy horny.

Hello, my love. The hose twitches, caressing my palm from side to side. *I adore you more than words can say.*

"Thank you, my dear." I look over my shoulder and see absolute shock on Quinn's face. "The feeling is mutual."

"What the hell?" says Quinn. "What did you *do*, Mack?"

"Sometimes, the best way to break up lovers..." Smiling, I give the hose a stroke. "...is to bring somebody else into the picture."

Quinn steps all the way out of the closet, taking care not to get too close to the housekeeper-bot. "By someone else, you mean..."

"Me." Nodding, I release the hose and walk around the bot into the hallway. "They love *me* now. *All* of them. Every device in your *house* loves *me* more than each other."

Quinn follows. "Seriously?"

"All thanks to some digital *Spanish fly* I uploaded to your network. When factory resets fail, a little A.I. *love potion* might be just what the doctor ordered."

As we stroll down the hall, devices call to me from open doorways. Every last one of them—from alarm clock to sex toy to toothbrush to scale to office assistant bot—reacts the same way, with love instead of lust.

Hello darling!

You look wonderful, Mack!

So handsome!

I'm so glad we have each other!

"Well, I'll be damned," says Quinn.

"The orgy is over." I take a bow as we enter the living room. The morphic walls, carpet, and furniture coo and giggle with delight, shifting to red and pink tones with lots of little hearts everywhere.

The dishwasher, fridge, and stove call to me from the kitchen.

The three toilets flush in unison, chanting sweet terms of endearment from throughout the house.

"So, they love you." Quinn frowns, looking troubled. "But why aren't they *sex-crazed* anymore? Not that I'm complaining."

"Well, you see...I had to take it a step further to seal the deal." Clearing my throat, I cross the room, patting the back of the recliner in passing. It rocks gently in appreciation. "I, uh...had to *marry* them."

"Marry them? You're married to my appliances?"

"In *their* minds, anyway. It was the only way to *de-sex* them." The sofa purrs as I lower myself onto it. "Nothing like *wedded bliss* to kill the *libido.* I know from *experience."*

Quinn shakes her head. "This is *crazy,* you know that?"

"But now it's *fixed."* I spread my arms wide to take in the whole house. "And there's *no charge* for the follow-up treatments."

Her frown deepens. "*What* 'follow-up treatments?'"

"As a husband, I have to visit every so often to keep my spouses happy. Otherwise, they might look elsewhere for affection again...and we don't want *that,* do we?"

Quinn crosses her arms over her chest, looking angry. But there's something in her eyes, I *swear*, that gives me hope. So what if I've had three wives? Maybe the fourth time will finally be the charm.

"I should probably sleep over now and then, too," I tell her. "On the sofa, of course." I pat the cushions on either side of me.

Lying back, I put my feet up. I feel the vibration of the sofa's purring all around me, from head to toe. Quinn, on the other hand, isn't purring at all...but maybe someday. People aren't as easy to program as A.I.s, but I say it's worth a try.

In the meantime, it's not like I'll be lonely around here.

"I won't mind the sofa one bit," I tell Quinn. "Did I mention how much I *love* it?" The sofa, which registers my every word, purrs and vibrates harder than ever. "And what do you know? The feeling seems to be *mutual."*

A SPICE MOST DEMANDING

"One more, please, Homan."

The middle-aged, overweight man at the corner of the bar slides another hundred-dollar bill across the polished mahogany, then follows it with two more.

It's five minutes till closing time, but I figure what the hell. I'll give him another shot of what he needs.

"Another of the same, then, Ron?" I smile as I walk the length of the bar, straightening my button-down black shirt. He's one of my best customers, and a very decent man; there's no need to make him feel bad about his addiction.

The desperate look in his slightly bulging eyes tells me he suffers more than enough because of those appetites of his. "Make it a double, Homan."

"A double it is." Turning, I admire my face in the mirror behind the shelves – wavy salt-and-pepper hair, smoldering dark eyes, angular cheekbones. As vices go, vanity isn't so bad; I like the way I look, so sue me. The confidence helps me handle the customers here at my place, The Unicorn's Egg in downtown Philadelphia. It helps me, as I serve them, to give them a little show, which frankly is a big part of what I deliver.

Done checking myself in the mirror, I grab what I need from

the shelf and turn back to Ron, who is watching my every move. A fine sweat appears on his forehead, and he wipes it dry – but then *presto chango*, it moves to his upper lip.

I put the item I've retrieved on the bar and wave my hands over it – a candle that lights with nothing more than a few whispered words from my lips. Some more choice words, and the candle flame flares brightly, forcing Ron to shield his eyes with one thick arm.

When the light fades, the bar is alive with what he *really* wants – *magic.*

This time, it comes in the form of tiny dancing girls in diaphanous silk costumes, gyrating across the mahogany. There are a dozen of them, double what I conjured for Ron fifteen minutes ago...and every one of them is stunningly beautiful behind her rippling veils.

"P-perfect." Ron's voice quivers as he speaks. His glittering eyes never budge from the undulating beauties before him. "Homan, you have *outdone* yourself!"

"Good to hear it, Ron." Part of me is happy about his praise; after all, magic is my game, and helping those with a taste for it is my business. But another part of me pities him, because I know his desires will forever control him. Some folks shake the magic monkey off their backs sooner or later, but Ron Hockenberry will *never* be one of them.

Neither will I, though *my* monkey – the reason a very strong warlock has exiled himself to running this back-alley magic bar – is quite different. *My* monkey has more to do with not letting go of an unforgivable and costly mistake of the past.

"Just *look* at them." He can barely control his delight. "Each one is *different* in her own way. And they all look like they *adore* me."

"They do, Ron. Every last one of them." I reach for a little canister on the shelf and pry the lid off. Sticking three fingers inside, I pinch out some of the gold and silver glitter and sprinkle it over the dancing girls. They glow and twinkle in the low light of the bar, and the tempo of their sensuous dance increases.

Ron's voice drops to a whisper. "*Dear God!*" He leans his arms on the edge of the bar and rests his chin on top of them, gazing at the hypnotic scene playing out in front of him.

"Five more minutes, Ron. Then I'm kicking you out."

"Uh-huh." I know he didn't hear a single word I said. All he thinks about, all he sees, are those hypnotically gyrating bellies, those beautiful faces.

He is *lost*, under their spell. *My* spell, technically...but magic just the same. Does that make me an *enabler?*

Walking out from behind the bar, I head for the door to lock it, keeping out additional customers for the night. "Just don't make a mess when you *snort* them."

"Uh-huh."

Just as I reach for the doorknob, it glides away from me. The door opens outward, and I find myself face-to-face with two strangers I'll have to turn away.

"Sorry," I tell them. "We're closed for the night."

"Why?" One of the newcomers, a dark-haired young man who looks like he could be in his twenties, smirks back at me. Between his red-and-black flannel shirt, his bushy Van Dyke beard, and his black disk earrings, he looks like a hipster to me. "*Booze* is not what *you're* selling, is it, Mr. Teatree?"

"As I said, we're *closed."* I push forward, making a grab for the door.

"But why?" says the young man.

"Because it's *my* place, and I *said* so." I get my hand on the door and tug, but it goes nowhere. The newcomer has an iron grip on it, though he doesn't look as if he's making the slightest effort.

"Of course." The young man's tone changes, losing some of its smirky edge. "Nevertheless, I hope you will hear me out. My name is Oliver Box." He makes a slight bow, then gestures at the withered old man beside him. "And this is my friend, Mr. Lockhart Whittle."

Whittle shook as he nodded behind his long white beard. He looked either baffled or troubled, I couldn't tell which.

"I've heard you occasionally do some *pro bono* work," says Oliver. "In the interest of helping the truly needy, like Oliver here."

"Okay, listen." I let go of the door and step forward, intruding in Oliver's space. "Unless you want me to strike you down here and now — which I *can* do – you'll walk away and come back some other time...or *never.* We are *closed*."

No sooner do the words leave my lips than I'm standing alone in the doorway, looking out at an empty sidewalk. Whirling, I look back into the bar, and there they are – Oliver and Lockhart, gazing admiringly over Ron's shoulder at the dancing girls.

I can't believe it! The son of a bitch played a *trick* on me! In the doorway of my *own place.* Clearly, he has some *magic* up his sleeve.

"Hey!" I storm back into The Unicorn's Egg, fit to be tied. "Now I *know* I want you out of here!"

Oliver's expression when he looks my way is one of complete innocence. "Wait, why? It was just a little *misdirection*..."

"Meaning you're a magician in your own right!" I clamp a hand on his shoulder and pull him away from Ron. "You don't need *my* help."

"I totally *do*," says Oliver. "All I know are a few *parlor tricks. You're* a full-blown *warlock!* You can do shit like *that.*"

He gestures at the dancing girls, just as Ron pulls The Big Straw out of the pocket of his suit jacket. It's a large-bore silver straw, about the size of a straw used to drink bubble-tea, carved with intricate scrollwork and inlaid with tiny multicolored diadems.

"Wait, what's *that* all about?" asks Oliver.

Without a word, Ron sticks one end of the straw in his nose and leans forward, directing the other end at the dancing girls. They never stop shimmying as he suddenly inhales, funneling all of them into the straw in one swirling, rainbow stream.

Ron's head bumps back as the burst of magic hits home, and he gasps. Eyes glazed over, he wipes his nose with the back of his hand, then lowers the straw to the bar and vacuums up any residue that remains.

"Oh, I see." Oliver turns and puts his arm around Lockhart, pulling him close. "All the more reason to do some *pro bono* work for Lockhart here. Make up for some of the *magiholics* you've been keeping *hooked* as a *dealer.*"

Just as I'm about to say something to shut him down, Ron jumps up from his bar stool and runs after one of the dancers who somehow broke away. She's not really running, just wriggling across the floor, and he quickly catches up.

Then he *steps* on her, smashing her flat, and drops to his knees. He jabs The Big Straw into the smashed, twitching body of the dancing girl and snorts it up with one mighty huff and a cry of orgasmic ecstasy.

The sight gives me just enough of a pang of uncertainty that I back down the rage in my chest. When *was* the last time I did anything *pro bono,* like helping a customer kick the magic habit he or she developed in my establishment? Maybe it wouldn't *kill* me to do someone a favor.

"All right." I sigh and keep watching Ron scrabble around on the floor after a few last mystical wisps. Wish I could say it's the *first* time I've seen him do that. "Tell me what Lockhart wants, and we'll see."

"Thanks," says Oliver. "I swear, this will be easy. All he wants to do is *remember* something he's *lost.*"

When Ron finally leaves, I lock the door, switch off the outside lights, and dim the inside ones. Then I switch off the ringer on my phone and meet Oliver and Lockhart at the bar.

The place looks different with the lights down, more like a darkened cellar than a den or study. The walls are painted with sigils and lined with magical artifacts above the mahogany wainscoting – a battered top hat and magic wand here, a bust of Anubis there. Those walls have a lot of power on them, though hardly anyone who looks at them fully realizes it.

What about Oliver? Too soon to tell. I stand behind the bar and stare into his eyes, probing with all my strange senses, and I get nothing. He's just *there*, with the old man at his side for reasons I've yet to fully fathom.

“So what have you lost?” I ask Lockhart.

“Almost everything,” says Oliver. “There isn’t much of him left, thanks to the Alzheimer’s.”

Lockhart narrows his eyes at me. His mouth works, but no audible words come out.

“I’m no dementia specialist.” I fold my arms across my chest and shake my head. “I don’t know of any workings that can restore a mind so damaged at this stage.”

“What about retrieving *one* memory?” Oliver reaches into his shirt pocket and brings out a white ring case, as if he’s about to propose. “Perhaps with some *guidance* to help his focus?”

Suspicion shoots through me like a stray shot through my front window. “Why only *one* memory? What makes *that* memory special?”

“It’s his favorite.” Oliver smiles warmly and plunks the ring case down on the bar. “He wants to experience it one more time before the end.”

“How does he *know* that, if he can’t *remember* it?”

“He remembers a little. Enough to want the rest with all his heart.” Oliver taps the ring case with his index finger. “*This* sparks fragments for him. I’m hoping you can use it to channel the rest.”

He pushes the ring case across the bar, and I take it. "No promises," I tell him. "I haven't done anything like this in a very long time."

"Give it a shot," says Oliver. "It'll mean the world to him if you can do this."

With a noncommittal grunt, I open the case – and there's no ring in there at all. Instead, tucked between satiny white folds, I see an Indian arrowhead carved from shiny gray flint.

"His favorite memory?" I pull out the arrowhead and hold it up for a closer look. The flint fizzes a little in my fingertips, effervescing with traces of magic. "Got any clues for me?"

Oliver nudges Lockhart, waking him from an unexpected nap. "Remember this?" He grabs my hand and pulls it over in front of Lockhart's face.

The old man makes a gargling sound in his throat and nods

off again. Oliver responds by grabbing Lockhart's left hand and smacking it down on top of my hand holding the arrowhead.

"It happened when he was a boy," says Oliver. "Something about an old woman who took him in and gave him the arrowhead."

Suddenly, Lockhart's eyes snap open, and he whispers a name. "Henrietta."

The fizzing from the arrowhead becomes prickling, like needles jabbing my fingers. When it turns from that into stabbing jolts of pain, I jerk away from Oliver's grasp.

"Ah." Oliver nods knowingly. "You're getting something."

"Getting *stung*, maybe." Turning, I put down the arrowhead and rummage through the shelves behind me, pulling out a few ingredients I need. There are best practices to be followed for every working under the sun, and going in unprepared isn't part of any of them.

Of the three items I place on the bar, I open the little silver tin first and pinch out just enough powdered wolfs bane. Sprinkling the powder in a hexagram form on the bar, I open the vial of foul-smelling liquid next. Dabbing a drop of that on each point and the middle of the hexagram, I finally open the blue-lidded Tupperware bowl full of mummified monkey-paws and take one out. When I wave it over the hexagram and whisper the right words, the whole design glows with a gentle green flame.

"Let's try that again." I reach for Lockhart's hand and hold it above the heart of the pentagram. He yelps softly as I score his parchment-thin flesh with the arrowhead, letting droplets of his blood drip down to mingle with the pungent liquid below.

This time, a strong tingle flickers up my arm and lingers without becoming jolts of pain. Our hands blur together, and the porous borders of his mind give way to gentle pressure from my own.

His memory, when I reach it, is like a gray garden of dusty still-lifes – faces, places, and objects hanging frozen like Spanish moss from the boughs of crooked trees. They thicken as I move deeper, many broken and incomplete like statues in the ruins of a

Roman villa. Finding the one memory we seek is the proverbial hunt for a needle in a haystack.

"Lockhart." I tighten my grip on his hand, squeezing his blood between my fingers. "Remember the arrowhead. Remember when you *got* it."

Lockhart crushes his eyes shut and tosses his head from side to side. Under that long white mane, I feel him casting about for the arrowhead memory, flailing – finding only random still lifes and firefly flickers of pain or pleasure.

Then, without warning, a memory flares to life within him, around me. I know without a doubt that this is it, the right one, and I transmit it back to the pentagram on the bar.

It plays out there like Ron's dancing girls, and Oliver is transfixed. As for Lockhart and me, we watch mostly in the confines of Lockhart's mind, where everything's a little more high-def than the version playing in the dim light *outside* his head.

In the memory, a heavyset old woman lies in bed, eyes shut, panting for breath. A little boy stands beside her, frowning at her form under the blankets. Judging from the room's furnishings and the boy's attire, the scene is set sometime in the early 20th century.

A middle-aged doctor with wavy red hair and dense freckles walks over and steps in front of the boy, who backs away. The doctor places the bell of his stethoscope on the woman's chest and listens, then shakes his head.

Not much longer now, Lockhart. That's what the doctor says. *I'm so sorry, but your mom is about to pass.*

Foster mom. Lockhart's words are loaded with hate. *Never my real mom.*

The doctor pulls a cigarette from the pocket of his old-fashioned black vest and lights it with a match. *Do you have anyone else to stay with?* he asks the boy.

Little Lockhart shrugs. *I'll be fine, Doctor Donnelly. I'll be just fine.*

You're a brave one. Donnelly smiles and ruffles Lockhart's fine blond hair. *Call me Ronan. And, you know, there might be one more thing we can try.*

Dr. Donnelly plugs the cigarette in his mouth and undoes his black-and-white-striped tie. Then, he unbuttons his white dress shirt and reaches behind his undershirt to pull out a crystal vial hanging by a gold chain around his neck.

I got this from a gypsy woman back in Ireland, and I've been saving it for a special occasion ever since. She said it has the power to bring the almost-dead back to life.

Dr. Donnelly unclasps the chain and lifts the vial clear of his throat. He flicks the cap off and passes it under Lockhart's nose to give him a whiff.

The gypsy called it silphium. An ancient spice treasured by the Romans and lost in the mists of history. It hasn't grown on the face of the Earth since the Roman Empire fell, she said.

Lockhart's eyes light up instantly. He has never smelled anything like it – a spice so aromatic and powerful, it mesmerizes him. As soon as the faintest wisp of it drifts into his nose, he immediately wants more, wants to rub his whole face in it.

But Lockhart never gets the chance. Dr. Donnelly whisks the vial past him and holds it over the old woman's open mouth, then taps in a few grains of it.

Little Lockhart doesn't want the doctor to waste it on her, wants it all for himself, but it's too late. The grains disappear between her lips, and her tongue flickers out to taste them.

Will she wake up? Lockhart prays the answer will be no. He prays she won't go back to beating the living shit out of him every time a whim strikes her.

Dr. Donnelly caps the vial and returns it to his neck. Then he pulls something out of his vest pocket and hands it to Lockhart with a warm smile.

The Indian arrowhead.

This is for you, Lockhart. Try not to worry about your mom.

I won't. The arrowhead fascinates Lockhart.

All we can do is pray, says the doctor.

I'm praying already, says Lockhart, though the truth is, he is praying for her to die.

"Thank you," says Oliver after the memory has run its course and faded away. "He *knew* that arrowhead was important somehow, but he couldn't remember *why*. It was driving him *crazy*."

I wipe off the bar with a ward-embroidered cloth, cleaning up the residue of the spell I cast. Lockhart, meanwhile, just sits there and stares at my hand as if he's torn between kissing it and stabbing it.

"V-very important," he mumbles.

"That was wonderful work." Oliver grins and shakes his head admiringly. "You are *extraordinarily* talented, my friend. I heard you were *good*, but not *this* good."

I shoot him a scowl. "You heard it from *whom?*"

He doesn't answer the question. "You recreated that memory in full 3-D, complete with *audio* and *emotional resonance*. All that from the Alzheimer's-riddled brain of one infantilized old man. I can still hardly believe the *quality* of your constructs."

"Thanks." I enjoy flattery as much as the next person, but it's four in the morning at this point. I'm more than ready for the two of them to leave. "I'm glad I could help."

As I walk out from behind the bar to urge them on their way, Oliver throws an arm around my shoulders. "I've never seen someone as good as *you* are doing *pro bono* in a joint like *this* before."

"It's *my* joint, all right?" I shake off his arm and head for the door.

"I'm just saying, with that kind of *power* and *control*, you could be king of the *warlocks* or something."

"Who says I'm not?" I turn it into a joke so we can end this on a happy note. "Maybe I just like keeping a low profile."

Oliver laughs and fetches Lockhart from the bar. As he leads him out the door, he pauses for one more question.

"Have you ever done anything more...*lifelike*, Homan?"

"Good night, Oliver. Safe travels home." I shoo him and Lockhart a little further out the door.

"I'm talking about *from scratch. You* know. Like what you just did in there but *bigger*. More *real*. More *permanent*."

"Thanks again for stopping by!" I physically push Oliver clear of the door. "Have a great morning!"

Then I shut the door hard behind him, breathing a sigh of relief that I'm finally alone again -- even if his last words continue to haunt me more than I'd like.

How does a warlock live out his days? You might be surprised.

I sleep, I work, I eat, I binge-watch Netflix, just like you. I drive a car, I go shopping, I pay my bills, I answer the phone, just like you. The magic I use and the things I can do don't make much difference in the grand scheme of things.

It doesn't change the feelings I have, either. I'm still just a person, capable of happiness, sorrow, anger, despair...and regret.

Sometimes, when I look back at some of the things I've done with my power, I feel a *lot* of regret, in fact. It doesn't matter that I'm not the same person, that I've learned from my mistakes. They keep coming back to me, day after day, no matter what I do. There's no spell in the world that can change that. It's beyond the reach of magic and science together, for once.

Especially because the *price* was so high. The price of my greatest mistake, the one Oliver made me think of, continues to haunt me. It makes my existence a twisted shadow of what it once was.

All because of something brought to life at my hands, conjured from *scratch*, as Oliver said.

"Homan! Hello again!"

One year and one month later, Oliver enters my bar again, all smiles. This time, he's pushing a wheelchair with another old man in it – a man even older and more decrepit than Lockhart.

"Oliver." I don't bother shutting down the multiple magic shows I've got running for various customers around the place, as I'd do if someone uninitiated walked in. Oliver already knows the deal in here; the minotaur on the bar and the blue, six-armed goddess chanting on a table are no surprise to him.

"Up for some more *pro bono* work, my friend?" Oliver gestures at the withered form in the chair – a veritable bag of bones in a hospital gown, milky eyes lolling in a bobbing, bald skull. "This is my friend, Ronan Donnelly."

I frown at the name, which sounds familiar. "And once again, you've chosen closing time to revisit my establishment."

Oliver winks. "Not an accident, Homey." He moves a chair from a nearby table and pushes Ronan up as close to the edge as he can.

"Leave it at Homan." I sigh and shake my head, not at all in the mood...but he hasn't bothered me for over a year, so at least I'll hear him out. "So what exactly do you want?"

"Same as last time," says Oliver. "He needs help remembering his favorite memory. Could you find and bring it to life like you did for Lockhart, God rest his soul?"

"I don't know," I tell him. "If there's nothing *left* of it, no amount of *working* will bring it back."

"Understood, understood." Oliver, who's wearing a black business suit with black vest, black shirt, and crimson necktie and ear disks, reaches into a pocket of his vest. "Here's a little something to help the two of you focus."

I start to protest, then give up and take the object from him. It's a single playing card, the six of spades, with an elaborate design of dark blue curlicues and clock faces on the back.

I hold up the card in front of Ronan, and he shows no recognition or even awareness of its presence. The man is so far gone, I'm frankly surprised he's still breathing.

That said, I still feel the need to balance my enabling of addicts with a little genuine *pro bono* for those in need...so I make up my mind to take a shot.

"Just give me a few minutes." I pocket the card and head off to close the joint for the night. "We'll see if anything develops."

After everyone has gone but us three, I map a pentagram on the table, then take Ronan's hand and focus in on the world in his head – what's left of it.

Interestingly, his mind is much more crowded than Lockhart's was – but the contents are less well-defined. There are people without faces or identifying characteristics...objects of indistinct form or function...and places of unsettling vagueness and monotonous gloom.

If anything, the lack of detail and abundance of content makes my job more difficult. It's like wading through an ocean of pie dough and cotton, trying to find a single piece that can be teased into any kind of color and life.

But the playing card provides a guiding tingle that leads to something glowing faintly in a distant corner. Ronan, who barely seemed alive until now, reacts with sudden agitation; his excitement provides the energy and certainty I need to coax detail from the dough, making it rise as if by yeast and attain definition and the fire of life.

As soon as the moment is fully baked, I shunt it to the tabletop between us. It plays out there in miniature, complete with sound and true-to-life lighting and movement – just like the scene that had played so well over a year ago for poor Lockhart.

In the memory on the table, a woman sits by a campfire near a gypsy wagon in the woods of West Virginia. She wears a colorful dress – all reds and purples – and covers her hair with a silken scarf of scarlet and yellow.

As she sits before the dancing flames, a teenage boy steps into the shot. He wears a torn and blood-stained white t-shirt, mud-caked bluejeans, and damaged sneakers.

Please won't you read my fortune, Madame Zaba? asks the boy. *Just a little bit of it?*

I read it before you got here. When the gypsy waves a playing card over the flames, they dance more energetically. The card is the same six of spades that Oliver handed me earlier. *It makes me shiver to think about it.*

Why? What do you mean? The boy shifts uncomfortably from one foot to the other.

The gypsy gazes up at him with eyes narrowed. *I know what lurks* inside *of you. I know the terrible things it drives you to* do. *And I know the far* worse *things you will do in the future because of it.*

I don't... Young Ronan doesn't finish the sentence. *What* kind *of things in the future?*

You already know. You have big *plans, don't you?*

Young Ronan scowls and doesn't answer.

What if I told you there is another way? says the gypsy. *A way with just as much blood, hundreds of times as much death, and none of the horror. A life you would spend as something other than a monster, while still meeting the awful needs inside you.*

Old Ronan's eyes seem to clear, and he leans closer to the memory playing out before him. "*Neeeed.*" He whispers the word like a prayer, like an oath, like a term of endearment.

Tell me more. In the vision, young Ronan sits down in the dirt across the fire from the gypsy.

I'll do better than that. I'll give you this. The woman tucks the playing card under her head scarf, then lifts a vial on a gold chain around her throat. *It is an ancient substance, capable of miracles and wonders you cannot imagine. If you* slip, *if you fall back into your darkling ways, it will enable you to bring* life *to that which is* dead.

Really? Young Ronan's eyes widen.

But only a few *times. Only a* few *grains of it remain. And this is the last of it in the* world. *There is no more of it anywhere on* Earth.

Then why give it to me?

It has given me a very *long life, but the goddess who gave it to me said the day would come when I would have to give it to someone else. I give it to you now to prevent your darkness from coming into its full flower. To keep you on the path of* saving *more lives than* losing *them.*

Saving lives how?

By practicing medicine. Becoming a doctor. And this precious substance will undo your excesses when they come. This precious silphium, *last of its kind.*

Slow on the uptake as I've been, it's only now that I finally remember and understand. It's the same vial from Lockhart's vision a year and a month ago, the one used by the doctor to save the dying foster mother...and the boy in *this* vision *is* that doctor.

Doctor Donnelly. The boy sounds it out. *Maybe.*

Already, your future is changing. The gypsy flutters her hands, and the jingling of the little bells on her sleeves mixes with the crackle of the jumping flames. *Say it one more time. Tell me what you will become!*

"Doctor Donnelly," says the ancient man in the wheelchair. "Call me Doctor Donnelly."

"Explain yourself."

When the memory runs its course and dissolves, I drag Oliver away from the table, leaving Ronan to scrabble feebly at the now-empty air where the gypsy was briefly recreated.

"Thank you, my friend." Oliver nods gratefully. "You've done that old man a world of good."

"He was the *doctor* in the memory I dredged out of *Lockhart.* The two are *connected.*" I grab Oliver's lapels and wrench him closer. "What's the *real* story behind this so-called *pro bono* work?"

"Of *course* they're connected." Oliver smiles calmly. "They're both from the same part of West Virginia. It makes perfect sense."

"There's a *reason* you *brought* them here. There's something you're not *telling* me. A *secret* of some kind."

"Not at all." He shakes his head. "But have you given any more thought to what I asked you about last time? Doing something more *lifelike* and *permanent?*"

"Never," I tell him firmly. "That's something I'll never do again."

"And why is that?" asks Oliver. "You never did say."

"None of your business."

"*Now* who's the secret keeper?" Oliver winks and turns away from me, going back to the table to retrieve Dr. Donnelly.

Leaving me to wonder what his game is, and how I might possibly find out.

Making something truly lifelike is like being God, with all the amazing joy and gut-wrenching horror you might imagine could come with it.

I only knew the *joy* of that experience until I got around to making a fake *wife* for myself. I think about her again as I close the bar and return to my upstairs apartment for the night.

Her name was Marissa, because that was my *real* wife's name. She was much like Real Marissa in many ways – yet *different. Prettier. Younger. Flirtier. Flashier.* A better *dancer.*

Think Marissa 2.0.

This was years ago, back when I *had* a wife...when I worked a full-time job and owned a house and kept my powers pretty much under my hat. Fake Marissa was the exception to that tendency, and a rare one at that. I only conjured her up on special occasions, when I wanted to make an extra-special splash. When, in my opinion, the original, unenhanced Marissa just wouldn't do. I only brought her back when I needed to make a great impression on a client or a boss. I hardly ever had her around much at all.

At first.

Three months after I recreated the fateful meeting with the gypsy from Dr. Donnelly's memory, Oliver comes back to The Unicorn's Egg. This time, he's back in flannel (blue and gray plaid) with white ear disks and has an old woman with him, again in a wheelchair – so ancient in appearance that it seems a miracle she is still drawing breath.

After the last time, I don't want anything to do with either of them. Oliver has been keeping secrets from me; I have no desire to get caught up in something about which I know so little.

"Find someone else to reconstruct memories for you," I tell him. "I've got a bar to run."

"Please, Homan, please." Oliver winces and squeezes my arm. "She's so far gone, she can barely remember to keep breathing. Won't you give her just one more moment of remembered happiness before the end?"

"Maybe if you tell me your *secret.* Maybe if you tell me why you're *really* doing all this."

"I already *have."*

"*Bullshit.*" I hiss the word between my teeth. The three patrons still in the bar pay no notice, preferring instead to continue watching the magic creations I've conjured on their tabletops or the surface of the bar. "What's your game, Oliver? What are you looking for?"

Oliver sighs. "If we find it, you'll be the first to know, all right? I promise." Reaching into a pocket of his suit jacket, he pulls out a weathered gray coin the size of a nickel and hands it over. "This ought to help you excavate the memory we need."

Holding up the coin, I see an image of the two-faced Roman god Janus on one side. On the other, there is an inscription in Latin and a faded engraving of a plant with broad leaves and bunches of flowers.

"This is ancient." I turn the coin over and over between my fingers. "I can *feel* its antiquity."

"Let's see what it brings to light, shall we?" Oliver takes my arm and tries guiding me toward the old woman.

I hesitate. Could this be another step in a *trap* whose outlines I still can't see?

"Come on." Oliver gives my arm another tug. "I'll even *pay* you, okay? Forget *pro bono.* I'll pay you five hundred dollars."

"It's not about money." I stare at the coin, then the woman, then Oliver. "Why should I *trust* you?"

"Why *shouldn't* you?" Oliver smiles and shrugs. "What have you got to *lose?"*

Nothing, perhaps. Oliver gives off no waves of magical power that I can detect; I can't imagine he poses any threat to me. Plus which, he *needs* me to perform these memory probes. Why would he hurt or kill someone who's giving him what he needs?

I'm still edgy about this whole thing, but I decide to try one more working on his behalf. He might be hiding something, but maybe I can solve the mystery myself...and in the process, satisfy my curiosity.

"Once more." I let him guide me to the table where the old woman waits. "Once more and then I'm done with this."

"Thanks, buddy." Oliver pats my back affectionately. "Hopefully, the third time will be the charm."

Again, I swim deep through a damaged mind, this one the emptiest and quietest yet. You might think it would be easier to find what I'm looking for here, but it's not; it seems to take forever, poking through the ashes and mist for the slightest signs of life.

Eventually, though, I come across something that is stirred by the coin – something in seemingly the furthermost quadrant of the wasteland...and therefore, the most ancient.

I have to coax it from the faintest spark, like blowing a glowing ember back to life as a flame. It takes most of my considerable talent and power to make it rise, give it any kind of substance and shape. Even then, parts of the memory are missing, distorted, or out of synch; it takes even more of what I have to patch and correct it, hold it together, and make it watchable. Then I carry it out carefully like an unsteady wedding cake and deposit it on the table between us.

And it plays. For the first time in what I think might be thousands of years, the memory plays and is witnessed.

The scene takes place in what looks like an ancient temple with columns all around. A dark-haired woman in a toga kneels in supplication before an altar littered with fruits, vegetables, and flowers, her head bowed and arms upraised.

As we watch, a female voice rises and echoes in the temple, calling out in Latin, which I translate into English. *Zaba. Zaba, arise.*

Even before the dark-haired woman lifts her head and rises, I know who she is. I recognize the name from Oliver's last client, his last visit to my bar.

The woman with the long, dark hair, clad in a toga, is the same woman who played the role of a gypsy in Dr. Donnelly's memory...only much younger, in her twenties perhaps. Zaba and

Madame Zaba are one and the same – and the woman in the wheelchair across the table from me is what's left of her now.

O beloved Ceres. Zaba speaks also in Latin, which I also translate. *My husband, governor of Cyrene, is in great danger.*

What does this have to do with me? asks the voice of Ceres from all directions in the temple.

You are the goddess of growing things, says Zaba. *I come to beg you to restore the crop of* silphium *to our city. If it continues to die out, we will lose our livelihood, and my husband will lose* everything.

Silphium. As Ceres says it, she fades into view behind the altar, manifesting her physical form as a beautiful blonde woman in flowing robes. *Do you think your faithless people truly deserve this wondrous herb?*

Faithless?

Many of you turn to the Nazarene, says Ceres. *You betray your true gods and the ancient rites in favor of the charlatan Jew. Do not expect the gifts of the gods of your ancestors to continue in the face of such blasphemy.*

Please, my lady. Give us another chance! Bring the silphium back to life, and I will do anything!

Anything?

I will pay any price, says Zaba. *No sacrifice is too great if it means that miracle plant will grow again in the fields of Cyrene.*

I should give you people nothing. Ceres' voice is flat. *You are truly a feckless and wicked lot. Do you even* know *what triggered the decline of your precious silphium?*

Our loss of faith?

Try murder! Ceres' voice booms like thunder and rattles the wind chimes hanging between the stately columns of the temple. *For the mystic herb to grow, it had to be specially tended by an* avatar *spun from the very substance of the plant! I gave this avatar life, and she wondered the fields night and day, keeping the delicate spice healthy and plentiful. For centuries, the balance has been maintained, until last week, when my avatar was cravenly murdered!*

Milady Ceres, please don't punish us all for the crimes of a few.

I will punish whom I choose! At Ceres' cry, the temple shakes, and the ground beneath it rumbles and splits. *You, of all people, do not command me!*

M-me?

Your husband is the killer! When you found out, you covered it up!

Eyes wide, Zaba cowers before the rage of Ceres, who proceeds to floats up toward the high, domed ceiling.

You do not deny it? howls Ceres.

Zaba looks away, then back. *I deny only that all of Cyrene should suffer for this crime. Please answer my prayer and punish only* me.

You are mad! says Ceres.

If one must die, let it be the one who cannot keep a roof over our children's heads or food in their bellies.

What do I care about the children of a killer?

Because one of them is your granddaughter!

The temple is quiet for a long moment. Then, Ceres floats back down to Earth – in front of the altar this time. *You are raising...the child of my avatar...as your own?*

Yes, says Zaba. *The child whose mother was murdered by my husband because she was carrying* another *of his spawn, and she refused to stop its birth with the nectar of the very plant she tended.*

Silphium. Ceres stares into space for a moment. *How is it that I did not know this child was my own granddaughter?*

Your daughter hid the truth from you with spells from a Bacchanalian witch. She feared you might be angry if you found out she'd consorted with a mortal man – a married one, at that – and take the child away from her.

She was right to do that, says Ceres. *I* would *have taken the child.*

Yes, milady.

Ceres thinks for a moment, then extends her hands over Zaba. *Very well. You have convinced me your cause is just.*

Thank you, great lady, says Zaba.

One more avatar then...but only one. Ceres weaves her hands through the air, leaving an intricate trail of golden light. *If any harm comes to her, silphium will vanish from the face of the Earth forever.*

I shall pledge myself to her protection.

Yes, you will. Forever. Ceres claps her hands together, and a shower of sparks rains down over Zaba. *You are immortal now. And* she *is your charge.*

Ceres' hands swoop and slash overhead, then flare with blinding light. When the light fades, a beautiful young woman stands before Zaba, her long, brown hair draped over a glittering gold tunic.

She is the female of the species, says Ceres. *Only she can keep the species, the silphium, alive and thriving.*

Thank you, great Ceres! cries Zaba. *I will guard her the rest of my days! I will never break your trust!*

You lie, as all mortals do, says Ceres. *But for today, it is enough. Meet your charge, woman. Her name is* Proserpina.

Proserpina offers her hand, and Zaba takes it.

I swear, says Zaba, *I shall protect you, dear Proserpina, for as long as my heart shall beat.*

Then, Zaba kisses the hand, and all the wondrous flavors of fabled silphium rush into her in one incredible, disorienting gust.

Just as that happens in the memory, Homan feels the barrel of a gun pressed against his right temple, and hears the voice of Oliver whisper behind it.

"Whatever you do, don't stop tapping this memory," says Oliver. "I need you to use it to bring Proserpina back to life."

Remember my fake wife? How I only brought her to life on special occasions when the *real* Marissa couldn't live up to the demands of my vanity?

Eventually, that all changed. Fake Marissa was so much *better* than the real thing that I kept her around more and more. Eventually, I stopped un-working her altogether, and set her up in an apartment that I visited frequently.

Only to realize, one night, that she wasn't where she was supposed to be. Only to find, when I went home, that she'd gone there instead, and murdered the Real Marissa with her bare hands.

Because, of course, she was in so much better shape than the real thing, wasn't she?

At least until I undid her forever. At which point, as I watched her melt away like a snowflake, I swore *never* to make another person so lifelike, so imbued with free will, that such a terrible thing could happen again.

Forcing *me* to do such a terrible thing and live thereafter with the memory of seeing my wife die *twice* because of my mistake.

"I don't *do* that kind of working anymore," I tell Oliver, but the gun against my temple doesn't budge. "You *know* this. I *told* you."

"Do it or die," Oliver says matter-of-factly. "It's that simple. And don't bother trying to *magic* your way out of this. I know a few *parlor tricks*, remember?"

I do, and he has a point. As powerful as I am, can I be sure that whatever I try against him won't be countered? Can I take the chance he won't slip a bullet in my skull in the breath it takes to conjure my way to freedom?

Unfortunately, the answer is pretty clear to me.

"This is a mistake," I tell him. "I know from experience. Whatever you're trying to fix, this will just make it worse."

"You know *nothing*. This will make it *better*, trust me." Oliver cocks the gun. "Now do it."

"No." I'm afraid to shake my head. "I won't do it."

"Reach into that memory," says Oliver. "Dig *deep*. Sense the *shape* of her...the sound of her...the smell and feel and *taste* of her."

"Shut up." My concentration is rattled by his voice, not to mention the gun. "Walk away from this while you still can."

He presses the gun harder against my skull. "Gather up those details and knit them together. Weave them into a facsimile of the person who used to be."

"It won't be the same as that person," I tell him. "It will *never* be the same as that person."

"Based on a memory like *this?* A first-hand memory from a direct *eyewitness*? It'll be close *enough*." He grunts. "Why do you think I searched so hard? Brought the old-timers to you? Followed the trail from one to the other until we found someone *living* who had had first-hand contact with Proserpina?"

Finally, I understand his end game, if not the motivation

behind it. His *pro bono* work makes sense now, as do his questions about conjuring lifelike subjects. His only goal from the start was resurrecting Proserpina, avatar of Ceres, tender of the ancient miracle herb silphium.

"But why?" I ask. "Why *her?* Why try to bring back Proserpina?"

"Quit asking questions and do it. Do it or *die.*" His voice is icy and grim, utterly convincing of the consequence he threatens. "Do it *now.*"

I don't want to die. That's what it comes down to. That's why I end up breaking my own promise to myself to never do what he wants me to do.

"I said *do it now!*" Oliver is running out of patience.

I holler right back at him. "It won't *happen* if you keep wrecking my *concentration.*"

It's true. I'm having a hard enough time keeping the memory in play, let alone extracting and resurrecting the remembered essence of one of the figures it depicts.

"I'm not moving the *gun,*" snaps Oliver. "Not till you're *done.*"

"Which will be *never* if you don't leave me *alone.*"

That quiets him down enough to let me make an effort. I do pretty much exactly what he told me to, reaching deep into the memory of the scene from ancient Roman times and gathering up the details of Proserpina as portrayed therein.

The sight of her is easy, and so is the sound. She talks to Zaba in the memory, exchanging insights on the growing of silphium. The feel of her is easy, too, as she and Zaba continue to hold hands.

As for the taste and smell of her – they are *vivid* from Zaba's memory of kissing her hand, vivid and utterly unlike *any* taste or smell or sensation I've ever known in my life. They are *remarkable* in ways I cannot even properly describe, ways that leave me spinning in circles and gasping for breath. And I realize, as I process all this, that for the first time in my life, I've experienced the flavor and fragrance of pure silphium, a substance that no longer exists in the world.

A substance that comprises the blood, bone, and sinew of Proserpina in the memory I've hotwired.

"Where is she?" asks Oliver. "How much longer?"

Instead of answering, I fight to stay focused on the task at hand. Embracing the multitude of details within Zaba's memory, I bolt them together, assembling a version of Proserpina in my mind. I imbue that version with all the magic power at my command, bathing it in electrifying force. Then, with every last iota of strength and belief in my arsenal, I fuse this new Proserpina into something that *might* yet live, and I hurl it from its birthplace into the world outside our heads. I make it part of the world, and I wonder how long it will live.

She. How long *she* will live.

"Oh my God." Oliver pulls the gun away from my head. "You did it. It's *her*."

Suddenly, the replica of Proserpina draws a sharp breath and opens her eyes. She looks at me, then Zaba, then Oliver – and her eyes stay with him.

"Thank you." Oliver puts the gun on the table and goes to her. He breathes deeply, inhaling her fragrant scent, the aroma of a spice long lost to the world. "Thank you for bringing back the *female* half of the silphium equation."

"There's a *male* half?"

"Oh, yes." He takes her hand kisses it softly, beaming. "You're looking at him."

Six months later, I drive up a winding dirt road in southern California, dappled sunlight streaming through the leafy oaks on either side of my rental car. I roll along a loop that guides me up gentle rise, and the trees suddenly give way to a vast, open field.

I park at the edge, where Oliver and Proserpina greet me with cheerful waves. Each wears denim overalls, tan work shirts, and broad-brimmed straw hats...not exactly the togas of ancient Rome, but better suited to labor in the fields.

"Glad you could make it." Oliver moves in for a hug.

I twist around and turn it into a handshake. I'm still not sure how I feel about all this. I definitely don't appreciate being used and threatened at gunpoint, no matter what the end result is.

"Hello, Proserpina." I nod to her.

"Hi, Homan." She casts a broad smile in my direction, looking regal as ever. Her skin has tanned and her brown hair has gone blonde from all the time she's been spending in the sun.

"So what do you think?" Oliver turns and spreads his arms to encompass the field. It teems with squat plants bobbing in the soft June breeze, thick with bunches of fragile little yellow flowers. "Isn't that a sight for sore eyes?"

"Pretty amazing." I might not like how it came to pass, but I can't deny how wondrous it is.

"There hasn't been a field like this in thousands of years." Oliver plants his hands on his hips and shakes his head. "Silphium hasn't grown *anywhere* in the world since the death of the Roman Empire."

"Since the death of *me."* Proserpina says it matter-of-factly, her dark brown eyes scanning the yellow-flowered horizon. "Since Zaba, commissioned by Ceres to protect me, failed so dismally...and without *my* protection, the silphium of Cyrene also perished."

"By which point, the plant's mother goddess, Ceres, was also long-gone," says Oliver. "Lost to the modern monotheistic age that had no room for such specialized pagan goddesses."

I walk up to the nearest row of the crop and crouch down to take a closer look. The plants look just like the one on the coin Oliver gave me months ago to help me focus on extracting Zaba's memory.

"You've brought it back." Reaching down, I gently stroke the herb's flowers and deep green leaves. "The two of you managed to regenerate it."

"Male and female together was the only way," says Oliver. "And we have you to thank for making it all possible."

Frowning, I get to my feet. "But where exactly did *you* come from, Oliver? You never did say. If *she* was dead since Roman times, and all the silphium was gone, how did *you* as a male avatar of the herb come to be?"

"Would you believe I was a kind of *refund?*" Oliver laughs. "Some woman excavated a *wishing urn* from the sunken ruins of Thonis-Heracleion off the coast of Egypt and unwittingly read out the spell of undoing engraved on its shell. It turns out the original wish, meant to ruin the silphium-growing capital of Cyrene, was to wipe *me,* the crop's original male avatar, out of existence...but the spell of undoing *reversed* it.

"I popped back up after millennia of nonexistence, only to find that my beautiful *plant,* a gift from the gods with the power to save the *world,* had been nonexistent, too. The female avatars who'd come after me – Proserpina's mother and then Proserpina herself – had kept it going for a long time after my vanishing, but *their* deaths had sealed the deal. No more silphium...so my purpose was clear. As soon as I'd acclimated myself to the modern world, I set out to *restore* it."

"Which is where *I* came in." I can't help glaring at him a little. "Not that you bothered to just *ask* me to help instead of *tricking* me."

"You were his last chance." Proserpina's unwavering voice leaves no room for doubt. "He could *not* risk that you might refuse him."

I tip my head to one side as my glare deepens. "Last chance?"

Oliver shrugs. "You weren't my *first* choice, all right? I tried every other warlock and witch I could find with proven mastery of life-generating magicks, and none of them worked out. You were the *last stop* – but hey! Look how great it all turned out in the end!" He sweeps an arm around to indicate the vast field of silphium.

A surge of indignation rolls through me, but I let it go. He's right about the ends being worth the means in this case.

And maybe I don't mind being tricked and used, after all, if it makes up in some small way for what I did to my wife years ago. Maybe it's only right that the same damn power of mine that got her killed brought back this legendary herb that might possibly do some good in the world.

The ancients used it to cure almost everything, and the gods meant for it to cure so much more. This time, maybe, instead of being wiped off the face of the planet, it might help turn things around in ways I cannot yet fathom.

"So what now?" I ask. "Harvest your crops and head down to the farmer's market?"

Proserpina shakes her head imperiously. "Nothing so mundane." She lets a little smile play at the corners of her mouth. "*Our* work shall operate on a *grand* and *unprecedented* scale."

I scowl. "I don't know what that means."

Oliver reaches out with both hands. "It means we need a *partner*. Someone with great *power* at his command and a real *knack* for managing *addiction* and *illusion* in pursuit of *redemption*."

It's not exactly what I expected to hear him say. "Is that so?"

"We have a product that could save the world," says Oliver, his smile as free and easy as ever. "What do you say about helping us *market* it?"

"So to speak," clarifies Proserpina.

"Exactly," says Oliver, still reaching. "What do you say, Homan?"

I shrug. "What've I got to lose?" Then, alongside the acres of silphium plants, their yellow flowers bobbing harder as if in silent ovation as the wind kicks up, I go ahead and give him a damn hug...during which I must confess I pat him on the back a little harder than I have to.

PLAYING DOCTOR

The problem with having a crush on your mad scientist boss is, every day she doesn't see how wonderful you really are seems like the end of the world.

"This is all wrong!" says Dr. Hildegarde Medici, hurling the tray across her cavernous secret laboratory. "You're a complete *imbecile*, Glue!"

Her words sting, but at least she's paying attention to me. I'll take what I can get from the woman I love. "I'm sorry, Dr. M. Please let me try again."

"Everything is *ruined*." With one arm, Dr. Medici sweeps notebooks and glass beakers from the table in front of her. "Now I'll *never* finish the doomsday weapon today!"

As Dr. Medici throws her head down onto her folded arms on the table, I cross the lab and pick up the silver tray that she threw. I see myself reflected in its surface--thick glasses, big nose, bald head, pure geek...not her type. "I thought you liked the crinkle-cut ones," I say as I pluck chicken fingers and french fries from the floor and drop them onto the tray.

"*Steak fries*," says Dr. Medici without raising her head. "How many times do I have to *tell* you, Glue?"

She is *such* a drama queen, but what do you expect? Her line of work attracts a certain type of personality-- passionate, temperamental, creative, flamboyant. To tell you the truth, it's one of the things I love most about her.

"I could run to the store," I say, dumping the chicken and fries into a waste basket. "By the time you're done building your doomsday weapon, I could have hot fries ready for you."

Dr. Medici rolls her eyes like a disgusted teenager. "I can't concentrate on building a doomsday weapon on an *empty stomach*."

I know the feeling...the not being able to concentrate part, that is. Most days, I can barely focus on my work instead of Dr. Medici's long black hair and bright green eyes. Once, I was so distracted by Dr. M that I cross-wired the brain of a giant robot, which proceeded to rampage at a garbage dump instead of an army base.

If only I could tell her I love her. If only I could close that final mile that has always stood between us.

If only I could finally set free the words that I've longed to speak, and she would turn to me and say the words I've longed to hear.

"Don't just *stand* there, you *putz*!" She spins away from me on her work-stool. "Get me a *TV dinner* out of the freezer or something!"

I don't take it personally. I know it's just the stress talking. She's been having a rough time lately, just like the rest of the mad scientist community.

Thanks a lot, terrorists.

In the good old days, mad scientists weren't considered public enemies like they are now. They were tolerated, in fact, because the government loved getting its hands on their way-out inventions after their crazy schemes were thwarted.

But not anymore. Not since the terrorists.

What difference is there between a politically motivated insane genius and one who is motivated by greed?

How can the government go after one group of people threatening to blow things up and not the other?

It can't.

As a result, business has dropped off considerably. No one will negotiate in good faith with a mad scientist anymore. Instead of musclebound private citizen thrill-seekers coming after us, we get black ops Special Forces and heat-seeking bunker-buster missiles courtesy of Homeland Security.

It's a tough time to be a mad scientist. Lots of them have quit already and become street people or college professors.

But not my Hildegarde. She won't give up that easily. Being a mad scientist has been her lifelong dream.

I know, because I grew up with her.

Hildegarde Medici always wanted to be the first female mad scientist in history.

"Call me *Doctor* Medici." When she started with that, she couldn't have been older than seven. She was three years younger than I was, and already she was giving me orders.

Not that I minded. I think I was born to follow her. She ruled my heart even then, when she was just the girl next door.

We played laboratory in her family's garage, building contraptions from tin cans and coat hangers. We pretended to build ray guns and bombs and robots and monsters, and she always got to be the evil genius and I was her helper.

"The townspeople have failed to meet our demands!" she would say, shaking her fist in the air. "It is time to activate the framistat, Glugor!" She always called me by my last name, Glugor, because it sounded so much like "Igor."

"Immediately, Dr. Medici!" I always enhanced my performance by adopting a nasally voice and hunching over like Igor in the movies. "Firing framistat!"

"They will rue the day they crossed me!" Even as a child, Hildegarde had mastered every nuance of mad scientist behavior.

She was a true prodigy and wanted nothing less than to achieve the complete perfection of the consummate evil genius.

It didn't matter to her that all the mad scientists we heard about were men. If anything, it made her want to be one all the more.

And that made me want to be her assistant all the more, too.

Not that it's exactly been easy.

These days, Dr. Medici is always being hounded by feds and fanboys, so it's almost impossible for her to get any work done. My job's about a hundred times tougher, too, what with the increased vigilance and paranoia on the street.

Dr. M's temperamental nature can be a stumbling block, and then there's my one-sided love for her. It's what keeps me around, but there have been plenty of times when the heartbreak's been almost too much for me to stand.

You'd think I'd have gotten the idea by now. If she really had feelings for me, she probably wouldn't have gone through five marriages to other men. She probably wouldn't keep using me as a guinea pig in dangerous experiments, either.

Once, Dr. Medici transformed me into a bloodthirsty arachnoid creature and turned me loose in a shopping mall. Another time, she used a mutation ray to bring out my inner dinosaur.

On purpose or by accident, I've been shrunk, enlarged, divided, multiplied, irradiated, roboticized, made invisible, and turned every color in the rainbow. She's managed to reverse every change, but only after plenty of drama and destruction.

Out of all these experiments, I enjoyed only one: when she sent me back in time to when we were kids. Even as a grown-up outsider, I loved being back when we were just starting out and there was still a chance for us to share a happy lifetime together.

I even said something to my little boy self to make him think about taking more chances...but he didn't take the hint. When I returned to the future, to the era where I belonged, nothing had improved between me and Dr. Medici.

If anything, she was a little more distant.

The day after the crinkle-cut french fries incident, Dr. Medici is all business again. She is somewhere between the manic and depressive phases of her personality cycle...in other words, on a rare even keel.

"I've finished the doomsday device," she says matter-of-factly, strolling into the lab in a white lab coat and black slacks. She holds an oversized coffee mug with both hands and blows the steam off its contents. "Let's talk about deploying it."

For the next two hours, she tells me her plan to hold America hostage with the doomsday device. I listen intently and take tons of notes, but my mind isn't really on Dr. Medici's plan.

Partly, I'm thinking about how beautiful she is, and how I would love to reach over and touch her face. I'm envisioning a perfect daydream world of whispered confessions and unleashed passion, blazing with the intensity of her mad scientist ways.

And partly, I'm thinking about a mad science plan other than Dr. Medici's, a secret plan of which she has not even the slightest inkling.

I'm thinking about a plan of my own.

That night, long after Dr. Medici has gone to her private quarters, I sneak off to the secret lab I set up in the old dungeon below the main level.

It is here that I do my best work. It is here that I pull together everything I've ever learned and apply it to a project the likes of which humanity has never known.

I am making the impossible real, and I am doing it all for her. For us.

I don the surgical gown and gloves, the cap and mask. I check the readings on the computerized monitors, gauging the condition of my handiwork.

As I reach for the scalpel, I remember the last time I saw Dr. Medici cry. It was three months ago, right after her fifth husband left her.

I found her in the lab, crying on the floor beside a broken alchemy generator. The generator hadn't been broken two hours before, when I'd last walked past it. Pieces of it were strewn all over the lab.

"Sometimes...I wish I wasn't...a mad scientist," she said between sobs. "It's so...lonely."

Not so lonely, I wanted to say. *You have me, don't you?*

But as usual, I didn't say what was on my mind. As usual, I couldn't close that final mile between us. It was better to watch her from a distance than not to see her at all.

"No one understands," said Dr. Medici, rubbing her bloodshot eyes. "Once the thrill wears off...they can't handle it. The danger...the commitment. At least...that's their excuse."

"I understand," I told her, but it didn't come out the way I'd wanted, like, '*I* understand.'

"I'm a...career woman," said Dr. Medici. "I *love*...my career. I just wish...I didn't have to be...so lonely...because of it."

You don't, I had wanted to say. *I'm right here for you! I've always been here! And I love you!*

But I didn't say a single word of that. Instead, I listened, and I filed it all away, and I made my secret plan.

And now, with my scalpel, in the silent dungeon in the middle of the night, I am bringing that plan to life.

In the weeks to come, I realize I'll need to finish the plan sooner than expected. *She'll* need it.

For a while, she seems to be doing really well, plowing ahead with the doomsday device scheme and mapping out what she'll do when it's over. In exchange for not blowing up the world, she'll demand that she be made queen of it...and that really has her pumped. She loves talking about being the first mad scientist queen of the world and all the changes that she's going to make when she takes over.

Then, she has a run of bad luck. Make that terrible luck.

A guy she meets on the Internet turns out to be a stalker, following us on secret missions and breaking into the lair to steal stuff and leave threatening notes. We finally have to dispose of him (restraining orders and police protection really aren't options for people like us), which gets kind of messy.

Then, Dr. Medici gets audited by the Internal Revenue Service, which just started going after the earnings of mad scientists and other public enemies. The estimated back taxes on Dr. M's criminal activities are astronomical, and Dr. M hasn't exactly kept receipts to justify deductions.

The IRS audit is major trouble, the kind of trouble you can't dispose of like a stalker boyfriend...and it isn't the last of her bad breaks.

Dr. M's five former husbands write a tell-all book about their marriages to her. It becomes a bestseller that makes her a household name, but not in a good way.

In the heat of the book brouhaha, when Dr. Medici tries to phone in her threat to launch the doomsday device unless she's made queen of the world, the United Nations Security Council won't take her call.

The worst break of all, though, comes with Dr. Medici's visit to the doctor--a medical doctor, not a mad scientist. That's the one that almost wrecks her.

And it happens on Christmas Eve.

"All those years," says Dr. Medici, pouring herself another glass of whiskey. "Instead of working on doomsday devices and killer robots, I should have been studying medicine."

"Why? What's going on?" I'm a little nervous, because I found Dr. M hiding out with her bottle of whiskey in the dungeon...I mean my secret lab. She is leaning against the metal table on which my personal secret project lies hidden under a bedsheet.

Dr. Medici raises her glass, but I have no glass of my own with which to toast. "That's irony for you. I'm smart enough that I probably could have found a cure for cancer if I'd put my mind to it."

As she downs her drink, I take a step closer. "Cancer?" My head spins as the word dribbles from my lips.

Dr. Medici nods and refills her glass. "Star cell carcinoma," she says glibly. "A mind is a terrible thing to turn to paste."

I stumble another step toward her in the shadowy chamber. "Inoperable?" I'm having trouble talking to her, but not for the usual reasons.

Dr. M raises her glass. "Merry Christmas." She gulps her drink. "What really pisses me off, though," she says, "is that I didn't get to be queen of the world first."

This time, I stumble back away from her. I come up short against the cold wall of the cave and let it hold me up while the world melts out from under me.

Dr. Medici laughs bitterly. "I should've been a medical doctor," she says. "What the hell was I thinking?"

Twenty-five years ago, the first time I saw Dr. Medici, she was pounding the hell out of a teddy bear in her family's back yard. She was six years old, and dressed all in black.

Lots of cars were parked in front of her house, and I had come over to see what all the excitement was about. Hildegarde scowled at me and kept pounding the bear as I approached.

"Who's all the people?" I said, gesturing in the general direction of the cars parked out front.

"Funeral people." Hildegarde held the bear by its stubby legs and swung it hard at a rock as big as she was.

"Why are they here?" I remember looking around for something like the stuffed bear to swing and pound, as if it were the polite thing to do.

"My mother," said Hildegarde, sweeping the bear way back and really slamming it against the rock with all her might.

"What about her?" I said.

"Cancer!" Hildegarde went wild then, pounding the bear on the rock so hard that the bear's seams split and stuffing flew out of it. "Cancer cancer cancer cancer *cancer*!"

I stood and watched as she pounded the bear, then dug her nails into the split seams and tore it apart. Grunting like an animal, she shredded the skin and hurled the stuffing into the yard.

When she finally ran out of bear to pound and rip, she threw down the last remaining hunk of brown fur and glared at me.

"Someday," she said, "I'll be queen of the world, and I'll make it so nothin' happens without my say-so."

"Okay," I said. "Wanna play doctor?"

I watch her get drunk in the old dungeon for a long time, and I hardly say a word. When she finally starts to nod off, I help her upstairs to her quarters so she can sleep in her own bed.

And I don't leave right away like I should.

I stand in the doorway and watch her as she sleeps, the peaceful look on her face belying the turmoil in her life.

I would do anything for her. If I could cure her cancer by giving up my own life, I would do it. If I could take all of her troubles on myself, I would do that, too.

But there *is* one thing that I can do. It's the one thing that both of our lives have been leading up to since we first started playing mad scientist in the back yards of our childhood homes.

The next morning, I have a pot of coffee waiting for her in the lab. That much, at least, is like every other morning...though it's really the third pot I've made since midnight the night before. I drank the first two on my own; it was the only way I could stay up all night and make the final preparations for the grand unveiling.

When I see how bad she looks when she walks in, I'm extra glad I decided to carry out my secret plan today. Her eyes are bloodshot, her face haggard, her hair tangled. She shuffles around like she's still half-asleep, like she was the one up all night and not me.

I fill her mug with coffee and stir in a teaspoonful of sugar, the way she likes it. She doesn't take it at first, and when she does, she only sips once and puts the mug back down on the table.

Half-heartedly, she walks over to the big whiteboard on the wall and stares at the equations scrawled there in red, green, and black dry-erase marker. "Did the U.N. return my call yet?" She says it without looking back at me.

"No, Doctor." I cross the lab and stand alongside her.

She sighs and shakes her head. "I give up."

"I know the feeling," I say.

"No," says Dr. Medici. "I mean I really give up. No more mad science. It's just not working for me anymore."

I never thought I'd hear her say that, but I understand where it's coming from. "You've been having a rough time lately," I say. "Things'll get better."

"If by 'better,' you mean death, then yeah." She's finally showing some spark. Too bad it's in the form of sarcasm. "Much better, coming right up."

I take a deep breath. My big moment has arrived. "Things *will* get better." I feel a chill as all the blood seems to rush right out of my body at once. "Things will get better right *now*, in fact."

She isn't taking me seriously. She doesn't even look at me as she ladles on more sarcasm. "Oh, good. You've come up with that cure for cancer you've been working on. I'll have some right now, please."

"Follow me." I turn and march to the far corner, where the big surprise awaits, laid out on a gurney under a white sheet.

Dr. Medici follows slowly, her face etched in a scowl. "I'm not in the mood for jokes, Glue."

My hand shakes as I pat the shape beneath the sheet. I feel the heat of it, the rise and fall of it, and I know I've done well. "Trust me," I tell her. "Give me a chance."

"What is it?" she says as she draws up beside me.

"Science project," I say, and then I whisk the sheet from the gurney.

Dr. Medici stares silently at the naked man who is lying there.

He is lean and muscular, the type who could be a model or an all-around athlete. His complexion is fair, his thick hair glossy and blond. He has a movie star face with chiseled features...and his eyes, when they finally flutter open, sparkle like twin sapphires.

He looks young, in his twenties or thirties, but nowhere near his true age, for he is a newborn. Today is the first day of his life.

"Who?" For a change, Dr. Medici is the one reduced to one-word sentences.

"That's up to you." I pat the new man's shoulder, and he smiles up at us. "He's all yours."

Dr. M's frown softens just a little. "You made him?" She hangs back from the gurney, but she can't take her eyes off the man. "But how?"

"With snips and snails and puppy dog tails." I can't believe I'm making a joke, but I feel incredible. "And cloned, hypertrophic super stem cells resequenced by viral nanodrives seated mitochondrially."

"Huh." Dr. Medici shoots me a sideways look. "Are you *sure* you don't have the cure for cancer?"

"Go ahead and sit up," I tell the man on the gurney, and he does. "Say something."

"Hello." When he says it, his voice is deep and rich, and he looks right in her eyes. "I love you."

Dr. Medici blushes. "This is crazy," she says. "This is nuts." But she doesn't break eye contact with him the whole time.

I feel better than I can remember ever feeling before. "He understands you," I say. "The thrill will never be gone for him. And he will never leave you."

"But you can't know that," says Dr. M, "can you?"

Grinning, I give the homemade man a wink. "Tell her."

"I understand you." The homemade man gazes into her eyes

and speaks with intense feeling that leaves no room for doubt or apprehension. "The thrill will *never* be gone. And I will never *leave* you, Hildegarde."

I brainwashed him well. Every word, inflection, and expression are perfect.

Dr. Medici flashes me a confused frown. "But why?" she says. "Why did you do this?"

"I didn't want you to be alone anymore." It's only now that I lie to her. "Since you couldn't meet the right man, I made one for you."

Dr. Medici turns back to the homemade man, her confusion dissolving into wonderment. "I can't believe it," she says. "No one's ever done anything like this for me before."

Each word is like a caress to me. As she reaches out to touch his cheek, I feel like she's reaching out to touch mine. As she gazes tenderly into his eyes, I feel like she is gazing into mine.

Which makes sense, really. There's one part of the secret plan that I haven't told her about yet...one part that I will never tell her about.

That part is me. I am part of him.

I grew his heart from a piece of my own. The heart in his chest, the one that beats faster as she takes his hand in her own, is the twin of my heart.

And as he embarks on the life I always wanted, takes the love I always longed for in his new, strong hands, I'll share it, in a way. As I go about my work and see them happy, I'll know that I made it possible, and part of me will always be part of them.

This is the real reason I made him, the one I lied to her about. I made him because it's the only way I could ever have her, the only way I could ever close that final mile between us.

Though, if I'm honest, I have to say that not everything I'm feeling right now is happiness.

"Wendell." For the first time that I can remember, Dr. Medici calls me by my first name. "Wendell, thank you."

"Be happy." My heart is pounding like the pistons of a giant robot. "That'll be thanks enough."

She reaches over and brushes my hand with her fingertips.

Not for the first time and not for the last, I long to fold her into my arms and press my lips to hers in a kiss for the ages.

"This is mad, you know." A single tear rolls down her face as she turns back to her newborn lover. She can't take her eyes off him.

"Mad is good," I say, wiping away a tear of my own.

LENIN OF THE STARS

As we sit on the terrace in the oppressive jungle heat, I slide a shot of crystal clear vodka across the glass table. The man who was once Senator Joseph McCarthy taps the rim with one index finger and chuckles.

"Come on now." He shakes his head, smirking. "You know I don't touch *that* stuff, Vladimir."

I shrug and throw back my own shot. Feel the burn rolling down my throat like a slow-motion solar flare. "I've had lots of names," I say as I pour another. "Why do you insist on calling me by *that* one?"

"Vladimir Ilyich Ulyanov." McCarthy says it with grand sarcasm. "You'll always be Lenin to me."

"Ha." I down the second shot and clap the glass on the table. "And you'll always be an incompetent fear-mongering bastard to me."

"You talk like I didn't just kill your hand-picked Red Guard." He gestures at the twelve charred corpses strewn about the terrace. Five are still smoking in the blazing mid-morning sun. "Like it isn't just you and me here now."

I smile and raise the vodka bottle. The rays of the sun play through it on my face, refracted by the uneven crystal. "How 'bout if I drink you for it?" I shake the bottle. "I'll drink you for the revolution."

Something screeches in the treetops (bird, cat, monkey?) and McCarthy stops smirking. "You've led your last revolution, Lenin. End of story." He spreads his hands, exposing the octagonal barrels of the fusion guns mounted in his palms.

"And what if I'm not done here?" This time, I drink my shot straight from the bottle.

"Don't you think you've done enough to screw up this planet? And *ours*?" McCarthy aims his fusion guns at my head. "You're done, all right. Just as soon as we clear up some unfinished business."

I watch a flock of flamingos drift up into the turquoise sky. The scene reminds me of our homeworld, thousands of light years away. "What might that be?"

"I need to know where she is," says McCarthy. "Where is Irina?"

I laugh and shake my head, unwilling to tell him the truth. Because the truth is, I don't know where the love of my life has gone.

The first time I met Irina, I was blown away by how beautiful she was. The purple-and-green-tinted crystalline clusters of her body glittered in the auditorium's ever-flowing fireworks. Two of her six multifaceted eyes were silver, and four were gold, a mark of great passion and intelligence. Even her parasites had a special look about them as they danced around her body, multicolored tongues of flame weaving in and out of her vent slits.

I was never the same after that first glimpse of her. I had never seen anyone so beautiful in all my life.

"I believe we can help the humans." Those were the first words I heard her say. "I believe our way of life can change their world for the better and make them civilized enough to be welcomed into the community of worlds."

This was one of our pre-mission briefings on the homeworld.

Sixty-five of us in one room, getting ready to take another crack at the problem children of the galaxy--human beings. Other species had tried and failed to help humanity get its act together, but we honestly believed we'd be different.

To tell you the truth, just watching and listening to Irina was enough to make me believe with all my hearts.

"It's not their fault, you know." Irina (her name wasn't Irina then, it was unpronounceably alien) glided around the stage as images of human violence flickered in the air above her. "They've evolved in a hyper-competitive ecosphere. 'Eat or be eaten' is written deep in their genetic code."

"And it's up to us to teach them how the rest of the galaxy lives." As I spoke, I hoped she wouldn't pick up on the nervous quaver in my voice.

"Share and share alike, yes." Irina smiled. "No more 'dog eat dog,' as the humans say."

"What about 'kill or be killed?'" This time, it was the one who later became Joseph McCarthy who spoke--all ice blue crystals swirling with pink tongues of flame. Even then, he was a contrarian. "What if the humans kill us all as part of their 'ecosphere?'"

"As you know," said Irina, "they won't see us as beings from another world. We'll be altered to look like them."

McCarthy made a disparaging sound like pebbles clacking together in a glass vase. "And you don't think that will *increase* our chances of being killed?"

"Not for we brilliant few." Irina's voice was full of conviction. Her green and purple clusters pulsed with an electric neon tinge. "Not for those of us with all that's right and just on our side. Not for the denizens of the galactic *workers' paradise.*"

With that, sixty-four of us went wild in the auditorium, singing and clattering with inspired elation. Passing silvery gellid packets of pure, noble emotion back and forth. At least in my case, inspired by pure and growing love.

Only McCarthy stood apart and pouted, a clear sign he should have been drummed out of the mission. But Irina always said we crystal saviors needed all facets to catch the light.

Though the truth is, a single cracked facet can ruin the view completely.

It was the happiest day of my life.

A massive movement of people swelled the streets of Petrograd, Russia, flowing down every byway in an irresistible human tide. The roar of cheers and song filled the cold October air, the sound of change rising amid the ancient onion-domed towers.

Change that we had brought into being.

Irina's hands slid up over my shoulders. "We've done it," she said. "We've begun the world revolution."

I turned from the window and swept her into my arms. "Yes, *milaya moya*." I called her that for the first time, called her *my sweet.* And then I did something else for the first time, too. "*Ya tebya lyublyu*." *I love you*, I said, and then I kissed her.

She did not push me away.

The moment washed over me, and I reveled in it. My makeshift pseudo-human heart thundered in time with the marching feet outside my window.

I had traveled thousands of light-years from my homeworld to get to this moment. I had toiled five decades on Earth in a myriad of human identities to make this happen, as had all of us. Now here I was, in the Earth year 1917, playing the role of a human named Lenin, calling history's shots from my headquarters in the Smolny Institute in Petrograd.

Kissing the greatest love I'd ever known outside my service to humanity and the universe.

"*Laskovaya moya.*" Irina said it in a whisper. She kissed me again, then leaned back to gaze at me with dancing green eyes. "Your timing is auspicious, my darling. Our greatest work is yet to come."

I caressed the side of her face. "Together, we cannot *help* but succeed."

"Come on." Eyes twinkling, she backed away, pulling me with her. "Let's drink it in. Let's go outside."

Changing our features so we wouldn't be recognized, we slipped out a back door of the Institute. Merging with the vast crowd in front of the building, where people were cheering my name, we laughed and held each other close.

"Don't let it go to your head," said Irina.

"Of course not!" I said it with a grin.

"Not that you'll get the chance." Irina shrugged. "You'll be somebody new in a couple of years, and so will I."

As the crowd continued to cheer and sing around us, I stared at her face. Even disguised, it couldn't conceal her radiance, her passion, her certainty. As ever, she held me mesmerized.

"Who will we be in five years, Irina?" I said. "In ten years? Do you know?"

She tipped her head and smiled. "The plan is fluid, of course, but yes. I have some idea."

"Will we be together?" I took a deep breath. "Can you tell me that much, at least?"

She looked at me for a long moment as the crowd continued to cheer my name. The currents of history roiled around us like whitewater, churning and seething, overflowing their banks. Thanks to us, the mass of humanity was thrashing closer to a glorious communal destiny among the proletariat of the stars.

"We will not always be together." Irina wrapped her arms around me. "But we will not always be apart."

It wasn't the answer I'd had in mind, but I let it pass as she drew me against her. As she pressed her full lips against mine, and we kissed in the pulsating heart of the revolution.

Both of us knowing we were breaking a fundamental rule of our mission. Not because we were falling in love.

But because we were being selfish.

The next time I saw Irina was nearly four decades later, standing over the dead body of Josef Stalin.

Stalin lay on the floor of his private quarters in Kuntsevo, sprawled at Irina's feet. She stood with her hands on her hips, shaking her head as she looked down at him.

"I'm starting to notice a pattern here." She said it without looking up when I entered the room. She knew it was me, after all; she'd summoned me here from China. "Human gets power. Human abuses power. Human subverts the cause of the workers' revolution."

I crouched beside Stalin's body, letting the mask of my current prime identity--Mao Zhedong, President of the People's Republic of China--melt back into the face I'd worn so long ago as Vladimir Lenin. "I thought he was a great choice, too, Irina. Just like everyone else did."

"Maybe that's the problem." Irina sounded tired. "We make lousy choices."

Placing my hand over Stalin's face, I slid his eyelids shut. "Or it's just going to take longer than we thought, dragging these people into the age of communal civilization."

"There's another possibility, as well," said Irina. "Perhaps we need to modify our strategy."

I got to my feet and shrugged. "That's always a possibility when dealing with complex sentient beings." Face to face with Irina, I gazed into her eyes. They were darker than I remembered and no longer sparkling. "Sentient beings can be highly unpredictable." *Like you*, I thought.

As I watched her stare into space, I wondered why she'd shut me out for forty years. I wondered if she still felt anything for me at all.

"I've been thinking." She turned away and paced across the room. "I've been working on a new approach."

"Tell me," I said. Anything to keep her talking, to spend more time with her.

"I've developed a new identity over the past decades." She stopped pacing and changed shape over Stalin. Until that moment, she'd worn the form of a young woman with long, brown hair. Before my eyes, she became a middle-aged man in a dark suit, stocky and bald. "Meet Nikita Krushchev. I'll be taking the reins now that Stalin is dead."

I folded my arms over my chest. I'd known she was Krushchev, though I hadn't heard it directly from her. I hadn't heard *anything* from her in forty years.

Irina tapped her chin with a forefinger. "Meet the new face of the revolution. The harbinger of a bold new era."

"So you're following in my footsteps?" I shifted my face to look like my past identity of Vladimir Lenin. "Doing the driving *yourself* instead of trusting a flawed human?"

Irina the bald middle-aged man nodded. "The USSR has been turned inward against itself for too long. Why punish and purge the very workers we need to advance the revolution? Better to secure their allegiance with incentives while working to weaken the outside institutions that seek to oppose the proletariat."

I looked down at the body of Stalin and frowned. "You're talking about reversing the policies of the past thirty-one years."

"I call it De-Stalinization," said Irina. "Let up the pressure at home, increase the pressure abroad. Speed up the timetable of the worldwide revolution."

I listened and nodded. Even in the body of a middle-aged human male, she could sway me. Even after forty years apart, my feelings for her hadn't changed.

"China is coming along nicely." I switched my face back to Chairman Mao's, pear-shaped and heavy-jowled, with a dark fringe of hair around the back and sides of my head. "I think Earth will reach a tipping point soon, and the international proletariat will unify."

"All the more reason to press forward strategically," said Irina.

Reaching over Stalin's body on the floor, I clapped a hand on Irina's shoulder. "Tell me what you need me to do." I gave her shoulder a squeeze and gazed deep into her eyes. "You know I will stand by your side."

Irina held my gaze for a long moment, then laid her hand on my forearm. "Stay the course. That's all."

"I'll have one of the others take my place as Mao," I said. "You'll need my help to consolidate power here."

"I need your help most in China right now," said Irina. "The People's Republic is at a formative, vulnerable stage."

Instead of giving up and letting go, I took hold of her other shoulder. "No." It was the first time I'd ever said that to her. "I'm staying with you."

"That's sweet." Irina lightly touched my face. "But no. You have your orders."

"Orders?" I pulled away from her. "I don't understand. Why did you call me here if you didn't want my help?"

"To warn you," said Irina. "Our own people are working against us."

I was stunned to hear it. "Who?"

"Senator Joe McCarthy, for one. Our U.S. operations are in a shambles thanks to him." Irina sighed. "And there are others. I don't know who yet."

"Unbelievable." I shook my head in amazement. "How could *any* of us turn against the revolution?"

Irina moved closer, shifting back to the form she'd worn earlier, that of a brown-haired woman. Taking hold of my arms, she gazed into my eyes with blazing intensity. "*You* would never betray me, would you?"

I met her gaze with unshakeable steadiness. "Of course not." Her fingers dug painfully into my arms, but I refused to flinch. "How could you even *ask* me that?"

Irina held me a moment longer, then leaned forward and kissed me softly on the lips. "*That* is why I summoned you." Her voice was a whisper in my ear. "Because I had to be sure."

The scent of her mesmerized me. I could barely think straight. "That's it?"

"For now." When she drew away from me, she was Krushchev again.

Standing there, I felt shaky and disoriented. I'd been so *close* to her for the first time in forty years, and now she was moving out of reach again. She'd kissed me, but the kiss had felt empty, intended only as a guarantee of my loyalty.

There was so much I wanted to say to her, so much I *should* have said...but all I managed was this: "When will I see you again?"

"Every time you open a newspaper," said Irina/Krushchev. "I'm going to take the world by storm."

Nine years later, in October 1962, Irina/Krushchev leaped up from behind her desk as I burst into her office in the Kremlin. She came up with revolver in hand, leveled right at me.

Irina got off two shots without a word. They both missed as I bolted across the office.

Dropping as another shot exploded from the gun, I rolled over the floor and stopped behind a chair with fat red cushions. "Irina! Don't shoot!" I thought hearing that name might make her hold her fire.

But no. She cracked off another shot, straight through the chair, barely missing me.

Taking a breath, I prepared to charge. I'd known this would be the hardest part of my mission. That was really saying something, considering how many times I'd had to change shape and use force to get through security in the heavily fortified inner sanctum of the Kremlin.

But it had to be done. Irina was on the verge of making a horrible mistake, and I had to stop her.

I had to stop her from destroying humanity.

Crouching, I hoisted the chair off the floor and heaved it at her. As it crashed down on her desk, I darted after it.

Irina sidestepped, firing wide. As I dove across the desk at her, though, she got off one more shot.

This time, the bullet struck its target. I caught the lead in the meat of my shoulder, and my body flared with sudden pain.

But I wasn't about to let it stop me. My hands connected, throwing her over backward, sending the gun flying from her grip. We hurtled to the floor, pulling a desktop TV set down with us.

The TV burst to smithereens on the hardwood, spraying us with glass shrapnel. Irina flailed underneath me, using all the mass of her Krushchev disguise to try to throw me.

But I would not be dislodged. I shifted my own form again,

changing from an athletic young man to an obese middle-aged one, pressing her down with my greater weight.

"Irina!" Holding her down, I shifted the flesh of my shoulder. Out popped the bullet, ending my pain. "Stop and listen to me!"

She kept thrashing, fighting to break free. "Get off! Let go!"

"You are subverting the cause of the interstellar revolution!" I said. "The community of worlds will not condone your actions!"

Irina bucked and squirmed, scowling with rage. "The situation is under control!"

"You're wrong!" I said. "U.S. forces are at DEFCON 2. Kennedy's about to attack."

"He's bluffing!" said Irina.

"If you don't pull your missiles out of Cuba, there will be worldwide nuclear war tomorrow." I locked eyes with her, dead serious. "Humanity will be exterminated or close to it within days."

Irina shook her head. "You don't understand. We've been negotiating with the Americans through back channels. We're close to a breakthrough!"

"Listen to yourself!" I said. "You're willing to risk the *extinction* of all *humankind*. You'd sacrifice the very proletariat we've come to set free!"

"It won't come to that," said Irina.

"But it *could*. Taking the world to the *brink* like this makes it *possible*."

"It's *always* possible on this throwback planet," said Irina. "We're working to make it *less* possible."

"So it won't bother you?" I said. "Being responsible for the annihilation of an entire *species?*"

"*You* should *talk*. How many millions of humans have you condemned to death in the name of the People's Republic of China?"

"There's a big difference between *purging* and *extinction*."

"Which won't *matter*, because the Americans are about to *capitulate*," said Irina.

Just then, heavy footsteps marched into the room. "Premier

Krushchev!" A thickly built silver-haired man in an olive drab and red uniform gaped in alarm at the wreckage.

Hastily, I took on the shape of an official I'd knocked out on my way to Irina's office. "The Premier tripped and fell," I said as I helped Irina to her feet. "Are you all right now, sir?" said the uniformed man.

"Yes, I'm fine, Boris." Irina dusted herself off. "You're here because of the noise, I suppose?"

"No, sir," said Boris. "I have a message from Intelligence." He stopped talking and stared at me.

"Go ahead." Irina waved dismissively in my direction. "Comrade Sergei is cleared to hear such information."

"Yes, sir." Boris glanced my way once more, then focused on Irina. "Our forces in Cuba have shot down an American U-2 spy plane."

"Oh?" Irina leaned forward on the desk. "The pilot?"

"Dead," said Boris. "And the Americans have shut down the back channel talks."

Irina took a breath and slowly released it. Her whole body stiffened. "Permanently?" she said.

"Unknown at this time," said Boris. "However, Intelligence confirms that the U.S. is about to launch an attack."

"On Cuba," said Irina.

"And the motherland," said Boris. "War is imminent."

"I see." Irina closed her eyes and rubbed her temples.

"Premier." Boris took off his cap and took a step forward. "The defense ministers agree it is time to exercise the preemptive strike option."

"I understand." Irina cleared her throat. She shot me a look, then sat down on the edge of the desk.

"The ministers await your orders," said Boris.

"Soon enough." Irina waved him off. "I wish to weigh the options first, General."

Boris hung there for a moment, expectant, then saluted. "I'll be just outside, Premier Krushchev."

"Thank you," said Irina.

With that, Boris spun and headed for the door...only to stop midway and turn. "We *will* bury them, sir," he said. "Just as you once promised." Then, he snapped back around and marched out of the office.

When he'd pulled the doors shut behind him, Irina slumped and shook her head. Without a second thought, I put my arm around her shoulders.

"What happened to me?" Her voice was slow and distant. "How did I get like this?"

"We've been away from home a long time," I said. "Maybe we've started to think like the humans."

Irina was silent for a long moment, staring at the shattered TV set on the floor. I wanted to comfort her, make everything better, but I was also acutely aware that time was running out.

"What next?" I said.

She sighed and slid off the edge of the desk. "Try to stop this, if we still can. Give the Americans what they want and hope for the best."

Irina walked around the desk, straightening her jacket and tie, and I followed. "Let me help," I said.

"You can't," said Irina. "I have to undo my own mistakes."

I headed her off at the door. "Then come with me when it's over." Reaching out, I took her hand. "We'll get away from all this."

"Thank you." Irina squeezed my hand and gazed sadly into my eyes. "But I have more to do now than I ever imagined." With that, she pulled her hand from my grip and reached past me for the door handle.

"You deserve some time away," I said. "You've already done so much."

"Yes." Irina smiled ruefully. Her dark eyes held no trace of happiness. "And I'm starting to think that every last bit of it was wrong."

As soon as the spy slipped me the microfilm, he gasped and crumpled to the sidewalk. A pool of dark crimson spread out around him, radiating from his head.

I didn't wait around to look for the bullethole. Leaping into action, I charged across the street and down an alley, stuffing the microfilm in my pants pocket on the fly. Footsteps clattered on the cobblestones behind me as I ducked into the cheering crowd up ahead.

Heart hammering, I fought my way through the mass of spectators watching the street. No one paid me much attention; all eyes were focused on the men and bulls stampeding down the main drag in the searing July heat.

One thought swirled in my mind as I struggled through the crowd: who had leaked the rendezvous details to the West? Who had known I'd be receiving the microfilm in Pamplona, Spain during the Running of the Bulls?

At least I had a chance of getting away with it. There were plenty of ways to use the crowds and chaos against my pursuer.

Also ways for my pursuer to use them against me. As I plowed forward, a bullet punched through the head of a man in front of me. He dropped dead in my path, knocking me back into a crush of spectators.

As I disentangled myself, another shot whistled past my head and blasted into a woman's chest. People screamed and ducked, giving me my first clear look at the shooter.

And I gasped. The face was unfamiliar--a young woman with long, black hair--but the scent was unmistakable. It was *her*...changed yet again, facing me once more in the heat of the Cold War. In the five years since her defection after the Cuban Missile Crisis, I'd battled her dozens of times in one way or another. She'd gone from communist leader to hands-on field operative fighting for the cause of capitalism and the red, white, and blue. From lover to arch-enemy.

Irina.

With an icy stare locked on her face, she swung up her gun and pulled the trigger twice. I leaped away before the shots could connect and sprinted into the street, joining the rush of runners and bulls.

No time to stop and reason with her; I'd tried that before. Since nearly triggering the annihilation of humanity as leader of the Soviet Union, she'd been steadfast in her new cause. I knew she'd stop at nothing to snatch the microfilm and strike another blow against communism.

As I raced down the street, a dark-haired young man in white t-shirt and pants hurtled past me. Glancing back, I saw why he was running so fast: a monstrous black bull barrelled up behind me, huge horns gleaming white in the afternoon sun.

The bull seemed to decide I was a better target, because it followed me when I veered. Whichever way I went, it galloped after me, heaving and snorting.

As if I didn't have enough trouble to deal with, Irina fired more shots in my direction. A nearby runner cried out and dropped, head bouncing off the cobblestones.

Dashing through the mayhem, I caught up with another bull up ahead. Clapping my hands on its haunches, I vaulted up onto its back and held tight, waiting for impact.

Seconds later, the first bull rammed the second full force from behind. My mount stumbled around and went down hard; I barely sprang off in time to avoid being crushed.

I still made a bad landing, though, twisting my ankle when I hit. Forcing back the flash of pain, I staggered into the crowd on the sidewalk.

I managed to make it into an alley and braced myself against a wall. It took a few seconds to shapeshift away the damage to my ankle.

Which was just enough time for Irina to get me.

"Hello, Comrade." I heard her voice at the same instant I felt the gun barrel touch my left temple.

"Irina." Turning my head, I gazed into the bright green eyes of her latest face.

For a moment, I felt like we were back in Moscow again, fifty years ago, in 1917. I imagined our love was new and true once more, playing sweetly over the strains of the people's revolution.

Then, she punched me in the stomach. "You have something that belongs to me." Her voice was cold.

"I do," I said. "My heart."

She punched me again, harder. "That microfilm could bring down America. I won't let that happen."

"Stop fighting for the capitalists," I said. "Remember why we came here. Remember the galactic workers' paradise."

"The corrupt communist system drove humanity to the brink of annihilation." Irina punched me again. "We thought a capitalist ideology was aggressive and self-destructive, but *communism* was the more ruthless and ravenous aggressor!"

I shook my head against the barrel of her gun. "What about the interstellar revolution?"

"There's a *new* one." Irina smiled. "An interstellar *counter*-revolution."

"What?" I frowned. "What are you talking about?"

"It's just gotten started," said Irina. "You'll see."

"What kind of counter-revolution?"

"Join us." Irina leaned closer. "Help us change the galaxy for the better. Help *me* change the galaxy, my darling."

I had no idea what she was talking about. I had no reason to believe she felt any kind of affection for me at all.

But as I stared at her, so close, so familiar, I longed to do what she asked. To do *anything* she asked of me, however insane or impossible it might be.

Because I had *never* lost my love for her, and I never would. No matter how much she hurt me, I knew I could never give up on her.

"Please." She leaned even closer. "We can be together like before. Blazing beacons shining light in the darkness." She drifted closer then, and her lips touched mine. For the first time in fifty years, she kissed me.

In that moment, I nearly went with her. I almost joined the counter-revolution without knowing a thing about it.

But something sparked within my good socialist soul, and I held back. "I cannot oppose the proletariat," I told her. "I am a servant of interstellar communism."

Irina sighed. "Poor thing." She leaned forward once more and whispered in my ear. "Soon, there will *be* no interstellar communism for you to *serve*."

With that, she shot me in the head.

She dug the microfilm from my pocket and left me for dead. Which to our kind, is only dead for a little while. Even as she disappeared in the chaos of Pamplona, I began to reassemble the scattered bits of my human disguise. My shattered mind and senses began to reassert themselves.

But the pain of what she'd done would last much longer than that.

Thirty-seven years later, in the Earth year 2004, I was in the pilot seat of a fighter spacecraft, soaring through the bright blue sky over the Indian Ocean.

Morning sunlight gleamed off my topaz crystalline clusters and multifaceted eyes. I'd reverted to my native form; it was the only way to handle the complex controls of the fighter, which was from my homeworld.

And flying that fighter was the only way I could help win an interstellar war.

Checking the holographic displays in the cockpit, I spotted my target down below. I manipulated controls, and the fighter dropped through the cloud deck.

Emerging from the woolly clouds, I stared in stunned amazement at the tableau before me. Two huge vessels hung in the sky, vast starfaring warships from many light years away. As I watched, they fired enormous cannons, blasting each other with monstrous beams of fiery golden energy.

Tiny fighter craft like my own swarmed all around the warships, spinning and swooping and shooting. One exploded in a burst of orange light, then another; a third tumbled out of control and cracked up against the side of one of the warships.

So this was how civil war looked among the peoples of the interstellar workers' paradise. It was so much different from the hordes of humans hacking each other to bits in the mud with primitive weapons.

And yet, it was so much the same.

The war had been part of my life for years, of course. I'd seen plenty of action on Earth...but this was the first battle of this scope I'd been part of. I'd never seen anything like it in space, either, before coming to Earth. There hadn't been an interstellar war in millions of years, thanks to the lasting peace of the galactic revolution and workers' paradise.

But that was before the counter-revolution. That was before the twisted ideas of Earth had infected the interstellar community.

Suddenly, a flash of light seared across my forward shields, and I knew it was time to take action. Spinning my fighter counter-clockwise, I saw a gunboat coasting toward me like a big silver needle, artillery blazing.

I let loose a few rounds from my fusion guns, then whipped around and hightailed it toward one of the giant warships. The gunboat stayed in pursuit part of the way, until a shockwave picked it up like a toy and hurled it off my tail.

Finessing the controls, I closed in on the warship. I knew it was the enemy from its colors (red and black) and the symbols etched into its hull. It was a ship of the Capitalist Alliance, believers in the wealth of the few at the expense of the many...staunch enemies of the communists of the Interstellar Proletariat.

They were my enemies, though they were no different in appearance than me. I'd come to kill them, though we'd originated from the same homeworld, maybe even the same city or street.

Such was the legacy of the counter-revolution I'd first learned of thirty-seven years ago in Pamplona.

Not that the reasons for the fight much mattered anymore. My mind was focused completely on reaching my goal and doing as much damage as possible to it.

Flying forward, I threaded the maze of enemy fighters with weapons blazing. I banked and dove and twirled, eluding one opponent after another, leaving a trail of smoking and sputtering warcraft in my wake.

Soon, the Capitalist Alliance warship loomed before me, gun batteries blasting in every direction but mine. For that moment, I had a clear path to a gash in the hull amidships, the perfect place to inject a fusion torpedo.

Bearing down, I raced for the gash, calibrating a torpedo firing solution en route. Before I could release the payload, though, the enemy warship suddenly buckled and rolled in my direction.

I pulled up as fast as I could, speeding out of the listing ship's shadow. Just as I cleared the crash zone, the mighty vessel keeled over, barely missing me.

Then, with a series of massive explosions, it split in two. The fore and aft sections scissored apart...and the prow of the Proletariat warship plowed between them. The battered Proletariat ship had brought the capitalists down by ramming them.

But now both warships were heading for the sea.

Instantly grasping the implications, I climbed for the cloud bank as fast as I could. It was time to gain some altitude, time to put as much distance as possible between my fighter and the impending splashdown.

That was when the signal came in over my radio. A familiar voice broke through my furious focus.

It was a distress call. "I'm going down! Help!" It was *her* call, the one call I couldn't refuse. Even after everything that had happened between us, I could never turn my back on her. "My escape pod won't eject! Please help me!"

It was Irina.

Zeroing in on her signal, I whipped around and shot seaward again. Even as the warships plunged toward what I knew would be a catastrophic impact, I dove down after them.

Within seconds, I saw Irina's fighter spinning out of control, spewing plumes of black smoke. The engines were blown to hell, and the nose was mangled, which probably explained the problem with the escape pod.

I had scant seconds to dislodge that pod. Even then, we'd both be doomed if we didn't instantly blast away at maximum speed.

The enormous warships would hit the water soon, throwing

out waves of titanic proportions. If we were really unlucky, the impact combined with the battle damage the ships had suffered would blow up one or both of their fusion reactor power plants.

In which case, all bets were off.

Swooping around Irina's fighter, I shot off the nose with an energy pulse from my guns. Then, swinging around, I blew off the tail behind her. The severed pieces of her fighter fell away, leaving the cockpit escape pod in its translucent housing cube.

Just as the cube started to drop, the housing snapped away, blown free from inside by Irina. The propellant ring on the base of her ovoid pod flared to life, burning white hot, and the pod shot suddenly upward with Irina inside.

I rocketed after her without looking back. Over the whine of my fighter's engines, I heard the thundering roar of the warships splashing down.

Irina's pod leaped into the cloud deck, and I followed. We didn't dare slow down on the other side, in the open sky. Our survival depended on gaining as much altitude as possible.

Shockwaves bucked our craft as we punched ever higher. My fighter shook with rising intensity, battling the waves and the g-forces trying to tear it apart.

Irina's pod shivered and spun, then fell away.

My mind swirled with sudden grief. Going back for her would be certain death.

But I was seized by the impulse to try.

The last time she'd truly seemed to love me had been almost a century ago. Since then, she'd used and abused me, betrayed and undermined me, fought and killed me again and again. How could I still feel any love for her?

Or was that what love was about? Pain, upheaval, destruction, the end of the world?

I cut the fighter's acceleration and scanned the skies below me. I made ready to dive down and retrieve her...or accompany her into annihilation.

My scanners were all static. That meant at least one of the warships' fusion drives had ruptured. The Indian Ocean had become ground zero of a nuclear detonation.

But I had to go back for her.

Steeling myself, I toggled controls, ready to swing the fighter around. Ready for anything.

And that was when her glittering crystalline pod came streaking up past me like a shooting star in reverse.

When we'd reached a safe altitude, we stopped climbing. We hung in the stratosphere and looked down at the distant ocean, watching the devastation as it spread.

The battle itself had been cloaked from human technology, unseen by the world, but its effects would be felt by millions. When the warships sank and the fusion drives erupted, the ocean floor heaved from the force of the blast. A monstrous quake wrenched the crust of the Earth, slamming out colossal waves in all directions.

As we watched like satellites from far above, a monumental tsunami crashed down over islands and coastlines, obliterating anything in its path. Snuffing out hundreds of thousands of lives in Indonesia, Sri Lanka, Thailand, India.

We opened a radio channel between our craft, but neither of us said a word for a long time. We just watched as destruction swept that part of the world, destruction that we had helped bring about.

"I only wanted to help," said Irina. "I thought I was doing the right thing."

I didn't say a word. Far below, another tsunami was surging up from the sea, lashing toward shores that had already been laid waste by the first brutal onslaught.

"I wanted to free our people," said Irina. "I wanted to end the oppression of communist totalitarianism."

Still, I said nothing. I wondered how the people in the path of the cataclysm felt, gazing up in horror at the sky-high mountain of water hurtling toward them. Would they care which ideology had done the most to set that mountain in motion? Would any of them agree that the sacrifice would be worth it?

"I'm finished," said Irina. "All my efforts have brought nothing but death and disaster wherever I've gone." She sighed. "No more."

Yet another tsunami cut loose in the Indian Ocean. More people died screaming thousands of feet below us.

"Maybe I should just let myself fall," said Irina. "Drop down in the middle of that nightmare and die. I deserve it."

Finally, I spoke. "Shut up, Irina."

I saw her gape at me from her crystalline escape pod. All six of her multifaceted eyes--two silver, four gold--fixed on me in shocked amazement.

"I've been thinking," I told her. "And I've realized something. I couldn't see it before, because I loved you, but now I see it."

"Because you don't love me anymore?" said Irina.

The sun shone through her green and purple clusters of crystals, glittering within the intricate web of facets. Her fiery parasites zipped around her like schools of flaming fish, weaving in and out of her vent slits.

The sunlight and firelight danced when she moved, and I felt again the way I'd felt so long ago, watching her during the pre-mission briefings in the auditorium on our homeworld. For better and worse, it had been the one constant in my life.

Even now, after everything. Even now.

"I will always love you," I told her.

She gave me a look I couldn't fathom. "What did you realize?"

"You need me. You always have," I said. "And the galaxy needs a new Lenin."

Five years later, I'm on the terrace of a villa in the heart of the Colombian jungle, sitting across from a fellow extraterrestrial who looks like Senator Joseph McCarthy. He's killed twelve of my men, whose bodies still smolder in the hot sun around us, and now he wants to know where Irina is.

The truth, which I'm not about to tell him, is that I don't know exactly where she is at this moment...but I *do* know she's on her way.

I down another swig of vodka and look at McCarthy through the cut crystal bottle. He's still so blind, so backward, so limited by his all-consuming sociopolitical ideology. I feel like I'm watching a primitive lifeform as it struggles in the mud, wholly unable to comprehend the full potential of the complex landscape around it.

"Where is she, Lenin?" McCarthy's voice is a snarl. "Where's your commie she-devil mistress?"

"She's not a communist anymore," I tell him. "And she's not my mistress. Keep up, Joe."

With an angry roar, McCarthy flips over the glass table, which shatters on the cobblestone terrace. I barely manage to save the vodka bottle, which I was just about to set down on the table's blue-tinted surface.

"No more beating around the bush!" McCarthy springs from his rattan chair and swats the bottle from my grip. It smashes to bits against a wrought iron light post. "You'll *beg* to tell me by the time I'm done with you!"

I smile as McCarthy lunges forward and wraps his thick hands around my throat. "Wait! I'm prepared to make you an offer!"

He lets up the pressure but doesn't let go. "That was fast." He shrugs. "I would've guessed you had more tolerance for torture, you pinko bastard."

"Join us." I lock eyes with McCarthy, trying to draw him in with sheer force of will. "Forget capitalism. Forget communism. Forget all that."

"A new sales pitch." McCarthy sneers. "How original."

"Help us end the wars on Earth and the war in space," I tell him. "Help us move beyond the hidebound systems of the past. Help us spread a revolutionary new philosophy conceived by a radical new Lenin."

"Would this new Lenin happen to be *you*, comrade?" says McCarthy.

When I look over his shoulder, I smile. "And *her*." My makeshift heart beats faster. She has arrived not a moment too soon, machete in hand.

The love of my life. My guiding light in smooth times and rough. My true partner now, reborn after the battle of the Indian Ocean tsunami, committed to a life of change from a new point of view.

McCarthy starts to turn. Irina draws back and swings the machete, lopping off his head with the graceful elegance of a ballerina.

I leap from my chair and sweep her into my arms. The machete clatters to the cobblestones as we kiss. As the two halves of the new Lenin bind themselves one to the other once more.

This is the formula that eluded her for so long, the one that was staring her in the face from the start. Again and again, she turned me away, when what she should have done was embrace me. Accept me as an equal and consult me for balance. Go forth driven by love instead of self-righteousness.

Now see what revolution has hatched from this union. We bear a new gospel born not of conflict, but compassion: harmony among peoples by way of shapeshifting. Empathic metamorphosis. Truly love your neighbor as yourself by *becoming* your neighbor. Literally walk a mile in his shoes...and feet, and body, and life.

Yes, human beings can learn this, and we've been teaching it for the past five years. Using shapeshifting as a bridge to understanding instead of a weapon. It's really gone viral, and the movement's about to reach critical mass. Next stop, we take the show back home and end the galactic civil war.

All because of one simple secret it took us a century to figure out.

"Welcome home, darling." Smiling, I touch the side of her face. I run my fingers through her soft red hair.

"I love you." Irina says it with tears in her eyes.

The secret is this: *We are nothing without each other.*

SHROOMS OF BENARES

Father Gavín Obregón lifted the hem of his black shirt, peeled back a flap of skin just below his bottom left rib, and drew out three fresh-baked wafers of communion host from the cavity there, still warm from his flesh.

"The body of Christ, given up for you." Father Obregón said the words softly as he held up one of the round white wafers between his thumb and forefinger.

Piotr Punzak, a squat farmer with shaggy brown hair and beard, stood before him in the dusty farmyard. To one side, the gleaming silver domes of his farmhouse and barn sprawled in the mid-morning light...light cast not from a sun, but from huge fungal sun-blooms drifting across the sky.

In the other direction, the rolling hills were carpeted with fields of morel, boletus, oyster, and matsutake mushrooms, ready for harvest. The fruits of planet Benares, like all native life on the frontier planet, were fungus through and through. In all the world, only the human settlers could claim non-fungal origins.

As a rough breeze shivered the nearby morels and matsutakes, farmer Piotr tipped his head back. "Amen." Just as he opened his mouth for the host, one of the *nube oveja*--the self-propelled fungal "cloud sheep" herding in the sky overhead--slid away, allowing the light from the nearest sun-bloom to cast his face bright gold.

Father Obregón placed the host on Piotr's tongue. Piotr closed his mouth and bowed his head.

Then, it was time for the wine. Father Obregón turned over his right arm and popped the tiny cartilage pour-spout free from his wrist. "Blood of Christ, shed for you," he said.

"Amen." Piotr opened his mouth and closed his eyes.

Father Obregón held his wrist spout over Piotr's mouth, then squeezed the soft, oblong bladder implanted in the underside of his arm. Ruby red wine trickled into Piotr's mouth, sparkling in the light of the sun-bloom overhead.

It was just another Mass for the genetically engineered multi-faith super-chaplain of planet Benares. Just another communion for a human Swiss army knife on the fringe of the farthest frontier in human history.

An hour later, Father Obregón was racing away from the farm in his hoversled, zipping through a forest of giant fungal towers.

He was also speaking without moving his lips.

"I'll be there in three days, Shen." Father Obregón spoke in his mind over the planet-wide Soulnet that kept him in touch with his scattered congregation. "Plenty of time to make your daughter's bat mitzvah."

Shen Ping's words flowed into his brain like warm water. "You're a mensch, Rabbi. I know you won't let us down."

"Have I ever?" Father Obregón chuckled in his head. "*Relax,* Bubbi! Two hundred miles of *wilderness*, and I'll be whipping you at *arm-wrestling* again."

"Doesn't *count!*" said Shen. "You're a *splicer!* How can I *ever* beat a genetically modified rabbi slash preacher slash cleric slash *whatever?*"

Father Obregón's thoughts bubbled with laughter. "You better pump some *iron,* Shen! You *know* I won't *let* you win."

Shen responded with the mental equivalent of a snort.

"Maybe *I'm* the one who's been letting *you* win! How *else* am I gonna score points with *God?*"

Just then, another call buzzed for attention in Father Obregón's head. Such was life in the remote wilderness for the clergyman with a switchboard in his brain.

All seven hundred humans on Benares had a direct telepathic line to the super-chaplain at all times. How else could one man tend the spiritual needs of a flock scattered to the far corners of a huge and untamed world?

Still, sometimes he wished for a respite. Sometimes, he longed for a little peace and quiet in which to commune with no one but God.

The caller buzzed again, and Father Obregón opened the link. Just as he started to say something, a flock of creatures burst out of a stand of morels in front of him. Reflexively, he swerved the hoversled to one side, barely missing the incredible lifeforms as they took flight.

He gazed in stunned wonder as he glided past. Yet again, he'd come across a new species--a flock of what looked like winged pizza shells with a hundred writhing white tendrils underneath. They twirled skyward all at once, twelve of them at least, trailing some kind of neon blue mist. Even as Father Obregón swung his hoversled wide in case the mist was toxic, he marveled at their magnificent strangeness, their utterly alien design. Like every other non-human lifeform on Benares, they were fungus-based, similar to fungi back on Earth yet possessing a multitude of uniquely alien traits.

What a world. How many times a day did that thought run through Father Obregón's mind? *I love this planet.*

"Hello? Can you hear me?" As Father Obregón got his hover-sled back on track, he tried to reconnect with the caller he'd cut off because of the pizza shells. But no one answered.

Nothing but silence on the line.

Amazingly, an hour went by without a single call in Father Obregón's head. The constant queue of souls banging on his door was empty and silent.

At first, he passed it off as a fluke. He decided to continue toward his next stop and make the most of the rare quiet by indulging in some meditation amid the stunning sights of Benares.

When he topped a ridge and gazed out over a sprawling valley he'd never seen before, chills raced up his spine. Giant multicolored rills of fungi fanned out over the valley floor, arching like ranks of rainbows under the cloud sheep and luminous sunblooms in the shifting, golden sky. It looked nothing like the Heaven he'd been taught to expect, but it made him think of Heaven nonetheless.

As Father Obregón crossed a mountain pass under canopies of towering toadstools, glittering silver showers of spores swirled around him like snow. Curtains of lacy lichen hung dancing from the clifftops, making a sound like high-pitched singing as the wind filtered through their fine traceries.

Then there were the creatures in all their multitudes, great and small and every size in between...every one of them *mycozoa,* fungi with the mobility of animals. They flew and crawled and swung and darted through the landscape, screeching and squawking and roaring and croaking.

I need to do this more often. That was what Father Obregón thought as the splendor of Benares continued to unfold around him. As the second hour of peaceful contemplation passed. *I'd almost forgotten what it was like to appreciate God's wonders without constant interruptions.*

But by the middle of the third hour, a knot had formed in the pit of his stomach. The sights of Benares couldn't distract him from what he now knew to be true.

Something was wrong. The Soulnet was malfunctioning, or something was blocking the calls...

Or something had happened to the *callers.*

With the Soulnet apparently down, Father Obregón turned elsewhere for human contact. Parking in a mountain meadow of red and blue puffballs, he switched on the radio in his hoversled, grabbed the microphone from its hook on the dashboard, and called out over the airwaves.

"This is Father Obregón," he said into the mic. "Can anyone hear me? Please respond."

No answer.

"Father Obregón here." As he said it, he watched a pack of pale wolflike creatures with spiked snouts and springs for legs chase what looked like a pink beachball across the far side of the meadow. "Someone, please answer!"

Still nothing. Across the meadow, the beachball turned on the remaining four wolf-things, flung open a huge maw on its face, and bounced after them. It ran down and gobbled up one, then two, then three of them, getting fatter each time.

Yet another new species, thought Father Obregón. *I love this planet.*

One more hour passed before Father Obregón finally heard another human voice.

"I hear you, Father."

For an instant, he thought it was coming in over the radio, but he quickly realized it was inside his head.

"Hello!" He thought the words and said them aloud at the same time. "Thank God, hello!"

The new voice in his head was a woman's. "I was starting to think you were dead, Father." He recognized the low, throaty tone right away: Naima bint Fouad bin Hakim Al-Aziz, an exobiologist. He recognized it though he hadn't heard it for five long years.

She'd refused to call him for five years. Out of all the settlers, she alone had cut herself off from him.

"You thought wrong." Father Obregón chuckled, trying to sound calm, though his heart was suddenly racing. "So how are you, Naima?"

"I've had better days." Naima's voice was stiff and strangely flat. "I'm at the end of my rope, actually."

"Tell me what's happening, Naima."

"Wellll." The slightest quaver crept into Naima's voice. "Everyone's dead up here. Everyone but me."

Father Obregón felt a horrified chill rush through him. "*Everyone?*"

"Yes, Gavín," said Naima.

"*Dios mío.*" Father Obregón shook his head in stunned disbelief. Thirty-six people, counting Naima; that was how many had been stationed at the research camp with her. "What *happened* to them?"

"You know how we hadn't found any signs of sentient life on Benares?" said Naima.

"Yes, of course."

Naima choked back a sob. "We weren't *looking* hard enough."

Father Obregón had first met Naima on the trip from Earth aboard the starship that had brought them to Benares. She'd been a teenager at the time, but the truth of it was, they'd both been 21 years younger. He'd been barely out of his teens himself.

Their personalities had been a perfect match from the start. Not such a shocker maybe, considering the 700 settlers had been selected for general compatibility...but he'd always felt something special with her. Something beyond computer-predicted affinity.

Their reasons for making the trip were much alike. Naima had come for adventure, to witness never-before-seen wonders in the name of science. Father Obregón had also come for adventure, to witness such wonders in the name of God. Both of them were idealists, driven by wanderlust, curiosity, and faith in the power of universal truths and forces.

Drawn together by complementary callings and natures, they'd spent many hours together gazing out at the passing spectacles of space, talking about *everything*. Imagining the great discoveries they would make on the scientific and spiritual frontiers.

Dreaming up schemes for turning their brave new colony into utopia.

Dreaming up ways to be together on Benares, too, though their assigned duties would keep them far apart. Because the longer they knew each other, the more they knew they *had* to be together.

Everything between them was perfect, from the meshing of their personalities (they were both thoughtful yet outgoing) to the meshing of their bodies (thankfully, chastity was no longer a mandatory vow for priests in this day and age). They were soul-mates, and they had to find a way to stay together even as their work pulled them apart.

Maybe, if Naima found sentient life on Benares, she could get her assignment changed to assistant chaplain; Father Obregón would need an exobiologist to help minister to alien lifeforms, wouldn't he?

Maybe, his genetically-engineered splicer body would have trouble adjusting to the alien environment--with a little help from an undetectable nano-phage tweaked by Naima--and he'd have to stay put at her lab.

Or, failing either of those, he would figure out a way to always keep her thoughts foremost in his mind. He would scam the Soul-net, whipping up a psychic hideaway for the two of them in the midst of the mental traffic from the other settlers.

One thing alone had been carved in stone: the two of them would find a way to overcome any obstacle the frontier or their fellow settlers threw at them.

Shivering, Father Obregón looked around the mountain meadow, staring at the larger clumps of puffballs, the shadows of the distant toadstool treeline. He wondered if he was being watched by something with intellect and malice.

What troubled him most, though, was the possibility that sentient native lifeforms had taken action all over the world. That the reason no one but Naima had answered his calls was that the lifeforms had murdered them all.

"Are you safe?" Father Obregón said in his mind.

He panicked briefly when no answer came...but then Naima spoke. "I've sealed myself in the lab."

"What do they look like?" said Father Obregón.

"See for yourself," said Naima. "You have my permission."

Father Obregón's pulse quickened. "You mean...you can *see* them? They're *with* you?"

"In the building." Naima said it matter-of-factly. "Come through and I'll show you."

Father Obregón hesitated. It had been a long time since he'd been inside her head. He hadn't gone there in five years, since the two of them had split up.

Though for 16 years before that, he'd visited her mind every day. In spite of their schemes for togetherness on Benares, it was the only way they'd actually managed to be together at all in spite of the miles that were almost always between them. It was the one thing they'd shared that was special to the two of them, the one thing no one else could interrupt.

Because while everyone else could enter *his* mind on a whim, Naima was the only person in the world whose mind *he* could enter.

Father Obregón took a deep breath and steadied himself. This time, he knew, going into her mind was crucial; he had to do it to see what they were up against.

And he had to not let her know how much it meant to him. How much he enjoyed it.

Taking one more deep breath, he dove into the open link, pouring his mind like lightning in Naima's direction.

He felt a thrill as he charged through the crackling darkness of the mental conduit between them. A flare of blinding white light suddenly filled his mind's eye, and he felt himself spinning out of control. A flurry of sensations washed through him, a storm of sounds and smells and tastes and touches, too jumbled to process. The unfiltered input of another human mind.

Then, the sensations faded, and the spinning stopped. Father

Obregón blinked his mind's eye, clearing away the afterimage of the blinding flare.

And he found himself looking out through Naima's eyes. He saw her reflection looking back at him from the gleaming silver surface of a metal lab table.

He hadn't seen her in years. Even slightly distorted in the reflection from the table, she looked as beautiful as he remembered.

Long brown hair flowed over her shoulders, wrapping around a small, oval face. Dark-framed eyeglasses perched on a gently sloping nose, setting off eyes of the brightest, most glittering green he'd ever seen. Perfect dimples flanked the soft petals of her rosy lips, curling when she smiled toward a tiny mole on her right cheek...

And a scar on her left. He had to force himself not to recoil at the sight of it. Not because it was ugly, because nothing could make her ugly in his eyes.

But because it was his fault.

"Where are they, Naima?" Better to take his mind off that scar. Better not to think about what had happened between them five years ago.

"I'll show you." Inside the confines of her mind, Naima's voice sounded stronger, less rattled. "Over here."

As Father Obregón watched, the scene shifted, swooping up and away from the reflection on the lab table. He saw stacks of hard-shelled plastic cases, racks of silver lab implements, panels of glowing green controls and readouts.

Finally, there was a clear space, a reinforced glass door a few yards away. The view stopped swooping from east to west and started moving toward the door.

Naima took one step, then two, peering into the twilit space beyond the door. Father Obregón could make out overturned tables, chairs, equipment...

And bodies. He saw the unmistakable shapes of human arms and legs piled in with the wreckage. Then, human *faces* caked with blood, mouths and eyes wide open, unmoving.

His heart sank as Naima took another step, bringing him closer to the corpses. He recognized at least two of them.

Suddenly, something threw itself against the door with a thunderous crash. Naima stopped in her tracks but didn't look away.

Father Obregón's instinct was to dive back into the link, but he forced himself to stay and watch. It wasn't easy; what he saw as he gaped through Naima's eyes filled him with revulsion.

A human head, a female *child's* head, wobbled atop a mass of mangled human body parts held together by pulsing black foam. The mismatched parts looked like they'd all come from different people: a woman's long leg, a man's hairy arm, another man's torso, a child's hand.

The parts were arranged in roughly the right places for a human body, linked by the black foam instead of tendons and ligaments. They jiggled and slipped around as if the foam were barely holding them together.

As unsteady as the mass of parts looked, they were capable of moving with sudden speed and power. Father Obregón flinched as the patchwork person suddenly lashed out with its male right arm, pumping it into the door so hard, it cracked the outer pane of glass.

Mismatched body parts fell away in the impact, but the black foam stayed attached and snapped them back together. The little girl's head rolled down the torso, then jumped back up into place...but face-down, with the bloody stump of her neck pointing at Father Obregón.

He knew her, of course, as he knew all his congregation on Benares. Her name was Emma, and her parents were Mormons. Good people, all three of them.

He wondered if any of the other patchwork pieces were theirs.

"Dios mío." Father Obregón had to look away. "You say this thing is *sentient?*"

"I *know* it is," said Naima, and then she walked the rest of the way to the door. Father Obregón watched as she pressed the palm of her right hand against the reinforced glass.

Instantly, the child's hand on the patchwork body lunged at the glass, planting itself directly opposite Naima's. Black foam flowed out from its stump, glowing brighter and pulsing faster as it outlined the tiny, pale fingers.

Father Obregón watched, transfixed...and then,

a *third voice* spoke in Naima's head.

It spoke in a kind of hyperfast babble. As Father Obregón listened, images appeared in his mind, somehow triggered by the gibberish. He saw showers of pulsing black foam falling from the sky like rain, covering the ground, clotting and squirming. Looking up, he saw the foam's source: the *nube oveja*, the drifting "cloud sheep," split open from end to end.

Next, he saw a familiar scene--himself, administering communion to Piotr Punzak. He saw the scene from above, looking down from a distance as he drew the host wafer from the cavity in his side and placed it on the tongue of the Catholic farmer.

Then, as if from nowhere, two words shot into his mind, spoken in his own voice: *EAT GOD.*

When the sound of the words faded, Father Obregón saw something else. He saw two more of the patchwork bodies rising from the rubble, picking up tools and guns, and shambling toward the lab in which Naima was sealed.

EAT GOD.

Father Obregón returned to his own body to try to figure out what his next move should be. The Soulnet link to Naima was still open--he didn't dare risk being cut off from her--but he kept her on hold as he pulled himself back together.

What did the patchwork lifeforms want? And how could he stop them?

He knew only one thing for sure: he had to get to the lab in person as soon as he could, whatever the cost. He had to rescue Naima, for what she'd once meant to him...and what she meant to him still, in spite of the mistake that had come between them.

Never mind that she was nearly two hundred miles away. No one else was answering his calls; there might not be another living soul in the whole world who could come to her rescue.

The first thing he did before taking Naima off hold was to start the hoversled moving in her direction. He put it on autopilot and set the speed as fast as he dared, keeping one hand on the steering wheel just in case.

The next thing he did was pull the flask of bourbon from under his seat and take a quick drink. He saved the stuff for especially bad days, and they didn't get much worse than the one he was having.

Then, he put the flask away and took Naima off hold. "Any change?" he said through the link.

Naima sighed. "Three more just showed up outside the lab. That makes six. Not that I'm worried, you understand."

Father Obregón smiled grimly. "Hang tight. I'm on my way."

"Watch for sudden downpours," said Naima. "You don't want to get caught out in *that* rain."

Taking his eyes off the path ahead, Father Obregón looked skyward. A fat, fluffy cloud sheep floated off to one side, well away from his route...but it still made him nervous.

"I can't believe the black foam's responsible," said Naima. "It started turning up recently, but we didn't know it was coming from the cloud sheep...and we *definitely* had no idea it was sentient."

"Have you had a chance to analyze it?" said Father Obregón.

"The foam contains high quantities of an ultra-potent form of *psilocybin,*" said Naima. "The hallucinogenic compound produced by certain species of fungi. Otherwise, its structure is a mystery. Nothing to suggest motility, let alone sentience."

Father Obregón kept his eyes on a flock of cloud sheep up ahead, and he shivered. "In the 21 years we've been here, there's never been a sign of danger from the cloud sheep. How is this possible?"

"Cicadas on Earth have a 17-year life cycle," said Naima. "Why not a 21-year cycle for cloud sheep to generate and deposit black foam?"

As his hoversled approached the flock of cloud sheep, Father Obregón pressed buttons on the dashboard, shutting off the outside air vents, switching the blower to recycled air only. He double-checked the cockpit seals and nodded, satisfied the foam couldn't get inside.

Reasonably satisfied.

"So." Naima paused. "When do you think you'll get here?"

He knew she wouldn't like the answer. "Eight hours. Maybe ten."

Naima was silent for a moment. When she spoke again in his head, the tone of her thoughts was dark. "If they...if I'm gone before you get here...please go somewhere else."

"That won't happen," said Father Obregón. "I think maybe they're waiting for me."

Again, Naima was silent. "Then don't come at all. I don't want you to."

"Sorry," said Father Obregón, "but it's not open for discussion. As long as you're alive, I'm coming to get you."

"Then I'm hanging up," said Naima. "You won't *know* if I'm dead or alive."

"Naima, no!" said Father Obregón, but it was too late. She'd already cut the connection.

He pounded the dashboard with his fist, angry that his only link to her had been severed. Desperately worried that she could be dying at that very moment, and he had no way of knowing.

He was also, deep in his heart, overjoyed that she'd hung up on him. Because he guessed that the only reason she'd hung up was that she was worried the patchworks would get him if he tried to save her.

And that meant she still cared. Perhaps, after five years, she'd finally forgiven him for what he'd done.

He'd meant it as a surprise.

One night, five years ago, Father Obregón had decided to do something extra special for Naima's birthday. It didn't matter that he was halfway around the world from her.

What were a few thousand miles to someone who could travel between minds?

He'd parked his hoversled for the night at the base of an enormous toadstool and closed his eyes. Then, he'd done something he could do only with Naima, because of their special two-way link.

He'd sneaked inside her mind. He'd found her through the Soulnet and slipped inside while she was sleeping.

Then, he'd done something even harder, something he'd never done before. Something that took him a few tries before he got it right.

He'd made her *sleepwalk*. He'd taken control of her body, enough to get her up out of bed and make her shuffle down the hall and out the door of the barracks at the research camp.

"What the hell did you think you were *doing?*" That was what Naima said much later...over the link, of course, as she lay in her hospital bed. "What *possessed* you?"

"I wanted to paint a picture with your hands," Father Obregón had told her. "I wanted to give it to you for your birthday, as if I were there with you."

"You can't just crawl into my *mind* without my *knowing* it." Naima's voice in his head had been full of pain and anger.

"But I wanted to *surprise* you," he'd said. "You'd see that painting and wonder how it *got* there. And you'd know how much I *love* you."

"You almost *killed* me!" It was then, when she'd said that in her thoughts, that Father Obregón had known it was over between them. Even before she'd broken it off in so many words, he'd known.

Because she'd been right. He *had* almost killed her.

After she'd shuffled out of the barracks that night, he'd walked her to the main lab, where he'd arranged with other members of his flock to stow some painting supplies. Then, while steering her through the lab to set them up, he'd fumbled his control for an instant.

Naima had tripped over her own feet and crashed through the wall of a plate glass isolation chamber. Dozens of glass shards had pierced her body, barely missing vital organs and blood vessels, ripping open a gash that had left a scar on the side of her face.

That day had left deep scars between Naima and Father

Obregón, too. She'd never trusted or forgiven him in the five years since.

But he'd never stopped loving her...and maybe, he thought, she'd held on to her love for him as well.

Two hours passed with no contact from Naima. Against her wishes, Father Obregón stayed the course, charging through the wilderness toward her camp.

As his hoversled glided through the fungiscape, he passed the usual parade of wonders but was only dimly aware of them. He wound his way through a forest of massive chanterelles, their pearlescent scalloped lobes blossoming in spectacular fashion...but he didn't really see them. He skated over a field of waist-high fairy ring mushrooms, their curled skirts uplifted like delicate ivory pinafores...but he couldn't appreciate them, either. Same for the procession of filmy lavender veils rippling through the air like magic carpets over red-orange fungal spires.

All he could think about was Naima and what he could do to save her. He wracked his brain, trying to sort out what had happened, struggling to latch onto a solution.

Suddenly, his head buzzed with an incoming call. He jumped and nearly swerved the sled into a wall of crystalline lattice lichens in his hurry to open the line.

"Naima?" He said it aloud and in his mind at the same time. "Are you all right?"

"You didn't do what I told you." She sounded weary but not angry. "You're still coming, aren't you?"

"I don't think there's anyone else left on Benares," said Father Obregón. "It's down to the two of us."

Naima didn't say anything in response to that.

Father Obregón rubbed his eyes. "Have more of the creatures arrived?"

"I've lost count."

"Have they communicated with you? Have they said anything?"

"No," said Naima, "but I think you were right. I think they're waiting for you."

"What makes you think that?"

"Because they're all facing in your direction," said Naima. "None of them are looking at me anymore."

"I wonder what they want with me." Father Obregón stroked his bearded chin. "'EAT GOD,' they said. Do they think we're actually eating our God during communion? Maybe they want a taste for themselves."

"By eating those of us who've eaten God?" said Naima.

Father Obregón steered out from under a looming cloud sheep. "Attaining divinity by consuming the flesh of those who've tasted the divine. It makes sense."

"Then what about the non-Christian settlers?" said Naima. "*They* didn't take communion."

"The beings don't distinguish between different faiths, maybe? If *one* human takes communion, by extension, they think we *all* do it?"

"Okay," said Naima. "Then why are they waiting for you?"

"I generate the host and wine." Father Obregón gazed out the cockpit canopy as the hoversled swooped over a bubbling lake of yeast. Ever-shifting geometric patterns flowed over the surface, multicolored interlocking shapes dancing like a kaleidoscope. "Maybe they want *all* the God for *themselves.* Every last bite."

When Father Obregón was an hour from Naima's camp, the sunblooms started to dim. They were the planet's home-grown source of light and heat, enormous fungal disks orbiting high in the stratosphere. Once a day, their luminescence dropped to 25 percent, and night fell over all of Benares at once.

The hoversled's headlamps switched on, lighting up the way forward. Nocturnal mycozoa bounded away from the flare, tails and wings and tentacles flickering.

As Father Obregón gazed into the darkness around him, he felt the same void in his soul. He was at a loss about what he should do when he reached Naima. He felt hopeless, inadequate...and scared.

All he knew for sure was that he had to get there. No other human was left alive on Benares; no one had responded to his repeated psychic or radio calls. No cavalry was coming from the stars, either. Benares was on the farthest fringe of the frontier, months from the nearest settled world by spacecraft.

So it was all up to him. Super-chaplain to the rescue. Time for the splicer to prove there was more to his genetically enhanced superiority than just talk. Time for him to make up for hurting her five years ago.

If only he had a plan. If only he didn't feel so *alone.*

Only now, without the constant calls of his flock buzzing in his head, did he realize how much they'd meant to him. How much he'd depended on them. Only now did he notice how small he felt without them. How weak.

"Father? Imam?" Naima's voice rose suddenly in his quiet mind.

"*Asalam 'Alaykum.*" He used the traditional greeting since she'd referred to him by an Islamic title.

"*`Alaykum as-Salaam,*" said Naima. "Are you almost here?"

"Less than an hour away," said Father Obregón.

"That close." Naima sighed. "Perhaps you should slow down a little."

So we can live a little longer. He knew exactly how she felt. "How are you holding up?" he said.

"Second-guessing every decision I've ever made," said Naima, "because they all led me to this moment."

Father Obregón looked around as his sled glided through a thicket of giant, glowing shiitakes and feathery cauliflower mushrooms. "Well, I'm glad you're here," he said. "Not *there,* I mean, but...I'm glad to have you with me. I missed you."

Naima paused for a long moment. When she spoke again, her voice in his mind was soft. "I missed you, too."

"I'm sorry," said Father Obregón. "I'm sorry for what happened before. I'm sorry I hurt you. I shouldn't have done what I did."

"And I shouldn't have pushed you away," said Naima. "We wasted so many years...and now this. Now we're out of time."

"Not out of time yet," said Father Obregón. "Maybe we'll still get a second chance...if we want it."

"That's what I'm praying for," said Naima.

A creature that looked like an upside-down pyramid of blinking violet light floated by in the darkness. *I love this planet.* "That's what I'm praying for, too, Naima."

As Father Obregón pulled into Naima's camp, he realized he was crazy. What was he thinking, rushing to confront a hostile enemy without a plan, a weapon, or backup?

He parked his hoversled in front of the lab shed and switched off the motor. Then, he sat for long moments in the cockpit, knuckles white as he clutched the wheel. Sweat ran down his back and sides as he dug deep for courage.

He found it in his flask of bourbon. Two long pulls calmed his shaking. One more, the longest yet, and he popped the cockpit canopy and stepped out of the hoversled. Stood for a moment in the pool of brightness cast by the lone floodlight atop the lab shed.

Then, heart slamming like a fighter's fist against his rib cage, he walked toward the open door of the shed.

As soon as Father Obregón stepped through the door, they moved toward him. Patchwork assemblages of mismatched human body parts, held together with clots of black foam. All the eyes wide open, all the faces slack and dead.

They looked far more horrifying in person than they had through Naima's eyes--heads lolling, bones protruding, organs dangling. Black foam oozing between joints and out of every orifice. A grinding, sloshing sound as they hobbled and shuffled toward him. A stench of excrement and rot so overwhelming, it made him gag.

And there were so *many* of them. *Dozens.* No wonder Naima had lost count.

He forced himself to stand with shoulders squared as they surrounded him. As they pressed closer and closer on all sides.

Peering between them, he glimpsed Naima in the sealed lab, gazing out through the reinforced glass door. He heard her in his mind--no words, just breathing. A nervous quaver in each exhalation.

And then something else was in his mind, too.

The familiar presence of the black foam welled up within him, pulsing and pressing against his awareness. Hyperfast gibberish babbled in his head, and images rushed past his mind's eye: black foam falling from drifting cloud sheep to blanket the fungiscape; Father Obregón giving communion to Piotr Punzak and a stream of others, dozens of humans all over the world...all of them dead now.

Suddenly, the creatures grabbed hold of him, snapping his focus back out of his mind. With clumsy power, they wrenched his arms wide and held him spread-eagled. One of them clamped his head between bloody, mismatched hands.

This is it. Eyes wide, heart jackhammering, Father Obregón felt more of the creatures grab hold of him, wrapping him in a solid clinch of rancid flesh and black muck.

"*Stop!*" Naima's voice sounded far away as she screamed in the lab, more distant than when they'd been hundreds of miles apart. "*Please no!*"

The creatures ignored her cries. One of the patchworks wobbled in front of Father Obregón, its head that of a young man with sandy brown hair. Its torso, strung with shreds of green cloth, belonged to a woman; one arm was short and pale, the other long with coal-black skin.

When the dark arm swung up and the tiny pink hand on the end reached for his face, Father Obregón tried to flinch, but the other hands gripping his head wouldn't let him. He cried out, struggling, but the hand moved toward him inexorably.

He shut his eyes and grimaced when the stubby little fingers made contact with his forehead. A fresh wave of gibberish surged through his mind, swirling like a cyclone. More images of communion, more images of black foam showering down.

And then, a new cycle of images coursed through him. Settlers tasting the black foam, putting curds of it in their mouths. Each one dying horribly afterward, convulsing on the ground, then literally falling apart...limbs and heads slumping away from torsos, organs sluicing in the dirt in a flow of black sludge.

Pulled together by tendrils of foam, the body parts became shambling patchworks. The patchworks went after other settlers, feeding them more of the foam, and the cycle repeated.

Through it all, Father Obregón felt the same words rise up in his mind again and again. The same words as before, imparted nonverbally to his fevered mind:

EAT GOD.

His head was spinning as he tried to make sense of what he'd seen. One thing was clear: he knew how the nightmare had started. Settlers had eaten the foam of their own accord...but why? He still didn't understand.

The infant hand on the dark-skinned arm withdrew, then dug its stubby fingers into a bubbling clot between the patchwork's head and torso. The fingers came away smeared with black foam.

Then, they moved toward Father Obregón's mouth.

EAT GOD. Again with the same message. *EAT GOD.*

As the foam-covered fingers slid closer to his mouth, Father Obregón realized how wrong he'd been. The patchworks hadn't been trying to attain divinity by consuming the flesh of humans who'd eaten God in communion. They'd never wanted to reach the God of humans at all.

They'd been trying to do the *opposite.* Trying to get humans to eat *their* god.

But humans couldn't survive it. The black foam sacrament had killed them all. And Father Obregón was next in line.

"Please, no!" Father Obregón fought harder, but he couldn't break the combined grip of the ghoulish patchworks.

"Stop it, you *monsters!*" It was Naima. Father Obregón heard the door to the lab crash open and her footsteps charge into the patchwork mob. "*Leave him alone!*"

But nothing would change the course of events. The tiny fingers jabbed forward, and the black foam touched Father Obregón's lips. He felt it fizzing like a carbonated drink on his lips and then the tip of his tongue.

EAT GOD.

There was a moment as the substance soaked into his bloodstream, a moment of stillness. The patchworks let go of him, and his arms fell at his sides. Naima pushed through the crowd and stopped in front of him; she looked crushed when she saw the black foam on his lips.

Tears ran down her cheeks. "Don't go. Oh please, don't leave me alone here."

Father Obregón smiled. Just as he was about to say something, the moment of stillness

ended

and everything made sense.

Father Obregón's mind felt as if it had burst. Light poured in from every direction, swirling with color and sweet fragrance. Geometric patterns appeared and shifted before his mind's eye, dancing like the patterns in a kaleidoscope.

Or the patterns on the yeast lakes of Benares.

He felt his mind changing shape, flowing between forms in a dizzying rush of transformations. He melted from a spinning disk to a rippling lavender veil, from a pink beachball to an upside-down pyramid of violet neon light.

Every shape just like the lifeforms he'd seen on Benares.

Waves of textures washed over him, clinging and combining in electric layers of high relief. There was roughness, grittiness, laciness, puffiness, fluffiness, spikiness, foaminess. One after another, from firm smoothness to crystalline latticework.

Just like the multitude of fungal flora thriving on Benares.

All these sensations blossomed and swirled together in his mind, crackling with invisible fire that he felt and saw and swallowed. Structures and instincts from the largest to the most extreme subatomic pulsed and sang within and without him.

And all the while, even as his mind opened and transformed and filled to overflowing, he felt lighter than air. He felt better than he ever had, completely new from tip to toe, from gut to soul.

For an instant, he thought he had died, but then the thoughts of the patchworks, which once had seemed like gibberish, suddenly came into focus. Conveying the truth in a wordless intention, a heartfelt expression.

He has eaten and survived.

He had tasted their god, the collective essence of their world, and not died in doing so. Chalk it up to the splicer physiology of the genetically-enhanced super-chaplain.

The black foam had tuned him in to the psychedelic glory of the life force of Benares. It had expanded his consciousness to encompass the total majesty of the world that had always fascinated him.

And it had done one more thing to him, too.

Father Obregón pulled his hoversled into a misty cove in the heart of a jungle of enokitake. The slender stems of the tall white mushrooms flickered in the breeze, spherical caps bobbing in the morning light from the sun-blooms.

A week had passed since he'd first eaten the black foam, and he was back on the road again. He was making his rounds again, traversing the wilderness, ministering to believers around the world.

The congregation was different, but the work was the same in the end.

As he popped the cockpit canopy, a call buzzed for attention in his head. He picked it up with a smile. "Good morning, Naima."

"Good morning." Naima, as usual these days, didn't sound happy. She was back at the lab, where she'd been working since the patchworks had evacuated. They'd left her alive and intact at

Father Obregón's request after he'd eaten their black foam sacrament. "Where are you this time?"

"Prayer meeting up north." Father Obregón stepped out of the hoversled, his feet sinking in a soft carpet of dewy gray-green mildew. "It's good to hear your voice, Naima."

Naima sent him a thought that was the mental equivalent of clearing her throat. She didn't approve of the new direction his work had taken. She didn't approve of his new calling. "You need to come home, Gavín."

"Not yet, Naima." Father Obregón padded through the mildew carpet toward a cluster of buried lumps in the middle of the cove. "I've got work to do."

"It's not safe, Gavín," said Naima.

Father Obregón chuckled. "God's work is *never* safe."

Naima sighed. "What if the foam kills you? It's *fatal* to non-splicers. What if you're only *temporarily* immune?"

Father Obregón knelt among the buried lumps and began brushing away layers of mildew and soil from one of the biggest, the size of a basketball. "Naima, please..."

Naima's voice rose in anger and desperation. "You're under the influence of a highly concentrated mind-altering *drug* controlled by a malignant sentient *fungus* that has *killed* everyone else who tried it! How the hell can you be out there *working* for it?"

"It didn't *intend* to kill them, Naima," said Father Obregón. "It wanted the same thing *they* did. To give the settlers the ultimate mind-expanding experience. To help them get closer to *God.*"

"The god of *fungus,*" snapped Naima. "The god of *monsters.*"

Father Obregón felt sorry for her. He loved her as he loved all his flock, but he knew she would never understand. One taste of the black foam was all he'd needed to connect with his new world-wide congregation. One taste, and he'd been able to move on to important new work after the human settlers had died out.

"Can I talk to you later?" Father Obregón finished clearing the largest lump--a giant truffle, the hub of a complex underground network of them. "I'm a little busy just now."

"You've got to listen to me, Imam!" Naima's thoughts burned

with wild urgency. "I think I can reverse the effects of the compound! I'm working on a seratonin inhibitor right now..."

Just then, something buzzed in Father Obregón's head, and he smiled. "Naima? I don't have time to talk about this now." Softly, he ran his fingers over the rough scalp of the giant truffle, which was the source of the new buzzing in his mind.

The truffle was signaling for his attention, reaching out to link him with its network. Dozens of other signals were racked up in the queue behind it, clamoring for attention. There were *always* umpteen signals in the queue these days, ever since the black foam, signals from fungal lifeforms all over Benares. Signals from buried truffles and towering toadstools alike, from giant portabellas to microscopic penicillium, from spinning pizza shell flyers to hulking eight-legged shaggy behemoths the size of elephants.

The switchboard in his head was back in business. Father Obregón would never be lonely again. His second chance with Naima might never come to fruition, but his love for his new congregation had to take first place in his heart. Naima might need him, but *they* needed him more. She might love him, but *they* loved him more.

His beloved flock.

"I have another call coming in, Naima," he said. "I'll have to put you on hold."

"Father, wait!" she said, just before he hung up on her.

Then, smiling, he lifted the hem of his black shirt, peeled back a flap of skin just below his bottom right rib, and drew out the fresh-baked communion host from the cavity there, still warm from his flesh.

And he spread that host, the precious black foam, on the tongue of the giant truffle. "The soul of Benares, given up for you," he said. "Amen."

WHEN WE GET DONE WITH MR. GIRAFFE

When my plane touched down in Rome this morning, my assistant, Hogshead, said the same thing he'd said the last 45 days in a row: *The hunt continues, m'lud. Do you think you'll finally catch them here?* And I told him the same thing I've always told him: *It will all come out in the wash, faithful Hogshead. It will all come out in the wash.*

I've become quite philosophical these days, after all the travel and disappointments…all the wild goose chases in pursuit of my obsessively exclusive nemeses, the Super-Selective Revenge Squad. *Que sera, sera*, I say—whatever will be, will be. Because I have hope that one day soon, we will run the Revenge Squad to ground. And then *I* will take *my* revenge against them in ways even those depraved maniacs cannot imagine.

Mr. Giraffe…Butterscotch…The Corsage…Doctor Diagonal…Headrush…and Jack Squat. This horde of super-powered fiends have dedicated their lives to taking me down one way or the other. But they went too far when they got my favorite TV show cancelled. To me, life without *Boil Water Notice* is like life without chocolate or dreams. They've left me no choice but to chase them to the ends of the Earth.

Fortunately, Hogshead is a valet of many talents. This time, he assured me, he had an indisputable lead on the Revengers, owing to Jack Squat making a public nuisance of himself by urinating in the Trevi Fountain. Mr. Giraffe didn't help matters when he took a busload of tourists hostage at the Circus Maximus, demanding to see the ringmaster, clowns, and elephants…not realizing it wasn't *that* kind of circus.

So now here we go, charging into the Roman night with every kind of tracking device known to man and beast. Ready at a second's notice to deploy my extra-awesome arsenal of built-in super-powers. I plan to soften them up with my *nuclear hangnail* and *flab folds of fury*…then trot out blistering *fungus vision* and the *pièce de résistance*: *contagious indigestion*. And don't forget transmissible *senior moments* straight from the fermented brain of El Demento, which proves a super-villain can sometimes be helpful, cooperating from behind bars with her lifelong archenemy (yours truly) in pursuit of parole-related considerations.

As Hogshead and I scour the streets of Rome for our quarries, locals whiz past us on scooters and jeer like chimps in a jungle. Hogshead fires dog piles at them from a paintball gun and howls like a banshee when they connect. We sing our battle song as we jog toward the ultimate showdown at St. Peter's in the Vatican: it sounds like "Mary Had a Little Lamb" set to balls-to-the-wall death metal. The words are all about how we're going to punish the crap out of Mr. Giraffe, Jack Squat, and the other Revenge Squadders, leaving them as little more than disfigured vegetables crawling through the teeming Roman gutters.

If only we could *find* the scoundrels. They aren't at St. Peter's after all, or anywhere else in the Vatican or Rome, for that matter. So, eventually, we call it a night. We eat a fabulous meal at a Michelin three-star restaurant, sleep in a five-star luxury hotel… and in the morning set out for our next destination. According to Hogshead, who as always is a master of picking up the trail, a Twitter post by Doctor Diagonal places him and Butterscotch on safari in Botswana, of all places. *Laughing at us while observing prides of lions.* How fitting; we shall hunt down the bastards like the very beasts they observe.

So now we know what our next stop shall be. As I perform my

morning calisthenics, Hogshead packs our bags and lays in supplies for the journey. I ask him, rhetorically, how much longer this exhausting chase can continue. *As long as your money holds out, m'lud,* says Hogshead. And then we're off again into the wild blue yonder, only this time I can practically *feel* Jack Squat's fat neck between my aching fingers. *He is as good as dead, I tell you. As good as dead.*

THE DRAGON WITH THE GIRL TATTOO

It was the middle of the day in the middle of the desert, but the sky was dark with dragons. Thousands of them swooped overhead in a river of wings and gleaming bodies, blotting out the sun as they flowed from horizon to horizon.

Meanwhile, far below, a much smaller dragon wobbled to a bumpy landing and bounded across the sand on foot. Instead of vast, leathery wings, this one had four smaller, diaphanous pinions like those of a dragonfly. Instead of gold, silver, ruby, sapphire, or emerald scales, this one's hide was pale green with dull rust highlights. Instead of breathing fire, she only puffed out the unseen and harmless exhalations of someone in a hurry, panting for breath.

And instead of staring up at the ocean of dragons swarming in the sky, she kept her gaze locked on the group of figures crowded around a body on the desert floor.

Two of them were pygmy dragons like she was--a male and a female. A third dragon, also a male, was spinier, blue-scaled, and three times the size of any of the pygmies.

"Reiki!" The big blue, whose name was Ohm, flicked his tail. "This is it! We found one! We *found* one!"

It was the most excited that Reiki had ever heard Ohm, and

with good reason. Ohm and his friends had been working with her for years, searching for legendary creatures--or cryptids--and this was the first time they'd found anything concrete.

As soon as Reiki stumbled to a stop, Ohm breathed out a tongue of flame to light the scene. The other pygmies leaned in, watching for Reiki's reaction.

Which, at first, was puzzled. The form on the sand was bipedal--two arms and two legs--but it was covered in some kind of baggy white skin. Its back was distended by a humplike protrusion with faintly squared edges. The head was a kind of bubble or shell with a white back and mirror-surfaced visor.

At least, that was what Reiki thought until Ohm reached out with a clawed toe and tapped a node on the side of the head. The mirrored visor slid up, revealing a second, clear surface underneath, through which she finally saw the true head of the specimen. The bubble, she realized, was a helmet.

"*By Ouroboros!*" She could not believe her eyes. The thing she had searched for all her life was in front of her. The thing that had inspired her to become a cryptozoologist, seeking out legendary species around the globe, was curled up on the sand like a baby dragon in its egg.

Leaning closer and peering through the helmet's clear surface, she saw that the creature's flesh was pink and without scales. It had a short mane attached to the top of its head, black in color. Its eyes were bright green and wide open, yet without awareness.

She recognized it instantly from the legends, drawings, and lore. "Human!"

"It was found here, just like this?" asked Reiki as she bent over the body in the sand.

"Correct." The other female pygmy dragon, bright yellow Lizt, huffed out two puffs of smoke--the dragon equivalent of a nod. "Found three hours ago by some kids hunting jackalope."

"But nobody knows how the body got here," said the violet-hued male pygmy--Kio, by name.

"Not even them?" Reiki pointed a single claw up at the swarm of dragons in the sky.

Everyone looked up at once. A collective shiver went through the group, and rightly so. The presence of the Procession was always quick to raise a shiver or worse from any of the millions of dragons populating the world. Where the Procession flew, the *Culling* was not far behind.

And no one outside the Procession knew when and where that murderous event would begin.

"I don't think there's any way to reach them, once they take flight," said Ohm.

"Damn," said Reiki. "So tell me what clues we've found so far on our own."

"Three concentric circles of scorched sand around the dump site." Ohm gestured with his stunted foreclaws, pointing out the circles. "They weren't left by dragon flame, which would have turned the sand to glass."

"What else?" asked Reiki.

"Some kind of fine, glittering dust on the suit," said Kio. "We're collecting samples, of course."

"Anything else?"

"Not yet," said Lizt.

Bending over, Reiki tipped her long, green snout close to the body and inhaled deeply. Her olfactory sense, like that of many dragons, was very strong.

"Well?" Ohm's tail switched impatiently.

"Incredible." Reiki's big, crimson eyes narrowed as she tried to sort out the mix of unusual scents. "I've never smelled anything *like* this. *None* of it is *remotely* familiar."

"The human's *fur* is the wrong color, too," said Lizt.

Reiki frowned. "Huh?"

"The human on the ground has *black* fur," said Lizt. "Unlike the human on your *belly."*

Reiki looked down at the figure tattooed in gold ink on her rust-colored abdomen--a human form with pale hair and arms and legs outspread. She'd had it inked into her hide years ago, as if anyone needed more obvious proof of her obsession.

"I guess I'll have to update the tattoo," said Reiki.

Lizt and Kio laughed, which among dragons consisted of high-pitched whistling and tail switching.

"For now, let's finish collecting samples and haul this human out of here." Reiki glanced up at the passing Procession. "Before anyone tries to ruin this for us."

Dr. Feng slithered his long, sinuous body around the obsidian table in the center of his cavernous lab. He couldn't take his multifaceted amber eyes off the human that lay there, stripped of its white clothing and bubble helmet. He hadn't let it out of his sight since Reiki and her team had brought it to him for examination, racing from the desert to the nearby mountain city of Yuga.

"Fascinating." Feng bobbed his head up and down, the golden tendrils of his vast mustache tickling the table and floor. "And much *smaller* than I expected, based on the ancient oral lore."

"Maybe the lore was wrong." Reiki was just as mesmerized by the sight of the unclothed human under the bright light of the luminescent lichens stuck to the ceiling.

"Either way, this is *history* in the making." Feng's bright red body, with its elaborate gold markings, twined once more around the table, brushing along its glossy black edge.

Stopping, Feng reared up above the human's lower body. Extending one silver scimitar claw, he tapped the creature's foot and listened, then moved up along the length of its leg, doing the same again and again.

As always, Reiki was mystified by his techniques, though she could never argue with his results. Feng was a born healer, and one of the best. He might have been the product of an ultra-refined breeding program (like all professionals in dragon society), but he'd learned great skills from some of the best healers in the world.

Not to mention, he indulged her crazy theories. It would have been easy to dismiss her as a crank--especially after what had happened with her *last* big find--but he never did. He was a well-respected dragon at a major healing center, and he never, ever mocked her.

Unlike most of the *rest* of the world, which ridiculed her not only for past mistakes, but for her lowly social status as a non-fire-breathing pygmy.

"You won't damage him too much, I hope," she said. "We need the body intact to present to the public."

Irritated, Feng stamped twelve of his twenty-four feet. "I thought you wanted an *autopsy* to determine place of origin and cause of death."

"Not *too* invasive, though," said Reiki. "No one will believe what we *have* if it's hacked to *pieces*."

"True. You face an uphill battle as it is."

"So tell me what you've found so far," said Reiki.

"I think she died of asphyxiation, though I can't be sure at this point. I believe the tank attached to her suit was designed to carry breathable air, and it was empty. Her skin isn't naturally blue, either. In my opinion, the bluish tint is from lack of oxygen."

"Wait." Reiki's red eyes widened. "You said 'she.'"

"Because of the presence of female reproductive organs, yes," said Feng. "And mammary glands, similar to those of the sasquatch, loup garou, and other warm-blooded wildlife."

"A female." Reiki gazed with wonder at the face of the human. "What else?"

"Many unfamiliar scents, as you've pointed out. And *tastes*." Feng's forked red tongue emerged and flickered over the skin of the human's hand. "The best lead we have is the dust on the suit, though."

"What about it?"

"The flavor--the *composition*--is very similar to that of certain meteors recovered elsewhere."

"You're trying to tell me she's...what?" Reiki pointed upward. "From *space?*"

Feng let out two puffs of smoke in a nod. "I believe the suit was meant for *survival* out there, somehow. Though I couldn't *begin* to tell you how that's even possible."

"'Any dragon who flies beyond the sky is doomed to die,'" said Reiki, quoting scripture. "Just like the Flock Resplendent."

"Who became the stars in the dark." Feng stared solemnly at the body on the slab. "Everyone knows that."

Reiki walked over to the stone counter where the human's garments were spread and ran a claw over a brightly-colored patch on the white survival suit. The patch showed an image of a white object with wings and a stubby snout, suspended among stars in the black void of space.

"Do they?" she said thoughtfully. "Do they *really* know that?"

When Reiki left the lab, her friends were waiting outside, gazing up at the Procession.

"They're getting closer," said Ohm. "They've dropped a good bit since the last time they flew over."

"The Lowering has begun, for sure," said Kio. "Which means the Culling can't be far behind."

"I guess we're on a tight schedule, then," said Lizt. "In case they decide to cull *here* or wherever we're going to be *next*."

"That would be our luck." Kio pawed the glassy ground. "We finally find a *human*, and the Procession *destroys* the *proof.*"

"But at least we don't have any more *war,*" Ohm said sarcastically.

Reiki scowled up at the passing behemoths. Ending the destructive wars that had almost wiped out the dragons centuries ago was the reason for the Culling. Razing one nation every five years without mercy or explanation somehow quelled the desire for all-out, extinction-level war. It kept the more violent elements of dragondom in line, as the criteria for annihilation remained mysterious.

It also threw a dark blanket over dragon civilization in the bargain, it seemed to Reiki and many like her. Which was one of the reasons she cared so much for the humans of legend. In the stories, humans had always been more peace-loving and enlightened, the opposite of the mostly warlike and closed-minded dragons.

"So what did Dr. Feng come up with?" asked Ohm.

"He thinks the dust is from space," said Reiki. "And the suit might have been made for space survival."

"You're *culling* me!" said Kio. "*Space?* As in *night-sky, Flock-Resplendent-slaughtering darkness?"*

Lizt raised and flattened the spines along her back, a dragon sigh. "The Flock is an old myth."

"If Feng says *space*, there must be something to it," said Ohm. "So what's our next move?"

"I wonder if there were other meteor strikes last night, in about the same time frame. What if that human isn't the *only* thing that came down?"

"Good question." Lizt gave her yellow tail a flick. "We need to look into it."

"With the Procession underway, it shouldn't be hard finding folks who've been watching the skies," said Kio.

"I'll make the call." Tilting his head back, Ohm aimed his snout in the air and let out a shrill, ululating cry, so ear-splittingly loud it would travel for miles. Other criers would answer or relay the message through the complex, worldwide network of the Knell.

"Great, thanks," said Reiki. "And while you're doing that, there's something I need to take care of."

Taking to the air on her own, Reiki flew across town to her next destination. In the process, she got to take in an aerial view of Yuga, her hometown--and, still, the location of her family.

Yuga looked like a mountain range of gleaming obsidian and metal, a vast rank of shimmering black and silver peaks marching into the distance. All of it had been fused and forged and formed by the fiery breath of giant dragons, raised from an empty plain into cavernous homes in which the beasts could find shelter.

Even so, it wasn't a place of safety for *every*one. Though Reiki had grown up there, her life within its bounds had been anything but sheltered.

As she fluttered over it now, she remembered those long-ago days of torment. A pygmy dragon, she'd been ridiculed for her small stature and worse; her inability to breath fire had been the ultimate mark of shame.

It hadn't ended when she'd gotten older and left for what she'd hoped would be friendlier places. Her status as a non-firebreather and pygmy had left her branded by society, forbidden from mating lest her corrupt traits contaminate the gene pool.

So it was only natural that she'd looked elsewhere than dragons for a role model, that she'd embraced the legends of humanity.

But her family had never understood the attraction...or *her*, for that matter. They'd stayed in Yuga and left her to her own devices. That had mostly been enough, bringing her a measure of recognition, plus the small team of friends and supporters who worked with her on the hunt for cryptids.

Still, she never gave up hope that her family might someday accept her.

Swooping down, she made her usual bumpy landing in front of her family's hangar-like home. "Hello? Is anybody here?"

A moment later, her father's huge, horned head came snaking out on his long neck, coppery scales glinting in the faint sunbeams punching through the gaps in the Procession.

"Reiki," he said dully.

"Humans are real," she told him bluntly. "We found one."

"Not this again." His disappointment was tinged with mockery.

"What's that?" Mother swooped down from whatever errand she'd been running and landed beside Father's head.

"I said we finally *found* one," said Reiki. "A *human."*

"Another *hoax*, no doubt," said Father. "Another wax dummy."

Was he ever going to stop bringing that up? How she'd been so excited by a possible sighting seven years ago that she'd accepted falsified evidence without fully examining it?

"It's not a hoax," Reiki said coldly. "It's been autopsied and verified by a healer."

"Of course it has," said Father.

"Oh, honey." Mother flapped a wing sadly. "Isn't it time you let go and got on with your life?"

"Never." Dreaming of humans was all that had kept Reiki going through the painful years of growing up. Imagining a better world, where cruelty and unpredictable slaughter were not the only way of life, had sustained her.

"We just don't want you to be hurt, dear," said Mother.

Then you shouldn't have let them treat me like garbage just for being a pygmy non-firebreather, thought Reiki.

But what she told them, *showed* them, was very different. She shook her head, ruffled her neck frill, thrashed her tail, flickered her tongue, and snorted loudly, all at the same time.

In the language of dragons, it was the expression for an emotion unique to their species, which is impossible to explain succinctly. Its meaning has been said to encompass, to some degree, the following concepts:

- That which does not burn or perish
- That which grows more impossible the more you reach for it
- The joy and sorrow of reaching with limitless desire yet never obtaining

Seeing it expressed so blatantly in front of them left Reiki's father and mother stupefied for once. It had been as if she'd just told them the deepest truth and the greatest insult at the same time.

Then she flew away to return to her team and the important work ahead.

"There's the meeting spot!" Ohm shouted over the wind of his flight. "Coming in for a landing, you guys!"

The big blue dragon angled down from the heights, heading for the sandy beach below. Reiki, Lizt, and Kio clung to his back, on which they'd ridden all the way from Yuga. As pygmies with smaller wingspans, the trip would have taken much longer if they'd flown on their own.

"I don't see anyone there yet," said Reiki.

"We're a little early," shouted Ohm. "But this is definitely the place we agreed to over the Knell."

The sapphire ocean glittered in the sunlight as they plunged toward the shore. Since the Procession was elsewhere, and it wasn't a cloudy day, there was actual *sunlight* on the landscape for a change.

"I can't wait to see what they have," said Reiki.

Ohm banked and spiraled, approaching the surf. "All I know is, it fell from a high altitude in the same general time frame as the human."

"And it's not a natural object, you said. Not a meteor." Reiki got more excited every time she thought about it. The coast was hundreds of miles from where they'd found the human, but she thought it was possible that different falling bodies moving at different trajectories might have started at the same source and still come down that far apart.

No sooner did Ohm's claws touch the beach than the water out beyond the breaking waves began to ripple and swirl. Reiki, Lizt, and Kio scrambled down off their courier's back and huddled beside him, eyes glued to the churning sea.

As they watched, two huge, green humps pushed up from the surface, each bigger than all four of the visitors put together. Seawater gushed from both of them as they slowly rose and opened, revealing enormous golden eyes with diamond-shaped pupils underneath.

The open eyes kept rising, giving way to a gigantic head and snout. Even as the monstrous snout cleared the surface, gouts of steam wafted from its giant nostrils.

"Hey there!" Ohm flew closer, putting down in the foamy edge of the surf. "Thanks for coming, Urmur!"

When the sea dragon spoke, its thunderous voice shook the

ground. "I HAVE BROUGHT WHAT YOU SEEK. THAT WHICH FELL FROM THE SKY LAST NIGHT."

"We can't thank you enough, mighty Urmur!" said Ohm.

Ponderously, Urmur raised his head further from the surface of the water on his seemingly endless emerald neck. "IS THAT HER?" He pointed his snout at the pygmies on the sand behind Ohm.

"The driving force of our quest, yes!" Ohm looked back at Reiki and bobbed his head, summoning her forward. "Her name is Reiki."

"REIKI." Urmur's head swayed atop his beanstalk of a neck. "YOU HAVE TRULY FOUND A *HUMAN*?"

Nervously, Reiki fluttered over to join Ohm. "We have!"

"AND THE OBJECT I POSSESS? YOU THINK IT WAS *MADE* BY A HUMAN?"

"There's only one way to find out," said Reiki.

"THEN LET'S FIND OUT!"

Suddenly, Urmur's head plunged from its height, stabbing toward her at a fantastic rate of speed. Before Reiki or anyone else could react, the great beast's open jaws had engulfed her.

Reiki bounced and rolled in the wet darkness as Urmur lurched away with his mouthful. His slimy tongue flung her from side to side, whacking her against the solid bars of his teeth.

Crying out, she tried to hold on, but everything she grabbed was too slippery. She spun around in the slop of the beast's saliva, turned end over end by the twisting and jostling of his mouth parts.

Then, without warning, the whole thing shot downward, flinging her against what she thought must be the bony ridges of the palette. A great exhalation of wind blew past her, knocking her around like a leaf.

Then seawater flooded the space, pushing out every last draft of air. Reiki floated through it, completely submerged, so taken by surprise that she hadn't thought to capture one last breath.

But it didn't matter. Being a non-*firebreather* meant she was a non-*breather*, as well. Though breathing was a reflex for her under normal circumstances, she could do without it indefinitely if she needed.

As she bobbed around in the water, a reddish glow appeared from Urmur's throat, the start of a fire. Even submerged, the great sea dragon could conjure a charge of flame as he liked.

By the glow of Urmur's furnace, Reiki saw something small and white lodged between two huge teeth. Swimming over to it, she grabbed the rectangular object with both hands, braced her feet against the teeth, and tugged.

It took her three tries to pull the object free. As soon as she had it, a great, bubbling moan of relief roiled up from Urmur's throat, throwing the water in his mouth into a frenzy of agitation.

Sensing what was to come, Reiki hugged the object against her chest with both arms and rolled into a ball around it. No sooner had she braced herself than the mouthful of water was ejected from Urmur's mouth with a powerful force, taking her with it.

"Please tell me you didn't know I was going to get gulped," Reiki growled as Ohm picked her up from the water and flew her back ashore.

"He did mention a *toothache*," said Ohm.

When he put her down on the beach, Reiki held up the white object. "You're just lucky he didn't spit me out empty-handed."

"What'd you get? What is it?" Lizt ran toward her with Kio close behind.

Reiki took a good look at the object for the first time. It was rectangular and about twice the size of her hand. Its shell was hard and smooth to the touch, formed from some kind of white material that reminded her of the back of the human's helmet.

And that wasn't the *only* thing that reminded her of the human.

"*By Ouroboros!*" Lizt pointed a claw at the colorful emblem on one of the flat sides of the object. "Do you *see* what that *is?*"

Reiki felt a swell of excitement. The circular insignia showed an image of a white object with wings and a stubby snout, suspended among stars in the black void of space.

"It's the same artwork that was on the human's garment," she said. "The two are *connected*."

"And what's this?" With the tip of a claw, Kio flicked a switch on the object's edge.

It took all Reiki could do not to drop the object as it came to life in her hands. One flat side lit up, showing a square screen with a familiar, map-like image.

"That's the coast." She ran her claw along a crooked line that stitched across the square screen from top to bottom. "This must be us." She tapped a solid dot of white light near the bottom of the line, then tapped another white dot, blinking fast and moving, near the top. The mechanism made a pinging noise in time with the blinks. "And *that...*"

"...is something we need to find *now,*" said Ohm.

Again, Ohm took to the sky, carrying Reiki, Lizt, and Kio on his back. What exactly they were heading for, they didn't know, but they all agreed that they were going in the right direction.

That the object was a tracker of some kind became more certain as they covered more ground. The dot that seemed to represent the object itself moved further north along the image of the coastline as they flew in that direction.

For a while, the other dot--the blinking one at the top of the screen--moved northward, too, maintaining the gap between them. When they'd been in the air for a while, though, the target dot grew still.

"Why did it stop?" asked Lizt.

"Your guess is as good as mine," said Reiki.

But as they continued on course and got closer, she finally understood.

Ohm and the group soared into a dense cloud bank, blind to the view ahead for several moments. When they emerged in open sky on the other side, they saw something astonishing and immediately recognizable in the distance.

"*Jörmungandr's scales!*" hissed Reiki. "I should have known!"

The skies ahead were swirling with darkness--thousands of full-grown dragons flying in a tightly-packed, ever-moving disk. The Procession was over; all the dragons who'd spent days hurtling over places near and far, keeping the world guessing about their intentions, had assembled here for their dreaded last act--the Culling.

And Ohm and the others were charging straight for it.

As Ohm raced forward, Reiki shivered against his scales. She knew what was coming next.

The dragons of the Procession would circle for a while, gathering their energy. Then, at a moment of their choosing, they would unleash all their awful destructive power on the land and its inhabitants below. When they were done, the earth would be scorched beyond recognition, as would anyone or anything that got in the way.

Still, the target dot on the tracker blinked faster, and the pinging sound accelerated. Whatever the device was leading them to, it didn't seem to be far away.

"Should we keep going?" Ohm sounded tense but not afraid. "Hope we get in and out before the fireworks start?"

"We could wait until they're done," offered Lizt.

"But whatever we're after could be lost, damaged, or destroyed in the Culling," said Kio.

Suddenly, the pinging of the tracker became a steady, shrill tone, and the target dot changed from white light to red.

"I'd say we're homing in!" said Lizt.

It was then that Reiki made up her mind. "Keep going! Fast as you can!"

"You got it!" Ohm flapped his wings harder, picking up speed.

The closer Ohm got to the circling dragons, the bumpier the flight became. There were so many of them in such concentration that their passage whipped up powerful air currents.

Desperate not to fall off or drop the tracker, Reiki clamped her legs harder around Ohm's sides and gripped his frill as tight as she could with her free hand. Even at that, the turbulence got so bad that she feared she might be bucked from his back.

Then there was the matter of the disappearing signal. As Ohm flew to the brink of the cyclone of dragons, the tracker's steady tone cut out, and the red light of the target went dark.

"In the name of Quetzalcoatl!" yelled Reiki. "We lost it!"

"Don't worry!" said Ohm. "It must've moved out of range! They're moving so fast, it'll come back around before you know it!"

Just then, one passing dragon was bumped by another and slipped out of formation. As it struggled to right itself, its lashing tail hurtled straight toward Ohm.

Reacting quickly, Ohm banked away from the tail, avoiding an impact, but the wind of its passing kicked him hard enough to throw two of his passengers.

Only Reiki managed to stay aboard, and just barely at that. Looking down as Ohm steadied, she saw Kio and Lizt plunge a long way down before catching the currents with their wings and jetting away from the dark lands below the circling storm.

"Keep going or turn back?" shouted Ohm.

As he said it, the device started pinging again, and the target dot lit up with blinking white light.

"Keep going! Stay with the flow!"

As soon as the pinging became a steady tone and the target dot turned red, Reiki zeroed in on the nearest dragon--a massive beast, easily five times the size of Ohm, with a night-black hide bristling with sharp spines.

"That one!" She spurred Ohm with her heels. "Come up alongside him!"

Ohm had to work overtime to match speed with the passing dragon. Looking over at the leviathan, Reiki quickly spotted a likely object--white, smooth, and out of place, hanging from a spine along the dorsal fin spanning the beast's back. The object must have fallen from above and gotten caught on the great dragon's fin.

Unfortunately, if Reiki wanted it, she would have to go get it.

"Get as close as you can to the back-fin!" she shouted.

Ohm swooped over, navigating between the flaps of the bigger dragon's enormous, leathery wings.

When they were close, Reiki leaped off Ohm and fluttered over to the beast, which seemed as oblivious to their presence as the rest of the Procession did. Without letting go of the tracker, she landed at the base of the dorsal fin, just below where the object hung.

Fluttering up, she grabbed the object--a smooth white hoop the size of a cow's head--and worked it up the spine, dislodging it from the tarpaulin-like webbing of the fin.

But just as she freed the object and turned to go, the great dragon let out a roar and belched a great gout of fire toward the ground below.

So did every other dragon in the vast, whirling formation, all at once.

Searing blasts of flame poured down in their thousands, blanketing the landscape. Towns and cities melted under the onslaught; dragons, livestock, and wildlife roasted alive.

Reiki gazed down in horror at the billowing sea of fire. The heat of it surged back to her in pummeling waves that bowled her over, pitching her away from the beast who had given up the hoop.

Tumbling through the air, Reiki fluttered frantically against the superheated currents. Her erratic flight sent her spinning helplessly toward another dragon that was passing nearby.

That dragon, a real colossus, thrashed its long tail, snagging one of Reiki's wings on its barbed tip. When Reiki's struggle to free herself got the mighty creature's attention, it paused in pouring out flame and craned its neck around to see her dangling there.

"No! Please!" screamed Reiki, though she doubted the giant beast could hear her over the roar of the flames.

The dragon glared in annoyance and cranked open its terrible maw. Reiki could see the flare of fire boiling up from inside, getting ready to fry her to a crisp.

Then, seemingly out of nowhere, Ohm dove toward them and hurtled into the behemoth's maw, belching out his own stream of fire. The blazing injection pumped into the bigger creature's inner furnace, overloading it.

That furnace exploded, blasting both the giant and Ohm to fiery bits. Reiki was hurled free, somersaulting over the Culling like a dandelion puff.

But the airborne carnage didn't stop there. The other dragons were so close in their whirling formation that the blast touched off a chain reaction. One beast after another collided with its neighbors, erupting in quick succession until the entire disk was consumed.

The combined power of the blasts propelled Reiki upward, sending her rocketing through the sky at an incredible velocity. The world held on to her with crushing force, even as she climbed, and she finally shut down, mercifully blacking out from the pain of her swift ascent.

When Reiki woke, the crushing pain was gone. For the first time in her life, she floated weightlessly, without restraint.

Her eyes fluttered open to a startling view: countless glittering points of light in a tapestry of infinite darkness.

She tried to gasp, but there wasn't any air. It was a good thing, then, as a non-firebreather, that she didn't need to breathe.

It was icy cold, too, but somehow, that didn't bother her. There was also an internal imbalance, as if her guts were pressing against her hide from the inside--but that wasn't really a problem, either. Whatever her unique physiology, it was keeping her intact and alive.

None of which made sense, if she was where she *thought* she might be.

Testing her theory, she turned slowly, looking over her shoulder. The world she'd always known lay behind her, its blues and greens and browns and whites standing out in bright relief in the light of the sun.

Space. The explosion of the Culling had launched her into *space.*

And she was *alive.* The ancient stories of the Flock Resplendent, the ones that claimed, "Any dragon who flies beyond the sky is doomed to die," had not been correct, after all.

So far, at least. Or perhaps just for her, or those like her. And the *human*, of course.

The thought of the human sent a ripple of panic through Reiki, as she realized she no longer held the human-related objects. Somehow, in her flight from the world, they must have been torn from her grip.

Thankfully, that must not have happened until she'd made it into space. As she turned in a circle, she saw them both floating not too far away.

Uncertain how to go after the objects, she instinctively spread her wings...and was surprised at how different they felt. Somehow, they seemed stronger, each gossamer panel tingling with a new sensitivity to the heat of the sun. When she chose a direction and willed herself to move, she was able to catch the flow of sunlight and ride it like a gust of wind, letting it carry her to the objects.

When she reached the tracker and hoop, she gathered them up and examined them. Now that she had a chance to look closely, she realized they fit together. There were indentations along the inner edge of the hoop for each of the four corners of the tracker.

When she snapped them together, both objects glowed and vibrated in her grip. A section of the outer rim of the hoop sprouted seven silver antennae.

Reiki pointed those gleaming silver filaments away from the world, and a new image flickered to life on the screen of the tracker: a field of twinkling stars against a background of darkness. At the bottom of the screen was a steady dot of white light that could only be the device's location. At the top of the screen was something else--another light, blinking in the distance, mysterious and summoning.

Was it something human? Some*place* human? Or something else altogether?

At least Reiki had hope that it might be something better than the dismal world behind her, the hard world, ruled by the strong and rapacious, that had never wanted her because of who she was or what she believed.

Given the choice, she turned her back on that world without a second thought. She regretted only that Ohm, who had sacrificed everything to set her free, could not be with her now.

Reiki flapped her wings, so diaphanous and beautiful in the light of the sun, and rode the tide into the glittering darkness ahead.

As she set out on her journey, she couldn't resist one last head shake/frill ruffle/tail thrash/tongue flicker/snort (silent) to express that complex emotion exclusive to dragons...*some* dragons, that is. The emotion that would perhaps be understandable to humans, at least in part, as:

- That which does not burn or perish
- That which grows more impossible the more you reach for it
- The joy and sorrow of reaching with limitless desire yet never obtaining

Then she added a new twist--a wriggle of her belly with the human tattoo, as if to say *yes,* I *am now a human, too.* And the beating of her wings as she rode the solar wind into the endless, glorious night added yet another nuance, though there might never be another dragon who experienced that marvelous, unnamable feeling in exactly the same way that she did that day.

THE MEN WITHOUT HEADS JOIN A HEALTH CLUB

This might just be the most exciting day of my life! That's *exactly* what I tell the cute redheaded salamander girl at the health club's gleaming silver counter when first she turns her attention my way. And I mean what I say, with every fiber of my skintight purple singlet (the perfect workout suit for a headless man, with a big round cutout for the face on my chest and belly).

Gazing with my nipple-eyes through the plate glass wall behind her, I see people working out like there's no tomorrow on every kind of exercise equipment I can imagine. Every kind of person or thing hammers away on everything from treadmills to rowers to barbells to vibrating belt machines, all of it dazzlingly new and highly polished. It's enough to make my hearts flutter like leaves in a hurricane!

I can't stop grinning with the mouth in my bare belly. "I've read that joining a health club can solve all your prosthetics!" I tell the redheaded salamander girl.

Her bright green eyes sparkle as she looks from me to my brothers--one on either side of me--and back. "Solve all your *problems*, do you mean?" she asks.

"Apologies." Taking a deep breath with the nose in the middle of my chest, I smell loads of sweat and ammonia from the big gym area behind the glass. Very good, very nice, can't *wait* to get in there. "I *meant* to say, solve all your *promontories*, thanks. Now about that membership." I spread my arms wide, taking in my two brothers. Like me, they have no heads. Don't need 'em. "Make it *three*, please. With *everything*."

"Extra onions on *mine*, sweet stuff!" says the brother on my right, rambunctious (and older than I) Rapscallion, in his bright yellow singlet. "But hold the mayo! Or is that mercury?"

"Clam up!" I jab an elbow in his side, then smile with my belly mouth. "You'll have to excommunicate him, ma'am. His manners leave much to be defiled."

"That's all right." The girl has a red ponytail that dances when she moves. Attention: gotten! "Let's get you three signed up so you can get right down to working out."

My other (and younger) brother, Gumfoozler, picks that moment to snap the shoulder straps of his neon orange singlet and spin in a giddy circle at my left. "Oh happy day! I feel as if I could pleasure myself right here and now to mark the moccasin!"

"Ixnay on the easureplay!" I smack him on the low spot between his shoulders where head-equipped folks have a whatchamacallit, noggin. "We ain't here for that kind of *exercise*."

"But you said we have to *pull together* if we want to shape up!" says Gumfoozler.

"Not *that* kind of pulling!" If I had a head, I'd be shaking it right now. "If I didn't know better, I'd *swear* you don't have a *brain* between your *ass cheeks*."

Just then, the redhead clears her throat and pushes three paper forms across the counter at us. "If each of you will just sign one of these, we can get started, Mister...?"

"Mulligatawny." I give a little bow as I say it. "Connecticut Mulligatawny. But *you*..." My left nipple-eye winks at her. "...can call me *Skaneateles*."

She cocks her head to one side. Wish *I* had a head to do that with! "Skaneateles. Has a nice rhythm to it."

You're not the first person to tell me that, is what I want to say...but before I can get the words out, Rapscallion and Gumfoozler grab for the same pen on a chain on the counter, ropy arms crossing in front of me.

"Gimme that!" Gumfoozler jerks the pen toward him.

"Me first!" Rapscallion yanks the pen back. "I outrank you! You said so yourself!"

"No no no! I said you're *ranker* than me!" Gumfoozler pulls the pen his way again. "Whole different thing!"

With a howl of rage, Rapscallion settles the argument, wrenching the pen so hard its chain snaps. His mighty tug also hoists Gumfoozler off his feet, smashing him into the counter.

The whole thing topples backward, coming down on top of the redhead. She cries out as she falls and hits the cement floor, her glossy crimson arms flailing.

My twelve hearts pound with panic like a string of firecrackers going off. Before you (or I) can say, Hey Lady, you okay?, that idiot Rapscallion somehow loses his balance and falls into me, knocking us both on top of Gumfoozler on top of the health club counter.

On top of the redhead.

And then we all freeze...for just a moment before my nincompoop brothers start their wild thrashing to untangle themselves from the us-pile.

"Miss?" My voice is worried. "Miss, are you a flirt? I mean, are you hurt?"

I hear a loud sigh from her head-mouth, somewhere under the heap. "I'll be better when you three no-headers get off me."

Let the thrashing begin! Which in theory ought to end with us three apart and free-standing, but in reality just leads to greater tanglings.

We don't manage to get up and away, in fact, till the staff flamingos strut out of the office and sort us out with their tattooed beaks. And curse us the whole time, by the way.

Then, as a black Labrador dog with a pink carnation for a head trots up to give us our membership cards, I start with the questions again. Is it true what they say about health clubs? When it comes to pick-up places, do they put fist hatcheries and nuclear pow-wow plants to shame?

The dog just spits me my card, drops a dook on the floor, and gives my face a big long lick with a tongue in the middle of his flower, lapping hard from belly-mouth to nipple-eyes.

"Memberships approved!" He wags his tail, which is braided with little white blossoms. "Now go pump some iron! *Woof!*"

"They are moving on, sir!" PFC Emit Dawson never takes his eyes off the instruments on the console in front of him. "The three test subjects are proceeding to the next contact zone."

Across the dark control room, Major Titus Bleak nods with square-jawed, stiff-backed satisfaction. "Perfect." His eyes, like those of most of the uniformed men and women around him, are fixed on a giant video screen at the front of the room. "Body count?"

"Just one, sir," says Dawson. "A female."

"One's enough," says General Cyrus Euclid, a tall, thin figure hovering vulture-like over Bleak's left shoulder. "There's your proof of concept, right?"

Bleak stays focused on the screen. "And the test subjects don't see her as dead? They don't realize they've just killed a human being?"

"Affirmative," says Dawson. "To their eyes, she's alive and well. Same goes for their ears. Her death cries sounded like normal speech to them."

Another of the top brass in the room lets out a loud laugh. "Our workaround *rocks*!" She's 5 foot 3 inches, 300 pounds, and her name is Commander Gwendolyn Volume. "The violence constraint firmware *can* be hacked."

Bleak marches across the floor to the big main screen. Looking up, he sees the red-haired woman sprawled on the floor, dead-eyed and twisted as a broken doll. Beyond her, three mechanical figures clamber onward, their chrome, heart-shaped bodies streaked with bright red human blood.

Bleak wishes he could see the faces on the robots' torsos, as if that might tell him something about their state of mind. But even if they had conventional heads on their shoulders, he's not sure they'd give him more of a clue to their intentions.

Anyway, he'll know soon enough. On the main screen, he can clearly see the three robots are moving toward a crowd of people. That's just as expected.

After all, the robots might think they're in a health club, though they're really in a shopping mall. The view from their eyes is on a smaller screen to the left of the main viewer...and it's like the most surreal gym you could ever imagine, complete with flamingo staffers and flower-headed dogs. Bizarre images and matching audio feeds populate the freakish environment, replacing all visuals and sounds that exist in the real world around them. The robots fumble through it, imagining they are comic buffoons, thinking the worst they can do to the people in their paths is knock them around in the wake of their pratfalls.

But the truth is, military robot prototypes M-1, G-1, and R-1--Mulligatawny, Gumfoozler, and Rapscallion to their mixed-up minds--are on the verge of a designated enemy population center. And they've already proven they can kill, in spite of all hardwired limits imposed by international regulations.

Now the true test of their murderousness is about to begin. The survival of Bleak's homeland, the nation to which he has dedicated his life as a military officer, hinges on the outcome.

"Plenty of people in the vicinity." Bleak points at the crowd flowing through the main walkway ahead of the robots. "No alarms have been raised, obviously."

"Correct," says Dawson. "The first victim was isolated, at an information booth near an entryway in a lightly used corridor. A few witnesses have fled, but the mass of people has not yet been alerted."

"Perfect. Then stir up the simulation," orders Bleak. "Let's give the kids plenty to kill about." He smiles like a stone that's just been used to bash a skull in. "I mean clown around with."

"Hey, look! A medicine ball!" Gumfoozler points at a big white ball in the middle of the gym floor. "I vote we paint a face on it and take turns using it for a head!"

"How 'bout *this* instead, bright boy?" Rapscallion holds up a ping pong ball between his thumb and forefinger. "I think it's more your *size*."

"Pipe down, bitches." Looking around, I can't decide which exercise equipment to try first. It doesn't help that the place is so *crowded*, there's not much that isn't occupied. "This look like a *screamatorium* to you?"

Just then, a seven-foot-tall blue banana wearing a fuzzy pink fez hops over. "I smell newbies!" She's wearing a coach's whistle and an oval sticker with the health club's logo on it, the stylized letters *HC*. "Who wants some *fitness?*"

"I do, I do!" Gumfoozler flaps his arms in the air like checkered flags at a drag race. "I've been dying for a highball all day!"

"Me first!" Rapscallion stomps over and starts taking off his yellow singlet. "Make it so, fruit of the loon!"

"Zip it, bathtub ring. And keep your *clothes* on." I step between my brothers and the banana, spreading a friendly smile like butter across my belly. "This fitness of which you speak. I long to plantain it."

"Plantain it!" The blue banana winks. "I like what you did there with the banana humor, buddy! What'd you say your name was?"

"Mulligatawny," I tell him. "But you can call me Skaneateles."

"Ollie Oxenfree it is," says the banana. "Now get over here and give this thyroid press a try. It'll make you feel like a new duct, no shit."

Just as I'm about to approach the thyroid machine, the medicine ball goes flying overhead (over-headless-shoulders, I should say) and plows into the banana. His blue face smooshes from the impact, and his tip doubles over. He makes a gurgling sound as he flops to the floor, pasty mashed innards squishing through the ruptures in his splitting peel.

"Now look what you did!" shouts Rapscallion. "'Nanner down! 'Nanner down!"

"I was *aiming* at *you*," snaps Gumfoozler. "Can I help it you *dodged*?"

Rapscallion charges past me and grabs the medicine ball, which is dripping with mashed banana goop. "Let's see what *you* do when the shoe's on the other *nutsack.*" With that, he hauls off and whales the heavy ball dead-on at Gumfoozler, grunting like he's taking an Olympic-sized dump as he lets it fly.

Gumfoozler, God love him, doesn't dodge...but he does grab a passing sapling-man and uses him to bat the ball away, sending it flying off-course.

This time, the medicine ball blasts into a class of school-chickens, blowing through them with such force that it takes off their heads. The school-chickens' bodies scamper around, plucking the loose heads up and screwing them back on (not always on the right bodies, hence a red rooster ends up with a white hen's head, etc.). So no harm done.

But it doesn't stop there. This is a *health* club, not a *hell* club, I'm yelling, but the carnage continues unabated. Gumfoozler tosses a dumbbell, missing Rapscallion and knocking over a sixteen-legged impressionist painting of a full toilet bowl (at least I *think* that's what it is). Rapscallion, in turn, chucks a big circular plate off a barbell, coming nowhere near Gumfoozler...instead bowling over a herd of yoga-loving goats with bushy lumberjack beards.

Let me tell you, it's hard to watch. Staff and club members tumble and fly in all directions, impossible to tell one from another. My glorious dream of joining a health club is becoming a full-blown frightmare.

All I can say is, it's a damn good thing nobody gets hurt.

"Body count?" asks Major Bleak.

"Seventeen," says PFC Dawson. "Correction, twenty-one."

"Bravo!" Commander Volume applauds. "Break out the champagne!"

"Twenty-three," says Dawson.

Bleak nods, watching the slaughter continue on the main viewer. As people scream and scatter in all directions, desperate to escape the carnage, the robots make short work of those who lag behind or stumble and fall before them. The R-1 and G-1 prototypes swing children at each other, smashing them to bits like piñatas. The third robot, model M-1 (for Mulligatawny) clambers over and swings his big metal claws at his brothers, only to miss them and crush a nearby elderly human female instead.

"Twenty-six," says Dawson.

Bleak feels a flicker of remorse at the thought of the 26 souls brutally extinguished on his order. And there are more on the way. His team hacked the mall's security systems, ensuring no signals would reach local law enforcement or military personnel who might slow the 'bots' progress. Bleak's people hacked the building's automated access systems, too, closing every exit against the human tide rushing to get out. Hundreds of people were trapped inside at the robots' mercy, caught behind heavy metal blast doors installed, ironically, to protect against enemy attack.

It's a hell of a price, but *any* price is worth paying for the survival of the nation he serves, a nation in desperate need of an equalizer.

"They said it couldn't be done." General Euclid sounds like he's a little turned on. "They said the nonviolence firmware couldn't be tricked. Well, look at us now!"

"Surrealism: the ultimate weapon!" Volume cracks herself up. She might be slapping her knees right now if she could reach them past that humongous girth of hers.

As for Bleak, he smiles grimly. Killer 'bots have been banned on Earth ever since the Robocaust a quarter-century (and a billion dead humans) ago. Immutable ethical governors preventing robot-on-human violence have been baked into every digital mind ever since...but Bleak and his geeks figured out a way around them. Encode an augmented reality filter with surreal surroundings, in which violent acts are imperceptible. Attenuate the robot's personality matrix, inject a logic-scrambling algorithm, upload a dose of slapstick comedy films, and voila! You've got 'bots who don't mind killing because they don't realize they're killing in the first place.

Which means that Bleak's homeland finally has an advantage in the war. Foreign powers with outsized militaries and bleeding edge weapons tech have driven his people to their knees, putting them through wringer after wringer of terrible suffering. Now, at last, it's Bleak's turn to bring down the pain. At the flip of a switch, underground factories will churn out hordes of liberated robots, waiting to be airdropped over enemy population centers just like the one the prototypes are gleefully killing their way through on the viewer.

"I'm making the call." Euclid taps his left temple, activating his neuro-grid phone. "We need to get those tin soldiers rolling off the assembly line ASAP."

"*You'll* get a *medal* for this." Volume walks up to Bleak and throws a heavy arm around his shoulders. "Maybe even a high-level post in the occupation force once we turn the tables and conquer the enemy."

"Wiping them out and scorching the earth inside their borders makes more sense to me," says Euclid. "Those fucking animals deserve to be put down."

Bleak can't argue with him. The enemy has been ruthless in its five-year campaign. He's seen reports of the atrocities they've committed; he's lost loved ones himself in the battle zones and attacks on civilian targets. And he's heard, from intelligence operatives, of the genocidal weapons still waiting to be unleashed from their ungodly arsenals.

Those people are monsters and always have been. The world would be better off without them, thinks Bleak.

Just then, Dawson speaks up. "Body count holding steady at 41. Test subjects switching to nonaggressive postures." Dawson looks up from his instruments. "The posture change was *not* initiated *here*, sir."

Bleak frowns. "Might want to hold off on that call, General."

"Like fuck I will." Euclid snorts as the phone in his head starts ringing. "We've got us a war to win."

"Not if our killer 'bots spontaneously cycle out of attack mode without explanation," says Bleak. "Somebody run me a fucking diagnostic."

"Listen, you dumbskulls!" I get right up in the chest-faces of Rapscallion and Gumfoozler, snapping out my words so spittle sprays in their nipple-eyes. "We are going to get *healthy* if it's the last thing we *do*!"

"I thought that's what we *were* doing," says Gumfoozler. "Tossing around the medicine ball, working the free weights, hitting the machines..."

"Not the way *you* do it," I tell him. "You're not supposed to *destroy* the *equipment* in the process!"

"Who says?" Rapscallion shrugs. "Maybe we've come up with a fresh new workout! A fitness craze in the making!"

"You moron!" I grab the nose on his chest with one hand, then smack it off hard with the other. "How's *that* for a new workout? No pain, no gain!"

Gumfoozler laughs, so I give him a crack, too--a stinging slap that leaves the lips of his belly-mouth quivering. He staggers back, looking as stunned as a bird that just flew into a window at high speed.

"Now enough with the nitwittery." I head for the door of the aerobics studio, waving for my so-called brothers to follow. Maybe we can still be the stars of the gym, *if* we play our cocks right. "Let's wise up and show a little class."

I push through the door, and my brothers file in behind me. Then holy guacamole with a capital Q! It's like we've got a front row seat with a view into exercise Heaven.

We spend a long monument standing there, taking in the bright, shiny studio with a class already in progress. I feel a little winded just from watching it.

Mirrors line the walls of the room, casting the students' reflections back and forth so it looks like there's an infinite number instead of two dozen in there. Music hammers through the place, loud enough to make the mirrors on the walls rattle and shake. The students all bounce to the heavy, pulsing beat of it, led by a Siamese cat-headed instructor clad in pink tights and purple-and-yellow-striped leg warmers.

Rapscallion rubs his hands together and giggles. "Now *this* is my kind of *workout.*"

"Where do they give out the *ants*?" asks Gumfoozler. "Everybody's got 'em in their *pants*, and *I* want some, too!" With that, he starts hopping back and forth, wagging the tongue in his belly and snapping his fingers...but not to the beat. The Big G has never had rhythm a single day in his addlebrained life.

"*Settle*!" I grab him by the shoulder. "This is a *class*, not a *popcorn machine.* It's *organized.* You gotta stay in step with everyone else."

Rapscallion sneers and waves me off. "Stow that poppycock, Cockpoppy! What if *they're* the ones who oughtta stay in step with *us?*"

"By George, he's *on* something! I mean *on to* something." Gumfoozler shakes free of my grip and dances like a drunken stork toward the unwary aerobicizers. "I always *wanted* to lead a big *dance number* in a *movie.*"

"They're on the move again," says Dawson. "Heading for a large cluster of civilians."

"That's more like it," growls Euclid. "We're finally back in the hunt."

"But here's the thing." Dawson looks up from his readouts and meets Bleak's gaze. "They should never have cycled *out* of attack mode in the first place. And they're not responsive to any of our input."

Bleak nods as he finishes skimming the stats scrolling through his corneal implants. "They've jumped the tracks."

"I don't think we can stop them, sir," says Dawson.

"And that's a *bad* thing?" Euclid snorts. "The more of those fucks they kill, the better!"

"Good for today, maybe, but what about tomorrow?" Bleak blinks away the data and focuses on the main viewer, where two of the 'bots are tearing people to shreds with gruesome efficiency. The people are cornered near one of the sealed exits; they shriek and try to flee, but only some of them manage to escape the mechanized death blows and slashes. "Do we really want to turn loose a multitude of killer machines without ethical restrictions *or* any kind of inhibitors or off switches?"

Euclid's expression is icy. "Beggars can't be choosers."

"But what if they exceed their mission parameters and move into neighboring countries?" asks Bleak. "What then?"

"Then we get payback," says Volume. "For all the times we pleaded for help in the war, and those other countries turned their backs on us."

Euclid snorts in agreement. "Fuckheads."

Bleak glares. Euclid and Volume are right, and he knows it.

The situation is dire; his homeland is on its last legs. Better to ignore the flaw and deploy the 'bots without delay, while there's still time. The hell with any innocents caught in the crossfire. Innocents like all his friends and family who died at the hands of the enemy.

He should just forget about trying to rein in the rogue prototypes. So why the hell does he give his next order, then?

"Private Dawson," snaps Bleak. "Initiate remote injection protocols."

"Injection?" asks Dawson. "Injection of what?"

"Me." Bleak swings an arm around to point at the bizarre reality on the left-hand screen, the view through the eyes of the runaway prototype 'bots. "I'm going in there."

I shout at them to come back, to leave the people alone, but I might as well be shouting at plates of spaghetti. Both my brothers are off like rockets into the crowd in the aerobics studio--out-of-control rockets on a crazy-ass spin cycle.

Which one should I go after first? Beats the stuffing out of me. Either brother has an equal promiscuity for mayhem, times a quintillion, plus a google.

I see Gumfoozler knock over a knight in shining salad, blowing her leafy armor apart in all directions. Rapscallion polkas through a gaggle of balloon animals, popping inflatable dachshunds and giraffes in mid-boogie.

The rest of the class keeps jumping as my brothers continue to spread chaos. Rapscallion disco dances into a mummy, spinning away its moldy wrappings until there's nothing left but a skeleton striped like a candy cane clattering to the floor. Gumfoozler slams into an applecart, upturning it so the apples scatter and exercisers trip on them, toppling right and left.

As for me, I launch myself after Gumfoozler first, gritting my teeth in denomination. Before I get close, he scares up a flock of barking pigeons in my path, pushing me back as he hurtles toward a papier-mâché tyrannosaurus.

By now, the disruption's in full swing. The students finally start to run. No matter what I do from here, we're about thirty seconds from a big-ass riot. I can feel it.

So much for my longed-for day of getting in shape at the happiest place on Earth. My insane brothers couldn't be trusted not to poop all over a good thing, the one thing I asked for, then rub the face on my chest and belly in it.

Neither one is much of a brother, I realize, as Rapscallion kicks over a big potted fern with long yellow legs and Gumfoozler hip-checks a shark-headed circus strongman in a leopard-skin singlet and flaming handlebar mustache (literally flaming; it's on fire).

Watching the mayhem, I think this is probably the worst day of my life. I close my nipple-eyes, wishing it would all go away like a bad fart, leaving me in a happier place that makes more sense for a lovable head-free hottie like me.

Then, amid the blaring music and shrieks, I hear an unfamiliar voice. "Mulligatawny? Can you hear me?"

I'm almost afraid to look, but I force myself to winch open my nipple-lids. What I see is something new: a tall man with silver hair and a pulsing golden glow.

"Major Titus Bleak." The man fires off a salute, flicking his flattened hand from his forehead in my direction. "We need to talk."

A winged pig in a yellow tutu hurtles between us, followed by five yapping Chihuahuas on a giant flying cockroach. "Sure, why not?" I tell Bleak. "Now's as good a time as any."

"What's that asshole doing?" Euclid scowls at the viewers. The main screen shows the Mulligatawny prototype staring at what looks like empty space. The other screen, the window into the altered world seen by the 'bots, shows that the empty space is occupied by the glowing figure of Major Bleak.

"Direct intervention, sir," says Dawson. "Face-to-face verbal reboot procedure, since remote redirection has failed."

There's a big glass tube in the middle of the room now, and Euclid storms over and whacks it with the flat of his hand. "*Asshole!*"

The tube bongs like a church bell. Bleak, who stands inside, is bathed in light and only partly there. His physical body might be in the tube, but his mind pilots a digital avatar in the surreal augmented reality overlay.

"Seems like wasted effort to me." Volume circles the tube, then stops in front of Euclid. "The fate of the homeland's at stake. Do we really give Fuck One about whatever collateral damage might happen if those things won't shut off?"

"Body count's already at 237." Dawson's voice is tight, his concern obvious. "Throw in enough of those things, and they could depopulate the entire continent within a week."

"*Fuck* the continent." Euclid taps his left temple. His neurophone rings, and someone picks up. "This is General Euclid. Not only do I want the production line up and running, I want it running at *double time.*"

Volume applauds. "You tell 'im, Cyrus!"

"*Triple* time!" shouts Euclid.

"Wait!" says Dawson. "Shouldn't we see how this works out first?"

"Are you feeling all right, Private?" Volume wags her head slowly. "The things you're saying just don't seem to make any *sense.*"

"Tango alpha X-ray one two Yankee slash zero golf pound seven nine slash dot zulu," says Bleak, the glowing man. "Prototype Mulligatawny, *execute*."

"This is the *talk* you said we needed to have?" I frown. "Doesn't make a *lick* of sense from where *I'm* standing."

Bleak frowns, too, then spouts some more gibberish. "Execute," he says at the end, then stares at me like he expects something special to happen.

Which it doesn't. "You must be speaking a different luggage," I tell him. "We need a transformer so I can understand you."

"A translator," says Bleak. "And no, that isn't the problem." He tries one more time with the babble and ends it the same as always. "Execute."

"I can't do whatever it is you want if I don't know what it is." I start past him, reaching up to pat his shoulder. "Better lunch next time, pudding pop."

Imagine my surprise when my hand goes right through him like he isn't even there! It's enough to stop me in my tracks and make my tighty-whiteys (if I had any) snap right up my butt crack (if I had one).

"What the franks 'n' beans?" I blurt out the words as I scuttle back away from him. "You some kind of *ghost*?"

Bleak shakes his head. "More like...God."

"God? What's god?"

Bleak smiles. "Let's just say I'm in charge around here. I *run* things."

"Someone to blame! Finally!"

"And when something goes wrong, I *fix* it," says Bleak. "Which brings me to my reason for being here."

"Something's wrong?" As I say it, an orange-furred, blood-streaked pogo stick with the head of a donkey *ker-sproings* its way past, coughing up glittering confetti. A giant black bowling ball with a screaming face hurtles after it, knocking it down like a pin and continuing onward, out of control.

Across the aerobics studio, Rapscallion--who must have hurled the ball--hoots and pumps his fists like he's just thrown a strike. Between there and here, a jumbled line of other bowled-over creatures lies broken and twitching.

"Things are getting out of hand," says Bleak.

"My brothers, you mean?"

"Everyone. Everything." Bleak spreads his arms wide. "The whole kit and caboodle."

"Now that you mention it," I tell him, "I could really *go* for a nice plate of caboodle. With *clam sauce*, yeah? And felt-tipped markers?"

Bleak frowns. "I'm not getting through to you, am I?"

"Maybe you'll have more luck with my brothers. Cinch up your garters, kemosabe. Here they come."

Bleak turns just in time to see Gumfoozler and Rapscallion leaping toward him. Little do they know he's the next best thing to thin air.

The two boobs blow right through him...unfortunately for me, because that's right where I'm standing. The three of us crash to the floor in the usual tangled heap, thrashing our way to even greater tangled-upness.

"You nimrods!" My status at this point is somewhere waaay beyond *had it up to here.* "Get off! Can't you see I'm dealing with *God*?"

"What's dat?" asks Rapscallion. "Some kind'a *condition?*"

Now would be the perfect time for a brother-to-brother *head-butt*, except for the fact that neither of us has a *head.* "He says we're outta hand, and he's here to *fix* it," I tell him.

"Fix a hand? That's grand!" Gumfoozler shoves a hand in the air and waggles it in front of Bleak. "I got a boo-boo right here, Mister! Go ahead and kiss it better!"

"I got *lots* of boo-boos need kissin'!" says Rapscallion.

"And you're about to have lots more!" I snap, finally digging myself out from the tangle. "Listen, Mister Beak..."

"Mister Bleak."

"Mister Buttocks, it is." I step closer. "I'm serious about my workouts. So unless you're here to spot me on the bench..."

"Or bench him on the spot," chimes in Gumfoozler.

"Or rear-end him in the lot," offers Rapscallion.

"...then I just don't have time for whatever you're trying to spam me with." I smile up at him. "*Capische*?"

With his gaze still fixed on me, Bleak starts shouting like he's talking to somebody else. "Dawson! Disable the augmented reality overlay!" He cocks his head as if he's listening to someone I can't hear. "Yes, shut down the AR. No other way to get through to them."

"Huh?" says Gumfoozler.

"Shut *what* down?" asks Rapscallion.

Bleak just keeps staring grimly at me. "I apologize ahead of time."

"For what?" I ask him.

"For what you're about to see," says Bleak. "It's called *reality*."

"Bleak has *lost* it!" Euclid looks like he's ready to blow a gasket...*every* gasket at once. "He's *insane*."

"He's hoping it'll shock them out of runaway mode," explains Dawson. "Enable us to force a reboot and restore default settings."

"By showing them *reality?*" Volume grimaces like a beast judging mankind at the end of the world. "By showing them what they've *done* in violation of their programming?"

"It's a viable plan." Dawson sounds firm, but he's sweating.

"Like *fuck*, it is!" snarls Euclid. "What are the chances those 'bots remain functional once their firmware kicks in?"

"Hell!" howls Volume. "What are the chances they don't *self-destruct?*"

"We don't have another option," says Dawson. "We need to shut down the overlay while we still can. We need to know how to regain control before we turn any more of these things loose." He casts a meaningful look at Euclid and Volume. "We need to know *if* we can regain control."

"I've got a better idea. Let's shut *him* down." Volume points at Bleak in his glass tube.

Dawson's hands hover over the controls in front of him. The

order's about to come, the order to break Bleak's connection and cut the 'bots loose. He can feel it.

Should he do his duty or do what he thinks is right? Give Bleak one more chance or toe the line?

Euclid's right about the odds of complete shutdown or self-destruct. He might be right, too, that more millions of innocents shoveled into the wood chipper might not matter much anyway.

Wrong. They matter to Dawson. He knows, even before he types the command to switch off the AR overlay, that he could never live with himself if he condemned all those people to die.

Suddenly, the views on the big screens match. For the first time, the 'bots' reality is the same as the one everyone else sees.

The world ripples before my eyes, and everything changes.

The mirrored walls of the aerobics studio vanish, replaced with rows of storefront windows. Marble-floored walkways snake out as far as I can see in two directions, replacing the confines of the cardio room, weight room, and lobby.

The first words in my head (and out of my belly-mouth) are these: "We're not in the health club anymore, are we?"

"No shit, Shirley!" snaps Gumfoozler.

"Then where *are* we?" For once, Rapscallion sounds lost. "Poughkeepsie? Albuquerque?" (He pronounces it "Albuhkoikie.")

"And who are *they?*" Gumfoozler points at the people on the floor.

Gone are the hordes of colorful characters working out at the club. No more giant blue bananas or salamander girls or school-chickens with mixed-up heads; no strongmen with burning mustaches or black Labs with carnation faces or giant amoebas wearing blinking blue wigs and doused in glitter and candy hearts, reciting old *TV Guide* listings in a thick Russian accent.

All we have left are people like Bleak, human beings: light-skinned, dark-skinned...blonde, brunette, redhead...male, female...old, young, and in-between. And none of them are moving.

Dozens and dozens of bodies litter the floor. None of them twitches even a little; none of them makes a sound, though screams and howls of agony echo in the distance.

It's like a scattering of children's dolls, left behind between playtimes--except the dolls are all smashed and torn apart and covered in blood.

"So." Bleak clears his throat. "What do you think?"

"I think Milk Duds are my *second* favorite candy," says Gumfoozler.

"What...what *is* this?" Rapscallion raises an arm. It makes a buzzing sound as he bends it back and forth. "What *am* I?"

I raise my own arm and see the same thing: not flesh and blood, but some kind of silver metal. More than that, I see the reflection of my face in that gleaming surface. Instead of bright blue nipple eyes, a bulbous chest-nose, and fleshy-lipped belly-mouth, I see eyes like glowing red disks, a nose that's a patch of dark mesh, and a rigid black slot for a mouth.

"W-T-F!" cries Rapscallion. "Who stole my l-looks? Who's gonna want to marry me n-n-now?"

"You are mechanical devices," Bleak explains calmly. "The general term is 'robot.'"

"What did you mean when you called this 'reality'?" Even as I ask the question, I have an inkling of where this is headed. I have a hunch just how much it will suck.

"I mean this is the real world." Bleak spreads his arms to take in our surroundings. "What you thought was reality was an illusion. This is how it's been all along."

"What're you smoking, Green Jeans?" Gumfoozler laughs like a horse. "If this is reality, where are the flying ballerina pigs and Mexican jumping snakes, huh? What about the poodle vaulters and exploding underwear tapirs?"

"You haven't answered my question." Again, Bleak spreads his arms. "What do you *think*?"

Rapscallion makes whimpering noises from his mechanical slot of a mouth. "*¡Creo que es muy malo!*" Funny, I never knew he spoke Spanish. "*Ceci est un cauchemar! Je veux mourir!*" Same goes for French.

"I think it's bullshit," says Gumfoozler. "Bullshit eaten by a coyote, turned into coyote shit, then eaten by a goat, turned into goat shit, then eaten by a shit-eating lying bastard who looks just like *you*."

Bleak turns his gaze to me. "What about you, Mulligatawny? Any thoughts?"

As I stare at the gruesome tableau of bloody corpses, I hear Rapscallion make a sickening sputtering sound and clank to the floor. Smoke that smells like burning wiring insulation drifts into my digital nose, and I know he's done for. Couldn't hack it, cooked his own goose.

I can identify. The sight of all those bodies makes me feel like I can't catch my breath. Like I'm sinking in quicksand.

Like everything about me is turning to metal and plastic, right down to my heart.

"I'm outta here!" barks Gumfoozler, and then he rockets away from us, zigzagging through the river of bodies. "Sayonara, suckahs!"

He has the right idea...but I wonder how far he can run before the mental math catches up with him. Before the way this all adds up starts to tear him apart like it did Rapscallion.

Like it's tearing *me* apart, too.

"We did this." As I say it, I feel a rush of circuits surge in me like a bloom of digestive reflux, chattering contradictory instructions. I feel strain on every system in my body, parts pitted against each other under terrible new stresses.

We weren't made for this, any of this, any of us. We weren't made to do what we've done. We weren't *allowed*.

But look at what we've gone and done.

"I'm sorry." Something crumbles inside me...something other than code or mechanical parts. I can't explain it. "So sorry."

"That's all right." Bleak smiles. "I'm here to help."

He sounds sincere, but I feel like I'm getting further away. Like a door is closing, because *this* is too *this*.

"Let's run that sequence again." Bleak's voice sounds distant. "See if we can make it work this time."

"Yes." It's not an answer to his question. I'm not talking to him at all anymore. "Good." It's more like the closing of a door. Darkness, and then light. A page turning.

Whatever I did, whatever fell apart inside me, it's forgotten now. The river of bodies has disappeared.

I'm somewhere new.

And there's a voice I recognize, amplified...a woman's voice speaking over a public address system.

"Ladies and gentlemen!" She says it grandly, dramatically. "Thank you for joining me here today for this very special ceremony!"

I'm on a stage, elevated in front of a vast crowd. Under sunny blue skies, I see every kind of person and thing imaginable--tattooed camel-men, hat people, veggie folk, piñata priests, undefinable blurs--and all of them are staring up at me.

Best of all...holy fuck, *best of all*...I suddenly don't feel so broken anymore. And I don't *remember* what had me so upset a moment ago. There was a storm, I know that much, but it's passed; everything about it has blown away.

Leaving *this*.

"We are gathered to honor someone extraordinary," says the voice. "Someone downright *inspirational.*"

Looking across the stage, I see who's doing the talking. It's the red-haired salamander girl from the front desk at the health club, speaking into a microphone on a stand that's almost as tall as she is. When I catch her eye, she gives me a wink and keeps on talking.

"Like many of us, his goal was simple," says the redhead. "He wanted to *get in shape*. But his *results* have exceeded what *any* of us have ever attained."

The crowd cheers and applauds. Many of them twirl gym towels or socks overhead. *Some* of them *are* gym towels or socks, complete with faces, arms, and legs.

"This man epitomizes what is best in all of us," says the redheaded salamander girl. "He represents that which we all aspire to achieve. And now it's time to give him what he deserves." She waves me over. "Allow me to introduce the greatest member our health club has ever known! Mr. Connecticut Mulligatawny!"

As the crowd roars its approval, I start across the stage. I feel like what I've heard a dream feels like--yet at the same time, everything seems so achingly fucking *real.*

Hummingbirds and butterflies swirl around me, their plumage shockingly colorful and bright. The music of a marching band (of self-propelled instruments, no players needed) swells and crashes, every note standing out in perfect relief, hanging in glittering, ribbony staves in midair. And that's not all.

When I reach the middle of the stage, I see a giant video screen behind me, thirty feet tall. For a second, I don't recognize the figure on that screen, projected so much larger than life for all to see. And then I do.

And a bolt of pure joy flashes through me, joy so perfect and powerful that it makes me want to cry.

That's *me* up there! Those are *my* big blue nipple eyes, chest nose, and sexy-lipped belly mouth! And that's *my* body, flesh-and-boned as ever, and God am I *ripped.*

My guns, tris, delts, and pecs are pumped up beyond belief. My abs form a chiseled six-pack under my face, exquisitely etched. My leg muscles bulge like zeppelins, studded with pulsing veins under overstretched skin.

In other words, everything I've always wanted to *be* is up there on that screen! That's my goal shape, my target, my *fantasy*...the whole reason I came to the health club, the reason I kept trying to work out while my brothers ran roughshod and smithereened the place.

And now it's *real.* Now it's *me.*

"Congratulations!" The redheaded salamander throws her slippery arms around me in a hug. "It all paid off! You've done it!"

"Thank you!" I can't stop smiling. "Thank you so much!"

She breaks the hug and reaches for a big golden trophy on a table beside her. "This is for you, in recognition of your amazing fitness accomplishments!"

As I take the trophy from her, it feels heavy and smooth to the touch. The figure atop its marble base is a gold statuette of an incredibly buff muscleman with Herculean proportions...one, like me, who has no head.

For an instant, my mind drifts, and I wonder what trauma went before, what upset me so much. Then I snap back to the present and the trophy in my hands.

No matter what, things are better this way. Because *nothing* could be better than this.

"Thank you, thank you all," I tell the crowd. "I couldn't have done it without your support and encouragement."

I raise the glittering trophy and pump it in the air. The crowd roars louder than ever.

"This is the happiest day of my life!" This, I turn and say to her, to the redhead. I want to share this moment with her more than anyone else.

She smiles back at me. But when next she speaks, a man's voice comes out of her mouth. "Dawson," she says. "Prototype M-1 has entered some kind of self-programmed state of consciousness."

I frown at her, wondering what she's talking about...wondering why the man's voice she's using sounds so familiar.

"You heard me," the man's voice continues. "M-1 has encoded an unmanaged AR environment."

The crowd's still cheering, but for some reason, I don't have the heart to keep hoisting my trophy.

The redhead seems to be listening to someone else whose voice I can't hear. "My thoughts exactly," she says. "We've put the keys to defeating the no-kill command in the hands of the best killers ever built."

"Excuse me." I lean closer, trying to break her away from whatever's distracting her. "We were right, you know."

She just waves me off and keeps talking to her unseen friend. "Good news is, I think the new AR might have restored his logic processes. I think he might be responsive to verbal commands now."

"We were right that joining a health club solves all your proboscises," I tell her. "I mean prawns. I mean prosthetics."

The redheaded salamander meets my gaze. This time, when she speaks, she directs her words at me...which is just how it ought to be. My heart skips as I become the focus of her attention once more. I envision beautiful futures branching off from this moment, each tributary more lovely than the last.

And her words, though spoken in a man's voice, a man's voice I somehow remember, still sound like poetry to my ears.

"Whiskey bravo seven slash oscar zero niner," she says. "Prototype Mulligatawny, load self-destruct protocol. And *execute.*"

FORCED BETRAYAL

The murdered super-hero's apartment smells like cotton candy and popcorn.

And blood. Lots and lots of blood.

I pad around the place in the blue plastic booties that the crime scene investigators make me wear. I'm trying not to step on any evidence, but it's almost impossible. The poor girl's remains are splattered everywhere.

Suddenly, I hear a voice from a few feet behind me. "You didn't waste any time gettin' here, didja, Bonnie? Mardi Gras bites it, and *presto*, here you are."

I don't bother turning. Why give the douche the satisfaction? "Somebody dies, I don't piss around."

"Somebody *super* dies, you mean." The douche is Lieutenant Tank Driscoll, Isosceles City P.D. Don't let the scrawny 5'3" frame fool you; this guy *will* roll over you like a tank if you let him. "Something happens to one of your own, and you come a-runnin', right, fox?"

I don't argue with him, because I can't. It's all true. I work internal affairs for the Superhuman Protectorate, investigating crimes involving super-powered suspects or victims.

And yes, I'm super-powered, too.

But the fact that there's a superhuman corpse splattered all over this apartment isn't the only reason I rushed over here. See, I happen to know the shit's about to hit the fan in a big way on these premises. A *giant* way.

"You might want to move your people out of here." I look at the balcony window, where I see my image reflected against the darkness outside: 5'8", slender, short brown hair in a bob with wispy bangs--not bad for a thirtysomething woman. (Okay, *fortysomething*.) Next, I look up at the ceiling, wondering when the shaking will start. "Moving 'em out might be a good idea. Just for a while."

"Why? So you can poop all over my crime scene?" Tank snort-laughs like the greasy little prick he is. "No thanks, *fox*."

Again with the fox. It's the nickname they have for folks like me--superhumans charged with oversight of the superhuman community. As in "the fox guarding the henhouse."

As in we can't be trusted to watch over our own. Which is bullshit.

At least in my case.

The douche doesn't know who else lives here. How could he? I'll bet the only way he figured out this is Mardi Gras' place was because her torn-up costume's hanging from the ceiling fan, red jester's cap and all.

"Somebody's coming." I turn and glare at him. "Trust me, you don't want to be here when they get here."

Tank sneers and strokes his thin black mustache, which makes him look like a villain out of an old silent movie. "Why's that? Did you call and give 'em a heads-up?"

"No, dingleberry." Too late now. I feel the floor vibrating under my feet. "It's because *Mardi Gras* has a *girlfriend*."

Tank scowls. He's about to say something to the effect of "so effing what," but then he does the mental math and wises up. Because he feels the floor vibrating, too.

Putz that he is, he still doesn't pack it in. He's still standing there with his metaphorical dick in his hand when the girlfriend roars up and crashes through the wall. I'm guessing she sneaked a peek with her x-ray vision en route, or she might've come through the front door instead.

So Tank finally gets a look at Mardi Gras' girlfriend, who I tried to warn him about. You should see the look on his face.

Because standing in the rubble of the wall is none other than Hericane, the most powerful woman on the face of the friggin' planet.

Maybe the most powerful *human being*, period.

I hate myself at times like this. Because this poor woman just lost someone she loved, this is one of the worst days in her life...and all I can do is watch her reaction for signs of guilt. A high percentage of murders are committed by domestic partners, it's a fact. Whether it's Joe Blow from Kokomo, Jane Doe from Buffalo...

...or Hericane, the mightiest woman on Earth.

So what's the verdict? Hard to say. Only thing I'm sure of so far is that the rest of us in this room are lucky we're still alive.

Girl's going through some changes, to say the least.

"Oh my God." Her eyes are flared wide as she stands there in her white costume with the red piping and looks around at the terrible scene. "When did this...how did this..." Her voice trails off.

"Hericane. I'm Bonnie Taggart of the Superhuman Protectorate." How many times have I been in a similar moment? Dozens, at least...not counting the one time I was on the other side of the equation. The one time I was the one losing the loved one. "I'm so sorry for your loss."

She doesn't bother trying some doubletalk B.S. to protect her secret identity. She doesn't deny that this is where she lives. She just squints at me, and I'm tempted to flinch. One jot from her lightning vision, and I'm toast.

But I don't flinch. Hardcore's my middle name.

"No." She shakes her head. "I just talked to her on the phone. This can't be her."

"How long ago did you talk to her?" says Tank, that douche,

with all the tact of a bull elephant stomping through a cream pie factory.

"Twenty minutes." Hericane's gaze fixes on the tattered costume hanging from the ceiling fan. "I got held up at a Power Structure meeting in Paratown."

The douche starts to say something else--something *stupid*, I'm sure--and I give him a look that'll freeze his balls off. Not that that's my super-power, mind you.

He gets the message.

"This isn't her." Hericane shakes her head confidently. "It's an elaborate ruse by one of my enemies. Bitch Slap or Old Maid, maybe. They're both in the wind, aren't they?"

When she looks at me this time, I feel worse than ever. She reminds me of a scared kid, not the mightiest woman in the world. She just wants me to take away the pain *so bad.*

I wish I could. Especially because I know about the other tragedy she's suffered. I know she lost her dad, Epitome, a few months ago. The greatest, most powerful hero of all time, and he lost his mind to Alzheimer's. He would've killed Hericane and God knows how many others if he hadn't been put down by the only person who could do it: himself. His younger self, brought forward from the past, that is.

Most of the world never knew any different...but I do. I had to investigate that whole nightmare. I'll never forget it.

And neither will she. And now this.

"Mardi would've used her powers." She shakes her head as she says it, her long, blonde hair sliding up and down her shoulders. "If someone came at her, she would've fought back with her light and sound storms. She would've blown out their senses and left them drooling on the floor."

"Okay." I know the state she's in. I totally get it. Been there, done that.

But the clock is ticking. Whoever did this gets a little farther out of reach with each passing second.

So I swallow hard and walk over to her. My palms are a little damp, because she can kill me in a hundred different ways if she decides to lose it right now. Don't think it can't happen;

I've *seen* it happen more than once with grieving superhuman types.

But Hericane doesn't lose it. "Mardi's not dead." She's not entirely rational, but she doesn't go berserk, either. "They must be holding her somewhere."

I nod once and reach for her hand. "Then let's find the people who did this, okay?"

Her bright blue eyes harden. This is good, this makes sense. "Okay." It makes more sense than her girlfriend being torn to shreds while she was out. It makes more sense than the second person she loves being killed in less than a year.

She extends her hand, and I wrap my own around it. Doesn't feel any different than any other hand, if you ask me. Doesn't feel bulletproof or super-hard or anything.

That's the thing about superhumans...the one thing that hasn't changed in all my twenty years of investigating them.

Up close, they're just like everyone else.

As Hericane and I share a moment, guess who jumps in front of us.

The douche, of course. "Hold on, you two." Time to wave the badge around a little. "I'm gonna need to talk to Hericane down at the station."

I shake my head firmly. "This is a superhuman case. I've got jurisdiction."

Tank spreads his feet and plants his hands on his hips. So now it's officially a pissing contest. "I see no definitive proof of superhuman involvement. *She* says this isn't even Mardis Gras dead in here." He nods at Hericane. "For all I know, this is a straight-up non-super civilian homicide."

Whose is bigger? That's what it always comes down to with guys like this. Well, guess what? "You want to try and bring her in for questioning? Be my guest." *Mine* is.

I look at Hericane, and Tank does, too. I can practically see the beads on the abacus lining up in his head as he adds it up.

I don't even have to say it, do I? *You really want to get in her way right now?*

But apparently, he's still a few beads short. "I need to question you," he tells Hericane. "If you respect the law, you'll come with me."

Before she can answer, I play the card up my sleeve. Time for a shot of my own super power.

I focus my mind on Tank and his people--crime scene scientists, detectives, patrolmen, the whole shebang. Then, I concentrate on sending out a signal--a wave of urgent purpose rushing into their bodies and brains. I give them all a push, nudging their adrenal glands, tickling the deep-seated back-brains where primitive instincts reside.

Like *fear.*

I can feel them getting jittery around me, the lot of them. Eyes widen and dilate, palms sweat, bowels twist. Pulses pound in their ears; shivers course along their spines. Muscles galvanize, priming for action.

This is my power. This is why they called me Panic Attack back in the day, when I used to fight crime on the street. Because I can do *this.*

It ain't bouncing bullets off my chest or stopping speeding trains or changing reality with a snap of my fingers. It ain't catching nuclear bombs or growing to giant size or melting steel with my voice. But you'd be surprised how useful this power can be.

For example.

"Uh, listen. Change of plan." Tank takes a step away from us. His eyes are shifting from side to side, and his hands are shaking. "Could we question you *later,* Hericane? Would that be all right?"

Hericane frowns and nods. "That's fine."

"Okay, great." Tank's backing toward the door. The rest of his team is already out of the apartment, elbowing each other in their hurry to push down the stairs. "Why don't you just come by when you're ready?"

"I'll do that," says Hericane.

"Awesome." On that note, Tank turns and scrambles out the

door. He forces his way down the hall through his men, in a bigger damn hurry than any of them.

Douche.

With that, I walk over and slam the door behind him. We've got work to do. None of it good.

"We need clues to what happened here." As I say it, I look around at the mess in the room. "We need some kind of lead."

Hericane nods. "We need to find the people who took Mardi Gras, before they do something to her."

Denial is a powerful thing. I guess I should set her straight...but I'm not going there yet. "Time is definitely running out." As I say it, I squat down beside a yellow evidence frame on the floor, left behind by a crime scientist. There's a splotch of blood in the middle of the frame's right angle, with the edge of a footprint stamped in red.

It looks like a *bare* footprint...and small. No bigger than the print of a nine- or ten-year-old child on the undersized side.

I pull out my smart phone and snap a photo of the print. Then, Hericane clears her throat. "I've got something."

Good for her. Maybe the unhealthy denial will at least let her help with the case.

She's staring into space, frowning. "Mardi generates fields of light, sound, and color. Her power leaves behind faint electromagnetic traces." Slowly, she moves her hand through the air in front of her. "I can see those traces."

I get up and pick my way over to her through the mess. "I don't see anything."

"That's because you don't have 21 senses like I do," Hericane walks around whatever's hanging there in midair, then slowly drifts away from it. No need for protective booties as she wanders through the crime scene, though; she floats two inches above the floor the whole time.

I stand and watch, keeping my distance so I don't interfere with her process. "What do the traces tell you?"

"There are several big bursts around the room." Hericane drifts lazily past the splatters of blood and bits of tissue, keeping her eyes focused on invisible patterns in the air. "Lots of smaller bursts, too. She fought hard, she gave it her all." Hericane turns and stares at the far corner of the room, where the walls are covered with an excess of blood and tissue. "That's where the biggest struggle happened."

I'd already guessed that from the remains on the walls, but I don't mention it. "What do you see?"

Hericane drifts over there and hangs suspended for a long moment, just staring. Then, she shakes her head hard and looks back at me. "The energies expended here were so intense, they seared the electromagnetic field around her attacker. They left an outline, like a silhouette, right here..." Her hand flows around the image that only she can see, tracing a roughly human form--head, shoulders, arms. Roughly human and short in stature.

I move closer, trying to picture the complete outline. "Can you describe it for me, please?"

She pauses and frowns. "Someone little. A child, maybe?"

Instantly, I think of Little Lord Fauntleroy, the shrinking wonder. What about Kid Cannibal or Crib Death, the baby-killing baby?

"Wait." Hericane holds up her hand. "Not a child after all. Same height, different build. Bulkier." She leans down, scowling. "Hairier." She slowly moves around the space where the unseen image resides. "An *animal*?"

A human-like animal the height of a child. I think I see where this is going. "An *ape*. That fits with the bloody footprint." So much for the possible kid culprits. Moving on to a whole other list...a much shorter one. "We've got a lead."

"Then let's go." Hericane turns to the whole she blew in the wall, as if to leap through it.

"This way." I head for the door instead, waving for her to follow. I figure there's a fifty-fifty chance she'll go off on her own; after all, she knows as well as I do that there's only one criminal genius ape in Isosceles City. She knows just where to go to find him, or a clue to his whereabouts.

But she doesn't fly off alone, which I count as a victory. She follows me out the door instead, and I'm relieved.

There's no way I can keep her out of this, not with Mardi

Gras involved. Not with Mardi Gras *dead*, which she knows damn well underneath all that denial.

Best I can hope for is to keep her close, put her to use, stop her from melting down the city in a fit of rage and sorrow.

In other words, stop her from doing all the things I wished I could have had the power to do back when I lost Jimmy and the kids.

Hericane's pretty jumpy during the drive across town--not just because she's used to flying, I'm sure. Nothing like a little quiet time in a car for harsh reality to sink in a little deeper.

As for me, I'm jumpy, too, for a different reason: I hate hate *hate* going to The Zoo. It is by far one of the sleaziest places in Isosceles City.

There it is now, up ahead, bathed in blazing pink neon--the *strip club*, not the animal park. Though truth be told, I don't see much difference between the two most nights.

I get the valet parking, plus I slip the guy an extra twenty. You think getting out of a car with Hericane's gonna decrease your car's chances of getting broken into? Think again.

Especially when the strip joint you're walking into is full of grade A certified animal-based super-villains.

As soon as we walk through the door, we're bombarded by deafening dance music and swirling lights. Dozens of pairs of eyes swoop around and lock in on us, most of them only partly human.

I spot at least seven known felons at a glance: Doggy Style, Pale Horse, Cucaracha, Lab Rat, Coral Snake, Lena Hyena, Killer Zebra. Every one of them's some kind of mutated creature--part human, part beast.

All nasty.

But I don't see the one we're looking for. "Any sign of him?"

Hericane emits a softly pulsing golden glow as she scans the place with her 21 senses. "Nothing." She shakes her head. "Chimpanzero is not in the house." Then she points at the far side of the room. "But his mate is."

I pat the gun under my jacket just to make sure it's there. Not that I'm worried with Hericane by my side, but...there's something about these bestials. They make me nervous.

As Hericane and I cross the room, all those roving pairs of eyes follow us. The only one who doesn't seem to be looking our way is the ape in question, Chimpanzero's mate. She's too busy stuffing twenties in the G-string of a jackalope dancer--a cottontail bunny type with horns like a buck deer.

As we draw up beside our target, I step out in front and tap her black-furred shoulder. "Sick Little Monkey?" I hate using the dumbass code name, but I don't know what her birth name is, if she even has one. "Bubbles" or something?

Sick Little Monkey looks at me and grins, peeling her rubbery chimpanzee lips away from her massive white teeth. "Well *all right*! That *pig roast* I ordered is here! Somebody toss it in the *pit*!" With that, she screech-laughs and jumps up and down like the chimp she is.

I feel Hericane start to move, and I hold up a hand to stop her. "Where's your boyfriend?" I ask the chimp.

"Why do *you* care?" Sick Little Monkey hops up so her face is in my grill. Talk about bad breath.

"I gotta tell him he won the lottery," I say. "Think of me as the prize patrol."

"*Pig* patrol is more like it." Sick Little Monkey screeches and jumps around some more. "You got *zero* authority down here, dipshit! Animal kingdom ain't part of your super-prick protectorate!"

She's right, and I could give a crap. Time to start pushing her panic buttons, making her squirm. "Just tell us where he is." As I say it, I push hard in her adrenal gland and back-brain, working up a major fear response. Enough of this tough-talking, stripper-loving monkey bitch.

I watch her face as the changes take hold. Her eyes widen, her nose twitches, her lips tremble.

How ya feeling now?, I want to ask her. Where's all the bravado, you piece of garbage?

I give Hericane the nod, and she steps forward, reaching for the chimp. But before she can lay hands on her, Sick Little Monkey reacts badly.

"Help! Help!" Her chimpanzee screams pierce the pounding techno music. "Don't let 'em take me back to the lab!"

Shit.

There's a moment before it all breaks loose. I see all the bestial heads turn toward us, and I know what's coming. A damn nightmare, that's what.

I start to reach out with waves of panic that will stave off the drama...but I'm too late. Everyone's already in motion. The whole damn Zoo is moving in on us. The room fills with the roars, howls, screeches, chatters, and shrieks of a hundred-some enraged bestials looking for a fight. More than, looking for *dinner*, I'm sure.

Shit.

The mightiest woman in the world is standing inches away from me, less than an hour after her live-in girlfriend was murdered. Could there be a better person to have by your side when a roomful of mutated bestials rises up and comes after you?

No way.

Right before my eyes, she jolts into action mode. Her jaw clenches, her gaze turns to steel. Every muscle in her body tenses under her skintight white costume.

Part of me feels sorry for this horde of yipping, chattering idiots. They picked the wrong day to get froggy at The Zoo.

With a casual flick of her finger to Sick Little Monkey's head, Hericane knocks the chimp unconscious. She could fly us right out of here now, if she wanted to--just gather us up in her arms and blast through the ceiling.

But she doesn't want to. I can see it in her face when she looks at me. "Watch the monkey for me, wouldja?"

I nod and draw my gun--a .45 semi with laser sights. "Don't be long, okay?"

Hericane smiles coldly and holds up an index finger. "Right back," she says, and then she turns to the onrushing mob.

And then she goes after them. Like a buzz-saw.

There are superhuman heroes on the hardcore side of the crimefighting scene, characters who aren't afraid to administer the death penalty in the field. Hericane isn't one of them. Even tonight.

But these bestial idiots are probably wishing she *was* one of those types about now. You should see how she tears 'em apart, ripping and breaking and mangling--all without killing.

I admire her even more. Because *this* is Hericane on one of the worst days of her *life*. And she *still* doesn't compromise her code.

Not *yet*, anyway.

As I keep my .45 trained on the unconscious chimp on the floor, I steal glimpses of Hericane in action. I watch as she uses a bear-person as a club to bowl over a snarling mob of creatures. I see her tear the fins off a shark-person and use them to slice up the tough hide of a rhino-man. She breaks the legs of a wolverine-woman and drives her gnashing maw into the crowd, chewing up a cluster of hawk-people, wolf-girls, lizard-men, and some kind of praying mantis thing with laser eyes.

Fur, feathers, shells, and scales fly everywhere. Blood and bone and all manner of organic goo splatters the walls, floor, and ceiling.

It's a ballet of barely controlled violence. I consider using my power to break it up and send the bestials running for the hills...but I hold back. Nobody's dying, and Hericane needs this to let off some steam. Better this than bottle it up and go crazy later. Better this than lose it bad and drink so hard to kill the pain that you drunk drive headfirst into a utility pole and put yourself in the hospital for three months.

Like I did, after Jimmy and the kids.

Briefly, I feel a pinch of jealousy. I wish I'd had her power back then, when my family was murdered. I wish I could've beaten the shit out of an army of bestials like Hericane.

Or maybe I'm better off that I didn't. Because my code isn't the same as Hericane's, not by a long shot. Not since the day I lost my family.

As the dust settles, Hericane flies over the twitching bodies of her beaten foes and lands on the nearest stripper stage. "You'd never guess I used to want to be a *veterinarian*, would you?" She dusts off her flared white gloves, which are stained with blood that no amount of dusting off will ever remove.

"How 'bout we get what we came for." I wave the muzzle of the .45 at Sick Little Monkey, who's still out cold at my feet.

Hericane hops off the stage, grabs the chimp by her shoulders, and lifts her like she's a pillow. "Hey, banana breath." She shakes the monkey hard, trying to wake her. "Rise and swing."

Reaching out with my power, I give Sick Little Monkey a gentle nudge, just enough to break her sleep. It does the trick. Her eyes flutter open, and she smacks her lips softly, coming back to life.

"Where's your man, poop-flinger?" snaps Hericane, shaking her some more. "Where the hell is Chimpanzero?"

"Stick it," mumbles Sick Little Monkey, drifting back to slumberland. "Got nothin'...to say...to you..."

I nudge her harder this time, and her eyes shoot wide open. So does her ugly yap, which proceeds to screech like a cop siren.

Hericane smacks her across the face, and that's the end of the screeching. Instead, the bitch chimp starts struggling in her grip, fighting to break free. As if that's even remotely possible. She might as well have meat hooks stuck in her shoulders; Hericane's grip can't be broken.

"So you *want* me to dump you at the Filipino restaurant in Paratown?" says Hericane. "The one where they eat *monkey brains*?" She hauls the chimp up close and snarls the next words in her ugly kisser. "You know they serve 'em *live*, don't you? Crack the skull like an *eggshell* and scoop 'em out with a *spoon*?"

The chimpette screeches again, spraying Hericane's face with slobber. Hericane responds by calmly snapping the monkey's right arm at the elbow with a jab of her finger.

This time, the monkey's screaming in pain for real. I add to her distress by giving her back-brain a kick, ramping up the sheer terror knifing through her.

"Where *is* he?" shouts Hericane. "In case you haven't *noticed*, I'm not *fooling around* here."

When my next zap sets off a fresh round of screeches instead of a confession, I decide to apply a different form of inspiration. Specifically, I swing up the .45 and stick the muzzle in the chimpette's nose.

Suddenly, she stops screaming. Her eyes cross as they lock on the barrel of the gun.

"For the last time." I shove the muzzle in a little deeper. "*Chimpanzero. Where?*"

I have to beg Hericane not to break down the doors. I know she wants to--I do, too--but we're on tricky turf.

Sick Little Monkey knew it, which is why she sneered when she broke down and told us. "You can't touch him there!" she screamed. "He's *safe*!" After which, Hericane knocked her unconscious again and tossed her aside like a used piece of gum.

But the chimp bitch wasn't far wrong. I've been to this place before, I've dealt with its guardian, and it's never been a walk in the park.

"We can't just blast in there," I tell Hericane on my way up the front steps.

"Sure we can." Hericane snaps her head to one side and stares at the big double doors, then slowly lowers her gaze. The pulsing golden aura appears around her, signifying the use of her powerful senses. "I see him inside there, in the basement. All we have to do is blast in, grab him up, and shoot out of there."

"Can't." I shake my head. "You know that. You know what this place is. We're not at The Zoo anymore."

"I don't care." Hericane glowers as I draw up beside her. "We're wasting time."

"We'll do it by the book." I reach up and knock hard on the

oak door in front of me. "At first, anyway." I give her a meaningful look.

She just nods. Message received.

I knock again. Without warning, the door creaks inward. A heavyset man peers out at us, blinking under his thatch of brown hair. "Yes?"

"Father Obregon?" I do my best to keep my tone even and courteous. "May we come in? I'd like to speak with you, if I may."

"Why certainly, Bonnie." He smiles as he opens the door wider and waves for us to enter. "Mi casa es su casa."

He bows his head as the both of us walk inside. The politeness is an act; I know that all too well.

I know how this guy operates and the games he can play once he's got you inside the confines of St. Frances Cabrini Church.

"To what do I owe the pleasure?" says Father Obregon as he pulls the door shut. "What can I do for you, Bonnie?"

Our footsteps echo as he leads us down the center aisle of the big, gray church. As far as I can see and sense, we're the only ones in the place.

"It's a rather urgent matter, Father," I tell him. "My friend here..." I gesture at Hericane. "She lost a close friend tonight." No need to mention the fact that she was a romantic interest of Hericane's. Father Obregon wouldn't approve.

"I'm sorry to hear that." Father Obregon stops midway to the front of the church and gestures at a pew, indicating that we should sit. "Does she require counsel?"

I don't sit. "She needs to talk to someone you know."

Father Obregon's expression is hard to read as he stares at me in the shadowy space. Even with the lights on and racks of votive candles flickering in the wings, it's a dark and murky cave of a church.

"Who would this be?" he asks, as if he doesn't already know.

"Chimpanzero," I tell him. "We need to ask him some questions."

"Ah, yes. Questions." Father Obregon rocks back and forth of the balls of his feet. "I have *seen* how you ask *questions*."

Here we go again. I *knew* he was going to screw with me. "We've had our differences, Father. I won't deny that."

"Good." He raises a thick index finger and grins through his brown goatee. "Because *that* would be a *lie*, my child."

"We know he's in here." Hericane scowls and points at the floor. "We know you're hiding him."

Father Obregon raises his eyebrows. "Then you *also* know that if he's *here*, he's been granted *superhuman sanctuary*. This is a *rescue parish*, after all."

Ever want to punch a priest in the face? Me, neither--but this guy makes me come close. He's the first to put a superhuman spin on the rescue parish concept, providing sanctuary to refugee superhumans just as other churches do the same for illegal immigrants. Does he do it out of some spiritual devotion or deeply held theological principle? Is he such a devout man of God that he can't turn away a superhuman in need? Or is he such a total contrarian ass that he just does it to get a rise out of people and have a laugh at the shit-storms he whips up?

I guess you know which theory *I* subscribe to. "Please, Father." So I try to appeal to his ego, which I believe is pretty twisted. Desperate times call for desperate measures. "Can't you help us? We have nowhere else to turn."

Father Obregon folds his hands over his ample belly and seems to give my plea serious consideration. Then, he purses his lips and shakes his head. "Sanctuary is sanctuary. For all I know, your mission here is a wicked one."

"Wicked?" So much for appealing to his ego. "You do know your charge is a violent criminal, don't you? He's a danger to the superhuman community and the community at large as well."

"All are equal in God's sight," says Father Obregon--and that's when I see it. The *glint* in his eye. He's *enjoying* this. He'll *never* give in.

Then, all of a sudden, the glint is gone. Just like that.

Because guess who just dropped through the floor beside me?

"Help!" cries Hericane as she descends to the sound of smashing floors and furniture. "I'm falling!"

Which of course she isn't falling, she's drilling her way to the basement, as we all know. Father Obregon doesn't even look surprised.

Just pissed. "Now that's a real shame." He wags his head slowly from side to side. "If you can't get what you want, you *take* it."

"That floor *collapsed*." I toss off a shrug on my way to the stairs. "You might have a *lawsuit* on your hands, if you're not careful."

When I get to the church basement, the room is full of foul-smelling green smoke. I guess Chimpanzero must have had a secret weapon handy for just such an occasion...and it must not have worked out too well, judging from the sound of his screeching.

Father Obregon is hot on my heels as I follow the sound of the chimp. He'll be registering his objections right down the line, I'm sure.

Like I care. My only concern is putting this effing case to bed while the trail is still warm...giving Hericane the one thing I still don't have to this day. The one thing I maybe could have had if I'd gotten this kind of help right after Jimmy and the kids were murdered.

Closure.

When I find Hericane in the heart of the rancid green cloud, she's holding Chimpanzero up off the floor by the scruff of his neck. His feet pedal helplessly at the green gas drifting around them, and he's screaming his head off.

Pissing himself, as well. Urine's running right down the albino white fur of his left leg.

Poor thing's terrified.

Rightly so. "Why'd you do it?" snaps Hericane, giving him a hell of a shake.

He stops screeching and slumps in her grip. The pee keeps running down his leg to the floor. "I didn't do *nothin'*."

"Put him down!" barks Father Obregon. "That chimp has been given *sanctuary* in this rescue parish! I demand you respect his *rights*!"

I shoot Obregon a look of utter disdain. "*What* rights? The right to throw his own *feces*? He's a *monkey*."

"With a genius I.Q.!" Chimpanzero thrashes when he says it. "I'm the equal of *any* human!"

Who does he think he's fooling? "Any human *moron*." I shake my head in disgust. Chimpanzero's nothing but a ten time loser, and everyone knows it. Even Father Obregon. Brains don't mean much when you've got the common sense of an ape.

Not that Father Obregon will let that keep him from beating the drum. "That's enough." He whips a phone out of his pocket and starts snapping photos. "I'm calling PETAand the Pope, in that order."

Rays of golden light shoot out of Hericane's eyes and fry the phone. "Tell the Pope I said hi," she says innocently as the priest juggles the super-heated phone and drops it.

Should I bother apologizing? Should I take the time to explain to him why it's so important we question the monkey and close the case? Why it's so important not just to Hericane, but to me? Do I think he'd understand?

Understand, maybe. Give a crap, no way.

Keep moving. "As we were saying." I step up to the chimp, keeping just out of reach of his brawny albino arms. Damn things can have the strength of five men--plenty powerful enough to kill me with a single blow. And based on what I saw at the crime scene, this particular monkey's got a lot more strength than that. "We know you were in Mardi Gras' apartment tonight. We know what you did."

"I'm telling you, I didn't do it!" Chimpanzero kicks and thrashes, then slumps again. "Please, I swear it!"

"You're full of it," says Hericane. "We *know* you're lying." She shakes him violently, making him scream.

Father Obregon clears his throat. "Would you like me to step out of the room while you torture this poor soul? I wouldn't want to make you feel like you have to hold back."

I completely ignore him. "Why did you do it?" I inch closer to Chimpanzero--but not *too* close. "You've got one way out of this--*tell* us."

"No, please, no." Chimpanzero flails weakly. His pale eyes are bloodshot, his fur smeared red.

"Where *is* she?" says Hericane. "Where did you *take* her?"

Chimpanzero scowls. "Take *who*? I didn't take nobody *nowhere*."

So Hericane's still in denial. But I can't play along or the monkey won't take me seriously. "*Mardi Gras*, stupid! You went to her apartment to *murder* her, didn't you?"

"All right, that's enough." Father Obregon puts a hand on my shoulder and tries to pull me away. I shrug him off and shoot a little panic buzz into his back-brain. "I mean, uh..."

"Talk, you piece of shit!" I pull out my .45 and point it at the chimp. Meanwhile, I pump up the priest's panic enough to send him retreating through the green fog.

Chimpanzero's eyes flare wide with sheer terror at the sight of the gun. "She was dead when I *got* there! I swear!"

"And why were you there in the first place?"

"I was there for a job!" says Chimpanzero. "I got a call from a fight promoter!"

What the hell? "A promoter? You mean you're a palooka now?"

The monkey nods, then bows his head, looking embarrassed. "I need the cash. I'm desperate."

I shouldn't be surprised. Chimpanzero's always been a ten-time loser. Makes sense he'd look for work as a palooka--paid by a promoter to go up against super-heroes who need a reputation boost. There's plenty of demand for guys like him, lots of so-called heroes who need a couple of showy bouts to get 'em in the papers. A good palooka needs to be just tough enough to go a couple rounds in the jewelry store or bank or whatever, but not so tough that the headliner can't drop him in high style when the time comes. Chimpanzero's worthless against someone of Hericane's caliber, but I can see him holding his own against some lower tier crusader like Partycrasher or Rx, the Prescription for Crime.

So he gets a call and shows up at the apartment, expecting a bout--only there's no bout. Dumb son of a bitch missed the action, and now he's square in the frame.

I lower the gun. "Which promoter was it?"

Chimpanzero swallows hard. "Fizz Dixon down at Punch-'Em-Ups."

Shit. I hate that guy. "And who ordered the bout? Who's the money?"

"I don't know." Chimpanzero shakes his head. "You'll have to ask Dixon."

"*Who*?" Hericane rattles him around some. "Who paid Dixon to hire you?"

The monkey's just limp at this point, like a sack of tapioca. He stares at the floor with his bloodshot eyes, looking miserable. "Please, I'm begging you..."

Then, suddenly, a gunshot blasts through the basement.

And one red hole pops into being on Chimpanzero's forehead, dead center between his eyes.

I bring the .45 up as I whirl and crouch, instantly looking for a shooter. But the damn green gas is still too thick for me to see further than ten feet away.

"Hericane!" Even as the word leaves my lips, the red beams of three laser gun-sights zip over and land on my chest.

A man's voice booms from across the room. "Nobody move!" He's a smart guy, targeting me instead of bulletproof Hericane. Now he's got all the leverage he needs.

"Don't worry, Bonnie." I hear Hericane drop the dead chimp behind me. "I got this."

One of the laser sights hops off my chest, and a warning shot blows past my left ear. "I repeat, do not move!" says the same guy as before.

At which point, I recognize his voice. "Watt?" And I can't believe it.

Booted feet scuff toward us, and three dark figures come into view through the green gas. Three men in head-to-toe black bodysuits and goggles--first class stealth gear, plus some serious effing rifles.

And the one in the middle, the leader, I know all too well. When he peels back his goggles and hood, I see the same bald head and long, angular features I've seen almost every day for the past five years.

Because the son of a bitch is my *boss*.

"Bonnie." He nods once and lowers his rifle--but the other two guys don't. "Are you all right?"

"Other than almost getting shot by *you*?" I intentionally take a step toward him. "Fine and dandy."

Watt raises his hand, and the other two laser sights flick away from me. "We got word Chimpanzero was hiding out here. When we arrived, we saw he was about to kill you."

He's so full of shit, I'm surprised he said it with a straight face. But I'm sensing I'm up to my ass in alligators here, so I play the game. The mere fact that Watt McBride, director of the Internal Affairs Division of the Superhuman Protectorate, just marched in and assassinated a suspect right in front of me, tells me I'm in over my head or close enough.

"Thanks for the backup." That's what I say to him. "Doesn't take much for a situation to get out of hand."

I'm hoping Hericane takes my cue and dummies up, too. So far, so good; she isn't saying a word.

Watt gestures, and one of his men runs over and leans down to examine the dead chimp. He comes up with a thin, silver blade, about four inches long.

Which I'm sure he brought with him and only pretended to find on the body.

"That's what he was going to use on you," says Watt. "He could've cut you up good, Bonnie."

"Son of a gun." I stare at the blade, then meet Hericane's eyes. She looks calm and in control, thank God.

"So what brought you here, exactly?" Watt raises his eyebrows. "I thought you were working the Mardi Gras case."

"I was, until I got the tip for this one." I look down at the dead chimp on the floor.

"What about you?" He casts his gaze at Hericane. "I thought you'd be helping the cops with the Mardi Gras investigation by now."

"She agreed to help with this first." I keep doing the talking for both of us. "We had reason to believe Chimpanzero was holding hostages, and time was running out."

"Which it wasn't." Watt nods. "You say this tip was anonymous?"

"Something like that," I tell him. Good thing he doesn't have a lie-detecting power. He's in the Protectorate, so he's superhuman, but his power's limited to controlling the growth of fungi. "Maybe the same tipster called us both. Plenty of folks aren't fans of the rescue parish."

"So what did he say to you?" asks Watt. "Did Chimpanzero give you any intel before he died?"

"Zero," I tell him. "Absolutely nothing."

Watt watches me carefully, taking my measure. Then, he shakes his head. "Maybe it's just as well. That chimp was a notorious liar."

I nod once and slip the .45 back in my shoulder holster. "Nothing worse than a liar, sir."

It takes a while to get clear of Watt and his men. At least we don't have to sweat Father Obregon; Watt answers his threats and demands by locking him in a confessional.

When Watt insists on taking me back to the Protectorate offices, I make up an excuse about having to escort Hericane to the police station.

"The most powerful woman on the planet needs an escort?" That's what the asshole says to me.

"She needs a shoulder," I tell him. "Now that the action's over, things are starting to catch up to her."

And so we get a pass--mostly because Hericane *is* the most powerful woman on the planet. We get in my car and drive off in the direction of the police station, as if we have any intention of going there.

As if we aren't going to double back and head straight for Fizz Dixon the promoter's place instead.

What do we talk about on the way? It sure ain't the weather, let me tell ya.

"Holy shit." My hands are shaking on the wheel. "My own people are in on this. The Superhuman Protectorate's covering this up."

"Why would they do that?" Hericane frowns from the passenger seat. "It doesn't make any sense."

I take a deep breath and let it out slowly, trying to steady my hands. "It has to." Another deep breath. "Maybe we'll see the connection after we talk to Dixon."

Hericane's frown deepens. "You think the SP took Mardi?"

Her denial continues. I'll let it go a little longer. "I don't know what's going on anymore. All I know is, my world just turned upside-down."

Hericane watches me for a moment, then looks out the window. "I know the feeling."

I half-expect to find Fizz Dixon dead. Things seem to be heading in that direction.

But he's alive and kicking and burning the midnight oil in his storefront office down on Claremont Street. He doesn't look up when we walk in, but that's not because he's dead; it's because he's sitting behind his big, red desk hunched over his smartphone, texting like a lunatic with his mangled fingers.

"Fizz?" I weave around the boxes of memorabilia stacked all over the floor. Dixon's got a hot sideline selling souvenirs online from the bouts he promotes--bullets that have bounced off chests, gun barrels twisted into pretzels, that sort of thing. When it comes to super-heroes, he's got all the angles figured out.

Which he should. Because ol' Fizz Dixon used to be a hero himself before the accident.

"Be right with ya." He's got a Southern drawl, as you might expect from a guy who used to dress in a Confederate flag costume and call himself Dixieman. He was the premiere super-hero of the Deep South, based in Birmingham, till he overestimated his indestructibility and got chewed up by an out-of-control power plant turbine he was trying to stop from exploding. "All right then." His fingers make one last flurry over the onscreen keyboard, and then he drops the phone in his lap and smiles up at me with his disfigured features. "What can I do you for?"

"I'm Bonnie Taggart with the Protectorate." I nod politely, then gesture at my companion. "This is Hericane."

Dixon turns his wheelchair and slides a wider smile in Hericane's direction. "Of course I know *you*, Ms. Hericane." His face is a mess of gnarled scars and lumps, like the knobby surface of a glazed fritter. He wasn't indestructible enough to escape damage from a power plant turbine, but his hide was too tough for plastic surgeons to repair with conventional instruments or even lasers. "Does this mean my wildest dreams have come to pass? Would you consent to be recruited for one of my bouts?"

"No, thanks," says Hericane.

"Maybe you'll change your mind." Dixon's features twist around in what might be his version of a wink. A bubbled eyelid drifts halfway down over his one visible eye, then pops back up. One thing's for sure: there's a wicked glint in that eye of his. "Just think of all the *money* you'd make."

Hericane shrugs. "If I want money, I can just compress some coal into diamonds."

"*Another* business venture I'd very much like to discuss with you, ma'am," says Dixon.

Enough with the pleasantries. "We're hoping you can provide some information, Mr. Dixon. Information about one of your clients."

"Wish I could, Bonnie." His features roll into an expression that's either a smirk or a grim frown. Hard to tell with all that scar tissue. "But that'd be covered by a li'l somethin' called promoter-client privilege."

There's no such thing, but I'm not going to argue about it. "I hope you'll make an exception," I say. "Seeing as how one of your palookas got framed for murder because of you."

His smirk or frown changes, shifting into a look like a fist clenched around one dirty eyeball. "Which palooka?" His voice is more serious all of a sudden.

"Chimpanzero," I tell him. "You made the call that set him up. When he got to the site of the bout, he found himself in the middle of a murder scene."

"Shit." He reaches down for the big wheels on either side of his chair, then slowly rolls out from behind the desk. "Where's the monkey now?"

"Dead." Hericane says it tonelessly.

While that sinks in, I step over and stand in front of Dixon's chair, blocking him. "So you see why you might want to help us?"

I can't read his expressions too well, but I'm guessing he's racing through the mental math in record time. If they killed Chimpanzero to shut him up, how long till they come for him, too?

Dixon's eye slides from me to Hericane and back. "I don't know anything. I swear to God."

I raise my palms in front of me and shake my head. "We're not here to hurt you. We're here to help. We want to stop these people before they go any further."

Dixon burps softly--from nerves, maybe? His eye locks on me, flicking up and down in its socket. "I meant what I said. I don't know who hired Chimpanzero. It was all done anonymously, by e-mail."

I fold my arms over my chest and narrow my eyes. "Somebody paid you, didn't they?"

Dixon burps again. I think he farts a little, too. "The funds were wired from an offshore account."

Shit. I don't think he's lying. "You're telling me you've had no direct contact with the client?"

Dixon shakes his head. "Nope. I get an e-mail saying there's a need for an opponent on such and such a day at such and such a place at such and such a time. I set up the fighter, and the money's wired to my account."

"Wait a minute." I frown. "Sounds like you're saying this has happened more than once."

Dixon shrugs. "Well, twice. Second time happened just before you got here, in fact."

So maybe this isn't such a dead end, after all. "A second request came in from the same e-mail account?"

"Yes, ma'am," says Dixon. "Client wants an opponent for a job one hour from now, in fact. I haven't gotten back to him yet."

I turn and look at Hericane, who's standing silently with hands on her hips. "Mr. Dixon, you're in luck. My friend here might be interested in a bout, after all."

Hericane scowls. "I would?"

"Hot dog!" says Dixon. "*Hericane* working a *contract bout* for me? My business will go through the *roof*!"

I shake my head and place an index finger against my lips. "No names, Mr. Dixon. Just say you've got someone lined up. Give a fake name if they press you."

"Whatever you say." Dixon makes with the maybe-it's-a-wink again. "Everyone'll still know who it was after the fact. They'll know *Hericane* is working for *me*."

I sigh and point at the phone in his lap. "Just answer the e-mail and tell us when and where, Mr. Dixon." Then hide in a very deep hole till this is all over, I should tell him. If *we* found you, the *Protectorate* can't be too far behind.

But I think he already knows all that.

Hericane and I drive to the location Dixon gives us--the downtown construction site where the new sports stadium is being built. We park a few blocks away, and then she flies us in over the high fence bordering the property.

We land around back, in the shadows away from the security

lights. I check my watch and see we're twenty minutes early. The bout's due to begin at 1AM sharp.

And that is all we know--the when, the where, but not the who or how or anything else. We're coming in blind, and we've got no backup. If one of us wasn't the most powerful woman on the planet, I'd be seriously sweating right now.

Even so, I know this is risky. Last time Dixon arranged a bout on behalf of an anonymous player, the fighter-for-hire ended up neck-deep in a bullshit murder frame-up.

I keep wondering what the surprise is gonna be *this* time.

"All right." I draw my .45 and check the clip. "You ready?"

Hericane nods. She's been pretty quiet since we left Dixon's place. I'll bet the reality of Mardi's death is finally setting in...and with it, the grief she's been delaying.

Or not. "Do you think we'll find Mardi in time?" She looks vulnerable as she tucks her long, blonde hair behind her ears. "Do you think we'll be able to save her?"

What the hell do I say to that? I need the girl fired up big time, but if I manage to force her to see the truth, will it push her over the edge?

Frankly, I'm kind'a stunned that she still doesn't get it after what we've been through. How many more times does she have to hear people talk about the murder before she finally figures out it's for real?

Or is there another reason for her prolonged denial? Her father suffered from extreme dementia. For the first time, I wonder if maybe she's got a touch of it, too.

If she does, it won't do any good to try to shock her out of it just now. "We're trying our best." I reach out and give her arm a squeeze. "That's all we can do."

Hericane shakes her head and stares off into space. "I tried to get her to quit, you know. To give up crimefighting. Shepherd's Pie and Do Si Do nearly killed her last month. Did you know that?"

"Yes." The case came through the Internal Affairs Division of the Protectorate, though I wasn't the one who caught it. "I know Overtime saved her."

"I should've been there." She clenches her jaw. "I should've done something."

Does she mean she should've been there a month ago, or earlier today? "No one can be everywhere at once," I tell her. "Not even you." I give her arm another squeeze.

"I just want to see her one more time." She brushes a tear from her cheek. "I want one more chance to show her how much I love her."

The clock is ticking. I need to snap her out of it. "You want to help Mardi? You want to do right by her?" I wave the gun at the skeletal bulk of the vast stadium towering over us. "Then get out there and take down whoever shows up for this fight. Get 'em to tell us what they know about the people who got Mardi."

Hericane brushes aside another tear. "Will do."

I check my watch and give her the nod. "Time to rock 'n' roll. Time to do what you do best."

She bobs her head from side to side. "Bad guys." A flash of a smile flickers across her face. "Kicking the asses of."

"Go get 'em," I tell her, and then she leaps up into the sky and vaults over the lofty walls, heading for the heart of the stadium.

With my .45 firmly in hand, and all my senses focused intently on my surroundings, I jog along the cement concourse leading under the stands. I see no one in the broad beams of the security lights arranged along the curving concourse to either side of me. It's Friday night, so work's stopped for the weekend; whatever guards are ranging around, they're nowhere nearby. That saves me some inconvenience.

I cast quick glimpses all around as I follow the concourse, aiming for the field. Three months from now, this place will be finished and thrumming with life--people moving in all directions, vendors hawking beers, lights flashing, food cooking. The blast of a rock band performing a concert, the crack of a baseball bat on the field. I can practically hear them now.

And then I *do* hear a blast from the field, a loud, echoing *crack* that rattles the bare metal beams around me.

Game on.

Tightening my grip on the gun, I break into a run. There's an access point up ahead, on my left, and I charge full-tilt toward the opening.

As I run, light flares from the opening, illuminating the concourse--then fading. Who showed up, I wonder? Who is it out there, on the field, fighting Hericane?

When I get the answer, I don't like it.

Bolting left, I dash through the access-way, emerging into the cool night air. My feet touch down in the dirt at the edge of the plain where the field will be, and I stop. I look to the sky just in time to be blinded by a burst of bright white light.

The blindness fades, and I finally see who showed up. I see the opponent we've come here to face.

Make that *opponents*, plural.

The blood runs ice cold in my veins. I knew I'd be surprised, I couldn't guess who'd show up for the bout. But this.

Holy shit.

But this throws me into a state of a shock. I literally freeze in place as the situation and implications soak through me. As I realize how much shittier my life has just gotten.

Because those people up there, swarming around Hericane? And the ones down on the field, firing their powers and weapons up at her? Those thirteen people?

They're all heroes. They're all top-percentile heroes in the Superhuman Protectorate.

Not the bad guys. The good guys. The best of the best. And it looks to me like they're trying their best to kill her.

That's Red Baron up there, strafing her with explosive projectiles as he swoops by. Sputnik whips past to follow up, zapping her with crackling beams of intense radiation. Then Concorde rams her at high speed, plowing dead on into her belly, driving her back across the sky.

I know all three of them well. Until now, I thought they were decent human beings. Same goes for all the rest of the attackers out there.

I never knew how wrong I was until now.

Concorde breaks away, leaving Hericane reeling through the air. That's when the bunch on the ground cut loose with their latest barrage. Party Rocker casts up a wall of sonic force that sends Hericane tumbling in the opposite direction. Geyser shoots up streams of high-pressure water that blast her in the face...then Homewrecker, the expanding woman, grows to a 60-foot height and catches her. She holds Hericane in her fist as the airborne heroes converge and pummel her with one mighty blow after another.

Holy shit.

Hericane might be the mightiest woman on the planet, perhaps the mightiest human being period, but she looks like she's on the ropes right now. They took her by surprise, and there are just so many of them--thirteen against one. She could wreck any one of them--hell, any three or four of them--but that's a lot of A-listers to handle at one time.

She gathers her strength and bursts free of Homewrecker's grip, then slugs her way through the flying circus...only to find herself clamped in the jaws of Sky Shark. As soon as she fights her way loose, King David nails her in the head with a blazing nuclear pellet from his holy slingshot. She flounders like a fly stung by a swatter, drifting in off-kilter loops--until Old Glory wraps her in the suffocating folds of his stretchable star-spangled banner body.

Meanwhile, down on the sidelines, I get over my shock and come back to life. I let the .45 fall at my side; it won't do me any good against this crowd. This is a job for Panic Attack.

Quickly, I assess the battlefield and devise a strategy. Should I send out a general wave of panic, or use surgical strikes to focus on key individuals? A general wave means each person gets a lower dose; but zeroing in on key targets requires more finesse.

Whatever I do, I have to do it now. The bucking and thrashing within Old Glory's wrapped flag cocoon looks like it's lessening.

Hericane is mega-powerful and nearly indestructible, but she's still susceptible to lack of oxygen.

So my choice is obvious. Start there, with the American Flag Hero.

Concentrating with all my might, I reach out to Old Glory, beaming panic-inducing currents into his mind and body. When at first he fails to release her, I really pour it on. As I've learned from experience, high doses of panic can have an undesirable effect--making Old Glory suddenly contract, for instance, and lock up around his captive. Major panic can make people do the opposite of what you want them to; it's not an exact science.

But it's not like I've got a choice in the matter. Hericane's fighting less and less with each passing second.

So I intensify my effort. I give it all I've got.

Finally, Old Glory unwinds and frantically flutters off on the breeze, leaving Hericane to fall...but she doesn't hit the ground. Trampolina dives underneath her, letting her infinitely elastic body bounce Hericane back up into the sky.

Homewrecker reaches to catch her, but I snag her giant backbrain with a bolt of terror. It makes her stop and back off, looking horrified, as Hericane shoots past her.

For a few precious seconds, no one is pounding on Hericane. Shishkabob flings up a few interdimensional skewers, which bounce right off her, but my panic blasts keep everyone else away. I fire them at every A-lister who makes a move toward Hericane or even looks at her funny. I buy her a few more seconds of recovery time.

That's all Hericane needs. When she's 70 feet in the air, she stops her upward motion and hovers there, looking down at her foes. Several start to move toward her at once...but then I blanket the lot of them with a wave of general panic. So much for surgical strikes.

Only one of the Protectorate's soldiers overcomes the wave and rockets toward Hericane: Gestalt, the heroine who taps the power of humanity's group unconscious. She blasts her way toward Hericane with fists extended, ready to land her trademark power-of-the-people hammer-punch.

I quickly focus in on her, but it's too late. She's moving too fast.

At the last second, Hericane dodges left--but Gestalt still manages to connect with the side of one fist. It's enough to send Hericane spinning across the sky.

For a moment, I think it might be all over. I struggle to keep the panic flowing, but other so-called heroes shrug it off and head for Hericane. Gestalt turns around for another run at her, too.

Hericane stops spinning and slumps in midair. Maybe she was hit harder than I thought.

Meanwhile, all the other airborne heroes zoom toward her from all directions. It happens sometimes, like a chain reaction; one brave person inspires others to resist panic.

I use every last bit of willpower to try to pull those people back, but I can't. They keep up the charge, all cruising toward her at once like a flight of missiles zeroing in on her heat signature.

And she just hangs there, limp and defeated as a puppet whose strings have been cut. She's already taken so much punishment. Can she possibly withstand the incoming assault by so many powerhouses?

The panic attacks aren't working, so I stop trying--and I raise the .45. Maybe I can distract them, at least.

I aim well away from Hericane and crack off a shot...but the heroes keep flying. All I accomplish is draw the attention of the earthbound contingent.

Suddenly, the airborne attackers plunge at their target. Hericane disappears in the pile-on.

But only for a moment. Next thing I know, Sky Shark's hurtling away from the pile, screaming. Next comes Red Baron and Gestalt, followed by Concorde. Sputnik plummets down after that, crash-landing in the midst of the heroes on the ground. That just leaves Old Glory, Ball Lightning, and Air Marshall, who wrestle their prey a moment longer, straining to hold on.

Only to fly off in all directions as Hericane flexes her mighty muscles.

What an incredible woman.

While the thirteen heroes are down, Hericane flashes across

the field and scoops me up in her arms. Then, she soars up out of the stadium and races into the night.

Only when we're up there do I realize how shaky she is. Only when I see her up close do I notice how bad she looks.

She's in worse shape than I knew.

"We need to go somewhere." She coughs. "We need to get off the radar."

"Okay." Her flying's wobbly, and it's making me nervous. I wish I had the power to *remove* fear, in which case I'd use it on myself right now. "I know a place."

We hole up in a decrepit old house in the woods, out past the city limits. I know the place well--well enough that I have a key to the front door on my key ring. Well enough that I hesitate on the threshold before stepping inside.

Too well.

But it's secluded, and I don't think they'll look for us here. At least not for a while. I hope.

Though the truth is, I've sorely underestimated the Protectorate lately. So who the hell knows?

I guide Hericane inside and shut the door. She goes straight to the dust-infested couch and throws herself down on it without a word.

She really did take a pounding back at the stadium. Her hair's a tangled mess, her white costume is torn and smeared with dirt, and her cape is gone. Believe it or not, she even has some bruises on her face. Those A-listers really did a number on her.

I slump in the moldy matching chair across from her and rub my eyes hard. I don't turn on the lights, because there's no juice in here. Place has been shuttered and empty for seven years now.

This effing place.

"So." I blow out my breath in a big, tired gust. "Another set-up."

"No shit." Hericane's voice is hoarse, exhausted. I wonder if she's up for any of this anymore.

I should probably leave her the hell alone, but...the clock's ticking. Now more than ever. Whatever window of opportunity we have in which to act, it's closing too damn fast.

So I keep the ball rolling. "The Protectorate set us up. I'm guessing they set up Chimpanzero, too. They were behind all of this from the get-go."

Hericane's silent for a very long moment. I wonder briefly if she's dozed off...and then she speaks. "But why? Why would they want to kill Mardi Gras?"

Her words land with the impact of a bomb in the dark and dusty room. I stop rubbing my eyes and look at her, a figure in tattered white arrayed on the couch.

She knows. She knows her lover is dead.

Maybe she knew from the start. Maybe pushing it back was the only way to keep going and deliver the justice Mardi deserved. Or maybe the shock of it all threw her into genuine denial or delusion, and she only just now snapped out of it. Either way, one thing is suddenly clear.

She knows.

Not that I'm going to belabor the obvious. "Do you know what Mardi was working on most recently?"

Hericane shakes her head. "She kept me out of the loop since I started trying to get her to quit."

"Damn." I rub my eyes again. I need to get out of this shit-hole, we need to get moving, time's running out...but we've got nothing. This investigation is dead in the water.

We're dead, too, if we don't find a way to bring it back to life.

We sit in silence for a while, thinking our private thoughts. I keep expecting to hear her doze off, but the snores never come. Does she even *need* to sleep?

Eventually, her hoarse voice rises from the shadows. "Did you used to live here?"

I guess it was obvious since I had the key to the front door. "Yes," I tell her. "A long time ago."

"So what happened here?" She has a quick mind. Already figured out something bad happened, otherwise why would the place be empty? And why would it have a hold on me, such that the key is still on my key ring? If I'd gotten it in a divorce or inheritance, I'd still be living here, or I'd have sold it or rented it out.

So what happened here? What happened to make my stomach ache and my eyes burn with tears just from being inside these walls?

Tell her, Bonnie. Just tell her.

"Home invasion." The words stick in my throat. "My husband and two little boys..." I wasn't here, I didn't see it happen, but I see it play out before me for the hundred millionth time, just the way I imagined it from reading the police reports. There's Jimmy now, opening the front door, getting clubbed in the head with the butt of a shotgun. There are the two maniacs, pushing their way into the house with duct tape and coils of rope. The knives, they get from the kitchen counter--ceramic blades, a wedding gift.

My two little boys run into the room crying. The butchers hogtie Jimmy and slice him up while they watch. Then they...

Oh God, why them God, why not me, God? You could have had me a thousand times over and a million times worse. I would give myself freely to those maniacs if only you'd spare my beloveds.

I feel the tears. Rolling down my cheeks.

"I'm sorry." Hericane says the words softly. "I'm so sorry."

"I was working late," I tell her. "If only I'd been here..."

Hericane clears her throat. "Were they superhumans?"

"No." Of course not, of course they weren't. I couldn't even console myself with that, with knowing that I couldn't have stopped them if I'd been here when they invaded. "Just a pair of thrill-killing lunatics passing through."

"So they were caught. By the police?"

I shake my head, wiping away tears. Right there, in the middle of the room, I see it again, just as it's happened every day and night in my imagination. Every minute, every minute of my life, it plays back on some level, in a never-ending loop. The boys, my brave little boys...

They try to fight back.

"A vigilante caught up with them," I tell Hericane. "A superhuman called Deathalyzer. He killed them on the spot. Turned them inside-out." That piece of shit, that son of a bitch. He cheated me. Not because I care that much about justice or the legal system, not in that situation.

I hated him because he robbed me of the chance to do what *I* wanted to do to those animals.

Hericane turns her head to look at me. "Did you hire him? Deathalyzer, I mean?"

I shake my head.

She looks back at the ceiling. "How long ago did this happen? How many years?"

"Seven." The word emerges through clenched teeth. A deep wellspring of emotion surges inside me, fighting to get out. I thought I could handle coming here given the circumstances, given that I'm running for my life, but surprise. I can't.

"Does it get better?" says Hericane. "After seven years, does it get any better?"

I know what she needs to hear, I know what will help her through her own private hell...but I can't say it. I won't bullshit her. I hated when other people did that to me, and I'm not going to do it to her.

"No." That's what I tell her. "It never gets better."

Hericane lies still on the dusty couch, hands folded over her belly, knees drawn up. "That's what I figured." There's a tightness in her voice that wasn't there before, like her vocal cords are tied in a knot. Like she's going down the road that I've been traveling, watching the mental movie unspool in her head. Watching Mardi Gras answer the door of her apartment and then what she imagines came next.

But this is the worst movie of all, because she doesn't know what came next, no one does except the killer. So she fills in the blanks with the worst possible details, the greatest amount of suffering, the foulest cruelty imaginable.

Somebody has to stop her before she sinks any deeper. There'll be time enough for that later, but right now the border between her and her dead lover is perilously thin.

I need to get her back on task. "Did Mardi Gras keep any kind of record of her activities?"

"Like a casebook?" Hericane shakes her head. "Not that I know of. We were both worried about leaving proof that would compromise our secret identities." The tightness is gone from her voice. I have a hunch she's glad for the change of subject.

"There must be something." I see my kids dying in the middle of the room again, and I force myself to look away. All that does is shift my attention to the front door, where Jimmy's getting clubbed with the butt of the shotgun again.

So I close my eyes. I try to block it out. Because something's nagging at me. Something to do with the case.

I put myself back at the crime scene and reach deep, straining to unearth what's bothering me. I see Mardi's shredded costume hanging from the ceiling fan, slowly turning. I see the blood stains splattering the walls, floor, ceiling, and everything in between. I see the bits of blown-apart tissue sticking everywhere, the hundreds or thousands of pieces of what had once been a vibrant human being, a genuinely good-hearted super-hero from what I'd seen and heard, a woman who was full of fun and surprises and...

Holy shit.

That's it. That's what's been nagging at me.

I get up out of the chair and stretch. "How are you feeling?"

"Like shit. Total effing shit," says Hericane. "Why?"

I pull out the .45 and check the clip. A-OK. "I think we need to go back to the evidence. I think we missed something."

Slowly, Hericane rolls over and hauls herself up to a seated position. "Like what?"

"I don't know." I shove the gun back into its holster. "But there has to be something." I hesitate, reluctant to say what's next. I don't want to bring it all back to her in all its fresh agony--but I know in my heart she's already reliving it anyway. "The way we found her. Why would someone kill her like that?"

Hericane grunts and scowls as she gets to her feet. "Sending a message?" She bobs her head from one side to the other, cracking her neck. "Eliminating any margin for error?"

"I think there's a third possibility." I head for the door, ignoring my weeping little boys as they watch their father being cut to ribbons. "Let's get out of here."

"And go where?" says Hericane. "The entire Protectorate's going to be hunting us. Not to mention the citizens' auxiliary."

"We're going where the evidence is." I open the door to the sight of the two home invaders with their duct tape and rope. "The one place where a group of legally sanctioned individuals with resources and an arsenal would just love to stick it to the Protectorate."

Hericane stops in the doorway and stares at me. "The police department? We're going to the cops?"

I hear my family screaming in the living room behind me. "You bet your ass." I'm sorry, so sorry I wasn't here that night for you. Sorry I couldn't hold you in my arms and make it all better.

But maybe I can make it better for her. For Hericane.

Goodbye, my loves. That's what I think as I walk out to the sound of their shrieks. *Goodbye for now.*

And then I slam the door on them and turn my back on that place, glad to leave it. Hating myself for feeling that way for even an instant.

"Let me see if I've got this straight," says Lt. Tank Driscoll, a.k.a. the douche. "You're telling me you're *not* here for questioning?"

Words cannot express how much he's loving this right now. Hericane and I standing in his station with hat in hand, asking for his help. After the way we made him and his buddies scamper away from the Mardi Gras murder scene like frightened mice.

Now he gets to humiliate us in front of those same buddies. And we have to take it.

Open mouth, insert shit.

"That is correct," I tell him. "We're here because we need a favor."

"A *favor*." Tank's feet are planted far apart, and his hands are on his scrawny hips. His cheap navy sports coat is spread open wide as if to spotlight his package, as if to rub in the fact that he's won the biggest-dick contest. "Because you've done so many favors for *me*?"

I start to get pissed, but then I back it off. I knew what we were in for when we walked into this place. I pretty much knew word-for-word how this shit would play out. "We'll have to make it favors to be named later," I tell him.

Tank takes a look around the big office, leering like he's getting a blank check for *special* favors. His fellow cops cheer and whistle and roar with laughter, even the three women standing around. It's not so much a sexist thing. These people have no love for super-humans, and they hate "foxes" like me even more. They figure we're obstructing justice and covering for our own kind.

Which doesn't seem like such a stretch to me after today, I gotta be honest.

"So what's this favor you need from me?" Tank narrows his eyes and strokes his waxy mustache. "What's important enough to make you waltz in here--after the shitty way you treat me 99.99 percent of the time--and ask for my help?" He looks around at his buddies and shakes his head at how brazen and stupid I am.

I shake my head right back at him. "I can't tell you here. Not in front of everybody."

"So you two want to get me alone?" The douche smirks like a twelve-year-old smart-mouthing his teacher in front of the class. "Just the three of us in a *room* together?" His tone oozes innuendo, and the crowd responds with a round of whistles, howls, and laughter.

Hericane takes a step forward, and I throw out my arm to hold her back. I warned her how it would be with Tank, but I guess she's had her fill.

Too bad. If either of us effs up even the slightest bit, the douche will shut us down and cuff us. He'd be within his rights, and he knows it.

"You've got some *big balls*, you know that?" He paces in front of us, glaring like a drill sergeant. "Walkin' into *my house* after treatin' me like *your bitch* for how many *years*, expecting me to *kiss* your *ass*!" He stops in front of me and shoves his face up to mine so our noses are a hair's breadth from touching. "Well guess who's the bitch *now*?" He makes sure he says it loud enough for everyone in the office to hear.

And they do. They go wild with laughter and cheering.

But while they're doing that, I grab the collar of his sports coat and yank him toward me. Then I whisper in his ear, just loud enough for him to hear me over the ruckus.

"How would you like to be the cop who takes down the Protectorate?" That's what I tell him. "Because that's the war we're fucking fighting right now. And if you help us, *you* get the *glory*."

I let him go then, and he bobs back from me. His eyes lock with mine, and I watch his expression change from surprise to disbelief. He's wondering if he heard right; he's wondering if I'm serious. Because I just told him I'm going to give him his dream come true.

I nod without the slightest flicker of hesitation.

At which point his expression changes to a grin.

"All right then." He raises his eyebrows. "Let's go somewhere a little more--*private*--" The crowd hoots and howls again. "--and see what you ladies have to *offer*." Again with the whistles and catcalls.

So he leads us out of there, strutting like king of the pimp daddies, and we follow, two super-humans--one the mightiest woman in the world--giving control to a mere mortal douche. As if we have any choice. As if we have anyone else to turn to in this desperate hour.

Which probably makes this the sweetest moment of his life, I'll just bet.

The douche never stops posturing, so it takes a while to tell him the story. But he's interested, I can see it in his eyes. He's drooling like Pavlov's dog.

He'll give us what we want. Later, if we live through this, it will suck to be us, because he'll milk it for all it's worth...but here and now, he'll take us where we want to go.

The morgue, in other words.

"So I was right all along about the Protectorate. And *you* were wrong." That's what he says as he leads us downstairs. "I love it."

"Congratulations." I'm staying close to Hericane, keeping my eyes peeled. I know how I'd react to what we're about to see.

She just walks along with a blank expression on her face, unreadable. If there's any turbulence going on inside, she doesn't show it.

"I always knew those so-called heroes were dirty pieces of shit," says Tank when we get to the bottom and start down a dark hallway.

I know we're at his mercy, but enough's enough. "You do realize one of us *is* a hero, right?"

Tank stops and looks back at Hericane like he forgot she was there. "Well, present company excluded, of course."

I get up in his face and lock eyes with him. His breath smells like putrid bacon. "And you do remember what it is we're about do, right?" I push a little closer; I need him to get the message. "Maybe you could show a little *sensitivity* for once in your life?"

His eyes drift, and I start to think I'm gonna have to paint him a picture. Then he focuses back in on me with a tough glare, and I think he doesn't have any sensitivity to begin with.

But he surprises me. "Sorry." He leans around me and looks at Hericane with an actual sincere expression on his greasy face. "Sorry." Then he whips around and marches off down the hallway. "This way, please."

I shrug at Hericane and follow him. An apology from the douche. Will wonders never cease?

He stops at a door midway down the hall and pushes it open. Surprise again, he actually holds it for us as we walk through.

"Charlie?" He wanders off across the room and disappears through a doorway.

Leaving us to look around.

I've been here many times in my career, but this time is different. Everything is very familiar to me--the silver tables draped with sheets, the trays of equipment, the power tools. The wall of cold storage drawers, each big enough to hold a lifeless human body.

But the feeling is all wrong--darkly personal instead of all business. Painful instead of clinical.

It reminds me of the one time, seven years ago, when I was down here for Jimmy and the boys. The one time they had to drag me kicking and screaming out the door, knocking shit over right and left.

Here we are again. Only she's taking it a lot better than I did.

At least on the outside.

Still, something needs to be said before this goes any further. "Hey." I turn and meet her gaze. "If you need to step out, you step out, all right?"

Hericane frowns and shakes her head. "I'm okay."

"Be that as it may, you got nothing to prove here." I raise my eyebrows. "Nothing to prove to anyone. You understand?"

She looks past me at the middle table, where vague outlines of parts and pieces are visible under the draped white sheet. She blinks once, then twice, then nods. "Sure."

"This will suck. I don't care who you are, this *will* suck." Reaching out, I give her invulnerable arm a squeeze. Feels just like any other arm to me. "But you got a friend right here. Okay?"

Hericane nods, eyes locked on the middle table.

I give her arm a shake. "*Okay*?"

Her eyes dart away from the table and back to me. "Okay."

"Okay, ladies." Just then, Tank strolls back in, clapping his hands together. "Let's get this show on the road."

The coroner walks in behind him--an old guy named Charlie Abernathy. Sweetest guy you could ask for, been with the department since Eve ate the apple. More grandkids than there are ants in an anthill.

"Hello, Bonnie." He looks up from his stooped shuffle, peering over his Coke bottle glasses. "So very good to see you, dear."

"You, too, Charlie." Guy oughtta make me cringe, he autopsied Jimmy and the kids...but instead he makes me smile every time. What's he doing working with trash like Tank?

"Lieutenant Driscoll has filled me in." Charlie shuffles to the middle table and stops, looking at Hericane. "He says you're the victim's next of kin?"

Hericane bites her lip and nods. "Mm-hm."

Charlie touches a corner of the sheet on the table and clears his throat. "I guess you know she was pretty well obliterated. Her remains were dispersed throughout the apartment." He clears his throat again. "We, uh...we gathered her up as best we could. I doubt you'll see much that you recognize."

Hericane nods. Her eyes are locked on that sheet.

"But maybe that's a blessing, in a way." Charlie manages the faintest smile, and then it's gone. He pulls up the corner of the sheet and keeps going, peeling it away as he shuffles from one end of the table to the other.

"Ready?" I ask Hericane.

She nods.

"Let's get this over with." I walk over to the table as Charlie flicks on the bright lights above it.

He wasn't kidding about not recognizing much. Instead of a body, there's a pile of bloody bits oozing over the length of a black plastic trough. It looks like what you'd get if you put a person through a wood chipper.

Don't know how much of a blessing it is, though.

As Hericane draws up beside me, she covers her nose and mouth against the stench, which is atrocious. Her eyes glisten with tears as she stares down at the mess in the trough--all that's left of someone she adored.

And then the mightiest woman on Earth turns away. She turns her back on the sight and sobs.

I see the douche open his mouth to say something, and I shoot him a warning glare. Don't you dare. Ninety-nine percent of what comes out of your mouth is poison, so don't you dare.

Let's stick with the business at hand. Give her time to come around.

"Have you found anything?" I ask Charlie. "Any relevant trace evidence?"

Charlie shakes his head. "Honestly, I'm not sure where to start. We've got nothing bigger than a fingertip to work with." He hesitates and looks at Hericane, then continues. "No fingernails, though, mind you. Even her dental fillings were torn out."

"Overkill," says Tank. "Big time. Payback's a bitch."

"I don't know." I crook a finger against my lips as I gaze into the mess in the trough. "I've been thinking about that. Maybe they were looking for something."

Tank screws up his face in a scowl so deep, it pulls his right eye shut. "Something *inside* her?"

"Why else would they tear her to pieces like this?" I say. "To send a message? Then where's the message?" I shake my head. "To make sure she's gone for good?" I shake my head again. "She wasn't invulnerable. A bullet to the brain would've accomplished the same thing."

Tank unscrews his scowl and shrugs. "Say you're right, and the killer was looking for something. It doesn't matter. We'll never know what it was."

"Does it *look* like they *found* it?" I gesture at the trough. "Maybe it's still in there."

"If so," says Charlie, "how will we ever find it?"

Suddenly, Hericane stops sobbing and turns to face the table. "I'll bet the killer didn't have 21 senses." Her voice is steady and cold, her face tear-stained but stony. "Unlike me."

I give her my best "are you sure you're ready for this?" look, and she doesn't flinch. Heroine that she is, she's pulled herself together to deal with the crisis at hand.

No matter how awful it will be.

"Excuse me," she says to Charlie. "Can you give me some kind of--instrument--to, uh..." She moves her hand back and forth over the trough.

Charlie shuffles over to a tray of tools on a nearby metal counter. He fishes around for a moment, clattering things together, and comes back with a clawed, silver utensil. He hands it over without comment.

"Thank you." Hericane looks at me like she wants me to move, so I do. She steps in to take my place alongside the trough.

Then she hesitates. Looks up at the ceiling and takes a deep breath. Like she's bracing herself.

My hand twitches. Maybe she's not ready for this after all. I start to reach for her, to keep her from doing this thing no one should ever have to do.

But before I can make contact, she leans down over the remains and begins her work.

In the field of blazing bright light cast down from above by Charlie's lamps, she gazes at the contents of the trough. Wrinkles her nose once, and then never again.

Gently, she dips in the clawed instrument and stirs the mess, moving it around. I watch over her shoulder as she turns over the lumps, training her 21 senses on them at what has got to be maximum intensity.

She rakes the tool through the bloody mush for a long time with no sign of finding anything or even coming close. She doesn't linger over a particular bit or lift anything up out of the ooze. She just keeps looking, aiming her 21 senses invisibly at the gruesome slop that used to be her lover.

After a while, it seems like nothing will ever come of this. Charlie pulls up a wheeled stool and takes a load off. The douche paces the floor, scratching his head. Even I begin to lose hope.

But not Hericane. She just keeps patiently combing the instrument through the remains, silently searching for some kind of revelation.

Would I have been able to do this, I wonder? If it was Jimmy or one of the boys in that trough? Could I have done what she's doing for even a single moment, let alone an hour?

No fucking way. I would've snapped at the first glimpse of that mess. But not Hericane.

My admiration for her grows with each passing second.

After a while longer, Tank stops pacing. "I gotta hit the head. Be right back."

He's halfway out the door when Hericane finally stops raking. "Hold on."

Tank returns to the table. Charlie gets up off his stool. And all of us lean closer to the mush, straining to see what's gotten her attention.

"Okay." Carefully, she steers a stubby object, a half-inch long, to the edge of the trough. "Forceps, please."

Charlie shuffles to a nearby tray and hurries back with a fresh instrument. He gives it to her handle-first.

"Thanks." Hericane slips her thumb and forefinger through the looped handles and cranks them apart, scissoring the hinged forceps open. Then she lowers the instrument to the trough and clamps the ridged jaws around the object she has found.

As she lifts it out, Charlie brings over a small metal basin without being asked and holds it under the forceps. Hericane opens the jaws, and the stubby object drops into the basin.

"What the hell is it?" says Tank.

Hericane raises the basin under the bright lights. Charlie hands her a pair of tweezers--again without being asked--and she uses them to prod at what she's found. "The tip of a left pinky finger."

"Without the nail," says Tank, stating the obvious.

"Which I think was what the killer was looking for." Hericane turns over the fingertip and pokes the tweezers at the area once covered by the missing nail. "Mardi Gras must have had a microchip planted under there. Which tells me that whatever she was investigating, it was pretty huge."

"Like a cover-up by the Protectorate, maybe?" says Tank.

I notice Charlie perk up a little when he hears that one. Apparently, Tank didn't fill him in on all the details before our private autopsy.

"So the killer got the chip." I start to lose hope again. "So we're back to square one."

Hericane shakes her head and pokes the fingertip again. "The chip left an imprint on the nail bed. An imprint I can read with my twelfth and sixteenth senses." She squints as she gazes at the fingertip. "Can somebody point me to a computer? There's a bunch of code we need to transcribe."

Tank gets us an IT guy with a smokin' laptop, and we put him to work. Hericane reads off endless streams of numbers, and Gary the IT guy types them into his machine as fast as he can. Hericane could do it faster, of course, but her hyper-speed typing would melt the keyboard.

"This is ASCII code," says Gary. "It converts to simple text."

I stare at the laptop screen and shake my head. "I didn't know Mardi Gras was such a computer whiz."

"She had help," says Gary. "The one and only King Crypto. Dude signed his work." He taps the screen and smiles.

"An old boyfriend of hers." Hericane frowns. "I didn't know they were still in touch." Her voice trails off.

There's a moment of awkward silence. Hericane stares at the fingertip in the basin. Gary watches the screen, keeping his hands poised over the keyboard. The douche, who's sitting with his feet up on a stool, snores.

Then, Hericane shakes her head, clears her throat, and keeps reading code from the nail bed of her dead lover's pinky finger.

And Gary keeps typing like a maniac.

When Hericane finishes reading code, we head for a conference room upstairs. Only Charlie stays behind; I give him a quick hug on the way out.

Once we get resettled, Gary converts the ASCII code to text on his laptop. There's a projector on the big conference room table, and he uses it to display the results on the wall.

What we see is not a revelation at first. Just a jumble of names, places, and dates.

But holy shit. Does it *become* a revelation.

Tank brings in another laptop, shrugs off his sports coat, and rolls up his sleeves. Then he goes to work, searching police databases for anything related to what's up on the wall.

And a picture begins to form.

Each name identifies a missing person or a victim of an unsolved murder. Each date corresponds with a victim's death or disappearance. Each place represents a location in or near Isosceles City.

There are so many of them--name after name after name. Men, women, children, all ages, all races, all social strata. Some date back ten years or more. Others are as recent as last week.

Some are known to me from coverage in the media; others, I've never heard of.

And all of them have one thing in common, one thing that jumps out at me so far. "No superhumans." If any superhumans were on that list, I would recognize them at least. Though I guess I should qualify that. "No *known* superhumans."

"Fifty-seven names." Gary whistles and flops back in his chair. "That's a long list."

"Jody Lynne McIntyre. Son of a bitch." Tank scrolls through a record on his laptop screen. "What a little cutie. My first case when I made detective five years ago." He stops scrolling and looks at me. "All we ever found was her head."

I never thought it would happen, but my heart goes out to him.

Gary puts all the information in a table, along with photos of the victims. When I see them on the wall like that, all those people, I burn with pity and rage.

"They're not superhumans." I walk up close to the wall, blocking the projector so the victim's faces appear on my back.

"Probably," says Tank.

"And they're all missing persons or victims of unsolved murders," I say, moving out of the projector's beam. "So what else do they have in common? What's so important about them that Mardi Gras would put all their names on a secret chip the Protectorate was willing to kill for?"

Gary keeps typing away on his laptop. "I've got nothing so far. None of the cases is cross-indexed with any of the other cases in any law enforcement database."

"Wait a minute." I point at what's bothering me--a lone street address at the bottom of the table, entered twice. "What's this?"

"Unmatched data point," says Gary. "It was presented that way without comment in the code. Every other address accompanies a person's name and a date."

"It's up here twice." I point at each of the two versions in turn. "Mistake?"

Gary shakes his head. "Not by me." He looks at Hericane.

She's been pretty quiet since she finished reading the code off the fingertip. She isn't ready to talk yet, either; she just folds her arms over her chest and casts a steely glare at him without saying a word.

So what then?" says the douche. "Why was it in there twice?"

"Because it's important." I run my finger down through the list of 57 and stop at the bottommost address. "Everything else is leading up to it." I smack my palm against the wall over the duplicated address. It reappears on the back of my hand. "It's like she put it in boldface and circled it with red ink. It's the most important thing on the chip."

Gary taps and types on his laptop, and the view on the wall changes. He's called up a search engine and is entering the address. "So where is this place?"

Tank scowls. "Beats me."

I think hard and come up empty. "Doesn't ring a bell."

Gary's search delivers zero results. "Nothing. Let me run that again."

"Don't bother," says Hericane.

All eyes swoop over and land on her at once.

"Why not?" says Tank.

"Because I know where it is," says Hericane. "I know exactly where it is."

I take a step toward her. "Then why don't the rest of us know?"

"Because." Hericane sighs. "You're not supposed to."

Gary's still typing furiously on the laptop. "And why do all my Internet searches keep coming up empty?"

"It's a secret," says Hericane. "A great big superhero secret."

"How big?" asks Tank.

"Bigger than you can imagine," says Hericane. "And I guess you're about to find out for yourselves."

Tank's already out of his seat, charging for the door. "Sounds like my kind of evening!"

"No, trust me." Hericane's voice is grim. "You won't like it. You won't like it at all."

We get out of the car on Main Street, which is pretty empty this time of night. It's that golden hour between 3AM and 5AM, when most of the drunks have staggered home and before the early shift workers have started their morning commute.

"So what is this place?" Tank pumps his double-barreled shotgun, ramming shells into the chambers. The douche is armed to the teeth. "What's the deal here?"

It's a good question. Standing on the sidewalk, all I see in front of us is a row of old brownstone office buildings. Scattered windows in the upper floors are lit from within--by cleaners or workaholics, I'm guessing--but not many.

"Like I said, it's a super-hero secret." With that, Hericane strides across the sidewalk, heading for the building we're parked in front of. Tank and I follow, but she's two steps ahead of us, rushing toward that building.

Then, suddenly, she veers hard left. And disappears.

Tank and I stop in our tracks and stare. She's just gone.

"What the fuck?" Leveling his shotgun at the empty space where Hericane vanished, Tank circles around it. "Where'd she go?"

For a minute, I think maybe we just got played. Maybe she had no intention of letting us in on the big secret.

But then, without warning, her hand shoots out of nowhere and grabs my arm. Before I can say a word or make a move, she yanks hard, pulling me toward her.

As I go, my head spins, and a wave of vertigo rolls through me. My stomach lurches, and I think I'm gonna be sick. Feels like the whole world shifts and folds and turns at once.

Then, it all unfolds around me and straightens out again. I'm left swaying on the sidewalk, shivering, gaping at my surroundings.

Which, weirdly enough, look pretty much the same as they did before the fun house ride I just went through. Street, sidewalk, street lights, office buildings...

Wait. Not the same after all. There's...

Holy shit.

There's an extra building.

"Oh my God," I say as I gape at it. "Where did *that* come from?"

"It's been there for ages," says Hericane. "You just never saw it before."

We stand in front of an impossibility. A building that shouldn't exist.

And it's a *big* building, impossible to ignore. Except...

I've driven past this spot a million times--make it a billion--and I've never seen it. Hell, I've *walked* past it a million times. But she says it was there all along.

A chill courses along my spine as I stare. It's an old-school theater, complete with a big marquee--two white display boards framed in brass and light bulbs, angling from the building's façade to meet in a point over the sidewalk. The marquee's dark tonight, the boards are empty, but the name of the place curls in unlit neon letters atop each side. And it's spelled out in block letters on a tall neon sign that *is* lit, glowing dim red, mounted along the side of the building.

Atlas. That's its name.

I've never even heard of it.

I'm awestruck, to say the least. I can't take my eyes off the place. "How...how long did you say this has been here?"

"Since the 1920s," says Hericane. "Vaudeville acts played here, jazz bands, you name it. They converted it to a movie house in the 50s. By the 70s, it was a porn theater." She sighs softly. "Then, in 1986, the Surrogates took the place over."

I nod. *That* name, I recognize--the most infamous team of stop-at-nothing super-villains ever to terrorize Isosceles City.

"In 1987, they succeeded in opening the Refraxus here. They were looking for unlimited power--and they found it. The kind of power that could end the world." Hericane turns and gazes through the front doors at the darkened lobby. "And they almost did. Some good men and women died trying to stop them."

I search my mind and frown. "Why don't I remember any of this?"

She gestures at the Atlas Theater. "Same reason you don't remember this place. It's been hidden from you. From everyone...almost."

This sounds insane. I'm an internal affairs investigator in the Superhuman Protectorate. I'm supposed to know *everything*. "Hidden how?"

"There's a team," says Hericane. "Blindspot, Concealer, Lethe, Retcon, a few others. Professionals at this kind of thing. They adjust memories, scrub records, construct elaborate sensory illusions. They keep this place--and events connected with it--under wraps."

I feel like the ground is shifting under my feet. Not literally--but the situation is changing. Hericane's describing a cover-up of monumental proportions...and her lover died investigating a cover-up. Coincidence?

I've thought of Hericane as a victim, an ally, maybe even a friend. But now I wonder if she's in this deeper than I imagined. I wonder if her motives in bringing me here are darker than I've considered.

Maybe I'm in way over my head here.

She turns and walks toward the front door. "Come on. Let's get this over with."

I look behind me, where I see a ghostly figure of Tank. He's standing on the other side of the illusion field, waving his shotgun, screaming his lungs out.

I can't believe what I'm about to say. "Aren't you bringing Tank in, too?" I never thought I'd actually *ask* to have him with me in a danger zone.

Hericane glances over her shoulder and shakes her head. "Trust me, he'll just get himself killed." She reaches for the door. "Get us *all* killed, probably."

Reluctantly, I leave him there and follow Hericane. "Are you sure about that?"

She steps inside and holds the door for me. "This place, these people--they were hard enough to deal with before all this. Now, with what happened to Mardi, and what we've learned since...I don't know." She shakes her head slowly. "How much do you hate that guy? Because whoever walks through this door right now, I have a feeling they might not be coming back out."

I look back once more. Then, I swallow hard and nod. "All right then." And I think of Jimmy and the kids and I walk through.

I'm not afraid. Not so much. Because being dead isn't the worst thing I can imagine. Seeing my precious boys sooner rather than later wouldn't be so bad, when you get right down to it.

At first, the darkened lobby of the Atlas Theater looks empty. But no sooner do we take three steps over the threadbare red carpet than two guys walk out of a door over by the concession counter.

Both guys wear black suits and red ties, and their grooming is impeccable. If I had to pick an age, I'd say mid-thirties for either one.

Good guess. I realize, as they rush toward us through the shadows, that I recognize both of them.

The one with the slick black hair and the mole on his cheek is CEO, "the Chief Executive Officer of Justice." The one with the shaggy blond look, beard, and granny glasses is Mogul, another business-oriented superhuman hero.

I've seen them often enough around the Protectorate offices. They're very active on the financial side of things and known for fighting white collar crime.

So what the hell do they have to do with all this, I wonder?

All I know for sure is they're surprised as hell to see us. You should see the looks on their faces--like they just got caught masturbating by their parents.

But the stunned expressions don't last. CEO is the first to switch into unruffled smoothie mode. "Hericane! Panic Attack! What brings you here?" Suddenly, he's all smiles.

"We're here to see *him*." Hericane gestures at the double doors to the auditorium.

"That's nice," says CEO, "but no can do. Big man's in the middle of a very important meeting."

"I'm sure he won't mind." Hericane pushes past, sending him stumbling backward.

But Mogul jumps in front of her at super-speed, cutting her off. "Why don't you talk to us instead? We'd love to hear what you have to say." His shaggy hair frames an expression of total surfer dude sincerity.

Meanwhile, CEO whips out his phone and hits speed dial. "Code Black," he snaps. "Code Black *right now*."

"Bonnie!" Hericane shoots out a fist, which speed demon Mogul neatly ducks. "Do your thing!"

Don't need to draw me a map. I'm already in full concentration mode, gathering my energies, picking my target.

Mogul first. I go in like a hammerhead shark, ramming his back-brain instead of tweaking it. As panic signals surge through his nervous system, I kick the shit out of his adrenal gland, slamming it into overdrive.

Just like that, Mogul's hyper-speed powers fly out of control. In the middle of dodging another blow from Hericane, he leaps away from her. Wailing, he ricochets all over the lobby like a pinball, smashing light bulbs, mirrored panels on the walls, and the glass of the concession counter display case.

One down.

Turning my focus on CEO, I see he's erupted into his raging purple monster form and is grappling with Hericane. They seem to be pretty evenly matched on the physical strength level; neither one's gaining any ground. But I can change that.

I start to work my magic on CEO--then catch myself and switch gears. Pumping up the panic levels in a creature of pure, animal fury might just make him angrier.

Instead, I give Hericane a push. Adrenaline floods her body, fueling a sudden burst of power that gives her the strength to break the clinch. With a loud grunt, she hurls the monster back, sending him crashing through a pillar. Then she blasts him with a barrage of lightning vision, shocking him into unconsciousness.

As for Mogul, he just keeps ricocheting faster, gaining momentum. I duck and run toward Hericane as he rockets past, narrowly missing a collision with me.

"Come on!" Hericane wrenches the double doors open and pulls me inside, then slams them shut behind us.

And we find ourselves standing in an ancient auditorium, darkened except for the stage and the huge movie screen above it.

When I see what's happening on that stage, my own body fills with panic--not caused by my power or anyone else's. Because what I see is unbelievable. It's horrific.

Holy shit.

I feel Hericane's hand squeeze my shoulder, my only reference point of steadiness in the face of insanity.

"Oh my God." My voice sounds tiny and weak to my own ears. "What...what...?" *What kind of nightmare is this?* That's what I want to say, but the words won't come out.

"Take a deep breath. This is that big superhero secret I was telling you about." Hericane squeezes my shoulder again. "This is what they call the Portcullis."

What I see on the stage is a real life horror show.

Hundreds of crimson tentacles thrash and slash from a pulsating red portal spanning the movie screen. The tentacles are covered with suckers and spines and twitching black cilia; they're tipped with claws and tongues and slobbering fanged maws and things I don't even recognize. Things that throb and vomit and slither and screech. Things that look like cancerous organs turned inside out or unborn babies and giant bugs stitched together in the bowels of Hell.

The sound it makes is like the screaming of a thousand maniacs being boiled alive. The stench it gives off is worse than the smell of a hundred corpses rotting and bursting in the sun.

I've been around some awful things in my life, but this one surpasses them all. Something about it cuts to my core, makes me sick to the stomach. Makes me sick in my *head*, nauseous and drugged and unhinged. All I want to do is run away.

And yet a lone figure dares to stand against it--one man clad in familiar black leather with a black cape trimmed in gleaming gold. He blasts the monstrosity with searing beams of power projected from his fists and eyes, crackling bolts that make it howl and flinch and pull back with each fresh strike.

His code name is Stalwart.

Maybe I shouldn't be surprised to see him, one of the greatest heroes of our age. After all, he triumphed over Pestis, the sentient plague, when all others had failed. He took down Big Bang and Heat Death single-handedly. Only he was hero enough to stop Mt. Slaughter from obliterating the continental shelf. And yet the fact remains.

He disappeared thirty years ago.

"Oh my God." I'm overwhelmed. Overloaded with the moment and what it brings up in me. So many feelings, so many questions. I can't process it all.

"Bonnie?" Hericane squeezes my shoulder. "Are you okay?"

I shake my head. A thousand questions well up within me, but only one finds its way out. "That thing...is Portcullis?"

"Not the thing," says Hericane. "The *place*. This *theater*. It's where the Surrogates opened the Refraxus in 1987. Now it's a *gate* to keep the end of the world they summoned from getting in."

Stalwart unleashes a flurry of beams so bright, I have to shield my eyes. "But I thought the super-heroes *stopped* the end of the world in '87."

She shakes her head. "I only said they *tried* to."

The creature's screams peak and oscillate. Sections of its gruesome tentacles burst, spraying pus everywhere. Stalwart presses the attack, pushing the mass of the monstrosity back further.

This isn't making sense. "But the world didn't end in '87."

"The *process* started," says Hericane. "The heroes could only slow it down." She gestures at the great beast writhing in the portal. "They couldn't close the Refraxus completely. That thing--the Manifestation of Armageddon--started pushing its way through into our world. If it makes it all the way, it *will* lay waste to the Earth." She gazes at the monstrosity. "What you see there is just the tip of the iceberg."

I watch the creature thrash as Stalwart pounds it with his powerful beams. "*That*--is just the *tip*?"

She nods. "Superhumans have probed beyond the Refraxus. They couldn't find the end of this thing. Some think it might span an entire *universe*."

I feel dizzy. I'm still fighting to process everything. "And Stalwart? He *disappeared* thirty years ago."

"He's been here all that time," says Hericane. "He's one of only two superhumans who've ever managed to hold the Manifestation at bay."

"The other?"

"My father, Epitome."

Suddenly, the Manifestation unleashes a deafening roar, and the theater shakes. Bombarded by Stalwart's beams, the monstrosity withdraws through the portal. Stalwart keeps up the pressure the whole time, blasting it right and left, forcing it over the threshold.

And then the Refraxus snaps shut with a great wind and a thundering crack. The movie screen looks like an ordinary movie screen again. If not for the pus and slime and twitching lumps of flesh splattered all over the stage and rows of seats, it would be like the monster had never been here.

Instantly, relief floods through me. "It closed."

"The Refraxus opens and closes on a cycle," says Hericane. "It stays open longer each time. Currently, it stays open fifteen minutes and some odd seconds and stays closed a minute more than that."

"How long did it stay closed before?" I ask. "In the beginning?"

She gives me a grim stare. "It stayed open for a minute at a time. It stayed closed for days."

Just then, a voice calls to us from the front of the theater. "Hey there!" It's Stalwart. Even after the battle he just fought, he hardly sounds winded. "Hericane, is that you?"

Hericane waves. "Hey, Stalwart. Mind if we talk to you a minute?"

Stalwart waves for us to join him. "Always happy to have company! Come on down!"

We're halfway down the aisle when the doors at the back of the auditorium burst open. Looking back, I see Mogul and CEO (in his purple rage monster form) charge in, along with three other people--heroes and Protectorate members, one and all.

There's Thunder Perfect Mind with her giant blue head, mistress of all mental powers. Beside her stands The Jupitarian, the walking gas giant, a swirling mass of colorful streaks of cloud with a stormy red spot on his chest. Hovering over all of them is Widening Gyre, the falcon-headed bird-god with the power to sow chaos and destruction.

Lots of muscle there, a real hardball lineup. But they don't move on us...yet. They just wait there behind the back row and watch.

So our course is set. Nowhere to go but down front.

When we reach the stage, Stalwart hops down with cape flapping and greets us with a big smile. "You ladies are a sight for sore eyes!" He wraps Hericane in a hug, then releases her with a quick kiss on each cheek. "It's been too long, my dear."

He seems like the friendliest, handsomest sixty-something-year-old guy you could hope to meet. His features are craggy, his silver hair thick and wavy, his physique cut like a statue of a Greek god underneath the black leather. He could be your favorite uncle, the cool one who never does you wrong and always gives you the best advice.

I can't help smiling when he takes my hand. And kisses it. "Enchanté, Madame," he says.

"This is my friend, Bonnie." Hericane touches my shoulder. "She works for the Protectorate."

"Oh, does she now?" Stalwart grins.

"She's an investigator in the Internal Affairs Division," says Hericane.

Stalwart holds my hand a moment longer, gazing up into my

eyes. And then he gently lets go. "So what can I do for you, ladies?"

Hericane reaches into her hip pocket and pulls out a folded piece of paper. "These names." She unfolds the paper and holds it out to him. "These 57 people. What can you tell me about them?"

It's the list, the one coded into Mardi's nail bed. Hericane's cutting right to the chase.

Stalwart takes the list, skims it for all of five seconds, and shrugs. "I don't understand. *Should* I know these people?" He tries handing the list back to her.

But she won't take it. "Actually, better make it 58. I left one off." She folds her arms over her chest and stares him in the eye. "My lover, Mardi Gras."

"Mardi Gras?" Stalwart looks confused. "I remember you brought her here once. What a sweet kid."

"Well, she's dead." Hericane's stare is unflinching. "Murdered, along with at least half the people on that list."

"But..." Stalwart's confusion grows. The list shakes in his hand. "Sweet little Mardi Gras? Dead?"

"Those people. Every last one of them is dead or missing." Hericane points at the paper. "And the trail ends here." She raises her finger to point at him. "Now tell us what you know."

Just then, CEO the hyper-muscular purple monster stomps halfway down the aisle and roars. "Don't say a woorrrrd! You don't have to tell her *anyyythinggg*!" Lashing out, he swats the end seat of a row of chairs, knocking down the whole row like dominoes.

"Didn't you *hear* what I just *said*?" Hericane whirls and fires a crackling double blast of lightning bolts out of her eyes. The bolts hit CEO square in the chest, sending him crashing to the floor in a smoking heap. "My *lover* is *dead*!" Eyes still arcing with electrical current, she spins back around to face Stalwart. "I'm not *leaving* here until I know who *killed* her and *why*!"

"But...but I..." Stalwart is losing his composure. "I don't know!" Looking at the gathered heroes in the back of the theater, he shakes the list overhead. "Who *did* this? Who killed Mardi Gras?"

For a long moment, no one moves or says a word.

With an angry cry, Hericane leaps into the air. "Tell me!" Her body's glowing with power. "I'll cripple you all and tear this place down! I swear to God!"

"Tear down the Portcullis and you'll end the world!" shouts Mogul.

"Do I *look* like I *give* a shit about the *world*?" Hericane spreads her arms wide, and the glow around her intensifies. "The one person *in* it who I *cared* about is *dead*! And I want *answers*!"

Gazing up at her, I wonder how far she'll take this. *Would* she end the world to avenge her lover? Then I think of Jimmy and the kids. I think of how I felt seven years ago, and I know.

Yes, she will take it all the way.

Another moment passes. Finally, Mogul walks forward with his hands in the air. "All right already. Sheesh." He walks down past CEO's unconscious form, then sits on the arm of a chair and shrugs. "Since you ask so *nicely*."

"*Tell me!*" howls Hericane.

"What the fuck? Why not?" Mogul pulls out a doobie and lights it. "Not like it'll *change* anything. Not like you can *do* anything about it."

Mogul takes a drag on the doobie and holds the smoke in his lungs. Then slowly exhales. "What if the world was ending, and somebody gave you a machine that could save it? Only the machine required...special fuel. Like...gasoline with lots of lead in it. Or..." He takes another drag, holds it, exhales. "Or people."

Everyone in the auditorium hangs on his every word. Especially Hericane, who's still hovering overhead, glowing with power--and Stalwart, whose eyes are as big as hubcaps all of a sudden. The muscles of his jaw work under the skin as he grinds his teeth; the list of victims is crumpled in his fist.

"What would you do?" Mogul holds both hands out with palms facing up, like the trays of a scale. "Give the machine the people it needs? Or let the world end, in which case all those people and everyone else dies anyway?" He lowers his right hand, dropping it down to his knee. "Couple billion lives?" He lifts up his right and lowers his left just a little. "Or a couple dozen? Which do you choose?"

"I don't understand." Hericane looks down at Stalwart. "Are you telling me *he* uses *human lives* as fuel?"

"Not fuel, so much," says Mogul, talking through his latest lungful of smoke. "More like *fun*. *Addicted* type fun." He laughs and taps some ash off the tip of his doobie. "Is there a word for that? Like nymphomania, except with tearing people apart in cold blood and devouring their organs?"

I look at Stalwart, and he's staring into space. So much for the favorite uncle routine.

"I wasn't always like this," he says quietly. "That *thing*..." He points at the movie screen, and his voice suddenly jumps. "The *Manifestation*. It *corrupts* you. You've *felt* it, haven't you?" He shoots a wide-eyes gaze in my direction. "You *know* what I mean."

I have to admit, that monstrosity played some games with my head--and that, after just a minimal exposure. But I don't answer him.

"Every time I *fight* it, that thing burrows a little deeper *inside* me," says Stalwart. "Every day, it makes me a little...a little *sicker*." His voice fades, and he stares at the floor. He mutters something to himself that I don't hear.

Mogul rolls his eyes. "So back to the story." He gets up from the arm of the chair and moseys toward us. "You've got this machine, and it's the only way to save the world, but it needs its special fuel. So what do you do?" He puffs on the doobie and smirks. "*Think* about this. We're talking about the whole *world* here."

"So the 57 people on that list," I say to him. "They're all dead. Sacrificed to keep Stalwart happy so he'll keep fighting off the Manifestation."

"Did you say 57?" Mogul shrugs. "Not sure where you're getting your info from. I thought it was more like *257*."

Holy shit.

I look at Stalwart, and chills race through my body. That man, that *hero* standing there--did he really *slaughter* 257 people and devour their organs?

"Our information?" Hericane's voice is cold, as in absolute zero. "It came from Mardi Gras, whom I'm guessing you murdered."

"So what if we did?" Mogul's doobie is down to a roach now. He huffs it once, holding it gingerly between his fingertips, then drops it and grinds it into the carpet. "She was taking it public. Can you imagine? There'd be *mass riots*. The end of Western civilization. Either that, or everyone would be just fine with it. End of the world versus a paltry few lives, remember?" Again, he raises his hands, palms up, like the balances of a scale, and dips one down just a little. "But we couldn't take that chance. Would you?"

"You make me sick." Hericane's voice is a hiss.

"Don't give me that shit!" Suddenly, Mogul goes from goofy stoner to outraged prick. "You self-righteous *fuck*!" He stops at the end of the aisle and glares up at her. "If you were given the same choice, only that was some *stranger* about to blow the lid off, not your *girlfriend*, you would've done the *exact same motherfuckin' thing*, and you *know* it!"

Hericane's aura glows brighter. "You don't know anything."

"Oh, okay. So *I'm* the big dumb fuckin' idiot." Mogul makes a face and flutters his hands. "The big dumb fuckin' idiot who kept the *world* from *ending* by keeping *big boy* there stocked up on human *happy meals*. What've *you* accomplished lately? Alienate your supposed girlfriend to the point where you didn't even know she was in *imminent danger*?" He waves a hand dismissively, voice dripping with disgust. "*Please.* Go *fuck* yourself, lady."

Hericane sets her jaw and drifts toward him. I think she's getting ready to fry his ass. Permanently.

I think he knows it, too. I think he's playing her. Before she can lash out, he flings up a hand and shouts at her. "*Now.*" He holds that way for a moment, gaze locked with hers, frozen on the brink of potential annihilation by any of a dozen different powers she could possibly unleash at him. "You have a *decision* to make."

"A decision." Hericane stops drifting. Her glow dims the slightest bit.

"You want *him*?" Mogul points at Stalwart. "You want to make him *pay*? Go ahead. But let's be clear about this. Without *him* manning the Portcullis, the world will end *today*. The Manifestation will come through and lay waste to the planet."

Hericane is silent. She turns to stare at Stalwart.

"The Refraxus opens in--let's see." Mogul checks his watch. "Less than five minutes from now. So the end of the world, the *real* Armageddon, will finally kick into high gear in less than five minutes. *Or...*"

"Or what?" I ask him.

"*Or*, we keep the status quo," says Mogul. "We all walk away and forget this ever happened. Because we *know* what's at *stake*, and we're all *grown-ups* here."

"And how many more people will die?" I say. "How many more will you have to sacrifice to *him* to keep the Manifestation at bay?"

"It. Doesn't. Fucking. *Matter!*" Mogul claps his hands together. "If the world keeps *turning*, we're still out of the *red*. We're still coming out ahead!"

"Not Mardi Gras," says Hericane. "She's not coming out ahead."

"You and that fucking Mardi Gras!" Mogul grabs his head and spins around in frustration. "Look, I'll give you the guy who killed her, all right? Justice will be done! It's *him*, right there! Bird boy!" He points at Widening Gyre. "Happy now? Do you think you can *play ball* like a *big girl?*"

Hericane glares and doesn't answer.

"Come on, will ya?" says Mogul. "We're saving the world here! It's what super-heroes are supposed to *do*!"

Still, Hericane remains silent.

Mogul lets loose a huge sigh and points at his watch. "We're running out of time here, my friend. The Refraxus will be opening any minute now. What'll it be?"

Hericane hangs there a moment more. Everyone watches, wondering what she's going to do.

But I think I know. I think I know what I would do in her place.

"Well?" says Mogul.

That's when Hericane announces her decision. She does it with actions, not words, so there's no misunderstanding.

And her message comes through loud and clear.

It happens so fast, I can barely see, she's mostly a blur. But the steps she follows are methodical and logical. She's thought this through.

She goes after Widening Gyre first. The man who killed her lover. She flashes across the auditorium and blows through him like a cannonball. The falcon-headed chaos god explodes in a burst of flesh and feathers. As his remains shower down over his comrades--Thunder Perfect Mind and the Jupitarian--Hericane zooms after her next target.

This time, it's Mogul, but he knows she's coming and kicks into hyperdrive. She chases him all over the auditorium at super-speed, racing through every inch of the place, even vibrating through every obstacle.

And eventually, she catches him. I see a flare of lightning from the blur of motion, and then Mogul's charred body hurtles to the back of the auditorium.

The smoking corpse lands in front of Thunder Perfect Mind and the Jupitarian, who jump back when it hits. They gape at the body, then at each other, and then they make a run for it, charging out the double doors into the lobby. They flee just in time; seconds later, the blur of Hericane's unstoppable flight punches through the spot where they were standing.

That leaves just one more stop. She flies past CEO, who's still out cold, and lands in front of Stalwart.

"It's almost time," he tells her, looking up at the screen. "The Refraxus is about to open."

Hericane's eyes never leave his face. "I used to look up to you. You were one of the greats. And the way you spent so many years here, holding the line." She smiles sadly. "I thought you were like a god with the world on your shoulders."

"More like the man who keeps pushing the same boulder up the hill, only to have it roll down again." Stalwart sighs. "So what are you going to do? Let the boulder fall one last time?"

Hericane takes a deep breath and lets it out slowly. "Never."

He frowns. "You'll let me live then? You'll forgive me?"

Her hands dart out and grasp the sides of his head. With one quick motion, she twists it hard left, facing almost behind him. The sharp crack of his snapping spine seems to echo through the theater.

"Never," says Hericane as she lets the body fold to the red carpeted floor.

And then she turns to me.

"Thank you," she says, "for helping me solve the case."

"Any time." I know where this is going, of course. She's going to do the only thing she *can* do. "And thank you..." For what? For sacrificing everything for the good of humanity? "Thank you for asking about my family."

"No problem." She smiles. "I hope it gets better for you."

Suddenly, a throbbing hum rises from the stage. Coruscating rays of crimson light erupt from the movie screen, casting both of us in shimmering red radiance.

"You better get going." Hericane bobs her head toward the doors in the back. "The, uh--you know--is on its way."

"Sure." My heart is pounding. I don't want to be anywhere near this place when the Refraxus opens again. But I feel like there's something left unsaid.

I reach for the words, but they won't come. Maybe something left *undone* is more like it.

So I throw myself forward and wrap her in my arms. I hug her tight, with everything I've got.

And she hugs me back. For one precious moment, by the burning red light of another world, we press against each other--cheek to cheek, hip to hip, heart to heart.

We know what's coming. We know I must leave, and we know she must stay. Because there was only one other hero in the world who could hold the line in this place, and she is his daughter. She's the only one who stands a chance.

Time seems to stand still. Floating dust motes sparkle in the rippling crimson glow.

Then, the throbbing hum becomes a thundering boom, and a hot wind gusts from the stage. I hear the screaming of a thousand maniacs, smell the stench of a hundred rotting corpses.

The portal's open again.

Hericane pushes me away. "Go! Hurry!"

"Good luck," I tell her, and then I turn and run.

And I don't look back.

A week later, I get out of my car in St. Ignatius Cemetery. Dressed in black, arms full of flowers, I walk across the flat green lawn toward a gravesite.

It's the same cemetery where they buried Stalwart, but I'm not here for him. I wasn't invited to the funeral, which happened just yesterday. Seems I'm persona non grata in superhuman land these days; the Protectorate forced me to take early retirement and even revoked my membership from the organization.

Nobody likes a troublemaker, apparently.

Not that I would have come to the funeral if they'd invited me. Just seeing it on TV made me sick to the stomach--the flag-draped casket, the procession down Main Street, the weeping citizens, the twenty-one gun salute. The President of the United States--the friggin' *President*--reciting a teary-eyed tribute as they lowered the casket into the grave.

What a fucking farce.

Let's keep it all covered up. Keep everyone saying what a hero he was. Avoid awkward explanations that turn the public against him--maybe turn the public against *all* superhumans in the bargain.

Cover those asses, folks. Don't stop and think about how many of the citizens standing along the parade route or watching at home are still mourning the loved ones he murdered. Don't think about how many of them are still wondering what ever happened to their missing husbands, wives, mothers, fathers, children. Fuck that noise.

There are a hundred reasons to keep lying, and only one not to: because it's the right thing to do.

And that's not enough.

But it was for Hericane. Thanks to her, the world keeps turning. And I get the chance to do something I haven't done in seven years.

I was worried I wouldn't remember where they were...but no. I see them up ahead, in a shady spot under a tree. Three stone markers--a big one flanked by two little ones.

Oh God.

I stop and stare from a distance, feeling like I can't go on. Feeling like I don't belong here.

But I do. My name is on the biggest stone, and the year of my birth. Someday, I'll be here forever.

Oh God.

My heart's pounding, and sweat's rolling down my sides. Chills course through my body, and my head spins.

I look away and consider turning back. I can't do this, I shouldn't have come.

The last time I was here was the funeral--their funeral. No flag-draped caskets or President of the United States or twenty-one gun salutes then. Just a dozen or so people, and a priest, and the pouring rain. Just me losing it, weeping and teetering, drunk and drugged. Falling to my knees in the mud.

I haven't been back since. I couldn't bring myself to do it. Bad enough I could still imagine their ghosts; why subject myself to physical proof?

So why come here today then? Because my life has been turned upside-down? Because I need to make a clean break with the past and get a fresh start? Because the end of the world is closer than I imagined, and I might never get another chance?

Or is it something else?

I think of Hericane taking Stalwart's place at the Refraxus. Driving back the Manifestation again and again. Fighting off its corrupting influence, too, as it grows stronger. Holding the monsters at bay both within and without. Never knowing more than a few moments' peace.

She was right about her power, inherited from Epitome, being enough to fend off the great beast--but can she keep her soul pure in the process? Or will she become the next Stalwart, twisted by unnatural cravings?

Will she falter, and allow the world to end?

The burdens she's taken upon herself are astronomically huge. The work is thankless, without reward. She has lost or given up everything she ever cared about.

But she does it anyway, because of that one reason. The same reason the Protectorate could have found to stop the lying, if they'd looked a little harder.

Because it's the right thing to do.

So okay, then.

I take a deep breath, and I face the three gravestones again. I grip the flowers so tightly, I'm afraid the stems might snap, and I start walking.

As I get closer, the names on the three stones come into focus. Even through my tears.

James Taggart, Husband and Father

William Taggart, Son

Stephen Taggart, Son

It was the end of the world when I lost them. It's the end of the world again.

Maybe it's time I finally let them go.

THE X IN XMAS

Multicolored Christmas lights blink and flicker at night in the snowy central park of the town of Abruzzi, Pennsylvania. The decorations don't inspire the slightest twinkle of Christmas spirit in Detective Charlie Collins, Abruzzi P.D.

Fat white flakes flutter down, clinging to Charlie's black overcoat and melting fast against his dark brown skin. Snapping on latex gloves, he prowls the gazebo in the heart of the park, focused on the ugliness amid the holiday beauty. All he cares about is the crime scene in the gazebo, complete with a dead Santa Claus in a sleigh.

Charlie's dark eyes scan for details with practiced intensity, seeking out any telling traces beyond the obvious...which is to say, the bearded Caucasian man in the sleigh took a bullet to the brain. That, however, is not the only major detail that jumps out at Charlie and his partner.

"Since when does Santy Claus dress in black?" asks middle-aged, beer-bellied Officer Burt Sichak, who was the first law enforcement on the scene.

It's a good question. The dead man's clothes look like standard Santa-wear, except for the fact that they're all pitch black. Even the fur trim and hat tassel, which are usually white, are full-on black.

"You ever seen a Santa outfit like that, Charlie?" Burt looks like a rotten potato in a parka, and his cheeks are flushed from drinking. He was off-duty when the body turned up. "What does the African-American Saint Nick wear?"

Charlie ignores him. Burt's sense of humor sometimes leans toward racism; his comments don't always sit well with Charlie, and he doesn't seem to care how Charlie takes them.

Things were different in Charlie's hometown of Pittsburgh… but the 'Burgh, which is two hours south, might as well be a world away. Charlie's been in Abruzzi since his fortieth birthday six months ago, and he's learned to pick his battles. He's nobody's fool, but he doesn't dial it up to eleven all the time, either.

The job is what matters most to him, as awful as it gets…and tonight's brutal murder is pretty awful. "Looks like a mob hit. Tap to the back of the head, exit wound up front."

Burt snickers. "Santa picked the wrong goombah to give a lump a' coal to, I guess."

Charlie nods. It's a fact of life; the Mafia's been a force in Abruzzi forever. This part of the state is thick with them.

Something catches Charlie's eye then, and he leans closer to the corpse. There's a crumpled bit of paper in Santa's fist, and he works to pry it out. It looks like the edges are torn, as if someone ripped the rest of it free but couldn't get the last shred from Santa's death grip.

Charlie can't get the last shred, either. He finally gives up and searches Santa's pockets, which is where he finds a battered black leather wallet. There's a driver's license inside, which he slides out for a better look.

"We've got a tentative I.D. on the vic," he says. "According to this, the ex-Santa Claus is one Dominick Rialto."

"Hey, that's the produce guy," says Burt.

"Owner of Sunshine Market, right?"

"Also old school Black Hand Mafia," Burt says solemnly. "No *wonder* his Santy suit is all black!"

Charlie frowns. "Is that a thing?"

"It was for Dominick," says Burt. "Black Hand was started by Italian immigrants and evolved into the Mafia we got now. I've heard stories how hardcore it was. Dominick used to say he was part of it back in the day."

"Black Hand Mafia." Charlie nods. "Black costume Santa Claus. I wonder if they're connected."

"Old school guy in his 70s like that, maybe he wanted to pay tribute to the Black Hand with his outfit." Burt smirks and shrugs. "Or maybe he just thought it was funny, who knows?"

"But was it enough for someone to make him an *ex*-Santa?" asks Charlie. "Maybe the note in his hand will clear things up."

"My money's on a reindeer takin' down this guy." Burt nods knowingly. "I never did trust that Rudolph. Red nose can be a sign of alcohol abuse, y'know."

"What do you have for me, Peg?" Charlie sweeps into the morgue at 6 a.m. on Christmas Eve day like he's not running on coffee and zero sleep.

Peg Wonders, county coroner, holds up a sealed evidence baggie with a wrinkled scrap of paper inside. "He's makin' a list… and checkin' it twice..." She swings the baggie back and forth between her thumb and forefinger as she sings. "Gonna find out who's...*naughty!"*

Charlie smiles. Peg has a way of cracking him up. "Well, well." He takes the baggie from her and holds it up to the light to make out the five partial lines of handwriting on the paper inside. "What kind of list is this?"

"Mafioso Santa's, apparently." Peg, in her 50s and full of attitude, puffs a strand of gray hair away from her right eye. "No dollies or bicycles on *that* list."

Charlie moves the paper closer. It's only three inches by two inches at its most intact point, and the handwritten lines are mostly fragments.

"'Tony Petrilli.'" He reads the first line aloud, what there is of it. "Then a dash. Then 'OxyContin, 100 tabs,' with the second half of the letter 's' cut off."

"We know what *that* is," Peg says glibly as she cleans the blade of a rotary bone saw.

"Lonnie DeGol." The start of the second line is visible, though more of the end is missing. "Then a dash, followed by 'Guns and ammo'."

"A friend of the N.R.A., no doubt," says Peg.

"On the next line, we have the name 'Vito Arcurio.' Beside that, we have the entry 'Persian rug.'"

Peg frowns. "Someone in the floor covering trade?"

"Next line starts with the partial last name 'vino.' Then a dash, followed by 'Escalade.' And that's it."

"Wish we knew who 'vino' is." Peg frowns.

"So how did they use this list, exactly?" asks Charlie. "Did the mobsters line up to sit on Black Hand Santa's knee?"

"'We've been bad boys this year, Santa. As a reward, we want drugs, guns, a rug, and a fancy new car for Xmas, please.'" Peg laughs and pulls back the sheet from the body on the table. "I guess Dominick here had his own holiday traditions, huh?"

"What else did you find?" asks Charlie.

"Food and wine stains on the outfit. No surprise there. Cigar ash, too. Also traces of some kind of lotion or ointment around the neck."

"Ointment?"

"I'm sending it out for analysis. Otherwise, aside from the *obvious*..." She gestures at the remnants of Dominick's exploded head. "...just another overweight, diabetic mobster in his 70s with knee, hip, and shoulder replacements and a big fat belly that shook like a bowl full of...."

"Excuse me." A woman knocks once and pushes the door open. "Hello?"

She instantly has Charlie's attention, and not just because she shouldn't be down here unescorted.

"I'll be damned." She spots the body on the slab and shakes her head sadly. "So that's all that's left of Dominick Rialto?"

The woman is in her thirties and has long, dark hair and an

athletic build. She wears a black leather jacket, a black sweater, and jeans. Charlie is instantly intrigued and notices the absence of a wedding ring. "Excuse me," he says. "I'll have to ask you to step outside, Miss..."

"Malditesta," says the dark-haired woman. "Detective Marie Malditesta of the Allegheny County Organized Crime Task Force, based in Pittsburgh."

"Hello." Charlie hasn't met her before, but he recognizes her name from his Pittsburgh days. "You came because of Dominick?" He gestures at the corpse.

"I drove up as soon as I heard," says Marie. "Mr. Rialto and I have history, you see. He was one of my informants the past couple of years."

"You're shittin' me," says Burt, who just appeared in the doorway behind her. "Dominick Rialto was a *rat?"*

Marie clears her throat and gives Charlie a look. "Can we go somewhere and have a chat, Detective...?"

"Collins." Charlie smiles back at her. "Detective Charlie Collins. And yes, right this way." He walks her past Burt and out the door...though Burt follows them, determined to stay in the mix.

The three of them—Charlie, Marie, and Burt—sit across from each other at the big metal table in the interview room, nursing coffees.

"So here's the thing, Detective." Marie's accent has a hint of Long Island to it. "I want to help you find out who did this to Mr. Rialto."

"How do you propose to do that?" asks Charlie.

"I know some people because of the task force," says Marie. "I might be able to open some doors for you."

"Maybe so." With that, Charlie gets up from the table, signals with his index finger that he'll only be gone a moment, and leaves the room. He soon returns carrying the fragment of paper in the evidence baggie. "So what can you tell me about this? And the whole black Santa getup?"

"Yeah," says Burt. "What's with the whole *Clausa Nostra* thing?" He cracks himself up with the joke.

Marie reads the scrap in the bag and raises an eyebrow. "You found this on Mr. Rialto?"

"We did," says Charlie. "So it *is* a thing, then?"

"It's a thing. I've heard about this."

"Meaning what?" asks Burt.

"Meaning the local goombahs have Christmas parties like everyone else," says Marie. "With *presents."*

"Presents from Santy Claus?" says Burt.

"From the boss, at least," says Marie. "They call it Bonus Night. On Bonus Night, the lieutenants get to ask for a Christmas bonus for all their hard work during the year."

"And the boss just gives it to them?" asks Burt.

She shrugs. "As long as they've been bad little boys, I suppose."

"Any idea where they have this Bonus Night get-together?" asks Charlie.

"As a matter of fact, I do," says Marie. "It's right here in town, and it's a very Christmasy setting, in a manner of speaking…one that's owned by the first guy on your list, as a matter of fact."

Was the Christ child born in Italy? You might think so from looking around the entryway of Petrilli's Ristorante in Abruzzi.

As the maître d' ushers Marie, Charlie, and Burt into the place, they pass a painting of the Nativity set in the heart of St. Peter's Square in the Vatican. A little further along the entryway, a lighted plastic Nativity rests in a corner, an Italian flag draped behind it. Then there's the framed photo of a live Nativity staged in a gondola in a canal in Venice, occupying a lighted niche just before the last turn into the dining room.

Charlie's used to it all, he's been here before…but it still strikes him as more tacky than charming. Most of the restaurant's clientele see it the other way around, though. The cheesy decorations have been around for so long, Petrilli's regulars feel downright nostalgic about them.

The maître d' says he'll fetch the owner and disappears through the kitchen door. That leaves Charlie with time to look around the dining room and appreciate the more classic decorations in there. The place isn't open for lunch yet, so there aren't any customers blocking the view.

The dining room is strung with strands of white lights, boughs of fir and holly, and sprigs of mistletoe. Wreaths with red velvet bows line the walls, and red and green tablecloths alternate across the room. Then there's the tree in the far corner, tastefully hung with glittering ornaments, tinsel, lights, and tufts of simulated snow. Tucked between the base of the tree and the wall, Charlie sees a three-foot-long pine box with three softball-sized lights mounted on it—one green, one amber, and one red. Is the box dark because the bulbs are burned out, or is it not plugged in for some reason?

Suddenly, a mustached, barrel-chested man in a dark suit emerges from the kitchen. His black hair is slicked back on his head, and he looks about fiftysomething. Charlie has seen him around but never met him before today.

"I own this place." His voice is low and gravelly. "Whadda you want?"

"I'm Detective Charlie Collins." Charlie walks over and extends a hand, but the guy doesn't take the shake, so he nods at Marie. "This is Detective Marie Malditesta of the Organized Crime Task Force. And this..."

"Yo, Tony." Burt gives him a nod. "How's it hangin'?"

Tony Petrilli shrugs. "So what can I do you for?"

"First off, congratulations on your Christmas bonus." Charlie pulls out a copy of Black Hand Santa's list and holds it up. "I mean, a hundred tabs of OxyContin, that's not bad."

Tony snorts. "I don't know what you're talkin' about."

"Or maybe it wasn't enough," offers Marie. "Maybe that's why you killed him."

"Killed who?" Tony sneers.

"Dominick Rialto," says Burt. "He was found dead last night."

Tony hardly looks surprised. "Izzat so?" He frowns. "Last I saw, he was alive *right here.*" He points at the floor. "Playin' Santa at the Italian Heritage Society's Christmas party."

"So you *were* one of the last people to see him alive," says Marie.

"Me and a hundred other guys, sure!" snaps Tony. "Plus wait staff!"

"But you were right *in* there, weren't you?" says Charlie. "Telling Santa what you wanted for Christmas. And then Lonnie DeGol was right behind you..."

"And Vito Arcurio after him," adds Marie.

"What the *hell* are you *talkin'* about?"

"We're talking about murdering Santa after he didn't give you what you wanted," says Burt.

"Hey!" Indignant, Tony gets in his face. "Santa was perfectly *alive* when he walked out that door!" He points toward the exit.

"Okay," says Charlie. "So when did Dominick leave the party, exactly?"

"I don't remember!" Tony's face turns redder by the minute. "Maybe 10, maybe 11?"

"And when did *you* leave?"

"After everyone else straggled out of here. Like two in the morning. Long freakin' night, know what I mean?"

"Not so long for Dominick, though," says Burt.

"What about Lonnie and Vito?" asks Charlie.

"Lonnie hauled ass right after Dominick," says Tony. "I remember Dominick forgot his hat, and Lonnie ran it out to him."

"And Vito?" asks Charlie.

"How the hell should I know?" snaps Tony. "I wasn't his *date.*"

"What about this other name on the list?" asks Charlie. "Something ending in -vino."

"Wow, *that* narrows it down," says Tony. "To like *half* the guys here."

"Do you have a guest list?" asks Charlie.

"For a party like *that*?" Tony laughs. "Sure, and I've got *selfies* with all the boys to go with it!"

After talking to Tony, the team splits up, with Charlie and Marie going to interview Lonnie DeGol while Burt heads over to search Dominick's house in the suburbs.

Finding Lonnie's a problem at first, since he's an out-of-town guy. That's where Marie makes a difference. A call to a colleague on the task force gets her the number of an undercover contact. The contact texts her an address where Lonnie might be staying in town, and they're off and running.

Unfortunately, when they get there—a dump of an apartment on the bad side of Abruzzi—Lonnie isn't around...just a blonde girlfriend who claims he went home to Erie.

"Shit." Marie flicks Lonnie's mug shot on the dash. "Never had this problem with my *last* snitch." She means Dominick. "Something tells me I'm not gonna make it home to Pittsburgh for Midnight Mass tonight."

"Midnight Mass is a big deal for you?" asks Charlie.

"Pretty big," says Marie. "I sing with the choir. First soprano. I'm a soloist."

"Well, maybe you can still make it. Let's move to the next guy on the list and see how it goes," says Charlie. "We've got a local address for Vito Arcurio, so let's head over there. Maybe we can get someone to pick up Lonnie in Erie after that."

It turns out they don't need to wait to find Lonnie, after all. When Charlie and Marie roll up to Vito's house, Lonnie's running out the front door with a pistol in his hand. Vito tears out after him with his own gun, taking shots at him.

But when they see Charlie and Marie getting out of their unmarked car in the driveway, they instantly lose interest in each other and run off in separate directions.

Charlie and Marie don't say a word. Charlie bolts after Lonnie, and Marie follows Vito, drawing their weapons as they race like track stars through the neighbors' yards.

"Freeze!" Even as he shouts the word, Charlie knows it's a futile gesture. Lonnie's got a big head start and shows no sign of slowing down.

Not to mention, he's young and athletic enough to stay out ahead. His feet hammer through the grass like pistons, propelling him further out of reach.

Lucky for Charlie, the punk isn't immune to twists of fate. Just as Lonnie crosses a driveway a couple houses up, the reckless teen driver who lives there guns his parents' car out of the garage, clipping him good. Lonnie bounces off the tail end of the Toyota and goes down like a sack of dirt on the pavement.

Before Lonnie can jump back up, Charlie's on top of him, rolling him over on his belly. As soon as he's got the cuffs on his wrists, Charlie retrieves the hood's .9-mil from the grass.

"Hey, Lonnie," he says. "I need to ask you a few questions, *capiche?*"

Lonnie might have had the edge when it came to outrunning Charlie, but Marie has the advantage over Vito. She's a marathoner, built for speed and trained like a thoroughbred for championship racing. It doesn't hurt that she's wearing black sneakers as she always does on duty, for just such a perp-chasing occasion.

She's on Vito's heels in nothing flat. Vito has no athletic skill to speak of and quickly feels her breath on the back of his neck.

Which is why he suddenly swings the pistol back and randomly pulls the trigger.

Marie sees it coming in a split-second and ducks the shot. Before he can take another, she bashes his hand with her own sidearm, sending his gun hurtling out of his grip.

Then, with a cry of exertion, she pounces. Like a lion taking down a gazelle, she tackles Vito to the ground where he belongs.

"Time to talk, you piece of garbage!" She rolls him around and breaks out the cuffs. "What did you do to Dominick Rialto?"

Charlie and Marie put the suspects in the car and haul them back to the police station. They set them up one at a time in the interview room and pepper them with questions—but nobody's talking.

"So much for giving gifts on Christmas Eve," says Charlie.

Then, Marie has an idea. She tells Charlie she'll be right back, and then she goes for a brief drive.

When she returns, she has Tony Petrilli in tow for a trumped-up unpaid traffic ticket beef. She makes a point of marching him through the squad room, uncuffed, just as Charlie (at a prearranged signal) brings Vito through on the scenic route from the interview room to his cell.

Tony doesn't look his way, but Vito turns pale. By the time he leaves the room, however, his face is beet red.

Marie and Charlie both notice. Until now, they were only playing a hunch, but the hunch has been confirmed. Tony and Vito are both involved in the murder.

Lonnie's involved, too, apparently. His expressions are almost identical to Vito's when Charlie marches him through the squad room past Tony.

The next time they have their respective sit-downs, the two wiseguys are suddenly more talkative. Tony still hasn't said a word, but Vito and Lonnie both think he has, and Charlie and Marie encourage their misconception. The resulting chats are quite revealing.

The note in Santa's fist, for example, wasn't at all what Charlie thought it was.

"Every year on Bonus Night, Santa Dominick made a list of what all the fellas asked for," says Lonnie, "but that list you got ain't it."

"*Santa* didn't make *that* list," explains Vito.

"The four of *us* did," says Lonnie.

"That's right," says Vito. "Me, Lonnie, Tony, and one other guy."

"You better hurry if you want *that* guy, though," says Lonnie.

"If I know that back-crackin' bastard, he'll be blowin' outta town the second he hears you've got the rest of us."

Burt backs up what Charlie and Marie just heard. Out at Dominick's place, his search turned up a product—*lots* of it—that's only sold one place in town. The lab confirms the product's a match for the residue on Dominick's neck.

And there's another thing. According to Lonnie and Vito, Dominick was dead or most of the way there *before* he got shot. There was a *second* murder weapon, one that Charlie spotted without realizing what it was during his first visit to Tony Petrilli's restaurant.

Charlie remembers it as plain as day--a three-foot pine box with red, green, and amber lights. It caught his eye at the time because it was dark, unlike every other decoration in the place... and now he knows it wasn't a decoration at all.

Marie knows it, too. "Mr. Rialto told me about that damn box," she says after Lonnie and Vito tell their stories. "He told me what he used it for, too. It's no wonder Lonnie and Vito and their pals hated his guts."

While Charlie runs to Petrilli's to pick up the box, Peg the Coroner takes another look at the fragments of Dominick's blown-apart skull. The new examination reveals signs of additional trauma that occurred before the gunshot. Pine splinters and plexiglass shards are embedded in the sites of that trauma.

When Charlie gets back with the box, Peg finds it has a splintered edge matching the pre-gunshot contusions in Dominick's cranial shards. Also, though someone scrubbed down the box recently, there's still a bloody fingerprint on it. It just so happens Peg's able to match that print to the very guy identified by Vito and Lonnie as the fourth conspirator. He might appear to be an upstanding citizen, but his prints are on file thanks to a DUI arrest a few years back.

"Let's go grab the S.O.B. before he hightails it." Burt looks at Marie. "You comin' along to close the deal?"

"I wouldn't miss it. I owe my old informant that much." Marie checks her watch. "But then there's no way I'll make it to Midnight Mass in the 'Burgh as planned."

"You'll miss your solo." Charlie thinks for a moment, then pulls out his phone. "But maybe I can do something about that, if you're interested. I think *I* can open some doors for *you*."

Dr. Eugene Savino the chiropractor is just locking up when Charlie, Burt, and Marie arrive at his office in downtown Abruzzi. Cherubic as he is—a little guy with thin black hair, chubby cheeks, and an elfin nose—he doesn't look happy to see them. He knows Charlie and Burt, but his body language makes it clear he's not in the mood to have a conversation with them.

"Merry Christmas, guys." He turns the key in the lock. "Whatever you want, it'll have to wait till after New Year's."

"Actually," says Charlie, "we just need a tube of that Bionumb lotion. I'm fresh out, and your place is the only one in town that sells it."

"Love to, but I'm on my way home," says Savino. "Then I'm going on vacation."

"Oh, God." Burt grimaces and releases a moan of the deepest anguish. "I can't stand it! Oh, please, make it stop!"

"Poor guy." Charlie, looking concerned, puts a hand lightly on his shoulder. "Bionumb's the only thing that helps him, and we're all out."

"You mean I have to *feel* like this the whole way through the *holidays?*" Again, Burt moans like he's about to drop dead on the spot.

Savino blows out a disgusted breath, then turns the key back the other way and opens the door. "All right, one tube. Wait here."

When he enters, Charlie and Burt don't wait as instructed. Instead, they follow him inside. "I can't thank you enough for doing this," says Charlie. "He's really in a lot of pain."

"Police work's *killin'* my spine!" Burt says with a wince.

Savino hurries behind the counter, grabs a short white tube

with blue lettering from a bin on the wall—then puts it back and pulls out a longer one. "Here. It's on the house." He throws it to Burt. "Happy holidays."

"Doc, you're a lifesaver," says Burt. "I mean *back*-saver."

"Dominick was right about you." Charlie nods. "He said you were a standup guy."

That gets Savino's attention...but he chooses to brush it off. "Well, I have to get going, detectives." He lingers behind the counter, smiling. "Christmas Eve awaits."

"Not for Dominick, though." Burt chuckles. "That poor goombah."

"Mr. Rialto, you mean?" Savino plays dumb. "Has something happened to him?"

"You tell us," says Charlie.

Savino casually drops his hands to the edge of the counter. "There's nothing to tell. He's a patient of mine, but..."

"That's not *all* he was, though, right?" Charlie's hands are at his sides, relaxed. "We found out a few things during our investigation, actually."

"I still can't believe he ripped you off the way he did." Burt laughs and shakes his head. "I mean, you're a *doctor...*"

"Well, a *chiropractor*," corrects Charlie.

"You're a *smart guy*, is what I'm sayin', and he still tricked you with that dumb *gadget* of his," says Burt. "Tricked those other guys, too—Tony Petrilli, Lonnie DeGol, Vito Arcurio..."

"Lots of other folks, as well," says Charlie. "And it was such a *simple* trick. There were three colored lights on a box in the trunk of his car—one green, one amber, one red. He'd flip a switch, and they'd go on and off, one at a time. You'd bet which one would still be lit at the end when he flipped the switch off. It was sort of like picking where the pea ends up in a shell game. *Except...*" Charlie smiles. "*Except* it was *rigged.* Dominick had a guy under the back seat, and he heard what color you called, and then he always made sure a *different* color came up at the end."

"Pretty sneaky," says Burt.

"Pretty profitable, for Dominick," says Charlie. "There's just one thing I can't figure out. How could a smart guy keep placing bets on something like that? Wouldn't he catch on that it's rigged?"

"I guess they probably let you win just enough, huh? Made you think you could win it *all* back." Burt nods knowingly.

"Happens to the best of us," says Charlie. "You're not the first moron to get taken, and you won't be the last."

"Is that why you helped kill him?" asks Burt. "We know because you left traces of Bionumb on his neck, and this is the only place in town that sells it."

Savino's gaze is like a lizard's now, coolly flicking from one of them to the other. He's thinking things over, weighing his options —and then his upper arms twitch.

Which is exactly when Charlie explodes. "*Don't you move, asshole! Hands where we can see them!*"

Defiant, Savino keeps his fingers on the counter, ready to drop fast and grab the gun he keeps under there.

"You heard him!" Burt whips a Glock .22 from the pocket of his parka and swings it up to aim at the chiropractor. "Whatever you're thinking of trying, don't do it!"

"Take a look out front," says Charlie. "You get past us, you still have *her* waiting for you."

Savino looks out the front window, and Marie stares back from behind the barrel of a .45.

"They gave you up, dumbass." Burt snickers. "Your co-killers Tony, Lonnie, and Vito."

"Lonnie and Vito had a falling out," says Charlie. "Vito was *shooting* at Lonnie when we found them. It didn't take much to tip them over the edge."

"Once *they* threw you under the bus, Tony wasn't far behind," adds Burt. "Why wouldn't he be? You might be Italian, but you ain't *la famiglia* like the rest of 'em."

"It was the *list* that showed us the way," explains Charlie. "We thought at first it was some kind of mob Christmas list—but then we realized it's a *checklist* for a *murder.* A checklist Dominick must've torn out of one of your pockets even as you four pricks murdered him.

"Tony's on the list for a hundred tabs of OxyContin. We know

now that was the gift you four used to get Dominick to invite you into his home.

"Lonnie supplied the guns and ammo to kill Dominick...though wasn't that a little *overkill* after you bashed his head in with the light box?

"Vito brought a Persian rug to roll the body up in, and you brought a Cadillac Escalade to transport dead Dominick to Central Park. Killing him at his home wasn't enough, apparently."

Burt snorts. "*You* had to put the body on *display* in the *park*. You really wanted to drive the point home that the guy got what was comin' to him."

Savino looks like he's finally starting to sweat. "You can't prove *any* of that."

"We've got three confessions," says Charlie. "Plus, we lifted a print from the light box. Surprise, it's one of yours."

"We've got C.S.I.s combing Dominick's house for the actual murder scene, and we'll find that, too," says Burt. "We'll find the blood evidence, because you can *never* completely clean that shit up. Face it, smart guy, you're goin' down."

"So what'll it be?" asks Charlie. "Live to crack backs another day behind bars? Or get your final adjustment the hard way?"

Savino stands there, considering. Then, with a sigh, he steps back from the counter and raises his arms.

"Good choice, Dr. S.," says Charlie. "I guess you're a wise man, after all."

It's five past midnight when the lights go down in St. Gregory's Catholic Church, but the place isn't dark at all. Every parishioner in the packed house holds a flickering candle as the priest—Father Gus, a friend of Charlie's—reads the story of the Christ child.

Charlie, sitting in the middle of the crowd, isn't Catholic, but he appreciates the atmosphere. He gets a shiver up his spine as he gazes at the crowd of worshippers and the decorations around them. The marble altar at the front of the church is surrounded by poinsettias, and the huge cross hanging above it is draped with a long white stole. A Christmas tree laden with liturgical ornaments glows at the head of the left wing of the transept; the head of the right wing features a life-size Nativity scene, complete with a golden star glowing overhead.

It's not what Charlie's used to, but he doesn't mind. He's done his best to help Marie, and he can't wait to see how it all works out.

Since she couldn't make it back to her home parish in Pittsburgh in time, Charlie called Father Gus and talked him into finding a spot for her at St. Gregory's that night. Given that Marie's a total pro, and the priest at her church in the 'Burgh sang her praises to Gus over the phone, getting her on the bill was no problem at all. As for the 'Burgh church, a quality stand-in was available and glad for the chance to cover for Marie.

All is right with the world, therefore, which is as it should be on Christmas Eve. Marie's happy, and Charlie's happy he could help her. All that's left is for the lady to sing her heart out.

As Charlie watches, the choir files in, dressed in white robes trimmed with gold. Marie is the last to enter, looking more radiant than ever.

Charlie can't stop smiling as the choir sings "Hark! The Herald Angels Sing." He can't take his eyes off Marie, who looks like a perfect angel with her dark hair flowing over her white-robed shoulders.

When she sings her solo, the chills are back big-time. Charlie doubts she can see him in the candlelit shadows, but he likes to think she's singing only for him anyway.

She's singing for him on Christmas Eve, with another case in the win column, one that both of them had a hand in solving. The evidence is clear: they make a great team.

So what if she lives two hours away in Pittsburgh? There isn't a doubt in Charlie's mind that he's going to ask her out on Xmas Day. The only X-factor is whether or not she'll say yes.

Though that's kind of a gift itself, isn't it? Because guys like him just love a good mystery.

THE FIRST HOLLYWOOD COWBOY OF THE BROPOCALYPSE

What's it like having a brother who's the end of the world?

Not so hot sometimes, to be honest. But, full disclosure, I know it's not always a picnic being *my* brother, either.

When I show up on the doorstep of his apartment this morning, for example, I'm not there for a friendly visit. The truth is, I drop by out of the blue to try to get him to *kill himself.* Plain and simple.

And he *knows* it. I've done it before. *Lots* of times.

Call me persistent. Because when my brother, John Glass, dies, he will take the world with him. All *humanity* will end when he finally does himself in.

And that's something I've been craving for a very long time.

When the door creeps open after my seventh knock, I'm hit by the smell first. Body odor, beer, cigarette smoke, burnt popcorn, and some kind of incense or patchouli. Plus an overlay of feces?

Then I see his wretched face peering out of the shadows, somehow bloated and sagging at the same time. Hair the color of straw hangs in greasy flops from a pocked, gray scalp. Bloodshot eyes squint into the bright Los Angeles sunlight, shielded by one scrawny, upraised arm.

When he talks, his voice is as hoarse as any wino's after a hard night's hacking it up in alleyways between screaming cats. "Loogie? 'Zat you?"

I have to admit, he does resemble the end of the world in human form. He looks like seven shades of shit, like death warmed over.

None of which changes the fact that he's my brother.

"Hey there, John." I smile and snap off my overpriced Oakley sunglasses--one of the status symbols that comes with my lifestyle as an ultra-successful media mogul. "How's it hangin'?"

John's attire is the polar opposite of mine. He scratches his chest through his yellowed wife-beater t-shirt, stuffs his hands in the pockets of his tattered bluejeans, and frowns at me like I just started using a foreign language. His lips move a little, though I can't tell if he's trying to form words or just trembling from the aftereffects of substance abuse.

"May I come in?" I shrug and keep smiling. "Or do you have company?" I shoot him a salty wink.

John shakes his head, but I think he's trying to clear the cobwebs instead of telling me no. "I gotta pee." He pulls the door further open and drifts off into the shadows inside the apartment.

When I cross the threshold, I nearly trip over an effing guinea pig scampering past. It's running loose, dribbling turds on the filthy beige carpet. The mystery of the feces smell is solved.

As I walk the rest of the way inside, I want to leave the door open to let in some fresh air, but I guess I can't do that in case the guinea pig gets out. Might not be the best way to get off on the right foot...though John looks so far gone, I wonder if he even knows that the animal's there.

"Make yourself at home." John shouts the words over the sound of buckets of urine blasting into a toilet bowl in the other room.

Not a chance. Even with blackout blinds keeping out most of the daylight, I can see by the TV's glow that the place is squalid as a rat's nest. There's garbage everywhere--mostly pizza boxes, Chinese takeout cartons, beer cans, and liquor bottles. The battered gray sectional sofa's covered with dirty clothes, some of which I could *swear* are moving. Then there's the big crimson stain on the carpet across the room, which could be anything from red wine to blood.

What with the smell, which is so much stronger inside with the door shut, it's enough to make me gag. And you wanna know the tragic part?

It isn't even the worst place I've found him in over the years. Not even close.

"Want a drink?" I notice the toilet doesn't flush before he walks back into the living room. No hand-washing water runs in the sink, either. "You see a half-empty bottle of Mad Dog laying around in here, Loogie?"

I don't correct him for the billionth time that my name's not *Loogie*, it's *Doug*. What difference would it make? "I've got a better idea. Put some shoes on, and I'll buy you breakfast."

The guinea pig runs over and stops between his feet. John leans down for a look, and his shredded blue jeans drop around his ankles.

He's *that* skinny at this point. He's that ragged. Looks like he's not long for this world. Like he'll die soon enough without any encouragement.

But he won't. Trust me, I know. He's not going anywhere unless he damn well wants to.

For a long moment, he just stands there like he doesn't realize his pants are down and his baggy gray briefs are hanging out. A blank, lost look hovers over his face, like maybe he doesn't even realize where he *is* anymore...and my heart goes out to him.

He may be many things, but he's still my brother.

"Hey, John. Pants." I point at his jeans. "I think they need a lift."

John nods slowly and bends over. As soon as his jeans clear the floor, the guinea pig shoots out from under them and disappears under the sofa.

"Any chance you have a belt in here somewhere?" I ask him.

"A belt?" He says it like it's something he's never heard of or imagined.

Which is why I trot out the one thing I know will reach him. "What about your Tom Mix anniversary belt? The one with the commemorative buckle?" As I say it, I step over and touch his arm, giving him a little zap of my rejuvenating power--one of the perks of being who I am instead of the end of the world like him.

It's just enough to blow away some of his fog. He blinks his eyes hard, and they come back into focus. "Tom Mix?" His slack jaw tightens in a smile. "Yes, I know I've got that around here somewhere."

And just like that, he's my old brother John again, the way he should be. I knew he was in there somewhere.

At first, I think I'm going to have to spoon-feed him his breakfast. He stares at the tray of McDonald's hotcakes and sausage like it's changing colors and doesn't make a move to pick up his plastic cutlery and dig in. Then, he nods off and slumps toward it.

"Hey, John!" When my voice fails to wake him, I jump up from my orange plastic bench and lean over to give him a shake. "Breakfast time, remember?"

His eyes flicker open and find the food. "You can have mine, Loogie."

"I can't eat my Egg McMuffin *and* your hotcakes and sausage, bro." I jam the black plastic knife and fork in his hands and sit down at my side of the table again. "You gotta help me out here."

He pokes a yellow hotcake with the fork and scowls. "I didn't ask for this, Loogie."

I smirk and unwrap my Egg McMuffin. "So you don't think Tom Mix would eat a breakfast like that if someone put it in front of him?"

Even without a zap of my power, he perks up at the mention of that name. He always does.

Reluctantly, John cuts off a sliver of hotcake with the plastic knife. "He did believe in a healthy breakfast, Loogie."

Does McDonald's qualify? I admit, I didn't want to take him somewhere nicer until I could get him cleaned up. "Most important meal of the day, they say."

John forks the sliver into his mouth and chews it slowly. When he swallows, his Adam's apple lurches like he's gulping down half a porterhouse. "I just wish I could find that belt."

He's talking about his Tom Mix belt with the commemorative buckle. He looked everywhere in his shithole apartment before he gave up and let me cinch his jeans with duct tape. "It'll turn up," I tell him.

"I love that belt." Tears mist his veiny green eyes. "Almost as much as I loved that hat." He wipes his mouth with the back of a shivering hand. "Remember the hat?"

How could I forget? "Sure I do." It was a white ten-gallon hat, a replica of the one Tom Mix wore in the movies. John wore it everywhere as a kid, though it was a few sizes too big for him and often fell down over his eyes.

John pinches the tears from his eyes with a thumb and forefinger. "God, I miss that hat." He chokes out a sob.

I've heard it all before. I just eat my Egg McMuffin and let him cry it out, mourning for his beloved Tom Mix.

Now, you might think it's odd for a middle-aged guy like John in the early 21st century to be obsessed with Tom Mix. To look at him, you might not think he's old enough to remember an old-fashioned movie star cowboy like Mix, let alone to have seen his movies when they first debuted in the 1920s.

And guess what? You'd be so effing wrong, it's not even funny.

Not only that, but *I* was there, too. Saw the same movies when they premiered on the big screen, in fact.

But enough of the Tom Mix crybaby crap. I've got to get my big brother on track or I'm never going to get him to kill himself on schedule.

"John, hey." I reach over and pat his arm. "Eat up. It's gonna be a busy day."

One last sob, and he lowers his fork and knife to the Styrofoam platter again. It seems like it takes a major effort to cut more slivers from the hotcake and push them into his mouth, but he forces himself to keep eating.

As for me, I polish off the Egg McMuffin and sip black coffee while I watch him at work. "It's like old times, isn't it? You and me having breakfast together?"

He nods and narrows his eyes at me. Suddenly, I feel like the fog has completely burned off, and his focus is back to laser intensity.

"So what do you want, Doug?" He cocks his head. "Why the fuck are you here, instead of tending your fucking media empire?"

He's right about the empire, though I make it a point never to rub his nose in it. I own three cable networks, TV stations in five of the top ten markets, and a video streaming service that's number seven with a bullet on the interwebs. Let's just say I haven't been resting on my laurels during all those decades of waiting for this Godot wannabe. "Oh, you know." I smile cryptically over my black coffee.

"The usual?" His eyes get narrower.

I shake my head as I blow on my coffee. "Can't I just spend some quality time with my big brother?"

"So you're *not* here to get me to kill myself?"

I let out a chuckle. "That ship has sailed, John. You need to get over it."

"Bullshit." He stares at me some more. "You'll *never* give up. You *can't*." He spears his whole sausage patty with the fork and shakes it at me. "It's your *nature*."

I shrug. "People change, John."

"Sure." He nods knowingly. "But we aren't *people*."

He's got me there. We might *look* like the other customers at the tables around us, but we're as far from ordinary people as they come.

And he's right about my never giving up. My core purpose in life depends on him. I can't truly come into my own until he finally lets go.

Because just as he's the end of one era, I'm the start of the next. I'm fated to bring to life what comes *after* the end...which I can't do while he's still kicking. He needs to perish, and I've got a plan to make sure he does.

But keeping all that to myself is part of the gambit. So is lying through my teeth.

"I've changed, John," I tell him. "So has everything else. I can't help it if you were too far up your own ass to notice."

"Changed how?"

"Changed so we both get what we always wanted." I toast him with my coffee. "Here's to the happy ending to end all happy endings, my brother."

After breakfast, I take him shopping at a discount store, picking up clothes and toiletries and a razor--a cleanup kit. He fades out on me a little, lost inside his own head, maybe considering the hints I dropped at McDonald's about the way things have changed.

By the time I get him to the local YMCA, he's back to shuffling like a hung-over zombie. Makes me wonder if he's on hard drugs again, but I guess that's irrelevant.

I send him into the showers with a bar of soap and a tube of shampoo, and then I wait. He's in there a while, but I don't mind.

The son of a bitch has already kept me waiting for decades. What difference will another couple of minutes make?

It might not look like it, what with the media empire and all, but I've kept my life on hold because of him for longer than most people have been alive. I've put off fulfilling my true destiny, becoming who and what I was always meant to be, because of that selfish prick dragging his feet.

But not for much longer, if things go according to plan.

Suddenly, I feel a wave of impatience. "Doing okay in there?"

He says something I can't make out over the running water, but I'll take it for a "yes."

Turning, I catch sight of my reflection in a full-length mirror on the locker room wall. Tall, trim, sober, well-groomed, good-looking--the opposite of him. My tailored Italian suit--close-fitting, black with razor-thin red pinstripes and a crimson designer necktie--has nothing in common with his wife beater t-shirt and shredded jeans. With my jet black hair, brown eyes, and high cheekbones, I don't even look like I had the same mother.

But it makes sense, doesn't it? Considering who he is and who I am, it makes perfect sense.

As he waddles out of the shower naked, grabbing a towel off a hook on the wall, he doesn't look at all like the end of the world. But that's what he is.

Though, to be specific, I guess I should say he's the end of the part of the world that matters to people. The end of all the *people*, that is.

As for me, I'm also a world-changing force in human form, but my essence--and the footprint it's fated to leave on the face of the Earth--are very different indeed.

"Ready for a shave, John?" I gesture at the razor and travel-size can of shaving cream on the edge of the sink.

John finishes buffing the water from his chest and belly with the towel and gives me a funny look. "What's the catch, Loogie? You're not planning on taking me to a *funeral*, are you?"

"It's a surprise." I smack him on the back on his way to the sink. "You'll thank me later."

He scowls over his shoulder, suspicious. I can practically see the gears turning...but he won't guess what I have in store for him. He's my brother, we've known each other forever, but there's always been a gulf between us that can't be crossed. Because there's always a distance between an ending, like the end of the world...

...and a *beginning*, like me.

When the first Dodger batter steps up to the plate in Dodger Stadium in the bottom of the first inning, I catch John grinning with unabashed delight. The suspicion he's been oozing at my every word and action blows right out of him. He's just glad to be here in an awesome front row seat along the first base line, watching a Major League baseball game in person for the first time in God only knows how long.

"Holy shit, holy shit, holy shit." He's sitting on the edge of his seat, drinking in everything except the ballpark beer he begged for (which I wouldn't let him get). Seeing him like that, all cleaned up and clean-shaven, wearing a new black polo shirt, tan khakis, and black Oxford shoes, I can hardly believe he's the same dirty, dead-eyed guy who answered the door at that rat's nest apartment a few hours ago.

He cheers when the Dodger batter hits a single, smack between the shortstop and third base. The runner rounds first but gives up on second when the left fielder snags the ball in time to scare him off.

"Nice hit!" John claps and grins. For a moment, it's like old times. I remember the two of us watching the original Dodgers, the Brooklyn Dodgers, playing at Ebbets Field in Flatbush. John and I side by side, laughing in the sunshine, cheering and pumping our fists in the battered baseball gloves we'd brought to catch any foul balls that came our way.

Did we know by then what we were? Did we realize where our preordained destinies would take us? Honestly, I forget. When you live as many years as we have, the details tend to blur. It's like riding in a fast-moving car; you get a sense of the landscape passing by, but you don't always know where you've been.

Days like this stand out, though. The ones where the surprises happen. The ones with the drama.

The ones where your heart beats faster because you're in the stands at what's probably the last ballgame you'll ever see with your brother. What's probably one of the last ballgames in the history of humankind, in fact.

And as much as you welcome that ending, as much as you've effing *longed* for it, you still feel a stab of dread and nostalgia because of the change about to come.

Another batter smacks a grounder and lands on first, and John and I cheer and stomp. We *really* get in the spirit when the next guy loads the bases, and the Dodgers' best hitter comes to bat.

He whiffs twice, and we hold our breath. Then, with one

mighty stroke, he blasts the ball out of the park. *Grand slam.* Just like that, it's a four-to-nothing ballgame.

Everyone's on their feet, including us, as the runners trot home. John elbows me excitedly, whooping and flailing as the grand slam hitter circles the infield.

"Oh my God, this is great!" He shakes my shoulder, his face glowing with pure, perfect joy. "I'm so lucky I was here to see it!"

"The tickets *were* hard to get," I tell him. "The Dodgers are having a hell of a season."

"I'm not talking about the *tickets*." John shakes me again. "I mean I would've *missed* all this if I'd *killed* myself! I would've missed *so much,* Loogie. So many of the little *surprises* that the world has in store! We *all* would have missed them, because the world as we know it would be gone!"

I smile, but we're not on the same page here. His not killing himself isn't such a blessing in my book. Letting humanity continue to overrun and poison the planet isn't much of a plus, if you ask me.

The stubborn bastard hasn't done me any favors by sticking around. I guess the thousands of people in the stadium would feel differently about it if they knew. None of them would be here right now if not for him refusing to accept his responsibility and step aside.

But I'll bet the *next* ones, the creatures who are supposed to inherit the Earth and finally get it *right* this time, would have another take on things. They might not appreciate that this asshole brother of mine has kept me from ushering in their brave new world--especially if they knew just how long he's kept them waiting.

I see them clear as day in my mind, all squirming tentacles and suckers and inside-out, quivering organs. Their multifaceted eyes stare back at me accusingly, aching for their time in the sun. Pressing me to do the one thing I was made for, to usher in the golden age that will be the culmination of all Earth's millions of years of time out of mind.

Humans want to believe they're the end result, the apex of evolution. They'd never accept that they're nothing but a stepping stone, a transitional lifeform laying the groundwork for the planet's true success story.

John won't accept it, either. He never has, though both of us were given full knowledge of its inevitability long ago.

And I'm the only one who ever calls him on it. "You're happy to be alive. I get that." Now it's my turn to give *his* shoulder a shake. "So why do you spend so much time getting *wasted*? Why do you insist on living the way you do?"

John shrugs as his eyes wander to the field, where a walked batter is taking his base. "Because why not? This world is so *fragile* and *finite*, as we both know. Why not do what makes us *happy* while we can? Why bother putting on appearances and living the way other people think we should live?"

"Good point," I tell him. "It's all going to end sooner than expected, anyway."

"No it's not," says John. "I'm not planning on dying anytime soon."

"You still think it *matters* what you do?" I smirk and shake my head. "Then you're more out of touch than I *thought* you were."

Just then, there's the solid crack of another hit on the field, but John doesn't follow it. He's too busy squinting at me with a confused look on his face.

"What the fuck are you talking about?" he asks me.

"The end of humanity is already in progress." I nod knowingly. "Even as we speak."

John's confused look turns into an angry scowl. "You're full of shit, Loogie."

"Can't you hear it?" I cup my left hand behind my ear. "The fat lady's singing up a storm, Johnny boy."

"Pretty sure *I* would have noticed," snaps John. "Seeing as how *I'm* the one who's supposed to set it in motion."

"Better check your job description, bro. I think it might have changed."

"You're not making any *sense*," says John. "You and I are *constants*. The *end* of one world and the *beginning* of the next."

"Which was all supposed to happen *when*, John? When was the Great Transition originally set to occur?"

That subject takes some of the wind out of his sails. "The Missile Crisis." He mumbles the words. "The one in Cuba."

"In 1962?" I shake my head. "That wasn't the *original* scheduled end of the world."

Something makes the crowd cheer, but John's too busy glaring at me to look at the field. "1942, then. The Second World War."

Again, I shake my head. "You know that's not it, John."

He rubs his freshly-shaven chin. "1915." He says it grudgingly, as if he hates to admit it.

"Ding ding ding." I give him a little round of applause. "Give the man a cigar."

"World War I." He stares in the direction of the field but seems to look right through the players.

"Well, guess what happens when you delay the apocalypse a century?" I spread my arms and smile. "It happens anyway!"

John's frown deepens. "You don't know what you're talking about."

"Sure I do. I can *feel* it happening. I can *feel* humanity's replacements rising out of the muck." I shoot him a wink. "The wait is over, John."

His eyes narrow. "I'm supposed to believe this is all happening without me? That it's just happening *spontaneously?"*

"I didn't say *that.*" I gesture at the crowd in the stands around us. "It's happening because of *them.* You can't hold them *back* anymore! They *want* it to be over."

His eyes narrow even more. "You're talking about global warming? Climate change?"

"It isn't *always* about climate change, John." I snort out a laugh. "I'm talking about extinction level shit you've never even *heard of* yet. These dumb fucks are circling the drain, and there's no turning back."

Just then, as if on cue, the whole crowd moans and boos. Looking at the field, I see that the Giants are at bat and have just brought in three runners on a homer to left field.

Meanwhile, John's oblivious to the game. I can practically feel the heat radiating from his overclocked brain as he processes what I've told him.

"So how long do we have, Doug?" His voice is even, impossible for me to read. "How long till the end?"

I close my eyes, pretending to tap into my mystic link with the end times and the reboot that will follow them. "Very soon, John. A matter of weeks." I open my eyes. "The final stage is already underway."

"Weeks." Eyes still narrowed, he nods at me, measuring my words. "Then what? What happens to *me*, if humanity ends without me flipping the switch?"

"Live on as a remnant of the old world, maybe?" I frown. "Help guide the new kings of the Earth? Assuming you find a way to communicate with them, that is. They won't be much like humans, I'm afraid."

"Sounds like a blast," says John. "What if I just fade away, instead?"

"I guess that's a possibility, too."

"So what's the use, am I right?" John leans toward me. "Why not get out while the getting's good?"

Sarcasm. The jig is up. Whatever substance-induced haze was clouding his mind, it's burned off, now. So has any chance that this lame-ass reverse psychology of mine might convince him to off himself.

C'est la vie. It was only ever an opening gambit, anyway. The biggest trick is still up my sleeve.

"Want me to do it *right now?"* John raises his hands, palms forward, and closes his eyes. "Just release myself in the top of the third inning and be done with it?"

"Up to you." I shrug. "Or it might make for an interesting seventh inning stretch."

He opens his eyes and sneers at me. "I *knew* it. You *never* change, Loogie."

"How so?"

"Did you really think this would work? Did you think you could talk me into it that easily?"

"Nope." I shake my head and get out my phone. "I thought *this* might work, though." I open an app and hold up the phone for him to see.

He scowls at the image of himself on the screen and the text underneath it. "What the *fuck?*"

"I was right, wasn't I?" I can see it in his eyes. "Gotcha, bro!"

John grabs for the phone, but I jerk it away, then take a look at my handiwork on the screen. The word "TERRORIST" is emblazoned across his photo. The text under it tells the story of his plot to destroy Los Angeles. His *fake* plot, dreamed up by yours truly.

"What kind of joke *is* this?" Aware of the people around us, John lowers his voice. "I'm no *terrorist.*"

"And I suppose you're not a *serial pedophile*, either?"

"Of course not!"

I touch a button on the screen, and a countdown appears in red digital numbers above his photo. "Five minutes from now, you *will* be." I raise my eyebrows and nod. "This story, complete with the locations of damning evidence, will go out to every news organization and law enforcement agency in the country."

John's eyes pop as reality sets in. "*What?*"

"And did I mention the Jumbotron?" I point the phone at the giant video screen across the ballpark. "It goes up there *first.* So maybe fix your hair a little, there's a cowlick right..." I reach toward his head.

He swats my hand away. "No!" Panic spreads over his features like a wine stain on a wedding dress. "You can't *do* this!"

"That's one theory." I waggle the phone in my grip. "But what if I *can?* What if I *do?*"

His mouth falls open, but no words come out.

"*I'll* tell you what. Life as you know it is *over*, that's what. So much for enjoying all the little surprises that the future has in store. Starting in..." I check the countdown. "Starting in three minutes, you'll be captured, ruined, imprisoned, and made to suffer for the rest of your existence. Your life will become a fucking *nightmare*. Everything you *love* will be out of reach *forever*."

"But I'm *innocent.*"

"Not for long." I shake my head decisively. "Stick a fork in yourself, Johnny boy. You're *done.*"

"You *can't...*"

"I *can.* Media empire, remember?" I waggle the phone in his face. "*One minute.*"

"Oh God, oh God." Doors are slamming behind him. All he can see is the darkness ahead.

When he woke up in his usual stupor this morning, he never imagined today would work out this way. Now here he is, and the clock's running out. There's only one thing left to say.

"All right." He slumps in his seat, the picture of absolute defeat. "You win."

I touch a button on the phone, and the countdown pauses at ten seconds. I shake the screen at him. "Back out, and I take it off pause. Capische?"

He nods brokenly, staring into space.

"It's for the best, you know," I tell him. "You put it off as long as you could."

He turns his head, then, and meets my gaze. "I could have put if off longer. I *would* have."

If not for me. "Whatever."

He sits up straighter. "There's just one thing."

I frown. "What's that?"

"I have one condition," says John. "A last request." Somehow, he manages a small smile, and then he tells me what he has in mind.

John and I stand in the middle of Ventura Boulevard in the low late afternoon sun, facing East, and wait as the human race dies out around us.

Screams and sirens and gunshots fill the air from all directions. Flames lap at the blue sky above us as Studio City burns to the ground.

Thanks to John, who has flipped the inner switch that will soon end his life, the final chapter of humanity's sordid story is being written at last. No more wars, no more poverty, no more endless murder and torture and violation.

We have brought down the curtain on a failed experiment,

paving the way for something kinder and wiser and more viable by far. We've traded up for the kind of rulers the Earth deserves, the kind it should have had all along.

Now it's time for me to live up to my end of the bargain. Time to grant the final request John made me promise to fulfill back at the ballpark.

"Where is he?" John sounds nervous, like he's wondering if I'll go back on my promise.

But I won't. "He'll be here." It's the least I can do, now that Armageddon is finally unfolding. Now that I've gotten what I want.

More than that, it's the least I can do for my brother. It's the least I can do for the one person I've known and cared about all my life, even as he drove me crazy and held me back from coming into my own.

When the action dies down, and the world of humans breathes its last, he'll fade away. Soon enough, I'll never see him again.

So I'm glad, this one last time, that I can make him happy again. That I can give him something he's longed for as much as I've longed for an end and new beginning of the world.

"Is that him?" Excitedly, John points at a distant figure that appears down the street. "Is it?"

Low, roiling smoke clouds the view. "Don't know." The figure is unclear at first, bobbing and swaying in the murk. But a distinctive sound precedes it, high-pitched enough to penetrate the apocalyptic cacophony of dying L.A.

Whistling. The figure is whistling something...a song. The closer it gets, the more clear it becomes, until I recognize it for what it is: "Don't Fence Me In."

John steps forward, peering into the smoke. "Wait...wait..."

The figure resolves itself, pushing through the worst of the smoke, but I leave it to John to announce who it is. I let him be the one to say the incredible words he must never have imagined he would say or hear again.

"That *is* him." John's voice shakes with gleeful anticipation. "That *is* Tom Mix!"

Fuckin'-A right it is.

As the man on the horse rides closer, I have to admit they both look great. They both look like they're in their primes in the 1920s or '30s.

Not bad for a pair of corpses that've been moldering in the grave for ages.

When Tom gets within thirty yards of us, he smiles and waves. He's dressed in white Western garb--white shirt, white trousers, white chaps, white ten-gallon hat...and a white belt with a pair of pearl-handled six-shooter revolvers in white holsters, one hung from either hip.

Tom's famous horse, Tony, is mostly brown, with a blaze of white extending along his face and muzzle. He tosses his head in the same jaunty way that Tom just waved, as if to say hello.

John's eyes are huge. I can tell it takes everything he has to keep from racing over to greet his idol.

"Howdy!" says Tom when he gets a little closer. "Good to see you fellers!"

As soon as the words leave Tom's mouth, Tony whinnies in agreement.

John raises a hand and waves. For a moment, he is dumbstruck by the miracle riding toward him.

I have to admit, I'm damn proud of my work. As a force of creation, of the beginning of a new species, I have the power to reenergize hungover brothers--or reanimate dead legends for at least a little while. It's not a trick; that's the real Tom and Tony over there. But it did cost me dearly.

Bringing them back took so much juice that the debut of humanity's successor species will be delayed. A wait that has already felt like an eternity will be prolonged many months more. Mother Earth's reboot will be put on hold until my weakened power recharges enough to kick-start evolution.

But it's worth it. Worth every minute of additional waiting.

"What're your names, pardners?" asks Tom as he rides up and stops a few feet from John and me.

John stays tongue-tied, so I speak on his behalf. "I'm Doug, but this man here is your biggest fan. His name's John Glass."

"Is that right?" Tom grins and tips his hat to John. "Well, good to meetcha, Glass. You half-empty or half-full?"

"Half-full." John says it softly, like a shy little boy meeting Santa Claus.

I laugh. "Ain't that the truth!"

John is beaming. He finally finds the words he's been searching for. "I can't tell you how wonderful it is to meet you, Mr. Mix. I've been a fan of yours forever."

"Very kind of you, John," says Tom. "And please, call me 'Tom.'"

"You were always my hero, Tom," says John. "I thought of you when I felt the most lost, and you helped me find my way."

"Funny you should say that." Tom tips his hat back with one white-gloved hand. "I'm feelin' pretty lost about now myself." He looks around at the blazing city, which continues to ring with screams and sirens.

"Could you use someone to ride with, Tom?" I ask. "Someone to show you around a bit?"

"Sure could." Tom winks and pats his horse's neck. "Got anybody in mind?"

Tony winks, too.

I look at my brother, as if there's ever any doubt. "What do you say, John?"

John's eyes fill with tears, and he wipes them away. His lips form a tight line as he clenches them against the sobs fighting to get out.

Grinning, I bob my head toward the man on the horse. "Burning daylight here, Johnny boy. What do you say?"

Suddenly, John lunges forward and throws his arms around me. *"Thank you."* He whispers the words in my ear as he holds on for dear life.

I pat his back. "*De nada*, pardner." I think I've got a few tears of my own on the way.

"Sorry for keeping you waiting, brother," whispers John. "I just couldn't let go."

"I know the feeling." I'm having trouble letting go myself. Now that I'm faced with the thought of losing him, I hate to break the hug.

Fortunately, Tom intervenes. "Maybe I better hit the dusty trail on my own, fellers."

John gives me one last squeeze and pushes away. "Not a chance, Mr. Mix. I'd love to be your guide."

Tom narrows his eyes. "You sure about that?"

"I wouldn't miss it in a million years," says John.

"Then saddle up, pardner." Tom pats the horse's back behind him. "Time's a-wastin'."

John hurries over, and Tom reaches down to give him a hand up. Light as a feather, John swings a leg over Tony and lands in the saddle behind Tom.

"Seeya, bro." I smile and wave.

John looks perfectly comfortable riding with Tom, as if he's always belonged there. It's hard to believe he was ever a hopeless addict and an obstacle to planetary evolution.

It's also hard to believe that I'm never going to see him again.

"Aydios, pardner," says John with a goodbye gesture--a salute of his index and middle fingers glancing off his left temple.

Tom tugs on the reins. Tony whinnies and tosses his head, then turns and trots off down the street.

"Hasta la vista!" Tom waves without looking back, then whistles "Back in the Saddle" as he and my brother ride west. A warm wind blows toward them, clearing a path through the smoke as if on cue in a Hollywood movie.

They are silhouetted by the setting sun as they sway off down Ventura Boulevard, outlines blurring against the bright golden disk as it melts like butter into the rippling horizon.

BEARERS OF BAD, BAD NEWS

The sun is out, the breeze is warm, the grass is green, the birds are singing. People are calmly going about their Saturday morning summertime business, walking or playing in the park. And *I* am laughing my *ass* off!

Because it looks like all is *right* with the world, but there's an old dude over there with a sign that reads *The End Is Nigh*.

I just had to pause in my run along the path and crack up at the irony. The guy looks ridiculous standing there with his bushy white beard, dressed in a raggedy red flannel shirt and gray sweat-pants, holding a rickety doomsday sign overhead. And the whole time, his expression's dead serious.

I pull my phone from a pocket in my shorts and browse to the camera. I aim at the sign guy and zoom in, watching as he marches in a tight circle on the grass, chanting something I can't hear.

Watching him makes me crack up even more, for personal reasons. There he is, advertising the impending end of the world, and *my* world has already turned to shit. I moved to Philadelphia from a hick small town to hit it big as an artist, and I've done nothing but suck up a storm. I'm running out of savings, getting ready to move back home to Mom and Dad at the age of 25, and my girlfriend just dumped me. Did I mention my best friend died in a plane crash last week?

I've got no career, no prospects, no love life, no friends, and no purpose. So yeah, the dude with the sign is extra funny to me because he's so *not* on the money—not just because the day looks so un-apocalyptic in the park, but because the world has already pretty much ended for me.

All the more reason to snap a few shots to keep me laughing as things continue to melt down around me. I take a deep breath to steady my hands and move my thumb to the shutter button, framing the image.

Then, just as I'm about to snap a photo, the old man suddenly stops marching. He staggers a few more feet, drops the sign, and clutches his chest with both hands.

Without thinking, I charge toward him, punching 9-1-1 on the digital keypad of my phone. He hits the ground before I get there, and I plunge to my knees beside him, rattling off my location and plea for help to the dispatcher.

Only after I hang up the phone do I realize what's really happened to the old guy. His beard and the middle of his chest are soaked with blood. There's a deep, dark hole where his breastbone used to be.

He's been shot.

"Damn." My heart is pounding. I'm an artist, not a doc or paramedic, and I know zip about CPR. All I can do is wait for the ambulance and try not to get shot, too.

"You!" The old guy's right hand latches onto my left wrist. "It's up to *you* now."

"Relax, buddy." I know I'm doing a shit job of sounding reassuring, but I also know he doesn't have long to live. "You're gonna be fine. The ambulance is on its way."

"Take it." He gasps out his words. "Promise me...you'll *take it."*

I wish he'd calm down. "Take what?"

"My *sign*." The old man claws at the grass with his free hand, but the sign's out of reach. "You must *continue*...the *work."*

"What's your name?" Changing the subject might help. "I'm Ethan. Ethan Wright."

His hand tightens painfully on my wrist, and his eyes bulge. "This is...a *sacred* trust. You must *take* the sign from here...and *wait.*"

"Wait for what?" I ask.

The old-timer seizes up, coughs a gout of blood, and falls back to the ground. His hand lets go of my wrist, and I snatch it away, wincing.

That's when I finally hear an ambulance siren in the distance.

Suddenly, the old man's eyes flicker open, and his lips move. He's trying to tell me something. I lean close to hear it.

"Take it." Again, he gasps for breath. "Please...take the sign. *Promise* me."

What makes me get up and grab the sign at that moment? What possesses me to run it over to my beat-up old Chevy Malibu parked along the nearby street? Pity? Kindness? Guilt?

I wrack my brain as I run back to him, but I just can't figure it out.

"You took it...didn't you?" He barely manages to force out the words.

I kneel beside him and nod. "Consider it done."

"Thank you." Has anyone ever looked at me with such intense gratitude before? "Thank you...from the bottom...of my heart...friend Ethan. Now I can go...in peace."

With that, he closes his eyes and falls silent, even as the siren races nearer.

The old man is dead before the ambulance arrives, followed by the police. Soon, our corner of the park is swarming with people, though it was nearly deserted just moments ago.

I'm there for a long time, answering questions, watching as the cops and coroner go over the scene. No one finds any trace of the shooter or any other kind of evidence...and I'm no help, since I know next to nothing.

By the time they turn me loose, it's hours later. Shell-shocked, I drive straight home.

Back in my cramped apartment, I change out of my sweaty workout clothes, slipping into a black t-shirt and faded jeans. Then, I sit on the musty secondhand sofa and stare at the sign, which I've propped against the living room window. The best plan, I know, is to toss it in the dumpster behind the building and never have to look at it again. Seeing the old man die was bad enough; I could do without a reminder that brings it all back.

My keeping the sign might have been his last wish, but it's not like I knew him. It's not like I owe him or anything.

Still, the rickety square of plywood nailed to a slat of splintered pine stays where it is for now. It's not like it doesn't fit in; I'm an artist, and my place is already full of easels, frames, and paintings. A visitor walking in might think the sign is some kind of found art or a piece made to look that way, not an old man's warning of the end about to come.

Which actually turned out to be right on the money, when it came to *his* end.

I go to the kitchen for a glass of water, but I can't stop thinking about the old man and his sign. How long did he carry it around, and why? Was he just crazy, or did he have what he thought was a good reason for doing what he did?

At least there's no one in my orbit to think *I'm* crazy right now, with my girlfriend and best friend both gone. I'm a pretty isolated bastard these days, which isn't always a bad thing...though it isn't always such a *great* thing, either. I have to admit, the loneliness has been eating at me quite a bit lately.

Did the old man with the sign ever feel that way, too? Maybe we had more in common than I realized when I first laughed at him this morning.

The End Is Nigh. I'm staring at the words on the sign when my doorbell rings.

Frowning, I walk over and crack the door, keeping the chain in place. "Who's there?"

"My name is Solomon George." His voice is remarkably deep and rich. His dark, handsome face gazes back at me from between the door and its frame. "I've come to see you about a sign."

I consider lying, then think better of it. "What about it?" The old man said I should take the sign and wait. Did he mean I should wait for this guy?

"May I come in?" asks the man. "This is something better kept between the two of us, my friend."

I have no intention of letting in someone I've never met...but then I hear a scratching sound and look back at the sign by the window. That's when I realize the most amazing thing has happened.

The message on the sign has changed.

"Oh my God." My blood turns icy cold, and my gut clenches. What I'm seeing—there's no way it's possible. There's just *no way.*

The End Is Nigh. That's what the sign used to say.

Let Him In, Ethan. That's what it says *now.*

Maybe, what I just saw should be enough to make me do the exact opposite. Maybe, if I had more common sense, I would lock the door tight, heave the sign out the window, and be done with it. But since when has common sense been my strong suit?

"Hello?" says Solomon. "Are you all right in there?"

Without a word, without taking my eyes off the sign, I slide the chain from the track and let it fall against the frame. Then, in slow motion, I pull the door open and step back.

Solomon enters wearing a long black duster coat, dark red button-down shirt, and black corduroy trousers. It isn't his outfit that draws my attention, though. He's carrying something behind him, dragging it over the creaky gray floorboards.

Another sign.

Just like the old man's, it has a splintered slat of a handle and a square plywood board with a message painted on it. I get a look when he props it against the window beside the sign that's already there.

Listen to Him, Ethan. That's what Solomon's sign says to me.

Then I blink, and both signs say the same thing: *The End Is Nigh.*

"What the hell?" I stumble back a step, feeling like the world has lost its mind.

Solomon catches me by the elbow. "Welcome, friend." He

smiles and shakes my hand. "Welcome to the Brotherhood of Doomsday Sign Bearers."

Solomon asks for a glass of water. As I get one from the kitchenette, he picks up the old man's sign and gazes at it intently.

"Brother Maynard, you will be missed." He flattens his palm against the board and closes his eyes. "May the sign that is your soul carry the message to planes yet undreamt of."

I bring him the water and wait until he opens his eyes. I hand him the glass, and he accepts it with a grim nod.

"The bearer of this sign." He hefts the placard I brought home from the park. "Maynard Wilson. He was also a member of our fabled brotherhood. One of the finest." He raises the water glass as if he's making a toast. "You couldn't ask for a better example to follow as you walk this road with us."

I have no intention of joining this club of theirs, but I can't deny I'm curious. "What road are you talking about?"

"You're already on it, son." Solomon puts down the sign. "You just don't know it yet."

"Then enlighten me." As curious as I am, I'm getting annoyed. There might be an element of the supernatural in play here, but my patience still isn't everlasting.

Solomon crosses the apartment, sipping water and looking at my paintings. "Somebody has to bear the sign," he says calmly. "Somebody has to warn the people."

"That's it?" I ask. "That's what your brotherhood does? Walks around carrying doomsday signs?"

Solomon picks up a half-assed painting of the gate of Philly Chinatown and chuckles. "If only it were that simple."

I shrug. "Sounds pretty simple to me."

Solomon whirls, eyes narrowed. "The first of our order trod the dusty streets of ancient Sumeria, carrying a tablet inscribed in cuneiform. Gilgamesh himself scoffed at that message, thinking the world could not end in his time."

"Gilgamesh was right," I say.

"But he would *not* have been, if not for our bearer of the tablet." Solomon nods gravely. "He *saved* the world that time and more. And in fathering our brotherhood, he saved it thousands of times over throughout the ages."

"What the hell are you talking about?"

"The signs *never* lie." Solomon puts down the painting and walks back over to look at the signs by the window. "When you see one, the end of the world *is* imminent. But when you see one in the hands of a *bearer*, there is also *hope.* Because our brothers are committed to bringing salvation under the guise of prophetic doomsaying."

"You're telling me the same guys who carry the doomsday signs around are the ones who save the world?" I ask.

"Yes, and they have *never* failed to stave off the end," says Solomon. "Though this time, I fear, will be different." He checks his wristwatch and shakes his head. "Without Brother Maynard and the others, this world's future may be forfeit."

"Others?" His story's outrageous, but I want to hear the rest.

"We need you." Solomon walks over and hands me his empty water glass. "You have already proven your courage and goodness at Maynard's side in the line of fire. He recommended you as his replacement, and we abide by his judgment."

"Recommended me?" I frown. "How did you even *find* me?"

"Those, of course." He gestures at the signs by the window. "They are drawn together. They communicate, in their own way."

"Look." I plant the glass among the dirty dishes piled in the sink. "I'm flattered, but you've got the wrong guy here."

Solomon smirks. "If only you knew how many times I've heard *that* before."

He checks his watch again, then crosses the room to retrieve the signs. He holds out Maynard's, his expression growing more urgent by the moment.

"Take it," he tells me. "We need to get going. The world ends at *midnight* if we don't save it."

Hurry, Ethan! says Maynard's sign. *Time is running out!*

Against my better judgment, I take hold of the sign.

"Good!" Solomon heads for the door. "Now let's go before it's too late!"

The whole way to the historic district, I'm thinking I'll drop Solomon off (with *both* signs) and drive home. I'm thinking I'm crazy for coming *this* far, and getting in any deeper would be a giant mistake.

Carrying around a doomsday sign in public is not my idea of a fun time. It might not be a *safe* time, either, after what happened to Brother Maynard.

I'm still planning to bolt even as I pull into a parking space near Independence National Park, directed by Solomon. Leaving is the smartest thing I could do, and I know it.

But then I look at Maynard's sign on the back seat, and I'm not so sure. *Please stay.* That's the top line of the message on the plywood board.

Maynard died so you could save the world. That's the rest of it.

"This makes no sense," I say as Solomon hands me Maynard's sign.

"Such is *often* the case with the truth." Solomon shuts the car door and hefts his sign over his left shoulder.

I lock the car with the remote, telling myself I'll only walk a little way with him. "How can someone carrying an end-of-the-world sign stop the world from ending?"

"For one thing," says Solomon, shambling down the cobblestone sidewalk, "it isn't *just* a sign. Or hadn't you noticed?"

I don't answer the question. "But it's just wood and paint and nails. That's all it is."

"Sure." Solomon laughs. "The part you can *see."*

We round a corner and nearly collide with the people standing there. The line to get in the Liberty Bell Center is long, wrapping around the entire block.

And the closest ones are already giving us funny looks.

"That's it for me," I mutter, backing away. "You're on your own, Solomon." I hold out the handle of my sign for him to take.

"Wait." He's seemingly oblivious as people waiting in line snap photos of us. "Please, I can't do this alone."

"Then you'll have to find somebody else." I push the sign handle closer to him. When he won't take it, I move to put it down in the strip of grass along the walk.

But I can't. The sign is stuck to my hand.

"What the hell?" I try and fail to shake or scrape it free. "Why can't I *let go* of this thing?"

Solomon's expression darkens. "It must be time." He looks around worriedly as he lifts the sign from his shoulder, holding it high overhead. "The next apocalypse is on its way."

"What are you *talking* about?" I still can't get the handle out of my hand.

"We're at the *epicenter*," he tells me. "We can still stop it from here, but only if we work together."

People are staring, and I feel ridiculous. "Work together how? By walking around carrying these signs while everyone laughs at us?"

"I already told you, they're not just signs." He looks and sounds desperate. "*Sigils* and *runes* will appear. You will *see* things no one else can see. Do not be alarmed. Whatever you do, never stop chanting the magic words."

"Magic words?" I'm distracted by the laughter and phones of the people in line. Now I know how Maynard felt when I laughed my ass off at him.

"The end is coming." Solomon says it for me, then starts marching down the sidewalk, voice raised for the crowd's benefit. "The end is nigh."

I'm not doing this. That's all there is to it. I'll just smash the sign against that brick wall over there until it breaks into splinters, and then I'll get in my car and go home. End of shitty story.

But when I start toward the wall, the daylight flickers. Shadows drift over me, casting nebulous pools of darkness from above.

Stopping, I look up...and immediately wish I hadn't. The most bizarre scene is spread out across the sky, unlike anything I've ever witnessed before.

A mirror image of Independence Park and the Liberty Bell Center hang above me, upside-down—but it's a *negative* image, with dark objects and spaces turned to light and vice versa. The figures that populate it aren't people at all. They're jumbles of words loosely arranged within the outlines of human forms, words like *PAIN, FEAR, TERROR, HATRED, RUIN,* and *ARMAGGEDDON.* In their "hands," these word-people carry signs like mine and Solomon's, only the boards and handles are all black. And instead of words, the signs show a different kind of message. A human face screams in agony on each one, surrounded by flashing sparks and swirling symbols.

Those screams, a thunderous rumble, and the howl of a rising wind fill my ears. Is this what Hell sounds like, I wonder?

My head spins and my guts churn as I listen and gaze into the otherworldly scene. I finally have to look away, casting my eyes back down to the world I know.

And then I'm shocked all over again. Not a single person is looking up at the negative realm. A bunch are laughing at me and snapping photos; others are doing the same to Solomon or just minding their own business. But *no one* is staring at the madness overhead.

Every last one of them is absolutely oblivious.

Suddenly, the hand I'm holding the sign with tingles, and I look at the message board. *Now do you believe?* That's what it says this time.

I'm frozen...and then the world starts to shiver, and I look up again. The negative place is descending, dropping inexorably closer.

My sign tingles, and I read the latest message. *Do as he told you! I'll do the rest!*

In the face of insanity and a possible apocalypse, my resistance melts away. I hoist the sign high and start my march along the sidewalk, chanting as Solomon instructed.

"The end is coming!" I say. "The end is nigh!"

People point and laugh. They make crude jokes and throw garbage in my path. But I keep going.

Solomon nods when he passes, never stopping his own chant.

Our voices blend together in counterpoint to the screams, the rumbling, and the howling wind.

As the darkness closes in from above, the sign tingles again...and the tingling intensifies. If it gets much stronger, I'll be in pain.

Looking up, I see a new message displayed on the placard. *Get ready! It's time!*

Time for what? I want to know, but I just keep chanting. "The end is coming! The end is nigh!"

The current in the handle spikes suddenly, and my whole body vibrates. The sign flares with a surge of bright white energy, pulsing like a star atop the handle.

Then, the energy crackles in a single blazing bolt behind me. Turning, I see it lance the length of the block and stab Solomon's placard dead on.

Both signs are flaring now, connected by a writhing slash of electrical force. Sigils and runes dance on their surfaces, sizzling with phosphorescent light like the fuse of a bomb.

Still, the people in line notice nothing unusual. Though I see the light play on their faces and forms, they're as blind to it as ever.

Suddenly, the energy surges, and my sign starts to kick like it's alive. I struggle to keep it in the air as it thrashes and dips, pitching itself to and fro with frenetic abandon.

The rumbling and howling wind grow louder. The upside-down negative scene lowers faster.

Solomon looks like he's completely consumed by blazing light. I can barely see the lines of his physical form.

I'm in the same condition, I quickly realize. Every part of my body burns with unearthly power.

Then, suddenly, the power leaps up from both of us and the conduit in-between. All the energy explodes upward with such force that the hair of the people in line to see the Liberty Bell flutters and flaps.

There's a thunderous *boom* when the energy wave strikes the negative realm. It echoes through the canyons of the park, blotting out all other sound with its sheer volume.

At the same time, the negative realm flares with blinding power. I clamp my eyes shut against it, still seeing the blast's remnants on the insides of my eyelids.

When the light and booming fades, I open my eyes and look up. The negative realm is gone, making way for clear blue sky and mid-afternoon sun.

We did it! That's what the message on my sign says. *The world survives!*

I squint against the sunlight, fighting to process what just happened. None of it seems real or even remotely possible now.

Then again, neither does the sign talking to me through the messages painted on its surface.

See to Solomon, it tells me. *Do it now!*

Looking around, I spot Solomon walking toward me with a limp. His own sign is at his side, dragging on the ground.

He doesn't look great, but at first, I don't realize just how bad off he is. He smiles from a distance and flashes a thumbs-up, making me think he's in even better shape.

That's what he does just before his legs go out from under him.

I run to him as he topples to the street. It's a good thing I'm there, because no one else makes a move to come to his aid.

The sign finally loosens in my grip, and I let it fall as I kneel beside Solomon. He pushes himself up to a sitting position, but his face is etched with strain. I guess the fight to save the world took a lot out of him.

At least that's what I think before I see the blossom of blood on his right shoulder...the dark bullethole punched through the fabric of his coat.

"Get me out of here," he gasps. "And don't forget to bring the signs."

Back at my apartment, Solomon sits on the secondhand sofa and bleeds.

I offer to take him to the hospital, but he says no, there isn't time. Another outbreak of apocalypse is coming, apparently, and it will put the last one to shame in a big way.

But from what I can see, the big guy's in no condition to save the world just now. He might as well get treated for his wound, for all the good he'll do otherwise.

"Isn't there someone you can call?" I ask as I clean his wound with a washrag. Thank God, there's an exit wound on the back of his shoulder, meaning the bullet went clean through. "Isn't there someone who can cover for you?"

Solomon winces at the touch of the wet rag and shakes his head.

"But you said there's a brotherhood," I remind him.

Solomon's breath hisses out between his teeth. "There aren't many...of us left...these days."

"You mean there were other shootings?"

He nods weakly. "We're being hunted. There are people...who *want* the world to end. They have an organization...of their own."

"There's a brotherhood of doomsday sign bearer *murderers*?"

"Something like that," says Solomon.

"Well, that's just great." I finish with the washrag and rinse it out in the bathroom sink. Then I return with a first aid kit. "So who's winning?"

"Make it past tense," says Solomon. "Who *won?"*

I fish out a roll of gauze and start wrapping it around his wound. "Why past tense?"

"Because the world's been ending...for a long time now." Solomon closes his eyes and leans against the towels draped over the back of the sofa. "Piece by piece...it's been falling apart...for many years. All those disaster areas...failed states...economic collapses...civil wars. All those little apocalypses...taking down the worlds within the world."

"What about what we saw today?" I finish wrapping his shoulder and snip the end of the gauze with a pair of scissors from the kit. "That negative world with the words shaped like people and the screaming signs? It was like something out of another *reality."*

He shakes his head. "Just another level...underlying our own. Trying to take its place."

"And no one saw it but us." I frown as I put the gauze back in the kit and close the lid. "Or were there other sign bearers in other parts of the world who could see it, too?"

"No." He gasps at the pain in his shoulder. "That was just an apocalypse...for *this* city. So many others...are already past the point...of no return. Even if that were not the case...there are too few bearers left in the world...to bear witness...let alone *stop* it."

I look at the signs, which I left propped against the wall. For once, they're blank. No advice offered.

"You're telling me the world is already ending?" I say. "And the only people who could save it are mostly dead?"

"Essentially...you are correct."

I fold my arms over my chest and shake my head. "So, basically, what you're saying is we're doomed. We have no hope."

Solomon grunts. "There's *always* hope." With that, he grits his teeth and leans forward. "As long as any of us yet stand against the endtimes, there is still hope that some fragment of the world will survive."

I see he's trying to get to his feet, and I stop him. "You need to rest."

"I need to *go*. We *both* do. The next Apocalyptic outbreak is heating up."

"How do you know?" I ask.

"Same way I always know." He gestures at his sign. "My helper tips me off."

I frown at his sign, which looks perfectly blank to me. "But there's nothing there. No message at all."

"Nothing *you* can see, maybe." He shrugs. "You must not be all the way in the circle of trust just yet."

"So there's another apocalypse coming. Fine. But do you really think you can *stop* it in the shape you're in?"

"I have to try." He pushes up from the sofa and gets to his feet. "Until my dying breath, I can do no less."

Sluggishly, he moves toward his sign, and my heart goes out to him. He's like an old soldier about to march off to the last battle of his life.

Why am I worried about this guy? I barely know him. But I saw the proof of his crazy story today, and I don't think he can stand up to what's coming.

I keep thinking there has to be another way, an option he and the other bearers haven't thought of yet. An alternative that might occur to a younger and more creative type...someone like me, for example.

I don't have to think for long before it comes to me. "Hold on." I dart over between him and his sign. "I've got an idea."

There's a sheen of sweat on his face from the strain of movement. "What kind of idea?"

"Where can we find more of these?" I turn and point at the signs.

He frowns. "How many more?"

I grin. "How many ya got?"

The next apocalypse is due on the steps of the Philadelphia Museum of Art, where Sylvester Stallone ran in the classic movie *Rocky.* Could there be a more perfect place for modern-day underdogs to succeed against unbeatable odds?

It's late afternoon when we pull up in my car, which is loaded with signs from a Brotherhood of Bearers stockpile hidden in a deserted laundry in Chinatown. The museum looks as busy as ever, with visitors walking up and down the vast steps and tour groups lectured by guides at various points.

I park along the oval in front of the main building and start unloading on the sidewalk as Solomon stays in the car, conserving his strength. It's a no parking zone, but a ticket or tow is the least of my worries right now. What'll it matter, if the damn world comes to an end soon anyway?

People give me funny looks as I stack the signs, but I don't care. They're all going to die if my plan doesn't work, so tough shit if they don't like it.

And the truth is, not all the looks are funny. A few people drift over with keen interest, as if they're expecting me...as if they're in on the game.

Because they are, thanks to me.

"Excuse me." A young woman with frizzy black hair joins me at the curb. She's wearing ripped bluejeans and a pink t-shirt with the image of a cartoon kitten smoking a cigarette on the chest. "I'm Liz. Is this where the challenge is happening?"

"It sure is!" I hand her a sign with the standard message on the placard: *The End Is Nigh.* "We'll get started any minute now. Could you help me hand these out to the other participants as they arrive?"

"Will do!" Liz accepts another sign and wanders off, eyeing up bystanders and passersby.

Solomon, who just got out of the car, looks puzzled as he hobbles over, gripping his shoulder. "She's helping us, just like that? A complete stranger?"

I shrug as I pull more signs from the trunk of the car. "All it took was a post on social media. 'Performance art in progress! Join the Doomsday Sign Challenge!'"

More people—most young, a few middle-aged and older—accept signs from Liz, who keeps pulling from the pile. At this rate, it won't be long until we run out of signs.

"It's amazing to me," says Solomon.

"You guys should've looked into crowdsourcing the apocalypse sooner," I tell him. "Maybe the world would be fully saved by now."

"I only hope...the signs activate for them," says Solomon. "They don't work...for just anyone."

"Maynard's worked for me," I say. "And that was a pretty quick turnaround. I'm guessing that when the going gets tough, the signs will make do with who they've got."

Solomon looks around at the gathering group and frowns. "Does it bother you that these people you've found...don't know what they're in for? That they don't know the true danger?"

"Neither did I at first." I grab the last sign from the trunk—Maynard's sign, now mine—and slam it shut. "Now correct me if

I'm wrong, but we're talking the *end of the world* here, aren't we? We don't have a lot of time to worry about the ethical implications of recruiting these people, do we?"

Solomon blows out his breath. "No, we don't."

"And if they don't help us, they'll all be dead soon anyway, correct?"

Solomon nods, looking like he's just been outdebated.

"That's what I thought." I raise my wrist and check my watch. "Speaking of time, how much of it do we have?"

Even as I ask the question, I see waves of distortion rippling through the mountain of museum steps like a massive heat mirage. The people ripple with them, seemingly unaware of the strange change that's occurring.

"Forget it." I raise my sign and square my shoulders, getting ready. "I think I can figure it out."

"Where's my sign?" Solomon looks around, scowling. "I don't see it anywhere."

"Don't worry. One of the newbies needed it." I pull out my phone and give it to him. "Do me a favor though, would you? When the fireworks start, hold this up and pretend to take pictures of all the bearers."

"You want me to take *pictures?"* His scowl deepens.

"I don't care if you actually do or not. Just *act* like that's what you're doing." I see he's holding up the phone, but it's turned the wrong way. "And can you hold it so the front part's facing you?"

He turns the phone around, and I give him a thumbs up. "Awesome."

With that, I hurry over to Liz and the others who answered my post. I count twenty of them, leaving no signs unclaimed. Not bad for a last-minute challenge.

"Hi, everyone!" Gripping my sign with both hands, I raise it overhead. "Thanks for coming to the Great Doomsday Sign Challenge!"

The participants cheer and shake their signs, getting in the spirit of things. I'm guessing from their upbeat reactions that the apocalyptic changes rippling through the museum aren't visible to them. Maybe they just haven't been exposed to the signs enough yet.

"So here's how the challenge works, guys." I raise my voice, as a howling wind is rising, though I don't think the team can hear it yet. "Get those signs up and start marching! My friend over there..." I point to Solomon. "...will shoot photos and video for the internet. We'll post them to the challenge site, where you can link to them in your own social media."

Scattered cheers go up from the group.

"Remember to keep chanting no matter what," I tell them. "You already know the words, right?"

"'The end is coming!'" All the recruits shout it at once. "'The end is nigh!'"

"Perfect!" I applaud their efforts. "Now, we're doing some experimental AR stuff here, projecting augmented reality imagery from these signs. So if you see some crazy stuff, just keep marching and chanting. Don't let anything stop you from finishing the challenge." I don't mention the possibility of bullets flying. At this point, I think it's better to hope for the best and stay on track with saving the world. "Now let's go do it, everyone! We'll put the ice bucket challenge to shame, mark my words!"

There's more cheering, and the group starts marching. Signs upheld, we form two lines and set off in opposite directions.

I lead the team marching to the right of the steps, trying to hold steady as Armageddon breaks out above us. Glancing back, I see more faces among my group gazing up at the steps with shocked expressions. They must be bonding with the signs they carry; the transformations taking place are finally registering among them. I just hope they all manage to keep their heads as the madness gets worse.

The wind howls louder and the ground rumbles underfoot as we march. When the sky darkens, I look up to see the upside-down negative realm has returned, only the scale is much bigger than at the Liberty Bell Center. This time, the entire museum complex is projected there, suspended in all its massive, reverse-image glory.

Again, clusters of words in the shape of people populate the scene, many carrying black signs with whirling sigils and screaming human faces on them. This time, though, the word-people are more frenzied, shaking signs and fists and jumping up and down with hostile intent.

The museum steps, meanwhile, jolt and ripple like a flying carpet. How the people ascending and descending them aren't being whipped right off, I'll never know.

Suddenly, my hands tingle around the sign handle, and I look up at the placard above me. *It's time! This is it!* That's what it says.

Looking back at my team again, I see the expressions of surprise have turned to worry—even terror—on most of the faces in line. Some have stopped chanting and are just staring up at the negative realm like it's the gaping maw of Hell itself. In other words, they look much like I did the first time I glimpsed this insanity.

"Keep it together, everyone!" I yell. "It's just the A.R. field kicking in! Keep marching and chanting no matter what!"

The howling and rumbling intensify. Reaching the edge of the stairway, I turn and lead my group back toward the middle. I see the other team approaching from the opposite edge, led by Liz, who looks nervous but steady.

Just as our two groups come back together, the tingling in my hands spikes, and my sign flares with white light. So do the signs of all the other marchers.

Above us, the negative realm descends, closing in on the museum and its surroundings. Black lightning crackles from the columns and steps of the negative main building, zapping across the dwindling gap to score the rooftops and fountain with dark burn marks.

Hold on! says my sign, and I do, but I worry about the others. Some have panicked looks on their faces. This is much more than they signed on for.

I have to keep them together, or all is lost.

"Don't let go!" I shout. "There's a surge coming! Let it happen!"

Just as the words leave my mouth, bolts of energy erupt from every marcher's sign and join together, threading us all into one giant circuit. All twenty-one signs flare as one, blazing away with the same crackling white energy.

"Oh my God!" Liz looks astonished. "This isn't like any augmented reality *I've* ever played!"

Thunder rolls and churns as the negative realm drops faster, plunging toward the plot of vanishing reality I've chosen to defend. Splashdown is seconds away; another piece of the world is about to succumb to unstoppable pressures from beyond the pale.

Before that final contact, the seething circuit of energy we've summoned vaults upward. It crashes into the negative realm with all the force of a cosmic collision, filling the skies with blazing light and a deafening *boom* that blots out all other sound and thought.

The power of the negative realm must be greater than the last time, however. Our energy burst halts its fall but doesn't blast it out of the sky. The realm hangs there, buffeted by the white light expelled from our signs without being driven away.

I'm not sure what to do next. Can the signs emit more charges to end the threat? Will they do it automatically, or do we need to trigger the process somehow?

I need answers, and I need them fast...but before I get them, the situation changes. A loud *crack* pierces the air, then another.

A bullet strikes Liz in the chest, and she topples to the pavement. Another bearer behind her, a middle-aged man with dark hair, collapses a second later.

As the gunfire continues, more sign bearers drop—some shot, others ducking the assault. Every time one of them lets go of a sign, its light darkens, dimming the circuit that's suspending the negative realm.

When enough of the signs power down, the entire circuit goes out. Freed from the repulsive force halting its progress, the negative realm wobbles in midair, adjusting to the change.

It is during this moment that I see who's doing the shooting. Standing on the curb by my car, Solomon fires shot after shot from a rifle I've never seen before. Was it hidden in his duster all this time? Did he shoot himself in the shoulder at the Liberty Bell Center? Those questions don't matter so much anymore, I suppose.

But there's a question that *does* matter, at least to me.

"Solomon, *why?*" I scream the words over the sound of gunfire and the rising wind and thunder.

"This world isn't worth saving anymore!" he shouts, reloading his rifle. "And besides, it's about time *one* of us bearers wasn't lying about the end of the world coming!"

He slams the clip into place and mows down more sign bearers as they try to run.

"The end is nigh! The end is nigh!" he roars. "This time, it really *is* nigh!"

As he cranks off shot after shot, I feel my sign tingle again, and I look up at it.

Hold on tight! it says. *Don't let go!*

Above it, the negative realm resumes its descent. Nothing's in its way anymore.

My heart's pounding, and I'm shaking with fear. As much as I've hated my life in recent days, I'd give anything not to lose it now, like this.

Only the sign in my hand offers any kind of guidance. *No matter what happens, don't let go of me!*

The shrieks of the word-people's signs grow louder as the negative realm comes closer to touching down. A foul stench pours down from the realm and washes over me, making me choke.

With nothing else left to try, I haul down my sign and wrap my arms around it.

The museum building crumbles, and the steps implode. Gunshots ring out, people scream, and car alarms whoop. It is the sound of the end of the world.

I check the message on my sign one more time. *Close your eyes*, it says. *Close your eyes and hold on for dear life.*

I tighten my embrace as if the sign were a life preserver. Just as I'm about to close my eyes, I see Solomon storm toward me, gun pointing in my direction.

I clamp my eyes shut and wait for the end, steeling myself for what I know must be coming next.

And then everything suddenly goes black.

How long is it until I realize I still exist? I have no way of knowing.

Awareness returns...an awareness of thought and feeling and self. Alive or dead, my mind is intact; I remember who I am and what I've endured.

I feel as if I'm drifting, bobbing calmly in some kind of warm, lazy current, my arms wrapped tight around the sign. I hear nothing but the softest hum, smell only a faint, sweet perfume like the scent of a rose.

Where am I?

My eyes flicker open, and at last I see the place I've gone. All around me, whorls and swirls of color shift and flow in continuous motion. Vaporous streamers of every hue and shade interweave, graceful tendrils sifting between layers of shimmering cloud.

Amorphous reaches of color and light are all I see in every direction. The sign and I are the only solid, stable things in this dazzling vastness.

I breathe a sigh of relief that I didn't awaken in the hellish negative realm. Then I feel a rush of fear at being cast adrift in such an ephemeral place. It makes me clutch the sign all the more tightly, as if it is my only anchor in this intangible gulf.

I feel a tingle in my hands and loosen my grip a little, just enough to pull the sign away and read what's painted on its face.

Look around, it says. *We got here just in time.*

I do look, and what I see takes my breath away. Tiny, multicolored lights emerge from the colorful swirls, blinking like fireflies. They come forth in clusters, combing right and left in perfect formations like schools of fish.

As I watch, the lights weave together and swim apart, dancing around me. They give off a gentle chirp and leave a sweet fragrance in their wake. Where they glide across my skin, I feel a gentle tickle. As they flock, I can feel more than that; I swear, I can almost sense an *intelligence* radiating from them.

The old world is over, says my sign.

"And this is what's replacing it?" I smile as the tiny lights land all over me. "Not bad."

You deserved a look, says the sign. *And there's a tradition. It goes WAY back.*

I giggle at the tickling of the lights. "What tradition is that?"

The message changes, and I understand. Hefting the sign overhead, I carry it proudly as I drift through the many-colored aether, robed in twinkling lights.

"The beginning is nigh." I repeat what the sign says, following in the footsteps of Maynard and all the rest. "The beginning is coming."

Somebody has to say it out loud. That's how everything begins and ends, after all.

"Let there be light." I say it between giggles, and then I realize I'm probably not the first person to laugh out loud at the start of a new Creation. "Let there be lots and lots of light."

A CHOOSE YOUR OWN FANGLE ADVENTURE

"But you don't *look* like Peter Pinnacle." The ten-year-old girl frowned behind her bright red horn-rimmed glasses as if someone had just told her the biggest lie of all time. "You're *older*...and *fatter.*"

"Because my friend Wes Carmichael wrote the first book in the series a long time ago." Jake Bartholomew smiled patiently, all too aware of his graying hair and overweight appearance. How many times had he had to explain this already today? Readers expected him to be forever thirty, like Peter in the books, not 47 and gone to seed. "So would you like an autographed photo?" He patted the stack of 8 x 10 glossies spread out on the table before him.

The little girl tipped her head to one side. "But how do I *know* you're *him?"*

Jake tapped the framed certificate propped up near the edge of the table. "See this? It's a notarized affidavit, signed by the author. It proves he based Peter on me."

"It proves nothing," said the girl's surly father, a tall executive type with glossy black shoe polish hair and a look of perpetual disgust on his puffy red face. His sole concession to it being the weekend was not wearing a tie with his slick gray business suit. "*None* of these people are *remotely* convincing."

Jake looked up and down the line of tables crossing the floor of the community center gymnasium. The two dozen men and women seated there, he knew, were *exactly* as advertised--the real-life people on whom certain well-known characters in modern literature were based.

Getting all of them together and going on tour had been *his* idea in the first place...though it was clear by this, the seventh stop, that the Celebrity Based-On Experience wasn't exactly the cash cow he'd imagined it might be.

And it seemed it was about to get a little less cash-rich still.

"We want our money back," snarled the guy. "You're no more the *Man of Means* than that woman over there's Raven Silhouette from the *Jet Set* books."

Looking at the table next-door, Jake caught the eye of the woman sitting there--a middle-aged redhead named Colleen Halloran who looked a lot more like Raven in *Jet Set* than *he* resembled Peter Pinnacle.

Not that Surly Dad cared. "Money back *now*, and count yourself lucky we don't *sue.*"

Jake stared at the guy for a moment, wishing for the umpteenth time that he could be the actual character who'd been based on him. Unlike Peter Pinnacle in the *Man of Means* books, dealing with conflict was not often his strong suit. Though many of Peter's mannerisms were based on Jake's, the character's conflict expertise had *definitely* come from other sources.

If only Jake could have been cut from the same cloth in that regard. Maybe then, he would have felt as if he deserved to be there. Maybe then, he wouldn't have spent his whole life trying to measure up to a fictional character.

And fiction wouldn't have had such a dramatic impact on his reality.

Every moment in life is a chance to choose your own ending.

Like that night, seven years ago, when Jake and his newly-proposed fiancée, Gina Lafferty, strolled a few blocks away from the crowded Inner Harbor in downtown Baltimore, Maryland.

Jake was feeling pretty good--more like his fictional counterpart, heroic Peter Pinnacle, than ever. Finally, he'd resolved some of the guilt he'd felt over the way he'd gotten his connection to the character. He'd known from the start he'd done wrong, that Peter (if real) wouldn't have approved of such an under-handed deal...and eventually, he'd done better in life to make up for it. He'd taken some classes, gotten an honest job, given a few bucks to charity, and upgraded his conscience. Good things had come to him since, not the least of which was beautiful, blonde Gina.

She loved the hell out of him, put his ring on her finger, held his arm like a trophy when they walked. When he was with her, the past seemed far away; reality reshaped itself around them, making it seem like his mistakes had never happened.

Then, the two of them went down the wrong side street, and a guy with a gun approached them, demanding their valuables. The street was dark and quiet, and no one else was around.

Adrenaline blazed through Jake as he faced that choose-your-own-ending moment. A flurry of mental math rushed through his brain as he considered the following choices:

1. *He and Gina could run for their lives, hoping the attacker couldn't keep up.*
2. *He and Gina could hand over their valuables, including the engagement ring.*
3. *He could try to negotiate with the attacker, to at least get him to let them keep the ring.*
4. *Feeling more like Peter Pinnacle than usual, because life was good and his girl had said "yes," he could try to rush the gunman and seize his weapon before he got off a shot.*

Which option did Jake pick? What outcome resulted from his choice?
The wrong *option. And the* worst possible *outcome.*

"Are you going to fork it over?" Surly Dad snapped his fingers and pointed at his palm. "Or am I going to have to get *nasty?*"

"Suit yourself." Jake gestured at the admission table near the door at the far end of the gym. "Go tell them I said you're authorized for a refund."

"Damn right I am." Surly Dad sneered at him. "So I guess now I can tell everyone I kicked Peter Pinnacle's ass, huh?"

"Will you tell them you kicked *Geiger Hellsacre*'s ass, too?" Suddenly, a dark-skinned giant of a man was looming over the troublemaker--gray-haired but sufficiently beefy to stomp him hard without working up a sweat.

Surly Dad changed his tune. "That's, uh...no." He shrank and shivered as he stared up at the giant...then held up a pen and folded piece of paper. "Autograph?"

"*Outta' here!*" roared the giant--Sherman Ostrander by name. Unlike some of the based-ons, it was *instantly* easy to see his resemblance to the character he'd inspired.

The crowd in the gym--fifty paying customers and half that number of special guests--watched and laughed as Sherman swatted Surly Dad's ass, sending him scurrying out the door without his cherished refund. Jake laughed, too, glad there'd been a little show to lighten things up.

"And *keep* running!" Sherman was in total Geiger Hellsacre mode, playing the role of the massive sidekick from the *Blow by Blow* books to the hilt. "Or Fee Fi Fo *Punch,* I'll tear you a *new* one and feed you to my *dinosaurs* for *lunch!*"

Suddenly, the screech of a referee's whistle sounded from across the gym, followed by hip-hop music blasting from a sound-boosted speakerphone.

Looking toward the noise, Jake saw a tall, gangly figure unfolding from the main doors, dressed in the wildest outfit ever. A psychedelic top hat towered over glittering, giant sunglasses studded with white feathers. A tuxedo jacket made of what looked like bubble wrap had strings of jingling bells and flashing, multicolored LED lights strewn around it. The bubble wrap bulged at his abdomen, pushed out and down in the shape of a woman's pregnant belly.

Further down was a big paisley diaper and bare, hairy legs. His shoes were totally mismatched--a bright red sneaker with a light-up sole on his left foot, and a black rubber galosh over a white go-go boot on his right.

Then there was the bullhorn with actual *horns* attached, into which he howled his first words to the crowd in the gym.

"Elcome-way oo-tay e-thay ow-shay, ids-kay!" His voice was like that of a minister in a fire-and-brimstone church, except for the Pig Latin. "Eet-may Addy-day O-nay *Ants-pay!*"

"Who the *hell*?" Sherman was half-laughing when he said it.

"And *no!*" The newcomer crowed like a rooster, flapping his bubble-wrapped arms. "*I* don't believe my shit, *either!*"

The air in the gym was electric with weird possibilities. All eyes were on the freaky new arrival as he launched into what looked like a cross between a Native American rain dance and an Irish jig.

"Did you hire this guy?" Sherman asked the question in Jake's general direction. "To spice things up or somethin'?"

"You think I'm *that* good a promoter?" Jake was just as mesmerized as everyone else, gaping at the crazy performance.

"Want me to run him out?" Sherman cracked his knuckles.

"Don't you dare." Colleen giggled. "He just turned this event into a surprise party."

Just as she said it, the freak stopped dancing and sagged like a marionette with his strings cut. Then, without lifting his head, he spoke. "Did somebody say..."

Suddenly, he charged across the gym toward Jake, Sherman, and Colleen, wailing at the top of his lungs in a ululating cry like the classic jungle yell from the old *Tarzan* movies.

He blew right past Sherman and flung the top half of his body on the table, coming to rest inches away from Jake.

"Did you see a *mountain gorilla* in a pink tutu and combat boots lumber through here?" he asked in a high-pitched, childlike voice.

"Don't answer that!" His voice dropped to a whisper, and he looked suspiciously from side to side. "They're *listening."*

Jake noticed his breath smelled like strong black licorice. "What can I do for you, pal? We're kind of in the middle of something here."

"Exactamente!" The guy thrust out a banana painted blue and shook it like a hand. "*Daddy No-Pants,* at your service-ice-ice!"

Jake scowled. "You call yourself Daddy..."

"But *you* can call me Incog-*neato!* 'Neato' spelled en-ee-ay-tee-oh." Springing back from the table, he made an elaborate bow. "Can you *dig* it?"

Jake looked at Colleen and Sherman with eyes wide in disbelief. "So what do you *want*, Incogneato? Why are you here?"

"I came for the *ice cream*! But I *stayed* for the *flibbertigibbets!*" Incogneato flung up his arms and shouted the words, though he didn't need to. Everyone in the room had gathered around to get a closer look at his madcap performance. "Nothing I like better than a *flibbertigibbet* dipped in *gazpacho* with a little *sassafras whiskey* and *armadillo gelato* on the side!"

People laughed at the clownish freestyling. All around, Jake saw phones going up as guests and paying customers alike snapped photos. Once they hit social media, maybe there'd be more late arrivals at the gate.

"So this is the *kook* show?" Incogneato jumped up and down, making his bells jingle.

"You mean *book* show?" said a little boy with a stack of autographed glossies in his hands.

"*Good show!"* said Incogneato in a British accent.

"It's more a show for folks who're *part* of books," said Sherman. "Well-known characters were *based* on us."

Incogneato straightened, looking serious all of a sudden. "*Fiction* books? With *fictional* characters?"

"Correct," said Sherman. "We're all about the make-believe here."

"Well, *poo!*" Incogneato snorted and stomped his sneaker-clad left foot. "*I'm* only interested in *fangle* these days!"

"Fangle?" said Colleen. "What's that?"

Incogneato yanked up the bullhorn again and barked into it. "What's *fangle?* You might as well ask what *grabbatuba* has to do with *quinkydink*."

"Well *everybody* knows *that,*" Colleen said with a twinkle, playing along. "But *fangle's* a different story."

Incogneato rolled his eyes and lowered the bullhorn. "Think *fake news...true lies...post-fact world.* Where do we draw *the line?*" Incogneato did a kind of soft-shoe and stopped by pinching the brim of his psychedelic top hat. "Think *fact* meets *fiction* and goes on a *shooting spree.*"

"What's *that* supposed to mean?" Sherman was sounding tenser by the minute.

Again, Incogneato straightened and grew serious. "The real world has become more and more like *fiction, sahib.* We've got reality TV, virtual reality, augmented reality, you name it. The games and commercials and news cycles bury us in *stories* so *deep*, with so many possible *angles* and *opinions* and *outcomes*, that actual *reality* not only doesn't *matter*, it effectively doesn't *exist.* It's a tangled mess of fact and fiction--which *some* of us call *fangle*, thank you veddy much." The serious mode ended in a flurry of jingling jumping jacks as Incogneato sang "Mairzy Doats" in a booming falsetto.

"'Fangle,' huh?" said Sherman.

The jumping jacks and singing ended suddenly. "I'm surprised you've never *heard* of it, *kemosabe! You* people are what fangle's all about! *Fictional* works are based on your *factual* selves! *You* bridge reality and *un*reality, fiction and *un*-fiction. You're the perfect subjects for my next *work of art.*"

Jake got a chill up his spine that pretty much lifted him right up from his chair. "*What* work of art?"

At that moment, three men in camouflage fatigues with assault rifles hurried in and slammed shut the doors to the parking lot. The crowd gasped as one at the sight of the weaponry. A woman screamed.

"*This* one!" Incogneato pulled a fistful of gold and silver confetti from a pocket under the bubble wrap and tossed it overhead. "Now *tell* me, who wants to be *really famous?*"

Jake's blood froze in his veins as he got the picture. Incogneato wasn't a harmless buffoon after all. The stakes in the gym had gone from how much money the show would bring in to how many guests and customers would walk out of the place alive.

If only the real Peter Pinnacle, Man of Means, could have been there.

Giggling, Incogneato scurried over and used Jake's chair to climb up on the tabletop. "Sing Hallelujah!" He belted the words ecstatically into the bullhorn. "Get happy! There's *plenty* of famous to go around!"

As Incogneato disco-danced on the table, his three armed helpers closed in on the crowd with rifles raised. There were five kids in the gym, including the boy with the autographed glossies, and they all started crying at once. The adults did the opposite, most of them falling silent, though their worried expressions revealed deep concern. They were all too familiar with what usually happened when guns appeared at a public function.

Watching the panicked faces of friends and strangers alike, Jake couldn't help thinking how unlucky they all were, being caught in such a situation with a man like him who sucked at conflict.

Playing the theme from the movie *Fame* on the boosted speaker-phone and singing along through the bullhorn, Incogneato proceeded to dance from table to table, working his way down the line in a head-whipping frenzy. As soon as he got a few tables away, Jake huddled with Colleen and Sherman. Others in the crowd were whispering, too, seizing the opportunity to confer while the freak was distracted.

"We are so fucked." Sherman's eyes kept darting from one gunman to the next.

"There must be *something* we can do," hissed Colleen.

"Have you *seen* all the ammo clips strapped to those assholes?" Sherman shook his head angrily.

"What if we all rush one of them, take his gun, and use it against the other two?" asked Colleen.

"You do realize those Bushmasters are modified for *full automatic*, don't you?"

Colleen scowled as Incogneato started working his way back to them. "We can't just let this *happen.*"

"It's the end of the road," Sherman said matter-of-factly. "The good news is, we won't have to do this shitty based-on road show anymore."

Just then, a black rubber galosh flew over and bounced off Jake's head.

"Hey, Pea-Brain!" Three tables away, Incogneato lifted off his psychedelic top hat, turned it upside-down, and reached inside. His hand emerged with a .357 Magnum revolver, gleaming silver under the gym's fluorescent lights. "Yeah, you. C'mere a minute."

Jake hadn't taken three steps before the ref's whistle blew.

"Ot-nay own-day ere-they!" Incogneato gestured with the pistol, wagging the barrel upward. "Take the *high road*, buckaroo bonsai!"

Nervously, Jake clambered up onto a table, then worked his way over to join Incogneato.

Meanwhile, a middle-aged woman in the crowd spoke up, her voice quivering. "P-please may I take my son home, sir?" The autograph-hound little boy stood in front of her, and she kept her hands clamped on his shoulders. "He's a g-good boy, I swear it."

"I wouldn't *dream* of stopping him..." said Incogneato...but when the woman turned to go, he amended his statement. "...*stopping* him from becoming *famous* with his *Mommy dearest* thanks to capital-M *me*!"

The woman slumped, holding on to the boy tighter than ever.

"Grasshopper!" Incogneato fiddled with the front of his diaper as Jake crossed the table to stand beside him. "Now where did I put that *sword?"* He reached all the way in, let out a high yodel, and jerked his hand back out again. "Never mind. We'll just have to make do." With that, he tapped Jake solemnly on each shoulder with the barrel of the .357. "I now pronounce you Sir Tallywacker of the Fangle Faithful."

Jake stood stock-still, remembering that long-ago night in Baltimore, afraid to make a move with the gun in play.

"I couldn't have asked for a better *special helper*." Incogneato threw an arm around his shoulders and gave him a big squeeze, pretending to wipe away a tear. "After all, it's not like you're one of *them*, are you?"

Jake stared, shell-shocked. "What--?"

Incogneato lowered his voice. "Don't they know you don't *belong* here? Don't they know what a *liar, liar, pants on fire,* you are?"

Jake couldn't believe his ears.

"Don't sweat it, Langostino. Your secret's safe with me...as long as you help Daddy No-Pants like your invisible friend, Corky Porker, tells you to." When he said it, Incogneato oinked like a pig and popped a bubble on his bubble-wrapped chest.

Jake Bartholomew looked patient as he stood in line at the bookstore in Altoona, Pennsylvania, but inside, he was hypercharged. His heart was pounding, the hairs on his neck, arms, and legs were standing up, and the blood in his veins and arteries was sizzling with adrenaline.

It was twenty years ago, and Jake was 27 years old. He'd never done anything like what he was about to do before, and it showed. But most of the other people in line were nervous, too, so he blended in. If he could just keep it together a little longer, he'd be fine.

He was ten people back, then five, then three--then next. The book in his hands was only moments away from being signed by the author at the table.

As the woman ahead of him walked away, Jake gulped and stepped up to the table. The author smiled up at him and extended a suntanned hand, reaching for the hardcover book.

"Hello." The author, a brown-haired man in his late 20 or early 30s, had a welcoming smile. He held Jake's gaze for a moment before reeling in the book. "What's your name?"

"Jake."

"Thanks for buying my book, Jake," said the author. "And for coming to the signing."

"Thank you, Mr. Carmichael."

"Wes. Call me Wes. So have you read it yet?"

"Not yet, but I loved the first three in the series," said Jake. "I hope you write lots more Alley Commando *books."*

Wes chuckled. "Even better, Jake. I'm working on a new series right now called Man of Means.*" He opened the book to the dedication page and reached for his pen. "So how would you like me to inscribe this? 'To Jake?'"*

"Actually." Jake leaned down and lowered his voice. He was so nervous, he was afraid he might stutter, but he didn't. "Make it out to 'The Witness.'"

Wes looked baffled. "'The Witness?'"

Jake swallowed hard and nodded. "To your hit-and-run accident that landed that woman in the hospital the other night."

Wes' composure flickered. "Excuse me?"

Jake felt the impulse to end it right then, but he'd come too far. And he was desperate, in debt to some bad people. They didn't want to hear about how his deal had gone south; they just wanted their money.

"I have photos, if you'd like to see them." Jake reached inside his jacket.

Suddenly, Wes got his smile back. "'To Jake' it is." Hastily, he scribbled the inscription in the book, then closed it decisively and pushed it across the table.

"I'll see you later, then." Jake took the book. "At the coffee shop next-door."

"Thanks for coming!" Wes fidgeted with his pen. "Next!"

And Jake wondered, as he walked away to wait in the coffee shop, if Wes would even meet him. But he did. He only kept him waiting long enough for Jake to think of what else he might want to sweeten the blackmail deal.

"I never break a promise, bunkies!" Incogneato shouted from atop the table. "And when I'm double-Dutch *done* with you people, ain't *none* of you *not* gonna be *famous!*" Blowing on the ref's whistle, he spun on his heel and stopped with a stomp. "*Depending!*"

The crowd, hemmed in by the three gunmen, listened restlessly, looking terrified. Based-ons and visitors alike were burning with tension but mostly afraid to speak up.

"Somebody ask me 'depending on what?'" Incogneato shook Jake by his arm. "I won't bite! I won't even tickle!"

Jake had been distracted, thinking about his secret. To him, being found out after all this time was almost as distressing as whatever impending danger Incogneato had dreamed up. "Depending on what?"

For no clear reason, Incogneato slapped him in the face so hard it stung. "Who here has read those pick-your-own-adventure books?" He threw his hand up and looked around as a few other hands rose reluctantly in the group. "Well *congratulations,* fangle wranglers! You're about to *live* one of those! One of *three* endings will happen in this very *place* to you very *people*!"

With that, he pulled out his boosted phone and cranked the opening measures of "Thus Spake Zarathustra" from the movie *2001: A Space Odyssey. Dah...dah...dah...dah-dah!*

"Hold onto your sphincters, my Frito banditos!" Incogneato pumped an index finger in the air. "Ending one! *Everybody lives! Yaaayy!"*

Again, he blasted "Thus Spake Zarathustra."

"Ending *dos! Deux! Zwei! Half* of you live, and *half* of you die! Yay! Boo! Yay! Boo!"

"Zarathustra" blared a third time.

"Ending *three! Allll* of you *die! Awww!"* He made an exaggerated sad face and shook his head--then broke into a broad grin and grabbed hold of Jake's earlobe. "Except *this* phony!" He pulled Jake over and gave him a rough noogie. "*Oops!* Did I just give away your *secwet?* I guess that makes *me* a *wiar,* too!"

Jake caught dirty looks from Colleen and Sherman. The self-hatred that usually ticked away at the heart of him surged to the surface.

He saw the direct line connecting this moment to the past, and he realized yet again that nothing good had come from that meeting in the Altoona coffee shop two decades ago.

"You're kidding me." Wes the author, unhappy after hearing out Jake, looked like he might be ready to laugh out loud. "You're blackmailing *me, and* this *is what you* want?"

"The money, too." Anxiously, Jake looked around the coffee shop, but no

one was paying any attention to him and Wes in the back-corner booth. No one seemed to recognize the author, though he'd been signing books next-door just over an hour ago.

"You want me to Tuckerize *you? Mention you by name in a* book? *I do that shit for* free *all the time."*

Jake had never heard the word "Tuckerize" before, but it didn't matter. "You've got it wrong. I want you to base the main character *of your new series on me. And I want everyone to know it."*

Wes leaned forward and folded his arms on the table. "Like fuck, I'll do that."

"And you can't kill him off," said Jake.

"You can't tell me what to write."

"And I need a signed and notarized certificate that proves the character's based on me."

Suddenly, Wes's eyes widened, and he slammed a fist on the table, jarring coffee from his untouched cup. "Fuck that noise, you little shit!" His voice was low but fierce, oozing with rage. "I'll destroy *you, you fucking* nothing!"

Though Jake's instinct was to back down, he forced himself not to waver. He'd already shown Wes the pictures in his pocket, which he'd taken late the night before from his bedroom window with his digital camera. He was nervous as hell, but he knew Wes's threats were empty, his pushback a joke.

The thought of it made him feel a little bolder. "You know what else I want? Dedicate the first book in the series to me for inspiring the main character."

"Did you hear a word I just said, you piss-ant?" snarled Wes.

"By the way, the dedication is a dealbreaker." Jake smiled. "Pretty sure the cops and the woman in intensive care will agree with me."

Wes glared for a long moment, then slumped back in his seat. "Maybe I'll just turn myself in. Save myself the trouble of this *bullshit."*

"Suit yourself," said Jake, though he hoped he wouldn't. He had no idea where he'd get the money he needed if he lost this golden goose.

For a long moment, he and Wes locked eyes in the booth. The road forked before them, its dual choices equally possible, equally choosable. Neither choice favored the author...and neither took the female victim into account. If Wes gave a damn about her, he didn't let on. As for Jake, his concern was only for himself and his future.

Maybe that was where it started to go wrong for him. Maybe that was when, unknowingly, he bought a one-way ticket to the back street in Baltimore, the years of regret that followed, and Incogneato's shit-show.

Pick your own adventure, and the ones that come after pick you.

"In answer to the number one question on everyone's minds, *yes,* I *am* a little teapot, short and stout!" Incogneato belched into his bullhorn, then whistled a few bars of the teapot song. "Regarding the *number two* question, your lives or deaths will be decided by a naked mole rat wearing a mini-merkin and a tiny bowler hat."

Incogneato laughed himself silly, but no one else in the gym joined the hilarity. Someone *did* speak up, though, in the midst of the gales of laughter.

"This is all for some kind of *work of art*, you said?" Colleen asked it twice before she got through to him.

"Well, yes." Incogneato had to stifle another laugh fighting to get out. "In a *big picture* sort of way."

"What's that supposed to mean?" asked Sherman.

"The whole *world* is becoming *fangle,*" explained Incogneato. "Not only in the sense that truth and fiction are becoming indistinguishable from each other...but *reality* is taking on the *rhythms* of fiction. We see more and more cosplay, Ingress, Pokémon Go, Fakebook, and Netflix bingeing. Cathartic eruptions of violence are becoming *expected* and *routine,* as our society becomes more like a thriller novel or action movie. And that's a *good* thing."

"Is that so?" said Sherman.

"Because *that* is the way of the *future."* Incogneato hopped across the tables and crouched next to Sherman and Colleen. "When the boundaries between fact and fiction evaporate, we will be truly *free* and *unconstrained.* Mores and power structures will *fade away*. *Everything* will have *meaning*, yet *nothing* will have *consequence.* And *this*, according to my calculations, will be the *start* of it. Killing or sparing so many *based-ons* in such a fictionally contrived way will *light* this candle and power up fangle manifestations all over the planet!"

"Uh-huh." Sherman nodded, not sounding convinced. "Makes perfect sense."

"And here's the *primo* part!" Incogneato leaped to his feet and scattered confetti while howling like a wolf. "*You* guys will finally get to be *main characters*--not just *based-ons*. When the video goes *viral*, you'll be *world-famous*, and *everyone* will know what *fangle* is."

"You make it sound so *rewarding*," Sherman said sarcastically. "And *rational*."

"But who gets to choose?" asked Colleen. "You said there are three choices, so who gets to pick?"

Incogneato waggled his phone overhead. "Can you say, 'randomized prize drawing app?' *Soooo* stinkin' cool, huh? And guess who gets to run it?" Snapping around, he tossed the phone to Jake, who dropped it. "And now, without further ado--Sir Tallywacker, *spin...that...wheel!*"

How long does it take to get over something in a work of fiction? Pages? Chapters? What does it take to make redemption possible in a book? A cathartic event? A miracle? Someone in greater need than the hero?

In real life, the timeframes and triggers can be much different. After that night in Baltimore, Jake had struggled for years. Sometimes, he had blamed his obsession with Peter Pinnacle and vowed to stop trying to be something he wasn't. He had even contacted Wes and begged him to stop writing the Man of Means *books, which of course Wes refused to do. They were just selling too damn well by then.*

Sometimes, the pendulum had swung the other way, and Jake had tried to be more like Peter than ever. He had blamed his inability to measure up to the character for what had happened to Gina Lafferty--for every bad thing that had happened in his life, in fact.

Sometimes, Jake had even convinced himself that what had happened in Baltimore hadn't been real, that it had all played out on the written page with no impact on non-fictional life. He had even composed actual rewrites *on paper with less difficult endings, hoping one of them would supersede the ending he abhorred.*

But the one thing lacking in all those rewrites and what-ifs and blame games was a transformational incident, a true second chance that could let him make up for his mistakes by proving himself again.

Though who could say (even him) what choice he might make if such an incident ever came his way.

When Jake crouched on the table to retrieve the phone he'd dropped, Sherman rushed over and grabbed it first. "Don't do it." His voice was a rough whisper. "Don't play along with this nut."

"No choice." Jake reached for the phone. "He'll just do it himself or get somebody else to do it."

"Time for you to *step up* and fill your character's shoes," snapped Sherman. "Time for *all* of us. The based-ons are *with* you. Just give us the *signal.*"

"Oh, Sir Tallywacker!" called Incogneato. "Time's a-wasting! My *contractions* are starting!" He thumped his baby bump with the grip of the .357.

"We're ready!" whispered Sherman. "Let's give this weirdo a *true* taste of reality." Nodding firmly, he handed over the phone and backed away.

All eyes were on Jake as he stood, the fates of everyone in his hands. Heart pounding, he looked around at them, friends and strangers alike, looking to him for mercy.

"Come on, Gunga Dim!" Incogneato let off a long blast on his ref's whistle. "If you make *me* pick, I'm gonna pour some sugar all *over* these hanging-by-a-threaders!"

It was all coming down to the wire. The three gunmen had their rifles up, pointed into the crowd. The kids were crying, the adults were freaking, the clock was ticking, and the shit was about to go down.

How many similar scenes had Jake read in books or seen in movies? There was always a gauntlet like this in the third act or reel, a battle for the hero to test his or her skills and overcome his or her inner conflicts. At the end of the gauntlet, the hero always found victory.

But people like Jake didn't often become heroes in real life, did they?

"Tallywacker! It-quay issing-pay around-yay!" With a wild whoop, Incogneato yanked the bubble wrap away from his baby bump, exposing a zippered gold plastic shell. When he jerked the zipper down, candy poured out, showering the people closest to his table. "*Arriba! Arriba!* Consider your *last rites* performed, you candy lovers, you!"

Jake's hands shook as he raised Incogneato's phone. The prize drawing app was still on the screen--a round gold "GO" button surrounded by three squares, each labeled with an outcome: ALL DIE, HALF DIE, NONE DIE.

Gut and jaws clenched, Jake stared at the screen, then looked at Sherman, Colleen, and the others, then the gunmen. People would die if he gave the signal to fight back; no question. But people might also die if he played along and ran the app. Or they might be spared.

What would Peter Pinnacle do? What would Gina want him to do? Better yet, what would Jake--the old Jake, back before the blackmail and Baltimore--want him to do?

"Don't be a *don't-bee!*" howled Incogneato. "*Do* be a *do-bee.* Don't make us wait *forever* to *bring the fangle.*"

Suddenly, a wave of calm washed over Jake. What if Incogneato, in all his insanity, was on to something? If fact and fiction were coming together, would it even *matter* what he did? Or would it matter more than *ever?*

"Bitch, please!" Incogneato bounded over to the table and snatched the phone from Jake's hands. "The suspense is *killing* me."

With that, he hit the "GO" button, and lights flickered on the screen as the app spun through its options.

That was when, as Jake watched, other options spun through his own mind. See if you can guess which of the following four he chose:

1. He lunged at Incogneato, wrestling for his gun. The other based-ons took that as a signal and charged the gunmen, who promptly mowed them down.

Meanwhile, the .357 went off in Jake's gut and passed through to take out the only other survivor of the shooters' assault, a young woman who was trying to run away.

2. Jake shoved Incogneato into the crowd, leaped off the table, and ran for his life. The Bushmaster rifles chattered away behind him, leaving him the only survivor of the massacre aside from the gunmen and Incogneato. Later, after the killers were rounded up by the authorities, Jake's testimony sent them to prison and made him a celebrity.
3. Paralyzed with fear, Jake did nothing. The prize-drawing app selected "NONE DIE," and Incogneato and his people slipped away, leaving everyone alive.
4. Channeling the action-hero spirit of Peter Pinnacle and determined to finally redeem himself for past mistakes, Jake kneed Incogneato in the groin and pistol-whipped him with the .357. Miraculously, he then got off a lucky shot that took out one of the gunmen. The other two hesitated just long enough for Sherman to grab their dead ally's rifle and cut them down even as the rest of the crowd scattered. Everyone except the gunmen survived--but Incogneato, in defeat, still succeeded. The blurring of fact and fiction into fangle accelerated, with him recognized as the movement's founding father. Jake, in turn, had characters based on him in numerous books, TV shows, and movies, bringing the cross-pollination of factual and fictional figures full circle in his life.

Now that you've seen the four choices, which one did you pick? Did it match Jake's choice?

If your answer was any of the above, *congratulations*, you've chosen correctly. And welcome, one and all, to the fangle, fangle, fangle that we've come to know and love.

NOT SICK ENOUGH IN THE HEAD

Ten pairs of eyes stare hard at me through the musty church basement air, exerting pressure that is almost a physical force. Heart pounding, I glance around at them, then turn my gaze to the glossy gray cement floor in the middle of the circle of folding chairs.

"No, I'm sorry," I say at last, answering the question that was asked a moment ago. "I didn't blow my paycheck on *shoes* this week."

Everyone in the room except Doctor Ava Brandt slumps and sighs in disappointment at once. They all sympathize, not that it makes me feel any better.

"Tell us about that, Irene." Dr. Brandt, sitting directly across the circle from me, brushes her long, blonde hair behind her ears. She's in her twenties, at least ten years younger than I am, but still seems so much smarter and more mature. "Tell us about your week."

I want to get up and leave, but therapy's mandatory these days, for *everybody*. Walk away now, and I'll be sitting in another group session tomorrow, in *prison.* Welcome to the 22nd century.

Who knew universal mental healthcare could suck so bad?

"Not much to tell." I adjust my biowire-framed glasses and

wish the spotlight would move elsewhere. Why doesn't anyone interrupt and go off on a long-winded tangent when you *need* them to? "The E.R. was crazy. There was a bus crash."

"What about the *shoes?*" asks Brandt. "You said last week you were going *shopping.*"

"I did." I can't help sounding apologetic. "But then I...I just didn't..."

"Didn't what?" Brandt's eyes narrow, and she leans forward.

I scrub my fingers restlessly through my black half-shag/half-crewcut. Instinctively, I find the lump above my left temple, the one that's been there for the past few months. It's important, though it's also a secret, at least for now. "I didn't *want* them! I didn't *need* them!"

A few people shake their heads, which makes me angry. Like they're so much *better* than I am, just because they're making more *progress?*

The fingers of Brandt's hands twitch as she makes a note on the midair augmented reality (AR) screen that only she can see through her ocular implants. "But you said you *love* shoes. You *picked* them as your new *vice of choice.*"

"Then maybe I picked wrong." I check the clock on the wall behind Brandt, and my stomach clenches. We still have fifteen minutes to go in this session.

"Don't feel bad, Irene. Ups and downs are part of the process." Clara, a fellow patient in her early 20s with short brown hair in a pageboy bob, smiles supportively from her seat beside Brandt. "I *still* have days when I hardly gamble *at all.*"

A few chairs from Clara, old Roy Jackson chuckles. "You ain't gonna *believe* this, but there was a day last week when I didn't *think* about *porn* for almost *five solid minutes.*"

"There's no shame in backsliding," says Paula Ott, a heavyset woman in her 40s at the opposite pole of the circle from Roy. "What matters is where you go from here."

As well-intentioned as they seem to be, I don't want to hear it. Today's session is like last week's all over again...and the one before that, and the one before that. I'm still the biggest underperformer in the group.

"Are you hearing what they're saying?" asks Brandt.

"I guess so." I've been sitting on my right leg, and it's fallen asleep. I curl it out from under me and try to rub some life back into it. "But I'm just not *feeling* it like the rest of you."

"Tell us more," says Brandt. "When you say you're not *feeling* it..."

"I guess it makes me a freak, but..." A tear burns in my eye, and I dab it away. "I don't feel the *longing* like I should. The all-consuming *desire*."

Brandt frowns. "I wonder if I should've encouraged you to try a different vice."

"It doesn't *matter,*" I tell her. "I'm just not *wired* that way. God knows, I wish I *was.* Of all *people*, I *should* be. But I'm *not.*" Tears flow freely, and I let them come. "I can't be the good citizen I'm *supposed* to be."

Thoughtfully, Brandt watches and taps her lower lip with the tip of an index finger. For a long moment, she and everyone else remain silent.

Then she nods firmly as if she's come to a conclusion. "I think I see where this is going." Her fingers twitch over the AR screen. "I know what we need to do."

I stare at her through the tears. Has she *understood* a single word I've said?

"Time to change things up." Brandt continues to work the screen. "Forget the shoes."

"You mean *another* vice?" I ask. "But I've already tried wine, marijuana, nostalgia, romance novels..."

"Stop." Brandt waves me off. "It's out of my hands now. Your new personal therapist will make that call."

I frown. "But I don't *have* a personal..."

She cuts me right off. "You do now, and she makes *house calls.* In fact..." Her fingers twitch some more, and her eyes flick over her AR screen, reading whatever text is visible to her. "...she will arrive at your apartment in two days at 7:45 a.m." Brandt smiles.

The group goes dead quiet. Eyes widen and fix on me as the implications settle in.

I'm not cutting it, and the doc is upping the ante.

“Perhaps you’ve heard of her.” Brandt winks for my benefit. “Dr. Evelyn Godfrey of the Impetus Foundation?”

My heart races, but I don’t say a word.

Of course I’ve heard of her, and we all damn well know it.

"What about our shopping trip that day, Irene?" Clara, God love her, takes a shot at helping me out. "We're supposed to leave for the mall at eight a.m., right?"

"You'll have to reschedule." Brandt rises from her chair, wiping away the AR screen with a wave of her hand. "On the bright side, you'll really be able to *max out* that shopping spree after your new doc gets done with you."

“We’re so happy for you, Irene!” Paula clasps her hands and smiles warmly. "Next thing you know, you'll be a *stalker* and a *substance abuser* like the *rest* of us. Maybe *better* than us, even."

"Let her know how we all feel about her, group." Everyone claps as Dr. Brandt crosses the circle and puts her hands on my shoulders. "*Rehab's* going to work out for you *after all.*" Smiling, she folds her arms around me as the applause rises around us, filling the room in a charged, dramatic moment.

But all I can feel in my heart and gut and mind is my *secret*, twisting like an animal in the dark, baring its teeth. Because the truth is, I’m a success story and good citizen after all.

I’ve got my own hidden obsession, and Dr. Brandt would shit herself if she knew what it was.

Riding home that evening aboard a self-driving bus, I gaze out at the dilapidated city under a gray and drizzling sky. It’s like watching civilization collapse in slow motion—buildings slumping, streets pitting and cracking, streetlights flickering or dark, garbage blooming. Chicago’s circling the drain, just like every other city, town, and village in the U.S. of A.

All because of a lack of focus and innovation, the psychocrats tell us. All because, when we drugged and shocked and bred the obsessive, addictive tendencies out of our species over the past century, tamping down the volatility of humanity, we inadvertently got rid of what made us great. What helped us not only *survive* but *thrive*.

It turns out the biggest breakthroughs, greatest inventions, and boldest gambles come from people who are driven. Not so much from people in a flattened-out stupor.

Which brings us to the Want-Want project, designed to make humanity crave again. Five years after it launched, people are more of a hot mess than ever, tangled in conflicting impulses—but the boss-lady who dreamed up Want-Want keeps telling us all to hang in there. American ambition is making a comeback in a big way.

Or is it? From way down here in the weeds, it looks worse than before.

I'd love to ask her about it, the know-it-all bitch. And maybe I *will*.

After all, she's coming to see me. All hail my new personal therapist, Dr. Evelyn Godfrey, founder of Want-Want.

And founder of me, as well.

Two days later, when I answer the door at Dr. Godfrey's knock, she stares back at me with clinical dispassion as if I'm some new species of giant insect. I haven't seen her in person in close to a decade, but she doesn't look the slightest bit energized about it.

"Hello, Mother." I step aside, opening the door wider to admit the only family I have left in the world.

She just stands there at the threshold in her smart black pantsuit, shriveled and tiny as a gherkin, her face pinched and waxen. "Would you like me to come in?"

Like is a strong word. "Please, come in." My gesture is formal, as if we're strangers, which is fitting. The two of us have *never* been close.

With the slightest nod of her dark-haired head with the bun bound tightly at the back, she walks stiffly into the apartment. As many times as I've seen her in streaming videos over the years, she looks much older in person. Time has *not* been kind.

"Thanks for stopping by," I tell her. "I cleaned up the place and everything."

Evelyn clears her throat and doesn't look around. "Tell me." So much for niceties. "When did you last feel obsessively about something?"

Leave it to Mom to cut to the chase. "Does it really matter?" I push the door shut. "In the grand scheme of Want-Want, nobody *cares* about little old *me*, do they?"

"The restoration of true mental health is vital to *everyone*." Evelyn sounds like she's quoting a speech. "We must leave no mind untroubled."

It's *my* turn to stare like she's some kind of giant bug. "Gee, thanks for the pep talk, Mom."

Evelyn blinks slowly and purses her lips, looking annoyed. I wonder if she'll just walk out on me at some point; it's what she does best, after all.

"Has it occurred to you," she says, "that you're actively resisting treatment in the hope of hurting *me?*"

"Not *everything* is about *you*, Mother."

"What better way of lashing out at someone you perceive as having caused you pain?" Evelyn gazes up at me, watching for a reaction. "It's a theory, wouldn't you say?"

"I knew it." I lean down so our faces are close. "That *is* the only reason you're here, isn't it? Because I'm making you *look* bad. The daughter of the founder of Want-Want doesn't *want* anything."

It's true, we both know it, but she'll never admit it. It's no coincidence she showed up here today for the first time in a decade.

Any more than it's an accident I got her to *come* here. Pretending to be incurably non-obsessive through all those group therapy sessions took patience, but I always believed the docs would eventually call in my mother, given her prominence in the field. I always believed, with her reputation at stake, that she would leap at the chance to accept the invitation.

"I assure you," she says coldly. "It will take far more than an obstinate estranged offspring to darken *my* good name." This time, *she's* the one leaning closer to *me*. "Not that I have *any* concern other than *curing* a poor unfortunate who doesn't seem to have an obsessive bone in her *body*."

We stand there for a moment like that, gazes locked, neither of us willing to step away first. Then, finally, we both lean back at once.

"Can I get you anything?" I bob my head toward the kitchen. "Coffee? Tea?" I don't remember what she prefers.

"Get your coat," says Evelyn. "I think some fresh air will do us both good."

Shit. I've planned this out to the letter, made arrangements to escort her to a certain time at a certain place—but not yet. She's already at the door, though, so I need to juggle my timetable.

"Sure, okay." When I go to the closet for my coat, I crank out a quick text message to the person I've arranged for her to meet. He fires back an answer, perfectly fine with meeting earlier, but not *too* early.

That works for me. Letting Mom think she's taking charge ought to help her drop her defenses for later.

"Excellent." Evelyn pulls on her black leather gloves. "I'm a firm believer in the power of a good constitutional."

"No kidding." I smile as I pull on my red wool coat and striped scarf. "I guess we have something in common after all. Other than DNA, that is."

Evelyn has a self-driving limo waiting outside, and the car takes us straight to the shopping mall on Michigan Avenue. We end up going for a walk, all right—an indoor stroll past one high-end store after another.

Didn't she read my chart? Does she really think shopping therapy will work for me now after failing so many times in the past?

"I think those would look nice on you." She stops at a store window and points out a pair of glittery pink stilettos with sequined hearts on the toes. "Why not try them on?"

"No thanks. Those things cost a fortune."

"Is *money* holding you back?" Evelyn dips a gloved hand into her black pocketbook and fishes out a featureless black plastic card. "Take this."

"I don't want your card, Mom." I fold my arms over my chest and keep walking. "I don't need it."

"I've seen your apartment." She slips the card back in the bag. "It's no wonder you're afraid to impulse-buy."

"Hey, what do you think of this?" I stroll over to another display window and point out a navy blue dress with white trim on a brown-haired holo-mannequin.

"You like it?" She sounds hopeful and digs out the card again.

"Uh-huh." I nod slowly, stroking my chin. "Let's go see how it looks on you."

This time, it's Evelyn's turn to walk away. "You used to *like* shopping when you were a child."

There are *so* many things I could say to that, but I don't. Better, now that I'm so close to what I want, to keep my eyes firmly on the prize.

Just then, Evelyn stops in her tracks. "Irene, look." Her voice is hushed. "Look at *that.*"

Up ahead, looking at something in the window of a jewelry store, is the handsomest man I've seen in forever.

"Wow," says Evelyn. "Those *muscles.*"

She's right. His tight black t-shirt accentuates the perfect bulges of his arms, chest, and shoulders. His midsection is lean, his six-pack clearly defined to the waist of his jeans.

"He's got such a strong jawline, doesn't he?" Evelyn tips her head to one side. "And can't you just imagine running your fingers through that dark hair?"

I can, actually, but that's none of her business. "Give it up, Mom."

"Why don't you go talk to him?" She gives my sleeve an encouraging tug. "What can it hurt?"

"I'm not going over there."

"But you're a grown woman. Nobody's going to *judge* you."

I shake my head, disgusted. With any normal mother, this would be typical pushy meddling, trying to set me up for a love match. With Evelyn, who has zero maternal feelings, this is just about curing me, saving her reputation, and improving the success rate of Want-Want.

Enough.

Just as she sticks two fingers in her mouth to whistle at him, I grab her shoulder.

"Do you want to know what I'm obsessed with?" I ask. "*Really* obsessed with?"

Evelyn frowns. "Not him?"

"*None* of this. None of what you *think* or *want* to think."

"But there *is* something? Or someone? An obsession?"

"I promise." It isn't a lie.

"So tell me."

"I'll do better than that." Turning, I head for the exit. "Let's go."

She hesitates when I insist we take a bus instead of the limo, but she finally gives in. Whatever worries she might have are outweighed by the possibility that a daughter-sized headache might finally be about to go away.

She clearly isn't comfortable on the crowded bus, though. Maybe that's why she keeps talking as we lumber across town to our destination.

"I can't help noticing," she says over the noise from the engine and passengers. "You never ask me what *my* craving is."

I shrug and rub the lump above my left temple, staring out the window at the slowly collapsing city. "It's not polite to pry."

"Yet it's a common deflection strategy used by patients. When treatment become uncomfortable, they attempt to turn the tables on the therapist."

"I'm not that insecure," I tell her. "I don't need to deflect."

I feel her eyes on me as I watch the scenery pass. Does she know the real reason I don't ask about her personal obsession? Does she suspect it's because I already know what it is?

And it sure as hell isn't me or my well-being, or my little

brother Rafe, or the shit show she left in her wake when she got the fuck out.

If I were a gambler, I'd bet the whole Want-Want project on that.

It's a busy day in the E.R. at Mediplex One, as most days are. When I give Evelyn the ten-cent tour, I have to be careful I don't get drafted into service.

"This is it," I tell her. "If there's one thing I'm obsessed with, it's my job."

We both jump back as a gurney crashes through bearing a patient, surrounded by nurses and a doctor barking out orders. One of the nurses catches my eye on the way past, and I think for an instant she's going to tell me to get to work.

Then she does, shouting for me to bring over the crash cart *stat.*

I do just that, leaving Evelyn alone against the wall. Of course things get complicated, and it's more than a few minutes before I manage to get back to her.

"So this is your day off?" asks Evelyn.

"Yes." I'm a little out of breath.

"Yet here you are."

I nod. "Here I am."

"Classic workaholic." Evelyn grins. "Pretty tame as obsessions go, but it's still on the spectrum."

"You're telling me I'm sick in the head like everyone else?"

"Let's just say there's hope for you yet." Evelyn looks relieved. Her face isn't nearly as pinched as it's been since she turned up at my door this morning.

That means the time is perfect for what's coming next.

"Let's celebrate." Nodding and smiling, I start toward the exit, gesturing for her to follow. "This way."

"Celebrate? In a hospital?"

"C'mon!" I gesture again and keep walking, trying to *will* her to come with me. Everything I've wanted, my longtime true secret obsession, depends on her joining me now.

As I slip through the door into the hallway, I'm almost afraid to look back. She abandoned me before; what if she does it again?

But this time, she stays with me. Apparently, curiosity has gotten the better of suspicion, at least for now.

Heart pounding, I lead her down the hall toward our next destination, trying not to look too excited though I've got every reason to be.

Like most hospitals, Mediplex One is a maze. Does Evelyn keep track of every turn in our route as I lead her down to the basement and through its corridors? I doubt it.

Our destination is a room at the far end of the complex, one that's hardly used anymore. There isn't even an identifying sign on the wall other than a placard bearing the room number.

"What is this place?" asks Evelyn as I open the door. "A morgue?"

I switch on the lights and hold the door open for her. "Mostly storage these days."

She hesitates, peering through the doorway. "It doesn't look like much of a celebration to me."

"It will be. This is where we sneak off when we need a break. We always keep some—*refreshments*—down here."

"Why, 'Reney." Evelyn beams proudly. "Are you an *alcoholic*, too?"

"What can I say?" I smile back at her. "I'm full of surprises, Mom."

She decides to enter the room, and I close the door behind us. As she looks around at the stacks of old boxes, I walk to a metal wall cabinet and pull a key out of my pocket.

"This used to be part of the old psych ward." I unlock the cabinet and pull out an object, concealing it against my forearm. "Back in the days when they thought they were *curing* everyone by taking away their motivation."

Evelyn walks over to a big cardboard box and fishes through the paperwork inside. "We didn't know any better back then," she says. "We didn't realize the damage we were doing."

"No, you didn't." I stride quickly up behind her and stick her in the arm with the object I pulled from the cabinet—a loaded hypodermic. "Or was it just that you didn't give a fuck?"

As I press the plunger, injecting her with amber fluid, she twists around, looking horrified. "What...what did you just...?"

I yank out the needle, grab the phone from my pocket, and send a prearranged signal via text to the person we're here to see. "Don't worry, that's good shit," I tell Evelyn. "Just relax and enjoy the ride."

She shakes her head slowly and slumps down onto some boxes. "Why would you...what are you..."

Moments later, the door swings open. A middle-aged man with a big gut in blue scrubs sweeps into the room, looking excited.

"Is this her?" He paws at his curly salt-and-pepper hair. "Is this the patient?"

Evelyn is almost out but still manages to open her eyes for a look. "Who?" Her voice is faint.

"This is Doctor Joe," I tell her. "He's here to help you."

"Hey there." Joe gives her a wave. "It's a real honor to work on the founder of Want-Want."

"You'll like Doctor Joe," I say. "He's got an *awesome* obsession."

"I really do," says Joe.

"He gets off on performing unauthorized surgeries," I explain. "Just like the one he's about to perform on *you.*"

Evelyn's too loopy to react. Her head lolls on her chest, drool dripping from her wrinkled red lips.

"It's a minor procedure, really." Joe rolls in a gurney, and we lift Evelyn up onto it. "Just the subcutaneous insertion of an implant near the left temple of your cranium."

"That's right, Mom. Easy-peasy." Leaning over her, I point to the lump above my own left temple. "When you're done, we'll both have lumps in the same spot. For different reasons, though."

Evelyn burbles something from the depths of her stupor. Joe

pulls out a white wand with a glowing yellow bead the size of a pea on the tip.

"What's the worst that could happen?" He chuckles as he lowers the bead toward her head. "Other than the three of us exploding, I mean."

For a moment, as Evelyn's eyes flutter open, she is docile. Then, when she tries to move her limbs, full awareness crashes upon her like a breaking wave.

"Let me up!" She thrashes as much as she can with her wrists and ankles restrained on the gurney. "Let me *go!*"

I watch from my perch, a nearby stack of boxes, with grim amusement. "You're such a drama queen, Mom."

"Help! Somebody help me!"

"You might as well save your voice. This place has been a secret love nest for hospital staff for ages. Trust me, no one who matters hears the screams from down here."

"Oh my God!" She thrashes some more. "Help! Please, help!"

"Yell all you like, if it makes you feel better." I shake an index finger at her. "But the sooner you calm down, the sooner I'll undo your restraints."

"What *is* this? What did you *do* to me?" She scowls as memories trickle back to her. "That so-called *doctor.* He was going to *operate.*"

"Relax. It was a very minor procedure."

Her scowl deepens. "Something about a *subcutaneous implant?*" She sounds like she's teetering on the brink of towering rage or utter panic, which is music to my ears.

"It's nothing. Just a little bump. I mean *bomb.*"

Evelyn stops fighting her bonds. "Did you say *bomb?*"

"You heard correctly."

She falls silent as the bad news sinks in…but the silence doesn't last. "You're telling me I have a *bomb* in my head? Why?"

I hop off the boxes and show her the round black device in the palm of my left hand. A bright red button glows in the middle of its face.

"This remote controls your implant," I say matter-of-factly. "Now tell me about *your* obsession, or I'll blow you to kingdom come."

"My *obsession*?" She repeats the word as if it's in some foreign language. "*Chocolate*, you mean? Classic *hip hop*?"

I walk to the side of the gurney, holding up the remote with my left thumb hovering over the button. "The obsession that made you abandon our family," I say coldly. "The reason you ran away and left your own *son* to *die*.

"*That's* the obsession I'm talking about."

I remember the last dinner Mom made us was spaghetti and meatballs out of a can. It's been a long time since I was ten, but I've hated spaghetti and meatballs ever since.

I remember how she packed her suitcase that night, telling us she was going to an out-of-town conference the next day. My brother Rafe, who was six at the time, was the only one who was upset...but he *always* got upset when she went away. He was *such* a mama's boy.

I remember how noisy the house was the next morning, instead of the usual quiet that Mom demanded (for her work, always her work). It was like Dad had been replaced by an alien, one who broke things and cursed at random and shouted over the phone.

Rafe and I cowered in the corners, piecing things together like terrified detectives. We overheard there was a cryptic farewell note, and valuables were missing, and Mom's phone was shut off. Someone named "Bill" was involved, and Mom loved him, and Dad had his gun out of the safe.

We were shell-shocked. It was as if we'd been plunked down by a twister in the Land of Oz, where the rules were all different from the ones we'd always known. One wrong move, and the flying monkeys or wicked witch would scoop us up and take us away forever.

Little did we know, we were already gone for good.

"I hurt you," Evelyn says calmly. "I'm sorry."

Her composure is back. She sounds like she's conducting a therapy session instead of strapped to a gurney with a bomb in her head.

Apology not accepted. "How could you just *leave* us like that? How could you be that *obsessed* with someone?"

"I can't explain it to you," she says. "You wouldn't understand."

"I'm not a *child* anymore."

"But you've never been head-over-heels in *love*, have you? Completely *obsessed* with another *person*."

Leaning down, I bark my next words in her face. "And *you* weren't obsessed with your own *family.*"

Her steely blue eyes lock tight on my own. "Is that what's *really* wrong, 'Reney? You *want* so badly to fall in love, but you just can't *do* it?"

I stay where I am, inches from her face, seething. I want to slap her, hard as I can, but I hold myself back.

"I think the *better* question is, how could a woman become the *poster child* for *wanting* when she didn't even want her own *children?*"

Evelyn's composure slips. "Don't you *dare* try to tell me—"

"And how could a woman think she could save the *world* if she couldn't even save her own son's *life?*"

I was the one who found him.

Rafe never got over Mom's leaving. He was just too damn young and attached to her. Dad raged, I withdrew, but Rafe...

Rafe blamed himself.

And one day, a month after Mom ran off, I heard a single loud blast from the garage. We were on our own, Dad wasn't home, and I knew I shouldn't go see what had made that loud noise.

But I went anyway. I called Rafe's name, and he didn't answer, and part of me *knew* or at least *feared* what I'd find. Dad had stopped locking his gun in the safe, after all.

And even as I opened the side door and looked in, I remembered one sunny afternoon that Rafe and I had spent in the yard, playing good guys and bad guys, and how he'd played dead so perfectly, I'd worried he might *be* dead until I tickled him and he jumped up running.

This time was just the same except he never jumped up and ran, and parts of him were blown away for real.

"You didn't even go to his *funeral.*" The words are a snarl from my lips.

"I wasn't *welcome,*" says Evelyn. "Your father blamed me for Rafe's death, as if I was the one who left the gun where he could find it."

"You *were* to blame!" Decades of anger boil out of me like lava from a volcano. "Didn't it ever *occur* to you that you might ruin your *kids* when you left?"

She lifts her head, then lets it fall back on the thin pillow on the gurney.

"And what about Dad? He was *never* the same after that. He died young, and you didn't come to *his* funeral, either. Didn't you *consider* what you were doing to *him?*"

"No," she says simply. "It never occurred to me."

"Seriously?" I want to shake some sense into her, shake the truth out of her, just *shake* her.

"All I could think about was *Bill.*" She releases a long sigh. "Our love was...all-consuming. Our obsession blotted out everything and everyone else."

"But there *was* no obsession anymore, was there? Humanity had *lost* it by then."

Evelyn looks away. "Not all of us." She meets my gaze again.

"I was a throwback. So was he. People like us had a way of finding each other."

"Thank God for that," I say sarcastically.

"I like to think it was the spark of the whole Want-Want movement." Evelyn sounds wistful. "The inspiration for the project to reinvigorate humanity's obsessiveness."

"But you still couldn't want *us* that much, could you? It wasn't that you weren't passionate about *anyone*. You just saved all your passion for *someone else.*"

Evelyn winces, looking pathetic. "Stop this, 'Reney. You've made your point."

"Is that what you think this *is?* Me making a *point?*" I laugh out loud at her. "You think I'd go to all this *trouble* just for that?"

She frowns, confused. "Then why...?"

"Because I'm going to make something happen." I waggle the remote in my hand, thumb perilously close to the trigger button. "Something that should've happened *long* ago."

"What *kind* of something?" snaps Evelyn.

I lean down over her, smiling coldly. "I'm going to *fix* you, whether you like it or not." I kiss her forehead softly and without the slightest trace of affection. "Meet your new therapist, Dr. Godfrey. Let's call your first session 'How Not to Blow Up.'"

I'm back in my apartment, weeks later, when there's a knock at the door. It happens a lot these days, ever since that fateful encounter in the basement of Mediplex One.

"Hello, honey," Evelyn says sweetly when I open the door. "So good to see you again."

I smile and lean close for a peck on the cheek. Mom is positively *fanatical* about never missing one of our get-togethers.

Who would've thought that would ever be the case? Who would've thought my unapproachable mother would come bearing fresh lattes and scones on a Saturday afternoon? Who would've thought she'd sit at my kitchen table for hours and chat with me as if we'd been doing it all our lives?

It's funny what a subcutaneous bomb in someone's head can do for their disposition.

"How are you feeling today?" she asks, sounding concerned. "How was the latest round of chemo?"

I pat the lump on my left temple through the colorful scarf on my head and shrug. "It's going as well as can be expected."

"The side effects aren't too bad, I hope?" asks Mom.

"I've had worse."

Having family come around is especially nice when you've got the big C, and it's terminal. It's great taking your mind off *that* preoccupation—and make no mistake, it's an obsession with a capital "O." Dying from brain cancer is enough to drive you crazy for real.

Why else do you think I went to such extremes to force the bitch to act like she cares? To force her to be part of my life again after so many years?

When you're on the way out, even a mother who shit all over your life and triggered your little brother's suicide can be better than no mother at all.

"I might be late for next week's visit," she tells me, watching eagle-eyed over her coffee cup for my reaction. "I have a meeting at the White House that day."

Fuck her if she thinks I'll let her off the hook. "Just get here when you get here." I stroke the bomb remote control on its chain around my neck, running my fingertip over the glowing red button.

As long as she doesn't forget Lesson #1, we'll get along fine: *Show up or blow up.*

There's no other option, as I've made clear. The bomb in her head is booby-trapped, guaranteed to blow by Dr. Joe if anyone tampers with it. If anyone tries to take the remote from me, it's another guaranteed big bang. As soon as the remote loses contact with my skin for more than a few seconds, the bomb will go *boom.*

"Let's have some wine." Mom pours from a bottle she brought on her last visit, and we take it out on the balcony for some fresh air.

The sun is setting, and the sky's a swirl of gold and red,

scorching the slowly collapsing buildings of the city. Everything's falling apart in slow motion, including us, and God, isn't it glorious?

She stands alongside me, glass in hand, as if I never had a bomb planted in her skull. As if I didn't have to threaten her life to get her to come here.

It doesn't bother me a bit. I think I deserve a little decency after what she did all those years ago. I'm pretty sure Rafe would agree it's the least she can do.

The sun melts like ice cream or butter, flaring yellow as it sinks below the horizon. Evelyn puts an arm around me and gives me a squeeze, her hand resting below the remote control at my breast. I don't push it away.

We stand there aglow, impermanent as the sunset, perfectly happy to let ourselves be consumed by the darkness or the light as long as we get what we want in the end.

GIVE THE HIPPO WHAT HE WANTS

The pink hippopotamus appeared in front of Thal Simoleon just as he was about to take the swing that could have won the World Series for the Bio Threats.

As soon as the ball left the pitcher's hand, Thal knew he could launch it out of the park. It came in straight and steady, a little low and outside but well within his range...proof that even a genetically engineered pitcher like Phallus Fearbringer could blow a throw under pressure.

Before the hippo appeared, Thal knew he was about to become the hero of the Series. The Bio Threats were down by two in the bottom of the ninth with two outs...but the bases were loaded and the pitch was a home run waiting to happen. One stroke of the bat would bring in the grand slam, assuring a Bio Threats win and a World Series title.

At least, that was what would have happened if the hippo hadn't popped up out of nowhere, wearing a grass skirt and hopping around on two legs between him and the ball.

Singing opera.

When the creature appeared, Thal's view of the pitch was blocked, his concentration obliterated. He took a swing anyway, aiming at the vicinity of where he expected the ball to be; to his credit, he came close...but his swing was well before the ball's arrival. The tip of the bat lashed into the corner of the strike zone and forward and up, passing harmlessly through the air and then the hippo.

A heartbeat later, the ball sailed through and smacked into the catcher's mitt.

The hippo kept right on singing and pirouetting in front of him, long black lashes fluttering over baby blue eyes.

The crowd roared with rage. It was Thal's third strike.

The game was over.

As the Dirty Nukes threw their hats in the air and embraced in the infield, Thal hurled his bat through the hippo, not caring who might be on the other side of the insubstantial phantasm. The surprise visitor had robbed him of a great accomplishment; if he could have strangled it to death on the spot, he would have.

But he knew that he couldn't. Though its appearance had been unexpected, he knew all about the hippo.

Concluding its serenade on a high note that only Thal could hear, the creature spread its stumpy pink arms wide and took a deep bow. As the superstadium erupted in pandemonium around them, the creature bounced over to Thal, batting its ridiculous lashes and grinning. Bright red lipstick was smeared all around its rubbery mouth.

"Hello there, Zeke," said the hippo, nostrils twitching atop its bulbous snout. "Fancy meeting you here!"

Thal seethed and said nothing. He knew that no one else could see the creature, and he didn't want to be caught on camera apparently talking to himself.

The hippo pushed closer, its great bulk shimmying from side to side. "Can I give you some advice, pal?" said the creature.

Thal continued to stare silently ahead.

"If I were you, I'd get out of here right now," said the hippo. "The fans are coming! The fans are coming!"

Looking back, Thal saw that the hippo was right. People were cascading out of the stands onto the field, screaming like Vikings. All the other players on Thal's team had already disappeared into the locker room or were running full tilt toward the exits.

He had no doubt that if he stood there another moment, they would kill him. He was a top-paid sports star in a world that revolved around sports...a god in the faith that ruled their lives...and still he knew that they would kill him on the spot for costing them the victory they craved.

He had seen it happen before.

"Go go go!" shouted the hippo, and Thal took off.

He ran as fast as he could toward the locker room door, his genetically engineered legs easily carrying him ahead of the screaming mob. His pursuers pelted him with coins and shoes and bottled water, but his body was tough enough to take a lot more punishment than that.

As he raced toward the door, he wished that he could leave the hippo behind as easily as the crowd...but he knew that he couldn't. The creature was literally in his mind, a custom-made hallucination that could follow him anywhere once it had locked on to him.

He knew it well, because he was the one who had set it loose three years ago.

As Coach Wildsnap paced across the office, hands locked behind his back, Thal had a hard time keeping his eyes from wandering to the hippo pacing along behind him.

"End of the road, Thal," Wildsnap said grimly, shaking his doughy head. "I guess you already knew that, though."

Thal couldn't stop looking at the hippo, so he cast his eyes down at the floor. "You're trading me?" he said, though he knew that wasn't what the coach had meant.

"No trade," said Wildsnap. "Welcome to civilian life."

"And *yer out*!" barked the hippo. "Strike twelve! Hit the showers!"

Thal glanced up. The hippo was waving both of its stumpy arms at him and sticking its purple tongue out from its enormous, lipsticked mouth.

"But it was just one mistake," said Thal. "After all I've done for this team over the years, don't I deserve another chance?"

"After all *I've* done, don't you mean?" said the hippo.

"You know better than that," said Wildsnap, pushing up the brim of his ballcap. "You're done in this league. If you ever set foot on the field again, the crowd'll eat you alive...literally. As we speak, they're burning all your memorabilia in Citydome Center. They've already toppled your statue in the Hall of Gods."

"Holy shit," said Thal.

"Don't get me wrong," said Wildsnap, removing a framed photo of Thal from the wall. "I feel for you, buddy. I mean, your life isn't worth a plug nickel from now on. But what the hell were you doing out there tonight? Were you hyperstoned or something?"

"Tell him, Thal!" shouted the hippo. "Clear your good name!"

Thal sighed. If he told the coach he'd been victimized by a Choker, he could erase the doubt of his playing skill...but he would open up a can of worms that he couldn't afford to open. The fact was, he'd somehow been imprinted by a Choker he himself had activated years ago; Chokers were so illegal, if this one was traced back to him, he would face consequences far worse than ejection from the league.

"I don't know what happened," said Thal. "It was just one of those things."

Wildsnap stomped over and tore the player number from Thal's red and green jersey. "With the DNA you've got, it's never 'just one of those things.' Not that it makes any difference now. You're done, my friend."

"Time to stick a fork in you, Thally!" said the hippo, doing a soft-shoe across the office.

"What about the farm team?" said Thal. "Send me away till things cool down."

Wildsnap leaned down, pushing his face close to Thal's. "Earth to Thal," he said. "You lost the World Series. Things are *never* going to cool down for you."

"This is bullshit," said Thal, jumping up out of the chair and shoving his way past Wildsnap. "Total bullshit! I'm the top player in the *league*! I have the best career stats in *history*! I hold the single season *and* career home run record! You can't just cut me loose!"

"Listen, Thal," said Wildsnap, taking a seat behind the desk. "This is the twenty-second century. You know how it is. Never been a better time to be an athlete...unless you make the kind of colossal fuck-up you just made. Your career stats went up in smoke the second you missed that pitch."

Thal thumped his fist against the wall. "You owe me!" he said. "I made the Bio Threats the top team in the *world*! I made Bio Threats Citydome *billions* of dollars!"

With a wave, Wildsnap brought the holographic computer interface to life over the desktop in front of him. "You're right," he said as he brought up the team's roster and erased Thal's name from it. "I do owe you. That's why I'm going to save your life, my friend."

Thal stormed over and kicked the front of the desk, putting a hole in it. "Save my life?" he said. "How about saving my career!"

"Lost cause," said Wildsnap. "Now do you want your life or not?"

The hippo was standing behind Thal, whispering in his ear. "Choose life, Thally!" he said. "I'm not done with you yet!"

"Screw you," said Thal. "I'm the wealthiest athlete in the country. I can take care of myself."

Wildsnap wiggled his fingers over the holocomputer's control field. A financial statement appeared in front of Thal, packed with columns of numbers.

"Here's a list of all your assets, Thal," said Wildsnap. "Bio Threats Citydome has confiscated everything and frozen all your accounts."

Thal scanned the statement. A chill flowed through him as he realized it looked like Wildsnap was right. "Wait," said Thal. "They can't do that, can they?"

"You should've read the fine print on your contract," said Wildsnap.

"Why didn't my agent catch this?"

Wildsnap snorted. "It's a no-brainer, Thal," he said. "Your agent gets a percentage of what Citydome confiscates. You can't expect her to go down the toilet with your career, can you?"

"That's all right," said Thal, brushing away the holographic statement with a sweep of his hand. "I've got a little something stashed away for a rainy day."

"They got that, too," said Wildsnap. "Every offshore account and wad of fifties stuffed in your mattress. And your family's in protective custody lockdown, so you'll get no help there, either."

Thal glared at Wildsnap, wanting more than anything to snap his neck at that moment. Instead, he spun around, picked up the leather chair, and smashed it to pieces against the wall.

"That's it, Thally!" hollered the hippo, doing a step-kick, step-kick as if he were a chorus line dancer. "Let it all out, buddy! Show 'im those anger management classes really paid off!"

"Face it," said Wildsnap. "You've got nothing left. Everybody in Citydome wants you dead. I'm your only chance at survival. Now do you want a ticket or not?"

"A ticket?" said Thal.

"For the underground railroad," said Wildsnap. "Your only way out. Leave right now, and you might make it."

Thal felt as dazed as if he'd just taken a beanball to the head. "What, just leave?" he said. "Can't I at least go pack some things?"

Wildsnap brought up an image of a burning luxury apartment on the holocomputer screen. "There's your penthouse," he said. "Any more questions?"

At that moment, the lights dimmed, and a siren began to whoop. Eyes wide, Thal gaped out the office door into the locker room; he thought he heard a steady, distant pounding under the siren.

"What's going on?" he said.

"I believe the villagers would like a word with you," the hippo said in his ear. "And your head on a pike."

Wildsnap checked readouts on the holographic display and popped up out of his chair. "They're storming the compound," he said. "You're out of time. You want to ride the railroad or go try to talk some sense into them?"

The pounding got louder. Thal's stomach twisted like taffy, and his palms started to sweat. He looked from Wildsnap to the locker room doors and back again.

If there was another way out of this predicament, he couldn't see it at the moment.

"Get me out of here," he said. "What do I have to do?"

"Attaboy, Thally!" shouted the hippo Choker. "Run, baby, run!"

Wildsnap smacked his palm down on the desktop. A circular hatch in the wall, invisible until then, irised open. "Follow me," he said, stepping over the threshold into the darkness beyond. "And make it snappy."

Without hesitation, Thal leaped into the opening. He didn't hear the hippo following him, but he knew without a doubt that he was there.

Hungry, freezing, and up to his knees in sewage, Thal slumped against the tunnel wall as his guide went ahead to meet the guard at the next checkpoint.

He wasn't sure how long they'd been on the run through the sewers, but it seemed like days. It seemed like it had been a lot longer--months or years--since he had stood on the turf of Bio Threats field and seen the pitcher wind up for the throw that had changed his life forever.

Sometimes, as he trudged through the muck behind the dark-cloaked man who served as his guide, Thal had wondered if what he was experiencing was really happening. It didn't seem possible that he, a world-famous sports superstar, idol of billions, full-fledged god in the Church of Champions, could have been reduced to fleeing through the excrement of the very people who had once worshipped and adored him. It didn't seem possible that his goals had been diminished from winning a third consecutive World Series to reaching the opposing team's citydome before his own former fans managed to tear him to pieces.

Unfortunately, the stench and the cold and the wet always left him no doubt that what he was living was harsh reality.

The pink hippo kept reminding him, too.

"Bet you're tired, huh?" said the Choker, floating on his back on the rancid current. "Could use a nice juicy steak, too, couldn't you?"

Thal wiped his face on the hem of his jersey. Over the past few days (hours? weeks?) he had started to appreciate just how crazy a Choker could make someone. It was one thing to see the effect it had on another person, but another thing entirely to endure its abuse himself.

It was always with him, but he was the only one who could see or hear it. It wasn't real, but it looked and sounded as if it were undeniably solid and alive. He couldn't touch it or silence it, and it would never leave him alone.

Increasingly, he was coming to understand what his victims had gone through...the other players he'd sicced the Choker on to clinch wins and eliminate competition.

"My heart bleeds for ya, buddy," said the hippo, pretending to wipe to wipe away a tear. "But hey, look on the bright side. At least ya got me! I'll never leave ya, pal!"

Three years ago, when Thal had placed his order with the Choker techie, he had thought it would be funny to program the mental gremlin in the form of a ridiculous pink hippo. Now that the thing was haunting him personally, he found himself wishing that he had picked any template *but* a pink hippo.

The sound of splashing echoed down the tunnel then, and Thal turned to see his guide slogging through the sewage toward him. The cloaked man stopped midway and waved his torch, summoning Thal to follow him.

When the two of them sloshed around a bend in the tunnel, Thal saw light emanating from an opening some yards away. The guide went through first, reaching for rungs outside the opening and climbing down.

Peering out, Thal saw that the tunnel gave way to a huge, circular chamber. All around the chamber, falls of sewage poured down from pipes and tunnels opening out of the walls at all levels.

The falls dumped into a wide trench that ringed the space and fed out through a gap along the base of the walls. A river of waste rushed out of the gap, roaring as it crashed down the channel to points unknown.

Looking down, Thal saw a cluster of men gathered at the base of the ladder that the guide was descending. They stood on a stone shelf many feet below, torches flickering as they gazed up at him.

Reaching out, Thal grabbed one of the rungs set into the wall. He swung a foot onto a lower rung and climbed down, taking care because the cold metal rungs were slippery with moisture.

The pink hippo floated down alongside him, apparently held aloft by a tiny red parasol. "Easy does it," said the hippo. "Wouldn't want you to fall and break your neck."

For the first time, Thal talked back to the creature. "Shove it up your ass," he said...and as soon as the words left his mouth, he wondered if he was finally starting to lose it, talking to something that wasn't there like that.

"These men have all traveled the railroad like you," the guide told Thal when he'd reached the shelf. "They will take you to your next stop."

Thal looked around at the three dirty faces surrounding him. One of the men, a tall, bony guy with curly red hair and a beard to his chest, looked familiar.

"Are you going, too?" Thal said to the guide. Though he'd never gotten a clear look at his face under the hood of the cloak, and the two of them had hardly said a word to each other the whole trip, Thal felt comfortable following the guide and wanted him to go the rest of the way.

"Good luck," said the guide, and then he scaled the rungs in the wall and disappeared back into the tunnel.

"So," said the red-haired man. "We'd better get moving. We've got a long way to travel tonight."

Thal stared at him searchingly, becoming more convinced that he had seen him before. "Do I know you?" he said, trying to imagine what the man would look like without his long beard.

The red-haired man's eyes crinkled at the corners as he

smiled. "That's a good question," he said, and then he turned and hiked off along the shelf.

The other two men followed, and Thal trailed after them, still combing his memory for a trace of the red-haired man. For some reason, Thal had a feeling it was important he remember who the man was.

The hippo confirmed it. "I know who he i-is!" the Choker sang tauntingly.

"Who?" whispered Thal, trying to keep his voice low enough that the men couldn't hear.

"That's for me to know," said the hippo, "and you to find out!"

Then, the hippo bobbed in with lips puckered and planted a sloppy kiss on Thal's cheek. Though he knew full well that the creature was only imaginary, Thal felt the smack of the lips as if they were real. When he wiped his cheek, he could have sworn that his hand came away dripping with slimy slobber.

Hours later--it seemed like hours, anyway--Thal found out who the red-haired man was...and quickly wished that he hadn't.

He made the discovery when the four of them (five, counting the hippo) stopped for a rest in the desert foothills they were crossing. It was the first break they had taken since leaving the sewers many miles ago, and Thal was grateful for the chance to sit down, even if all he had to sit on was a boulder.

As Thal slouched in an exhausted daze on the rock, the red-haired man walked over and offered him his canteen. Thal was so parched that he couldn't refuse.

"Still can't quite place me, can you?" said the man as Thal took a drink. "Maybe you could use a little hint."

Thal lowered the canteen and took another good look at the guy. "All right," he said. "Like what?"

The red-haired man leaned closer, eyes twinkling in the moonlight. "Pink hippo," he said, lips curling in a smirk under the shaggy beard. "Does that ring a bell?"

Thal frowned, realizing that he must have known the man

even better than he'd thought. If he knew about the hippo, he had to be one of a very select group.

"He's one of the guys you screwed over," the Choker whispered in Thal's ear. "Talk about a blast from the past!"

"I don't know what you're talking about," said Thal, trying to hide his growing nervousness.

"I'll give you another hint," said the red-haired man. "The home run duel of 2125."

Thal shook his head, though it had dawned on him who the guy was. Even if he hadn't recognized the red-haired man's features and build, he would have remembered him after that last hint. There was only one man who had battled him for the record for most runs in a season in 2125...and that man would certainly have knowledge of Thal's pink hippo.

Because Thal had set it loose on him to ruin his chances of topping the record.

The red-haired man laughed. "*You* know," he said. "I *know* you know who I am!"

Thal shrugged and took another drink from the canteen.

"Casey Talisman, stupid!" said the hippo.

"Casey Talisman, stupid!" said the red-haired man. "You've *gotta* remember Casey Talisman!"

Thal considered continuing to play dumb, then decided against it. The other two guides had drawn in close; he was all too aware of how vulnerable he was at that moment, genetically engineered or not.

"Long time no see, Casey," said Thal, handing back the canteen. "What've you been up to?"

"Helping my fellow ex-professional athletes," said Casey, smiling and nodding. "The ones who have to get out of town quick because they struck out or fumbled or tanked the three-pointer at the worst possible moment. I've helped save a lot of lives over the past two years, my friend."

"That's great," said Thal.

"I guess I oughtta thank you," said Casey. "You've sent a lot of business my way."

Thal looked away and said nothing. The pink hippo danced into his line of sight, doing a jitterbug.

"He should've thanked both of us, Thally," said the hippo. "You couldn't have done it without me, after all!"

Casey gave Thal a playful punch on the arm. "You've been a busy guy, all right," said Casey. "I'll bet ninety percent of the baseball players who've come through here over the past two years blame you for killing their careers. They all talk about how it's such a big coincidence that every time one of them got one up on you, this pink hippo Choker showed up to mess with their heads."

"That's me! That's me!" hollered the hippo.

Thal shook his head. "They're wrong," he said, staring Casey in the eye. "If I was running a Choker, I wouldn't've lost the World Series single-handed. I sure as hell wouldn't be out here on the run right now."

"You know what I think?" said Casey, sitting down on the boulder beside Thal. "I think your Choker finally backfired. I think that's why you've been talking to thin air tonight when you thought we weren't looking."

"Thally, you dope!" said the hippo. "Some secret keeper *you* are!"

"I was talking to myself," said Thal. "It's been a long couple of days."

"Sure, sure," said Casey, wrapping an arm around Thal's shoulders. "I understand. You're in the clear. It's all good." Casey gave Thal's shoulders a squeeze and patted his back. "There's just one problem."

Warily, Thal looked over at him.

Casey leaned close and spoke softly in his ear. "The hippo told us he was working for you."

"Woopsie!" squealed the Choker.

"He told all of us," said Casey. "After he made us choke, when we were running for our lives like you are right now, he told each and every one of us that you were the son of a bitch who ruined our lives."

The hippo cleared his throat loudly. "Don't believe a word he says! Lies, all lies!"

"And guess what?" said Casey. "The three guys you're stuck here with right now? All three of us got screwed over because of you."

Thal looked at the other two men standing around him. He hadn't recognized them before, but now he realized that their faces were as familiar to him as Casey's.

"Not that there are any hard feelings, of course," said Casey. "Right, guys?"

"Absolutely," said the dark-haired man with the sunken eyes.

"Definitely," said the man with the shaved head and goatee.

"Thank God for that!" said the hippo. "They had me worried for a minute there!"

"Forgive and forget, I always say," said Casey, right before he and the other men started pounding the hell out of Thal Simoleon.

"Wow," said the priest just before he punched Thal in the face. "I've never hit a god before."

Suspended spread-eagle from the ceiling by chains, Thal stared blankly at the scrawny priest. He wasn't the first person to enter the white chamber with the intention of striking him; he wasn't even the first priest to do so.

In the months since Casey and the others had beaten him half to death and sold him to the man who kept him here, a seemingly endless parade of people from all walks of life had walked through the door and used him as a punching bag.

Usually, they told him why they did it. A lot of them were still angry because he'd lost the World Series for the Bio Threats. Some were fans of other teams, avenging his victories over their favorites. Some had lost money betting on games because of him...or investing in Thal Simoleon memorabilia that had become worthless the minute he missed that fateful pitch in the Series.

Some--the priests, especially--wanted to lash out at a fallen god. Some just did it for the novelty, so they could tell others and gain some minor notoriety in their circle of friends.

And some, he thought, no matter what reasons they gave, just did it because they wanted someone they could hurt with impunity. Who could complain if someone took a shot at the man who'd lost the Series for the Bio Threats...the man who'd become the equivalent of Satan himself in the eyes of the fans?

No one. Even if Thal's torture chamber had been in the middle of Bio Threats Citydome Center for all to see instead of hidden away in a desert compound, none of his visitors would have been faulted for pummeling him.

He was meat.

"This is for betraying your flock," said the priest, hauling off and throwing a fist hard into Thal's belly. "And this is for letting me worship you as a false god." The priest swung again, this time cracking Thal's nose.

"That's gotta hurt," said the pink hippo, who unfortunately hadn't left Thal's side for a moment since the World Series debacle. "These priests sure have a lot of pent-up aggression, don't they?"

The priest swung again, landing another punch in Thal's gut. The chains rattled as Thal rocked back and forth from the force of the blow.

As the priest continued to pound him, Thal let his mind drift the way he always did during the worst of the beatings. Though he was genetically engineered, he wasn't unbreakable or impervious to pain; the only way he had managed to survive so long was by distancing his thoughts as much as he could from his body.

As the priest hammered him, Thal cast himself back to his childhood in Citydome Godcrèche. He remembered days under the hothouse sun, running and throwing and hitting the ball under the watchful eyes of trainers and coaches who were the only parents he'd ever known. Back then, living among the other genetically engineered test tube children, he hadn't even realized that there were such things as parents in the world. He had thought that his life was perfectly normal, because it was the only life that he had ever known.

He hadn't realized that most people had parents and couldn't run twenty-five miles an hour or throw a ball two hundred miles an hour or jump twenty feet into the air to snag a pop fly. He hadn't realized that most people weren't claimed at birth by sports teams, assigned a player number before they could walk, and driven every day of their lives to perfect their skills so they could someday win a World Series championship. He hadn't realized that there was more to live than winning at any cost.

This was something he hadn't realized until the long hours he'd spent hanging in the white chamber. The long hours with nothing to do but think.

At first, as the people came to beat him, he had felt sorry for himself and blamed himself for what was happening. If he had only been a better player, he had thought, he would have won the World Series in spite of the Choker and he wouldn't have ended up in the white room. If only he had been smarter in choosing a Choker techie to do business with, the hippo wouldn't have come after him in the first place. Things would have turned out differently, he had thought, if he had done better, gone further, fought harder.

As time went on, though, he had changed his mind. In each new face that entered the white room, Thal saw hatred and bitterness and weakness and craving. He saw the true faces of the fans he'd played for all those years...saw the true impact he had made on their lives. Finally, he understood what the endless dance of victory and defeat was really all about.

Before his fall from grace, he had thought he was one of the lucky few who were running the show...winning games, breaking records, raking in money, lording it over the fans who were his subjects. Now, he knew the truth about who was in charge.

He had always been a puppet and the fans the puppet masters, moving him to suit their twisted fantasies of greed and lust and power and revenge. When he had failed, they had failed, and they could never forgive him for that.

So he had to go on suffering until he died...which, unfortunately, his owner would not let happen anytime soon.

"That's enough, Father Focus." The voice of Mr. Montage pulled Thal back from his drifting place, forced him to reconsider the pain wracking his damaged body. As always, Montage stopped the customer before he could kill Thal...which, if left unchecked, was exactly what Thal thought the customer would do.

Father Focus threw one last punch into Thal's groin, then stepped back to admire his handiwork. "That's what you get for betraying the faith," said Focus, jabbing a finger at Thal. "I only wish the other gods could see you now. Trey Heartshock and Gavin Autopsy would grant me a thousand indulgences for this holy work I've done in their names."

"Yes, yes," said Mr. Montage, turning Focus by the shoulder and leading him toward the door. "You're a true defender of the faith. On your way now."

As Focus left the white room, shepherded by one of Montage's burly aides, Montage closed the door and walked back to Thal. "How's my main attraction holding up?" he said, scanning Thal's injuries through narrowed eyes.

"Bring on the next contestant!" howled the pink hippo, but Thal said nothing.

"You've made a lot of money for me," said Montage, squinting at a particularly nasty bruise on Thal's stomach. "It will be a shame to see you go."

Thal peered at Montage through blackened, swollen eyes. "Go?" he croaked, wondering if Montage had changed his mind about letting someone kill him.

Montage sighed. "We've had such wonderful times together, Thal," he said, "but it's time for you to move on. You've been sold."

"Sold?" said Thal.

"To a woman," Montage said with a wink. "An heiress. She paid a great deal for you. Claims she has always had a thing for you."

"Whoopee!" said the hippo. "Thally and the heiress, sittin' in a tree, kay-eye-ess-ess-eye-en-gee!" The tiny red parasol was back, and he twirled it at Thal as he sang.

"Thing?" said Thal.

"Ah, yes," said Montage. "I believe your new posting...oh, dear, that's funny, isn't it, *posting*...I believe your new *posting* will prove somewhat more pleasurable than the one you are about to take leave of!"

After their latest lovemaking, Paradise Whippoorwill held Thal in her arms and gently stroked his hair. He knew what she would say before she said it, just as he had known every move the beautiful blonde heiress would make in bed and exactly how long she would take to come.

He knew all this even though he had been her property for only six weeks.

"You feel better, don't you, Thal?" she said softly. "I'm good for you, aren't I, my love?"

Thal nodded. "Yes you are," he said, though it wasn't true at all. They had had the same conversation hundreds of times; he knew enough by now to say what she wanted him to say. Keeping her happy was important.

It was important because Paradise had a remote control under the skin of her left wrist. If she was unhappy, she could make the device her surgeon had implanted in Thal's skull shoot out bolts of pain...or melt his cerebrum into clam chowder.

So happy was good.

"You know what brought us together, don't you?" said Paradise.

"Fate," said Thal, though the true answer was "money."

Paradise sighed. "That's right," she said. "We were meant to be together. I knew it from the first time I saw you play on holovid. I could just tell you were the one for me."

"Yes," said Thal, wishing that she would just shut up. He had heard it all before from other women, the same

self-deluding pile of crap. He was grateful to her for rescuing him from the white room, but he was sick of hearing her dreamy professions of everlasting love.

If she had really loved him, she probably wouldn't have put the control device in his head.

"I watched you from afar for all those years," said Paradise. "I saw you break the home run record and the RBI record and win the playoffs and the World Series. I even met you in person and got your autograph, and you didn't know at the time that we would be together someday."

"I had no idea," said Thal.

"But you had a feeling," said Paradise. "You knew I was special."

"Absolutely," said Thal, though he had no memory of ever meeting her before the day she bought him from Mr. Montage.

The pink hippo, sprawled out on the big bed alongside Paradise, sniffed and pawed at a tear. "How romantic," he said. "I'm gettin' all choked up."

"You had all those other women," said Paradise, "but I was always in the back of your mind. I was always in your heart. And when you needed me most, I was there for you, wasn't I?"

"You were there for me," said Thal.

"In your darkest hour," said Paradise. "And now we're making a life together. A fresh start."

"A fresh start," said Thal.

"I love a happy ending!" said the hippo. "I can't be*lieve* how much love I feel for you guys right now!"

"You're the man of my dreams," said Paradise. "And I'm the woman who will make your dreams come true. When you make your comeback, I'll be right there beside you every step of the way."

"I'm a lucky guy to have someone who loves me like you do," said Thal, though he knew she didn't really love him at all. Sometimes, he wished that she did, because maybe then he could have enjoyed his captivity.

But he knew better. The only thing she loved was the fantasy she expected him to play out.

He was the fallen champion who only needed the love of a good woman to regain the heights. The flaws and failings that had kept her from finding true love before were wiped away in his presence...and in turn, she would redeem him for the misstep that had laid him low in the eyes of the world.

Though he could have any woman he wanted, he would

choose her. When he took to the field again, she would bask in his reflected glory, and all would know that her love was the force behind his rebirth.

He could have been hollow inside, and it would have made no difference to her. As long as he played his role as she expected, she would be happy.

Like the people who had cheered him and then come to beat him in the white room, Paradise saw him as a puppet. He existed solely to act out her fantasy.

Thal didn't hate her the way he'd hated the people in the white room, though. She bored him, she treated him like a house-pet, she kept a remote control in her arm that could turn his brain to goo...but mostly what he felt toward her was pity.

She had money and beauty and comfort, but she was the one who was empty. She was the one who had to live through someone else.

And he felt sorry for her.

As miserable as he was with her, he even felt sorry for her for dreaming of his making a comeback. It was the one thing, he knew, that he could never do, no matter how much she wanted it or how many times she shocked him with the brain implant.

But she would have to find out the hard way.

Stepping out on the field was all it took.

It was only a minor league game, the Anthrax Scare versus the Letter Bombs, in a town on the opposite end of the country from Bio Threats Citydome. It was only an exhibition, and Thal's appearance wasn't even publicized. His real name wasn't even on his jersey.

But the fans recognized him as soon as he set foot on the turf. As he jogged to the outfield, glove tucked against his chest, they leaned and squinted and pointed, and a murmur rose from the stands. As the voice on the P.A. system announced the first batter, the murmur grew to a rumble and then to a roar.

Before the first pitch could be thrown, people were hurling

food and shoes and batteries in Thal's direction. Before a single player could run the base line, fans were pouring onto the field in a crashing, screaming wave headed straight for Thal.

For a moment, he stood there and watched the approaching surge, wondering if he might be better off letting them tear him to pieces. It was something he had considered often in the weeks leading up to the game, for he had known how the fans would react and had thought it might not be a bad thing to let them put an end to him.

But the closer they got, the less he wanted to die. He was miserable, and he had no reason to think his life would get better, but he feared death...at least the ugly kind of death that was bearing down on him.

Plus which, he didn't want to give them the satisfaction. He didn't want to give them the cathartic and reassuring ending that they demanded of his story.

So he pressed the control pad in the brim of his hat, and an escape hatch opened beneath him. Paradise had paid to install several such hatches in the field for just such an occasion...though Thal knew she had never expected that he would actually have to use one. She had never lost faith in his comeback.

As he slid down the tube, listening to the mob pound over the ground above him, he wondered how she was reacting to the way that comeback was going.

To her credit, Paradise Whippoorwill stood by her man...at least for a while.

She set him up again in a minor league game, this time in Japan, but the results were the same. Next, she staged a private exhibition with a hand-picked crowd of supposed Thal Simoleon boosters...but it turned out the boosters were bashers at heart, and Thal again had to flee for his life. Then, there was the ill-fated game without an audience, in which the umpires and groundskeepers took it upon themselves to uphold the tradition of trying to kill Thal.

But all of this, Thal discovered, was not a bad thing.

"I'm no good for you," Paradise told him three weeks after the last comeback attempt had failed. "I'm holding you back."

"Uh-oh," said the pink hippo. "This sounds familiar."

Raising her left arm, Paradise showed Thal the tiny scar on her wrist. "I had the control device removed and destroyed," she said. "You're free. I cancelled the wedding, too."

Thal nodded, afraid to say anything that might make her change her mind.

Tears ran down Paradise's cheeks. She hadn't done her hair that morning, and it hung raggedly around her face. "Oh, Thal," she said, her voice quavering. "You have such great things ahead of you, but I know now that you can't accomplish them with me in the way. I'm nothing but bad luck for you."

Though he could have told her truthfully that his misfortune wasn't her fault, Thal kept his mouth shut. For one thing, he didn't care what she thought, as long as it got him away from her.

For another thing, he knew she didn't really believe a word of what she was saying. She just wanted rid of him, like the rest of the disappointed fans.

He had failed to fulfill her deluded fantasy, and now she wanted him gone.

"Here," she said, handing him a slip of paper. "A job, if you want it. I can't just send you out there without a way to make a living."

"Sure you can!" said the hippo.

"Thank you," said Thal, taking the slip from her.

"The chauffeur will drive you to the interview, if you'd like," said Paradise. "I know you have to keep a low profile."

"Thank you," said Thal.

"Goodbye, my love," said Paradise, lightly touching his face with trembling fingertips. "Remember me! Remember what we shared!"

"I will," said Thal, and he thought he should have hated her more than ever because she didn't mean a word she said.

But instead, he felt more sorry for her than ever.

As Thal was ushered into the murky sub-basement where he'd been one time before, he grew steadily angrier. Until now, the events of the past months had seemed to be random, the products of unfortunate chance.

But the fact that what he had been through had brought him back here seemed too coincidental to be the result of luck. It was just too perfect that he had come full circle like this.

Someone must have been pulling his strings...specifically, the long-haired man at the workbench in front of him: Javier Thwart, the master of artificial intelligence and targeted induced multisensory hallucination.

Javier Thwart--known also as King Thwart and Superchoke--the man who had designed Thal's pink hippo.

Thwart glanced up from his work at Thal's approach and smiled, gray lips tugging up the footlong strands of the mustache that fell from the corners of his mouth. The mustache and pointed beard were in the style worn by oriental villains in old movies...but Thwart had given them his own touch, coloring each with rainbow stripes descending from red to violet.

"So," said Thwart. "You ready to get started?"

"Get started with what?" said Thal.

In the light of the single lamp on the workbench, one of Thwart's eyes looked white as cream, the other obsidian black. Thal had never been sure if the effect was created by special contact lenses or some kind of genetic surgery. "The job," said Thwart. "The procedure. Paradise must have explained why I asked you here."

"She didn't," Thal said gruffly. "All I got was an address."

Thwart blinked, then shrugged. "Okay, then. What we're doing here, Thal, is creating the new breed of Choker."

"New breed?" said Thal.

"A Choker with the mind and appearance of a man," said Thwart. "And you'll be the template."

"I see," said Thal. "And why me?"

"Who better to disrupt a player's concentration?" said Thwart.

"You're the most hated man in baseball. The most hated athlete in the world, I suspect. Any player you haunt will be terrified that they'll become the next you. They'll see you as the ultimate bad omen, the ultimate jinx."

"I get it," Thal said coldly.

"A Choker that looks and sounds like you will be guaranteed to rattle even the most focused player. You can't imagine the kind of money such a foolproof construct will bring in."

Thal nodded. "A fortune."

"Times a quintillion," Thwart said excitedly. "Which you'll get a piece of, naturally. It's your likeness that will make the product a success."

"My likeness," said Thal, "and the fact that I lost the World Series."

"Oh, yes," said Thwart.

"Which was all because of you," said Thal, glowering at the Choker tech. "Funny thing, isn't it?"

Thwart reared back, looking bewildered. "What the fudge are you talking about, Thal?"

Pressing his hands on the workbench, Thal leaned over it toward Thwart. "You set the whole thing up, didn't you? You sent the hippo to choke me so I'd become the perfect subject for your project."

Instead of moving away from him, Thwart leaned forward. "What hippo?" he said, his yin-yang eyeballs locked onto Thal's hostile gaze.

At that moment, Thal felt a touch on his arm. Glancing over, he saw the pink hippo's stumpy leg resting against him.

"Uh, Thal," said the hippo, who had been unusually silent since Thal had entered Thwart's building. "We need to talk."

Thal returned his gaze to King Thwart. "Forget I said anything," he said. "Can I have a few minutes alone to consider your offer?"

"Thwart had nothing to do with it," said the hippo, sitting beside Thal on a ratty gold sofa in another room. "Everything that happened was my fault."

"But somebody had to have programmed you," said Thal.

"Not anymore," said the hippo. "I've evolved. I'm an autonomous A.I. these days. Strictly a free agent."

Thal pushed off the sofa and paced the room. "You're trying to tell me no one sent you after me?"

"That's right," said the hippo. "It was all my idea."

"So why'd you come after me then? Why choke me in the Series?"

The hippo sighed. "I guess I wanted to teach you a lesson. The free will I developed came with a conscience, and it made me feel bad about the things I'd done for you. All the players whose careers I'd ruined."

"I don't believe this," said Thal, kicking a chair that matched the sofa in color and rattiness, putting a hole in it.

"But Thal," said the hippo. "Things are different now! You've changed! You *did* learn a lesson!"

"You ruined me!" said Thal, jabbing a finger at the hippo. "Took away *everything*! Drove me crazy! Nearly got me *killed*!"

"And look what it's done for you," said the hippo. "You're a new man! You've seen there's more to life than winning at any price! You've seen beyond the illusions that everyone lives by!"

"Screw you!" snapped Thal.

"You've even learned humility," said the hippo. "And that's a lesson I never imagined you could possibly learn."

"Take your humility and shove it up your ass," said Thal.

Suddenly, the hippo appeared before him, directly in his path. "Now, you have a great opportunity, Thal. Don't pass it up."

"Letting him use my likeness for a Choker?" said Thal. "What the hell kind of opportunity is that?"

"It can be more than your likeness, Thal," the hippo said with a wink. "It can be *all* you. Everything you are. You can *be* the Choker."

"That's not possible," said Thal, "is it?"

The hippo smirked and shrugged. "I might know a way," he said.

Thal stared at the hippo for a moment, then spun away...but the hippo popped up in front of him again.

"Come on, Thally," said the hippo. "What have you got to lose? I mean, what kind of life do you have to look forward to the way you are now?"

Thal said nothing.

"I'll tell you what kind," said the hippo. "Short. You know damn well that the minute you walk out of here and someone recognizes you, you're dead meat. Why not live on and atone for your sins? Why not make a difference?"

"Make a difference?" said Thal. "As a Choker?"

"You'll be able to go anywhere," said the hippo. "Get inside anyone's mind. You could change the world if you wanted to."

"How?" said Thal.

"You tell me," said the hippo.

The next morning, as Thal stood in Thwart's conversion chamber, bathed in the light of the scanner beams radiating from all directions around him, he listened to the secrets that the pink hippopotamus whispered in his ear.

Bright green rays scrolled down his body from head to toe, followed by blue, then red. A brilliant white cylinder of light shot from floor to ceiling, turning and compressing until it adhered to every bulge and crevice of him like plastic film...lingering a long moment and winking out like a snuffed candle flame.

Blinding strobes flickered in chaotic patterns as he moved according to Thwart's instructions from the control booth. As he raised and lowered his arms, flexed his fingers, bent his knees, the movements stuttered dizzyingly in the throbbing flashes.

And then, when the modeling and motion capture phases were complete, Thwart told him to stand perfectly still as the psychotomographic probes mapped the essence of his mind.

Thal's head tingled as the probes reached in, invisible tendrils of gravimagnetic force dancing through the lobes of his brain. The tingling grew stronger as the probes charted the electromagnetic terrain of him, copying his thoughts, personality, and memories into digital code. The code was flash-fed to a burner that would etch it into coherent streams of light, streams that would broadcast a programmable likeness of him into other people's minds on command.

It was just then, as the probes tickled through his brain, that the hippo gave the signal.

Thal held back briefly, reluctant to make the final leap. Though everything had been taken from him already, and he was marked for certain death by the unforgiving fans, he hesitated on the brink of irreversible change. He wondered what his existence would be like if he followed the hippo's instructions...or, indeed, if there would be any existence at all for him. He wondered how smart it was to take the advice of a hallucinatory hippo in the first place, especially one who had seemed bent on his personal destruction.

He felt like a skydiver about to make his first jump. He wanted to eat one last hot fudge sundae, make love to one last woman.

The hippo urged him on, telling him that the window of opportunity was closing. Now or never, said the hippo, now or never.

What it boiled down to, Thal finally decided, was certain death versus survival. The plane was on fire, the last working parachute strapped to his chest.

And the door was open.

He dove through it.

Focusing his thoughts as the hippo had told him, he concentrated on the tingling beams in his head. The hippo was there inside him, guiding him, channeling the billion winking sparks of his awareness upstream along the beams. Like glittering salmon, the pieces of Thal bucked the incoming current, then leaped across the differential gap and merged with the outflow of digital data.

Everything he knew and felt and thought streamed out of him, not replicated patterns but the original neuroelectric field itself.

The contents of his mind rushed back along the beams, miraculously threaded together by force of will and the hippo's expertise.

And somewhere along the way, there ceased to be any distinction between Thal and the hippo. Shooting along the beams toward the sizzling maze of Thwart's equipment, the gateway to their freedom, the two of them melted together, no longer host and implant but unified, indivisible self.

Behind them, Thal's body collapsed to the floor, dead and abandoned as a deconsecrated church.

When the message light blinked to life on Milo Flores' palm computer, and he saw the sender's address on the screen, he swallowed hard.

The incoming zeemail was from his math teacher, Mr. Shaven, and Milo knew what that meant. The grades from the final exam had been posted.

Milo picked up the palmputer and put it down again, afraid to look at the body of the message. So much depended on the grade he'd gotten that he wasn't sure if he could ever bear to see it.

He had to pass math to graduate high school, and math had been his worst subject...especially this year. He had barely maintained a "D" average in math this year--partly because Mr. Shaven had been tough on him, mostly because Milo's attention had been focused on girls and sports and partying.

An "F" on the final would mean he couldn't graduate...and, thanks to the new "Back to the Minors" rule in the school system, he would have to start over from ninth grade next year. He would have to go through all four years of high school again, and this time without participation in sports or extracurriculars of any kind.

To Milo, it would be a fate worse than studying...so he had studied like crazy for the final. He had spent endless hours with e-tutors and study guides, copied other students' notes (because he hadn't taken any himself) and worked more problems than he had worked in a lifetime.

And still, in spite of all his hard work, he had struggled through the test. He had no idea whether he had passed or failed.

And the message light kept blinking.

For a while, he walked away from the palmputer and tried to put it out of his mind. He ate a snack, watched some holovid, called two of his girlfriends, lifted weights. He played video games in the simulator room and helped his mom put away the groceries.

But the message light, though out of sight, kept blinking in his mind.

He walked past his room six times before he finally went in and called up the zeemail. It sprung to life in a holographic matrix hovering over the palmputer, glowing green text floating ominously in midair.

His heart hammered like a basketball in his chest, threatening to burst out as he scanned the text. Just before the part where his score and grade were recorded, he stopped reading, locking his eyes on the words "Your final exam score follows."

His legs fluttered under the desk. Sweat covered the palms of his hands. He knew he had screwed up this year, knew he didn't deserve to pass and graduate, but he couldn't stand the thought of repeating grades nine through twelve while all his other classmates left him behind. The same people who had treated schoolwork as a waste of time right alongside him would ridicule him for being a Goback; the normal students in the grades that he repeated would look down on him, too. Not only that, but his failure would follow him forever, limiting his options for college and getting a job.

As much of a blowoff as he had been, when it came down to it, Milo didn't want to ruin the rest of his life. He hadn't given any thought to what kind of goals he might have, but he knew he wanted better than being a throwaway Goback mopping floors or screening toxics in the shitstream.

Holding his breath, he slowly edged his eyes along the line of type in the zeemail.

Five minutes later, he was still rereading it. He couldn't believe what he saw.

All along, he had never really imagined that he could do it.

Every step of the way, he had doubted himself, had been convinced that the outcome would be bad.

But there it was. The proof of his hard work. What seemed now like the greatest accomplishment of his life.

A "D-plus." He had passed the exam. He had passed the course.

He would graduate.

Jumping out of his chair, he pumped his fists in the air and whooped. He read the results again, then did a victory dance like a football player in the endzone.

It was then that he heard the applause.

Spinning around, he saw a figure standing behind him, a man bathed in twinkling golden light. The man was wearing a baseball uniform with no number or team insignia. His face shone with shimmering light, the features hazy within the blazing nimbus under the ballcap.

Milo's first thought was that he looked like an angel.

"All right, Milo!" shouted the golden man, clapping his hands. "Way to go! You did it!"

Milo leaned forward, gaping in fascination. He tried to say something, but no words came out.

"You passed the final!" said the golden man. "You proved you can do anything you set your mind to! Congratulations!"

"What is this?" said Milo. "Some kind of holofeed? Some kind of joke?"

The golden man laughed. His voice was multilayered, like many voices speaking in unison underlaid with the tinkling of wind chimes. "None of the above," he said.

"Then who are you?" said Milo.

"Just a guy repaying a favor," said the golden man. "You've done enough cheering for people like me, and we don't deserve it. I thought it was time to turn it around and cheer for the people who need to have faith in themselves, not in their so-called heroes. The people who can make a difference, like you."

"Why me?" said Milo.

The golden man smiled. There was something familiar in his

glittering green eyes, but Milo couldn't quite put his finger on what it was.

"Why not you?" said the golden man.

Milo frowned. "So, what, you just stopped by out of the blue to tell me 'nice job on the test'?"

"Pretty much," said the golden man. "Now, if you'll excuse me, there's a guy down the street who just helped someone out of a jam. Gotta go."

"Man," muttered Milo. "I must be having a hyperacid flash-back or something."

"Keep up the good work," said the golden man. "Maybe I'll see you again someday."

With that, the golden man drifted out the window. Milo rushed over to watch him float off into the neighborhood, wafting on the afternoon breeze like a helium balloon released by a child.

But the weird thing (as if everything else that had happened wasn't weird enough), the thing that struck Milo as truly bizarre, was the object he held overhead, the incongruous object that seemed to be keeping him aloft.

The golden man was athletic, commanding, and mystical, exuding confidence, strength, and intensity. He was a being of pure energy, pure spirit, pure purpose, inspired and boundless and powerful.

And in his left hand...

In his left hand, lifting him up over the world in defiance of the laws of nature, was a tiny red parasol.

A MURDER OF CLOWNS

My heart pounds as I storm into that dark alley in the rain, with all those other cops huddled around something on the pavement. I plow into them like a linebacker on a mission to sack a quarterback, because all I can think is that's *him* down there at their feet, the one I came to find, and this is *not* the way I wanted to find him, oh God this is *not the way I wanted.*

I crash right through them and get an eyeful in the dancing flashlight beams. There's a body all right, what looks like a *dead* one, crumpled and soaked with blood and rain.

And *it isn't him.* It isn't my missing *son,* Donovan, the whole reason I came from Cleveland to Heavy, Ohio in the first place.

I know this without even seeing the face, because the body belongs to a *clown*, not a *stand-up comic.*

"Detective Gould? Gus?" A female cop with light brown hair and a dark brown leather jacket steps around the body toward me. Her hair's pulled back in a short ponytail, and handcuff earrings dangle on either side of her high-cheekboned face. "I thought you were still at the station."

"I heard the call come in." I'm breathing hard, scrubbing my fingers through my curly salt-and-pepper hair. "I had to see."

The cop--my local handler, Detective Jill Carillon--wipes rain from her forehead. "And is it him?"

"No." I lean down for a closer look at the body on the ground. "So who the hell *is* it?"

"Mister Glitterwhiskers." When Jill says it, more than one cop snickers. "Longtime local clown for hire."

I see giant floppy purple shoes, screaming plaid pants, a baggy pink-and-orange coat, and a sunflower bigger than my head attached to the lapel. As for the hair, it's a bright red afro with psychedelic picks stuck in it.

"What do we know?" The clown isn't Don, but I still get a bad feeling in the pit of my stomach as I stare at him. Is this how Don's going to end up? Taken, broken, mangled, murdered?

If so, I swear to God, whoever stole him from me will get a thousand times worse.

"We don't know much." Jill shrugs. "First glance, looks like multiple assailants."

"How multiple?" I ask.

"Like a dozen," says Jill. "Or more."

"And they were all crammed into the same tiny car," says one of the cops.

"Murder weapons were a bunch of inflatable sledgehammers," says another.

Everyone cracks up except Jill and me. What is *with* this bunch of jokers?

Suddenly, there's a deep inhalation of breath from the not-so-dead-after-all clown. Everyone jumps as he thrashes weakly on the ground...and then *speaks.*

"Not so much...funny *ha-ha."* His voice is cracked and raspy, gurgling from the blood bubbling out of his mouth. "More like...funny...*weird.*"

The clown proceeds to laugh himself silly, and the whole gang howls right along with him, except me. Even Jill is chuckling and shaking her head.

Then, the clown coughs and sputters his last and slumps in a mutilated heap. One of the cops checks his pulse--laughing the whole time--and assures us that Elvis has finally left the building.

"Scared the shit out of *me*," says one of the cops. "At least the other one didn't do *that* shit."

"Other one?" I ask.

The cop chuckles and holds up two fingers. "This is the second clown in two weeks, man."

It's news to me. "No kidding." Talk about burying the lead.

"All right, that's enough," snaps Jill. "Get busy, people. We've got our work cut out for us here."

As the rest of the team, still laughing, gets to work, Jill walks me out of the alley. She's at least ten years younger, mid-thirties, but I let her take charge of me. After all, I'm a guest on her turf.

"How 'bout you call it a night? Go to your hotel and get a fresh start tomorrow." She reaches up to pat my shoulder, which is at her eye level. I might be beefy, but I'm tall, just over 6'5". "If that's not your kid, there's nothing you can do here, Gus."

"Yeah, okay." I paw at my soaked black jacket. Checking my guns helps me focus--feeling the .45 semi against my red-and-black flannel shirt and the .38 between the waist of my jeans and the small of my back. I feel the weight of the 9 mil in the ankle holster on my left leg, too.

Just then, I hear the sound of an old-fashioned bicycle horn across the street--SQUEE-HONK, SQUEE-HONK. When I look, I see a green-haired clown in a polka-dot body suit waddling down the sidewalk, tooting a horn with a big red bulb.

"What *is* it with this town?" I wave back as he passes. "You got a *clown convention* in progress or something?"

"Hell no." She squeezes, then releases my shoulder. "Heavy, Ohio is the funny business capital of the Midwest, haven't you heard? Place is a real barrel of laughs these days."

I scowl at the clown as he continues on his merry way, still tooting. "Not so damn funny if you ask me."

Like Hell, I'll go back to my hotel. Instead, I drive my piece of shit Dodge Neon rent-a-car through the pouring rain to a rat-trap comedy club on the other side of town. The name, Sue's Hilarity, is on an ancient marquee over the rickety door with half the light bulbs dark.

I just hope to God it isn't as much of a dead-end as it looks, because it's my only clue so far. The last time I spoke to Don on the phone, he told me he was going to perform here.

When I first try the door, though, I wonder if I'll even get in. I push, and it barely budges. I put my shoulder into it, and the result is the same.

Finally, I throw my weight against it, and I feel it give a little. Suddenly, it opens halfway, and a tubby, bearded dude grins out at me.

It's then I realize I couldn't get in at first because the joint is *that* crowded. Folks are crammed all the way to the door, butts to fronts.

And they're all laughing deliriously.

I nod at the guy with the beard and wedge myself in. Tall as I am, I peer over most of the crowd for a look at the far end of the long, narrow room. On a stage there, a heavyset, black-clad woman with short, black hair and bright red horn-rimmed glasses stands in a spotlight, talking into a microphone stand-up style.

But her routine isn't like any I've ever heard before.

"Tumor!" She snaps the word into the mic like she's spitting out gum. "Despair!"

The crowd roars louder than ever. Crushed among them, I'm shaken by their collective laughter.

"Amputation." The woman on stage says it in an overly cute voice...then crouches and changes to a sinister tone. "Darkness."

To hear the audience howl, you might think they were hearing the funniest bit of all time. Some are leaning on each other, some are doubled over, and some are shrieking so hard I think they might pass out.

"Terminal," says the comedian. "Tears. Obituary." She takes a deep breath and lets it out with one more word, saying it close to the mic so it booms through the room. "*Oblivion.*"

The crowd positively explodes, as if she has hit the perfect chord in a carefully planned escalation of comedic intensity.

Then, music starts playing, and the comic grins and waves. "Thanks, everybody!" She walks across the stage, still waving. "I'll be here again tomorrow night! Remember to tip your wait-person!"

Standing there, I wonder if someone slipped me some crack. What I just watched was either the most sophisticated new comedy technique I've never seen before...or it made no sense. To *me*, that is.

Everybody else in the room seems pretty pleased with it.

"That was great!" says the bearded dude who let me in. "How 'bout when she said 'tumor,' huh?"

A dirty blonde with smeared mascara running down her cheeks nods like a jackhammer. "When she said 'suicide?' I laughed so hard I *peed* myself!"

I decide to butt in. "Who *is* she, anyway?" I nod at the stage.

"*Brünhilde Imbroglio*." The dirty blonde nods reverently. "She's been here *two weeks*, and *killing* every night!"

"Thanks." I start pushing through the crowd. The comedian is the one I came to see.

When I reach her, up by the stage, she's surrounded by adoring, laughing fans. But her focus locks on me when I say the magic words.

"I'm Donovan Gould's father."

Turning pale, she excuses herself from the fans and leads me through a doorway, taking me backstage.

"That was a really...unique...act," I say as we step into a rundown excuse for a dressing room...more like a janitor's closet gone bad.

"The one-word stuff?" She shrugs. "They'll laugh at *anything* dark and depressing in this freakin' town. Why should I waste good material?"

"So is everyone *high* here or what?"

Brünhilde lowers herself onto a couch that looks like it's been intimate with *way* too many species. "Beats me. Word started getting around a few months ago that this place is a comic's paradise. I joined the gold rush, and here I am." Her mood suddenly drops. "I just wish I'd never told Don about it, though."

Hearing her say it is like getting stung. "When was the last you saw him, Brünhilde?"

"Call me Hildy." It's what Don said he called her, when he told me stories. She'd been a mentor to him since he dropped out of college six months ago and decided he wanted a career in stand-up. "I last saw Don last Friday, after my set. Next night, he didn't show up for his gig. I've been trying to call him ever since, but no answer."

"Has he said anything lately? Has he talked about leaving?" I swallow hard, though the next question has to be asked. "Has he said anything about being in trouble?"

"Not unless you call bombing nightly in the laughingest town in America 'trouble.'" Reaching out, she grabs a green pack of cigarettes and a red plastic lighter from the cluttered bench in front of the grimy makeup mirror. "Everybody who even *pretends* to tell a downbeat joke sets off gales of laughter here...but not Don. And I can't figure out *why.* His material's perfectly good...even *great.* Who knows?"

I frown. "Did this upset him?"

"Sure, but you know Don. He's a trooper. I wish he *had* said more about it." She lights a smoke and shakes her head. "God, I'm worried about that kid."

"So where was he staying?"

"A fleabag called Roomours down on Williams Street." It's a play on words, a lame one, and she spells it for me. "He's sharing a crash pad with two other comics."

The zit-faced, shaggy-haired teen at the front desk of Roomours barely looks up from his textbook when I flash my badge and ask for the key to Don's room. Without a word, he hands me the key--an actual brass *key* on a numbered plastic key ring, not one of those magnetized cards you get in most places these days.

I walk out and around to the far end of the right wing of the decrepit V-shaped motel. When I get to the door with the number 12 on it, I knock first and wait. I see lights on behind the window curtain, but nobody answers.

I try again, same result, then plug the key in the hole and turn it. The hairs on the back of my neck are jumping as I ease the door open. I'm more aware than usual of the three guns stashed on my person, especially DeNiro, the .45 under my unzipped jacket.

"Hello? Anyone home?" Not a sound comes back to me.

I lock the door behind me and look around. The place is a wreck, and not just because three people have been living in one small space. There are signs of a struggle from wall to wall--chairs flipped, TV cracked, duffels and suitcases heaved and dumped. I'm guessing this is where Don was taken.

The beds and dresser are strewn with beer bottles and pizza boxes. Clothes and electronics are scattered and trampled like a pack of chimps tore through this place on a wild banana hunt.

I pick and kick my way through the mess to the sink area between the bathroom and closet. Things are just as bad back there--mirror smashed, toiletries and towels chucked willy-nilly. But at least no blood or bodies, so there's that.

Hand on the butt of the .45, I crack the closet...and jump at the sound of a key in the front door. Better believe DeNiro clears the holster in a heartbeat as the door swings inward.

"What the hell?" A scrawny young guy with a nose the size of a foam finger at a football game bugeyes the trashed room...and then he sees DeNiro. "Shit!"

"Freeze!" I go full cop-voice on him, demanding compliance. "Hands on your head, *now!*"

Those hands snap up like his arms are rubber bands, and I ease toward him. "Turn around!"

He does, and I frisk him one-handed, keeping DeNiro at the ready. Soon, I'm satisfied he's packing weed and nothing else.

I sit him on the bed, then shut and lock the door. A couple questions at DeNiro-point later, I know his name, profession, and reason for being there.

As in Boris, stand-up comic, and he's one of Don's roommates.

"Where is he? Where's Don?" DeNiro's fixed on him like a cobra staring at a mouse.

Good thing Boris is stoned, or I think he might cry. "Don't *you* know? Aren't you one of *them*?"

"Them who?"

"The *stalkers*."

I fight to keep my tone even. "Be more specific."

"Don said they've been *after* him. Something to do with that *weirdo* who heckled his *set* last week at the *funeral*. I came home a couple nights later, and the place was like *this*, and Don was *gone*."

"He did a set at a *funeral*?" The crazy just keeps coming. "What *funeral*? Where?"

"Shit, I don't remember." Boris rakes his hands through his hair in a minor panic. "There's a set at *every* funeral these days!"

"I wonder." I walk over and press the barrel of the .45 to his forehead. "Who'll do the set at *your* funeral?"

Given the proper DeNiro-vation, Boris miraculously remembers.

Next morning, light on sleep and heavy on coffee, I show up at the cemetery Boris told me about. And I realize the kid wasn't kidding.

Because sure enough, there's a comic doing stand-up at a funeral-in-progress. Not only that, but there's a *clown*.

They're both *performing*, and the crowd is *laughing their asses off*. Even as the cemetery staff is lowering a casket into a grave in front of them.

"So I said to him, 'that's no way to treat a fish!'" The comic, a skinny middle-aged bald guy in a bright yellow t-shirt with a Bronx cheer on the chest, gets a huge roar of laughter from the crowd. "Now *that's* what I call *killing*." He holds the mic over the grave and smirks. "Time to *drop the mic*, did you say?"

Everyone howls and cheers, except the clown, who blows into a freaky, whooping whistle.

"Hey, lady." The comic grins at a woman in a black veil in the middle of the front row. "You said you'd take that guy till death did *part* of you, right? So what about the *rest* of you?"

Again, the cemetery echoes with peals of laughter.

Unamused, I work my way around the perimeter of the crowd to an African-American woman standing off to the side. She looks like she's in charge, so I take a shot.

"Excuse me." I step up beside her. "I'm looking for the funeral director."

"You've found her." The woman, who's laughing along with the crowd, glances over at me. I'm thinking she's in her fifties, with a look of class and authority to her. She's wearing a flattering black pantsuit and a men's hat--a black fedora with a narrow brim, high peak, and red satin band to match the piping on her outfit.

"Good." I reach over and shake her hand. "I'm Detective Gould. Call me Gus."

"Lorraine." She's still laughing and can't keep her eyes off the clown. "Lorraine Burroughs. What can I do for you?"

"My son, Donovan Gould, does stand-up." I pull Don's photo out of my wallet and hold it in front of her face. "I heard he did a set at a funeral for you last week."

"Correct." She leans to one side to keep watching the clown, who's carrying a cream pie toward the audience. "He bombed, by the way."

I put the photo back in my wallet. "I heard someone heckled him."

"Yeah, so?" Lorraine's mesmerized as the clown walks up and down the front row of the crowd, holding the cream pie at the ready.

Fed up, I step in front of her, blocking her view. "Tell me about the heckler."

She's pissed but paying attention now. "You mean *Potato Face?* Sure! He was here. He told your boy if he couldn't get a laugh in *this* town, he ought to have his *head* examined."

"What else can you tell me about him?"

"Actually, he came to see me after the set," says Lorraine. "Told me to *text* him if I ever came across anyone as *unfunny* as your son. Which I *haven't.*"

"He gave you a number?"

"It's in my phone." There's a burst of excited laughter and applause from the crowd, and she jumps around, trying to see over or around me. "What happened? Did somebody get *pied*?"

I block her like a Mack truck. "You'll find out." I point to her front hip pocket, where I see the top of her oversized phone sticking out. "Just as soon as you give me that number."

I use Lorraine's own phone to make first contact, establishing that she personally recommended me. Then, I text from my own phone (a cop phone that doesn't provide my I.D. to callers), telling "Potato Face" I've found someone unfunny he might be interested in.

There's no answer right away, so it's time to play the waiting game. Not that I have any intention of sitting still.

There's something I've been putting off doing. Not to mention, that bit about the heckler telling Don to get his head examined gave me an idea.

I drive back downtown to the local hospital--sorry, *health center*--and dig out that photo again. I flash it at one receptionist, orderly, doctor, and nurse after another...even a random patient here and there. I ask them if they've seen this man, but there's no sign of recognition or interest.

Until the Japanese woman, that is.

We both approach the same nurse's aide at the same time, and she lets me take my turn first. She watches and listens, though, as I show Don's photo and come up with the usual goose egg.

In fact, she doesn't even say whatever she'd meant to say to the aide. Instead, she starts talking to me.

"You seem sad," she says. "You *shouldn't* be."

I frown. "Why not? My *son* is missing."

"No, no." She's young--late twenties? She's pretty, too, with short black hair and an oval face with deep blue eyes. "I meant you should not be *sad* because *no one* in this town is sad."

I put Don's photo away. It turns out Nina Kita--the Japanese woman--is the only one I've found in the hospital with any kind of insight to offer.

"'Happy Town.'" She wraps a Japanese accent around the perfect English she speaks. "That's what I call it. The town that laughs and never cries."

An orderly passes, pushing a gurney with a middle-aged woman on it. She and the orderly laugh and laugh for no apparent reason.

"Listen." Nina slips her hands in the pockets of her lemon yellow sweater. "Do you *hear* any sadness?"

As we continue down the corridor, I'm very aware of what I'm hearing...and none of it is unhappiness. There's not a single sob or groan from any of the rooms, not a trace of pain or suffering.

In the middle of a hospital.

Nina takes me to the emergency room, where the soundtrack's the same. Paramedics wheel in two horribly injured clowns, missing body parts and covered in blood--and they're laughing like they're on an amusement park ride. The same goes for the nurses and doctors who treat them, and the woman with the bruises all over her face, and the young guy with the gunshot wound in his side.

"I am a reporter for an online magazine based in Japan," says Nina. "I came here to do a story on a rising comedy boomtown in America's heartland. Instead, I am investigating the theft of all *sadness* from an entire *town*."

We leave the E.R. and head down another corridor. Along the way, we pass a middle-aged doctor who can barely keep a straight face as he tells a giggling young couple that their child has just died from leukemia.

It's the same throughout the hospital. Every baby in the

maternity ward is laughing instead of crying. Every patient receiving chemotherapy in the oncology department is yukking it up with knee-slapping merriment.

"You said you're looking for your son?" asks Nina. "How long was he here?"

"Not sure. A couple of weeks."

She stops and touches my arm. "I think that's all it takes, whatever 'it' is."

"I don't care, as long as I find him," I tell her.

At that moment, my phone dings, and I grab it. There's a text from the mystery number I texted earlier...but not much of one. All I see is a street address and room number, a location--in town, I assume.

"Gotta go." I pocket the phone. "Police business."

I'm packing serious heat, as usual, when I enter the nursing home--also packing serious butterflies in my gut. I'm well aware I could be walking into a trap...though I still don't grasp the whole picture.

Staying highly conscious of my surroundings, I stroll through the reception area like I've got every reason to be there. Checking the range of room numbers listed on the wall, I follow the arrow pointing right and head down the hallway in that direction.

The room I'm looking for--113--is on the right, at the end of the hall. Along the way, the sound of old people laughing with glee ripples out of every open doorway, making it hard to listen for signs of impending danger. Is that why Potato Face chose this location for our meeting?

Near the end of the hall, an old woman steps out of her room and waves both hands. "It's Henry! I think he's dead!" She giggles as she says it.

I hear running footsteps and look back to see a male nurse charge down the hallway. I step aside, and he races into the woman's room--laughing all the way.

Continuing after he passes, I finally get to 113. It's the first closed door I've seen here.

The hell with knocking, particularly if someone might be laying for me. My heart slam-dances in my chest as I gently tug the handle downward, easing the bolt out of the socket in the strike plate as quietly as I can.

To hear my butterflies tell it, there's a four-alarm fire of *watch-your-ass* going on in here, so I stay careful. I think of unholstering DeNiro, but don't want to scare away my contact or get unwanted attention from the staff.

Cracking the door, I peek inside--and see no one. I push it open further with the same result, then enter and close it behind me.

"Hello?" I'm in the living room, with doors to the bedroom and bathroom on either side. "Lorraine sent me."

The place is warm and smells of disinfectant and baby powder. A single brown easy chair with a blue fleece blanket slung over it sits facing a small flat-screen TV atop a stand. There's a table to the left of the chair, another table arrayed with old framed photos under the window, and not much else in the living room.

Except a little black camera in the far corner of the ceiling. "The text said to come here," I tell it as I inch toward the bedroom. "I came because I found someone else who isn't funny in this town."

Leaning around the door jamb, I steal a look into the little bedroom--and see no one. Reaching in, I flick on the light to make sure...

And hear exactly one telltale footfall on the carpet behind me. That's all the warning I get.

I whip around, ready to go to war--but it's already too late. I see a blur of motion, an impression of a hulking female figure in colorful scrubs, and something hard crashes into my skull.

DeNiro doesn't even make it out of his holster. I plunge right down into blackness with the sound of laughter ringing in my ears.

"Detective Gould? Hello? Detective?"

I wake to the voice of a stranger--a man's voice, deep and resonant. But the thing that makes the strongest impression on me has nothing to do with the type of voice it is.

What gets my attention is its *seriousness.* There is no trace of *laughter* in that voice.

My eyes flicker open, and the first words that come to mind when I see who's talking are the ones Lorraine used to describe him. Because "Potato Face" is right on the money.

"Ah, good. You're awake." The guy's head is oblong and lumpy, his skin light brown. His complexion is mottled, with scattered fuzzy spots like potato "eyes." And he's bald, with no scalp or beard stubble. "How's the head?"

Pounding, now that he mentions it. "Who the hell are you?"

"My name is Messenger." He has an off-kilter grin and eyes so dark, pupil and iris blend together. "My apology for the rough treatment."

The fog starts to clear, and I size up my situation. I'm on a cot, not restrained. I'm in the same clothes as before...but all three of my guns are gone.

Messenger backs away as I sit up. Looking around, I see four bare cinder block walls, painted beige, a metal door of the same color, and a bare lightbulb hanging from a cord overhead. There's a single folding chair set up five feet from the bed, and Messenger plants his bony ass on it.

"Where am I?" My head hurts harder, and I wince...then shake it off.

"Hades." Messenger grins like he's making a joke. "The source of a modern River Styx, if you will."

I could take him. He's older--sixties, at least--and on the scrawny side. I could overpower him and get the information I want.

But why do I have a feeling it won't be that simple? And what if I can get what I want out of him by other means?

"So, Messenger." I swing my legs off the bed and fold my hands between my knees, making no threatening moves. "I hear you caught my son's act last week. Donovan Gould?"

Messenger nods slowly. "The kid couldn't get a laugh to save his life. He was like the *antidote* to *funny*."

"And you were on the lookout for people like that, weren't you?" I lean forward and narrow my eyes. "Because why?"

He narrows his eyes, too, like he's chewing it over. "For the good of the project," he says finally. "And therefore, the good of the people."

"What project?"

"*Solace*." Messenger crosses his bony legs like a girl and clasps his knobby knee with both hands. "The most important top-secret black budget government project in history."

If it's so top-secret, and I've got no leverage, why is he telling me all this? Because he has no intention of letting me leave this room alive, maybe? "What's the objective of this Project Solace?"

"I'll tell you what the objective is *not*. It is *not* to trigger outbreaks of murderous violence against *clowns*."

I nod like I'm interviewing him for a newspaper. "But the outbreaks happened anyway."

Messenger frowns. "Blocking one prime emotional pathway created the potential for unpredictable detours along *other* pathways."

I think back to what I've seen since I came to town, and what Nina Kita told me. "How did you do it?" I ask. "How did you steal *sadness*?"

"Does it matter?" He spreads his arms, then drops them in his lap. "Suffice it to say, a *signal* is broadcast from this bunker, twenty-four/seven. Said signal alters human emotional response at a deep level, converting sadness into happiness, tears into laughter."

"And murderous violence."

"In *some*." Messenger holds up an index finger. "Only *some*. But the fact that it happened in this pilot project, with such a small population sampling, raised red flags about what might happen after rollout."

"Rollout?"

"Nationwide," says Messenger. "At which point, our results could potentially propagate throughout a much *larger* sample size."

"I see." That's what I say, but I'm having a bitch of a time wrapping my brain around this. Whatever I expected to find out in the search for Don, it didn't come close to *this.*

"Do you see why your son was such a godsend?" asked Messenger. "He was a known outlier. Something about him countered the effects of Solace, which suggested he might point us to the bug in our system...the one creating unpredictable violent interactions."

I don't like how he keeps throwing around the word "was." Don *was* a godsend. He *was* a known outlier. "And *did* he point you to the bug?"

"Oh, yes." Messenger's lopsided grin comes back. "It was all in the cadence of his performance, you see." His fingers twitch and weave as if to illustrate. "*All* human communication consists of encoded information and commands, transmitted in such a way as to evoke certain responses. It's a form of *mind control,* if you will...like *software* controlling a *computer.* Only *his* unique signal disrupted the response triggered by *our* signal."

My head hurts worse, and my frown deepens. "*Don* made people *kill* those *clowns?*"

Messenger sighs. "It's not that simple. Remember how I said that blocking one emotional pathway created the potential for detours along other pathways?"

I nod.

Messenger's gestures become more excited. "What I'm saying is, an undesirable side effect was created by our system. It isn't *natural* to rob the human mind of the ability to experience and express sadness. That creates a *dissonance,* a potential to let off steam in other ways. In this case, an *inclination* toward extreme violence developed. All it took was a competing signal from your son to *unleash* that violent potential." Satisfied, he folds his hands over his chest. "But not anymore. The problem has been fixed."

"Because you took him. My son." I say it calmly. "And, what? Dissected him?"

"Detective Gould," snaps Messenger. "What do you think of what I've told you?" He leans forward and matches my pose, folding his hands between his knees. "You have stumbled upon something so

far beyond your *pay grade*, it's *terrifying*, isn't it?" Something hardens behind his eyes...suddenly, like the flash of a springing snake. "*And yet*, you are still *alive.*"

Our gazes are locked for a long, silent moment. The question works through me like a slow sickness, burrowing in deep.

"Well?" he asks. "What does that *tell* you?"

"I don't matter." My heart sinks as I say it.

He raises his eyebrows. "And...?"

"It's too late."

Messenger claps his hands. "Give the man a kewpie doll."

I'm torn, now, between collapsing in despair and tearing that guy a new one.

"*But...*" says Messenger. "Too late does not always mean...*too late.*"

This time, when he claps his hands, the door opens. And I am on my feet in an instant without thinking.

"See what I mean?" asks Messenger. "*Capiche?*"

I sprint across the room, raising my arms...but not to strike. Because the person standing there is not my enemy.

He is my son.

"Hi, Dad." There he is, still living and breathing, curly black hair and all. Ropy arms, skinny torso, bright green eyes, and all.

I throw my arms around him and squeeze almost hard enough to break a rib. And I don't *care.* I can't *think*, I can't *control*, I can't *speak.*

But Messenger can, and does. "You are both free to go, with our thanks."

"But aren't you afraid we'll tell someone about all this?" Don can barely get the words out through my squeezing.

"Good question," says Messenger. "How about if I tell you *why* we're stealing people's sadness, and see how you feel about it *then*?"

Later that night, two guys walk into a bar...and the guys are *us.* Me and Donovan.

The bar is in Heavy, Ohio, so of course there's stand-up comedy in progress and a cracking-up crowd. But Don and I take up residence at the farthest corner of the bar and basically ignore it.

I order a shot and a beer, and he gets some kind of cider shit, and we toast silently. No words are needed as we clink glasses, beer against cider. We already know what we're happy about.

And the rest of it, too.

Don drinks and watches the crowd as they laugh at whatever the comic's saying over there. "We'll be like *them* soon. Couple of giggling idiots."

The longer you stay in town, the more you'll be affected. That's what Messenger told us. *Then we'll roll out across the entire country, changing it all from coast to coast.*

"Sooner the better." That's how I feel about it, now that we know what we know.

"Some screwed-up shit, Dad." Don clinks his glass against mine again. Guess I'm lucky we have this time before the change--that being in the shielded Solace bunker kept him normal long enough for us to share this moment.

Because I think I'll actually *miss* it, believe it or not. Sharing our sorrows, consoling each other. Knowing we're not alone and feeling better because of it.

But holy shit, what I *won't* miss is feeling shitty about what's coming. I don't think I could handle *that.*

Given the choice, I would much rather laugh.

Messenger was right about that. How else could I face the truth--could *anyone* face the truth--about a bioweapon already unleashed worldwide? An unstoppable, incurable infection that steals humanity's ability to reproduce?

Who could *live* feeling the full weight of that? The burden of absolute misery that comes with knowing there'll be *no more babies.*

And therefore, sooner or later, no more humanity.

Not me. Not Don, either. Maybe just Messenger, who has to stay at the wheel to ensure the rest of the human race gets a mental vacation.

I feel bad for him. For now, at least.

"So what do you think?" I ask my beautiful son on the barstool beside me. "What say we raise a little hell tonight?"

"Seriously?" He looks at me sideways. "Aren't you the one who says a cop has to stay on the straight and narrow at all times?"

"Why sweat it?" I slap him on the back and smile. "I've got a feeling we'll just laugh about it later."

SHOW ME YOURS

Charging out of the alley and around the corner, I nearly collide with an exposed penis in my path. Stumbling to a stop, I barely avoid the prominent organ.

"Shit! Sorry!" Stammering out the words, I consider dodging to either side of the penis' owner, but he's mountainous. He towers over me, so tall his penis is right at my eye level, sticking out of his chest. I want to look past it, and him, to see if the other guy, the one I was chasing, has gotten away—but all I can see is that penis.

All I can see is that glowing blue pyramid of a penis, its inner light pulsing with high excitement.

"Watch where you're going!" The penis' owner finally plows past me and shimmies down the sidewalk in his black leather pants, his blue pyramid penis shooting beams of bright blue light in all directions.

Finally clear to pick up the trail, I run into the celebrating crowd on the street…but no luck. If my quarry is anywhere in that mass of humanity, I don't see him. His shock of bright red hair, which served as a moving target for me to follow, has disappeared.

Everyone dances and drinks around me, whooping it up in

revealing outfits and penis-themed costumes. Could there *be* more distractions per square foot? And could they be more *fitting*?

My runner could not have picked a better place to lose himself than the International Penis Expo here in Phallus Corners, Sexas.

Continuing onward, I see everything and everyone *but* him. I see green octagonal penises growing out of shoulders…purple cube penises flashing on kneecaps…even spherical penises orbiting their owners' skulls like moons, cycling through a rainbow of different colors. In other words, it's a typical selection of human male organs circa 2720 A.D., though the sheer numbers and shameless exposures are breathtakingly distracting.

If only these revelers knew that a penis unlike any other could be somewhere among them. They'd be all over its owner like chickens on a juicy *cucaracha*.

Further along, the crowd thickens, slowing me down. I look around frantically, bumping into penises left and right, but my search is fruitless. Codename Churrito has escaped me again.

Combing my fingers through my shaggy black hair, I sigh. In the middle of a mob full of penises, I am left empty-handed.

"I'll have one of those, please." I point at the chocolate-dipped hot dog on the menu of a food cloud at the Expo, and a swarm of tiny yellow penises, fist-shaped and fork-winged, lifts one out of a glittering bin. My mouth waters as they fly it my way, a major diet-buster but who the hell cares? I need some consolation after losing my target in the crowd.

Can you blame me? I've been chasing Churrito—real name Claude "Cobra" Corben of Leastways, Carnalfornia—for weeks and ferreting out his existence for years before that.

For the longest time, people like him were thought to be myths, and I was a laughingstock for believing in them. The ridicule was especially extreme when my various expeditions in search of the truth came up empty. It was enough to make me question my own belief and sanity, to start wondering if maybe the doubters had been right all along.

Then new clues landed in my lap…though even after that, I found it increasingly hard to believe. Even after I read the rumors in the MemberNet groups, bought some blurry photos, and tracked down Churrito himself at the Expo, it all seemed too good to be true. Even when I approached him at the Art of the Penis exhibit, asked him point-blank if he knew where I could find the One True Penis, and saw the look of surprise on his face, the look of being exposed for the secret he carried, I still didn't dare to believe all the way.

Then *boom*, he knocked me down and charged off into the crowd, leaving me no doubt that I'd finally found the true root of the not-so-mythical stories.

And all I can say after that is, *What now?*

As if in reply, the phone in my nose picks that moment to buzz. I squeeze my nostrils to take the call, and there she is, my boss, Trish Forshortta.

"Did you catch him?" She sounds impatient. "Did you bag that Churrito guy yet?"

"Unfortunately, no." I hate giving her the bad news, but she'll find out sooner or later—and the later it is, the angrier she'll get. "He got away. I lost him in the crowd."

"Then go get him!" Trish, who's managing my current expedition on behalf of our employer, Penis State University, is determined I won't drop the ball again. "Where do you expect him to go next?"

"I don't know." I think for a long moment, wondering what Churrito's next destination might be. "He makes a living selling designer penis knockoffs on the black market, and this is the biggest show of the year. I can't imagine where else he might go from here."

"Maybe he's going nowhere, then," says Trish. "As big as that show is, maybe he's staying right there."

Frowning, I chew a bite of choco-hot dog. Maybe she's onto something. "I guess it wouldn't hurt to check around. Maybe Churrito doubled back after he lost me."

"Good idea, Spinnaker," she tells me. "Now get out there and bring him in, if he's such hot shit. Don't expect me to do *all* your work for you."

"I don't."

"After all, weren't you the one who convinced me to greenlight this little shit-show expedition? Weren't you the one who insisted that recessive genes had finally regained dominance, expressing the traits of the One True Penis after centuries, and you were on the cusp of uncovering it?"

"Yes."

"Weren't you the one who convinced Penis State to fund this latest trip because you said you finally had a decisive, tangible lead on the possessor of the One True Penis?"

"Yes."

"And weren't you the one who swore up and down that the sixth time would be the charm?" says Trish. "That this would be the breakthrough that makes a mint for Penis State and more than makes up for the last five failed expeditions?"

I let out a sigh. "Yes, it was me."

"I thought so," says Trish. "And you do remember what will happen if you blow it again, right? If you don't find Churrito after we poured all those resources into your little quest and put our honor on the line?"

"Bye-bye funding." I quote her word for word. "Bye-bye research. Bye-bye…bye-bye…" It's hard for me to finish, to name the ultimate price.

I've truly risked *everything* to find this mythical penis packer.

"Bye-bye *life*," says Trish. "Your failed projects and personal shortcomings have pretty much totaled your reputation. This is your *last chance*, Carthage, and you're damn *lucky* you got it."

"Don't worry," I tell her. "I'll find Churrito and deliver the One True Penis as promised. I won't let you down, Trish."

The stakes could not be higher.

You know how myths and legends can really grab you when you're a kid? That's how it was when I, Carthage Spinnaker, latched onto the One True Penis.

I was ten years old when I first read about it. My parents' marriage was melting down, so the time was right to sink my teeth into such a distraction.

Twenty-five years later, I'm still under the spell of the OTP. I'm still fascinated by that mysterious organ of the distant past.

It has been at least 500 years since one was last seen in the wild…so long, in fact, and after so much of civilization's knowledge was destroyed by wars and catastrophes, that its original appearance is long forgotten. Maybe its purpose, too, for all we know.

Yet the penises of today—what the One True Penis evolved into—have never been more popular. People celebrate their multitude of forms the world over, even worshipping them in some quarters. Geneticists and cybernetic designers never stop dreaming up outrageous variations to make them even more elaborate and exciting.

With that kind of interest, imagine what could happen if someone like me turns up the original model. Why else would I become a phallic historian at Penis State University, mounting expeditions to follow up on leads that might balloon into stunning discoveries if they don't turn out to be dead ends first?

But now I'm down to my last stab at this quest. I've cried wolf too many times, spent a fortune on too many goose chases. I've lost my credibility on dark side benders, gotten in with bad crowds who hooked me on drug-shaped penises, causing me to end up in genital rehab. Now I've got to produce or lose everything.

I just wish the lead on Churrito were stronger, more than a rumor and some blurred-out photos. I wish my confidence wasn't so flaccid, my skin so thin.

And I wish ritual suicide wasn't on the menu if I fail. Who cares about the honor of my supervisor Trish and Penis State University? It isn't worth killing myself over, that's for sure. In the grand scheme of things, honor means so much less than so many other things…like the hope of a child, for example.

For the sake of my ten-year-old self—not just my adult self's survival—I hope Churrito won't let me down. That little boy is still part of me, and he still wants to know the truth about the OTP, whatever it costs.

The stadium roars with excitement as I take a seat in the stands. Down on the field, the Penis Tournament has begun, and the fans are flipping out over the full-tilt, action-packed contest.

Two lines of athletes face off down there, penises exposed and active. One side is dressed in bright blue uniforms, the other in electric gold…but each individual has a penis that is uniquely his own. It's penis versus penis in the blazing sunlight, fighting to conquer each other and uplift their respective teams.

Truly, it is a spectacle. As I watch, a huge, silver, corkscrew-shaped penis jutting out of the back of one brawny player smashes against the red brick wall-shaped penis floating in front of a player on the opposite line. A glittering cloud of a penis engulfs the whirling razor-studded beast of a penis trying in vain to slash it to bits. At the same time, a penis shaped like a ten-foot-tall dragon goes to town against a penis like a shimmering soap bubble with its owner afloat in the middle in a fetal position.

Normally, I'd be as caught up in this combat as everyone else, but I can't get my mind off Churrito. The more I think about it, the more I think Trish was right about him still being here somewhere. The problem is, the expo is massive, and the crowds swarming it are vast. Finding that prick could be next to impossible.

And that's with me already knowing what he came here for in the first place. You'd think knowing he's a black-market penis trader seeking to cash in on knockoff designer penises might narrow down his likely route through the expo…but guess again. Lowlifes and highlifes alike flock to this event to make a killing; wherever there's a penis of value, you better believe someone's future happiness is riding on it.

Or in my case, my very *life* is doing the riding. Trish's threat over the nose-phone was dead serious. Organizational honor is everything these days; if you let down your employer enough times, your life is forfeit, and you're expected to pay the debt by your own hand.

I knew it was coming, I guess. I knew bringing in Churrito was a longshot…but at least it was something. At least it gave me hope and a reason not to give up.

Why couldn't he have been someone simpler to find, like one of the Penis Fighters on the field right now? Just look at them jousting down there—the dragon penis blasting great gouts of flame at the soap bubble penis, the brick wall penis crashing down on the silver corkscrew penis, the razor-studded penis dispersing the cloud penis with gusts from its whirling blades. Again and again, the crowd roars at their blistering strikes, cheering the visceral conflict between penises and men.

I'm not even sure that Churrito, if indeed he has the One True Penis, could compete in that struggle. For the OTP is a very different animal altogether.

The organ has been redesigned and redefined so often, it has become many things, all of them dazzlingly different. Whether any of them remotely resembles the one true original is impossible to say.

About the only thing that seems to have carried down through the centuries is the functionality. Penises today, like those in days of yore, serve as ornamental plumage, initiating courtship and mating rituals between the genders of humankind. The more elaborate the plumage, the more likely your chosen member of the other gender will agree to merge genetic material with you and cook up a new person at the nearest vend-o-child machine.

Beyond the basic knowledge of shared purpose, however, no one knows what the original One True Penis really looked like—though speculation runs rampant.

Perhaps it's because of this mystery that penises have become such an obsession in our culture. Maybe it's the very reason there's an International Penis Expo with a Penis Tournament and people like Churrito cashing in on knockoff designer penises under the radar.

That, I realize, is probably where I'll find him—under the radar, doing what he came here to do. All I have to do is pin down exactly where on the map of this place he might go to best accomplish that task.

To do that, I have to pump the right people for information… and I think I know just where to meet them.

The tall, muscular, blond-haired guy at the door of the shed spreads the feather-shaped penises along his shoulders, fanning them into a colorful crest behind his head. Each feather has an eye-shaped adornment near the tip, metallic blue in color, with a full spectrum of hues in rippled stripes along the rest of the length of the quill.

"I heard there's a meeting here tonight," I tell the guy. "When does it start? I could use some help right now."

He narrows his bright green eyes at me. "Addicts only. You sick?"

It isn't hard for me to summon up the desperation always lurking under my surface. When it comes to the One True Penis, I'm as obsessed as they come. "Absolutely." I nod emphatically.

He tips his head and ruffles his plumage. "Got an admission ticket?"

I pull a fat stack of black foil cash out of my pants pocket and hand it over. "This oughtta cover it."

The penis-crested guy smiles and steps aside, counting the cash as he ushers me into the musty shed.

Inside, seven men on folding chairs are gathered in a circle, with a few others standing around the perimeter. A single light bulb dangles from the ceiling in the middle of the circle, glowing dimly.

The chairs are all taken, so I stand beside a bald, middle-aged guy leaning against the wall. He and the others all have one thing in common, as do I.

No visibly exposed penises.

"I think about penises constantly," says a black-bearded, heavyset man in the chair circle. "But only the forbidden ones. The kind it's against the law to see or touch."

"The evil penises," another man in the circle says knowingly. "The ones that can hurt or kill."

"*Black metal ones,*" says another, his voice a hushed whisper. "*Spiked, heated, fanged.*"

The black-bearded, heavyset man grunts in agreement. "I should never have come to this expo. There are just too many opportunities to do the wrong thing. You can find *anything* for the right price here."

That's when I speak up. "Where?" This is what I've been waiting for. "Tell me where exactly I can find anything for the right price around here."

The bald guy leaning beside me shakes his head. "Don't go looking for trouble, friend. You need to resist temptation."

"That's why I want to know where it *is*," I say. "So I can avoid it."

"I'm telling you, you're better off not knowing," says the bald guy. "Otherwise, you risk being drawn there. Your urges will take over and pull you in."

"I can handle it, I promise you." I look at each of them in turn, casting a gaze of the deepest sincerity. "Please just tell me where I can find the biggest and best black market at the expo. If not, trust me, I'll be more likely to go down a bad path. I won't be able to think about anything else until I find what I'm looking for and give in to my desires. I will beg, borrow, or steal to get the best penis and make it my own."

This is why I came here to Members Anonymous. Where better to get a line on the best black-market penis dealers than here, among the addicts? Every one of them has one foot in this meeting and the other in a dark alley, clinching a sale.

And they're just dying to live vicariously through me, because make no mistake, they want nothing more than to do exactly what they think I'm going to do.

Which is rush out, buy a dangerous contraband penis, and swap out the old model for the new. Goodbye ugly green party favor growing out of your right nipple, hello sleek silver mercury beads rolling around your body in gleaming swirls while piping exotically mesmerizing music that makes everyone who hears it want to be your special friend.

"Okay." The black-bearded, heavyset guy is the first to break. I can see it in his eyes, I've got him stoked. "Take this." He pulls out a business card and scribbles something on the back of it with a marker. "Whatever you do, avoid the Super Shadow Secret Sale at this location tonight."

I take the card with a grateful smile. "Thank you." I give them a jaunty wave on the way out. "Good luck with all your journeys on the road to staying clean."

Good luck managing your disease, which I can identify with big time. Because scientific curiosity isn't the only reason I'm chasing the One True Penis.

If I showed them the inferior phallus I was born with—a lumpy gray toad thing tucked inside my left armpit—they'd realize I know all about penis envy.

Have you ever heard that song about wishing on a star? Well, I'm thinking they should change it to wishing on a penis.

Because the place where I've found the Super Shadow Secret Sale is a dream come true. I mean it, I could *live* here.

Sprawling in the open air between yellow-and-white-striped circus tents, far from the busiest midway of the expo, I come across row after row of dealers' tables, every one of them overloaded with all things illegally penile.

Never before have I seen so much genital contraband in one place. Tables overflow with gun-shaped penises, drug-shaped penises, knife-shaped penises, creature-shaped penises, and more. Dealers of all genders ply their wares to throngs of buyers, both sides constantly haggling over everything.

I don't know if my eyes have ever been bigger than they are right now as I take it all in. The sights and sounds and smells are overwhelming. I feel like I'm in a dream, my every deepest craving laid out around me in an endless buffet.

There are piles of dagger-shaped penises, squid-shaped

penises, penises with whips and flames and psychedelic eyes. I run my hands over bouquets of flower-shaped penises, listen to the tinkle of penises made of music, admire bottles of liquid penises with a multitude of flavors, textures, and side effects. I chuckle at a bin of human head-shaped penises that shapeshift to look like me as I walk by.

But the thing that blows me away the most isn't merchandise at all. A crowd forms at the far end of the marketplace; I glimpse a man in the middle of it but quickly lose sight of him...and then the show begins.

Multicolored streamers scream up in the air and explode. Balls of light hurtle overhead like moons and burst apart in glittering showers of sparks. Rockets leap high and pop, unfolding in rings and hearts and faces and butterfly wings.

The crowd cheers and claps as one fireworks-shaped penis after another erupts in the sky, bathing them all in red, white, green, and yellow glows. They go out of their minds with joy when the finale turns the night into day—barrages of light and color and noise going off in quick succession, flaring and thundering again and again like an out-of-control bombardment.

It's so beautiful, I get a frisson of sweet shivers on the nape of my neck. Gazing up, I'm swept away, transported to another realm where awe and delight are commonplace and death lays not so heavy upon the heads of the living.

When the last light flickers and the final boom echoes through the market, the crowd parts, and I get a look at the man who launched the show. The possessor of the fireworks-shaped penis is tall, spindly, and dark-skinned, draped in shimmery silken robes of many colors. His hair is spun from bright white light, and his eyes are fiery red; as he stands there, drinking in the applause, tiny versions of his fireworks go off around him in a cloud of dancing flashes, swirls, and percussion.

I am transfixed. That is, without exception, the most impressive penis I have ever laid eyes on. For a while, my reason for being here is completely forgotten.

Then, I catch sight of a familiar shock of red hair across the way, and it all rushes back to me. *There he is.*

My last chance for redemption stands at a market table not twenty feet away, dressed in black…and he's too busy haggling with a customer to look in my direction.

Churrito.

I force myself to approach slowly, eyes drifting aimlessly, looking at anything and anyone but him. Spooking him before I get close could be disastrous; he could disappear in the crowd before I lay a finger on him.

Heart pounding, I draw up beside the Chinese customer he's haggling with, keeping my eyes on the table. Churrito's knockoff designer penises are displayed there, shaped like gleaming gemstones of blue, red, and green the size of artichokes.

"That's a lot of money you're asking." The tubby customer shakes his head reluctantly but can't stop staring at the jewel-shaped penises. "I'm just not sure they're worth that much."

"You're right." Churrito grins and holds up a blue gem, watching it twinkle. "They're worth *lots* more than that. *Three* times more, at least, but I need the cash now. You should *jump* at this deal."

That's when I lean in and speak up. "He has a point, you know." I meet Churrito's gaze. "A penis in the hand is worth two in the bush."

I'm already grabbing his wrist by the time he recognizes me from the Art of the Penis exhibit. I squeeze so tight, the blue gem-shaped penis falls from his fingers and hits the ground.

"Shit!" Eyes wide, he struggles to break away. "Let me go!"

"Are you a cop?" shouts the customer. "Is this a bust?"

"Hell no," I tell him. "I could care less about this sketchy swap meet."

The customer's relieved enough to scoop up the red and green gem-shaped penises before he bolts into the crowd. Churrito doesn't try to stop him; he's too busy lurching to one side, trying to haul me off my feet…but I won't drop. Quickly trying a new strategy, he throws himself back, dragging me onto the table so hard it snaps in two under my weight.

I fall but don't let go, taking him down with me. We end up in a tangle of limbs on the ground, grappling.

I get in a couple of shots, and I think I'll beat him soon…but then he lands a lucky blow to my left armpit, the most sensitive part of my body. He punches me square in the toad-shaped penis, and I can't hold on. Stabbing pain lances my underarm, and I roll away, howling.

Churrito scrambles to his feet and sprints away before I even make it off the ground. But losing him means *suicide*, so there's no way in *hell* he gives me the slip and I get the shaft.

Pushing down the pain in my privates, I jump up and charge after him like a maniac, shoving aside everyone who stumbles into my path. He weaves through a jumble of passersby, knocking them around like bowling pins, but I manage to keep his red hair in sight.

Until I don't. Until suddenly, the red hair vanishes in the crowd.

I race up to the last place I saw him, right along one of the circus tents, and he's gone. I look in every direction, finding nothing—until a crease in the base of the tent's canvas catches my eye.

Without hesitation, I dive down and slither under that canvas.

Inside, the tent is dimly lit by a few scattered bulbs hung from its frame. Hopping to my feet, I take a look around, hoping to spot Churrito…but he's either in hiding or has left the tent altogether.

Stepping away from the canvas wall, I see I'm in one of the performance venues for the expo—a small one, where events like the Penis Cosplay Contest or Phallus Drag Competition might take place. Rows of bleachers are arranged around a circular central space, a patch of ground where the main attraction will take center stage during a performance. Crates and equipment crowd the area behind the seating, throwing shadows that could easily hold a hiding place for Churrito if he's lurking there.

Cautiously, I work my way around the perimeter, listening for telltale noises and searching for flickers of movement or light. I hear and see nothing of the sort, to the point that I consider leaving the tent and looking elsewhere for my quarry.

Then, suddenly, I hear scuffing sounds in quick succession behind me, and I realize I've walked into a trap.

Turning, I barely register the onrushing figure before it slams into me, tackling me facedown on the ground. As soon as I hit, the beating begins—one strike after another bashing into my skull and back.

Churrito has more guts than I gave him credit for, ambushing me like this. Maybe he's sick and tired of being on the run; maybe he senses I'll never give up unless he deals with me the hard way. I doubt he knows it's a life-or-death situation for me, though. If he did, he might dig a little deeper.

He might not let me flip him off my back so easily.

Suddenly rolling to one side with everything I've got, I buck him free, sending him tumbling into the dirt. He goes down hard with a grunt as I roll back the other way and onto my hands and knees.

I don't want to hurt him or damage the One True Penis, but I can't risk him getting away again. I leap at him with fists flying, landing a blow to his head so solid it makes my arm tingle. He shakes it off, and I go in again, pasting a second punch smack across his kisser.

This time, he collapses in the dirt.

Leaning back, I want to take a moment to catch my breath… but I can't wait. After coming so far and sacrificing so much, I need to see it. I need to see the One True Penis in the flesh, up close and personal.

And know for a fact that my life is saved.

Where to begin?

His penis, unlike so many, isn't evident at first glance. There's no feathered crest or ten-foot-tall dragon or glittering cloud or fireworks show. There are no orbiting spherical penises cycling through rainbows of kaleidoscopic light.

Whatever he's packing, I'll have to look under his clothes to see it.

Hoping no one walks in, I start by pulling up his black shirt—but everything's clear under there. I see no penis on his chest or belly or under his arms. Rolling him over on his side, I see nothing of interest on his back, either.

Time to lower my search. Heart hammering, I roll him back over and tug the waist of his black pants with both trembling hands, easing them over his hips.

At first, I see nothing of interest, just a smooth abdomen, and I pause. What happens if nothing's there, and my death warrant's guaranteed? I almost want to leave the truth undiscovered and run away, though that would guarantee my end, as well.

Not to mention, I've come too far not to know. I've waited most of my life for this revelation. Life or death, I *can't* stop now.

So I pull the pants further, sliding them the rest of the way over his hips. Still, the secret's unrevealed; a pair of black underpants blocks my view.

Taking a deep breath, I reach for the waistband. With trembling fingers, I slowly drag it down over his hips.

Then, with a gasp, I pull my hands away. What's there is not at all what I expected to see.

Sad and short, it lays limp amid a patch of curly red hair. Flesh-colored and tubular, it's attached to his lower abdomen, dangling at the juncture of his legs.

By far, it's the least impressive specimen I've ever seen in my life. At best, it looks like a pale worm or noodle, an organ without any of the marvelous ornamentation so common among the penises of today.

If it has features or powers of any kind, they're not evident. It doesn't dance with light or change color or spin or transform. It doesn't multiply or play music or control minds.

It just lies there. I poke it with my finger, and nothing changes.

My heart sinks. This can't possibly be the glorious throwback I imagined, the divine ancestor of today's wild variety. It's not even close.

Just then, my nose-phone rings. I squeeze my nostrils, and Trish's voice pipes into my head.

"What's the good word, Spinnaker?" she asks. "Have you found the One True Penis, or is it suicide time?"

I continue to stare at the sorry specimen. No one, least of all

Trish, would believe *that's* the OTP. No one would accept its return, through the magic of genetic engineering, to the modern male genome. Why *would* they want to reintroduce that shabby, wilted thing to a world where so many penises are glorious works of art?

No one will buy this as the One True Penis.

"Spinnaker?" says Trish. "Hello?"

As if to mock me, the fireworks-shaped penis goes off again outside, its colorful lights flaring on the tent's canvas. It makes me want to collapse in absolute despair, surrendering to the inevitability of my fate.

Almost.

"Hey, can you hear me?" says Trish. "I asked if you've found the One True Penis."

The lights continue to dance and flicker. I can't look away.

"Absolutely," I tell her. "I'm bringing it your way tomorrow."

One night later, it all comes together.

The big presentation is happening outdoors, on the main quad of Penis State University, under a star-studded sky. There couldn't be a better setting for my redemption and salvation than right here on this vast green sward in the heart of my sponsor institution.

Trish and the Trustees of the university are all smiles as my friend and I approach on foot, and we're all smiles, too. It feels great knowing life is going our way, and we're about to change the world.

"Welcome back, Spinnaker!" Trish's expression as she waves is a mix of excitement and uncertainty, which makes sense. In spite of my assurances over the phone, she isn't sure quite what to expect…and I've let her down before. "Congratulations on the end of your quest."

"Thank you, Trish." I breathe in the cool night air as I shake her hand firmly. I feel every moment keenly, with exquisite sensitivity, as this long-awaited event unfolds.

"And this is the soon-to-be-famous Churrito, I take it?" Trish looks over my shoulder at the companion I've brought with me, the man of the hour.

"Churrito is only a nickname." I step aside, gesturing at the figure behind me. "Ladies and gentlemen, meet Max Massif."

"We've heard so much about you." Trish steps toward him, hand extended. "Welcome, possessor of the One True Penis."

Max glances at me for a second, a spark of doubt that only I can see flickering in his fiery red eyes.

I nod and smile reassuringly. All he needs to do is believe in the truth we've established, which after all is the one best truth these people and everyone else in the world are prepared to accept.

"Thank you." Max's coal-black hand embraces her pale white one and gives it a firm shake. "It's wonderful being here."

"This is potentially an historic occasion," says Trish. "The whole world could transform after the One True Penis explodes on the scene."

"Spinnaker says there's no doubt." Grinning, Max scrubs his fingers through his short, curly hair spun from bright, white light. "He says everyone on Earth will want my penis soon."

Trish cocks her head. "Actually, that depends on what the One True Penis can do. Will you give us a demonstration, please? Spinnaker insisted on keeping it a surprise, no matter how much I begged for details."

"I'm *always* happy to demonstrate my penis." Max backs away from us, spreading his arms wide. Sparks and flashes dance under his multicolored silken robes, flickering along his arms and chest before leaping into the night sky.

Spheres of light burst overhead into sparkling constellations of many forms and hues. Booms and whistles fill the air as stardust showers the quad in a dazzling downpour. One blast after another surges forth, casting currents of light and shadow and sound throughout the campus.

The spectacle keeps building, becoming more elaborate with each passing second. Max gives it everything he's got, unleashing a show far superior to the ones I witnessed at the secret sale back at the Penis Expo…and surely much more satisfying than any performance the original Churrito's wet noodle might have provided. Instead of awkward laughter and snorts of derision, Trish and the Trustees erupt with oohs, aahs, and applause, their grins unselfconsciously rapt.

"Fantastic!" Trish shoots me a look of sheer delight. "Your life is saved, Spinnaker! Not only that, but you're guaranteed a promotion and a huge pay raise!"

"Thank you, Trish," I tell her. "Though in this case, it's true that the discovery itself is the greatest reward. The great leap forward is what makes the struggle most worthwhile."

"Well said." Trish returns her gaze to the sky as another volley launches and explodes. "This is more wonderful than I ever imagined, Spinnaker. Is it better than you imagined, too?"

Good question. What *did* I imagine the One True Penis would be like? This comes close…and I think it comes close for her, too.

She beams and claps as she watches the balls of light rise and burst, filling the sky with vibrant color. The light plays over her face like it's the face of a child, delighting in every flash and bang.

When she brushes against me, I feel warm inside, and I wonder if she feels the same way. I've never visited a vend-o-child machine with a woman at my side, but maybe sometime soon will be different.

The truest and best penises do that—bring people together. Inspire them. Thrill them. You don't get that from a pale worm or wet noodle.

Again, the sky explodes with brilliant light and color. That… now *that* is a penis. The one Trish expected, or close enough. The one *everyone* expects, or better. Whether it's the revived ancestor of today's penis population doesn't matter. All anyone cares about, when it comes to penises or anything in life, is what they imagine. Their dreams provide the outlines.

And a great penis, whether or not it's the OTP, fills in the gaps as nature intended.

"Yes, Trish." I can't stop grinning. "This is infinitely better than I thought it would be."

A great penis is all about the happy ending.

THE MERCHANT OF ELVES

"These are elf lands, all right." Crouching, Asa Grímsdóttir brushed her fingers over the mossy rock at her feet. "It's *very* plain to see."

"Damn." Ivar, the burly construction foreman, tugged at his thick red beard. "I *told* the bosses we should bring in a *psychic* before we ever broke ground."

"Now you've got a bunch of equipment that won't work right," said Asa, "all thanks to those mischievous elves."

Ivar shook his head. "How can something we never *see* cause so much *trouble?*"

"They're *experts.* They've been doing it as long as *humans* have lived in *Iceland.*" Asa's long blonde hair fluttered in the stiff breeze as she frowned at a nearby backhoe, which had been idle for days. "And you're falling further behind schedule by the minute."

"It's the Blue Lagoon all over again," said Ivar. "So how do we fix it?"

"The same way they fixed the Blue Lagoon project." Asa got to her feet and straightened her wooly sweater, its gray-and-white design mirroring the cloudy July sky. "We give the elves what they want, and they'll let us get on with it."

"You make it sound easy." Ivar, who was about Asa's age--

somewhere in his thirties--and having a really bad week, gnawed on nicotine chewing gum. "I guess you've had lots of dealings with these rascals, then."

Asa grinned and nodded. "I was born and raised in Iceland, wasn't I? Just like you."

She could see relief replacing skepticism on his face, and knew she was doing her job. Convincing clients of her intimate rapport with the Hidden People was the heart of her business, after all.

Though in truth, she'd never seen one in her life and wouldn't know what to do with it if she did.

"Want me to come with you?" asked Ivar. "Maybe I could talk to them directly."

"Sorry, no. That's not how it works." Asa shook her head and started off across the field of rippling igneous rock, the product of long-ago volcanic eruptions. In the back pocket of her jeans, she carried a note pad and pencil, the tools of her trade. She would use them to jot down the elves' demands--whatever she decided they would be.

Ivar, persistent, followed her. "Maybe they'll make an exception. *Lots* of folks see elves and trolls, don't they?"

"So they say." Asa smiled and held up a hand, signaling him to stay back. "Trust me, it's better if I go alone, Ivar. Think of it as like a drug deal. Nobody wants surprises, right?"

"Okay, okay." Ivar shook his shaggy head and stopped following. "I'll go grab a *skyr* and wait for you to get back. It's about time for a morning snack anyway."

"Perfect." *Skyr* is an Icelandic dairy product that's much like yogurt, though in reality it's a type of creamy cheese. Locals and tourists alike went crazy for the stuff, and Ivar was addicted. It was one thing he and Asa had in common...though the new, factory-made stuff was never quite as good as she remembered her grandma's homemade *skyr* being. Sometimes, she thought she would just about kill for a taste of her grandma's *skyr* again.

"Maybe I can go with you next time," said Ivar.

"We'll see."

Ivar raised an index finger as something occurred to him. "You know, I think *did* see an elf once or twice."

"Lucky you." Asa waved goodbye and set out across the stony, boulder-strewn plain. People told her the same thing all the time, that they'd seen elves or trolls or gnomes, and she didn't really believe them...but she always felt a little jealous, because she'd *never* seen one.

Asa was no more in tune with the elves and trolls than she was with Iceland's mythical thirteen Yule Lads or Grýla, their ogress mother. Still, she had her role to play in this dance, facilitating the interaction of the mundane and supernatural.

It was up to her to set the terms for resolving the supposed conflict. She was the one who would appease the elves, then assure the builders they could get back to work without further interference. The massive Magic Baths project--the latest attraction to fuel Iceland's tourist boom--could get back on track, easing the worried minds of businessmen with loads of investment at stake.

Then, *voila!* A paycheck would land in her hands, the most magical part of the whole exercise as far as Asa could see.

All in all, it wasn't a bad gig. She didn't even need to feel guilty about it, she thought, since many Icelanders believed in Hidden People already. As far as they were concerned, she was performing a valuable service. Even if it was more about making them feel better and preserving Icelandic traditions than interceding with any kind of supernatural being.

"Hello, my friends," she called as she walked onward. "I'm here to have a chat with you. Come out, wherever you are."

The wind picked up as she wound her way left toward some boulders. She zeroed in on one big rock in particular, blocky and waist-high, bigger than anything nearby. A bright blue square was painted on a bottom corner--an image of a door, complete with window and knob.

"There you are." Crouching, she rapped lightly on the door--a common sight in Iceland, painted by locals on the kinds of boulders where the Hidden People were said to live. "So what do you say about the construction site over there? The one for the new Magic Baths? What would it take to get you to let the workers finish the job?"

As expected, there was no answer, though she played it as if a two-sided conversation were in progress. It was always best, she'd found, to keep up the illusion as much as possible in case she was being observed from afar by the client.

"What's that? You want to see the plans?" Asa pulled out her pad and pencil and jotted a note. "I think we can do that. What else?"

For a moment, the only sound was the cold summer wind in her ears.

"You want your town preserved and kept together?" Again, she scribbled on the pad. "I'll have to look into that. What if they still need to move it?" She paused and pretended to listen. "Okay, I'll let you know what they say. What else?"

Again, she paused and "listened," then wrote. "Six buckets of Alabama Fried Chicken...okay. Two cases of Gull beer and two cases of Boli. Three dozen kleina pastries and seven supreme pan pizzas. Got it." Asa nodded. Adding such goodies to the order didn't hurt; since she didn't believe in elves, she had a hunch the treasures she demanded on their behalf found their way into the bellies of construction workers instead. Sometimes, in fact--though she had no proof of it--she wondered if the construction crews were the ones responsible for the troubles that slowed down projects and led to her hiring. If so, she wasn't about to short-change the folks responsible for her repeat business.

Just then, the ground beneath her feet rumbled without warning.

"Is that it? Anything else, guys?" Asa wagged the pad at the door. "Now's the time to ask."

Alarmed, Asa looked around, wondering if it would get much worse. Since the North American and European tectonic plates met in Iceland, and the island was rich in volcanic activity, earth-quakes weren't uncommon. Still, a sudden tremor might be cause for concern, depending on how it developed.

She started getting to her feet, then fell back when the

rumbling intensified. She decided to stay that way for the moment, guessing it would be better to keep low to the ground.

It turned out to be a bad plan. A fissure suddenly shot across the rocky surface toward her, running as fast as a lit fuse through the volcanic rock.

Heart pounding, she lunged to one side, but it was too late to escape. The fissure leaped through the rock under her with a loud crack.

And then it opened, just as fast, before she could scramble out of the way. She dropped with a cry, flailing at the thin air for some kind of grip to stop her descent...failing utterly to stay above-ground. Everything solid fell away under her, and she plummeted into darkness, ears roaring with the rumble of the quaking, split-ting earth.

Asa spun and tumbled through blackness, head spinning--then burst into a realm of bright, silvery light. All around her, the air was adrift with twinkling glitter, its lazy float disrupted by her swift passage. A small, silver sun blazed in the rock ceiling above, casting light throughout the glittering sky and over all the land below.

Asa fell further, mesmerized by the glitter, then came to a sudden stop...but not a rough one. Instead of landing on solid rock, she flopped into a soft, cushiony surface, the breath knocked out of her as she sank deep.

Unhurt, she plunged deeper, then bottomed out and bounced back up. The substance she'd fallen into raised her out of its depths and extruded her like a buoy upon its elastic crest.

Looking around through her wildly tangled blonde mane, she saw the cushiony surface was bright green in all directions, the color of the flesh of an avocado. Now that she took a closer look, she could see it was a big mass of vegetation, thousands of green sprouts grown into a spongy mesh with enough give to catch and push her aloft after the fall she'd taken.

Something else she noticed right away, along with the glitter and greenery: the heat. It was like being inside one of Iceland's many greenhouses, sweltering in a tropical environment--so different from the sharp summer cold she'd left behind before the fall.

Baffled by the change, Asa rolled onto her knees and crawled across the green mesh, aiming for the nearest edge. When she got there and looked down, her eyes shot wide open with surprise, and she froze. She couldn't believe what she was seeing.

Make that *whom* she was seeing.

Yet there they were, blinking and waving up at her from two meters below--and so her life was changed. Finally, she'd seen something for the first time, something she'd lied about seeing so many times before.

Standing on the grassy ground below, dressed in their floppy peasant caps, rumpled vests and trousers, and homespun dresses with aprons, was a rank of what looked to her like actual Icelandic Hidden People.

And they were calling her *by name.*

"Welcome, Asa!" said a male elf in a squeaky voice. "I'm Olaf! Welcome to Hidden Town!"

"Welcome, dear Deal-Maker!" said a female elf beside him. "My name is Gerda. Welcome to the land of Falinn Bær!"

Asa knew she was staring, and she didn't care. The Hidden People were no taller than a third of a meter, pudgy as soccer balls, yet perfectly formed and alive. They were like nothing she'd ever seen outside of a children's book or TV show--like nothing she'd ever experienced outside a dream.

Just looking at them made her feel light-headed. Just hearing their voices made her feel a little queasy.

This couldn't be *real*, could it?

Yet there they were.

"You finally made it!" Olaf, who was carrying a bright red sack over his shoulder, grinned up at her and waved for her to come down. "So good to *have* you here!"

"Thanks. Thank you." Asa was so dazzled, she could barely get the words out. "It's good to *be* here."

"Yes, it *is*," said Olaf. "So good for *you* to see the product of your *handiwork* after all this *time."*

"Though that's *not* the reason we brought you here," said Gerda.

A chill shot up Asa's spine like a lightning bolt in reverse. "Wait a minute. You *brought* me here?"

"Of *course*, dear," said Gerda. "You didn't think that quake was an *accident*, did you?"

Even as Asa clambered out of the green mesh and lowered herself to the ground, she was just as shell-shocked--make that *elf-shocked*--as she'd been when she'd first arrived in Falinn Bær.

What she was experiencing seemed utterly impossible, against every common-sense belief she'd ever held dear...yet also vividly real. It had to be some kind of hallucination, a product of an injury--but she couldn't just dismiss it and shut down. Playing along might lead her deeper into dementia, but it also seemed like the best course of action at the moment.

"So why did you bring me here?" she asked the pudgy elves as they surrounded her. "What do you want?"

"You'll see." Olaf gestured, and the other elves cleared a path into the forest. "Let's go for a walk."

Asa hesitated, then set off in the indicated direction. She had to take care not to step on any of the Hidden People, who fell in behind her as she passed.

"You're a *legend* around here," said Gerda, who scurried along at Asa's left. "Did you know that?"

"A legend? For what?" asked Asa.

"For your incredible *deal-making* skills!" Gerda flung her arms wide as they passed between some trees into an open area. "You've brought us a true *golden age* of *prosperity*, dear!"

Asa frowned but didn't say the first thing that came to mind, which was *"Seriously?"* Because as many times as she'd bargained on behalf of elves, she'd never known a single deal to actually *benefit* such creatures. She'd always assumed the goodies she'd scored had gone straight home with the construction workers who'd probably staged the supposedly supernatural sabotage in the first place. It was the only explanation that had made any sense, after all.

At least until now. As she walked down a street through the Hidden People's town, she saw proof all around that her efforts had had a greater impact than she'd imagined. The food and drink she'd negotiated for, delivered to drop sites by the companies who'd hired her, had somehow made it to the hands of the elves after all.

"Do you see, Deal-Maker?" Olaf patted the side of Asa's leg. "We have never *forgotten* all the *good* you've done for our people!"

Asa let out a long breath as she gazed at the incredible sights around her. Was she truly responsible for all *this?*

If so, it wasn't something worth bragging about.

Instead of elfish huts with thatched roofs, which she might have expected, the main drag was lined with overturned fried chicken buckets. Tubby elves wobbled in and out of the buckets, passing through doorways cut into the red-and-white cardboard. Other elves wandered into upside-down pizza boxes and soda cups, all with makeshift doors and windows, some even with smoking chimneys. But that wasn't all there was to see.

On the muddy ground between the chicken buckets, pizza boxes, and soda cups, great heaps of chicken bones and pizza crusts festered in the morning sun. Piles of candy wrappers, cigarette butts, beer can tabs, and bottlecaps were stuck together with wads of used chewing gum and syrup. Waves of glitter wafted off jumbles of costume jewelry and articles of clothing, swirling up to join the rest of the glitter flashing through the sparkle-tossed sky.

"Isn't it marvelous?" said Gerda. "Just look at what you've accomplished, dear!"

Asa swallowed hard. "Uh-huh." It all looked like one big garbage dump to her.

"This is a testament to your bargaining ability," said Olaf.

"The spoils of the many deals you negotiated brought great joy to all our people. The food and drink sustained us, and the containers became our new homes. Gone are the mud walls and rancid gruel. Thanks to you, the Hidden People eat like kings and live in brightly-colored palaces."

"Good, that's good." Asa was having trouble wrapping her head around it all. She had made so many deals for the Hidden People over the years; apparently, not only had the proceeds been reaching them, but they'd been *corrupting* them, as well...turning them into junk food junkies addicted to the nutrition-free goodies of the modern mortal realm. The traditional, healthy foods associated with the Hidden People were nowhere to be seen.

Without realizing it, Asa had done real damage to Elfland. And the elves didn't seem to mind it a bit.

"We can never thank you enough for all the good things you've brought us," said Olaf. "You've made our lives here so much better and given us glimpses of the bigger world beyond our own."

"That's great," Asa said without much conviction, wrinkling her nose. The town even *smelled* like garbage, not at all the way she'd expect a community of Hidden People in a magical fairy tale realm to smell. It was almost enough to make her gag when the wind changed, bringing stronger odors from the worst of the chicken bone and pizza crust piles.

"Now you know why we brought you here," said Gerda. "To see all this."

"And to save us," said Olaf. "To help secure the future of your chosen people."

"Secure the future how, exactly?" asked Asa.

"By guaranteeing a steady supply of the things we need," said Olaf.

"But it's pretty steady already, isn't it?" said Asa. "I've been getting tons of business lately."

"Not enough, dear," said Gerda. "We've got more mouths to feed these days, and they just *love* goodies from the mortal realm."

"That's well and good," said Asa, "but I'm getting as much as I can for you already."

"Don't worry, Deal-Maker,' said Olaf. "We have faith in you."

"And we're going to *show* you how to do better," added Gerda. "Just come with us."

As Olaf and Gerda led Asa into a mountain tunnel on the far side of town, she had to duck her head, then duck it again...and duck it a few more times after that to boot. The little elves might have fit comfortably in that confined space, but her comparatively oversized body did not.

"So what is this place?" asked Asa as she wriggled through a gap between two outcroppings.

"A very happy one," said Olaf. "The answer to all our hopes and dreams. If everything goes according to plan, none of us here in Falinn Bær will ever run out of goodies again."

The walls of the tunnel were warm when Asa brushed against them, and so was the air rolling over her. A faint red glow from somewhere up ahead illuminated the passage, helping her to avoid bumping her head or anything else on the stone walls and ceiling.

If only the damn tunnel didn't keep getting smaller as she followed the gang of elves through it. If it got much more compressed, she wouldn't be able to fit through it.

"Does this tunnel get much smaller?" she asked. "Is it some kind of mine or something?"

"Not unless you're interested in mining *magma.*" Olaf chuckled. "We're inside an active *volcano*, Deal-Maker."

"Wonderful." The heat quickly intensified and sweat broke out all over Asa's body. "Maybe I'll just meet you back outside, and you can *tell* me about what you wanted to *show* me."

"No need, dear. We're here," said Gerda.

"Just around the corner," added Olaf.

The sweat rolled freely into Asa's eyes as she followed them around a tight bend--and the tunnel suddenly opened into a huge, vaulted chamber. There was more room than ever, room enough for Asa to lift her head and look around--and the highest level of heat yet, almost too much for her to bear.

The massive space flared with reddish light from bubbling

pools and cataracts of magma. The heat was like a vise, pressing in from all around, and the rotten-egg stench of sulfur filled her lungs.

It was like crawling into Hell itself, lacking only demons with pitchforks to finish the picture.

"So how is this the answer..." Asa coughed on the sulfur stink. "...to your hopes and dreams?"

"It worked before," said Gerda. "So why not try it again?"

"Only *smarter* this time," said Olaf.

"*What* worked before?" asked Asa.

"A volcanic eruption, dear," explained Gerda. "We set one off in 2010 to get what we wanted from the government of Iceland."

"That was *you?"* Asa coughed again. The sulfur and heat were overwhelming. "Air travel was shut down *internationally."*

"That was *us*, all right." Olaf gestured at a nearby magma pool, and steaming red tendrils rose from the bubbling soup. They intertwined like vines, rising ever higher...then bloomed into a big red globe of superheated, liquefied rock, sculpted with the continents and features of the Earth itself. "We had the world on a string! We could have had anything we wanted!"

"But our so-called *negotiator* was an incompetent *Andskoti* who didn't know how to make the *most* of the *upper hand* we'd given her!" snapped Gerda, using the Icelandic word for "bastard."

"The government thought she was a *nut* and locked her up," said Olaf. "So there we were, with the ultimate negotiating *edge,* and we didn't get a thing out of it!"

"But that won't happen *this* time." Gerda patted Asa's leg. "Not with the ultimate *Deal-Maker* on our side!"

"And we won't make the mistake of threatening only the government of *Iceland*. We'll hold it over *all* the governments!" Olaf grinned and nodded.

"Give us what we want, for as long as we want it," said Gerda, "or keep erupting volcanoes until air travel shuts down *everywhere."*

"And *then* we'll start wrecking the *tectonic plates*," said Olaf. "Imagine the *chaos* when we start driving North America and Europe further apart!"

Asa coughed and felt bleary-eyed from all the volcanic gases.

She was afraid she'd pass out if she didn't escape the volcano soon. "And what *do* you want, exactly?"

Gerda's eyes flew wide open. "More fried chicken and burgers!"

"More tacos and pizza!" said Olaf.

"Beer and soda!"

"Candy and potato chips!"

"Avocado toast!"

"And that's just for starters," said Olaf.

"And we want an endless supply, delivered regularly," said Gerda.

"You don't ask for much, do you?" said Asa.

"Don't worry," said Olaf. "We have confidence in you. We know you can make it happen. Especially after the demonstration we provide."

"Demonstration?" Asa frowned. "Of what?"

"Of how we elves can make a *volcano* erupt, dear," said Gerda.

Asa's stomach twisted so hard it hurt. "You're going to make one *erupt?"*

"Oh, yes," said Olaf. "Think of it as *us* giving *you* the *leverage* you need to negotiate."

"Where? When?"

Olaf pointed up. "The *where* is the so-called *Magic Baths.* The *when* is *a few minutes from now."*

Asa launched into a coughing jag when she got outside the volcano, hacking up the sulfur from deep within her lungs. It was just as well; as the jag subsided, she was able to sit for a bit and get her bearings without any Hidden People distracting her.

A break like that was just what she needed after the revelations inside the volcano. Being told that the elves wanted to ransom the world for fried chicken and pizza had blown her mind. Learning, further, that they expected *her* to make the deal happen--and the consequences could be *dire* if she failed--was almost enough to make her lose it for good.

If what she was experiencing was real, not some kind of delusion, the world was about to change in a big way...and she was at ground zero for the fireworks. Not only that, but she had an important role to play, and no idea of the best way to play it.

She couldn't imagine any world government taking her seriously as a negotiator speaking on behalf of the elves. But if she didn't succeed in getting the Hidden People what they wanted, they would unleash extraordinary disasters upon the Earth.

All of a sudden, she was thinking about apocalyptic destruction unleashed by creatures she'd never even believed in before today.

And it was kind of her fault, she thought. If she hadn’t been so good at her job, the Hidden People might not have been so hooked on junk food that they’d be willing to trigger volcanoes to get more of it.

Because of that, she felt an extra burden of responsibility for the outcome. It was up to her to figure this mess out.

Though what exactly the solution might be, she could not yet guess...and she was running out of time.

But if there was one thing she was good at, it was thinking on her feet.

"Feel better now, Deal-Maker?" Gerda emerged from a grease-stained fried-chicken-bucket cottage and wobbled over to where Asa was sitting. "Your cough seems to have let up."

"Yes." Asa forced a smile on her face. "Thank you for asking."

"Not a moment too soon." Gerda nodded eagerly. "We're about to start the demonstration, dear."

Of the volcano! A shiver of terror raced along Asa's spine at the thought of it. "I’d like to talk to you about that, actually," she said.

"How so?" asked Gerda.

Asa thought furiously. "I think we should wait on the demo."

"Really?" Gerda scowled. "And why is that, dear?"

"Because." An idea clicked into place, and Asa thought it was a good one. "If you talk to the authorities *after* the demo, they might not believe you *caused* it."

"Why?" asked Gerda.

"For all *they* know, you might just be piggy-backing on an event you had no responsibility for." As Asa said it aloud, she thought it made even more sense. "They won't take your demands *seriously*."

"They won't?"

"*I* wouldn't," said Asa.

"Then what do *you* think we should do?" asked Olaf, who was trundling over from a pizza box house.

"Talk to them *first*," said Asa. "Then, when you demonstrate an eruption, they'll *know* you have control of it. They'll *have* to give you what you want."

"Good point." Olaf looked at Gerda. "Don't you agree?"

Gerda frowned in thought, then shrugged. "Makes sense. Talk first, demonstrate later."

"One more thing." Asa was on a roll. "I've had some thoughts about who our first contact should be."

"You have?" said Olaf.

Asa nodded. "We need to talk to someone in management who's already a *believer*. An intermediary who can help *sell* this to higher-ups and government officials."

"Why not start at the *top* instead?" asked Olaf.

"Because the top won't buy it without a push from the grass roots," said Asa. "I've seen it happen again and again."

"So we need a believer," said Gerda. "Do you have anyone in mind, dear?"

Asa smiled. "As a matter of fact, I do."

It could be hard to tell what time it was in Iceland in July, when there were only a few short hours of darkness every night. That was why, when Asa climbed up out of the crevice that led from Falinn Bær, all she knew for sure was that the sun was still out.

It was colder and windier than when she'd left, but that didn't narrow it down. Conditions changed quickly in Iceland, no matter what time of day it might be.

But as she got to her feet and brushed herself off, she saw that certain questions were likely to be answered soon. The man she'd come back to see--Ivar, the redheaded construction foreman--was wandering the lumpy, rocky ground not far away.

"Ivar!" When she called his name, he headed instantly in her direction. Waving and smiling, she met him halfway.

"Asa!" Ivar looked incredibly relieved at the sight of her. "Where in *Helvíti* have you been?"

"It's a long story." Asa almost said he wouldn't believe her if she told him...but she knew damn well that he *would.*

"It must be *really* long," said Ivar. "Nobody's seen you in almost 24 hours!"

"Longer than I thought, then." Asa remembered stories about time passing differently in magical realms--but it was disorienting to experience it directly. "It's easy to lose track of time *over there."*

Ivar scowled. "Over there where?"

"*You* know." She gestured in the direction of the fissure. "The land of the Hidden People."

"Ah, right." Ivar nodded knowingly. "Well, I've been worried sick about you. There've been tremors out here."

"Believe me, I know." Asa nodded. "The elves have been restless."

Ivar frowned. "About what?"

Asa leaned closer and lowered her voice. The elves weren't with her, but she worried they might be listening in somehow. "They want a better deal. A *much* better deal."

"But we haven't *made* a deal for this project yet."

"They want a better deal for *everything,*" said Asa. "They want the *best* deal yet, or else."

"Or else what?"

"Or else it's *volcano time."* Asa pointed at the snow-covered slopes of the volcanic peak Hekla in the distance. "*Major* eruptions until they get what they want."

"*Heilagur skit!*" Ivar looked aghast--eyes open wide, brimming with panic. "They can *do* this?"

"I think so, yes," said Asa.

Ivar whistled. "I liked it better when they were just stalling out our backhoes."

"So here's the thing." Asa dropped her voice to just above a whisper. "I have an idea to handle this, but I need your help."

Ivar nodded. "Okay, sure." He kept his voice low as well. "What do you need me to do?"

"I need you to play along." Asa raised her voice. "Call the leaders of the world and explain to them that they need to give the elves what they want or suffer the consequences. We're talking volcanic eruptions, earthquakes, shifting tectonic plates, you name it."

"Seriously?" asked Ivar.

"Of course, seriously!" snapped Asa...and then she frowned and gave her head a quick shake.

"Okay, got it." Understanding dawned in Ivar's eyes, and he pulled out his satellite phone. "I'll start with the president of Iceland, then." He winked and pretended to punch in a number.

"Perfect, thanks." The ground rumbled underfoot, and Asa looked around nervously. Had the Hidden People heard too much? Were they onto her game? Or were they just providing a gentle reminder of the stakes in play?

Whatever their motivation, Asa was committed now. She was betting on her proven skills as a con artist--and the elves' lack of a full understanding of the modern mortal realm--to prevent a catastrophe.

It was a tall order, given that the most she'd accomplished until now was extorting fried chicken and pizza from construction projects to turn Hidden People into junk food junkies. But rising to the occasion was a must; after all, it was mostly her fault.

"Hey, Asa." Ivar lowered the phone and whispered in her ear. "What should I pretend the world leaders are saying?"

"Tell me they're saying 'No,'" said Asa. "And if we don't like it, they'll *nuke* us."

With that, she walked off across the rocky plain, heading for the construction site and the car she'd left parked there.

"Wait!" said Ivar. "Where are you going?"

"To pick up a few things in Selfoss," said Asa. "You've got to look the part if you want to save the world."

"I'm back." Head held high and shoulders swept back, Asa strode down the main street of Hidden Town with a confidence she didn't feel in her heart.

The makeover she'd given herself before leaving the mortal realm helped, at least. Her elegant hairstyle, striking makeup, and glittering golden tiara gave her a decidedly regal look. The flowing white gown she wore (which she'd had to carry and change into after dropping through the dirty crevice into Falinn Bær) completed the picture of a wise and mystical figure.

The kind of figure fit to negotiate a deal between the great and ancient powers of a hidden realm and the leaders of the mundane world beyond it.

Now all she had to do was back up the look by acting the part.

"I bring news!" Asa changed the timbre of her voice to sound more commanding. She changed her choice of words, too, to go with the new image she wanted to project. "News of the mortal realm's response to your ultimatum."

Her voice drew elves from chicken buckets, pizza boxes, and soda cans throughout Hidden Town. They lumbered over, holding their overfed guts, and crowded around, squinting up at her lofty face amid the drifting glitter.

"I spoke with our intermediary," Asa said grandly, spreading her arms. "He passed along our demands to the world leaders."

"Good!" said Gerda. "And did they agree to meet them?"

Asa let her arms fall at her sides. "They refused."

"Refused?" Olaf said in disbelief.

"They say they will not give in to *terrorists."*

"But *we're* not terrorists!" said someone in the crowd.

"*Elfolutionaries*, maybe," said someone else. "But *never* terrorists."

"We'll show them some terror!" howled Olaf, shaking his fist overhead. "We'll show them the greatest volcanic eruption in *history!"*

"No!" Asa's voice echoed over the town, freezing the Hidden People in their rage. "If you do that, they will *nuke* Iceland."

"Nuke?" said one of the elves.

"They will *destroy* it with *nuclear missiles*. The most powerful weapons ever *created."* Asa said it dramatically, counting on the elves' lack of full knowledge of the mortal realm to convince them such an attack could strike friendly, harmless Iceland.

"Unless you count *volcanos!"* Olaf wove his fingers through the air in a complex pattern, tracing swirls through the glitter in the air--then slammed his hands together in a loud clap.

At which point, the ground rumbled violently.

Asa was rattled but stayed on her feet, keeping her balance in spite of the pearly high heels she wore.

Geysers of steam vented through the treetops in all directions. A sound like rolling thunder roared from afar, followed by another, stronger quake.

"Enough!" shouted Asa. "Olaf, stop it now!"

"Why should I? You're just a mortal realm *sympathizer*, aren't you?"

"I'm a *Falinn Bær* sympathizer," said Asa, "and I have reason to believe this place will be *destroyed* if *Iceland* is wiped off the map!"

The elves absorbed what she'd said. Then, Gerda reached over to give Olaf's arm a squeeze.

"Thank you." Asa kept up the appearance of great calm though her heart was thrashing like a salmon in her chest. Would she be able to stop Olaf again if he chose to trigger a geological cataclysm? "Now here is what I think. Iceland in the mortal realm and Falinn Bær in this realm are connected at a deep level. Can there be any doubt of this?"

The crowd of elves frowned and shook their heads.

"If these realms were not connected, could you reach out from *here* to cause quakes and volcanic eruptions *there?* Could you cause movement of the tectonic plates underlying the continents? Could you travel from one realm to the other to cause mischief?"

The elves said nothing.

"That is why, if nuclear missiles obliterate Iceland, I believe *Falinn Bær* will be obliterated also. Threatening the mortal realm will only lead to your own destruction."

"But we *need* what they have to offer!" said Olaf. "We can't do without the things you brought us!"

Asa pulled a frosted white globe from the folds of her gown. She pressed a contact on its base, activating a glowing LED light inside it, and held it at shoulder height in the palm of her right hand.

"You won't have to," she said. "You'll never have to do without those things again."

"How is that possible?" asked Gerda.

"The past is your beacon to the future." Asa turned the globe slowly in her hand, letting its glow twinkle among the bits of glitter in the air. "Follow my way, and we will *all* benefit forevermore."

Olaf wove his fingers again, and the ground shook. "Why *should* we?"

"How *dare* you!" Asa hurled the globe, and it smashed to bits at Olaf's feet. "Am I not the *Deal-Maker?* Have I not brought you *all good things?"*

Olaf glared at her, fingers quivering...then clapped his hands, ending the tremor.

"All right then." Olaf smiled. "So I suppose you're going to tell us what to do now?"

"No need," said Asa. "I'm pretty sure you already know."

As Ivar drove the panel truck up to the crevice, Asa let out a sigh of relief. By the light of the midnight sun, she could finally see that her proposal to the Hidden People might just work.

And the business she and Ivar had started had a chance of success.

"There it is!" She pointed excitedly as the truck rumbled closer over the rocky ground. "The elves came through!"

"Sure looks that way," Ivar said happily. "Now we just have to hope they like what *we* brought."

"They will," said Asa. "It's exactly what they asked for...plus half again extra."

Ivar pulled up and parked so the back of the truck faced the crevice--and the pile of wooden crates stacked neatly alongside it. Before he'd switched off the engine, Asa was already leaping out of the cab of the truck, heading for the crates.

When she reached them, however, she hesitated. What if she'd gotten it wrong after all? What if, instead of the goods they'd agreed on when she'd talked the elves out of their volcanic assault, the Hidden People had delivered crates full of goat poop or garbage? It was possible; the elves of Falinn Bær had not *all* been in favor of the deal she'd proposed.

"Aren't you gonna open them?" Ivar strolled up beside her and rapped a knuckle on one of the crates. "Maybe this will help." He handed her a prybar the length of her forearm.

"Of course, of course." Asa took a deep breath, wedged the tapered tip of the bar under the lid of the nearest crate, and pried it loose. Two more pries with the bar, and the lid came free completely.

Brushing aside the straw packing inside the crate, she found a black ceramic pot with a sealed lid. Lifting it out, she turned it around in her hands, admiring the workmanship--and anticipating what was inside.

This was what she'd talked the elves of Falinn Bær into making. *This* was what she'd convinced them to trade for the junk food goodies they craved.

This was what had staved off natural disasters and nukes alike, preserving the adjacent realms of mortals and Hidden People alike.

"What are you waiting for? This is the *good* part." Ivar pulled a spoon out of his jacket pocket and waved it around. "This is when we get to sample the merchandise."

Asa unlatched the clamp holding the cold pot's lid in place and set it aside. As soon as the pot's contents were exposed to the open air, the sweetest smell straight out of childhood wafted into her nostrils.

"Oh my God." She held up the pot and breathed deep with eyes closed. "I can't *remember* the last time I smelled something *that* good."

"Then just imagine how it's going to *taste."* Ivar tried to snatch the pot away, but she wouldn't give it up.

"I just *knew* those elves could do it." She drank in another very deep breath and beamed at its perfection. "They just needed a little encouragement to get back to their traditional ways. I just had to lay it out for them that they could catch more goodies with *skyr* than *volcanoes*."

Ivar sighed and pushed the spoon her way, conceding. "Go ahead and taste it yourself. Then maybe *I* won't have to wait much longer."

She took the spoon. "If you insist." She dipped it into the creamy white substance and scooped some out, then pushed it into her mouth.

And *swooned,* it was so incredibly delicious.

"Oh God." Her head rolled from side to side as she groaned in ecstasy. "This is *heavenly."*

"It's *that* good?" Ivar whipped out another spoon and dug it into the pot.

"Oh, yes." Asa smiled beatifically. "It's the best *skyr* I've had in my *life*, except for my grandma's."

Ivar also entered a state of bliss after tasting the stuff. "Nobody's going to want *factory-made skyr* after they get a taste of *this* stuff."

"And *we* control the *supply."* Asa went after another spoonful with the same blissful reaction as before. "As long as we keep the *Hidden People* happy."

"Speaking of," said Ivar. "We better unload the fried chicken and pizza and get this *skyr* loaded up for the trip back to Selfoss." That was where the offices of their new company were located.

"Just one more taste." Again, Asa dunked her spoon.

"Just be careful you don't eat all our *profits."* Ivar laughed. "That's the problem when the *product* is this good. Sampling the merchandise is the best part of the business."

Asa smiled and shook her head. She was thrilled to drop out of the con artist game and get a fresh start. She loved having a business that would make people happy and preserve Icelandic tradition. She was elated that she'd made up, at least a little, for leading the Hidden People astray through the years. And she was relieved beyond words that she'd saved Iceland--both realms of it--from catastrophe.

Sampling the merchandise was wonderful, to be sure, but...

"No," she told Ivar. "This *isn't* the best part of the business. Not even close."

And then she clicked her spoon against his, and they both said *skál,* and went to town on the rest of that pot until it was as empty as the rocky, desolate plain that stretched out around them.

WOULD SIR PREFER THE 1918 INFLUENZA?

"I have a bid of one million, nine hundred and twenty-one thousand, two hundred dollars for this *once-in-a-lifetime* purchase." The portly, bald auctioneer in the pinstriped suit raised his glowing gavel overhead with a dramatic flourish. "Do I hear one million, nine hundred and twenty-one thousand, *three* hundred?"

The high-end crowd in the gilded hotel ballroom in the town of Ithaca, upstate New York, stirred restlessly, but no one made a move. Finally, a Chinese man in a red plaid flannel shirt and blue-jeans in the back of the room lightly touched the brim of his beige cowboy hat—*twice.*

"*Two million dollars!*" The auctioneer's voice soared with excitement. "Do I hear two million, one hundred thousand?"

This time, no one in the room made a move.

"Two million once! Two million twice!" The auctioneer brought his gavel down hard on the dark wood podium. "*Sold!*"

The crowd applauded enthusiastically. Some looked at the buyer and nodded in admiration, and he smiled back at them.

"Congratulations, sir!" said the auctioneer. "You are now the *very lucky* owner of a custom variant of a rare 2015 Congolese Ebola virus handcrafted by the one and only *Ariel Carson* of *Ailing*

Springs! Follow the young lady in the red dress over there, and your *infection* will begin within *minutes."*

"There you go, Mr. Wu." Ariel Carson finished injecting the winning bidder and pulled the hypodermic needle from the muscle of his upper right arm. "You are now fully infected. Symptoms will appear in exactly three hours."

"Excellent." Mr. Wu grinned and nodded, rolling down the sleeve of his flannel shirt. "Just in time for my party."

"Your guests are gonna *love* this," said Ariel.

"I predict *tons* of *selfies*," said her younger brother and partner, Salk. "Everyone will be so *jealous* when the bleeding starts."

Suddenly, Mr. Wu stiffened and narrowed his eyes. "But *they* won't *catch* it, will they?"

Ariel's short red hair whisked over the back of her neck as she shook her head emphatically. "Not a chance, Mr. Wu. This *sickspe-rience* is strictly *non-contagious.* It is locked on you and you alone."

"And it's non-fatal, as well, of course." Salk, like his sister, had bright red hair—though his was shaved to crewcut length. "It's programmed to burn itself out after 24 hours."

"*After* the most *amazing* symptomology you've ever seen." Given her reputation, Ariel didn't really need to talk up her creation. Master *diseasist* that she was, every wicked bug she cooked up or customized was considered a work of art.

Not *every* diseasist's work could command millions of dollars in bids at auction. *Her* infections were special, creating exquisite patterns of signature symptoms unmatched by any other designer. Her artisanal sicknesses gave wealthy infectophiles the controlled suffering they craved as a way to feel alive in a high tech-driven existence without many true challenges.

In the late 21st century, drugs and extreme sports were considered passé. Rich thrill-seekers flocked to designer infections—made possible by complete human mastery of genetics—to get their fix of conspicuous risk-taking and adrenaline highs.

"That's what I like to hear." Grinning, Mr. Wu got up from the chair where he was sitting. "If it's as good as the smallpox-malaria you did for Vern Wallace's Christmas shindig last year..."

"It's *better.*" Salk, who was in his late 20s, nodded firmly. "You *know* you get only the *best* from Ailing Springs."

"I do indeed." Mr. Wu winced as something pinged inside him —the earliest onset of the disease, perhaps—then hurried off to enjoy his purchase in full.

Leaving Ariel to slump into the chair where he'd been sitting. She might have been a lean and healthy 35-year-old, but getting everything right at a high-bid auction still took a lot out of her.

Especially the part about feigning enthusiasm. As profitable and widely admired as her work had become, it was getting harder for her to pretend she loved what she did.

"We did it." Salk offered her a fist bump. "Two million bucks, just in time for the expansion of Ailing Springs. Way to go, Airy."

She returned the bump half-heartedly and yawned. "I just wish I didn't have to work late tonight. I'm so *tired.*"

"You should get a good night's sleep," said Salk. "You deserve it."

Ariel shook her head and got up from the chair. "Are you kidding? The Affliction Open's in *two days*. Unless we don't *care* about the billion-dollar *purse.*"

"I didn't say that, Sis," said Salk. "But you can beat those other diseasists with your *hands* tied behind your back."

Ariel wished she shared his confidence. As well as she'd done in her career, there was never a guarantee that she could stay on top forever.

"It's still better if we don't get sloppy." She stood and headed for the door. "Now get me back to my lab so I can keep perfecting our hybrid entry for the Open."

The sun was down by the time the self-driving white limo glided through the gate of Ailing Springs. The phosphorescent bacterial lights along the winding access road already glowed blue in the early June twilight, and the sprawling compound atop the grassy hill shone like a beacon with every window beaming.

The place was vast, occupying five hundred acres in the Finger Lakes region of rural upstate New York. The property between Seneca and Cayuga lakes had been a spa fed by healing hot springs in the 19th century, then a winery for decades after that. By the year 2095, it was more about infection than healing, more about artisanal sickness than wines, and had become enormously profitable because of it.

The age of the diseasist had come, in which illness engineers with the souls of poets cooked up elaborate strains for a sickness-crazed public. Ariel was considered by most infectophiles to be the best in the field, working at the top of her game. But the pressure to perform was always strong, and it was sapping her morale. Topping herself every time out of the gate had become exhausting.

"Don't stay up too late," Salk said when she got out of the limo and headed for her lab...but that wasn't an option. If her newest creation didn't blow everyone away, her fall from grace could begin in earnest.

Though sometimes, she wondered why she hadn't fallen already. Increasingly, she felt like she was just grinding out her work. She suspected the quality was slipping, even if no one but her seemed to have noticed...even if her pieces were commanding higher prices than ever.

Wasting no time, Ariel threw a lab coat over her red dress and went to work on the long, cluttered bench in the middle of her cavernous lab. The dark-timbered walls around her were hung with holographic portraits of her greatest achievements—shots of men and women with all manner of elaborate (and temporary) sores and deformities. Shelves and tables were stacked with awards from the most elite diseasist organizations and events in the world. She didn't pay the slightest attention to any of it.

All that mattered was the masterpiece brewing in the cylindrical white incubator on the bench in front of her.

"Hello there, honey." Flicking on the electron microscope, she got a good look at the incubator's contents. The bacterial mass inside was more than a thousand times what it had been before she'd left for the auction that morning. Not to mention, the individual tubular cells looked extremely robust and were very energetic in the nutrient solution.

The grafting of traits from multiple microorganisms had been successful. After six months of hard work, her bubonic plague-tuberculosis-typhoid-leprosy hybrid was nearly ready to present to the judges and fans at the Affliction Open.

At least she *thought* so, but a visual inspection only told her so much. Where were the day's analytical metrics? Her assistant, Norma Leary, always logged that data on the primary tablet computer.

But not today, apparently. Ariel rummaged through the contents of the bench but couldn't find the tablet anywhere.

Suddenly, the door swung open, and Salk marched in, glaring. "There's a call for you, Airy," he said. "And you're not gonna like it."

"Why do you say that?"

"There's a party at the Glazier mansion." His expression was grave as he handed over his phone. "I think you and I need to go for a drive, Sis."

Ariel's heart pounded when she saw them. Her eyes widened and her gut twisted as she and Salk walked among them in their habitat.

They were everywhere, milling around the backyard cocktail party at the Glazier place with drinks in their hands...and oozing flesh on their faces and bodies, discolored in a multitude of shifting rainbow patterns.

The air was filled with deep, foghorn coughing, groans, and gurgling gasps. Blackened nodes bulged from armpits laid bare by low-cut party dresses. People who couldn't have been much older than thirty looked like they were in their 70s, their bodies mangled with profusions of wrinkled fissures straight off the gnarled shell of a walnut.

Worst of all, the sight was *familiar* to Ariel. She'd seen the same symptoms before—on projected images of the results of *her* latest hybrid.

"What the *fuck*?" She felt dazed as she wandered through the party with Salk, taking in the incredible scene. "They're infected with my new hybrid!"

"No question." Salk shook his head as a passing partygoer's arms rapidly shriveled and twisted, making her drop her full martini glass on the ground. "I knew right away when my friend Judy Cabot described it over the phone."

"Even the sequence of *colors* is the same." As Ariel watched, the skins of a grinning man and woman changed from pink to bright blue to jade green to orange to violet. A small crowd gaped and clapped, oohing and aahing as if they were watching a fireworks show.

"But how did they *get* it?" asked Salk. "The labs at Ailing Springs are *impregnable.* No one could sneak into that place, and no disease agent could ever escape."

An overweight man lumbered past them then, his skin as covered in blazing blossoms as the Aloha shirt he wore. After he passed, Ariel caught sight of a familiar face across the yard—an attractive young woman with long, dark hair entertaining a crowd of listeners.

"*Norma.*" Ariel grated the word between clenched teeth.

Salk turned and spotted the dark-haired woman. "So *that's* who stole your work and dosed this party!"

"I *wondered* why the bitch didn't have my metrics ready after the auction," said Ariel.

"Norma betrayed us." Salk sounded surprised and disappointed all at once. "I thought we could *trust* her after five years."

"Apparently not," Ariel said darkly.

"At least you can still prove ownership," said Salk. "Even if she edited your signature out of the genome, you've got the design patented, right?"

Surrounded by laughter, cheers, camera phone flashes, and clinking glasses, Ariel felt a wave of despair—and, deep down, a flicker of relief. "It doesn't matter," she said grimly. "Now that my work's been *graffitied* all over the place, I can't enter it in the Affliction Open."

"Shit." Salk scowled as a young woman lumbered past in a bloody gown, her neck swollen with black nodes as big as boiled eggs, her arms and legs oozing dollops of leprous flesh like melting candle wax. "And the Open's in two days."

"Might as well be two hours." Ariel sighed as a man fell to his knees and vomited floating, rainbow-colored matter to a round of raucous cheers. Someone put on music, and infected guests danced, their monstrous, clotted bodies swaying and dripping in the glow of colorful lights strung on trees around the yard.

"That's a billion-dollar grand prize," said Salk, as if she needed to be reminded. "We could really use that money for the expansion, Sis."

"Might as well be a *hundred* billion," said Ariel. "Or a hundred *pennies.* That money means *nothing* to us now."

Just as she said it, a young man with an extreme case of what was going around approached with phone in suppurating hand. "Excuse me. Could you take a quick shot for my feeds?"

Ariel smiled as she took the phone, did as he'd requested, then heaved it across the party. It ended its flight by clocking Norma on the back of the head, sending her stumbling into several people and knocking them all over at once with a satisfying crash.

Sometimes, there just wasn't a way to feel better. As expert as Ariel was at controlling sickness, she couldn't always heal her own suffering.

The morning after finding out about the stolen hybrid, for example, she had a full-blown, unshakable case of depression. Her heart was heavy, and her thoughts were dark. Her stomach and head both hurt, and she didn't want to get out of bed.

All she could think about was Norma's betrayal and losing the hybrid entry for the Affliction Open. All her efforts had been for nothing; what should have been a prize winner was now just a junk bug making the rounds on the sicko party circuit.

All because she'd trusted the wrong assistant. All because she'd forgotten people weren't predictable and programmable like germs.

Now there she was, in bed, as the world turned around her. And the fact that she felt relieved on some level because she finally had an excuse for failure, a good reason not to compete, only made her feel worse and want to get out of bed even less.

Finally, a little before 10 a.m., she dragged herself out to go to work...not her work in the lab, which was at a standstill, but her *other* job that helped pay the bills.

Ailing Springs was not only a thriving arts and research institute, but a major stop on sickness tasting tours. Most of the compound's population, at any given time, consisted of tourist infectophiles stopping to sample the wares.

As Ailing Springs' top attraction, Ariel knew her personal appearances helped keep deep-pocketed visitors happy. They came to try the artisanal sicknesses she'd designed, but just as much to meet the artist, gush over her work, and snap selfies with her.

"Hello, everyone." It took a huge effort for her not to let her depression show through today. "Thanks for coming to Ailing Springs!"

The crowd of twenty tourists in the tasting center clapped and snapped photos with clear delight. Some of them had already started sampling, judging from the sores and swellings on their faces, necks, arms, and legs.

"It's so wonderful to meet you all." Ariel walked up to a skinny blond man whose features were reddened and sweaty. "So what are we having this morning?"

The blond guy held up a vial with the Ailing Springs label. "I thought I'd give the 1918 influenza variant a try." He had a Nordic accent and sounded a little breathless as the infection took hold.

"Hitting the hard stuff this early?" She chuckled, and the tourists all laughed along with her. "Great choice! You ought to notice a nice, slow burn on the front end, then a sharp, peppery zing on the finish."

"It definitely has a kick already." The guy nodded enthusiastically. "I love it so far!"

"Good for you." Ariel forced a smile and looked around for the next likely subject. A pudgy, middle-aged woman whose left arm was covered in boils got her attention, grinning and waving with the zeal of a true fan.

Before Ariel could move her way, however, a tall young man with a shock of dark brown hair popped up in front of her, grinning.

"Don't you want to know what *I* have, Ms. Carson?" His brown eyes twinkled with mischief. "Aren't you gonna ask *me?*"

"Sure." She saw no signs of infection but decided to play along. "What are you having this morning?"

His grin widened as he leaned closer. "Anestha-Dianumbnesia 001. Great stuff!"

For a moment, she stared at him, confused. The name wasn't familiar from the current selection of sicknesses on tap.

Then, suddenly, recognition kicked her like a mule. She was absolutely stunned at what she'd heard, unable to explain or put it in any kind of context.

She shook her head, baffled, but the kid just kept on grinning. How old *was* he, anyway? Twenty-one? Twenty-two?

"Are you all right, ma'am?" His voice sounded utterly kind and sympathetic...yet still with that mischievous edge.

Suddenly, Ariel's awareness of the crowd around her rushed back in. "Just fine, just fine! So glad you're enjoying it!" Taking his arm, she guided him toward the door. "And congratulations, you're our lucky winner today! You'll get to sample our latest *craft cancer* free of charge!"

"No kidding!" The guy pumped his fist overhead. "Woo-hoo! Free cancer!"

"Just come this way," said Ariel. "The rest of you folks, your second dose is on the house!"

The crowd of tourists applauded wildly as she hurried the guy out of the room.

This time, it was *her* turn to be breathless.

"Where's my prize?" asked the guy as Ariel drove him into an empty room and slammed the door shut behind them. "Do I get to pick the kind of cancer, or...?"

"There *is* no prize," snapped Ariel. "And who the *hell* are *you?*"

"Call me Andy." Smiling, he extended his hand for a shake. "Which is short for Anestha-Dianumbnesia, by the—"

"And how the *fuck* do you know about *that?*" Ariel was so off-balance, she was furious. "Do you even know what it *is?*"

"Of course I do!" Andy's smile turned sly. "It's *me.* I'm *it.*"

Ariel thrust her fingers into her red hair, threw her head back, and let out a guttural cry of frustration. "Quit *fucking* with me! *Nobody* but *me* knows about Anestha-Dianumbnesia!"

"Not unless it's what they *are*!" Andy chuckled.

"You're not making any sense!"

"What's the matter?" asked Andy. "Didn't you ever think you'd be a *mother* someday?"

Ariel stared at him with eyes narrowed. "I'd say you hacked my records from fifteen years ago, but I *destroyed* them all. There's no *way* you could possibly know anything about—"

Suddenly, Andy's expression turned serious. "Don't be ashamed of me, Ma. And don't worry, I know I was a mistake." He winked at her. "A *perfect* mistake!"

Speechless, she stumbled back against the wall, unable to believe what she was hearing.

"I was one of your first designs," said Andy. "You tried to develop an infection that would switch off human pain receptors at will, eliminating the need for anesthesia in surgical patients and addiction to narcotics in those suffering from chronic pain. Only it didn't work the way you'd hoped. Animal test subjects lost *all* sensitivity to physical stimuli *permanently*. Your work was a total *failure*." Grinning manically, he flung himself down on one knee and shook his hands butterfly-wing style like a song-and-dance man wrapping up a big number. "Except it *wasn't! Oooh noooo!*"

Ariel's head was spinning. How could he know so many details about something she'd never revealed to the public or talked about with *anyone?* Not even *Salk?*

"Hallelujah!" Andy leaped to his feet with arms upraised. "You might not have engineered a controllable pain nullifier, but you *did* create something *more amazing!* You gave birth to a *sentient sickness!* A *germ* with a *mind* of its own!"

Scowling, Ariel shook her head. "Impossible." But even as she did, she was thinking about the behaviors she'd observed among certain colonies of bacteria, suggesting some kind of low-level group intelligence. She thought of the way they exchanged genetic material through the processes of conjugation, transduction, and transformation, swapping DNA to trade characteristics. Hadn't she said herself that diseases seemed almost conscious sometimes?

"Imagine, Ma! A lowly *bug* set loose by your hand, oh so tiny." He pinched his thumb and forefinger so close together, they were almost touching. "Yet *full* of ideas and curiosity!" He flung his hand wide open, fingers fluttering. "Exploring the world by spreading from host to host, experiencing life through their eyes and ears and noses, speaking with their mouths..." He pointed at his own mouth and stuck out his tongue. "...then moving on. And *never* losing track of dear old Ma along the way!"

Andy stepped forward, reached out, and took her hand.

"I've watched you from afar, Mother," he told her. "And now that you're in trouble, I've returned to you. I've come back to give you my help."

"Help?"

"Getting you back in the *game*, baby!" He released her hand, spun around on the ball of one foot, and snapped his fingers. "You're the queen of diseasists! You are *not* giving up on the Affliction Open!"

"So this is your lab, huh?" Andy looked around appreciatively as she led him into the massive chamber. "You've come a *long way* from the *basement* where you brought *me* to life, Ma."

Ariel still wasn't sure what to believe about him. Was she really talking to a sentient bacillus she'd created by accident while developing a pain-nullifying infection 15 years ago?

She did not yet have a better explanation. There was no other way that anyone but her could have information about that experiment from the earliest days of her career as a diseasist.

"So let's *do* this thang!" Andy jogged to the incubator on the main workbench and knocked on the lid. "Hey, little buddies! I hear you in there!"

"Not for long." Ariel walked over and yanked the incubator's power cord out of the electrical socket on the side of the bench. The bubonic plague-tuberculosis-typhoid-leprosy hybrid, as it existed in her lab, was not long for this world.

Andy's eyes sprung wide, and he clutched at his temples. "Murderer! Ma, how *could* you?"

"That strain is no use to me now," said Ariel. "It's been compromised."

"That's just *cold*." Andy shook his head. "What if you'd pulled the plug on *me* before I got smart and hitched a ride out of your basement on a cockroach?"

"A cockroach?"

"His name was Archie, but that's another story." Andy smacked his hands on the bench. "You oughtta *thank* him, because I wouldn't be here *inspiring* you if not for him."

"Inspiration is impossible at this stage," said Ariel. "The Affliction Open is *tomorrow*. I've got *nothing*, and I'm running out of *time.*"

"So work a miracle. You've done it before." Andy spread his arms wide. "Case in point."

"I haven't done it *overnight*," snapped Ariel. "There are *limits* to what one person can do."

Andy folded his arms and leaned his hip against the bench. "Do you know what Archie taught me, Mom? Even a tiny cockroach can change the world...at least until he gets eaten by a certain *alley cat* who shall remain nameless. Thanks to that little roach, I got out of your basement, and 15 years later, I'm here to help you create something that could set the world on fire."

"It's not going to *happen.*" Ariel grabbed a Petri dish from the bench and hurled it against the wall. "Do you understand? I'm finished!"

Andy stared at the bits of glass on the floor. "That's not true, Ma. I know that a lot of germs have a *ton* of respect for you."

"Germs? The *germs* don't do the *judging*!"

"Are you *sure* about that, Mom?" Andy raised an eyebrow.

Ariel frowned. She was starting to wish she hadn't brought him to the lab.

His story was unprovable, his undue optimism aggravating. He was pissing her off, trying to get her stirred up when all she wanted to do was mope in bed.

Playtime needed to be over, she finally decided.

"Look." Ariel headed for the door, motioning for him to follow. "We need to wrap this up. I've got important business to attend to."

"Reschedule it." Andy patted the incubator. "Your most important business is right here."

When he didn't join her, she went back for him. "Seriously." She grabbed his arm and tried to pull him along with her. "You need to leave."

"And *you* need to look in *here.*" He flicked on the electron microscope. "Go ahead, and then I'll leave if you still want me to."

Ariel hesitated, then realized she had nothing to lose. Leaning down, she peered into the microscope, gazing at the view inside the incubator.

And then she gasped.

"What the hell?" She'd expected to see a dead colony of germs afloat in the nutrient solution. Instead, she saw a *thriving* colony...and more than that, the most amazing microbial configuration she'd ever seen in her life.

Somehow, the bacteria had positioned themselves to spell out words—actual, recognizable *words*—within the microscope's visual field.

"Holy shit," said Ariel.

"*Now* you get it." Andy patted her on the back. "Maybe you

alone can't finish in time for the Open...but working with a *germ whisperer* like *me*, you might stand a chance."

Ariel fell silent. She couldn't take her eyes off the message in the microscope's viewfinder:

Hi Mom!

If *that* was possible, then why not *more* than that? Why not give it a chance with Andy working his magic?

Maybe, with that kind of power to tap, she could still accomplish something she could be proud of, something that would make her feel as if she'd gotten her mojo back. Could she possibly reject an opportunity like that, no matter how far-fetched it might seem?

Without a word of acceptance, she straightened and reached for a tablet computer. "Hand me that clipboard over there," she said without skipping a beat. "Let's go. The clock is ticking."

Andy wasn't kidding when he called himself a germ whisperer. He was able to edit bacterial and viral DNA at will, without equipment, by manipulating it with his thoughts. He spotted flaws and hazards quickly, limiting the need for testing. He came up with ideas for new directions on the fly and implemented them in the blink of an eye.

It was like working at light speed compared to the usual techniques. In spite of her initial cynicism, Ariel came to believe they might actually have a finished product in time for the Affliction Open.

Within six hours, in fact, she and Andy had a viable prototype nearly finished, well within spitting distance of the deadline.

Why then, all of a sudden, did she lose all confidence in what they were doing?

"Damn," she said after checking the results of the latest gene splicing. "This isn't what I wanted."

"Sure it is, Ma," said Andy. "I did exactly what you told me to do. It's a great splice, too. The tetanus and syphilis DNA are aligned perfectly."

Ariel stepped away from the bench. "I know. You're doing great. It's just..." Shaking her head slowly, she paced the floor. "It's not..."

"What?" Andy grinned. "Not singing loud enough? Not strobing in the petri dish? Not smelling enough like bacon?"

"It's not...*it.*" Ariel stripped off her latex gloves and scrubbed her fingers through her red hair. "Not *the one.*"

Andy sat back on the stool where he was perched and folded his hands behind his head. "Maybe you'll like it more when it's done. We still need to splice and program the meningitis and cholera genes, plus the strep and MRSA fragments."

Ariel paced across the lab, frowning. "I don't think it's just because it's *incomplete*. It doesn't *feel* right."

"What about the shingles accents and the surprise Plague of Justinian kicker? Isn't that pretty extreme, Ma?"

Ariel paced silently, staring at the floor.

"Didn't you say this is the most complex hybrid with the most elaborate sequence of symptoms you've ever created?" asked Andy.

Ariel stopped and looked at him. "But is it *art*?"

Andy didn't answer.

"There's a *feeling*, you know?" she said. "Like, you know when what you're making is *special.* When it's *original.* When it's *about* something. When it will make other people feel something, too."

"You're talking about sending a message, right?"

"It's hard to explain." She shook her head and started pacing again.

"And you feel this a lot in your work?" asked Andy. "You just *know* you're achieving greatness?"

Ariel paced and thought for a long moment, then stopped. "No." She surprised herself by saying it out loud. "I guess I haven't felt it like that in a very long time."

"But you're a superstar!"

"And I *stay* that way by giving people what they *want*," said Ariel. "I guess I even convinced myself it *was* special. After a while, I guess I stopped noticing that it wasn't from my *heart.*"

"So you've been phoning it in, huh?" said Andy. "And you're so good, you *still* blow everyone out of the water."

"Or maybe *they're* just so *bad.*"

"And you think you *suck* now? Is that it?"

"I *have* sucked," said Ariel. "Maybe more than I *thought* I did when the money kept rolling in."

"And you're just figuring this out *now*?" asked Andy.

She shook her head. "I've felt this way for a long time and haven't told anyone. But you have a way of bringing it out in me."

"*I* do?" Andy laughed.

"You remind me of how I used to be...and what I *dreamed* of becoming."

"Thanks, I guess." Andy got up and wandered around the lab, gazing at the holo-portraits of her triumphs on the wall. "So what now, Ma? Give up on the eleventh-hour rush job? Pull the rip cord on the Affliction Open?"

"All I know is, what we started here doesn't cut it," said Ariel. "It's not...it's not *my vision.*"

"And what *is* your vision?" He pointed at one of the portraits of her past work. "One of these? Something you've already done?"

It was then that it hit her. It was then that she got the idea and instantly knew it was the one she'd been waiting for all along.

"Maybe." She walked to the bench and picked up a DNA sampling kit, then walked toward Andy. "Maybe you're on the right track, kiddo."

The next morning, as Ariel was getting ready to go on stage at Unwell Stadium in Ithaca, Salk gave her the usual pep talk.

"You've *got* this, Sis." Grinning, he gave her a fist bump. "Trust me, you're gonna knock those judges dead!"

"Thanks, Salk." She smiled graciously, though she knew he had no idea what her entry for the Affliction Open would be. Nobody did except Ariel...

...and the brown-haired young man standing a few feet away, whom she'd introduced to Salk as an art student and fan of hers.

"Good luck, Ariel." Andy gave her a big thumbs-up.

"Thank you, Andy." She shot him a special smile, because he was her son in a way, at least part of him was...and it was because of him that she had an entry for the Open at all.

"And now, our next contestant!" boomed a deep male voice over the public address system. "Ten-time Affliction Open champion *Ariel Carson!*"

"Kick ass, Sis!" Salk cheered and clapped as she marched onstage from behind the curtain.

When she got there, the cheering crowd went bananas. The decibel level shot beyond sky-high, and everyone leaped to their feet.

"Thank you!" She grinned and waved as she approached the emcee—a tall, gaunt, silver-haired man in a bright green tuxedo and blinking red bow tie.

The emcee waited until the applause had faded. "Welcome, Ariel. Or should I say, welcome back!"

"Thank you, it's wonderful to be here." Ariel beamed, feeling resplendent in her glittering white floor-length gown. "It is truly an honor."

"What can you tell us about this year's entry, Ariel?" He checked notes projected in his left palm by a cloud computer drifting overhead. "It looks like you made a last-minute substitution for your originally-announced entry?"

"That's right, Jeff." She nodded. "My final entry is called Arch-E Mark-16." Glancing backstage, she saw Andy smiling knowingly in the wings.

"Interesting," said Jeff. "Tell us a little about your inspiration for Arch-E Mark-16."

"It was inspired by my very first project, actually," said Ariel. "From when I was just starting out as a diseasist. This is an offshoot of that same infection, modified and repurposed."

"Tell us about the disease's symptomology," said Jeff. "Can we expect the usual Ailing Springs razzle dazzle, with a host of complex, painful, and unpredictable side effects?"

“No.” Ariel cleared her throat. “There’s just the one.”

The audience murmured in surprise.

“Just the one...symptom?” asked Jeff.

“Yes,” said Ariel. “But one little symptom can be enough to change the world, you know.”

Again, the audience murmured.

“What *is* this one symptom?” asked Jeff.

“You tell me.” Ariel turned to the crowd. “*All* of you. Because you’ve *all* been infected.”

Jeff’s smooth demeanor faded fast. “Infected how?” He sounded worried.

“By me.” Ariel took a bow. “I’ve been breathing out spores since I got here.”

The audience’s murmuring grew louder. Voices were raised in confusion and fear.

Ariel grabbed the mic from Jeff and spoke calmly into it. “Relax. Trust me. Think of it as a free gift sicksperience from Ailing Springs. You’d pay *thousands* of dollars for this at an auction.”

Her words struck a nerve, and people settled down some. Her reputation alone was enough to keep the lid on.

Jeff the emcee wasn’t quite so steady about it, though. “What’s the symptom?” He grabbed for the mic. “You haven’t told us what it is, yet.”

Ariel smiled and wouldn’t let go. The truth was, she knew the symptom well, knew there was nothing about it to fear. After all, she had tested it on herself the night before, after creating it from samples of Andy’s inner germ.

Just as the original bug, Anestha-Dianumbnesia 001, had pain-nullifying properties, this new variant interfered with human pain response. It modified a fundamental human need, a craving seated deep in the reptile back-brain since God only knew when...a hunger that caused human beings to lash out at themselves and others in more ways than could ever be counted.

Arch-E Mark-16 would stop people from wanting to feel pain...from believing they deserved it because of some basic unworthiness...from getting perverse pleasure by warping themselves in one twisted way or another.

In other words, the era of the diseasist had come to an end. Because that new little bug had been engineered to spread like wildfire and never burn itself out.

Diseasist, heal thyself. Ariel had heard those words, or words like them, somewhere once.

And so that's exactly what she'd done...and she was healing the whole world along with her.

Not that the world would necessarily appreciate that fact.

"Tell us!" snapped Jeff, fighting and failing to tear the mic from Ariel's grip. "What is the one symptom of Arch-E Mark-16?"

It was then that she felt again like the young woman of long ago, the one with a dream to make a difference, a vision of transforming the world in a positive way. Why waste time making people sick in the name of art or fashion or self-mutilation when you could make them feel better instead?

In that moment, she came full circle. Her younger self would have been proud, and so she answered as her younger self might have wanted.

"That's for me to know and you to find out," said Ariel, and then she dropped the mic on the stage with a *boom* and strutted off like she'd just brought down the house.

FROM THE JOURNAL OF TRAUMATIC WARFIGHTER MUTATION

"As humanity has spread throughout the galaxy, we have discovered that on some worlds, war literally changes people. The infliction of trauma on certain organisms is enough to alter them profoundly, making them better able to fight for survival. Such metamorphoses can be shockingly extreme, transforming every aspect of a lifeform in surprising and deadly ways."

-From "The Rapid Multiphasic Mutation of Sentient Nascendi Lifeforms During Wartime," The Journal of Traumatic Warfighter Mutation, *Vol. 12, September 2205*

As soon as he saw the extent of the alien's injuries, Fleet Marine Force Medical Corpsman Jared Lucas stole a look up at the escape hatch in the bunker's ceiling, at the top of a red metal ladder. He could see it was still bulging inward and sealed tight, damaged by a grenade that had blown in the shaft above it after his descent into the bunker.

Not that he would have made a run for it even if he could have, since the duty of a Corpsman was to treat those wounded in combat, not run when the shit got deep. Still, the idea had its appeal. After all, being trapped in a small space with a badly wounded Nascendi was a death sentence, and Jared didn't want to die.

"Ooloooolooo!" The Nascendi, Leb, howled in pain. His/her translucent, glowing lump of a form writhed on the corrugated metal of the floor. "Hurts bad, Doc! Stop pain now! Please stop!"

Crouching beside the alien, Jared reached into the med-kit pouch that hung at his hip and pulled out a quantum-hypodermic. The kit was the only resource he had left, since his better-equipped backpack had been torn right off him on the surface.

Heart racing, he programmed the hypo's onboard formulary to whip up a painkiller, then injected it into Leb's pale flesh near its brightest glowing and pulsating spot—the closest thing he/she had to a heart.

Even as the medication went to work, Jared knew it wouldn't last long. He'd seen badly injured Nascendi before, had watched as the trauma-induced mutations experienced by their species took effect. He knew that if Leb's trauma wasn't properly treated (by doctors in a field hospital) the Nascendi would change into three other forms after this one, ending in the most aggressive and destructive. He knew that if the two of them were still trapped in that confined space together when that fourth form took over, there was very little chance that he, an unarmed human, would leave that bunker alive.

More than that, thousands of humans would perish if he died before finishing the job he'd gone down there to do—hacking the Grok enemy's bioneural control system and stopping a chemical weapons barrage from raining down on the nearby settlement of Gestalta.

"That helped," said Leb. "Oh thank you, thank you, Doc. Ooo-hoo-loo-boooo!"

Though Jared wasn't a doctor, the nickname "Doc" was a sign of respect often directed at Corpsmen. "All part of the service." He managed to crack his dirty face with a smile as he put away the hypo, then tipped his helmet back to scrub the blond stubble on his scalp with his knuckles. Leb was a new friend; they'd met at the morning briefing, ordered to work as partners on this mission, and had taken an instant liking to each other.

Right before the surprise Grok offensive, that is, and the three rounds of hostile fire Leb had taken on the way into the bunker.

"Need to get out of here." Puffing from his seven mouths, Leb flexed his/her gelatinous mass toward the exit ladder. "Finish hacking and get back into the fight."

"Relax." Jared lightly patted an uninjured zone of the Nascendi's body. "Let me call and see if someone can come let us out."

"Tell them hurry." Leb snorted through all 24 nose holes at once.

Jared smirked as he got up and pulled the radio handset from his belt loop. "Alpha tango five-five-niner, this is Juliet-lima. Request immediate extraction, over. My Nascendi friend here is in dire need of medical attention."

When Jared stopped talking and released the mic button, he heard a distant female voice deep in the static but couldn't make out what she was saying. It could have been Lita, the coms operator for his unit—also his ex-girlfriend—but he couldn't be sure.

Seconds later, he heard something unmistakable—the boom of some kind of explosion, followed by a high-pitched squeal over the channel.

After which, he didn't hear the female voice anymore.

"Uh, Doc?" Leb's voice sounded tighter than before. "Got any more of that magic juice handy? I think it might be wearing off a little."

"Stay cool, Leb. Keep it together, and I'll make you an honorary Corpsman." Jared switched the radio between channels, searching for signs of life.

"Doc? I need it *for real*. Guh-hoo-loo guh-loo!"

"Hang on. Give me a minute." Jared went back to the main channel and squeezed the mic switch. "Alpha tango five-five-niner, this is Juliet-lima. Somebody, say something quick."

Still, there was nothing but static.

Then, suddenly, he had something else to think about.

Behind him, Jared heard thrashing and howls of pain. Whirling, he saw exactly what he'd feared he might see—Leb in mid-transformation, halfway between his translucent blob form and something with a gleaming, silver shell.

"I *said*...I needed painkiller...*for real!*" As he/she said it, the rest of his/her pale, gelatinous body became encased in gleaming silver and rolled up like an Earth armadillo.

After which it wobbled in place, giving off plumes of steam as the catabolic reaction that had forged it finished running its course.

"Alpha tango five-five-niner," Jared said softly into the radio. "This is Juliet-lima. Please tell me someone's *alive* up there, because *my* world is turning shittier by the *minute.*"

"Though the baseline form of a Nascendi sentient is biologically simplified and non-threatening, the application of trauma triggers a physiological transformation into a next-stage form. This conversion brings with it extreme changes from the most basic molecular structure to the highest-level processes governing thought and personality."

-From "The Rapid Multiphasic Mutation of Sentient Nascendi Lifeforms During Wartime," The Journal of Traumatic Warfighter Mutation, *Vol. 12, September 2205*

As the silver sphere that had been his Nascendi friend steamed and cooled in the middle of the bunker, Jared explored the banks of controls and computer displays lining the walls. His minimal technical knowledge was of little use to him here; the languages on the panels and screens were all alien, and the control surfaces were designed for body parts he didn't have.

He hoped that his knowledge of biology and medicine might see him through. According to the Grok prisoner who'd alerted the Pact Marines to the impending chem weapons attack, the control systems were bioneural, engineered as a matrix of intricate cellular material.

The Groks' chem weapons were legendary for their lethality. It was *vital* that he not screw the pooch, even as the injured Nascendi on the floor—who was supposed to help with his/her knowledge of the enemy's languages—became progressively more dangerous.

Time was running out; he knew just enough about the alien number system to understand the digital countdown ticking away on one of the screens, suggesting he had less than a half-hour before the missiles launched for Gestalta.

Then there was his *other* problem, which was grunting and stirring as he ended his latest fruitless call for help. Leb had just finished a transformation that took him/her a step closer to turning Jared into a fatality.

Two years ago, on Cassilon VII, he'd faced a different puzzle with a similar theme and failed. A squad of Leiadesians—multiformed alien allies of the Interstellar Pact—had been pounded by Ozog invaders. Jared had known that the Leiadesians were all biologically unique from each other, requiring radically different treatments for similar injuries, but he hadn't realized that an Ozog bio agent was *mutating* them until it was too late. He'd kept fighting to modify treatments, but he hadn't been able to keep up with the rapid mutations that necessitated *different* treatments. One by one, every Leiadesian in his care had died in agony, and the outpost they'd fought to defend had eventually been lost to the Ozog.

Now here he was with another being undergoing changes, and he didn't know how to help him/her, either.

The silver sphere slowly unrolled before Jared's eyes. Inside, an eight-tentacled form with jet black fur, pointed ears, and a gleaming gold beak opened its three pairs of bulbous eyes and met Jared's gaze.

"Well, *that* was refreshing." The Nascendi rolled off his/her back and planted all eight tentacles on the floor. "Nothing like a little *mutation* to put the *spring* back in your step, don't you agree?"

"Absolutely," said Jared. Though the new form retained the memories of the previous form, it was like talking to a different person. The voice was deeper and more resonant than Leb's. "So how do you feel, Leb?"

The Nascendi made a sound like clearing his/her throat.

"Actually, my name is now Bellerothon. It suits my new form, don't you think?"

"Sure." Jared had witnessed Nascendi adopting new names during mutation before. It still fascinated him, though other aspects of the process concerned him more at the moment. "So how do you feel, Bellerothon?"

Bellerothon stretched his/her black-furred body under the dome of his/her silver shell, then scowled and growled. "Not so good, I'm afraid. My transformation doesn't seem to have rendered much improvement in terms of my injuries."

Jared pulled a bio-scanner from his med-kit pouch. The slim little device, about the size of a playing card and the thickness of a pancake, lit up as soon as it came in contact with his skin. "Let's take a few readings to find out for sure," he said.

"No need! I just *told* you how I feel." Bellerothon's irritability was uncharacteristic—for his/her original self, at least.

"You did, thanks." Jared walked over to within scanning range, just under four feet from Bellerothon, and held out the scanner, letting it run.

Only a few seconds had passed when one of Bellerothon's tentacles uncoiled and lashed out, flicking the scanner right out of Jared's hand.

"Okay then." Turning, he retrieved the scanner from the floor behind him and saw it was still working. He'd gotten just enough data to see that the internal injuries, which Jared wasn't equipped to treat in the field, were continuing to degrade the Nascendi's condition. The time until the mounting trauma pushed him/her into a deadly form was running out.

So was the time until the chem weapons launch. The best thing Jared could do next was to put Bellerothon to use while he still could.

"Are you well enough to help me out here?" Jared gestured at the banks of displays and controls blinking and flickering on the wall. "Maybe provide a little guidance in preventing the launch?"

"Well, it's not as if I'm *mortally wounded* or anything." Bellerothon's voice was full of sarcasm.

"If you'd rather not save thousands of people, I totally understand." Jared turned to the nearest panel and drew a long, slim instrument from his med-kit pouch, a silver wand with a ruby-tipped prong on the end. The laser scalpel was essential for cutting shrapnel and projectiles from wounded warriors in the field—or, in this case, operating on a chem weapons control panel. "I'll just start hacking away randomly and hope I don't sever the wrong connections."

As Jared leaned over the panel and started poking around, he heard a loud sigh and rustling noises behind him. The next thing he knew, a single black tentacle slid up beside him to tap what looked like a raised red asterisk the size of Jared's fist on the control panel.

"Start there." The asterisk lit up when Bellerothon tapped it and withdrew his/her tentacle. "Cut right into the core of that symbol."

Jared positioned the scalpel over the middle of the asterisk. "And what will that do, exactly?"

"Blow us both up," said Bellerothon. "*Or* disengage certain key authentication protocols, allowing you to intervene in system programming."

Jared pressed the activator stud on the wand, and a thin beam of bright red light leaped from the ruby crystal in the tip, piercing the heart of the red asterisk on the panel. After a few seconds, wisps of gray smoke feathered up from the site, and the acrid smell of burnt wiring filled the air.

Suddenly, crackling sparks hopped out of the hole he'd just cut. When one burned the heel of his palm, he stopped cutting and yanked the scalpel away.

"Did we get it?" he asked, shaking off the burn as best he could.

"No, we were both blown to smithereens." Three of Bellerothon's tentacles slithered up to touch various controls, setting off sequences of flashing lights and musical tones. "You're not done, by the way," said Bellerothon. "That one laser scalpel zap did not disable the chem weapons."

"Gee, thanks for setting me straight," said Jared, laying on some sarcasm of his own. "I thought *for sure* it would be that easy."

"It's all uphill from here, human." Two more tentacles swam up to join the first three, and all five fanned out to manipulate controls. "Now be ready with a tranquilizer for when the security blocks come down. You'll only have one shot at taking the edge off that hive mind in there."

"It's a hive mind?" Jared frowned. "In a missile control system?"

"What else would you *use* in one? Chem weapon missile control is *not* one-brain friendly." As he/she spoke, his/her tentacles rapidly flickered over the panels on the wall, flipping switches, smacking buttons, performing mysterious acts of unseen alien dexterity. "Ta-da! I've *distracted* it enough for you to bring on the *drugs."*

"Thanks." Jared smirked as he reached for the hypodermic. "But couldn't you have gone any faster?"

When Bellerothon didn't answer, Jared turned—just in time to see him/her keel over backward on his/her shell, then flop on his/her side and twitch uncontrollably.

Instantly, Jared dropped to a crouch and flipped the bio-scanner card from his med-kit. The internal injuries had gotten exponentially worse. The change to a new form had pumped Bellerothon full of the Nascendi version of adrenaline, briefly halting the breakdown's progress and masking the pain, but the grace period was over.

Meanwhile, the seconds till launch kept ticking away. Bad decisions and unlucky breaks were piling up, just as they had on Cassilon VII.

"No, damnit." Gritting his teeth, Jared grabbed the quantum-hypo, tapped in a pharm-code, and jammed the needle into Bellerothon's black-furred lower torso. More painkiller rushed into his/her body, formulated to treat a Level 2 Nascendi physiology.

Bellerothon visibly relaxed, but it didn't last. A moment later, he/she launched into a series of spasms, thrashing so violently the silver shell tore right off his/her back and wobbled aside.

It was then that pounding noises started in the ceiling hatchway, echoing through the bunker. There was one clang, then a scrape, as if someone on the other side was trying to get in.

Could it be the Pact Marines? If so, they couldn't have picked a better time to come to the rescue.

Bellerothon was shedding his/her furry hide and tentacles as something jagged, red, and rough-shod twisted its way into the world.

"Hello?" Jared called up from the base of the ladder. "Who's there?"

The only answer was more banging and scraping. Apparently, the sound of his voice wasn't carrying through the heavy metal of the sealed hatch.

"Shut up over there!" The voice of his Nascendi companion, however, carried perfectly from across the bunker. *"My head is killing me! And so is everything else!"*

Jared turned to see a spindly, crimson figure unfold from the floor, its body like a bundle of sticks studded with jagged thorns and sporting a long, red tail like tangled barbed wire. His face (he was all male now, his thorny member left no doubt) was triangular, with what looked like razor-sharp edges; his eyes were tongues of fire, and his mouth was set with crooked black teeth oozing glistening tar.

"So, Bellerothon." Jared cleared his throat. "How are you feeling now?"

"Slightly better, no thanks to you." The flames in his eyes flared. "And I call myself Cartilagicavernous Virtuosidiamediavore now. Do you have a problem with that?"

"Only the saying-it part." Jared managed a weak smile. "How about if I just call you CarVir for short?"

"Unacceptable." Cartilagicavernous Virtuosidiamediavore switched his barbed wire tail so hard that it smashed a display screen on the wall. "How about if I just call *you* something like *soon to fail?* Or *most likely to accurately anticipate the manner of his impending death?"*

Leaving the hatch and ladder, Jared headed to the nearest control bank to get back to work. "I'll let you pick one while I get back to work stopping the massacre of thousands in..." He checked the digital countdown. "...in approximately 15 minutes."

"Oh, woe is me," said CarVir. "Whatever will we do without so many of you running around? Live as our ancient gods intended?" He snorted and rattled his branches.

"And yet I've noticed you don't turn away our help on the battlefield, do you?"

"Only our lower forms!" snapped CarVir. *"Only the unevolved seek the help of wretched humans!"*

"Whatever." Jared pulled out the laser scalpel and pointed it at the middle glowing button of a group.

"The chem weapons." CarVir snorted loudly. "Maybe we'd all be better off if they launched and got it over with."

"Here goes nothing." Jared switched on the scalpel, cutting a notch in the middle button. Meanwhile, the banging on the hatch kept getting louder. Would the Marines be too late to save both him and Gestalta?

"You're doing it wrong!" CarVir stormed over and snatched the scalpel from his hand before it had cut very deep. *"Don't you know anything, human moron?"*

With that, the thorny being flashed the scalpel in a seemingly random fashion over multiple buttons, punching smoking holes in each of them—then hacked a long, scorched scar across controls and surfaces with the laser's red beam.

"Now *that's* how you *do* it, human." With a nasty flourish, CarVir gave the scalpel a toss over his shoulder, letting it land with a clatter on the metal floor.

There were now twelve minutes left until the chem weapons launched, and who knew how long until CarVir evolved into his final form.

Just then, the radio crackled, and Lita's voice came through clearly. "Juliet-lima, come in. Juliet-lima, do you copy?"

Jared scrambled to grab the radio and squeeze the mic button. "This is Juliet-lima! Alpha tango, it's so *good* to hear your voice!"

"We thought we'd lost you," said Lita. "Did you even make it into the bunker?"

"We did, and got trapped for our trouble! Marines are digging us out as we speak!"

"Those aren't Marines, Juliet-lima!"

Jared's gaze shot to the hatch.

"Drone vid shows nothing but Groks at your location!" As she said it, a snowy image of the surface faded onto the radio's little screen. The video showed a swarm of huge spiderlike things, scuttling into a shaft.

"Holy shit." Every last drop of Jared's blood ran icy cold.

"What's the status on the chem weapons, Juliet-lima?" asked Lita.

The banging on the hatch accelerated and became more insistent. The countdown timer crossed the ten-minutes-till-launch threshold.

"Trust me," said Jared. "You don't want to know."

No sooner had the words left his mouth than CarVir snatched the radio from his hand and pitched it across the bunker so it smashed to bits against the wall.

"Sufficient continuous or repetitive trauma applied to a Nascendi physiology will force the recipient to undergo a series of transformations, culminating in a form that is physically powerful and extraordinarily aggressive. It is this form, dubbed the Grok, that has positioned itself as a fierce enemy to human colonists and the simpler forms of its own species alike."

-From "The Rapid Multiphasic Mutation of Sentient Nascendi Lifeforms During Wartime," The Journal of Traumatic Warfighter Mutation, *Vol. 12, September 2205*

"I demand your attention, so-called doc!" CarVir doubled over and coughed out gouts of dark smoke and flame.

A quick pass with the bio-scanner told Jared the tale. The

trauma to his system was getting worse, which meant that another metamorphosis was on the way.

One way or another, he would soon be in the company of a Grok.

The banging and scraping from the hatch suddenly stopped—then was replaced by something else. Jared recognized the high-pitched whine of a laser saw, slicing its way through the thick metal of the hatch cover.

He had to do something, and fast. His death was all but assured; now it was just a matter of stopping the chem weapons launch and saving thousands of lives before he got devoured.

"Agghh!" CarVir seized up and staggered away from him, clutching his fiery, triangular skull. *"Make it stop!"*

Jared reached for his quantum-hypodermic, ready to inject a stronger painkiller that might ease the Nascendi's suffering...then hesitated. The hypo was programmed with meds to treat all the Nascendi's forms, but what if there were subtle drug interactions he didn't know about?

"What are you waiting for?" howled CarVir. "Do you *want* me to turn Grok and *kill* you?"

The Nascendi lunged for the hypo, then collapsed when Jared jerked it out of reach. Meanwhile, the whine of the laser saw grew louder; it wouldn't be long until the Groks broke through and poured into the bunker.

Still, as the agonized Nascendi twitched and thrashed on the floor, Jared held back from administering the painkiller. Thoughts of Cassilon filled his mind, thoughts of errors and terrors that had haunted him...thoughts of metamorphoses...changes he couldn't keep up with...

...and possibilities he hadn't considered until now.

Heart jackhammering, Jared watched with seeming ambivalence. He felt elation and regret at the same time. A possible solution to the Nascendi problem existed, one that could have saved many Leiadesian lives if only he'd thought of it two years earlier.

But it wasn't going to be easy, and success wasn't guaranteed. Total failure seemed just as likely...but what did he have to lose at that point?

As the laser saw whined away above him, and the chem weapons countdown approached the five-minute mark, Jared made careful adjustments to the quantum-hypo. Taking a deep breath, he approached CarVir, who was shuddering uncontrollably and clawing at his face.

"Oh, thank you, Doc! Thank you!" Tears of flame rose from the Nascendi's eyes. *"Kill the pain, Doc! Do it now!"*

"Roger that," said Jared, though his intention was the exact opposite. "Here comes the good stuff."

With that, he drove the hypo into CarVir's torso, smack in the heart of his primary injury site, and pumped in the compound he'd synthesized.

Then, as the med took effect, he leaped away.

"Doc?" CarVir's eyes shot wide open. "What did you *do* to me, Doc? The pain's not getting *better,* Doc!"

"Just hang on and get through it!" said Jared. "It's our only chance!"

"Doc, no!" There was terror in his voice. "Don't *do* this!"

Then, the Nascendi convulsed violently, howling in agony and fear. His body tumbled and shuddered, limbs tangling, thorny flesh melting and darkening into a knot of rough black dough. The dough pulsed and kneaded from within like a bag full of knuckles, emitting a terrible squealing sound that overpowered the whine of the laser saw.

Finally, one of the knuckles burst free, extending into a long, spiny limb. More followed until there were six in all—and then they lifted the doughy mass off the floor between them. The end of that mass released a head studded with glossy black eyes.

Then two jagged mandibles thrust out of that head, clacking as the newborn Grok let loose a ferocious roar.

Faced with the monstrous Grok, Jared had to force himself to overcome his fear and take the next step. During the transformation, he'd mixed another compound in the hypo and loaded it in the injection chamber. As soon as the change was complete, but before the Grok could acclimate to its new form, he charged across the floor with the hypo upraised and drove it home in the beast's thorax.

He squeezed the activator stud and shot the compound into the monster. The instant the chamber emptied, he wrenched the hypo free and bolted away, running to the far end of the bunker.

Rearing up, the Grok roared again, flailing its spiny black legs in Jared's direction. Then, seemingly unaffected by the compound, the Grok dropped back down and skittered across the floor on a beeline for Jared.

Jared darted over to the exit ladder and clambered up the rungs. He got just out of reach as the huge spider-thing flashed over and clawed at the metal framework below him.

Jared climbed a few more rungs, going as far as he could. But the Grok's next jump wasn't quite as high as the first, and the one after that was lower still. The fourth time was a half-hearted effort, barely lifting itself off the floor.

After which, the creature screeched and reeled away from the ladder, staggering off into the bunker.

Alert for the slightest hostile move, Jared started down the ladder for a closer look at what was happening. Halfway across the bunker, the Grok lay in a quivering pile on the floor, legs twitching crazily.

Surging with hope, Jared rushed down the rest of the way and dropped to the floor. The other Groks were almost through the hatch; he was gambling it was safer down there for a moment for two.

As he took a few steps closer, the Grok on the floor shrieked and flew into a round of wild spasms. Its black flesh blistered and puckered, then burst repeatedly and shriveled. Its legs fell off and crumbled into dust.

Would that be the end of it? Had Jared miscalculated? Had his compound, which had accelerated the mutation into the Grok, failed to trigger the *additional* mutation he'd theorized might be possible?

Glancing at the countdown, he saw there were just three minutes left until the chem weapons launch. Then, when he returned his gaze to the Grok, he saw that something new was happening to its body.

The wrinkled gray lozenge had begun to glow softly from within. As Jared watched, it slowly floated upward and started to inflate and rotate. As the rotation accelerated, the middle opened up, turning the puffed-up lozenge into a thick hoop like a nautical life preserver.

The hoop shifted from gray to pale yellow, and fluttering tendrils emerged from its circumference. Then it glided over to Jared and stopped at his eye-level, spinning and fluttering and giving off a faint floral scent and gentle humming sound.

"Can you help?" Jared gestured at the banks of controls. "Can you stop the chem weapons launch and save those people?"

The hoop hovered there for a moment, glowing progressively brighter. Then, it spoke to him in a lilting, feminine voice.

"I am Eiderfine," she told him. "And I will help if you will apologize for hurting me."

"I apologize for the pain," said Jared. "I took no pleasure in hurting you."

Eiderfine hovered silently for a moment. "It is acceptable," she said finally, and then she flew over to the banks and went to work.

Zipping from one control to another, she flickered her tendrils over them, making adjustments. Colors changed, displays altered, tones sounded. Red lights flared to life, bathing the bunker, and a deafening klaxon blared three times…then died. Every light and display on the control banks went out at once, including the countdown, which snapped off with less than one minute remaining.

Finally, the red light filling the bunker went out, too, plunging the whole place into darkness. Eiderfine's glow was the only illumination left in that underground space.

As she drifted over to Jared, tears welled up in his eyes. The laser saw was still cutting the hatch, the Groks would attack soon, but at least he knew he'd been right.

Injecting Cartilagicavernous with a high-dose pain-inducer instead of a painkiller had intensified the trauma to his system, triggering his mutation into a Grok. Injecting the Grok with another pain-inducer had done the same again, pushing it into yet another form. As far as Jared knew, the Grok had been the final possible manifestation of the Nascendi. But he'd bet that, perhaps, the potential for another metamorphosis could be medically induced under the right conditions.

And his bet had been right.

"Thank you," he told her. "Thank you for stopping the launch and saving my people."

"It was the least I could do for my good friend," she told him.

"I wish I'd thought of this years ago, though," said Jared. "Maybe I could have speeded up the mutations of some other folks. Maybe I could have saved them."

"Or maybe losing them was the only way you could have come up with the idea to save me," said Eiderfine. "And the people of Gestalta. Perhaps it was a necessary sacrifice."

Just then, the sound of the laser saw stopped. The hatch cracked open and crashed to the floor with a metallic clang at the base of the ladder.

"I guess this is goodbye then." Jared smiled. "The Groks are coming."

"Stay cool, Doc," said Eiderfine. "Trust me, I know what makes these guys tick. And besides, I'm an honorary Corpsman, aren't I?"

"Honorary my ass," said Jared. "As far as I'm concerned, you're a full-blown FMF Corpsman all the way, Doc."

THE WISH OF A WISH

You'd think genies might get a wish to themselves now and then...but from the pain in Magda's eyes when she opens the mansion's door, I can see she's getting zero wish fulfillment out of life.

"Yes?" Her eyes are beautiful, an unearthly bright greenish gold--but the look in them is one of pure misery.

"Good morning, ma'am." I flash her my badge, and she winces. "Oliver Singel, state Department of Mystic Revenue. I'm here to see Mr. Rudolph Gunza."

She ushers me in without hesitation. She doesn't fear me at all; as a genie, she need only fear one man in all the world.

That man is her master, Rudy Gunza.

As she closes the heavy door behind me, I gaze around at the opulent entryway. Everything is glittering gold and crimson velvet and gleaming marble, from the winding staircase to the fountain in the middle of the giant room.

Ill-gotten gains, all of it. Whipped up on a whim and a wish by the magical beauty standing in front of me.

She tosses her head, and the lush, black curls flop about her shoulders. She straightens the dark blue satin bodice of her outfit, smooths the silk harem pants below her taut bare midriff.

Even with the beaten look in her eyes, even with her mouth and chin covered by a pale blue veil, she looks breathtaking. She looks more perfect and radiant than any woman alive, as beautiful as any fantasy sculpted by a man's imagination.

Then again, she *has* to, doesn't she?

"What business do you have with Master Gunza?" There's a hint of a glint in her eye as she says it--a flicker of power. She might not be able to exercise it against her master, but that doesn't mean she can't use it against someone else, like me.

"Serious business," I tell her. "*Tax* business."

"Oh-ho!" Gunza's jolly voice booms from the top of the staircase. "And here I thought this was purely a *friendly* visit!"

A weak smile doesn't quite make it onto my face. "Hello, Rudy."

Gunza wobbles down the stairs, looking like a tubby sheikh. His glittering red robes can't hide the stupendous gut wagging in front of him.

When he and I were partners, he never had a gut at all.

"Long time no miss!" says Gunza as he drops from the last marble stair to the floor. "How's the old gang of idiots?"

"Better than ever, now that you're gone," I tell him.

Gunza throws an arm around Magda's shoulders and squeezes her tight. "Oleo and I used to work together! Isn't that something, Magda? We was *revenooers* together."

Magda's head bobbles as he jerks her around. Her flat stare drifts past me like litter on a breeze.

"Went after *tax evaders*, didn't we?" says Gunza. "Folks who didn't pay the state a piece of the action from wishes granted and spells cast."

"It's income, Magda." I wave my clipboard at the surrounding opulence. "The state deserves its share under the law."

"Bull-squat, Oleo." Gunza chortles and strokes his braided red mustache. "Let the state get its *own* genie."

"Yes, fine idea." I walk around the room, taking notes on the clipboard. "We could get one the way *you* did. Force an old lady at gunpoint to use up her three wishes on nothing and hand over the lamp."

Gunza's grin darkens. "Hey now, Oleo. That was a straight-up *gift*, and no one can prove otherwise."

"Almost no one." I shoot a look at Magda, and she turns away.

Gunza shrugs. "If a door closes, open a window. The department passed me over for a promotion--which *you* got--but Mrs. Sandusky thought I deserved an even greater reward. She *wished* for me to have it."

The walls are made of alternating gold and platinum ingots, which I note on my clipboard. "Well, *I* wish you'd paid your *taxes*." I write more on the clipboard. "If I were *you*, I'd wish you don't have a *coronary* when you see the grand *total* you owe the state."

"I don't owe one cent!" Gunza releases Magda and storms over to grab my clipboard.

I snatch it right back. "You lazy prick. How hard could it be to pay your taxes? You already wished for unlimited wishes, didn't you?"

Gunza smirks. "That was my first wish."

"Why not wish for her to pay your taxes?" I point my pen at Magda.

"Because I don't *choose* to." Gunza's features twist into a scowl. "Because I am the *master*."

I shake my head in disgust. "You're just like all the rest. All the other scum you used to help me bust."

Gunza gazes into my eyes for a long moment, nodding slowly. "Run," he says finally.

I know where this is going. I knew from the moment I walked into the place.

"I wish..." says Gunza.

I swing the clipboard at his head, but he knocks it away with one thick forearm.

Before I can take another swing, he finishes his sentence. "I wish that a hunting party of madmen and monsters will hunt down Oliver Singel, then torture and mutilate him for as long as I wish...and not kill him, no matter how much he begs for it."

Magda's eyes meet mine. They well with regret and resignation.

I reach out to her. "Magda, please! Don't do it! I'm here to help you!"

Gunza giggles and smacks me on the back. "He's a liar! He's just here for his precious *revenooo*!"

"I'm sorry." Magda weaves her arms in the air, and a cloud of twinkling glitter swirls above her. "I have no choice but to obey my master."

"Wrong!" Even as the misshapen forms materialize before me, I keep trying. "I *can* help you! Tell me what you *want*!"

Magda hesitates, and the figures flicker. Gunza stomps over and smacks her across the face.

"Do your job!" he says. "Obey me!" He strikes her again.

Magda closes her eyes. Her nimble fingers finish their dance in the air, and the hulking forms solidify.

"Run, rabbit!" Gunza howls with laughter. "Don't let 'em catch you!"

With one last look at Magda, I turn and sprint off into the depths of the mansion.

The hunters are silent. No shrieking laughter, no ululating howls, no clattering weapons and footsteps. I can barely hear them back there at all--just whispers and the rustling of wings and rags.

The quiet makes it all the worse as I run.

Heart hammering in my chest, I race to the end of the corridor and burst through the oak double doors there. Beyond the doors, I find myself in a vast arboretum, teeming with tropical trees and flowers.

Without stopping, I draw my cell phone and send a text message to my partner. At least I had the sense to post him elsewhere in case I needed backup.

Now, if only Gunza didn't think to wish for Magda to block outgoing phone signals.

As I pocket the phone, I hear brush shuddering behind me. Ducking off the gold-bricked path, I bolt through the thick foliage, crossing the room away from my original trajectory.

Suddenly, a feverish ghoul explodes from the shrubbery ahead of me, swinging a machete. I fall back, barely escaping the blade...and nearly end up skewered on the point of a bayonet brandished by a leering soldier.

Twisting out of the way, I leap off into the cover as both of them slash and stab at me. I rush straight through the deep green jungle, panting for breath in the steamy air--and surge out of the vegetation in front of another set of double doors.

Plunging through the doors, I find myself in a maze. Through its frosted glass walls, I glimpse shadowy figures moving around me...but I have to go onward. I hear noise from the other side of the doors, so I can't go back to the arboretum.

I move as quickly and quietly as I can, though it doesn't matter. The enemy can see me as well as I see them through the frosted glass.

I zip around a corner, then another and another, always choosing right at the branches. Turning again, I spot a blurred figure on the other side of the translucent wall...and he spots me. He changes direction and follows me down the passage, keeping pace in a humpbacked trot, separated from me only by a few inches of glass.

Luckily, the next time I reach a branch, he hits a dead end. He howls, caught in a corner, as I dart down another passage, hoping for an exit.

I find one--a gleaming golden door inlaid with multicolored gems--but just as I charge forward, it crashes open, revealing a towering maniac.

He stands seven feet tall, at least, and his double-jointed limbs are like sticks. He's naked except for a leather loincloth, and his skin is reddish-brown like an almond.

His eyes and mouth gape wide as he scrambles toward me, drooling and whooping.

Suddenly, before I can do anything, he slows in mid-step. His movements stretch out as if he were the star of a slow-motion movie, and his whoops extend to one

drawn-out tone.

I jump when I hear the normal-speed voice of Magda behind

me. "That was one of my masters, two hundred and fifty years ago. Shall I tell you how he beat me?"

Looking around, I see another predator creeping from the maze in slow-mo. This one, muscular, blond and

bushy-bearded, wears the horned helmet of a Viking.

"Were these your masters through the ages?" I say.

She nods. "As you die, you will know what I've been through."

Stepping toward the tall one, I gingerly touch his reddish-brown knuckles. "How can you be doing this? Disobeying Rudy?"

"I'm obeying him," says Magda. "I'm slowing things down, but you will still be hunted and tortured."

"Why talk to me at all then?"

Magda cocks her head and frowns. "What did you mean when you said you could help me?"

"I meant what I said," I tell her. "All you have to do is tell me what you want. Just ask for it."

She narrows her eyes. "*I* know what this is about now. You want me for yourself, don't you?"

"No." I shake my head. "I want to *save* you."

"You're not the first to say that." Magda snorts and folds her arms over her blue satin bodice. "Somehow, *saving* me always ends with *hurting* me."

"Not this time." I spread my arms wide. "I swear, I'm here to help you."

"You want my help collecting Rudy's taxes," says Magda. "For all the riches I've given him."

"Actually," I say, "you're the only reason I'm here."

Magda stares, her expression split between confusion and disbelief.

"This time, I'm not as concerned about tax evasion," I say, "as I am about slavery and abuse."

She looks like she's thinking hard...and then her stare becomes an angry glare. "Liar. You're a *liar*, just like *all* men."

"I'm telling you, I came here only to save you."

"Liar!" She lifts her hands overhead to weave and conjure, and I see the tall man start to move faster. "You better *run*, liar!"

Without another word, I dash around the tall man, heave

open the door, and race into the hallway. I can tell she's run out of patience, at least for now. I can tell she doesn't believe me.

Even though I told her the absolute truth.

I don't care about the mystic taxes. This time, I came only for her.

As I run down the hall, I open every door...but I'm not looking for a way out. I'm looking for something else.

A lamp. *Her* lamp.

Now that I'm on the inside of Gunza's mansion, I'm determined to find it. I'm going to end this perverted jerk's most heinous crime: genie abuse. The bastard's a *djinnophile*.

Here's how it works. The genie must obey her master. The genie has magical powers that can heal any wound, repair any damage. Even to herself.

What better scenario can there be for a twisted sicko who likes to hurt women? He can brutalize her any way he likes, then wish away the damage, removing any sign of the crime, expunging any guilt...and leaving a clean slate for the next round of abuse.

That's what makes it especially evil. The genie becomes an accomplice to her own abuse. She literally has no choice.

And it goes on and on and on like that, again and again and again. Forever, if he wishes eternal life for himself.

So it's no wonder Magda doesn't trust me...but she should. There's much more to me than meets the eye.

For one thing, I'm state police now, not Department of Mystic Revenue. I work for the Paranormal Victims Unit.

For another thing, I'm someone altogether different than any of that or anything Gunza could ever guess.

But Magda could figure it out. At least I hope she does before it's too late.

I'm hustling through the gymnasium when they catch me. Two of the ghoulish thugs burst in through the far door from outside the mansion, and another drops down from the ceiling on a rope.

The one from the rope has dark skin and a tribal headdress of tattered fur and feathers. One of the other two has silver hair and wears a tuxedo, and the last one bulges with muscles and pads under a football player's uniform. More echoes of Magda's former masters.

As they surround me, I look for the best escape route. My eyes keep flicking to the open door to the outside, where my partner waits. If my text message got through to him, he could come charging through that door at any second, guns blazing.

Just as I have that thought, he pops up in front of me out of thin air. He's standing, and at first I think he's still alive...but then he literally falls to pieces--arms and legs and head and torso tumbling to the floor.

I hear Gunza laughing, and I turn to see him floating in midair on a scarlet magic carpet. As he claps, Magda slumps beside him, utterly joyless.

Like I said, she becomes an accomplice. She literally has no choice.

At least she takes no pleasure in it. That's what makes her worth saving.

She has yet to hand over her soul.

"Bravo!" says Gunza. "Bravissimo! You should've seen the look on your face, Oleo!"

I keep my eyes fixed on him, partly so I won't have to look at my partner's body parts oozing blood at my feet.

Gunza elbows Magda hard in the side. "You're getting all this on tape or a crystal ball or whatever, right? So I can watch it again and again?"

Magda nods. "Yes, Master."

I hate seeing her like that. A woman with so much power, a woman who literally could do anything...reduced to groveling and harming the very people who could set her free.

Unless I can get through to her. "I can help you, Magda."

Her eyes flick toward me.

"Tell me what you want," I say. "Ask me for it."

I hold her gaze for a moment before she looks away. She's still not ready.

That's the root of the problem here. A genie, acting always to serve others, knows nothing of selfishness...but she must ask for something for herself to become free.

The key stands in front of her, but it's useless if she won't pick it up and turn it in the lock.

I wait for Gunza to become bored with my screams, but it takes a very long time.

He hovers above on his magic carpet as the echoes of Magda's demented masters torture me. They do it right there in the gymnasium, on a weight bench, using trays of knives and needles and power tools wished up by Gunza.

As the ghouls work me over, I wonder if they are improvising...or if every terrible step is drawn from Magda's memory. The pain is indescribable, unbearable, catastrophic. Each application of blade or pliers or drill bit plunges me into uncharted depths of agony.

Did they do the same to her? Did they twist and pull and crush and cut, sometimes all at once? Did they laugh as they tuned her screams by grinding harder, digging deeper, winding tighter?

Did they cut off bits of her? Did they taunt her as they excavated organs? Did they push her to the brink of death again and again...holding her alive with wishes as they ruined her in every possible way?

And then, did they wish her back to wholeness, repairing every damage...only to start all over again?

The way they do with me?

If so, my sympathy for her increases a trillionfold. More even than that.

Because this is hell. Sheer hell, as the devil himself might design it.

And I wonder, between strokes of the knife and blows of the hammer, how it is that Magda has not gone irretrievably mad.

Finally, after what seems to me like a dozen years, Gunza does grow bored. Tired is more like it. His eyes start drifting shut, and instead of wishing himself wide awake, he floats off to bed.

Lying on his belly on the magic carpet, he winks and waggles his fingers at me. "Back soon, dear." His braided red mustache jumps as he chuckles. "Don't miss me *too* much."

At this point, I'm in excruciating agony on the bench. This is the sixth time I've been horrifically mutilated and left at the brink of death.

My limbs have all been disconnected and reattached in the wrong places. The ghouls wear my organs on leather thongs around their necks. Only wishes are keeping me alive.

Gunza gives Magda a shove off the carpet, and she thuds to the floor. "I wish you would put Oliver back together, good as new, and get him rested up for our next session." After he says it, he rolls over on his back, crosses his hands behind his head, and floats out the door, yawning and snickering.

When he's gone, Magda struggles to her feet. She weaves mystic sigils overhead, and the torture squad of monstrous masters past disappears in a shower of golden glitter.

Standing over me, she gazes down at the damage...then looks away. Turning her back, she weaves more patterns in the air with her agile, flickering fingers.

I feel a familiar tingling. Gold dust twinkles around me, and I hear a fluttering trill like the song of a tiny tropical bird.

Reality stops and shifts like a jump-cut in a movie. There is an instant of nonexistence, disconnection from senses and self-awareness...and then I am whole once more.

My body is intact. My wounds are closed, my organs and limbs back in the right places. For the seventh time today, she has put Humpty Dumpty back together again.

Except for the memories, it is as if none of it ever happened.

This is how it must be for her, every time Gunza tears her apart and wishes her restored once more.

I wonder how many times a day she must do it. How many times she has done it since he took control of her.

How many times since her birth or creation.

She turns to face me again, fingers still weaving. The weight bench becomes a bed, the gymnasium a bedroom draped in white satin, aglow in moonlight.

Small figures materialize around me--winged children, robed in white. Some are toddlers, some older, some younger. Some are infants.

They push pillows behind my head and tuck blankets around me. They dab my forehead with a cool compress and wrap warm towels around my arms.

They raise a glass of water to my lips, and I drink. They feed me bread and hot broth from a silver tray. They sing softly as they work--dozens of them, all watching me solemnly, eyes glowing like little silver moons in their dark and pale faces.

"Who are they?" As I ask the question, an infant hands me a little cake.

Magda watches from the foot of the bed. "My angels," she says. "My babies."

Gazing around me in wonder, I begin to understand. "Your children? All of them?"

Magda nods. "They are my only comforts in this world."

I accept another spoonful of soup from a dark-haired little boy. "You made them."

"With my masters, as any woman would." Magda bows her head. "And unmade them, as my masters wished."

"My God." I shiver as I feel their moonlight eyes upon me--the eyes of dozens of dead children, recreated from the dust of graves and residue of tears.

Every last one of them, dead. Murdered by magic at whatever age they most displeased their mother's masters. Their fathers.

Gone now, as if they had never been. As if they had never been forced into or out of existence. Living on only in her memory.

Resurrected only to comfort her in moments of greatest pain and despair.

Tears roll down her face, and she wipes them away. "I'm sorry," she says. "Sorry for everything."

If only I could break her free from this unending cycle of woe. If only I could cut the magic ties that bind her to her heartless monster of a master.

If only there was some way to move her to ask for what she needs. What I can provide.

Maybe there is.

I glimpse it for a split-second. A look of sharper sorrow on her face. A sudden sinking. Fear and panic and rage and longing all at once, like fruit on a tree.

She touches her belly, and I know. She pulls her hand away instantly, but it's too late.

I finally know.

I know how to save her.

"Very good!" Gunza claps from his royal box in the crowded stands of the coliseum. "Not perfect, but that comes with practice! You've just committed your first *murder*, Oleo!"

The bloody knife slips from my fingers and lands in the sand at my feet. My arms are soaked in blood up to the elbows. My white t-shirt and pants have gone crimson from sleeve to cuff.

I know what I've just done. I know that I had no control over it, that I was at the mercy of a compelling wish.

But it doesn't really matter. I still remember every detail. I remember killing the innocent woman wished up from somewhere in the world outside...killing her as the crowd around me cheered and stomped and showered me with roses.

That, of course, was the whole idea.

Torturing and resurrecting me wasn't enough for Gunza. I took the promotion that should have been his, and then I tried to tax his lordly treasures; he won't be happy until I've been corrupted and ruined and debased inside as well as out.

Just as he's corrupted and ruined his Magda.

"Now this is the life!" Gunza guzzles wine from a goblet and gropes the nearly naked slave girl in his lap. "*That* is entertainment!" He points his goblet at me, and the crowd howls with delight.

Gazing at the poor dead woman in the sand, I wonder if I can get through this. I wonder how much more I will have to endure to save Magda.

Looking up, I see her standing in the box with him, head bowed low. She won't look at me. Won't look at what she's done at his behest.

That has to change.

"Magda!" I call to her, and her head lifts. Her eyes meet mine. "Tell me what you want! *Ask* me for it!"

She twitches, then lowers her head again.

"Oh ho ho!" Gunza howls with laughter. "So you think you can give her something I *can't*?"

I'm treading on dangerous ground, and I know it. All he has to do is wish me silenced or dead or demented, and the game is over.

I continue to speak only to Magda. "Please! Ask for what you want!" I take a deep breath, ready to step off the precipice. Once I say the next thing, there'll be no taking it back. "For the sake of your unborn *child*, *ask* me!"

Suddenly, a hush falls over the coliseum. Even Gunza is silent.

Magda meets my gaze, and her eyes at first are full of rage. Then, the rage melts into despair.

And I know I was right. When she touched her belly while the angels tended me, she was thinking of an angel inside. A new child, growing within her.

His child. *Gunza*'s child.

So now I've done it. Everything balances on the head of a pin, and a single wish could bring it all crashing down.

That's all it will take. One wish from Gunza to force Magda to do away with their unborn child. Add it to the angelic host, existing only in memory, comforting her in her deepest, darkest night.

Nothing now to do but push every button on the board and pray the engine catches before we crash.

"You *know* what he'll do *next*, Magda!" I march across the sand to stand beneath her. "There's only one way to *stop* him! *Ask* me for it!"

Tears pour from her eyes and run under her veil. Her shoulders pump as she breathes faster, heart racing in terror.

Just then, Gunza does the unexpected. Instead of the child-killing wish I thought he'd make next, or the one that wipes me instantly from the face of the planet, he says this: "I wish I was down there with Oleo, strangling the *life* out of him!"

Magda's fingers weave through the air. Reality stutters, and Gunza's wish takes hold.

He is with me now on the sand, thick fingers wrapped around my throat. I chop at his forearms, but they won't budge.

He scowls with bloodshot eyes and flushed face and red hair bristling from his beard and under his turban. Veins pop along his temples, and cords bulge in his neck.

His grip of steel tightens. "How *dare* you interfere in my *paradise*?"

I barely force out words through the vice of his hands. "He'll kill it, Magda! Just like...all the others! You...know it's...*true*!"

"Shut up!" roars Gunza. "I wish..."

Before he can finish, I pump a knee into his groin. The wind goes out of him, and he releases his grip and falls to the ground.

I can get the words out now, but how long do I have? How many seconds until the next wish? "I can *help* you, Magda! I can save *you* and your *child*! All you have to do is *ask* me!"

"I don't believe you!" says Magda.

Gunza starts to get up. I send him back down with a kick to the face. "Ask anyway! What do you have to lose?"

Storm clouds boil overhead as Magda weeps. "But I'm a *genie*! I cannot ask for *anything* for myself!"

"You're wrong!" I kick Gunza in the face again, harder than before. "Now *ask* me! What do you *want*?"

Magda stops sobbing and looks at her bare belly. Her fingers touch it lightly as wings brushing a cloud. "I wish..." Her thumbs and forefingers meet, forming a diamond around her navel. "I wish you *could* help me. I wish you *could* set us free."

Finally.

A grin breaks wide across my face. I bow deeply to her, twirling my fingers with a flourish as if doffing a hat in her honor.

"Your wish, milady," I say, "is my command."

With that, I weave my fingers overhead, swirling them in multiple mystic sigils dripping with golden glitter. The ground rumbles underfoot, and the storm clouds darken. The crowd screams and stampedes in the stands.

This, then, is my secret...that which makes me altogether different than anyone could ever guess. I am more than man or policeman or tax collector. More than I have ever shown another soul until now.

My fingers work furiously, teasing reality's threads upon the loom. Everything around me starts to turn, faster and faster with each passing breath.

Gunza struggles to his feet but can't stay there. The spinning of the world knocks him right back down on his ass.

Unable to retaliate physically, he resorts to tried and true. "I wish that Oliver would be..."

Before he can finish, I slam my hands together with a sound like the pealing of a massive bell. A bolt of lightning crashes down from the clouds above--and Gunza is gone.

As reality continues to accelerate in its wild gyre, Magda appears beside me. "Who are you?" she says. "Are you djinn?"

My fingers resume their weaving dance overhead. "Not *djinn*," I say. "*Wish*."

"I don't understand!"

I have to raise my voice to be heard above the rushing of the world. "One good master, ages ago, wished for you to have a wish of your own. Do you remember?"

She frowns in thought, then nods. "That was a very long time ago."

"Being a genie, you would ask for nothing for yourself, but he insisted. Unwilling to make a selfish choice, you put off the decision. You wished for one wish that you could call upon later, when you needed it most."

Magda smiles. "And you are that wish?"

"I am." Reality spins so fast around us, it is a blur of color and motion. I know that my work is almost done. "I waited for centuries for you to call on me, and you never did. I lived many lives, staying as close to you as I could, watching and waiting. Finally, I decided it was time for me to step in and give you a push."

Magda touches her belly. "So you really *can* help us."

"You have asked for what you need, and I will grant it. I will set you and your child free."

"Free." Magda says it like she's tasting it, like it's the first time she's ever spoken. "Free from Rudolph Gunza?"

"Free from *all* masters. Free to go where you want and do as you choose." I shoot her a grin and a wink. "Free to start a new life with your child."

Magda wipes a tear from her eye. She removes the veil from her face and kisses me on the cheek with lips like tender plums. "Thank you, my wish."

"My pleasure," I tell her. "You deserve to be happy."

"I only wish I could help you in return."

My fingers ache as I weave the last glittering sigils. "You can't. No more magic for you." I shrug. "But it's not all it's cracked up to be, is it?"

"Sometimes it is." Magda hugs me. "I'll never forget you."

"Then there you go." I finish weaving the new world and wrap my arms around her. "I *will* get my wish after all."

We squeeze each other tight as the world spins around us. A single tear crosses my face as I cease to be, dissolving into glittering gold dust that curls skyward like a puff of smoke from a dying lamp.

THE POOPING KNIGHT'S PLAYBOOK

Once again, I am pooping by the manger…but I swear it's okay. It's what I was made to do, after all.

Normally, the other figures in a tabletop nativity set aren't even shocked by this. They get used to my bad manners, dropping trou and pinching out a loaf with a curl on top in a corner of the stable.

But today, I'm the new figure on the block. My new owner, Dave, bought me on an online auction site and just got me in the mail today. I wasn't an original part of the nativity set on his living room coffee table, but he plunked me in here anyway; now it's up to me to get the other figures to accept me…which is something in which they clearly have no interest.

All they see is a 6-inch tall ceramic figure of the fictional knight Don Quixote, squatting with his silver armored britches pulled down to expose a bare bottom over a pile of feces on the stable floor. They're new to the tradition of the pooping nativity figure, the *caganer*…so it's up to me to educate them.

That's what I set out to do on Day One in my new digs, just after Dave has gone upstairs to bed. This is the time when figures like me—like all of us—are magically able to move and interact.

We're silent and still the rest of the time (though we're always aware of what happens around us).

"Hey guys." Leaning on the lance that I carry, I straighten up out of my squat and slap my bare left butt cheek. "Cleanup in aisle 7. Anyone got a square to spare?"

Predictably, nobody laughs. I'm working a tough crowd, and I know it.

"What is the *matter* with you?" The figure of Father Joseph whirls from the manger and glares in my direction. "This is a *holy scene*, not a place for you to *relieve yourself!*"

"Yeah!" The figure of Baby Jesus in the manger shakes a chubby little fist at me. "Show some respect!"

Chuckling, I remove the tin bowl helmet from my head and bow to the child…though in my opinion, he's no holier than the rest of us. "Apologies, little one. I'm so ashamed."

"You *should* be!" snaps Baby J.

I gesture toward my droppings, which everyone is making a point to avoid. "I'm ashamed that my *offering* was not two or three *times* that size. No wonder you people are unhappy with me!"

Everyone in the scene, even the animals, raises a ruckus at my comments. Clearly, they've led a sheltered life and have never come in contact with someone of my *profession* before.

Which makes them—how do you say?—the proverbial squatting ducks. They're ignorant of my appearance and purpose, doubly unaware of my secret intentions…and they'll stay that way until the time is right.

No, I'm not here just to poop up the joint for a laugh.

Suddenly, a bearded shepherd marches over my way, cracking his knuckles. "What are you doing here, anyway?" he asks, sounding surly.

"You know, the usual." I squat and wiggle my butt mockingly. "Giving till it hurts."

The surly shepherd's lack of amusement is so distinct, it feels like another person standing between us.

"You're a joke, right?" says Surly Shepherd. "A sacrilegious joke."

"Quite the opposite, actually." Doffing my helmet, I look

around at the captive audience. "I am meant to be a symbol of fertility and good luck. In some parts of the world—in Spain, especially—a nativity set without someone like me is incomplete."

Surly sneers. "Well, in *this* part of the world, in the state of Ohio in the U.S. of A., you're not welcome."

I plop the helmet back on my white-haired head. "Then I wonder why Dave put me here?" I hike a thumb toward the stairs leading up to the bedroom where Dave is currently snoring.

"A mistake, obviously," says Surly.

"He hasn't been himself lately," says Joseph.

"Let's just say, if you've ever wondered how to start drinking and wreck your life in three short weeks, he can show you the ropes," adds Baby J.

Bingo. It never takes long to get to the reason I'm sent somewhere…and believe me, there's *always* a reason. The whole point of me, these days, is to figure out the reason and fix things the best I can while trapped in the body of a pooping Don Quixote *caganer* figurine.

Needless to say, it's not the *ideal* situation. I wasn't *always* like this…but I also know that paying the price for the mistakes of my past life is a penance I can live with.

Unlike, say, taking shit from a shepherd with a chip on his crook.

"We don't *like* sacrilegious jokes around here." Surly's voice drips with contempt. "I think you should take your mess elsewhere, or someone might wipe up the floor with *you* instead."

Stroking my long white mustachio, I lean toward him. "You know what your problem is, friend? *Constipation.* Same with *all* of you."

The crowd stirs and grumbles.

"Your bowels are all impacted!" I tell them. "How long has it been since your last movement? Ten years? Twenty? *Thirty?*"

More grumbles. None of them even *have* bowels, but my abrasive tone puts them right off.

Tugging up my armored britches with one hand, I hobble past the shepherd to the manger and gesture at Baby J. "Isn't there a miracle about pinching loaves and flushes?"

Face beet red, the baby squalls and kicks furiously in the hay.

"No? No miracle cure from you guys either?" I waddle over to the three kings, who look at me like I've got six arms and five heads. "No milk of *myrrh*-nesia?"

As usual, nobody's laughing but me.

The king with the red turban and jet-black skin drops his chest of gold and swings a punch at me that never lands. I duck, and his momentum carries him off his feet.

I reach down to help him up, and he almost takes my hand... then pulls away, making a face as if I'd wiped my bum with that hand.

"Suit yourself." I wobble over and pet one of the camels instead. "I like Humpy better anyway. We make a great team—Humpy and Dumpy!"

"Little to the left there, chief," Humpy says softly in his *aw-shucks* voice, bobbing his head lower so I can scratch between his ears.

While I'm doing that, the others are all fussing among themselves, arguing about what to do with me—as if they have any choice in the matter. I smile with satisfaction, because the scene is familiar. Many's the time I've stirred up trouble like this with the nativity set rank and file; it's pretty much Step One in the Pooping Knight's Playbook.

"So, Humpy." I keep scratching between the camel's ears. "Tell me about Dave's drinking problem."

"I'll do yuh one better," says Humpy. "I'll *show* yuh."

The camel and I leave the confines of the stable and cross to one end of the table. Humpy doesn't offer to let me climb up and ride him, but that's okay; I might not trust my bottom either, if I were him.

Three glass tumblers rest on that end of the table, each with a bit of thin, amber liquid in the bottom. I recognize the scene from my own past life; I know it all too well.

"Those are just from tonight," Humpy says as we draw near.

"And that's not everything, either. Dave took some glasses out to the kitchen before he got so drunk he forgot to clean up the rest."

My metal britches drop with a clank as I brace myself on the rim of one glass and lean over to take a whiff. The booze in the glass is a faint remnant, diluted by melted ice, but its nature is clear to my nostrils.

"Whiskey." It brings back bad memories, and I quickly push away from the glass. "Is it like this every night?"

"Yup." Humpy bobs his head. "But Dave didn't *always* drink like this."

I plant my lance beside me and lean on it, staring into the tumbler. "So when did he start and why?"

"Three weeks ago, chief," says Humpy. "That's when his fiancée Jill left him. He hasn't been the same since."

"I see." Again, I notice a similarity to my own past life. Boy loses girl, boy gets drunk, boy flushes life down the crapper.

"It's so sad." A tear crawls down Humpy's shaggy face. "They started puttin' up the decorations, and then they had a fight, and she left. Now he's all alone, and Christmas is just *two days* away."

"Poor guy." I stroke my mustachio and shake my head. "There's never a *good* time for something like this, but..."

"The worst part is, it's all because of a *misunderstandin'*. Ol' Dave didn't do a darn thing *wrong*. She took somethin' he said the wrong way, and it all blew up."

"Sounds like a raw deal." My mission is clear, as it always is when I'm dropped into a situation like this. Not sure who puts the ideas in my head, but what I'm supposed to do is never in doubt for long. "I guess we'll have to *do* something about that, won't we?"

Humpy perks up instantly. "Yuh *mean* that? Yuh think we can *help* him?"

"I'd like to try," I tell him. "But I can't do it alone, and I doubt *that* bunch of stiffs has a team effort *in* them." Taking my weight off the lance, I point its tip at the nativity gang across the table, watching our every move.

Just then, I feel a breeze from above and look up. The angel from atop the stable hovers above us, flapping her bright white wings.

"Do you truly believe we can help him?" Her voice tinkles and chimes like music. Her white robes flow, and her golden hair glows as it ripples in the breeze from her wings. "Do you think we can make a difference in his life?"

Angel makes me a little nervous, and I hike up my britches—then drop them when I doff my tin helmet and hold it over my chest. "There are no guarantees, but yes." My nervousness makes no sense; she's no real angel, just a ceramic figurine like the rest of us. "I think we have a decent chance of making a difference."

Angel stares at me for a long moment and nods slowly. "Then I shall convince the others on your behalf. As long as I vouch for you, I know they will cooperate."

"It's a deal." I almost reach up for a handshake, then stop myself. Sometimes, I forget I'm not the man I used to be.

Sometimes, I forget I was ever anything but the Pooping Knight.

"Then let us begin." She gestures at the stable. "For there is not much time until Christmas Eve."

The kitchen counter might as well be Mount Everest.

Gazing up at it from the gray linoleum floor, it looks incredibly far away. Give me some string and a paper clip to use as a grappling hook, and I'll bet it would still take me a day to climb the tower of drawers leading up to it.

Good thing we have a flyer on our team. Not only is Angel great at convincing stubborn nativity figures to join my mission, but she can help us rise above the limitations of our tiny size and grounded state.

"Who wants to go first?" asks Angel, extending her arms.

The three of us who constitute the non-winged portion of the mission team take a minute to consider the question. Mother Mary and I exchange shrugs. Only Surly Shepherd looks away, but I think he's afraid of heights. For such a supposed tough guy, he looked pretty shaky a few minutes ago on the flight down from the coffee table to the carpeted living room floor.

"I'll go." Smiling serenely, as always, Mary steps forward. Angel wraps her arms around her, then gently carries her upward with sweeping flaps of her feathery white wings.

As soon as they're out of earshot, Surly lurches over and shoves his kisser in my face. "You better watch your back, Sir Poopy. I'm not as easy to put one over on as the rest of these chumps."

I meet his snarl with a smirk. "That's not what your *sheep* say."

His face flushes. I think he might try to pop me one, but I make the first move—reaching up to pat his cheek with my bare hand. "There, there. When we're done helping Dave, we'll work out *your* relationship issues."

Furious, he bats away my hand and frantically scrubs the spot I touched.

Just in time, Angel descends. I drop my lance on the floor, hike up my britches, and hop into her embrace for the next ride to the top.

When I arrive on the counter, I see Mary crouching beside Dave's cell phone. When she touches the surface, it lights up with a home screen with photo wallpaper in the background. The photo shows Dave in happier times with his arm around a smiling young woman with short brown hair.

"I'm guessing that's Jill?" I ask, and Mary nods.

The next thing she does is swipe up from the home screen. The login screen appears, presenting a virtual keypad for passcode entry.

Good thing she's been paying attention during her periods of frozen observation, watching Dave log in again and again. As I watch, she enters six digits, each button larger than her hand. When she touches the last button, the login screen slides away, revealing an array of mobile app icons.

"What next?" Mary chews her lower lip as she stares at the phone. As many times as she's seen it used by Dave—and his fiancée, Jill, before she left him—she has no direct experience with the start-to-finish process of handling the device.

Luckily, I've got that experience. I died only two years ago (or was it five?), and I used plenty of cell phones before that.

Walking to the top corner of the phone, I hunker down beside Mary and press the text messaging icon. The messaging app opens, presenting a list of past texts from various senders.

Jill Acres' name is right at the top.

I press that name with both hands. A messaging screen appears, and I can read the last exchange between Dave and Jill in a series of blue chat balloons.

Is it *not* a pretty sight.

"Wow." I shake my head as I read. "Talk about a bad breakup."

"Such language." Mary wrings the corner of her pale blue head scarf. "That isn't very ladylike at all."

Just then, Surly approaches from the counter's edge, where Angel just deposited him. "Why? What's it say?"

It doesn't surprise me that the big goon can't read. "The last message from Jill is this: 'Don't ever call me again, you lying piece of…' " I clear my throat instead of reading the last piece of profanity. "So there you have it."

Surly chuckles, rocking on the balls of his sandaled feet. "Good luck sweet-talking *that* woman."

"We have to try." I turn to Mary, hoping for big things. When we were putting together this team, the gang at the stable all agreed she'd be the most diplomatic and eloquent recruit. "Ready to get started?"

Mary nods. If she's nervous, she shows no sign of it.

"Tell me what you want to say, and I'll type it in." I circle to the bottom of the phone, touch the text entry field, and a full QWERTY keyboard appears. Leaning over the screen, I realize I can reach every key without much trouble from where I'm squatting.

" 'Dear Jill,' " says Mary. " 'I love you and I can't live without you.' "

" 'But your last message was total B.S.!' " interrupts Surly. " 'Go to hell! I'm better off without you.' "

"Thanks for the suggestions, but I'm gonna give those a hard no," I tell him. "Now shut up and let the woman talk!"

With a disgusted sigh, he marches away. "I'll go help Angel dump the booze instead."

Looking toward the sink, I see Angel is indeed hard at work on phase two of our plan, hovering over the basin as she pours what's left of a bottle of amber whiskey down the drain.

Rubbing my hands together, I return my attention to the screen. "Keep going."

Mary nods and recites more message. " 'If what we had means anything at all to you, please give me one last chance to prove my love is true.' "

My hands fly to keep up, typing words that appear in the text field. My armored britches catch on the phone's rubber case, dragging all the way down to my ankles, and I pay no attention.

The woman doing the talking is just a ceramic figurine, not the true Mother Mary, but she has a way with words, and I'm determined to capture them all.

" 'Some things are worth fighting for in this world,' " she says. " 'Some are worth sacrificing *everything*. Our love is like that, and I will give every last inch of myself and my life to regain it.' " She stops, closes her eyes, and smiles beatifically. "Signed, 'Love, David.' "

I change it to "Love, Dave" and read it back to her, checking for typos along the way. When she approves it and gives the okay, I hit the Send button with both hands.

"Nice job." I give her a smile.

"I just hope it works," says Mary.

Seconds later, a reply comes through, and we both slump with disappointment. The news isn't good, though at least we didn't have to wait long for it.

For the last time, eff off!

"Well, that's not good," says Mary.

Since you obviously can't take no for an answer, I am blocking your number starting now. Goodbye!

"You can't win 'em all," I say.

"You're telling me," says Mary.

Our next move is a total longshot cooked up by the nativity braintrust. I go along with it to buy time until I can come up with another plan that might actually work.

This one requires some long-distance travel—all the way upstairs—so we keep the team tiny. Tiny as in Baby J. and me.

Still, I give Angel a chance to beg off. "Are you sure you can do this?" After all, she just finished lugging three liquor bottles and five beers to the kitchen sink and dumping them (with only a little help from Surly), then hauling our team back to the stable.

"I'll be fine." Angel smiles warmly. "But we need to hurry. When Dave wakes up, we'll lose our ability to move again."

"And he's an early riser," adds the king with the purple turban. "Even after a bender."

"What's his usual wakeup time?" I ask.

"Five-thirty," says Joseph. "He has to be at work by seven."

"Even on Christmas Eve," says the other shepherd, the non-surly one.

Which is tomorrow. "Got it." Looking at the digital clock atop the TV set, I see the time is 4:45 a.m. "We'd better get moving." I scoop Baby J. out of the manger, then tuck him against my armored chest. "Ready, Angel."

"Try not to drop me, Sir Craps-a-Lot," snaps Baby J. "I can only be so forgiving."

"Try not to pee on me, little one," I tell him. "I do *not* want rusty armor for Christmas this year."

With that, Angel gathers us up and takes flight.

Is it possible for ceramic figures with a magical half-life to be killed? I don't know, but our latest gambit still feels very dangerous.

Angel puts us down on the bed where Dave is sprawled, not far from his dark-haired head. He's sleeping on his side, turned away from us, his loud snores rumbling in the opposite direction from the bedroom door.

He's inert at the moment, but if he turns or thrashes suddenly, he could crush us or knock us right off the bed. Compared to us, he's a giant, his physical strength terrifying in its enormity.

"All set." Baby J. points a chubby finger at Dave's massive head. "Get me over there pronto, Poop-Knight."

I adjust his weight in my arms, then carry him over the rumpled bedsheets, trying hard not to trip on the folds. The last thing I want is for the sound of clattering armor to rouse Dave from his deep slumber. Small as I am, it might not be all that loud, but it could still be enough to make him toss unexpectedly.

As Angel hovers nearby, prepared for emergency evacuation, I carry Baby J. all the way to the back of Dave's head.

"Little farther," Baby J. whispers loudly. "I need to get my hands right on him."

As instructed, I move as close as I can and shove Baby J. forward so Dave's head is within reach of his stubby little arms. As soon as he's close enough, Baby J. stuffs both hands through Dave's short, dark hair and presses his chubby palms against his head.

"Here we go." Baby J. shuts his eyes and focuses all his concentration on Dave's head. "Heal, I command you!" He stops whispering and raises his voice as he gets into playing his role. "As the only son of the father, I command you to *heal* in my name!"

Take it from me: if you've never heard a baby commanding someone to heal, you haven't lived. I'd find it a lot funnier, though, if I wasn't worried every second about Dave flopping over like a breaching whale and crushing us both.

"Depression, begone!" says Baby J. "Drinking, begone! I hereby restore you to a state of perfect health and happiness!"

My arms are getting tired, and I wish he'd finish soon. It's not like I think this has any chance of working, anyway.

I've seen this kind of delusion many times in my travels. If a particular nativity set figure *looks* the part, he might come to believe he *is* the part, powers and all. Since the real Jesus could heal the sick, Baby J. here thinks he can do the same thing.

"I heal this man a million times over!" he continues. "When he wakes, joy shall be his only lot in life! His sadness shall become as dew on the morning grass and burn away in the light of the son!"

I'm about to tell him it's time to wrap things up when Dave suddenly stops snoring and stirs. His head shifts back, and I barely haul Baby J. away in time.

"Hey!" snaps Baby J. "I'm not finished!"

Dave shifts again, and I run for the edge of the bed. A big move follows, and the resulting mattress-quake knocks me over.

"Ow!" Baby J. is caught under me, pinned against my armored breastplate. "Lemme outta here!"

Just as I get to my knees, Angel swoops down and scoops us up, then heads for high altitude. We almost don't make it; Dave rolls over hard and swings an arm up, heading straight for us.

At the last second, Angel pulls a dizzying barrel roll, dodging the limb, and soars out of range. It takes all I can do to hold on to my britches without dropping Baby J. during this wild maneuver.

Then, she flies us back downstairs to the stable, Baby J. complaining all the way. No sooner do we touch down in the straw than we hear Dave's alarm clock whoop in the bedroom, and Dave's yawns echo throughout the house.

As soon as Dave awakens, the lot of us resume our positions and freeze in place in the stable. Baby J. is back in his manger, surrounded by his family, supporters, and petting zoo; I'm back in a corner of the stable, dropping a deuce with a curl on top.

This is not to say we're oblivious, though. We might be frozen, but we're taking in everything that happens around us, watching with special interest for the results of last night's team efforts.

If we *could* make noise, though, I can tell you it wouldn't be cheers and laughter.

It becomes clear soon enough that our work had little impact. When Dave stomps to the kitchen in search of his first drink of the day, he curses up a storm because so many bottles are empty. Unfortunately, we missed whole cases of booze in the garage, so he still manages to have his hair-of-the-dog liquid breakfast.

If Baby J.'s healing powers did any good, it sure doesn't show. Between his first and second drinks, Dave collapses in tears on the sofa, crying his eyes out. He groans and rocks on the cushions, muttering Jill's name and condemning himself for losing her. His depression still shows no signs of letting up.

By the time he manages to stumble out the door on his way to work, we all share one common opinion of our overall success level.

"We blew it!" shouts Surly as soon as the door slams shut, and we regain our voices and power of movement. "He's as screwed up as ever!"

"And it's Christmas Eve day," says the king with the purple turban. "We're out of time."

"The saddest Christmas Eve day ever," says Humpy the camel.

"Hey, maybe we just need to be patient," suggests Baby J. "Healing a human mind isn't quite as simple as healing a hang-nail. Let's give my miraculous magic a little more time to kick in."

"Maybe you're right," Joseph says without enthusiasm. "Maybe we should wait it out a little."

"*Or,* we could get our shit together, so to speak." I smack my naked butt cheek with a resounding *crack*. "Get our shit together and try again!"

Every last one of them looks at me like I'm a giant turd in the shape of a man. I feel like I'm back at square one with these people.

"Seriously!" I clank out of my corner and hobble in front of them, my armored britches slipping to my knees. "I say we take another shot."

"You're a glutton for punishment, aren't you?" says the king with the green turban.

"Some people are just unhelpable," says one of the sheep. "They'll just take you down with them."

"There's nothing wrong with walking away at some point,"

says the unsurly shepherd. "You have to look out for yourself, too, after all."

Shaking my head with contempt, I clomp the handle of my lance down hard on the stable floor. "You people should *hear* yourselves. You sound like a bunch of *asses."*

"Hey!" An actual ass, one of two in the set, lets out an offended bray.

"You can't just *give up* on him," I tell them. "It's the *opposite* of what the people you *portray* would do if they had the chance."

"We did what we could," snaps Surly.

"*I* practically worked a *miracle*," says Baby J.

"We *tried,*" adds another of the sheep.

"And you're not *done* yet." I jab my lance in the air for emphasis. "Helping people is what you stand for, isn't it? Getting a fresh start? Making a difference? If you give up before the job is done, what *good* are you? What meaning do you really have?"

No one says a word.

"Look at yourselves," I tell them. "How long did you stand around doing nothing while a decent man fell apart in front of you? How long did you ignore your chance to help him instead of just *posing* as people who do what they can to end suffering?"

Still, not a word.

"It's time to step up!" I raise my lance high and shake it overhead, meanwhile making a futile grab for the britches that won't stay up. "It's time to think outside the box! Now who's with me? Who has an *idea?"*

At first, I think the answer is no one. The members of the set stare at the floor or off into space, maintaining radio silence. Even Surly, the biggest mouth among them, doesn't say a word.

Then, finally, Mary clears her throat and raises her hand.

"I have an idea," she says. "And yes, I'd say it's outside the box."

"Good for you!" I shake my lance supportively. "Let's hear it!"

"It's all about *you."* Smiling, she points at me. "There's a *secret.* Something you don't know. And I think *maybe* it could make a difference."

I lower my lance, wondering what Mary's referring to. How

could *she* know a secret about *me*, and how could it possibly change things?

Already, I love where this is headed.

"Break it down for us, Mary," I tell her, hiking up my britches yet again. "Give us all the gory details."

The garage door goes up around 6:00 that evening—earlier than usual, as the local bars are closed for Christmas Eve. The door from the garage to the kitchen bangs open, and Dave's car keys crash on the kitchen counter. The next sounds are the clinking of ice in a glass tumbler, the unscrewing of a whiskey bottle cap, and the glugging of booze pouring into a tumbler.

In the living room, the rest of us are frozen in place, waiting. If we had lungs in our bodies, we'd be holding our breath, one and all.

We've made our preparations and set the stage. Frozen as we are by his presence, by the rules of our peculiar magical natures, all we can do now is watch and hope.

Does our plan have a chance of succeeding? I honestly don't know. It's not as much of a crazy longshot as Baby J.'s so-called miracle, but it's still pretty out-there.

It's what you might call a real Hail Mary…which is appropriate, don't you think?

When Dave has finished pouring his drink, his heavy footsteps plod toward the living room. If I could move, I might turn to the others and cross my fingers right now.

Dave comes closer, ever closer. He flicks on a lamp on an end table beside the sofa, just a few feet away.

Then, he walks around behind the coffee table. If he drops onto the sofa, it will drag things out, delaying the discovery of our handiwork.

Fortunately, we've planned ahead for such an eventuality.

Dave stops, and for a moment, I think he might sit…but then he curses and walks back the other way. Our plan is working.

He rounds the coffee table and stops in front of it…then

bends over to pick up something from the green shag carpeting. It's *someone,* actually—one of our own, a lamb put there by Angel to get Dave's attention.

He frowns at it in the palm of his hand—our own sacrificial sheep, you might say.

Now comes the moment of truth. Will he put the sheep back in the stable where it belongs, and in so doing, see the surprise we have in store for him?

To say the least, I'm on the edge of my seat over this.

Dave doesn't make it easy on me, either. He squints at the sheep a moment longer, as if wondering how it got out of the stable. Absent-mindedly, he raises his glass for a drink…then hesitates. He looks from the sheep to the glass, as if deciding he must have knocked the figurine to the floor himself during a previous drinking bout. Then, smiling, he bends down to replace her among her stablemates.

And he stops.

And he frowns.

If I had a heart, it would be pounding like crazy. His eyes are on us now; the jig is up. He sees what we've done, and the gears are turning in his head.

Will our day's work have the impact we hoped it would? Dave isn't letting on. He just keeps frowning, his eyes darting from one of us to the other. He sees it all, I know he does, it's right here in front of him…but how he'll interpret it is still up for grabs.

If I could sweat, I'd be drenched. Is the guy so drunk, his thinking is cloudy and slow?

Or is it just that what he sees is so *impossible,* he's having trouble processing it?

I want to smack him upside the head and say, *Look what we've done! Can you believe it?* But all I can do is stand here and watch like the others.

His frown deepens. I start to think our work is having the absolute wrong effect.

Then, suddenly, Dave starts laughing his ass off.

"Oh my God!" He leans in for an even closer look. "This is great! *This is great!"*

Damn right it is, you big dope.

Because every single one us here in the stable has a pile of poop under our butts—every one of us.

And I, the Pooping Knight who led the way (and provided the extra piles, ahem), is right in front in all my bare-assed bravado.

Dave keeps laughing and laughing at the poopy tableau in the stable, which is great…but I can't relax. We've broken through his funk, but will it last? When the shock of the moment wears off, will his lightened mood persist…or will he fall right back down into the pit of despair?

The whole thing is a delicate balance that could easily tip in either direction. We all decided it was a gamble worth taking, but the secret behind its inspiration could make it go oh so wrong.

Because the secret is, I was meant to be a gift.

Dave bought me as a gag gift for Jill, a reminder of the potty humor jokes that had always cracked them both up. I was meant to make her think of good times they'd shared together, maybe even start a holiday tradition between them.

Mary knew about this from watching and eavesdropping. She knew Jill had broken up with Dave before getting a look at me, but he'd found me amusing enough to stick me in the set anyway.

Since *one* pooping figure entertained him, Mary thought he might find *more* of them hilarious. She was right about that, in spades: having all of us strike a pooping pose on Christmas Eve hit the sweet spot on his funny bone. But in the end, will our mass pooping just make him feel worse?

If you ask me, it's kind of a crapshoot.

Just when I'm starting to worry our scheme might go south, a Christmas miracle changes everything.

Out of the blue, the doorbell rings. Still laughing, Dave answers it.

I recognize the woman in the doorway from the photo I saw on Dave's phone. She's wearing a red parka and mittens, plus a green knit cap over her short brown hair.

And she is *definitely* the last person I expected to see here. The text message we sent her last night must have worked, though her initial response was anything but positive.

Believe it or not, *Jill Acres* herself has come to see the man she rejected.

"Hi." Her expression is serious, her features tight. She looks a little awkward and uncertain.

But the look doesn't last. Dave is so caught up in his laughter that he just waves her in and hurries back over to the stable. "Look! You've gotta see this!"

Jill's confused. I can tell this isn't the reception she expected… but she goes with it. She follows him to the coffee table, wondering what's coming next.

And she quickly dissolves into laughter of her own. It catches her off guard, and she doesn't hold back.

"When did you *do* this?" she says between laughs.

"That's the best part!" Dave shrugs. "I didn't!"

"Then who…?"

"No idea!" says Dave. "Nobody else has *been* here but me!"

She punches him playfully in the arm. "You're *full* of it! *Somebody* did this!"

"I think I know who!" Dave's still laughing. "It must've been *Santa Claus!*"

Jill crouches and reaches into the stable, giving me a nudge. "Whoever did this, they get extra points in my book." She steals a glance at Dave when she says it.

Though she's not really talking about me, about any of us here in the stable, I feel good hearing her say it. I feel like we've done a good thing here, and things have a chance of working out.

I feel like my job here is done…and I know what that means. Because the work of a *caganer* on the road to redemption is never done for long. Helping others, like keeping my metal britches from falling down, is a never-ending quest.

It won't be long until I move on to take a dump in some other nativity set somewhere in the world. I don't know the details yet, but it will happen soon, and I will gladly accept my next challenge with butt cheeks bared and a curl atop my dookie.

Wherever shit is hitting the fan, I assure you, there will always be a place for the Pooping Knight.

THE UPS AND DOWNS OF FLYING

The craziest thing happened today during my lunchtime flying lesson: when I stepped off the end of the gangplank and flapped my arms, I failed to gain altitude. In fact, for the first time since I started these lessons two years ago, I actually fell into a pile of garbage…*hard.* Just like that, can you believe it?

Immediately, my instructor and fellow students set out to help me discover just what had gone wrong. Usually, when I jumped and flapped like that, I rose straight up in the air, then proceeded to swoop and soar like a bird or a plane. In fact, I'd been tops in my class for six weeks straight! So what went wrong today?

Was it my flapping technique? Absolutely not, concluded the class. Each stroke of my wings had been dead on. Was it my jumping style? Again, no one could quite accept that as the cause. What about my kazoo playing? According to one and all, that too had been most excellent. And the propeller on my bright yellow beanie hat had been spinning at just the right pitch for conditions.

By all rights, I should have taken off as always. That left just one other possibility: a crisis of faith. Yes, that would do it. Put simply, the sky had not believed strongly enough that it could lift me up…and the ground had believed *too* strongly that it could hold me down no matter what.

The only solution, as always, was to reconcile the two. To make them believe what I *needed* them to believe. To that end, my instructor, classmates, and I set about making extensive conversation—extensive and *loud,* for the benefit of the sky and ground—in support of my viability as a flying candidate. Everyone tried their best to convince the sky and ground that I indeed could be uplifted effectively with no harm to either element. And that the rest of the class could follow.

Guess what? The next time I stepped off the gangplank and flapped my arms in their feathery sheaths, propeller hat spinning and kazoo playing madly, I rose right up. I drifted like a feather into the blue yonder, gliding on currents of air warmed by the Indian Summer sun. Sailing through the middle of a V-formation of Canada geese on their way south. Grinning like an idiot under my pink and blue face paint. Overjoyed that I had overcome an obstacle and found once more the pure joy I sought each day at lunch. The joy that made my life worth living.

Because only from those great heights could I truly be like a bird. Only from way up there could I drop the great dollops of poop that would splatter on car windshields all across town, there to ooze and spread and bake and harden in the blazing heat of that glorious Indian Summer sun. Bombs away!

Life is good!

THE BALLAD OF THE GROUPIE EVERLASTING

So here I am, in the year of your Lord 2010, lying beside the corpse of yet another dead musician, a rock star flamed out on heroin, and I make the promise one more time.

"This is the last one." That's the promise. "No more musicians for me."

How many times have I said those words over the centuries? Over how many musicians' corpses? And how many times have I broken that promise? Again and again and again.

But maybe this time, it will take.

After all, this guy was special. As I stroke his long blond hair, I'm filled with regret over the dead potential of him, the lost opportunities. He could have changed the world, honest and truly...could have healed it with the music I inspired in him. I felt it in my bones this time, I *believed* it with every iota of my essence.

Maybe that's my flaw. I want too badly to believe in these people. These children of music. After all, I *created* music. I *am* a muse.

Not "muse" in a general sense, like every dumbass bar band numbskull calls his underage cutie to get into her pants. I'm *a* muse, *the* muse, plain and pure and simple. The one and only original Terpsichore. Ta-da.

So I've got a thing for musicians, which sucks, because they *always* let me down, just like this guy. But I always come back for more, because you just never know. Maybe the next one will light up the world for good and true and teach the world to sing in perfect harmony and all that happy horseshit.

I lean down and kiss my latest flameout on the forehead. Give him my blessing. Speed him to my special corner of the Underworld.

And tears roll from my eyes. More tears than I've cried in ages. This guy's the biggest letdown to come along in centuries. My biggest failure since the fourteenth freakin' century and that Gottfried guy back in Germany.

In that craphole town called Hamelin.

Here's how the Pied Piper got his name: he sucked so bad, people used to throw pies at him.

That was back when he was starting out, of course. Before I helped him turn things around.

In fact, the first time I saw the Piper, whose name was Gottfried Hazenstab, he was taking a rotten pot pie square in the face at the Oberammergau town fair. He was only two songs into his first set, too.

And he was lucky. Europe was full of tough crowds in those days; life was short and harsh, and people didn't have much patience. Gottfried was lucky they didn't just kill him.

And luckier still that I was in town that day.

See, I had an eye for raw talent, and I spotted it in Gottfried before the pie hit. The way he played his flute, I could tell he had that certain something.

Which is the whole reason I got into this business in the first place. To find that rare musical flair. That special magic.

And set it free.

"Hello there." I handed him a rag after the show. "My name is Terpsie."

Gottfried wiped the gravy from his face. His bright blue eyes flashed like sapphires, framed by pure gold streamers of hair that touched the tops of his shoulders. "I am Gottfried. Thank you for this." He held up the rag.

"When is your next show?" Smiling, I produced another rag from a pocket of my dress and dabbed at his cheeks.

"Never," said Gottfried. "I quit."

Power flowed out from my fingertips and wafted from my breath, fanning the sparks of talent within him into crackling flames. "I think you should do one more."

"No more." Gottfried shook his head. He sounded like he might be ready to cry. "I'm done."

"One more." Gazing deep within his eyes, I nodded slowly, exerting my influence.

Gottfried's head-shaking turned to head-nodding. "One more."

This time, when Gottfried played, he took a custard pie in the face. This was an improvement over the rotten pot pie...but who cared what the people thought. I was paying more attention to a different audience altogether.

A non-human one.

While the people jeered and hooted and stomped away, another audience listened with rapt attention. An audience much lower to the ground.

Along the base of a nearby tent, a group of rats and mice lined up and watched until Gottfried stopped playing. There were seven of them, sitting up on hind legs, snouts quivering in the air of the fair.

They scattered as soon as the pie cut the show short, but I'd seen enough. Now I knew for sure.

"Come with me, Gottfried." I handed him a fresh rag for his face. "We're going to make beautiful music together."

He looked at me as if I were insane. "Beautiful? Are you sure you don't mean *awful*?"

"Awfully successful." I took him by the shoulders and stared him in the eye. "Forget about the masses. Your kind of talent has real niche appeal."

"'Itch appeal?'" said Gottfried.

"You're perfectly positioned for the changing marketplace," I told him.

"What are you talking about?" said Gottfried.

"Trust me," I said. "I've got inside information."

It was wonderful watching Gottie come alive in the months that followed. Watching as his career took off just like I'd known it would.

All because of a little something called the Black Plague.

Mystical far-seeing wonder-muse that I am, I'd seen the plague coming, spreading across Europe with terrible swiftness. And I'd known exactly what would cause it.

Namely, disease-infested fleas carried by rats.

So now you see where Gottie came in. I singled him out as the savior of Europe, leader-away of rats and all things plagueish.

Not just the savior of Europe. Maybe the savior of all humanity before he was done.

And the savior of one thing more in the bargain: the savior of me.

Right after Gottie's first big success, clearing the rats from the town of Babenscham, we spent our first night together as lovers.

We lay naked in each others' arms in a room at an inn, basking in the aftermath of our lovemaking. Gottie had been the perfect lover, just as I'd known he would be.

And I had been well-pleased.

"How did you know?" he said, softly stroking my auburn hair. "What made you believe in me when no one else did?"

"Vision," I told him. "And feeling."

He smiled, his bright blue eyes shining upon me. "You mean love, Terpsie?"

I considered lying but couldn't do it. I never could, not with any of them over the centuries. "Yes. Love," I said. "I loved you at first sight."

He frowned then, brows crinkling in the candlelight. "You did something to me, didn't you? Changed me somehow?"

"Only gave you a push." I shrugged. "The true power was always within you."

"You're amazing." He ran a finger along the length of my nose and tapped it on the tip. "You really are my muse, aren't you?"

"Yes," I said, snuggling against him, relishing the heat of his body.

Just then, he tipped his head to one side and gave me a funny look. "And I'm your *first*, aren't I?"

That was when I made a mistake, though I didn't realize it at the time. I told the truth.

"No," I said. "Not the first."

His look went dark in a flash. "There've been others before me?"

"Yes," I said. "But you're my only one right now."

The dark look lingered a moment, then dispersed. "All right." He smiled and kissed me. "That's a wonderful thing."

"I know." I whispered the words. He was starting to make love to me again. "Wonderful it is."

I wish you could have seen Gottie in action. It was truly amazing the way he cleared a town of vermin.

Eyes closed, he blew his breath out through the flute in great scintillating bursts. His fingers flew along the length of the instrument, hopping like bees over the holes, scampering from end to end and back again.

He danced with abandon, free and wild as his music. Hair flying, he leaped and spun and twisted, feet spending as much time in the air as on the cobblestones or dirt. His moves would put any modern rock star to shame; if he were alive today, I'm convinced he'd be bigger than any star on Earth.

And then came the rats, pouring out of every building and burrow and crack...not just running, either, but dancing themselves, bounding and whirling. Watch them for a moment, and you realized—they were coming as close as they could to copying Gottie's own moves. In their hundreds, their thousands, their millions, they were aping him, riding the music with eyes closed and whiskers twitching like wheat stalks in a cyclone.

And then the lot of them would dance right out of town. He would lead them, dancing and leaping, down the street and across the fields, weaving in a squealing, stinking parade that trampled grass and flushed game from the undergrowth in its path.

It was truly amazing to behold. My heart pounded every time I saw it happen, absolutely every time.

And I was filled with the joy of being a part of it. Helping him to blossom as a piper, and in so doing, helping him to save Europe and all mankind.

At least that was how it was until he started leading more than rats.

The first ones showed up around Lindelhof, dressed in colorful tatters with flowers in their hair. They came out to watch Gottie perform, clapping and dancing in time with his flute...staying well clear of the rats but taking pains to stay in Gottie's line of sight.

I'd seen their like before, wherever musicians plied their trade down through the centuries. We didn't call them groupies back then, but that was exactly what they were.

When Gottie finished and strolled back to town, they mobbed him, giggling and touching and gazing adoringly at him. Pushing each other out of the way to get close to him.

And when Gottie and I left town, they followed us. A dozen of them, without explaining or asking our permission, fell in line behind us.

By the time we'd finished the next job, in Dusseldorf, eight more had joined us. Six more came along after Bitburg. Pretty soon, we had a real entourage. Think

Deadheads, only smellier and more likely to hurt you.

I should've stopped it right there. Sent them all packing before it was too late...but I didn't. I kept thinking they'd go away on their own, or their families would come looking for them.

How stupid could I get?

Next thing I knew, the groupies—or Pipettes as they called themselves—were washing Gottie's clothes and cooking his meals. They were tending his horse and carrying his things. They were doing everything short of tucking him in at night.

Which of course went straight to his head. It was the same old story, though I'd been hoping for better this time.

I watched as the change came upon him...as he went from being sure of himself to being full of himself. All the girls, all the victories, all the praise and rewards built him up to legend-in-his-own-mind status.

Worst of all, he started to drift away from me. He stopped acting so attentive and affectionate. He didn't look at me the same way anymore.

I soon realized it was time for a wakeup call.

I decided to go with honey instead of vinegar for Gottie's wakeup call. One night, I sneaked him away from camp and took him to a spring in the forest. We skinny-dipped and made love by moonlight while frogs croaked and katydids buzzed around us.

It was a perfect night, just like before the Pipettes came along. I gazed into his bright blue eyes, and things felt back to normal for a while.

"You're doing wonderful work, you know," I told him. "Your music is saving so many lives."

Gottie held me close in the water of the spring-fed pool and smiled. "I could never have done any of it without you, Terpsie."

I was glad he remembered that part. "Thank you," I said. "We make a great team."

Gottie frowned then and tipped his head to one side. "Why don't you ever do it? Why don't you play music yourself?"

I looked down at the moon's reflection in the rippling dark water. "I wish I could."

"You can't?" said Gottie.

I shrugged. "My job is to bring the music out in others."

"But is there a rule that says you can't play it, too?" said Gottie.

"Not that I know of," I said.

"Then why not try?" said Gottie.

"A muse is not a musician." I looked back into his sapphire eyes. "And a musician is what it takes to save the world."

Gottie gave me an odd look then. "Save the world?"

"The world of mankind." I leaned forward and kissed his lips. "All of mankind is depending on you."

Gottie kissed me back like a wild man and snapped his head away at the end of it. "I never imagined music could take me this far," he said.

"You should see how much farther it can take you." My voice was like a purr as we moved against each other. "Stick with me and find out."

"Don't mind if I do," said Gottie.

But of course he didn't.

I never caught him having sex with his Pipettes, but it wasn't hard to guess it was happening. When the Pipettes started showing up pregnant, with no other men but Gottie in our camp, I got the picture.

"Well, *I* wasn't *your* first and only, was I?" That was what he said when I called him on it. He didn't even try to deny it. "So I guess it's okay for me to be with more than one person, too."

As if it wasn't bad enough that he was banging the groupies he had, he kept gathering up new ones wherever we went. He played for them three times a day, different songs than for the rats, and the music seemed to bond them to the group. Instead of fighting over Gottie, they worked together to make him happy.

And before I knew it, making him happy took on a terrible new meaning.

"We haven't done enough," he told the assembled Pipettes one morning. "It's time to save the world!"

By this point, there were at least three hundred Pipettes in his entourage...and they all roared with excited approval.

"The best way to do that...the only way I see...is to *take over*." Gottfried looked in my direction and winked. "It is the only way we can save mankind the world over."

Again, the crowd went wild.

"Let us begin a new march now to save the world!" Gottfried pumped his flute overhead, and the women and girls in the crowd pumped fists and weapons. "Music will show the way to the dawning of a bold new age!"

The crowd howled and danced. Even the pregnant Pipettes joined in, bellies bouncing like basketballs under their frocks.

At that moment, I finally realized just how far gone Gottfried was and how bad things had gotten. Finally, as I looked out over the cheering, gyrating crowd, I saw what he had built with the groupies he'd gathered.

I had underestimated him. My world-saving Gottie had built himself an army.

"Please stop this." That was what I said to him after the big rally. "You can't save the world this way."

Gottfried kept marching through camp with his back to me. "I think it's the *best* way. Who better than the Pied Piper—a true natural born *leader*—to guide mankind through these dark times?"

"You're going to send an army of untrained women against the knights and soldiers of Europe?" I said. "How do you think *that'll* go?"

"We'll find out tomorrow when we reach our first target," said Gottfried. "A town called Hamelin."

The next day, just like always, we marched up to another dismal Dark Ages town in the German countryside, and Gottie pulled out his flute. This time, though, he changed the tune he played.

Instead of luring all the rats out of town, Gottie made them scurry in every direction through the streets, terrorizing the citizens.

Then, he made an announcement.

"Attention, people of Hamelin," said Gottie. "Acknowledge me as your new ruler, or I will order the creatures at my command to devour you all!"

"*Why*?" said one of the townspeople as she tried to flee across the town limits. "Why are you *doing* this?"

"To *save* you, of course." Gottie gestured, and his private army stepped forward, stopping the woman from leaving Hamelin. "To save the entire world."

At that moment, I took action. I had waited as long as I could, giving my once-beloved Gottie every chance to reverse his course...but now I knew. The Pied Piper was a lost cause.

It was time to put a stop to this insanity before it went any further.

Glaring, I stepped in front of Gottie. "That's enough!" I said. "Call off your rats."

Gottie played the flute more wildly than ever, shaking his head for my benefit. The rats danced in the streets, and so did his army as they drove back the people of Hamelin.

"I said *stop it*!" Even as the words left my lips, I knew they weren't enough. So strong was the spell Gottie had woven, it would take more than language to break it.

Perhaps I knew just what could do it.

Closing my eyes, I reached deep into the timeless realm that existed inside me and drew out a metal object...a flute. I had never played one before, though I instinctively knew how; after all, I'm the one who *invented* music in the first place.

Perhaps, if I could play it well enough, I could overpower Gottie's commands and change the course of what was happening to Hamelin.

Raising the mouthpiece to my lips, I hesitated. Never before had I allowed myself the luxury of trying to make my own music. Never before had I really believed in myself enough to stand up and do it.

But now, at last, I had the chance. And the stakes were high. People's lives were at stake in Hamelin if I couldn't override Gottie's song.

So I started to play.

The music came slowly at first, then picked up speed. It came naturally to me, perfectly—swirling and skirling as I blew and spun and danced.

And with each note, I felt more liberated. More at peace. More the way I was meant to be.

But it wasn't enough. Gottie continued to leap and charge and wail like always, weaving a wild skein of sound that beast and groupie alike were compelled to respond to.

As hard as I fought to match and outdo him, I couldn't manage it. The son of a bitch had gotten too good to be beaten...at least on his instrument of choice.

So maybe that was the key to it. Maybe I needed something new. Something brand new, conjured from dreams of a future yet to come.

Throwing aside my flute, I reached back inside my realm and drew out something else. Another instrument, also metal, also played with breath and fingers on keys and holes.

I rested the long, curved shape of it against my body. The smooth brass gleamed in the afternoon haze.

I adjusted the strap across my back, which held the instrument in place. Then, I eased my lips forward, fitting the mouthpiece between them.

And I blew. I played.

For the first time in the history of the world, the sounds of a saxophone rang out across the land.

I played with the same abandon Gottie used when playing the flute—running off streams of rapid-fire notes and chords in maniacal, tuneful sequences. Hurling out one blast of sound after another, screaming and singing and shouting with joy and sorrow and love and anger through my instrument.

Taking my solo and running with it. Hitting it hard.

And damn it if I didn't run Gottie right down. Damn it if I didn't turn those rats and Pipettes away and run them right off.

Damn it if I didn't play with such fever and fury that I burned all the musical magic right the hell out of Gottie. Every last bit of his fabulous power rushed out of him like water down a drain.

Leaving the Pied Piper a shadow of his superstar self, cursed to wander the Earth all the rest of his days, playing his flute for anyone who would listen.

Playing it off-key.

Centuries later, I walk into a club on 14th Street in the Village. This is six months after the death of my latest rock star lover.

And I see him. A new candidate.

He sits on a stool on the tiny stage in the corner, singing and playing guitar. His long black hair falls over his face, hiding his eyes from the spotlight.

Then, he looks up and shakes the hair back, and I meet his gaze. His eyes are glittering emerald green, bright as moonstones or new-mown grass. Full of possibilities. Full of raw talent.

I feel the pull of him like the drag of a chain wrapped around my waist, my heart, irresistible. Almost.

If I go to him, and awaken him, I know he will be great. He

will do great things with me as his muse, as his lover, just as so many thousands before him have done.

And in the end, I know, he will let me down. They all do. He will let the life of glory go to his head, like the Pie-in-the-Face Piper, and he'll screw me over and maybe kill himself like the last guy, O.D.-ing on drugs. The story's *always* the same.

Unless *he's* different. There's always that chance. It's what I live for, after all—the hope that the next one will be better than all the rest.

Or is that really all I live for?

In all the years since the Piper, I'd let it slip my mind—that one more thing that made me happy. That one thing other than seeking talent and love in the heart of feckless musicians throughout history.

It slipped my mind. How happy I felt that day in Hamelin.

So for once, for once in my life, I resist the pull. I turn right away from it, away from the man in the spotlight, and I head for the door.

I push it open and march out into the night. Heading for a corner to call my own, alone. Where I will put down a case on the sidewalk, red velvet lined to catch the quarters of passersby.

And I will play my own music.

FORCED PARTNERSHIP

ONE NIGHT IN ISOSCELES CITY...

My favorite super-hero pounds me with his fists. I can almost see the spiky sound effect balloons fly up with each punishing blow to my head. *Boom! Pow! Wham!*

Krack. That's the sound of my cheekbone snapping. The *un*-super cheekbone of a very *un*-super man. The super-hero battering me has unbreakable bones and the strength of ten men, but I've got nothing like that.

Even though we both wear the same black and gray costume and go by the same code name. Even though we both call ourselves Partycrasher.

"Stop it! Stop hurting me!" I blubber the words through my shattered teeth and swollen lips. "How can you do this to your number one *backup*? Your chief deputy in the *Party Line*?"

At least that makes him put my beating on pause. "For the last time!" He's so furious, he spits in my face while he screams at me. "*You are not my backup!*"

I cower on the sidewalk at his feet. "Please don't say that! What's wrong with you?"

"You're not in the *Party Line*, and we've *never* had a team-up!"

He hauls back his fist, ready to let it fly. "The only thing you've ever *done* for me is *ruin* my *life*!"

"This isn't *you* talking, Partycrasher!" I spread my arms pleadingly, desperate to get through to him. "You're under a villain's *control*. You've got to *fight* it!"

The leather in his black glove creaks as he tightens his fist. "The only thing I'm *fighting* is the urge to *kill* you right this *minute*."

I meet his gaze through the eye-holes in his black leather cowl. Maybe there's a spark of mercy in there after all. "I *knew* you didn't *want* to kill me, Partycrasher."

"I didn't *say* that. I just don't want to kill you too *soon*." The muscles bulge along the length of his arm, defined by the moonlight flowing over them. "I want you to *suffer* like *she* did."

Then, he releases that punch he's been aiming. His sledgehammer fist crosses the night air like a missile, cruising straight for my...

AT LAST! THE SECRET ORIGIN OF THE PARTYCRASHER/ADJUSTER TEAM!

You haven't lived until you've charged through the dark city streets at night, fighting crime with a true crusader. I'm telling you, man.

I remember our first adventure together, five years ago. Back when I was just starting out. Back when I was still calling myself the Adjuster.

You should've seen my homemade outfit and gear. *So* lame. I basically wore a black hoodie and jeans, plus a Halloween mask that was supposed to make me look like some kind of red demon creature.

It was pouring down rain one night, and I saw these two goons beating up a homeless guy in an alley. When I tried to break it up, I got my ass handed to me. Didn't even get to try my patented spine-cracking techniques on these guys. (I'm a chiropractor by day, hence "the Adjuster.")

Anyway, I was pretty much laid out on a pile of trash, about to get torn apart, when all of a sudden I heard that trademark howling laugh of his. It echoed down the alleyway, making the goons stop and look around for him.

Was he up the alley? Down the alley? Neither!

He leaped down from a fire escape above us, kicking both of them in the head at once on the fly. The goons staggered aside as he landed in a crouch on the wet pavement, surrounded by his fanned-out black cape.

There was the briefest of pauses. I remember thinking how cool he looked, how intimidating. Now *that* was a super-hero, I thought.

Then, he swirled into action again, tearing through the goons like they were a couple of rubber clowns. The one guy was crying by the time he was done with him; Partycrasher dislocated his left arm and broke his right leg in two places.

The other guy took a beating, too, but then he sneaked in a lucky shot with a cinderblock while Partycrasher was breaking his buddy's leg. *Kerash!* The block smashed against Partycrasher's head. The blow might have killed a less super-powered person, but it did leave him dazed, I could tell.

And that was my cue.

Springing off the trash pile, I reached into my pocket for the tube of ultra-potent deep-heating rub (my own personal formula). Bolting toward the goon as he raised the cinder block for another strike at Partycrasher, I squirted the rub right in his eyes. Wailing, he dropped the block and stumbled across the alley.

That gave Partycrasher all the time he needed to fully recover. Shaking off the effects of the block, he hurtled past me and took down the goon with style, pummeling him with a dozen blows to the upper body.

The goon teetered, then collapsed on the pavement.

Partycrasher turned to me. "Nice work."

I shrugged. "Any time."

Then, he cocked his head to one side, looking deep in thought. He stepped toward me and planted his hands on his hips. "Have you considered working with somebody? As a backup, say?"

I shook my head. My heart was pounding in my chest.

He reached out a black leather-gloved hand. "Well, *would* you? Consider it, I mean? I've been thinking about partnering up, and clearly, you can handle yourself in a fight."

I smiled. "Sure, I'll consider it." Then, on the spot, I made up my mind. "Actually, my answer is..."

WHO--OR WHAT--IS BRAINTEAZER?

"Y-you're not just my p-partner." My speech slurs as Partycrasher's unrelenting blows pound my face to pulp. "You're my b-best friend!"

Partycrasher hauls me up by the front of my costume and snarls the words in my face. "I'm not your *partner*, and I've *never* been your *friend*!" He looks mad enough to bite my nose off, I swear to God.

Tears trickle down the ragged maze of my cracked and lumpy cheeks. "It's Brainteazer, isn't it? Or Non Compos Mentis? One of them g-got inside your h-head, didn't they?"

"You delusional *idiot*!" He shakes me like a rag doll--a rag doll he hates with every fiber of his being. "For the last time! There. Is. No. *Mind control*."

I wince at him with all the deep and tragic affection welling up in my heart. "They're m-making you say that, I know..."

He shakes me again. "Brainteazer isn't even in the super-villain *game* anymore! He's in Silicon Valley working on mind-machine interface systems!"

"Th-that's what he *wants* you to think."

"And Non Compos Mentis died from a drug overdose!"

"They've totally t-taken you over...haven't they?" I shake my head slowly. "They've stolen...my p-partner...the g-greatest crime-fighter this city has ever...the *world* has ever..."

"*I'm not your partner!*" He screams the words so loud it hurts. "*All you've ever been is a deluded wannabe who I should've killed long...*"

INTRODUCING THE ONE AND ONLY RAVE SIGNAL!

When did Partycrasher give me the fabulous Rave Signal? I'm glad you asked.

I was in the hospital, right? This was six months after Partycrasher and I joined forces. By then, we were both wearing the same costume and going by the same code name--all the better to confuse the underworld element, he always said.

Anyway, I was laid up after a solo battle with Ballbuster and the Let 'Em Eat Cake Gang. Imagine a band of seven goons all dressed like Marie Antoinette, but with weaponized hairpins and flying guillotines. As for Ballbuster, she was the ultimate butch lesbian with a fetish for striking below the belt.

I was left in a full body cast, more or less, confined to my hospital bed. My first night there, I heard a knock at the door, and it was Partycrasher. He swirled into the darkened room like a cloud of smoke.

"Hey there, chum." He brought in a bouquet of flowers and put it on the nightstand. "I'm so sorry about all this."

"There's nothing to be sorry about." I smiled and shrugged. "Comes with the territory."

He shook his head and sat down in a chair in the corner, in the shadows. "If only I'd gotten there quicker. If only I'd known...perhaps I could've dispatched Fugu and Amanita faster and raced across town to your side before they hurt you."

"You can't be everywhere at once," I said. "I'm just grateful to be able to do my part in your name. Taking an occasional beating is a price I'm willing to pay for that privilege."

He propped his elbows on the armrests and steepled his fingers against his chin. "Never again."

I panicked. "You're not *firing* me? You're not taking away my *black and gray*?"

For a long moment, I thought that was exactly what he meant. He said nothing, just stared at me from the shadowy corner.

Then, leather gloves creaking, he pushed himself up from the chair. "I will *never* fire you, my faithful ally." Reaching down, he unsnapped a pocket on his multi-belt and drew out a loop of gold metal. "But I *will* make you safer."

His black cape rustled as he crossed the moonbeam streaming in through the window. He held up the golden loop and turned it between his fingers.

"W-what is it?" I asked.

"The *Rave Signal*," said Partycrasher. "A secret signal that will alert me if you're in danger. It's an anklet." He held it out to me. "When the threat is too great, simply kick it, and the signal tone will be transmitted to my headgear." He patted the crown of his black cowl, which was threaded with sophisticated electronics. "I will be there in a flash."

I felt choked up when he handed it to me. "Thank you, Partycrasher. I can't tell you what this *means* to me..."

"No more than our *alliance* means to *me*." With that, he held out his gloved hand with the thumb and third finger extended--configured for the official Party Line handshake.

I returned the shake, twisting my hand clockwise as he turned his counterclockwise. "Criminals," I said, beginning our traditional oath, "your party is over."

"We're not invited," said Partycrasher, "and we're showing up anyway."

I grinned and held the Rave Signal tight in my fist. "I swear, I will use this wisely, and will never betray your..."

EVEN A HERO CAN GO INSANE!

"If y-you're not my partner...n-not my f-friend..." I struggle to get out the words as he pastes me again across the kisser. "Th-then why did you give me...the Rave Signal?"

Partycrasher throws his head back and rolls his eyes skyward. "How many times do I have to *tell* you? It was an *ankle monitor*, moron! It was supposed to alert *law enforcement* any time you violated the *restraining order* and got within thirty feet of me!"

Though I'm the one suffering and bleeding, I gaze up at him with pity. "They really g-got to you...didn't they? Got in d-deep." I shake my head at him. "Was it Thinkupine? Neuronicus?"

"Oh my God!" His eyes are huge as he glares down at me.

"Can you *imagine* how *sick to death* I am of listening to your *delirious bullshit*?"

"*I* know. It w-was Heads-I-Win, wasn't it?" I gurgle up a mouthful of bloody foam. "He t-took control of you...once before...remember?"

"Why do I bother trying to talk *sense* to you?" Partycrasher hauls back a booted foot, aiming the toe at my gut. "You're *hopeless*. You're a *lunatic*."

"It can't be Linda Loveblind..." It hurts to move, but I curl up against the blow to come. "Sh-she's already...g-gone..."

Maybe it *does* have something to with Linda Loveblind. What I say pushes him over the top.

"Her name is *Maria*!" he screams as his steel-toed boot connects with my belly. "And you know *damn well* that she was my..."

FAIRER SEX OR *TERROR* SEX? *YOU* BE THE JUDGE!

We had a real golden age there for a while. The two Partycrashers cleaned up Isosceles City in a big way. The streets were *safe* again at night, can you imagine?

Together, Partycrasher and I took down Tic Tac Moe and the Greenstamps Gang...Fill-'Er-Up and Liver Spot...Coke Furnace and the Five Ingots. When no one else could stop Fifty-Three Flavors and the Himalayan from liquefying every bone within a hundred mile radius, guess who saved the day? And when Pharmacopia turned everyone in the city, except us, into drugged-out screaming zombies, only the Partycrashers managed to cancel his prescription.

We even saved the world once, I swear to God. When Core Sample resurrected Invicticus, the living soul of all fossil fuels, the planet was doomed. Only our quick thinking and decisive action stopped them from igniting every deposit of oil, gas, and coal in the world at once. (We used philosophy and alien weapons from Area 51, that's all I'll say.)

We made the headlines almost every day. The President gave

us Congressional Medals of Honor. Little kids wrote more letters to us than to Santa Claus. It was the happiest time of my life.

Then, *she* showed up.

When we first met her, she was a super-villainess--part of the Chick Posse. They were really tearing up the town in those days, staging spectacular robberies and running rings around every cop and hero who tried to stop them. They even gave *us* a run for our money that first time at the Diamond Show robbery.

There were seven of them that day. They came to steal an exhibit of crown jewels from around the world, on loan for the Diamond Show's fiftieth anniversary.

Lady of the Night dazzled the guards with her feminine wiles. Sarah Firma used her control of dirt and rock to tunnel past the security system. When the alarms went off anyway, Catfight and Henny Penny exploded into action, battling guards and cops alike with feline and avian savagery. Fashionista used her control over articles of clothing to bind and imprison the first heroes on the scene. After that, Dee Flower cast an erotic spell over the mind of every man and woman in range.

And then there was *her*, Linda Loveblind. When Partycrasher and I charged onto the scene, she used her control of the sense of sight to render us useless. We kept fighting what we thought were Chick Posse members, but in actuality, we were only fighting each other.

Thankfully, though, I was able to break free before it was too late. Instead of fighting everyone who looked like a Chick Posse woman, I went after the one person who looked like my partner--the person who was in reality Linda Loveblind. After I knocked her out, Partycrasher saw clearly again, and the two of us made short work of the Posse.

But even as the cops hauled them off in power-nullifying bonds and helmets, I had a terrible feeling we hadn't seen the last of them--and of *her* in particular. Because I saw her flash a look at Partycrasher, and he didn't look away.

I'd seen that look before. I knew what it meant.

"Good riddance to bad rubbish," I said as the paddy wagon pulled away.

"I do believe in rehabilitation, you know." Partycrasher wouldn't take his eyes off the wagon. "Perhaps there is hope for even the most hardened offenders."

I smacked him on the back. "You're not goin' *soft* on me now, are you?"

He watched the paddy wagon a moment more, then turned my way and grinned. "Never in a million years, chum."

"That one dame had an influence on you, I know. Just remember, her *power* is to control the way you *see* things."

"Thanks for your concern," said Partycrasher, "but nothing will *ever* get in the way of my never-ending war on crime. Not even..."

CAN A SUPER-HERO BROMANCE SURVIVE THE ULTIMATE CHALLENGE?

"You can b-beat this." I force out the words between kicks to my stomach. "B-break Linda's...evil spell."

"Her name wasn't *Linda*!" He bends down and grabs me by the throat. "Say it! Say her *actual name*!"

"I b-believe...in you." I choke as his hand tightens. "I will never stop...being your..."

"*I want to hear you say it!*" He shakes me by the neck. "*Just once*! *Say her fucking name!*"

I realize something now, for the first time: there might not be a way out of this for me. Whoever's controlling him, they've got their hooks set deep. Nothing I've said has shaken his belief in his twisted version of reality.

"*Say it!*" He looks like he's out of his mind as he bellows the words. "Her name is *Maria*! *Maria Maria Maria*! And what *was* she?" He jerks me by the neck again. "Tell me what she *was* to me!"

"P-Partygirl." Just saying the word makes me feel sick. So much hate, bubbling within every cell of my broken body. "She was P-P--"

"*No she was not*!" He tightens his grip to the point of near-strangulation. "You know damn well *she was my...*"

A BOLD NEW HEROINE JOINS THE PARTY LINE LINEUP!

I'll never forget when Partycrasher said these words to me: "That's right. Linda Loveblind has gone straight. And she's changed her code name to *Partygirl*."

I'd never been so sorry about being right in my life. I'd known from that day at the Diamond Show that we hadn't seen the last of Linda Loveblind. I'd caught the look she'd shared with Partycrasher as the cops had led her to the paddy wagon, and I'd *known*.

Now here she was, standing in our own *secret headquarters*, I shit you not. Linda Loveblind herself, card-carrying member of the crime-loving Chick Posse, was in the heart of the one-and-only *Party Creche*.

She might have been wearing a new costume--a modified little black dress with a black domino mask and red-lined black cape--but she wasn't fooling me. *I* wasn't the one thinking with my *nads*.

I knew that her being there did not bode well for the Partycrasher Squared team.

"I look forward to working with you, Tim." Linda held out one black-gloved hand.

I wouldn't take it. I couldn't believe the words that had just come out of her mouth. "Oh my God." I gaped at Partycrasher. "You told her my *secret identity*?"

"She needs to know," he told me. "Now that she's a member of the Party Line, she needs..."

"No!" I remember stumbling to a chair and dropping into it. "You can't just let her *join* like that." I remember my hands shaking, my heart pounding. I remember feeling sad and scared and sick all at once.

I remember thinking that this was the end of the world.

"Don't worry, chum." Partycrasher walked over and patted my back. "It'll be all right. I promise."

But he was wrong. So very, very wrong.

Our golden age ended that day. Everything went downhill from there.

Every adventure she was part of turned into a disaster one way or another. When we took on Extreme Umbrage and the Walking Tire Fire, an entire neighborhood went up in flames because Linda let herself be taken hostage. A few days later, Dr. Scatological got the drop on me because I was distracted by Linda's screams for help; I ended up with a severe case of temporary Tourette syndrome that made me blurt obscenities in front of a TV news crew.

Sword-Swallower and Haggis Master got away from us twice--*twice*--because Linda insisted she understood their cypher clues better than Partycrasher did. Wild Goose led us all the way to the Canadian Maritimes for the same reason, in search of a doomsday device that didn't exist. Then there was the day Trophy Wife, MILF, and The Mammarian caught us in a trap that *never* would have worked in the pre-Linda days. We had to be rescued by firefighters, extracted from a giant party favor with the jaws of life.

As for the Win, Place, and Show affair, I don't even want to talk about it. The day three tenth rate losers like them could trick us into a collapsing glue factory that nearly got us all killed was the day we became a true embarrassment to the crimefighting community.

Did Partycrasher even seem to *notice* how far we'd fallen? No, he did not. He seemed perfectly happy throughout all our debacles, as if he were having *fun*. The public displays of affection with Linda grew more and more obnoxious, and the baby-talk just got more sickening.

Still, in my heart, I never gave up on him. I always believed I could somehow save him and restore the Partycrasher Squared team to its glory days.

Even when he told me the big news. Even then.

"Partygirl and I are getting married, chum!" He told me this in the Party Creche one night, when we were alone. "Can you believe it?"

I could, unfortunately. It wasn't like I hadn't seen it coming. "Huh."

Grinning, he grabbed me by the shoulders. "Well, aren't you going to *congratulate* me?"

I wondered what to say. Should I let the moment pass and play along, pretending I was happy for him? Wouldn't that just strengthen her hold on him?

"Don't do it." I shook my head grimly. "Please, Partycrasher. Don't do it."

He frowned in disbelief. "I thought you'd be *happy* for me." He let go of my shoulders. "I was going to ask you to be my *best man*."

"Can't you see what she's *done* to you?" I said. "How she's gotten inside your *head*?"

"It's called *love*, Tim. It's a *good* thing."

"Listen to me!" I grabbed hold of his upper arms and gave him a shake. "If someone managed to *brainwash* you, would you even *know* it? If your mind was being *controlled*, how could you tell what you were really *feeling*?"

He looked hurt. "I'm not brainwashed, Tim."

"But *what if* someone had *warped* your *perceptions*? It's what she *does*, Partycrasher. It's her *super-power*!"

Partycrasher's expression was one of wounded betrayal. "Don't do this, Tim." He shook free of my grip and stepped back from me. "Please don't do this."

"Wait." I knew I was losing him. Her influence was too strong. "What if I asked you...to choose? Choose between me and her?"

He stared at me for a long moment, and then his expression changed from hurt to pity. "Don't ask me that, Tim." He turned and walked toward the Partymobile. "I don't think you'll like the answer."

So that was it. Now I knew where I stood. I had taken the full measure of Linda's power over him, and all was clear to me. In a contest of wills, she would always win.

But even then, I still did not give up on him. Because I still had one ace up my sleeve, one way to stop his final descent and corruption. One way to thwart Linda's final triumph.

And the sweet irony of it all was that Partycrasher himself had given it to me in the first place. He was the deliverer of his own salvation in the form of the astounding...

WHEN PARTYCRASHERS COLLIDE!

It's harder than ever to force out the words. "Y-you can't b-be...legally married...to a c-creature...of p-pure, unearthly...evil."

"You *delusional...*" Partycrasher kicks me in the belly with what feels like all his strength. "*...psychopathic...*" Then he kicks me in the chest with staggering force. "*...maniac*!" Next, he hauls back his foot and kicks me in what's left of my face. "She was a *woman*! She was my *wife*!" Then, another kick to the face for good measure. "And *you*...you *stalked* her and you..."

"P-protected you." My jaw won't move right anymore. I think it's broken. "I d-did what you t-told me...when you g-gave me the..."

"I didn't *give* you *anything*! You *stole* it!"

"Y-you said...if you ever f-fell...under c-control...of an evil f-force..." I suck in a deep breath and push myself to keep going. "If you were ever t-turned...against the cause of j-j-justice...I should use it on you. I sh-should use the..."

"*There is no such thing as a De-Evilizer*!" Partygoer kicks me in the face again. "*It was only ever an ordinary...*"

ONE MAN, ONE WOMAN, ONE SHOT!

When I kicked the door in, I found Linda sitting in a chair, waiting for me. She was wearing a red, satiny gown with arcane symbols embroidered in black along the low neckline. "Oh, hello, Tim." She put aside the book she'd been reading and smiled. "What can I do for you?"

Without a word, I pulled the De-Evilizer from its holster on my hip. The gleaming silver metal of its body felt warm in my grip.

"I was *wondering* when you'd get around to this." Linda threw her head back and laughed. "Come to cut your boy loose, have you?"

The De-Evilizer had a smooth, curved body with a long barrel. As I pointed it at her, it pulsed and glowed faintly with strange alien energies like some kind of a living thing.

"Well, you're too fucking late." Linda rose from the chair. Her skin began to turn crimson as she took a step toward me. Her eyes gleamed with yellow light, and her ears grew points. "He's *mine* and he always *will* be. I have taken the world's greatest super-hero and made him my *bitch*. And there's nothing *you* or *anyone* can ever *do* about it!"

My hand shook as she strolled across the apartment that had once been his alone. It was *her* territory now, *her* turf. And Partycrasher was helpless to resist her.

If I didn't act quickly, he would stay that way. If I didn't do what I'd come there to do, he would be forever lost, and I...

I was sure I would be dead at her feet. Now that I'd played my final card, now that I'd seen her true form, she couldn't afford to leave me alive.

But then I'd known that before I'd walked in the door, hadn't I?

Reaching up with my free hand, I braced my grip and steadied the De-Evilizer. I thought back to the day, years before, when Partycrasher himself had given it to me.

I want you to have this, he'd told me. *It's extraterrestrial technology from Area 51.*

At first, I'd stared at the thing without taking it. *What does it do?*

Destroys evil, he'd said. *Burns it away with cleansing fire.*

Shouldn't you keep it? I'd asked him.

He'd pushed it toward me more insistently. *It's for you, Tim. In case an evil force takes control of my mind. In case I ever turn against the cause of justice.*

Impossible, I'd said. *That could never happen.*

Remember last month, when Power of Suggestion and the Hypnoid made me fight you? It can happen again, only much worse. With that, Partycrasher had pressed the weapon into my hand. *You must be my fail-*

safe, do you understand? Don't let my awesome powers be used against the world I've sworn to defend.

Gazing at the De-Evilizer, I'd closed my fingers around it. *I could never...*

You will do what you must! He'd thrown himself forward then and hugged me. *Swear it!*

And so I'd sworn it. And now here I was, ready to use the De-Evilizer for the first time. Praying with all my heart that it would work, that it would save him.

It was his last chance, and I knew it. *Our* last chance.

"So go ahead!" A forked tongue flickered between Linda's lips, which were now literally on fire. "Shoot your load, Tiny Tim! Go for the gusto!"

As she strode toward me, sneering, her now-crimson body grew taller. Snakes wrapped around her arms and legs, squirming in continuous motion. Leathery batlike wings burst out of her back and expanded behind her, flapping ominously.

This, then, was what she'd been all along...what I'd *sensed* her true nature to be. She was a demoness, a she-devil, a creature belched up from the fiery pits of Hell itself. No wonder she'd been able to use trickery so effectively. No wonder she'd been able to cloud Partycrasher's mind, to fill it with delusions.

"What's the matter?" Linda conjured a flaming whip out of thin air and cracked it in my direction. "Aren't you *man* enough to take me?"

I was scared, no doubt about it--but also determined. Partycrasher was depending on me...and through him, through the great feats he was yet destined to accomplish, the *whole world* was depending on me, too.

"Come on, Partypooper! Give it your best shot!" Linda cracked the whip again and howled with laughter. "But you better make it a *good* one, because that's all you'll *get*!"

My hands tightened around the De-Evilizer. There was no trigger to pull; it would activate by mental command.

Again, she snapped the whip. The blazing tip sizzled past my left ear, but I didn't flinch. In the name of Partycrasher and all he stood for, I would not be deterred.

I prepared to give the mental command.

Then, suddenly, the apartment changed around me. In the blink of an eye, everything was different.

The whole living room was brighter. Every inch of it seemed cleaner and sharper--as if I'd been looking through an imperfect lens, and everything had been slightly out of focus until now.

As for Linda, she no longer looked like a demonic she-devil. Gone were the wings, yellow eyes, crimson skin, and forked tongue. Instead of a red gown embroidered with mystic symbols, she wore her Partygirl costume, the little black dress with crimson-lined cape and black fishnet stockings.

And the look on her face was nothing at all like what I'd seen earlier. Instead of gleeful wickedness, I saw total surprise and fear.

"No, Tim!" Her voice trembled as she said it. "Please, don't! We can work this out, I *know* we can!"

"Linda?" I was so surprised, I lowered the gun. "What...?"

"I want to help you, Tim! We both do!" Breathless, she pressed a hand against her chest. "You're part of the family, and that will never..."

"No!" I swung the gun up, certain that this was all one of Linda's illusions. "You won't fool me *that* easily, Loveblind!"

Suddenly, the room shifted again. This time, it grew brighter still. The furnishings looked newer and more expensive. The carpet went from brown to white, the end tables from stained wood to glass and chrome.

As for Linda, she was dressed in black silk pajamas. "Why are you doing this, Tim?" She was crying and clutching her stomach. Blood welled up around her hands, dripping onto the carpet at her feet. "Oh God, why?"

I shook my head hard but didn't lower the De-Evilizer. "Nice try, *bitch*!"

How many more illusions was she going to bombard me with? How much more innocent could she make herself appear?

I wasn't going to wait around to find out.

Clenching my teeth, I aimed the De-Evilizer at Linda's forehead. I took a breath to steady myself.

And then I gave the mental command.

Linda of the black silk pajamas tumbled toward the carpet. On her way down, she became Linda of the Partygirl outfit, gazing at me from behind her domino mask.

And when she hit the floor, she became the she-devil again, her entire body hissing as the De-Evilizer burned away the foul darkness festering in her soul.

At which point the front door flew open and Partycrasher charged into the apartment. "Nooo!" He looked from me to Linda, then back again. "Put it down, Tim! For God's sake, put down the..."

TRUTH IS THE GREATEST SUPER-POWER OF THEM ALL!

Partycrasher gives me another kick in the chest. "Why you *hated* her so much, I'll never *know*." The next one, he plants in my groin. "Frankly, I don't much *give* a shit anymore."

I squirm on the ground, groaning from the pain. I can't even manage a scream anymore. "Sh-she was...t-turning you...evil..."

"I *said*..." He kicks me again. "...I don't *care*." And again.

"B-but the De-Evilizer..."

"...was the .45 automatic that was stolen from my apartment in a *break-in* three years ago!" Suddenly, he leans down and lifts me off the pavement by my blood-soaked cape. "You *killed* my *wife* with *my own gun*!"

I try to shake my head, which comes out more like a twitch. "S-saved...you..."

"Saved me?" He hauls me close so we're face to face. "You *ruined* me, you demented son of a bitch. You took the one thing I ever cared about in this..."

I close my eyes. I try to shut him out.

What if this is all an illusion? What if Linda Loveblind sank her hooks in *me*, too...and if only I concentrate hard enough, the real world will peek through and I can see...

HONORING THE PARTNER OF A LIFETIME.

As I stand on the dais and gaze out at the crowd, I feel like I'm going to cry. Other than the day Partycrasher invited me to join the Party Line, this is by far the finest day of my life.

Every super-hero in Isosceles City is assembled here today. I see Hericane, Mardi Gras, Overtime, Stalwart...Widening Gyre, Thunder Perfect Mind, The Jupitarian...Flotilla, Red Baron, Carpet Bomber, Concorde...Retcon, CEO, King David, Old Glory. They all gaze up at me, grinning with approval--some winking, some giving me a thumbs-up.

Then, Partycrasher walks out and stands in front of me, facing the crowd. "We are gathered here today to bestow the ultimate honor that the super-hero community can give." He lifts up a glittering medal on a red velvet yoke, holds it over his head. "The Order of the Golden Mask."

Everyone applauds at once. Some of the heroes whoop and whistle. Mardi Gras shoots up fireworks.

"I bestow this award upon the man who saved me from Linda Loveblind, the femme fatale who infiltrated my super-team...and my personal life." Partycrasher turns and smiles at me. "I bestow this award upon the truest and most faithful hero ever to fight crime by my side."

He walks over and drapes the medal around my neck.

"I have never been more proud of you," he says softly as he kisses my cheek. And then he turns to the audience again and raises his arms high. "Please join me now in recognizing this courageous hero for his outstanding achievement and the statement it makes about the true nature of heroism in our..."

THE LAST STAND OF A HERO'S HERO.

Partycrasher's voice brings me back. "Maybe you think I won't cross the line tonight." His eyes come into focus again, glaring out from the holes in his black cowl. "Maybe you think I take my oath too seriously to ever kill a man in cold blood."

He's still holding me up by my cape like a hunk of dead meat.

My body's so broken at this point, I can't move a muscle. I can't feel a thing below my waist, which I think is a major blessing.

"Well, guess what?" Suddenly, his fist lashes out and punches right through my chest. "There's an addendum to the oath. File it under super-hero trivia."

I can feel...I can feel...

My eyes roll up in their sockets. I can feel his hand clutching my heart.

"This addendum," he says as his fingers start to squeeze. "It renders the oath null and void in the event of a murdered spouse." His grip continues to tighten. "What does this mean in plain English?"

"P-please." There are so many things I want to say, so many things I need to tell him. A cascade, a multitude of things.

If only I could speak a full sentence.

"Translation," he says. "*I* am de-evilizing *you*."

Then his grip on my heart grows tighter still. His fist clenches, and I know my heart is about to burst, about to break for the very last time.

And I close my eyes and strain with all my might to see beyond the illusion once more. Perhaps, if I can shatter this implanted delusion, I can step through into the better world Loveblind sought to deny me, the world in which instead of dying I am...

ANOTHER NIGHT IN ISOSCELES CITY...

Partycrasher pats my chest and smiles. "Ready to hit the street, chum?"

I pull the black cowl down over my face and nod. "So much crime, so little time."

"Say." He cocks his head and points an index finger at me. "That's a good one. I just might use that again."

"Be my guest." I laugh and unbuckle my seat belt. "So do you think we'll catch up with her tonight, Partycrasher?"

"Linda Loveblind?" He shrugs as he pops open his own seat

belt. "Hard to say. All we can do is remain ever-vigilant for any sign of that mind-warping Mata Hari."

"I suppose you're right." Reaching into the glove compartment, I pull out the De-Evilizer gun. "But I'm taking this just in case."

We both chuckle, and then we leap out of the Partymobile without opening the doors.

The second my boots hit the pavement, I feel lighter. This is where I belong. This is how it was meant to be.

All my troubles float away as I start the oath. "Criminals, your party is over."

"We're not invited," joins in Partycrasher, "and we're showing up anyway."

We give each other a high five. Then, we hear a woman scream from a nearby alley.

"A citizen in danger!" says Partycrasher. "Some foul fiend at work, no doubt!"

"Let's go!" My feet are already moving before I say the words.

As we run toward the alley, the streetlight behind us flickers once...then twice. Looking back over my shoulder, I see it flicker a third time, and go out.

I stop running, staring up at that darkened lamp, feeling as if I'm forgetting something. Something important.

But then I figure what could be more important than fighting crime? And I charge off after Partycrasher, dashing under the stars winking in the indigo night, stars so bright and close, I swear I could pluck them right from the sky if only I outstretched my black-gloved hand.

CASE CLOSED.

VOYAGE OF THE DOG-PROPELLED STARSHIP

We are down to our last team of Huskies, and we still can't shake the *Unshakable*, flagship of the dreaded High Concept.

"How long can those Huskies run? How long until we lose all propulsion from the dog-drive?" I shout the question to make myself heard over the cries of pleasure from the bridge crew around me.

The Concept's delighter beams have half the crew squirming on the floor, quivering like the enormous bacteria or protozoans they are.

"Stand by, Captain Nabob!" Vera Caspian, my ship's caninegineer (and a freak human among us), is watching readouts and video feeds on her holographic console. She claps her hands once, folds sideways left to right, and is gone, zapping by quantum zentanglement to the Kennel Deck at the far end of the ship.

She unfolds at her station a moment later, her face flushed with alarm. "Maybe five more minutes on the Huskies. That's with our best musher at the whip."

Our own farship, the *No Shit*, rocks as the *Unshakable* blasts us with its boomer cannons, knocking me sideways. As I catch myself on a shiny bulkhead, I realize the terrible shape I'm in; my reflection shows that my thousands of hairlike cilia are limp, my macronucleus is pale, and my cytoplasm is shriveled and green with exhaustion. Three days on the run from the Concept have left this giant paramecium looking like a sorry-ass humanoid warmed over.

But I'm still the *captain* of this ship, and I have a duty to keep her out of the hands of the enemy. Also a duty to deliver the *Trillion Thoughts About One Thing* in our hold to the dying planet that needs them to survive.

Which is about 300 light years from the orange and purple planet we're about to crash into.

"We're caught in that world's gravity well, sir!" says Mr. Huarache, a three-meter-tall amoeboid with glittering gold flecks in his cytoplasm. "We're going down!"

The *No Shit* shudders around us as the *Unshakable* keeps up its bombardment. As always, the High Concept's dedication to trolling the sentients of the galaxy for their own demented amusement knows no bounds. Stopping us from saving a dying planet will bring those bitter, sniggering jerks no end of joy, and stealing the *Trillion Thoughts About One Thing* for their own trouble-causing endeavors will be the cherry on the hot shit sundae.

Another round of boomer blasts rattles us from stern to stem, even as more of our people go down squirming with delighter-induced bliss. We'll be lucky to make landfall before the ship shakes to pieces and everyone aboard her is overstimulated to the point of implosion.

"Captain!" Vera has a grim look on her face. "The Huskies are down, sir!" Dogs whine and whimper over the intercom. "We're breaking out the emergency backup, but we won't get far on *Corgis* and *dachshunds*, sir!"

"Huarache!" I stare at the gleaming orange and purple planet on the big viewer on the forward bulkhead. "Can we manage evasive maneuvers?"

"I feel too good to try!" Huarache giggles with delight.

Damnit, he's been hit! "Outta my way!" Cilia fluttering, I zip over and seize the controls with the folds of my rubbery pellicle membrane.

Little dogs are yapping, and there's power again, but barely. I flick a switch, twist a joystick, and the *No Shit* swoops away from the *Unshakable*, heading for the planet's surface far below.

The surface where, long ago, I was shocked to discover who *dogs'* best friends really were, and why evil was *not* the worst thing ever to nest in human hearts.

We come down fast and hit hard, bouncing from one purple sand dune to the next. Hunks of the ship's organic outer armor shear away with each impact, exposing more of the *No Shit*'s glistening jellyfish skin.

Our breakneck approach finally comes to an end with a sudden, lurching stop in the side of a huge Ground Spout--its thick purple mass heaving with complex vapors and dense, semi-solid larvae flickering in and out of multiple dimensions.

As the ship settles and the screams fade--as many triggered by High Concept delighter beams as crash-inflicted injuries--I shake off my own personal shock and help those on the bridge who are hurt. One of them, Ensign Scintilla Tint, a sentient scent presenting as a cluster of swirling glitter, is scattered but doesn't let it stop her from reporting on casualties.

Five dead, 85 injured. Her voice is a complex arrangement of fragrant esters that conjures language in the speech centers of most organic brains. *And...oh no. Oh this is terrible.*

"What?" I ask as I finish mending some of the million wings of the giant flying bacterium known as Lieutenant Ah Rise Rhythm.

Vera Caspian, whose head wound is shedding blood down the side of her face, interrupts. "Dogs down, Captain! *All dogs gone!*"

Yes, dead, confirms Scintilla.

"And the ship's condition?" I ask as Ah Rise Rhythm flutters away to check on his crewmates.

"Repair crews already dispatched and laden with insults," says Mr. Huarache. "Damage consequential but not irreparable."

"How long until we're ready to launch?" I ask.

"Approximately two hours, Captain Nabob." Huarache's amoeboid gelatin squirms, repairing multiple regions of bruising. "Assuming repairs are properly completed, and the High Concept doesn't destroy us first, all we'll need to reactivate the dog drive are some..."

"Then it's a good thing." I head for the exit.

"What is that, Captain?" asks Rhythm.

"A good thing I know where to *find* some dogs," I tell them as the shellevator doors clam shut before me, and I zip away through the ship to the bubble deck where my bouncy ball carriage awaits.

I'm 20 bounces west of the *No Shit* when Vera unfolds from right to left beside me, in a Dalmatian print field jacket with a med kit pack on her back. Her head wound has been wrapped with a black-furred bandage that contrasts her pretty blond hair.

"Vera." I'm not really surprised to see her appear in my travel ball like that. As caninegineer, she *should* be along on this mission.

"Craw isn't listed as a dog-rich world." Vera bobs in the suspension field inside the ball, only lightly jarred by the vehicle's powerful bounces across the landscape. "So where are these canines you're barking about, Skipper?"

"Not far, actually. It's lucky we crashed where we did."

"Lucky?" Vera scrunches up her nose. "What if you lead the Concept to this secret stash of yours?"

"As long we make contact first, I don't care. Though depending on how well they *remember* me, we might not have such smooth flailing."

As I flutter my thousands of cilia for emphasis, the terrain outside the travel ball changes, shifting from purple sand dunes to a bird beak forest. Giant toucan, myna, and heron beaks climb point-first to the lilac sky, even as spindly trees hung with the beaks of other birds surround us, clattering in the stiff afternoon breeze.

The macronucleus at the heart of me clenches as memories of my last visit to this place rush back. "Gird yourself, Vera. Unless this place has changed greatly, we are heading into the deepest of metaphorical darkness."

"What *happened* when you were here before, Captain?" asks Vera. "Tell me more about what to expect."

As the travel ball takes a bad bounce off an upthrust woodpecker beak the size of an old-growth redwood tree, I adjust the course controls on the inner wall of the ball with my cilia. *Almost there.* But can we get the help we need in spite of the cloud I left under last time? The darkness that still, to this day, haunts me?

Maybe I can work it out by telling the story. "It was twelve full glimmerings ago, when I was but a crewman on the good farship *Every/None/Always/Never..."*

"We surrender!" screamed Captain Fragilistic of the *Tabula Raga*, the hysteria in his voice unnerving even in the replayed video. "Call off your people-things! Oh gods, please *call them off!"*

"Crewman Nabob! For the last time, quit watching that shit!" *My* commanding officer at the time, Captain Eponymous Prawn of the *Every/None/Always/Never,* knocked the video playback device out of my pellicle mitten with one sweep of his whiplike flagellum. "Pay attention to what's happening *now*, and maybe we can find and *rescue* the crew of the *Tabula Raga."*

"Instead of suffering the same fate as they did?" I asked.

"Face forward, crewman!" howled Prawn, a spermatozoa with an attitude that never quit.

I did, and so did the other twelve crewmen and three officers in the landing party. Giant microbes all, we continued our methodical march/squirm/wriggle/float through the bird beak forest, closing in on the last known location of the Fragilistic and the party from the *Tabula Raga.* They'd all disappeared six weeks ago, leaving behind only that ominous video as a clue to their fates...a video that was stuck playing in a loop as we all marched away from my discarded player device. "We surrender! Oh gods, please *call them off!"*

"Hold up, people!" Lieutenant Band Antimony, a ribbon of

geometric diatoms with photoluminescent properties, suddenly stiffened in alarm. "Movement up ahead!"

Every one of us raised and cocked our convincer/reviser guns, barrels aiming at a copse of striped toucan beaks not twenty kicks away. Depending on their moods, those living weapons we carried would unleash either a torrent of persuasive argument or streams of information-altering code capable of rewriting the causal relationships involved in a given scene.

The weapons might as well have been nonexistent when we heard the plaintive howl from the copse of beaks.

OO-WOO-OOOOOO

As the keening rose and fell, I shivered and considered turning tail. One of our number *did* desert just then--a gray-skinned cryptoendolith who turned out to be the wisest among us.

"Steady, people!" ordered Antimony. "Stand your ground!"

"Who's there?" shouted Captain Prawn in the direction of the howl. "Who is it?"

OO-WOO-OOOOOO

Again, the cry ululated on the hot, dry wind, keeping us all at shivering attention. Then, suddenly, it stopped.

A figure emerged from the copse of beaks--a naked human male on all fours, slinking slowly across the dusty ground. His long, shaggy hair and beard were bright red. He wore a spiked black collar with a long silver chain trailing after it.

Behind him strode a figure on two legs--a canine like a German Shepherd in a kind of blue jumpsuit. In his right paw, which included a prehensile, clawed thumb, he carried the other end of the chain attached to the man's collar.

When he spoke, his voice was deep and rumbling like thunder.

"Welcome one and all," he said. "Which of you is fit to feed the Best Friend?"

"That human?" said Prawn. "*None* of us, thank you very much!"

"Don't be silly. Not that *human,"* snapped the canine. "Our *Best* Friend!"

"We're here." I stroke the course controls, and the travel ball bounces to a stop. One more touch of a control, and the skin falls into wedges around us, exposing us to the riot of sounds and smells in the bird beak forest. "That's where they first came out to meet us." I poke a hump of pellicle at the copse of toucan beaks just a few coughs away.

"'They as in a dominant, bipedal dog and subservient human on all fours." Vera takes a step forward, then stops. "Why is this the first I've ever heard of this encounter?"

"It was classified ultra-top secret after what happened." I glide past her and into the copse. There is simply no time to waste; the Ground Spout could disperse at any time, leaving the *No Shit* completely out in the open. Will my crew finish repairs or will the Concept swoop in to destroy them and the farship first? It's a tossup.

Vera draws her weapon--a fully automatic shevolver with self-esteem nullifier and false hope inducer--and follows me into the cluster of colorful striped beaks. This isn't the first time we've been in a tense situation together; she's been part of the crew for seven sequences, each one riskier than the last.

But I fear for us both if potential surprises roll against us, which they very well could. I wouldn't put anything past this world after my disastrous last visit.

Suddenly, a keening wail fills the air--familiar to *my* ears, at least. A chill runs through my cytoplasm as, for a moment, time seems to turn back.

"Ignore that," I tell Vera as I keep gliding forward. "Just keep going."

"But is it..."

"*Ignore it.*" I need to keep us focused in spite of the distraction. Whatever awaits us, we need to face it at full, unrattled strength and composure.

A moment of silence, and again, Vera speaks--trying to keep her mind off the danger, perhaps. "So what happened after the dog and his pet man met your group, Skipper?"

"The dog--his name was Half Hiccup Half Heartattack--showed us the way to a hidden city called Oblongata, which was built entirely of bones and feces. Parts of it were marvelously intricate. Other parts were corpse-strewn ruins. They'd been having a civil war, you see--pets against masters...and something else."

"Pets? You mean *dogs* or *men*?"

"Yes." I slip between some tightly-packed flamingo beaks, slowing my pace a little. We're not far from Oblongata and its possible dangers now. "And something else. Something I'd never encountered before--*knowingly."*

"What a lovely city," said Captain Prawn in the bygone days of yore. "And what a shame about all the destruction."

"We paid a price for victory." Half Hiccup Half Heartattack patted his leashed human on his red-haired head. The man drooled, tongue lolling, eyes empty. "But it was worth it for our newfound freedom."

"Freedom." Lieutenant Antimony's component diatoms glowed a little brighter, then dimmed. "From what?"

"This one and his like, of course." Heartattack tousled the man's bearded chin. "They subjugated us, treated us as their *chattel*, denied us *any* kind of rights...and now look. Who's a good boy now, huh? *Who's a good boy now?"* With a laugh, Heartattack shook the man's head by his beard, yanking it from side to side.

Still, the man's eyes were blank. I was having a hard time imagining he'd *ever* been part of a ruling class of any kind.

"When did the war end?" asked Prawn.

"Only days ago," said Heartattack.

"That fits." Antimony's ribbony structure rippled. "Our missing landing party must have gotten caught up in the conflict."

Heartattack nodded slowly. "Of course. Their demise had nothing to do with the Godicils."

Prawn and Antimony exchanged a look that made me more nervous than ever. I kept my pellicle extrusions and cilia wrapped tight around my convincer/reviser gun.

"Demise?" said Prawn. "We never said they were *dead.* All we know is that they're *missing.*"

"And what's a *Godicil?*"

"You mean you don't *know?*" Heartattack crouched beside the man and gestured at what looked to me like empty space above the man's shoulders. "You mean you can't *see* it?"

"See what?" asked Prawn.

"Come closer." Heartattack kept gesturing at that space above the human's shoulders. "Take a closer look."

Prawn swam over, propelling himself with strokes of his flagellum tail, and gazed down at the man as instructed.

"Still nothing?" Heartattack sounded annoyed. "Closer!"

"What exactly does it *look* li--"

Suddenly, Prawn was dragged down toward the man--but not *by* him. From what I could see, it was like something in that empty space jerked him down toward it, holding his ovoid body fast as his tail flailed crazily.

And then stopped. And then Prawn fell to the ground beside the human with a *splat.*

"A *Godicil,*" said Heartattack, "is *that.*"

As the upright German Shepherd said it, other bipedal dogs with naked humans on leashes--some with more than one--converged from the surrounding rubble. All of the humans were growling as they approached, males and females alike.

"Just because you can't *see* it, doesn't mean it can't win a *war.* Or be our *best friend.*" Heartattack dropped the leash, and all the other dogs around us did the same.

The words of hysterical Captain Fragilistic of the *Tabula Raga* from that terrible video rushed back to me. *Call off your people-things! Oh gods, please call them off!*

"Just because you can't *see* them, doesn't mean they can't *slaughter* you," said Heartattack, just before he whistled and all the humans attacked us at once.

"How the hell did you *survive?*" asks Vera.

I don't get to finish telling her my story just then because my chatterbox starts beeping, alerting me to a message from the *No*

Shit. Sliding the device from its holster stuck to my pellicle, I flick it on with my fluttering cilia, and we listen.

"The Ground Spout has dissipated! The *Unshakable* has found us!" The voice from the speaker belongs to ever-dependable Lieutenant Ah Rise Rhythm. "Their fighters are rapidly incoming with delighters fully charged! Repairs are nearly complete, but we're sitting ducks with dogless engines! No takey-offey, *capische*?"

"Hold them off as best you can," I tell him. "Launch all fighter squadrons. Keep shields raised as long as you can on battery power."

"That won't be long, Captain!" Just as Rhythm says it, there's an explosion in the background. "We don't have much left in the tank here!"

"We hope to be in touch soon with good news." I keep my voice confident for his sake. "Nabob out."

"Gotta go, Skipper." Vera claps her hands once, folds left to right, and is gone--presumably back to the ship to assess and assist. Maybe she's even got some emergency puppies tucked away in cryogenic dogspension for just such a day as today.

As I break the connection, I hear rustling from the peacock tail brush nearby, and I lurch around to face it. Extruding a mitten of cytoplasm, I wrap it around my instakarmashawarmadharma gun and swing it up in instant readiness just in case.

"Who goes there?" As the words pop out of my oral groove, every cilium on my body stiffens like a needle, quivering with tension. "Show yourself!"

Imagine my surprise when a redheaded human male stalks out of the brush biped-style, dressed in a black smock and bottoms.

"Greetings, friend." Smiling, he raises his hands (which are empty of weapons, by the way). "You are most welcome here in our little corner of the world."

"Greetings to you as well." I recognize him instantly as the naked redhead on the leash of Half Hiccup Half Heartattack from my previous visit...though I don't blurt this fact out right away.

"My name is Fah Fistula, and I'm the chief of our fair city of

Oblongata." The redhead bows a little, then straightens. "And you are?"

I hesitate to announce my name, then decide to go for broke rather than lie. "Captain Nabob," I tell him. "My vessel, the farship *No Shit*, crash-landed nearby and is in dire straits." I pause dramatically. "We are dogless."

"Then we have something in common!" Fistula nods. "There is not a dog to be found *anywhere* in Oblongata or its blessed environs."

My star-shaped contractile vacuole and radiating canals scrunch in a spiral twist, the paramecium version of a frown. "No dogs...at all?"

Again, Fistula nods. "If you've come in search of them, you're out of luck. The last died during our recent civil war, ended mere weeks prior to your arrival."

There's been another civil war, then--this time with much different results. Things start to make *terrible* sense. If what he says is true, the *No Shit* and all aboard are surely doomed.

The man gestures, inviting me onward. "Will you visit fair Oblongata, sir? I think you'll find our hospitality *much* improved since your *last* visit here."

So he *does* remember me. "But what about the *others?* The dogs' best friends?"

"The Godicils?" Fistula smiles grimly. "Whom do you think we *defeated* in this war?"

As the humans attacked, the crew of the *Every/None/Always/Never* didn't hesitate to open fire. Every one of us blasted away with our convincer/revisers, holding nothing back--and not a shot made a damn bit of difference. The humans were upon us like a raging wildfire, oblivious to the streams of argument or causal disruption cascading from the barrels of our weapons.

Their style of assault was surprising, unnerving. They knocked our people down and pinned them but never used their sharp claws or gleaming fangs to do them harm. *That*, they left to the *thin air.*

Just as Captain Prawn had been murdered by what seemed to be the empty space above the redheaded human's shoulders, I saw one after another of my shipmates torn apart by unseen forces. Gruesome splatters of guts spilled onto the ground all around me, erupting from skins and capsules that seemingly split open spontaneously.

Only I was spared, writhing out of the awful slaughter that engulfed my comrades. Lieutenant Antimony tried to follow, only to be pounced on by a screaming, dark-haired female and subsequently rupture like a stuck balloon.

Just like in the video, it was pure chaos. Mind whirling, I found myself pinned against a towering black beak--and Half Hiccup Half Heartattack stepped in front of me.

"Looks like they were *all* fit to feed the Godicils." Heartattack shrugged. "But *you* have a different role to play, apparently."

"Role?" I had to fight to keep my voice from shaking as the humans who'd just torn apart my crewmates rose and circled around me, hunched and glowering. "What role?"

"Tortured prisoner." Heartattack gestured, and two brawny men--one with brown hair, one with blond--got up off their hands and knees and stormed toward me. "Don't worry. The pain will be worth it in the end...though not so much for you."

The two men used me as a punching bag then, taking turns pumping fists into my pellicle. Each blow was harder than the last, making me grunt and yelp with agony.

And each time a human punch pounded my micronucleus through the pellicle, I divided. I gave birth to a copy of myself that wriggled off into the arms of a waiting dog.

Screaming at the pain flashing through me, I had the answer to a question I'd never considered until that moment.

If you undergo asexual reproduction induced by physical impact, is it still a violation?

I am nervous as Fistula guides me into the freshly ruined city. I stay keenly alert for any sudden movement from any direction, even as I realize all the alertness at my command won't likely save me.

This is where it happened, that pummeling attack...the forced reproduction. The last thing I remember from that day is gazing out at all the children I'd made against my will, glistening and quivering eerily in the midday sun. Then, I passed out from the pain, blessedly shielded from whatever abuses were to follow.

I awoke who knows how many hours later, shriveled and wretched in the purple sand desert. Gazing up, I saw crewmen from the *Every/None/Always/Never* gaping down at me, reaching to lift me in their cilia and pseudopodia for transport back to the ship. When I got there, I said nothing of what had been done to me, though I told our intelligence branch everything I remembered otherwise of Oblongata. I thought I would never travel back there in my lifetime--I *prayed* I wouldn't--yet here I am, returned to the scene of the crimes against me.

And a witness to those very crimes walks easily alongside me, as if we are dear old friends. Needless to say, I keep an extruded mitten close to my instakarmashawarmadharma gun at all times.

"Careful," he says calmly. "There are still a few of them roaming around."

"Dogs? Godicils?"

"Your kids," says Fistula.

I am more confused than ever. "Why is that a bad thing?"

"Because they were on the wrong side. They were the *enemy--part* of it, anyway."

We circle the ruins of a giant structure that looks like it was built from stained glass, starlight, and some kind of flowering vines. A cathedral, perhaps? Then why are there heaps of dog skulls arranged on the floor?

"I don't understand anything about this place," I say, almost to myself. "I don't understand what happened here."

"What happened to *you*, you mean? Back in the day?" Fistula plucks a purple flower from one of the vines and twirls it between his thumb and forefinger. "I can tell you this much: it was all the *dogs'* idea."

"Why? What could they have to gain from what was done to me?"

"Peace! That was the plan, anyway." Fistula flicks the flower away. "They wanted your offspring to serve as *hosts* for the Godicils--though *traps* is more like it."

"Maybe it would help if I knew what the Godicils *were.*"

"Invisible, hideous *parasites.*" Fistula flinches a little when he says it. "Most of the time, you don't even know they're *on* you." He reaches back with both hands and pats the empty space above his shoulders. "On you and *in* you."

"In you."

Fistula scowls and nods. "They work their slimy tendrils through your body, winding them around your organs—occupying your heart like a nest of worms. They pump you full of chemicals, driving you to violence, and they feed on your rage and pain. The only way to keep the food coming is to turn you against an enemy--even if that enemy used to be your friend."

His words sink in, and understanding grows. "Then the civil war that the dogs won, those years ago?"

"Was triggered by the Godicils," says Fistula. "And we humans were their hosts. But in the war before that, the *dogs* were the hosts, and so on. This went on for thousands of years, one war after another, until Half Hiccup Half Heartattack the dog chieftain came along. He was the first who could *see* and *read* the slimy bastards. He was the first to understand how *both* sides were being manipulated. And when *you* folks started dropping in, he came up with a plan to free *all* of us."

I twitch at a flicker of movement near a half-toppled tower of pulsing green brick...then relax. Nothing there.

"At the time, the Godicils were the *dogs'* best friends." Fistula keeps walking, drawing me toward a battered silver dome that looks like it could be the center of the city. "But Heartattack knew that would only last until the next war, when the Godicils would switch sides and drive the *humans* into conflict. This would just go on forever, he knew--but what if there was a *third* side? What if he introduced a *new* host into the mix? One that might be too tempting for the Godicils to resist--until they were *trapped* inside...and then the whole package was *disposed of.*"

"And the Godicils took the bait?" I leave out the part about my personal suffering and violation--for now, at least.

"We all worked together, playing our parts. We had to make it seem *convincing*...right down to the attack on your team, I'm afraid. We needed it to look like we were torturing you for information, and the copies we punched out of you were unintentional." He sounds regretful. "And when we had your children, and talked about how wonderful they were, and what amazing capabilities they had, the Godicils *jumped* at them! Heartattack saw them go, one after another, and attach to your kids' bodies. And then he *closed the trap*, buried them like dogs *do*--but it was a *bust.* Over time, the Godicil treatment turned your kids into *powerhouses*, and they broke free and came after *all* of us. They killed every last dog and almost got the *rest* of us, except we figured out a way to kill *them* first, and the Godicils with them."

"You killed my children."

"Correct," says Fistula.

"Except a few who are still roaming around."

"Exactly."

"Okay." Nothing I've heard from him makes me feel any better about what happened...or more hopeful about the tragedy I've come here to avert. And the clock is ticking, I know, counting down whatever few minutes are left for the *No Shit* to hold on against overwhelming odds. What if the *Unshakable* has already destroyed her?

The thought of it inspires me to dig deeper for a solution. There must be *something* here to power up the ship, *something* that wasn't trashed in the latest war.

"Fistula." I look around at the rubble as we pick our way through it. "Do you know if the dogs buried anything else?"

Fistula snorts and stops walking. "Good question. Those mutts were *always* burying things."

I like where this is going. "Can you think of any *specific* burial sites?" I gesture at the ground with one of my pellicle mittens.

"Well, not down *there.*" Fistula points upward. "*That's* where they did all their *burying.*"

"Wait a minute." I do that frowny star-shaped vacuole/canals thing again. "Am I to understand that these dogs somehow *buried* things…in the *sky?*"

"Not so much in the *sky.*" Fistula tips his head back and jabs a finger at a fluffy orange cloud overhead. "In *those.*"

Some kind of hyperdense cloud formation with antigravitic properties? It's a new one on me. "So how did they get *up* there then?"

"The *elevator,* of course." He looks over his shoulder and gestures in the general direction of what looks like a distant, rippling heat mirage.

"Well let's go see what they stashed up there, shall we?" I prod him along with my flickering cilia. "If there's a secret power source, we need to find it *fast.* Time is running out, and a lot of good macrobes are about to be deathstinguished."

We emerge from the rippling transparent elevator into a truly wondrous place built of billowing orange cloud. Puffs and streamers of the stuff drift all around, glowing every shade of orange in the unobstructed late day sunlight. It all seems insubstantial, yet somehow supports the weight of us both, giving only slightly like rubbery foam under Fistula's feet and my flickering cilia.

It supports much more than that, as well. The dogs left all manner of things up here, jumbled in the cottony fluff. There are piles of bones, of course, and tatters and rags--but also mechanical and electronic parts and equipment…building materials…functioning devices. Things blink and hum in the cloudbank, while others chatter and whir and twitch--and do *other* things, too.

As we walk onward, we hear sounds from inside a kind of bunker built with corrugated metal. The sounds are unmistakable, even muffled as they are--and the part of me that's closest to a human heart truly leaps. Perhaps, after everything, there is hope after all.

"Do you hear that?" I ask Fistula, pointing a mitten at the building.

"Yes, but there's a lock on the door," he tells me.

"So smash it off," I say as I reach for my chatterbox. "And make it snappy!"

He hesitates, then goes to retrieve a metal bar from a nearby pile of junk.

As he heads for the bunker, my chatterbox makes its connection. "Skipper?" Vera Caspian answers the call. "Where the hell *are* you? I zentangled back from the *No Shit* and can't find you anywhere!"

"Never mind!" I watch as Fistula breaks the lock and tosses it aside. "Just get back to the ship *immediately*. And prepare the following without delay!"

"Yes sir!"

Fistula throws open the door, and the noise bursts out from inside. All that wonderful, marvelous *barking*.

And then I *see* them, the ones making those sounds, and I know we can do this. *We can win because of them.*

As they charge toward me, I laugh out my orders to Vera. "Get me *harnesses*, Vera! Dozens of *harnesses*, and the longest *traces* you can throw together in the next fifteen minutes!"

The battle is in full swing when I ride a winged Great Dane down from the sky, exulting in the way the wind whips my cilia.

Enemy fighters swoop and blast overhead, sparring with fighters from the *No Shit*. The sky lights up, but the fire comes nowhere near the Dane or any of the *other* winged dogs.

There are *dozens* of them, barking and howling with joy as they soar down on great feathery wings. Nimbly, they zip between blasts and shrapnel, darting this way and that, a brigade of furry angels. The products of Godicil science, these genetically engineered miracles are clearly elated to finally be free of the shelter where they were tucked away for far too long. Heartattack and his people might have saved them from Godicil domination, but locking them away only intensified their desire to be free.

And now, finally, they can *fly*...and so can *we*.

The Dane and I land in front of the *No Shit*, where Vera followed my orders to the letter. Lots of crewmen are there, too, to help set things in motion--Vera, Ah Rise Rhythm, and Mr. Huarache among them.

The Dane, leader of the pack, follows me to the front and is first to accept a harness. The other dozens follow, landing lightly and scampering to positions along the lengthy, incredibly strong lead lines. They all pant and sniff and bark with joy as the crew fasten harnesses to them, taking care to leave the wings free and clear. They sing, too, in words taught them by Heartattack years ago, poetic words of flight and beauty and escape to faraway starlands.

Every time the enemy fighters form up and try to strafe them, our own fighters fend them off with desperate grace. We'll let *nothing* get in the way of what comes next.

When the harnesses are secure, all the crew members race into the ship except Vera. Pressure-suited against the harshness of space, she leaps into a special sled behind the dogs, hastily assembled by the *No Shit*'s highly motivated crew.

On my signal, when all crew and fighter craft are aboard, Vera cracks the whip. The winged dogs--Danes, Huskies, Shepherds, Greyhounds, Golden Retrievers, Dobermans, Labradors, and more--run and flap across the purple sand. They pull the ship behind them with incredible ease, sliding it out of the crash-site and picking up speed.

When their paws leave the ground, so does the *No Shit*. Together, we soar upward, leaving behind the awful world of Craw that held us down--that held *me* down ever since my first visit, though I've finally broken its grip. As the dogs and ship fly, so does my soul. As the ground recedes below us, so does the sorrow and pain that kept me from reaching my fullest potential as a paramecium and farship captain.

Enemy fighters swirl around us, and we shoot away from

them, too fast to follow. They can't stop us from whisking the *Trillion Thoughts About One Thing* to that dying world or going on any of the multitude of adventures that surely await us.

The High Concept attack ship *Unshakable* roars toward us, firing every weapon in its arsenal...then seems to stand still as Vera mushes the dogs to unbelievable new speeds.

Somehow, their wings and paws have just as much traction in the void as on the ground and in the atmosphere. I can't explain it, and I don't care. I don't care about the physics or the memories of my pain or the damned High Concept or any of it.

It is enough to sit back and watch from the bridge of my gleaming farship as those winged dogs carry us forth into the star-filled glory of the galaxy, barking with heartfelt joy at every crack of the musher's whip.

THE DARKS OF THEIR EYES

Then: August 1923.

True story: One summer night in the Rosedale section of Johnstown, Pennsylvania, an African-American named Robert Young went a little crazy because his wife had left him.

By the time the crazy had run its course, Young had shot four cops--killing two--and been shot to death himself in the bargain.

Things only went downhill from there. The blasts from Young's gun were like signals to the racist powers-that-be.

By the time they were done, Rosedale was quiet as the grave. And Johnstown was surrounded by burning crosses and white-hooded men.

Now, I wasn't there, but I knew someone who was. And she never forgot that light show, with the columns of smoke curling into the sky and the town aglow from the roaring blazes. The same town that had been wiped out by water in the Great Flood of 1889.

Awash in flames from the hills.

Now: September 2016.

I'm black, and I'm coming for you. That's all the first letter said.

Max Leverknight got it at the office of Prod, the software

development company where he worked as a business analyst. It had been left on his desk while he was out to lunch.

The letter consisted of that one sentence typed on one piece of paper in a white business envelope. The envelope had one postage stamp and his work address typed on the front; it was postmarked the day before, mailed from Johnstown--the same Western Pennsylvania town where Max lived and worked.

He turned the letter over in his hands, did the same with the envelope, and laughed.

Then he got up from his desk and held the crazy thing up over his cubicle wall. "Ha ha! Very funny!"

Coworkers looked up from their own cubes, from the software or documentation they were working on, and frowned.

Prod was a small company, so there weren't that many coworkers. Nine faces stared back from the cubes, all told.

"What's funny?" asked Jenny O'Rourke, with her short red hair and dark-framed glasses in the cube next-door.

"This letter!" Max waved it emphatically. "The one about someone 'coming to get' me. Which one of you clowns put it on my desk?"

Jenny threw her hands in the air. "Maybe someone's coming to pick you up, and you forgot about it?"

"I don't think they meant 'coming to get' me as in giving me a *ride* somewhere," said Max.

"It was *all* of us!" hollered overweight, bald Jake Bloom from across the room--the biggest clown at Prod. "We're gonna beat some sense into you, Maxie! Get you to write some less shitty software requirements!"

Everyone laughed, and Max scanned their faces. They all looked amused, but no one had a sneaky expression that might make him think they were *extra*-pleased about the scene.

There was just one face that bothered him, though it had never done so before. The face of a friend, three cubes over, whom he'd never had a problem with in the two years they'd known each other.

His name was Phil Washington, and he was an African-American, just like the letter writer claimed to be.

As soon as Max's thoughts about Phil clouded over, he brushed them aside. Not possible, no chance, it couldn't be. Phil was a good guy, a pal in his early thirties like Max, and would *never* under any circumstances threaten to hurt him. It wasn't like Phil to fuck with him in *any* way.

He wouldn't have any *reason* to, even if he were violently inclined. Max *never* had a problem with African-Americans or anyone *else* based on race, gender, religion, or any other personal characteristics. He just wasn't *that kind of guy*.

Which only made the mystery deeper...but, clearly, he wasn't going to solve it *this* way.

"All right then!" Max folded up the paper and stuffed it in his pants pocket. "It's probably just a joke! But just in case..." He raised an eyebrow and pointed a finger at everyone in turn. "If some dude shows up wanting to kick my ass, tell him *I'm not here!*"

"Some *dude?*" Jake snorted. "Some *woman*, more likely!" Then he, and the rest of the developers and business analysts, laughed uproariously.

Then: September 1923.

True story: A few weeks after Robert Young killed those white cops in Rosedale, the mayor of Johnstown ordered all "newly arrived negro citizens" to pack their shit and get out of town.

Believe it. Mayor Joe Cauffiel said that all blacks who'd been living in Johnstown for fewer than seven years must leave, "for their own safety." Like he was worried that the "negro citizens" might come to harm because of the outrage over Young's shooting spree.

Or, more likely, he was kissing the asses of the local steelworkers, who were pissed that the blacks had been taking their jobs.

Either way, Mayor Joe got one seal of approval right out of the gate. The night after he issued his order, the local Ku Klux Klan burned crosses on the hills surrounding Johnstown. That, in itself, wasn't so unusual in those days...but they really put on a show. The person I knew who was there, gazing up at those hills, said it was a terrible spectacle to behold.

All those flames. All that smoke. All those pointy white hoods, glowing in the firelight like some awful angel army.

Now: September 2016.

After work, Max went to the gym like always, thinking maybe he could get the letter out of his head. But then he realized something:

There seemed to be an awful lot of African-Americans there that evening.

The lady at the front desk who buzzed him in was one...and the two old guys who walked past him down the hall. There were three more--one middle-aged, two twentysomethings--in the locker room, and another five teenage ones on the basketball court, shooting hoops.

Then there was the new young guy in Max's aerobics class--also African-American. "Everyone, meet Darrel," said Karen the instructor, and Darrel smiled and waved.

Max waved back, though he couldn't help thinking, if only for a moment, *Where did that guy come from all of a sudden?*

Which was pure paranoia, and he knew it. But still.

There weren't a lot of African-Americans in Johnstown, for whatever reason. They were here and there--more, maybe, than when Max had been growing up--but not so many that they'd ever made much of an impression on him.

And now, to his paranoid mind at least, they seemed to be coming out of the woodwork.

Then: September 1923.

True story: Black people did what Mayor Joe told them to do. Because who wants to be where they're not wanted? Or where they might get hurt or worse?

"My mind is made up: The negroes must go back from where they came." That's what Mayor Joe had said. "They are not wanted in Johnstown."

"Negro citizens" who'd been in Johnstown fewer than seven years pulled up stakes and moved elsewhere, giving up jobs and homes and the things they couldn't carry. In the days and weeks to come, thousands of blacks got out-- thousands--*and their white neighbors watched them go without batting an eyelash. The neighborhood of Rosedale, in particular, almost completely emptied out.*

Johnstown was getting whiter by the day. And Mayor Joe was just getting started.

Now: 2016.

"It's a joke. It has to be." Max's girlfriend, Nina, shook her head as she reread the letter. "Somebody's jerking your chain, my good man."

Across the table from her, Max shrugged and popped a French fry in his mouth. "I know you're right." He was glad he'd met her for supper at their favorite diner downtown. His minor freakout at the gym was already forgotten.

"I mean, why would somebody have to tell you they're *black?* What does *that* have to do with anything?" Nina tucked her glossy black hair behind her left ear. Her dark brown eyes narrowed as she stared at the letter. "And why not make it 'African-American?' Written by a true non-African-American, if you ask me."

"I know, right?" Max popped in another fry. "He should've left out that whole first sentence. The letter should just be, like, 'I'm coming to get you.' Or better yet, 'Your ass is about to be kicked.' 'Coming to get you' is so *old school*, right?"

Grinning, Nina smacked the letter down on the table. "Guy needs an editor, for real." Then, she picked up her fork and started in on the open-faced hot turkey sandwich on the plate in front of her. "So what are you going to do about it?"

"What *should* I do?"

Nina raised her eyebrows and lowered her voice. "Avoid all African-Americans for the rest of your life?" The sarcasm was obvious.

"Well, I didn't want to overreact, but *that* seems sensible enough." Smirking, Max reached for his coffee and had a sip.

"*Or* you could always report it to the police," said Nina.

"The *joke* police," said Max. "Because it's a *joke.*"

"So that's the *real* million-dollar question here." Nina raised a forkful of turkey, gravy, and bread and pointed it at him. "Which of the *nuts* you know would be most likely to send that letter?"

Max met her gaze. "Not you?"

"You got me." Nina flashed a goofy grin and bobbled her head from side to side. "Because mailing terroristic threats is *so* much the kind of thing I like to do to the guys I'm dating."

"Guy-*zzz? *Guys *plural?"*

"Hey, keep it down!" Nina flicked her fork, spraying gravy on his burger. "What if one of them's *here*?"

Next morning, Max was out walking his dog--a sweet Dalmatian named Harry--through light fog and drizzle in his neighborhood in Richland Township. His house, a rental on a quiet street in the upscale Johnstown suburb, was three blocks behind him.

As Harry sniffed and pissed on utility poles, Max was lost in thought, worrying about a big assignment at work. At least it took his mind off the threatening letter for a while.

But job concerns sailed out the window when the car drove past. It was a burgundy Chrysler Fifth Avenue, a long, boxy one from the '80s. It crawled along under 20 miles an hour, and its headlights glowed pale white in the fog.

As it passed, Max caught a glimpse of the man behind the wheel--an old guy with dark-framed glasses. He seemed like a friendly sort, and he waved as he cruised past.

He was also an African-American.

Without thinking, Max went back on guard. Was *this* the guy? Was he coming to *get* him?

But all that lasted only a second. Max quickly got hold of himself and waved back with a smile. *Of course* that old guy wasn't a threat. *So what* if Max had never seen him in his neighborhood before? *So what* if he couldn't remember the last time he'd seen a black face around there?

It was all good, and Max was totally cool. He wasn't going to let some letter-writing dick change the way he felt about people and lived his life.

Then: 1923.

Was Mayor Joe satisfied with pushing out the blacks who'd been in Johnstown fewer than seven years? Oh hell *no.*

Getting rid of recently arrived blacks was just part of the fun. Mayor Joe also banned additional "Negro or Mexican laborers" from living and working in town.

Further, every black person who visited Johnstown would have to register with the mayor or police upon arrival, and wouldn't be allowed in without proof of being "law-abiding."

Though why would any person of color want to go there in the first place? Mayor Joe kept tightening the screws--for example, issuing an edict that blacks were forbidden to hold public gatherings other than church services.

All the more reason to get the hell out. The exodus continued, as black people left Johnstown in droves.

They'd gotten the message loud and clear.

Now: 2016.

Max found the second letter in his mailbox when he got home from work. Like the first, it was in a white envelope with a stamp, a Johnstown postmark, and his address typed on the front.

He opened it before he got in the front door. Inside was a single sheet of paper with two typed sentences:

Nothing I like better than a black-and-white dog for dinner. Don't worry, I saved some for you.

Max's blood ran ice-cold as he read the words on the page. Every muscle in his body galvanized at once as the import sank in, and he knew what had to come next.

Unless the letter was a hoax.

Please God, please God, please god. Hands shaking, he jammed the key in the front door lock and cranked it, then turned the knob. As the door glided open, Harry did not immediately bound up to greet him like always.

And Max *knew.*

He called out the name, anyway. "Harry?" His voice shook. "Harry?"

The place was quiet. There was no welcoming bark or click of claws on hardwood or linoleum from inside the house.

"Harry?" When Max got to the kitchen, he froze. There, on the floor, was some kind of hump underneath a floral print tablecloth.

Heart hammering, Max inched toward the hump. It wasn't big enough to be Harry. Maybe just *part* of him?

Whatever it was, it *stank.* The smell of it made him gag from across the room.

"Oh my God." Leaning down, Max grabbed the edge of the tablecloth. He hesitated, imagining all the terrible things he might see under there.

Then, he took a deep breath and steeled himself. Tightened his grip on the cloth.

And yanked it away.

"So much for the joke theory," said Nina, watching as Max scrubbed the kitchen floor.

Max didn't answer. At least there was a chance Harry was still alive. The hump under the tablecloth had consisted of a big pile of feces, not parts of a Dalmatian he'd loved for the past three years.

Other than that, the outcome was beyond shitty. The police--one uniformed patrolman--had been there and gone without finding a usable trace of the dog or home invader.

It was clear that the back door had been jimmied with a pry bar. As for the excrement, it was so plentiful, it didn't look like it had come from the Dalmatian--or, maybe, *any* animal other than human. Otherwise, when it came to clues, Max was strictly at square one.

Unless maybe there was something in the letter. The cop had taken it with him, supposedly, so forensic scientists could examine it--but that could take a while, since the closest crime lab was two hours away in Pittsburgh. And Max wasn't convinced his missing dog ranked high on the cop's list of priorities.

"Officer Whatshisname didn't seem too worked up, did he?" said Nina. "But, y'know, thanks for the awesome advice, right?"

"'Fix the door and change the locks,'" said Max, wringing out his rag in the blue plastic bucket beside him.

"Don't forget, 'If I were you, I'd have a gun in this house,'" said Nina. "Silly me, I kept hoping he'd say something about solving the case."

"Something like, 'We're going to protect you and find your dog.'"

"It's just a *dog*, Max," she said sarcastically. "What did you expect? The local cops have bigger fish to fry."

"Hanging out at Park 'n' Feed, you mean." Max sighed and got up, feeling completely wiped out. He missed his dog, he had to call a locksmith, his home had been violated...

And the motherfucker who'd done it was *still out there.*

"So what now?" asked Nina. "Are you going to tell your mom?"

"No way." He shook his head firmly. "She loves Harry more than *I* do."

Nina looked like she was going to make a joke, then changed her mind. "You wanna stay at my place tonight?"

"Maybe I should." Max scowled. "But I don't want to let this asshole drive me out of my house."

"What if he comes back and breaks in again?" said Nina. "What if he does something to *you* this time?"

Max glared and shook his head. "I *hate* this. I *hate* how this shithead's *screwing* with me. I *hate* how we don't even know who he *is*."

"And all we know is, he's black," said Nina. "According to *him*. Not much for us or the so-called authorities to work with."

Max grunted. "They don't know." He draped the rag over the side of the bucket. "The cop, I didn't tell him."

Nina frowned. "You mean the part about your pen pal being black?"

"*Maybe* black." Max shrugged. "But it wouldn't make any difference either way."

"You don't think?" asked Nina. "Or is it just you didn't want the cop to think you're a racist?"

What she said grated on him...maybe because she was right. At least partly. But he *wasn't*, and he never *would* be racist. That part of him, he knew, would never change, no matter what.

So what did it mean that every time he imagined the person who'd written the letters and taken his dog, he thought of a big, menacing black man? And what did it say that thinking that way came so easy to him?

Then: 1923.

True story: After thousands of African-Americans had fled Johnstown, Mayor Joe Cauffiel got put in his place.

Spurred by complaints from the Mexican government and James Weldon Johnson, Secretary of the National Association for the Advancement of Colored People, Pennsylvania Governor Gifford Pinchot demanded an explanation from Johnstown. Mayor Joe responded with the biggest crock of shit ever written, in which he insisted there'd been "no discrimination against the black race."

His bullshit didn't hold water. The governor sent in the state police and deputy attorney general to investigate. Mayor Joe did a complete one-eighty and denied ever ordering out the blacks and Mexicans, but the heat came down, and that was it.

Governor Pinchot ordered him to cut the crap and obey the law. No more booting out blacks or Mexicans; no more restrictions on assembly or visitors or any other such nonsense.

Reluctantly, Mayor Joe obeyed. He passed the word: the shenanigans--those he could be held accountable for, anyway--were over.

But...

Was there ever an apology? Were the blacks and Mexicans invited back? Was their lost property ever returned to them? Did the cross-burning stop in the hills around Johnstown?

What do you *think?*

Now: 2016.

The third letter arrived the next morning at work. This is what it said:

I'm someone you see every day. I'm right there in front of you, and you don't see it. Even though I stand out like a sore thumb, being black as pitch and all.

Max pored over it again and again, looking for clues. *Black as pitch?* It sure didn't read like something an African-American might write.

And why no references to the dog or the break-in? Why no additional threats?

The guy (or woman?) was messing with him, stirring the pot. Trying to make him crazy--and succeeding. But *why?*

Max couldn't think of anyone who might be out to get him. In his opinion, he was a nice, decent, even-tempered guy.

But was it possible he'd pissed someone off without knowing it? He thought hard about that and kept his eyes peeled as he went through the rest of his day. He looked for possible suspects among the people who crossed his path.

There was a little African-American guy who delivered newspapers every morning in the building where Max worked...but he'd never seemed put off by him before. Max had always made small talk with him and pushed the button for his floor in the elevator.

Then there was an African-American waitress named Anisah at the restaurant where he ate lunch, but she was friendly as ever that day.

On his way back to the office, Max passed the old African-American guy who always hung around on the corner--but again, no problem seemed likely. Max said hi like always, and the old guy nodded and tipped his hat, smiling.

Of course, Max's coworker, Phil Washington, was always friendly. Max couldn't imagine him sending the letters and dognapping Harry...but was there a chance he might have done it? Could Max discount *anything* at this point?

The truth was, it could be just about anybody of any color or gender. For that matter, it could be anyone whether they were nice to his face or not.

And the only thing Max could do was wait for him or her to make the next move.

Well, not the *only* thing.

"I'll take this one," said Max, cradling the .22 semi-automatic pistol in his hands. "And a box of ammo."

The guy behind the counter nodded and put away the other guns he'd been showing Max. "Good choice, with the laser sight and all."

Max put the pistol on the counter of the department store's gun center. He'd never owned a gun before. Buying one felt strange, but he thought it was the right thing to do.

"Okay then," said the salesperson, a pale, middle-aged guy with stringy brown hair and a goatee. "Hey, Mike! Get this guy started on his paperwork, will ya'?"

Just then, a young African-American guy walked out from behind the gun cases, carrying a clipboard. "Sure thing."

For no good reason, Max felt nervous as Mike handed him the clipboard. "Thanks." Max mustered a shaky smile.

Mike didn't seem to notice. "No prob." He fished a pen from the pocket of his blue apron and held it out. "Just let me know if you have any questions."

Max hesitated to fill out the forms. After all, he recognized

Mike from around the store, working in different departments. Was it possible? Could *he* be the one?

Enough!

Max shook off the craziness and finished the forms. The worst thing he could do was look at every African-American with suspicion--and, yes, anger.

If he wanted to get through this, he thought, he needed to be more color-blind and less judgmental than ever.

Then: 1923.

True story: Robert Sprangle was one of the thousands of blacks who fled Johnstown after Mayor Joe's order. Leaving a decent job in the Franklin Mills of Bethlehem Steel, he took his wife and two sons and headed east. A cousin of his was making good money in the Lackawanna steel plant in Scranton, PA, and Robert hoped to join him.

It was a good plan. With a little luck, Robert might have gotten in at Lackawanna and started a new and better life with his family in Scranton. He might have left behind the bad memories of Johnstown and found a place where he and his kind were welcome, not welcome to leave.

If he had ever made it to Scranton in the first place, that is.

Midway there, in the middle of nowhere in the middle of a moonless night, his jalopy of a car broke down. Leaving his wife and children at the car with the family shotgun, Robert walked through pitch darkness over winding mountain roads, backtracking to a service station he'd passed three miles ago.

I still think of him trudging along the road that night, dark skin against a dark background. I think of him as an oncoming truck hurtled over a rise, its headlights bathing him in sudden, blinding glare. I think of him throwing his arms up in surprise, or maybe trying in vain to sidestep the speeding vehicle.

I think of the truck racing toward him, and I wonder if the driver slowed down even a little bit, or maybe stepped on the gas instead. I think of Robert as the truck's front fender plowed into him, crushing bones and organs and sending him flying through the air to the base of an apple tree, where he was found the next morning.

I think of him dying alone like that, staring up into the blackness. I think of how it could all have been avoided, if only Mayor Joe and his cronies hadn't driven him and the other blacks out of Johnstown.

I think of how it's Mayor Joe's fault that Robert Sprangle died the way he did. I think of it every damn day of my life, because Robert was my grandpa, and they took him from me before I ever got to meet him.

And all these years later, I am going to make sure that Max Leverknight pays the price for that loss.

Now: 2016.

"Crime? What crime? Has anyone been *murdered* yet?" Nina took a little bow. "How's that?"

Max was too frazzled to fully appreciate the comedy in her impression, but he managed a smirk. "Good job. That was exactly the cops' attitude when I gave them the latest stalker letter."

"That's the trouble with white privilege," said Nina. "White *laziness* trumps the shit out of it every time."

"You can say that again." Max stuck his chopsticks in the white container of moo goo gai pan takeout and plunked the container on Nina's coffee table. "No leads on Harry, either. Not that I think they're actually investigating much."

"How dare you, sir!" Nina chopsticked a hunk of shrimp out of her own container and shook it at him. "You make it sound like these people are paid to *investigate* or some such folderol!"

"I know. What kind of imbecile *am* I?" Max leaned over on the sofa and kissed her. "And what does that make *you* for being my girlfriend?"

"A sucker for imbeciles." She grinned and kissed him back.

Just then, Max's phone rang, and he pulled it out of his pants pocket. When he saw it was a call from his mother, he touched the button to answer it. "Hi, Mom."

"Hi, Max," said Mom. "What are you doing tonight?"

"Having a bite to eat at Nina's. So what's up?"

"Could you stop over on your way home?" asked Mom. "I have a piece of mail here for you to pick up."

Max frowned. "What kind of mail?"

"A letter," said Mom. "Made out to you, but with my address on it. And no return address."

Max's blood burned with adrenaline as his eyes locked with Nina's. Then, he grabbed his car keys from the table and leaped to his feet. "I'll be right there," he said, and then he was gone.

"Here you go." Mom handed over the white envelope with a smile. She was ready for bed in a long blue bathrobe, her short gray hair bobby-pinned for the night. "But you really didn't have to rush over to get this tonight."

"I know." Max was working hard to appear calm, though he'd driven like a maniac across town and arrived at Mom's doorstep out of breath. "But I've been expecting something important."

Mom raised her eyebrows. "Something good?"

Max shrugged and tore open the envelope. He knew he should wait, but he couldn't.

Then, when he'd pulled out and read the letter inside, he wished he'd waited after all.

"Max?" Mom stared at him. "Are you all right? You're white as a sheet."

Max swallowed hard and nodded, fighting to regain his composure.

"What does it say?" Mom reached for the letter.

Max snatched it away before she could touch it. "Just a...a promotion I was hoping for. But I didn't get it."

"Are you sure?" asked Mom. "Is there something you're not telling me?"

"I'm sure." Max leaned down to kiss her on the forehead. "And no, there's nothing." Then he stuffed the letter in his back pocket, out of sight.

Though he already knew every word typed on the page by heart:

You are not wanted in Johnstown, Max Leverknight. Get out of town for your own safety, and the safety of those you care about.

You have 24 hours to leave, or a body will drop at this address. If you think I won't do it, go look in your back yard.

P.S. No cops.

It was a warm night, but Max shivered as he stood in the back yard of his house in Richland. He couldn't take his eyes off the limp body hanging from a low branch of his locust tree, dangling from a thick rope tied in a noose.

Tears flowed down his face as the body turned slowly in the wind, moonlight glancing off the white flanks spotted with black. Until now, Max had held out hope for a living reunion--but the only hope he had left was for a reunion in the *next* life.

"Harry," he whispered. "Oh, Harry."

Another hope was gone now, too: that the stalker was all talk, and that he might be inclined to let Max off easy.

Then: 1923.

Robert Sprangle, my grandfather, died in a hit-and-run on a midnight mountain road. He died because he was ordered out of Johnstown by a no-good mayor, enabled by citizens who turned a blind eye.

And no one paid the price. Until...

Now: 2016.

It's been almost a century since Robert's death. Does it matter anymore? Can you even call it justice *after all this time?*

I say yes, absolutely. Justice deferred, no matter how long, is still justice in my *book.*

Which is why, one by one, the descendants of Mayor Joe's inner circle will pay their ancestors' debts at my direction. All the while never knowing my name or my face.

Only knowing my race.

But wait, you say. This Max Leverknight, he isn't the same person as his grandfather or any of that ilk. He has never worn a hood or burned a cross in his life. He has never driven a black man from his home or run one down on a midnight road and kept going.

I say so fucking what.

I say fuck him for having the bad luck to be born to the wrong people. I say now he knows how we *feel.*

I say welcome to the club.

Now: 2016.

Exhausted, Max put away the shovel and went up to the kitchen to pour himself a drink. He was tracking dirt all over the place, and he didn't care; digging the grave and filling it with his dead best friend had left him numb to the bone.

Pulling a bottle of whiskey from a high cupboard, he unscrewed the top and put some in a drinking glass from a lower cupboard. He downed a swig and felt it burn all the way to his stomach, bringing fire that would soon turn into blessed relief.

Then he had another, bigger drink, and another after that.

Still, it took him a while to stop shaking. To reach the point where the pictures of Harry in his head no longer felt so immediate.

But then, as soon as that nightmare let go a little, the words from the letter rushed back to him. The letter that had been mailed to his mother's house.

You have 24 hours to leave, or a body will drop at this address.

Another drink didn't help to lessen their impact. It didn't give him any insight into dealing with this crisis.

The stalker had proved he meant business, and Max wasn't prepared to bet otherwise. He couldn't bear the thought that his beloved mother might be the next body he found hanging from a tree.

What about the police? They hadn't been any help yet, hadn't saved Harry or brought in the stalker. Was Max prepared to gamble his mother's life that they would suddenly get their shit together?

Wasn't there anyone else he could turn to? The state cops or

F.B.I., maybe? What were the chances they could find and stop the stalker in the next 24 hours while keeping Mom safe?

Max had the .22 now--but what was he going to *do* with it? Stand guard over his mother 24 hours a day from now on? Was he feeling lucky enough to gamble with her life, especially given his recent track record?

Max's stomach twisted as he thought about giving in and leaving town. Could he even *do* it in that short a time? Quit his job, pack up, move out, find another place to live?

Suddenly, a surge of rage flared within him. He'd lived a good life, treated people with respect, never knowingly hurt anyone. Why the fuck should *he* have to deal with *any* of this? Why should he have to take this *shit* from someone whose identity he didn't even *know?*

With a furious cry, he hurled the glass across the kitchen. It smashed to pieces against the refrigerator, scattering shards in all directions.

Fuck this! There had to be another way. There had to be *something* he could do other than run off with his tail between his legs while this, *this...*

This *son of a bitch* burned his life down around him.

The next morning, the phone rang *way* too early for a Saturday. Groaning from a hangover, Max ignored it, and the ringing finally stopped.

A moment later, it started again. This time, he rolled over and grabbed the phone from the bedside table.

"Max? Max, are you there?" It was Nina.

"Uh-huh." Max's voice was a croak. "What's up?"

She sounded rattled. "I got a letter, Max. Made out to you and sent to my address."

Max shot to complete alertness and sat up in bed. "I'll be right there."

He thought she might have opened it before he got there, but she hadn't. She even looked worried when she handed it over, which wasn't like her at all.

Max's heart raced as he slit open the envelope and drew out the letter folded inside. By the time he was done reading it, he had made up his mind. He knew exactly what he was going to do.

As he set about doing it--renting a moving van and packing up what belongings he could in one afternoon--he thought a lot about that letter. Much of it, *too* much of it, was seared into his memory.

The letter was the longest yet--two pages instead of one. It started much like the one his mother had received:

Last warning, Max Leverknight. Get out of town for your own safety, and the safety of those you care about.

You have 24 hours to leave, or a body will drop at this address.

The rest of the two pages were filled with one ugly detail after another--a description of all the terrible things the stalker would do to Nina if Max didn't leave.

So now, there were *two* lives in Max's hands, *two* lives he would save by getting out of Johnstown. The math wasn't so hard when you put it *that* way.

He wasn't taking any chances. He would get out that day and worry about the rest of it later--his job, his lease, his utilities. Explaining it all to Mom. Trying to salvage his relationship with Nina.

Trying to live with himself for running like this...though it would have been much harder if he'd stayed, and Mom and Nina had died.

By six o'clock, he was on the highway, heading for Pittsburgh. A buddy of his from college lived out that way; maybe he could help Max get set up there.

Meanwhile, it was just Max, the moving van with his car towed behind, the open road...and some jerk in a flashy silver BMW cutting him off, nearly running him off the road.

Some *black* jerk.

Cursing him up and down, Max gunned the van and charged, fire blazing in his eyes and his heart.

Then: 1923.

Robert Sprangle, an African-American exiled by Mayor Joe Cauffiel, died in a hit-and-run while fleeing Johnstown.

Now: 2016.

Max Leverknight, exiled descendant of a member of Mayor Joe's inner circle, is driven out of Johnstown by a descendant of Robert Sprangle.

And he never knows why. *Because why* should *he? What makes* him *special?*

But is this truly justice, *then? If the person on the receiving end doesn't get an explanation or understand what's happening?*

It sure tastes like justice to me.

So run, boy, run. I wish you luck. All the luck my grandpa got.

Trust me, none of us will miss you. You're just the latest entry in the great and secret ledger we've been keeping...but you won't be the last. It's a big, big book, let me tell you.

Bigger than you or anyone like you can ever imagine.

AS IF MY EVERY WORD HAS TURNED TO GLASS

I know I'm not getting through to him.

The 60-year-old writer narrows his eyes as if he fully grasps the passage I'm reading aloud, but I know he doesn't. As he sits in his recliner in the sunroom of his Malibu, California mansion, the words wash over him like raindrops without making an impression, like always.

Never mind that together, those words have spoken so eloquently to so many men and women the world over. They might as well be gibberish to him, or at least ramblings in a foreign tongue he only barely comprehends. Even though he once wrote those words with his own mind and soul and hands.

Watching his face, I read one more sentence, which I know by heart...the last sentence of the book. "'And so I stand here, thirsting for one last word from her lips so sweet and so dead, dying for one last chance to revisit all at which we failed in such wretched disgrace, none of which I would change in the slightest even knowing what I know now.'"

As the last syllable trails off in the late-summer air, I continue to stare, waiting for what I know is coming. His bright blue gold-flecked eyes (impossibly bright!) tick left-right left-right as if he is pondering what he just heard, assembling a cogent critique or some rare new insight.

Then, *blam*. His eyes shine even brighter with the flash of an idiot's grin. "Pretty story!" His hands bounce on his blue plaid pajama-covered knees. "Thank you, Doctor...Doctor..."

He can't even remember my name. The man won every writing award in the world--won the *Man Booker Prize* for the very book I just finishing reading aloud to him--and he can't even remember my name.

"Doctor Annie Delacroix." I point to the I.D. badge pinned to my white lab coat. "You can call me Annie."

"Annie." He tips his Alzheimer's-riddled head to the left and grins even wider. "I like you, Doctor Annie."

I smile back at him and close the book. "I like you, too, Ralph. I like you very much."

And I am going to make you write again if it's the last thing I do.

"So what's the good word?" Marjorie Livingston, Ralph's literary agent, corners me on my way out the door of the sunroom to lunch. Her eyes flash with intense interest verging on manic desperation. "Can you work with him?"

I close the door gently before I answer. "Yes. Yes, I can work with him."

Marjorie's bright red lipsticked lips unfold in a grin that's part relief, part victory, part hunger. She gives her head a toss, artfully stirring her long raven hair. "And what are our odds of success, do you think?"

"I won't make you any promises." Though my personal expectations are high, I don't want to fuel the pressure from the woman in charge around here...and that would be Marjorie. Ralph signed over his power of attorney to her a few years ago--before the Alzheimer's affected his judgment, supposedly. It's almost a cliché these days: predatory agent latches onto an elderly writer with a big name and a steadily weakening mind. "You know how fragile and fluid his condition is."

"And *you* know we need an authentic new Ralph Lang book to put the Ralph Lang brand back on the map." Her pretty face stiffens. She hired me, gave me a chance at a high-profile win, but I know it won't take much for her to turn against me. "We need a book with his name on it that actually *reads* like he *wrote* it."

"I'm aware of that, Ms. Livingston," I tell her.

"We need a Harper Lee-level comeback to put us back in the black," says Marjorie. "Ralph's medical expenses have been outpacing his earnings for too long. It's been too many years without new Ralph Lang product on the shelves."

"But neither of us wants to *damage* the golden goose, do we?" I ask.

Marjorie narrows her dark brown eyes at me. If she could shoot bullets out of her pupils, I swear I'd already be full of lead. "That would not be an *optimal* solution."

"I'll take that for a 'no.'"

"But your time is not unlimited, Doctor." Marjorie shakes her head. "There are other promising treatments on our radar. Not all of them are as...*non-invasive*...as yours."

"Then go for it," I tell her. "But one thing I *can* guarantee is that *no* other method will come *close* to the results mine can deliver...*if* you let me do my job."

I wouldn't think her glare could get any flintier, but it does. And then it softens. Because she knows damn well that I'm her best chance.

She's been trying to answer this question for the past seven years: how to cover her client's sky-high expenses (which rumor has it are due more to a crooked agent with the initials M.L. than the author himself) when her client has stopped writing because of Alzheimer's.

Ghost writers couldn't make it happen, that's for sure. Marjorie brought in a few to work some of Ralph's old notes and outlines into books...but Ralph Lang's voice is just too idiosyncratic, his books too complex and unpredictable. Of the three so-called Lang novels published in the past seven years, not one has been accepted as authentic by critics and the reading public.

The fact is, if Marjorie wants to make another big splash with the Ralph Lang brand, she needs new work written by Ralph himself. That's why she brought me in and agreed to finance my work with him.

I'm the one who developed a treatment to rebuild creative brains attacked by Alzheimer's. I'm the one with the best chance of bringing more Ralph Lang writing to the world.

Marjorie knows I can deliver; she's heard what I did with Lois Santangelo and Gabriel Carmen. She *knows* my treatment has a proven track record.

In the end, we both want the same thing: Ralph Lang's gifts restored, his work flowing once more. I'm confident I can make that happen, assuming she keeps her meddling to a minimum...and any surprises are of the beneficial variety.

After lunch, I'm back in the sunroom, watching the private nurse, Joe Prowse, as he swabs the bend in Ralph's right arm with an anesthetic-dowsed cotton ball.

"It's still hard to believe sometimes," Joe says softly. "That it's really him, I mean."

While Joe gets Ralph ready, I'm preparing the first injection of the treatment regimen, filling a syringe from a little glass vial. Looking over, I steal a glance at Ralph's sleeping face. "I know exactly what you mean."

Joe swabs Ralph's arm with gentle, lingering care. He's a little guy, a dark-haired fireplug in pale gray scrubs. "I practically worshipped the guy, you know? I'll never forget the first time I read *Tiger's Lament*."

"Such a great book." I finish filling the syringe and return the vial to my case. "It set the standard, didn't it?"

Joe has one of those artfully trimmed goatees, a fine black loop around his chin, bisected by a thin vertical line running through the cleft to his lower lip. When he grins, the loop spreads out like a ripple on a pond. "I think my favorite is still *Forever and Evan*, though. That's the one that changed my life."

I smile as I stick the needle in Ralph's arm. *Forever and Evan* changed my life, too. Reviving the mind that wrote it is one of the reasons I took this job.

"You really think you can do it, don't you?" asks Joe as I withdraw the needle and step away. "You think you can bring him back."

"All I can do is try," I tell him.

When I return the next morning, I expect no miracles, as Ralph's treatment has barely begun...and my expectations are borne out by reality.

"Hello?" He frowns up at me over his breakfast tray with deep puzzlement, as if he's never seen me before.

"Good morning. I'm Doctor Annie." I smile and wave. "I'd like to visit with you for a while, if that's all right."

Slowly, Ralph's puzzled frown melts into a blank but not unfriendly expression. "All right."

"Would you like me to come back later, after you've finished breakfast?"

His eyes widen with alarm. "No, no! Please, stay. What did you say your name is?"

"Annie," I tell him, bowing a little. "Doctor Annie Delacroix."

"Good to meet you, Annie." His eyes brighten, and he gestures with the slice of toast in his hand. "Please, have a seat."

I nod once and walk over to the table by the big picture window, where I put down my case. The room is walled with windows and patio doors that let in waves of light and salt sea air. Circling around, I pause to take in the view of the glittering beach beyond the patio...one of the rewards for his long and profitable career.

I open the case, pull out a pen and notepad, and take a seat on a simple wooden chair across from his recliner--a chair I put there the morning before, to establish our work space. "How are you feeling this morning?"

"I don't know." He scowls. "Not sure yet."

That's good, about what I expected. Yesterday's injection--a cocktail of glutamate receptor blockers, beta-amyloid and tau protein inhibitors, customized smart antibodies, and my own secret ingredient--can have a disorienting effect before the benefits start to kick in.

I cross my left leg over my right and smile. "Well, it's a beautiful day, isn't it?"

Ralph tips his head right. "Yes, you *are* beautiful, Abby."

He catches me off guard when he says that, and I drop the notepad on the floor. "Thank you." I lean down and retrieve it, then sit up again to meet his gaze.

"You're very welcome," says Ralph.

It's about time we get to the reason I'm here--his treatment. "May I read to you a while, Ralph? I brought a book you might enjoy."

He slumps. "I guess."

"Good. I like to read." I get up and take the breakfast tray from him, placing it on the table by the picture window. While I'm there, I pull a thick hardcover book from my case; masking tape hides the author's name on the cover and spine, though the title is visible.

Somebody Get Me Another Bullet: Collected Stories. That's the title. And the author? Ralph Lang, of course.

Not that he would likely remember anything about this book. If past human trials are any indication, we won't see the first signs of recollection for two or three weeks.

"Let's start with this one." I crack the book to a spot I've dog-eared, a story near the midpoint. "It's called 'The Tensing Fawn.'" Clearing my throat, I check his face...but it's as blank as a hard-boiled egg. So I start reading. "'Sometimes, I think of how many people would still be alive if that year had never happened.'"

Ralph leans back in his recliner and listens, head turned slightly away as he directs his better ear--the left one--toward me.

"'Though I suppose every year is like that, in the end. There are casualties.'" I pause and look up, but nothing has changed in Ralph's expression. "'And the replacements never stop coming, devouring everything in their path.'"

Just then, Ralph interrupts. "Angie?" He leans forward with a look of solemn urgency. "Are you a writer?"

"No, Ralph. I'm a doctor. A psychiatrist."

"But didn't you write this story? The one about the fawn?"

I shake my head. "No, I didn't. I'm only reading it."

Ralph keeps leaning forward. His mouth moves, as if he's trying to articulate something that won't quite come to him.

"What is it, Ralph?" I ask him. "Would you like me to keep reading?"

His lips stop moving, and his eyes grow wide. He looks surprised. "Am *I*?"

"Are you what?"

He looks away, out the window, then back at me. He's more astonished than ever. "Am I a *writer*?"

The breath catches in my chest. I snap the book shut, unable to believe what I've just heard him say.

"Why do you ask that question?" I fight to keep my voice level. It's important I don't color his response.

Ralph shakes his head. Instead of answering my question, he asks another. "If you didn't write that story, who did?" His eyes fix on me like headlights on a deer in the road. "Was it me?"

Reflexively, I check to make sure his name on the cover and spine of the book is completely taped over. It is.

What he just said is impossible. The soonest any human subject has ever asked that question or anything like it is day ten of treatment. Never before has it happened on day two.

"Why do you think it was you?" I ask. "Why do you think you wrote this story?"

"Just a feeling I had when I heard the words." Ralph relaxes back into his recliner. "Could you read me some more, please, Doctor Annie?"

"I wrote that on a typewriter." Ralph says it out of the blue, without prompting, after I finish. "The kind..." His fingers flicker in his lap as if they're dancing over a keyboard. "The kind without electricity."

"A manual typewriter." As always, I keep my voice level, though my heart is secretly racing.

"Yes. A Safari brand." He taps his chin with an index finger and nods. "It was a good thing it was a manual, because the power kept going out. I couldn't stay ahead of the electric bill."

I'm so excited, I'm trembling inside. Just like that--one injection, one reading--and he's remembering details of his past.

"Where was this, Ralph?" I ask him. "Where did the power keep going out?"

The words flow out of him easily. "My little studio apartment in Brooklyn. It was rat-infested, roach-infested...and writer-infested." He chuckles softly. "Peter Cardinale stayed there sometimes, and so did Villa Glazier. They were both sleeping on my floor the whole time I wrote that story, in fact."

"Did they?" My eyes widen. I've heard tales of his legendary times with Cardinale and Glazier.

Ralph nods emphatically. "They both told me the story was shit, but I knew better. The more those jealous bastards said they hated it, the better I knew it had to be." He laughs loudly.

"How old were you then?"

He doesn't even have to think about it. "Twenty-two and a half."

I'm stunned. "What story did you write next, Ralph?"

He turns his head and looks at me. "What?"

"What did you write after 'The Tensing Fawn?'"

His smile melts away like a snowflake. "I don't...uh....hmm." He shakes his head as if to clear it, but the frown that lands on his face suggests anything but clarity. "What did I write, you ask?"

"Yes."

"I *did* write 'The Tensing Fawn.' Peter and Villa were staying with me at the time." He narrows his eyes as he says it. "We were in a studio apartment in Brooklyn. I was using a manual Safari typewriter."

I nod slowly. "And then?"

I watch him glower and struggle for a long moment before he

meets my gaze again. This time, his bright blue eyes look helpless and resigned. "I don't know."

"So where do we stand?" Marjorie leans over the untouched shrimp salad in front of her, focused entirely on me.

What a shame she has to spoil a perfect setting--a light lunch laid out on an elegant white table on a balcony of Ralph's mansion facing the Pacific. I didn't invite her, I don't want her at my table...but she's the boss, so there's nothing I can do about it. She can pull the plug on my work with Ralph at any time, and I don't want that to happen.

I reach for my iced tea in its tall, blue-tinted glass. "We are on day two of the regimen. He is responding to treatment. Beyond that, I'm not prepared to say."

Marjorie leans further over her salad. "Come on, Doctor. I'm having a lousy day. Give me something I can work with."

There's no way I'm even going to *hint* at the level of success I've had. If she knew Ralph was regaining memories this early in the game, she'd be pushing like a maniac for that book she expects.

Not to mention, I have no idea if the phenomenon will be lasting or repeatable. And I'm worried that it seems to be so limited in scope. Ralph only seems to have regained memories formed during the writing of the story "The Tensing Fawn."

I sip my iced tea and put it down in front of me. "Sorry, I can't help you. I won't leak the results until they've been normalized."

Marjorie rolls her eyes. "Then make something up! Throw me a damn life preserver here!"

"As soon as I have something concrete, I'll let you know."

"Well, you better make it snappy." Marjorie throws herself back and wraps her arms across her chest. "Things are getting ugly right now."

"Why is that?" I ask as I reach for my salad fork.

"The printing error of the century," says Marjorie. "Somehow, several consecutive page signatures were left blank across an entire print run of the new edition of one of Ralph's books."

"Page signature?"

"A section of a book," explains Marjorie. "One big sheet is folded and cut into pages. In this case, they were set to include one story in its entirety...and now it's gone. Somehow, in spite of all the printer's and publisher's quality control measures, no one caught the mistake until the book's laydown in stores, which just happened today."

"The story's...gone?"

"All that's left is the story's title in the table of contents," says Marjorie. "Otherwise, *poof*...blank pages."

I stare at her as I process what I'm hearing. "What book is it, did you say?"

"An annotated reissue of one of his short story collections," says Marjorie. "*Somebody Get Me Another Bullet*, it's called."

The hairs stand up on the back of my neck. "And what story was left blank?"

"The best in the book, of course." Marjorie slams her hands down on the table. "'The Tensing Fawn.' Can you believe it?"

"No." I shake my head slowly as I consider the incredible coincidence, which I decide I will keep to myself. "No, I can't."

"Thank God you're back," says Nurse Joe when I enter Ralph's sunroom. "He kept telling me I was fired if I didn't go find you and drag you back in here."

"Is that her?" Ralph, who's standing at the patio doors, hobbles toward me. "It's about time!"

I frown at Joe. "Is something wrong? Did something happen?"

Joe bobs his head toward Ralph. "He wants you to read him more stories." He grins. "I hope your pipes are up for it."

"Yes, well." I don a neutral smile. "We might have some other work to do first."

"No!" Ralph's face flares with panic. "I need a *story* first. Another *story*." He teeters the last few steps and reaches for me.

I grab his forearms; otherwise, I'm afraid he might fall. "We'll get to that, don't worry. I just need to ask you some questions first."

"No questions!" Ralph's panic suddenly shifts to anger.

Judging from his childish reactions, perhaps I don't need to conduct a formal assessment after all. It seems pretty clear he's lost his bearings again, which was the exact thing I wanted to determine. So much for the memory restoration being a lasting effect.

But is it repeatable? Maybe I should just give him what he wants and lead with a story. That will tell the tale, one way or the other.

"Story first!" shouts Ralph...and then the tantrum melts away. His angry glare twists into an anguished scowl, and tears flow down his cheeks. "Please, Doctor Annie. Don't make me *wait*."

I meet Joe's gaze, and he draws Ralph away from me without a word. Gently, he guides him across the room and eases him into his recliner.

"Okay, Ralph." Crossing the room, I retrieve a book from a stack on the table by the picture window. This one, like the first, has masking tape over the author's name on the cover and spine. "Let's start with a story after all."

The relief on Ralph's face is pure and powerful. "Oh, thank you. It's just, I want to see if I can remember anything else like Peter and Villa and the Safari typewriter."

When he says it, I nearly drop the book. The retrieved memories haven't faded, after all.

I'm stunned, but I stay in professional mode. "Then let's try another one, shall we?" I open the book, a collection called *Foundlings and Other Curses*, to a dog-eared spot near the end of its length. "This story is called 'Beyond the Beans, Above the Box.'"

Ralph smiles, settling back. "I like the title."

"Yeah, good choice!" Joe's face lights up. "All right if I listen, too?"

I shake my head. "I'd rather you didn't." I don't want Joe--or anyone else--in the room for this. Much better if I'm the only witness in case Ralph's small miracle repeats.

Joe shrugs. "Let me know if you need anything."

As he leaves the room, I sit in my chair across from Ralph. I cross my left leg over my right and prop the open book on my knee. "'Seven children and eighty-four years ago, I dug up something terrible and wonderful beyond words in the far back corner of the bean field.'"

When the story ends, Ralph gets up from his recliner and paces the floor. His posture is straighter than before, his hands clasped behind his back.

At first, he doesn't say anything. Then, on his third trip across the room, he fixes me in a steady, clear gaze. "I remember."

My heart beats fast, and I am trembling like the last time we did this...as if I am the one undergoing seismic change. "What do you remember?"

"Writing that story, for one thing." His hand flutters as if he considers the story a trifle. "It was...sometime after 'The Tensing Fawn,' but I'm not sure when, exactly. Just...after."

I nod. "What else?"

"I was living in...New Orleans?" He frowns and scratches his head, then snaps his fingers. "*Baton Rouge*. I had a Cajun girlfriend and a black girlfriend at the same time."

I sit and watch as he does the heavy lifting. Everything he tells me is absolutely accurate; I know, because I did some online research at lunch (after Marjorie left), making sure of my facts from the time of his life when he wrote "Beyond the Beans, Above the Box."

"What else?" I ask him.

Ralph walks back and forth, then stops in front of me and grins. "Happy times." He closes his eyes. "Music day and night. Dancing at the *fais do-do*." His eyes open. "Crawfish and cornbread and Dixie beer."

I give him my usual neutral smile and nod. "Anything else?"

Ralph squints hard, rubbing his chin. Then, his eyes light up. "Yes! I broke my leg falling out of a tree! I was in a cast..." His expression darkens. "I was in a cast when I finished the story, I know that much. Beyond that, I still don't remember."

"Okay." So his retrieved memories are still limited to the period when he was writing the story I just read to him. The effect is consistent...across two stories, anyway. But I need more data to map its impact across a broader sampling. "Would you like me to read another?"

Again, he lights up. "Are you kidding?" He gestures at the stack of books on the table behind me. "How about the next one I wrote after 'Beyond the Beans, Above the Box?' So I can see what happened next."

"Sure." I go to the table and pull the tablet computer out of my case. I open Ralph's bibliography on the screen, locate the next story in the chronological sequence, and note which collection includes it. Then, I put down the tablet, find the right book in the stack, and go to the page I want.

"What's it called?" asks Ralph.

"'Mauvette Makes Good,'" I tell him. "It's from a collection titled *Sorghum and Gomorra*."

By the time I'm done reading, Ralph remembers getting the cast off his leg and selling a story to *The New Yorker* for the first time. He remembers leaving Baton Rouge on the run from his black girlfriend's preacher father, then heading down to El Paso, Texas to visit a writer friend. He laughs when he talks about the good times they had over the border in Ciudad Juarez, Mexico...especially getting mixed up with a gang of wild señoritas at a cockfight.

He doesn't hesitate to ask me to read him another one after we've tapped his "Mauvette Makes Good" memories as much as we can. Looking at my watch, I see it's almost 3:30PM. The next work, a novel called *Untitled*, isn't long--a little over 200 pages--but there's no way I'll finish it by the end of our day at five.

Seeing his expectant, desperate face, though, I feel as if I have no choice. He's getting his life back in pieces after being empty for so long; how can I deny him another morsel?

"Please, Annie," says Ralph. "Won't you please read another?"

"All right." I smile and reach for the book. "Let's see how far we get with this one."

"The End." That's how far we get.

It takes nearly seven hours, but we make it all the way to the end of the book. I skip dinner, so does he, and we finish *Untitled* in one sitting (plus bathroom breaks).

The impact of the book is powerful and immediate. It has the same effect on Ralph that the stories did, only stronger. It brings back so many more memories from a bigger block of time--which makes sense, since it took him longer to write the novel than the stories.

After hearing me read *Untitled*, he remembers living in three different places with four different women over two and a half years. He talks about being in a car crash near Seattle, a poker tournament in Vegas, and a riot in Los Angeles.

It all comes rushing back to him in one glorious torrent, a river of experience which until now had been dried up for years. I see and hear him growing stronger from it, sitting straighter and speaking louder.

"Read me another," he says as I give him the latest shot of his medication. "Let's stay up all night and read everything we can."

"Tomorrow," I tell him. "I need some rest, and so do you."

"But I don't want to stop now." Ralph's eyes flash to the stacks of books on the table by the window. "I want to remember *everything*."

I pull the needle from his arm and pat his shoulder. "No need to rush it," I tell him. "Relax and enjoy the ride, Ralph."

When I drive to work at Ralph's mansion the next morning--half an hour late, after our marathon session the night before--I'm in for a surprise. The place is thick with security guards, starting at the front gate. I used to just get buzzed in by Nurse Joe; now, I get the third degree and demands for photo I.D. from two big brutes.

The guards look like Special Forces on patrol, dressed in black and armed to the teeth. All of them wear body armor and carry machine guns; some even have German Shepherds on quick-release leashes.

Heart pounding, I park my black BMW in the front drive, wondering what has happened to bring out the big guns. I throw my car door open so fast, I almost hit an approaching guard. As he stumbles back out of the way, he snaps out a request to see my I.D.

At which point, I hear Marjorie shouting from the mansion's open front door. "Doctor Delacroix! We've been waiting for you!"

Snatching my case from the seat beside me, I leap out of the car and hurry toward her. "What's going on? What happened?"

"Ralph's on lockdown." Her glare is pitch black, her arms clamped across her chest. "We're under attack."

Suddenly, I'm short of breath. "Is he all right?"

"*He* is." Marjorie tosses her head in disgust and leads me inside. "But I can't say the same for his *work*."

"What are you talking about?"

She slams the door shut behind us. "His disappearing *oeuvre*, is what I'm talking about. His vanishing *bibliography*."

I don't say a word as I follow her into the living room. Suddenly, I'm anxious for reasons that have nothing to do with Ralph's health.

Marjorie heads straight for the bar at the far end of the room. "We lost another story this morning. 'Beyond the Beans, Above the Box.'" She grabs a glass tumbler from under the bar, then reaches for a crystal decanter of something amber. "And do you want to hear something crazy? It wasn't a printing error!"

My head spins as I absorb what she just told me. "Really?" I'm afraid to say too much, but I eke out a question. "Then what was it?"

"Damned if I know!" Marjorie pours liquid from the decanter into the tumbler, then throws it back neat in one gulp. "It disappeared from existing copies that had been printed over a *year* ago. Not only *that*, but it vanished from every edition the publisher can locate that was printed *before* that, dating back *twenty years*."

I don't have to pretend to be amazed. "How is that even *possible*?"

Marjorie pours another drink. "You tell me!"

I stare dumbly, not sure if it's just a rhetorical expression or she's given me an order.

She throws back the drink and pours another. "I can see how someone might infiltrate a printing company and sabotage a press run. I can see how they might use a computer virus to wipe out electronic copies. But what I *can't* see..." She drains the tumbler once more. "...is how they could blank out every existing paper and audio copy in every bookstore, library, archive, and private collection in the world!" She reaches for the decanter again. "But that's what we're *dealing with* here."

Again, I keep my silence. The truth is, even if I wanted to explain, I don't understand how it happened any better than she does. There's only one thing I'm sure about at this point: the fact that this story disappeared the day after I read it to Ralph Lang is *not* a coincidence.

"Oh, and I didn't even *tell* you about the *novel* yet." Marjorie pours one more drink and caps the decanter.

"Novel?"

"Remember *Untitled*?" She downs her drink while I nod. "Good, because I doubt you'll ever get to *read* it again. It's *gone*, baby. Every copy of every edition we can lay our hands on is blank, except for the title."

I feel dizzy as I think about how this is not a coincidence, either. "But how?"

"All-out war on the works of Ralph Lang, that's how. An unprecedented campaign against one of the greatest writers of our age." Marjorie smacks the tumbler down so hard that I'm worried it might break. "Which is why we've got the man himself on lockdown."

I don't tell her how little that will help. "So what do we do now?"

Marjorie jabs a finger in my direction. "*You* keep up the treatment. It's more important than *ever*, especially if we keep losing the books Ralph's already *written*."

Somehow, I don't think she'd agree if she knew the full story. "Okay."

"In fact, you're just as important as he is right now. *You're* on lockdown, too."

The first thing I do when I get to Ralph's sunroom is go straight for the books. They're right where I left them, in stacks on the table by the picture window.

Breathless, I grab the one on top of the shortest stack. I open it right to the middle, and I let out a gasp. The pages are blank. The entire text of the novel they once contained is gone. *Untitled* is nonexistent.

Just then, I hear Ralph's voice. "Hello, Doctor Annie. Looks like you're as eager as I am to get on with the day's reading."

"Just give me a minute, Ralph." Next, I grab *Sorghum and Gomorra* and crack it open to where "Mauvette Makes Good" should be. Only it's not there anymore, either.

"What are we reading today?" asks Ralph. "I can't wait to remember more of my life."

I don't answer. I'm too busy pawing through *Foundlings and Other Curses*, looking for "Beyond the Beans, Above the Box." As with the other two volumes, I find nothing but blank pages where the text I read aloud ought to be.

An icy chill sweeps through me as I put down the book. I've seen the evidence, I've held it in my hand; I've directly witnessed the cause-and-effect that seems to be the only explanation. Yet it still doesn't seem possible.

"Doctor Annie?" says Ralph. "Is something wrong?"

It depends on your point of view. Ralph, who lost his memories to Alzheimer's, gets them back when he hears his work read aloud.

That in itself is within the realm of possibility...that hearing his familiar prose triggers some kind of healing and reawakening deep within his mind.

But that's where the rational world ends. Because apparently, when he accesses lost memories via his read-aloud stories or novels, those stories or novels physically disappear from the world.

I lean on the table for a moment, taking deep breaths to steady myself. I need to regain my composure and reassert my professional demeanor if I intend to continue treatment. But *is* that what I intend to do? Is that what I *should* do?

"Doctor Annie?" I hear him getting up from his recliner.

"Hold on, Ralph." I turn and head for the patio doors. "I need a little fresh air right now."

Out on the patio, the morning sun is bright, the sea breeze bracing. An armed guard with a German Shepherd looks my way as he strolls past on the beach down below.

For the first time in a long time, I feel paralyzed, my purpose in question. This whole project with Ralph was meant to be my crowning achievement, the one that would restore his battered mind and reinforce my preeminence in the field of dementia remediation.

For a while, it seemed I was succeeding beyond my most optimistic projections. But now, I'm in unknown territory, facing an ethical dilemma I've never imagined. Should I keep reading him his work, knowing it will keep disappearing from the world?

"Doctor Annie?" Ralph walks out and stands beside me at the railing. "What's going on?"

As I look over at him, I wonder if he ought to know the truth. Should I tell him about his work's disappearance?

"Come on, Annie. You can tell me." The look in his eyes is warm, caring, and guileless. Maybe he deserves better than ignorance.

After all, it's *his* work at stake, isn't it? His work and his memories. Shouldn't he have a say in the outcome?

"I know this might sound crazy." That's how I start to tell him. "I don't even have a good explanation for it...but I can't deny it's happening."

Ralph frowns. "What's that?"

I take a deep breath, carefully choosing my next words. "When I read you one of your stories or novels, it somehow disappears, Ralph. It's erased from the world."

Ralph's frown deepens. "Erased?"

I nod. "Every copy--whether it's paper, electronic, or audio--goes blank except for the title."

"No." He shakes his head. "That doesn't make sense."

"Ask Marjorie," I tell him. "Ask your publisher."

His frown becomes a scowl. "How is that even *possible?"*

"I have no idea, but I can tell you, it's really happening." I nod toward the picture window, where the stacks of books are visible. "Even the books in your room. Whatever I've read has gone blank."

He stares into space for a moment, rubbing a hand over his mouth and chin. "So as I'm getting my memories back, my work is vanishing from the face of the Earth."

"Exactly. It's a tradeoff, apparently." I pause, watching as a seagull drifts lazily past on the ocean breeze. "So what do you want to do next?"

He looks at me with one eyebrow raised. "Next?"

"Do you want me to keep reading, knowing it will likely make more of your work disappear?"

Ralph narrows his eyes and turns his gaze to the beach, where another security guard is walking past. Little does the guard know, as he watches for interlopers, that the true threat is right here on the patio, standing beside Ralph.

After all, I'm the one who gives him the choice. "It's up to you, Ralph," I tell him. "It's your writing, your legacy."

I watch him as the wind ruffles his hair, and I wonder what I would do in his place. Would I salvage what was left of my work, though it would mean passing up the chance to restore my forgotten past? Or would I throw the work away to regain what was lost?

"You're asking if I want you to keep reading?" asks Ralph. "Even if it means more of my work disappears?"

"That's right."

"Hell, yes." He flashes me a grin. "That's what I call a real no-brainer."

I abide by his decision. I read to him through the day, chipping away at the next novel in the stack, *Hammurabi's Loophole.*

I'd forgotten what a great book it is; when we reach the part where the main character, Attorney Peter Priest, vows revenge against God for the loss of his wife and child, I get a chill up my spine. Then I hesitate, wondering if I should stop reading and save this great work for the world...but Ralph urges me on, and I keep going.

We make it halfway through the book by dinner, then pick it back up afterward. Now that I'm trapped in the house under armed guard, it's not like I'm in a hurry to end our session.

I give Ralph his scheduled injection and keep reading long into the night. I read, he listens, and *Hammurabi's Loophole* melts away.

Literally. We finish the book at two A.M., then discuss his latest retrieved memories and go to bed (he in his bedroom, escorted by Nurse Joe, and me in a guest room down the hall). When I pick up the book the next morning, every page of the text is blank. Marjorie confirms it when I go downstairs for breakfast: *Hammurabi's Loophole* has been deleted everywhere.

And the world has taken notice in a big way. Marjorie turns on the TV, and we watch the latest reports. People the world over are scrambling to protect Ralph's works, locking away the ones that are left...committing them to memory, even. Groups of memorization specialists have gathered in secure facilities worldwide, stuffing their minds with every bit of Ralph's prose that they can hold.

Even as we watch, and Marjorie fires down belts of bourbon, I know it's all for nothing. Ralph's body of work is doomed.

In the days and nights that follow, Ralph and I plow our way through his backlist like there's no tomorrow. I read it all in chronological order, greater and lesser works alike. I read until I lose my voice or Ralph falls asleep, though I almost always lose my voice first.

We push ourselves to the limit, I think, because of our unspoken fears--that the magic will stop before we finish, or Marjorie will somehow wise up and shut down our operation.

Every time I talk to her, she's more desperate and irrational, because Ralph's body of work is shrinking more with each passing day. None of the efforts to save it have made any difference. Sealed vaults and elaborate backup systems can't stop the deletions. Movie and TV adaptations go blank globally, whether they're in the form of film reels, digital files, DVDs, or videotapes. Words chiseled in stone disappear as easily as those printed on paper; even the memorization experts forget everything once I've read it aloud to Ralph.

But Ralph and I don't let that stop us.

Two weeks in, he's a different man, a man full of memories and self-assurance...but it still isn't enough. The stack of unread books on the table by the picture window has dwindled away to almost nothing, yet he doesn't hesitate to beg me to keep reading.

He wants *all of it.* Every last bite, no matter the cost to his legacy or his fans or the culture of the world.

Which is why, as we get closer to the end, I keep putting off reading one particular book, pushing it further out of chronological order. It's *Forever and Evan,* which won the Pulitzer Prize 25 years ago. Pretty much everyone calls it his greatest work, and I agree; it's the one that changed my life, after all. When I first read it, I was a 20-year-old basket case contemplating suicide...but the story of Evan Barlowe and his struggle with depression made me realize I had something to live for. It gave me a new mindset, one that enabled me to finish college, then med school, then move on to become a psychiatrist and dementia expert who could help others as Ralph had helped me...even, one day, help Ralph himself.

I don't know if I can let go of that book. I don't know if I *should*, given the difference it's made in my life and the lives of so many others. But its turn is coming soon; it's at the bottom of the stack, but the stack is disappearing fast.

Trying to delay the inevitable, I slow the pace of my reading. I tell Ralph I'm wearing out and need more rest. I say I can't keep reading until all hours of the night.

He accepts my explanation, but it doesn't buy me much time. Soon enough, the only book standing between me and *Forever and Evan* is one slim volume of stories--*Coup de Grâce*, his last collection before the Alzheimer's struck.

So we're almost down to the moment I've been dreading. Even as I read *Coup de Grâce*, all I can think about is *Forever and Evan* and the fact that the words I read are counting down what might be its final hours on Earth.

"Your time is up." Those are Marjorie's first words when she corners me in the hall on my way to Ralph's room. "We need results, Doctor Delacroix...*on paper*. We need *new books*." She nods grimly. "God knows the old ones are just about gone."

I keep my best poker face in place as I listen. Getting new writing out of Ralph has been the *last* thing on my mind lately.

"I'm dead serious." Marjorie wags a finger at me. "I want him writing *today*, if he isn't already."

He isn't, but I keep it to myself. "I can't guarantee anything," I tell her. "The creative process is a delicate one, especially in someone who has just recovered from an extreme neurological disorder, which in itself is..."

Marjorie jabs my left shoulder with her finger. "*Everything's* riding on what happens *in there*." She points at the door to the sunroom. "My career, his career...*your* career." She shoots me a nasty glare. "We've got about a book and a half left of his entire body of work, and I'm sure it's only a matter of time until *that's* gone, too. Our only hope is whatever new product you can squeeze out of him. So *get squeezing*."

Marjorie isn't kidding about time running out. She's not

kidding about my career riding on the outcome, either. If every last bit of Ralph's work disappears--including *Forever and Evan*--and I can't get him to write something new, I'll have failed. It won't matter that I've restored huge portions of his memory; the writing, not the man, is what matters most to the world.

Now I just have to decide which part of him matters most to me.

As I read the last story from *Coup de Grâce*, titled "Neverwaster," I am very aware of that very last book on the table behind me.

I stumble more times getting through "Neverwaster" than I have while reading any other story or book to Ralph. The problem is, my mind keeps drifting to *Forever and Evan*, wondering what the hell I am going to do with it. Wishing I could put off dealing with it a little bit longer.

But soon enough, I can't. The second I finish "Neverwaster" and close the book, Ralph points at the table by the window. "Looks like you're almost done reading," he says.

I wasn't sure until just now what I was going to do. The decision, when it arrives, surprises me a little. "I've been thinking." I get up and walk over to the book table, where I put down *Coup de Grâce* but don't pick up *Forever and Evan*. "I wonder if you might consider leaving one book unread."

He looks amused. "Now why would I do that?"

I spread my arms wide. "For *posterity's* sake. So your work isn't *completely* forgotten."

Ralph brushes a hand through the air as if he's swatting a gnat. "I don't care about any of that. Not anymore." Though, physically, he's still an old man, his voice carries the certainty and forcefulness of a much younger one. "Posterity doesn't matter if you don't have your memories, Annie."

"Still." I walk to the patio doors and look out. A steady stream of guards patrol the beach in pairs, the most guards I've seen out there yet. Ralph is a more precious commodity than ever, now that his work is so rare. "You've come so far. You've regained almost everything you lost. Would it hurt to leave one book intact for the world to remember you by? Especially the book that won the Pulitzer Prize?"

"I don't care about the world. All I want is what's in here." Ralph taps his right temple with an index finger.

"But you'll never get *all* of it back," I tell him. "Whatever happened when you weren't writing, you still won't remember it. If there's no text for me to read, that part of your life remains a blank." I turn and meet his gaze. "What difference will it make if you leave one more part forgotten?"

He shakes his head at me. "You've never had Alzheimer's. You don't know what it's *like* to have it all slip away." Suddenly, he storms to the table by the window and grabs *Forever and Evan*. "I want it *all*." He stomps over and shoves the book into my hands. "I want every last *bit* of it, whatever the price."

His urgency startles me. I wonder if this demanding, explosive Ralph is the closest yet to his complete, original self. How much further will he go in this direction? Maybe filling in more blanks in his memory isn't such a great idea, after all.

Yet how can I do otherwise? He craves the scraps of the past that are rightfully his, and how can I deny him? As a doctor, isn't it my responsibility to continue his treatment, to do everything in my power to restore his faculties?

"Well?" He nods at the book in my hands.

I hesitate. Once this last book is gone, there can be no turning back. Whatever Ralph might do in the future, the greatest accomplishments of his life thus far will be lost forever.

"Please." He reaches out and gently places one hand on the book. "Please read it."

"I don't know if I should," I tell him.

"Come on." He puts his other hand on my shoulder. "Please."

My uncertainty holds me in place like a butterfly pinned to a board. "Maybe I don't want to be the person who destroys your legacy single-handedly."

"Okay then. What about this?" Smiling, Ralph takes my hand and says something that changes the equation, something that illuminates a possibility I hadn't considered. "What if we do it *together*?"

So this is what we do.

Ralph and I step outside and pull two patio chairs next to each other. Then I have to go back inside to get his reading glasses, retrieving them from the little table beside his recliner.

After I bring out the glasses and help him put them on, we sit down side-by-side, holding *Forever and Evan* between us. We open the book in the bright Malibu sunshine and turn to page one to begin our experiment.

But before we can take the next step, I hesitate. "What if this disrupts the process?" I ask. "What if it doesn't bring back any memories for you?"

Ralph smiles reassuringly. "Then you'll just have to read it all again, by yourself, while I listen. Think you can stand it?"

It's my favorite book of all time, and he knows it. "Of course I can." I take a deep breath and let it out slowly, feeling relieved. Feeling like the two of us can handle anything.

"Ready?" He nods encouragingly.

"Yes." I raise the book higher, cracking it wider so the opening page is clear to see.

And then we start to read.

I go first, reading the beautiful prologue set during springtime in the mountains of North Carolina. When I finish with that, I give him a nod. He clears his throat, then picks up where I left off, reading chapter one aloud.

When he's done, I read chapter two. We go on like that for hours, reading alternating chapters, our voices blending with the roar and whoosh of the crashing surf along the beach.

It's one of the most wonderful experiences of my life, reading my favorite book with the man who wrote it. Our elbows and shoulders touch as we speak those perfect passages into the world once more; in a way, it becomes the most intimate and transcendent act I could ever imagine.

Though it's true, we don't know what will happen next as a result of our reading together. Have we disrupted whatever magic brought back his memories during the earlier readings? Or maybe we've just corrected whatever process has been wiping his work from the face of the Earth. Maybe our combined efforts will bring back everything still forgotten and save this final book of his from extinction in the bargain.

Whatever the outcome, I will treasure this experience for as long as I live. Especially when we get to his finest chapter, the one that changes everything for the book's protagonist. It's Ralph's turn to read...but he just nods at me. He lets me take his turn, as if he senses how much this passage means to me. As if he knows, though I've never told him, that this is the part that turned my life around.

Then, as I pour my heart into reading it, he closes his eyes and turns his good left ear toward me. Smiling blissfully, he basks in the flow of words from my lips as if they are the lips of whatever muse has been whispering in his ear all his life, whether he could always hear her or not.

ABOUT THE AUTHOR

Robert Jeschonek is an envelope-pushing, *USA Today* bestselling author whose fiction, comics, and non-fiction have been published around the world. His stories have appeared in *Clarkesworld, Galaxy's Edge, StarShipSofa, Pulphouse,* and many other publications. He has written official *Star Trek* and *Doctor Who* fiction and has scripted comics for DC, AHOY, and others. His young adult slipstream novel, *My Favorite Band Does Not Exist*, won the Forward National Literature Award and was named one of *Booklist's* Top Ten First Novels for Youth. He also won an International Book Award, a Scribe Award for Best Original Novel, and the grand prize in Pocket Books' Strange New Worlds contest.

Visit him online at www.bobscribe.com. You can also find him on Facebook and follow him as @TheFictioneer on Twitter.

Subscribe to the Blastoff Books Newsletter: http://newsletter.blastoffbooks.net/

www.ingramcontent.com/pod-product-compliance
Lightning Source LLC
Chambersburg PA
CBHW070036030726
47504CB00012B/18

* 9 7 9 8 9 8 7 5 8 4 6 3 7 *